A QUEST FOR A CHRISTIAN
IRELAND

THE BANKS
OF
THE BOYNE

DONNA FLETCHER CROW
AUTHOR OF *THE FIELDS OF BANNOCKBURN*

MOODY PRESS
CHICAGO

Four lines from "In Memory of Eva Bore-Booth and Con Markievicz" The Collected Works of W. B. Yeats, Volume 1: *The Poems,* Revised Editor: Richard J. Finneran U. S. rights, Simon & Schuster, used by permission.

Extracts from *The Land of Heart's Desire,* "The Stolen Child," "The Lake Isle of Innisfree," and "In Memory of Eva Gore-Booth and Con Markievicz" from The Collected Powems of W. B. Yeats. Permission of A. P. Watt Ltd. on behalf of Michael Yeats.

"Bind Us Together," by Bob Gillman, 1977 Kingsway's Thankyou Music. In North, South and Central America by Integrity's Hosanna! Music/ ASCAP. All rights reserved. International copyright secured. Used by permission.

"Rejoice," by Graham Kendrick, 1983 Kingsway's Thankyou Music/adm. in North, South and Central America by inegrity's Hosanna! Music/ ASCAP. All rights reserved. International copyright secured. Used by permission.

Quotations (letters) from *The Life and Time of Mary Ann McCracken 1770– 1866* by Mary McNeill. Permisson: Blackstaff Press Ltd., Belfast: 1988.

ISBN: 0-8024-7737-2

1 3 5 7 9 10 8 6 4 2

Printed in the United States of America

England my passion,
Scotland my joy,
Ireland my pain.

To all who have
suffered for Ireland

ACKNOWLEDGMENTS

Thank you to my lovely Irish friends, who opened their hearts, their homes, and their country to me. Especially to Caroline, David, and Ruth McAfee and Harry and Grace Stevenson.

I invite my readers to join me in praying for the many people and organizations working for reconciliation on both sides of the border, such as Billy and Mena Mitchell at the Local Initiative for Needy Communities (LINC Centre), Ivan and Isobell Miles at the Ark Family Centre, and Pastor Philip McAlister and the Oasis Coffee House.

Also thank you to Sir Jocelyn Gore-Booth for his tour of Lissadell House.

IRELAND

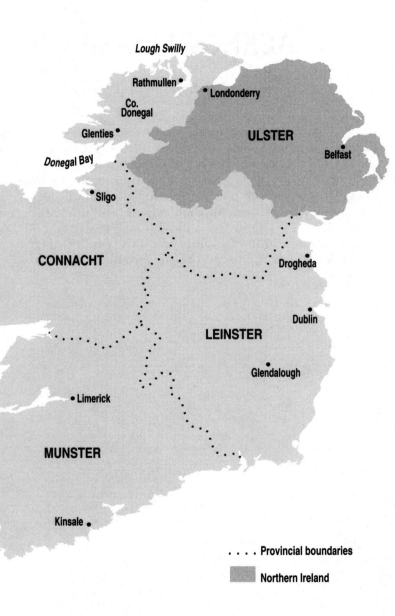

Lough Swilly

Rathmullen •

• Londonderry

Co.
Donegal

Glenties •

ULSTER

Donegal Bay

Belfast

• Sligo

CONNACHT

Drogheda

Dublin

LEINSTER

Glendalough

• Limerick

MUNSTER

Kinsale •

. . . . Provincial boundaries

Northern Ireland

NORTHERN
IRELAND

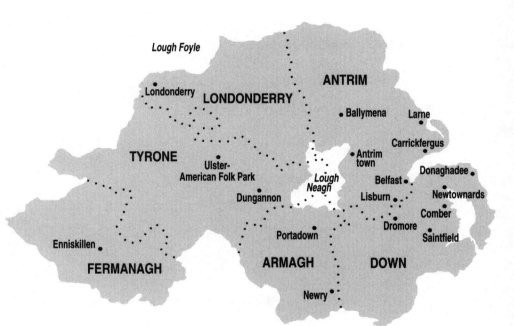

Lough Foyle

ANTRIM

Londonderry

LONDONDERRY

Ballymena

Larne

Carrickfergus

TYRONE

Ulster-
American Folk Park

Antrim
town

Lough
Neagh

Belfast

Donaghadee

Dungannon

Lisburn

Newtownards

Comber

Dromore

Saintfield

Enniskillen

Portadown

ARMAGH

DOWN

FERMANAGH

Newry

THE GENERATIONS OF NORTHERN IRELAND

Generation 1—The Plantations
  1607 The Flight of the Earls
  1610 The plantation of Ulster begins
  1611 King James Bible published

Generation 2—Cromwellian Ulster
  1625 Charles I crowned
  1639 The Black Oath required
  1641 The Uprising
  1649 Charles I beheaded
       Cromwell takes Drogheda

Generation 3—The Ascendancy
  1689 The Siege of Londonderry
  1690 The Battle of the Boyne
  1695 First of the Penal Laws enacted
  1717 First wave of Irish emigration to America

Generation 4—The Union
  1789 John Wesley's last visit to Ireland
  1791 Wolfe Tone forms United Irishmen
  1798 Rising against English rule
  1801 Dublin and Westminster Parliaments united

Generation 5—The Great Famine
  1845 First potato crop failure
  1859 Evangelical revival sweeps Ulster

Generation 6—The Birth of Northern Ireland
  1914 Home Rule for Ireland passed
       World War I begins
  1916 The Easter Rising
       The Battle of the Somme
  1921 Northern Ireland Parliament opened
       Anglo-Irish Treaty signed

THE GENERATIONS

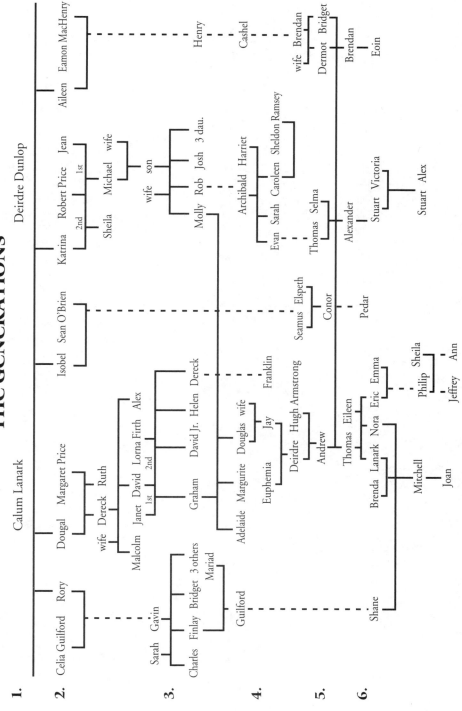

WORD LIST

Except where noted, italicized words are Irish Gaelic. Irish and Scots dialect words are Roman.

abecedarian—rudimentary alphabet book
athair—Irish for father
bairn—babe
bap—bread roll
Battle of Kinsale—1607; England defeated Spain
bawn—fortified enclosure
beannacht—Irish for blessing; a greeting
besom—Scots for obstinate female
biscuits—crisp cookies
Black Oath—oath abjuring the Covenant: required by Charles I
boll—of grain, 6 bushels; of cloth, about 30 yards of fabric
Book of Common Order—by John Knox; regulated worship of
    Reformed church
caidleagh; Scots ceilidh (kay-lee)—Irish for party; usually with singing
    and dancing
cailīn (colleen)—Irish for girl
carrick—man's fashionable greatcoat having multiple capes
chapman—peddler
clachan—cluster of cottages
clāirseach; Scots clarsach—Irish harp
Clandeboye—ancient Gaelic kingdom, now County Down
coo—cow, Scots dialect
copse—clump of trees, thicket
corbie—Scots for crow
crack—Irish for fun
croppies, cottiers—farmers occupying cottages and small holdings of
    land in exchange for rent or services
dearthāir—Irish for brother
deirfiūr—Irish for sister
dia duit—good afternoon

dreigh—Scots for gray, drab weather

farl—three-cornered oatcake

Fenian—member of Irish society dedicated to overthrowing English rule

Flight of the Earls—Gaelic lords of Ulster fled to the Continent in 1607, leaving vast lands leaderless

Garda—Irish police

Glorious Twelfth—holiday commemorating Battle of the Boyne (July 1 on old-style calendars; now July 12)

guineaman—gypsy engaged as horse trading agent

hedge school—school held in fields by priests when Catholic education was outlawed

hornbook—a child's primer having a sheet of transparent horn to protect the parchment

Huguenots—French Protestants who suffered persecution in France

inish—island

Jacobite—a supporter of King James and the Stuart line, usually Catholic

landau—elegant four-wheeled carriage

Leveller—political party aimed at leveling all differences of rank

Loyalist—more extreme Unionist

madra (madoo)—Irish for dog; used as proper name here

māthair—Irish for mother

National Covenant—Scots confession of faith and denunciation of Charles I

Nationalist—one who wants Northern Ireland to become part of the Republic of Ireland

Old English—English who settled in Ireland during Middle Ages and became Catholic

partizan—long-handled spear used by foot soldier

plack, merk, groat—small Scottish seventeenth-century coins

plantations—colonies of English and Scots planted in Ireland by British Crown

rackrent—rent raised on a lease

rapparees—ex-soldiers living as outlaws

Republican—more extreme Nationalist

Rī Sīogaī—Irish fairy king

rieved—stolen

roup—Scots for public auction

Sackville St.—Dublin's main street (now O'Connell)

Scots Confession—first confession of faith by Scots Reformed Church, written by John Knox in 1560

seanachaidh (she-natchee)—traditional Scots Gaelic storyteller *seanathair*—Irish for grandfather

servitors—former English army officers rewarded with lands to colo-
nize in Ulster

Sinn Fein ("ourselves alone")—Republican political party

stramash, stushie—uproar, Scots dialect

stravaig—to wander aimlessly or to enjoy oneself

tā—Irish for yes

taken up—arrested

termagant—an overbearing woman

the Pale—area of English influence around Dublin in early days
(about a forty-mile radius)

Travelers (tinkers)—Irish gypsies of Celtic descent, not Romany

uisce beatha ("breath of life")—Irish for whiskey

uncail—Irish for uncle

undertakers—Protestant colonists who undertook to settle large sections of Ulster

Unionist—one who wants Northern Ireland to remain part of the
United Kingdom

wane—baby (also wee'un)

wheesht—be quiet, Scots dialect

woodkerne—outlaw

wrack—seaweed gathered for fertilizer

wrackers—poor people (usually native Irish) who gathered seaweed

GENERATION ONE

THE PLANTATIONS
1607–1624

I will also make thy officers peace,
   and thine exactors righteousness.
Violence shall no more be
   heard in thy land,
Wasting nor destruction within thy borders. . . .
I the Lord will hasten it
   in his time. . . .
And his mercy is on them that fear him
   from generation to generation. . . .
The Lord shall reign for ever,
   even thy God, O Zion, unto all generations.
Praise ye the Lord.

Isaiah 60:17–18, 22
Luke 1:50
Psalm 146:10

1

All the way up from London, the sun had glistened on the North Sea. But just as they reached the outskirts of Edinburgh, the mists descended on Arthur's Seat, obscuring the welcoming greenness. Clouds swirled around the castle high on the rock outcrop at the center of the city, making it look more unreal, more distant, and more unconquerable than ever.

Mary shivered. Perhaps she shouldn't have come.

She jumped from the train with her two pieces of carry-on luggage and started up the street from Waverly Station, her heart leaping at the sound of the pipes. How comforting they were. She had come home. The piper still played on the corner. The castle still stood on the hill. Although no flags were now flying along Prices Street, Edinburgh seemed even lovelier and more spacious in the late spring than it had at Festival time four summers ago.

Still, Mary shivered. The mist had thickened to a drizzle. Where was he? By the bagpiper, Gareth had said. Then why wasn't he here?

The piper started the next verse of "Scotland the Brave," and the words repeated themselves in Mary's head: *Brave are the hearts that beat beneath Scottish skies. Wild are the winds that meet you. Staunch are the friends that greet you . . .*

So often her heart had leaped at the thought of being greeted by one certain very staunch friend, waiting for her beneath Scottish skies. But now . . .

A passing newsboy caught her attention. "Bomb in London!" He shouted and waved a paper bearing a heavy black headline. "IRA breaks cease-fire! Six dead!"

Mary shut her eyes. How awful! And after eighteen months of peace. She had always thought she would rather like to see Ireland. But if they had returned to throwing bombs at each other, no thank you.

She tried to force her thoughts back to Gareth, but her mind was as blank as if someone had turned off the TV. A moment of absolute terror gripped her. What if she didn't recognize him? She had an urge to dig in her wallet for the picture she carried. But there was no need.

All she had to do was close her eyes to see the springy black hair, the brilliant dark eyes, the strong cheekbones, and the warming smile.

But the memory brought its own fears. What if the sparkle in his eyes was gone? What if, after all, Gareth was really a very ordinary man? Perhaps that was what her father had been trying to warn her of when he hugged her at Newark Airport. He'd reminded her that several planes flew westward cross the Atlantic everyday.

Why *wasn't* Gareth here? Could she have mistaken the place? Could he have forgotten the time?

"Mary!"

She turned at the sound of her name being called with a slightly rolled "r."

But the Scotsman who called her was tall and blond, his light blue eyes covered with silver-rimmed glasses. It was her slightly distracted-looking, academic cousin.

"Brad!" She flew to him with a mixture of relief and dismay. "Where's Gareth?"

"Hello, Bradley, how nice to see you," he teased as he picked up her bag. "Gareth's exam schedule changed. Sharon's fixing dinner at the flat. Sorry the weather's so dreigh for you." He turned up the street toward the bus stop. "There'll be a number fifteen along any minute —or an eighteen. We sold the car—more important priorities—but it'd be handy at times like this."

A maroon double-decker bus soon lumbered along. Brad shepherded Mary and her luggage to a seat, talking all the while in his gently burred voice about his lecturing in geology at the University since he'd finished his degree and how very fine he found life now that he and Sharon were old married people.

Mary was happy for all her cousin's good news, and she made the appropriate sounds when he paused for breath. But the worry she felt pushing at her obscured all other thoughts. What if she had built it all up in her mind? The beauty. The people. Gareth himself.

"I'm coming back to marry you just as soon as I can" had been her parting vow. Who would have thought it would be so long? Four years of letters, phone calls, and not-very-patient waiting. And *were* they to marry? Gareth's letters, though maddeningly sparse, had been as warm and witty as the man himself but exasperatingly noncommittal. So she had made herself hold back after her initial gush of trans-Atlantic mail. She wouldn't continue to overwhelm him.

Then, strangely, over the past two or three months, his letters had almost stopped. Of course, that was because of the pressure he was under preparing for his exams. Wasn't it?

Mary lurched against her broad-shouldered cousin as the bus

turned down Lothian Road at the west end of the gardens surrounding the castle and headed toward the University district. She straightened herself and shook back her long, blunt-cut blonde hair in a gesture designed more to shake out distressing thoughts than to smooth the hair.

Could any land really be as beautiful as she remembered Scotland? But more important, could any person be as wonderful as she believed Gareth to be? They had spent less than two months together in all the time they had known each other. Yet, even apart, their love that had begun on their wild quest through the Highlands seeking the Stone of Scone had flowered and deepened. Hadn't it?

She glanced out the window, and the scene made her catch her breath. "It's so beautiful. Far better even than I'd remembered—the castle on the hill in the center of all this green and all the lovely architecture." Her voice caught, and she took a gulp of the fresh, moist air. "I just can't take it in. It's so good to be back. It's like a fairy tale."

But how long would the fairy tale last? She tried to stop the questions and relax, but the tightness remained inside her. Everything she wanted in the world was here. Would she still think so when Gareth arrived? Would Gareth think so? They had waited so long.

Seeing Sharon reemphasized how long, indeed, it had been. Brad's wife was as delicately beautiful as ever with her cloud of red hair, porcelain skin, and blue-green eyes, but her figure—

Mary squealed and embraced her cousin-in-law the best she could. "Why didn't you tell me?" She looked from one proudly beaming face to the other. "My mother, Auntie Val—they must know?"

"Oh, aye." Brad grinned and shoved his glasses back into place. "Swore them to secrecy, we did. We were saving the surprise. Good news is more fun in person than in a letter."

Mary agreed. And she hoped that would be Gareth's explanation for his recent silence.

A sense of loneliness washed over her as her smiling cousin cuddled his wife—in Scotland they always called it cuddling rather than hugging. When she left four years ago she had thought this was how things would be by now with her and Gareth. Suddenly she wondered if they would ever be.

Sharon ushered her to the sofa. "So, how long are you here for?"

That was what *she* wanted to know. "Forever. A week. As long as you'll have me."

"Well, you can have the nursery until Angus arrives." Sharon patted her abdomen. "So that much is settled."

There was a noise in the hall. "Ah, there you are. Come you in, man."

Mary's heart jumped. Then she stared at the young man who entered. Gareth couldn't have changed that much.

"Mary, I don't think you've met Gareth's brother, David."

She rose and offered her hand to a man who appeared to be a couple of years older than Gareth. He was a little taller, his hair lighter, but he had the same intensely brilliant eyes. And his presence made her all the more anxious to see Gareth.

Sharon gave them all tea, and somehow Mary managed to keep up her end of the conversation. But after the first few sips, her throat closed, and she couldn't take another swallow. Brad and David talked about Davie's work as a computer programmer, but Mary didn't pay much attention. It was obvious that David was a brilliant man, but he wasn't Gareth. And that was all she could think about.

When the men left the room to look for a book of Brad's, Sharon whispered, "Be kind to him. He's a lovely man but rather broken-hearted at the moment, though he doesn't show it. He was engaged for three years—she ran off with an Englishman just two weeks ago. That's why we asked him by tonight. He needs friends right now."

Mary nodded. The room fell silent. She took refuge in a long sip of tea.

The doorbell sounded like a shot going off. Her tea sloshed into her saucer and down her blue and brown plaid skirt.

Sharon glanced at her, then moved toward the door.

Mary couldn't stop herself following into the hall. Her own words rang back in her mind, *I'm coming back to you.* And she was back. She couldn't breathe. Then she saw him. Even blurred through the glass door she knew that dark hair, that brilliant smile.

Then she was in his arms.

Laughing, crying, squealing, she clung to him. "Oh, Gareth . . . Oh, I was so afraid . . ."

"Afraid? What's this?" His Glaswegian lilt was the most beautiful music she'd ever heard.

He pulled back, and they looked at each other.

"Your hair's grown" was all she could say before she was in his arms again.

Sharon's meal was excellent. The tangy sauce and lemon slices on the pork chops were tasty enough to catch even Mary's distracted senses, and the multitude of vegetables that always accompanied a proper Scottish dinner were as fresh and colorful as she remembered. Mary hadn't eaten since her economy flight to Heathrow, but for all that, she couldn't eat for reveling in being in Gareth's company. He looked wonderful. He sounded wonderful. He was wonderful.

She knew she had a foolish grin on her face every time he looked at her, but she didn't care. Fortunately, Sharon plied him with questions regarding the completion of his exams and the schedule for the graduation ceremonies.

Mary was delighting in his description of the anticipated pomp when she was brought out of her golden daydream by Gareth's answer—really his non-answer—to Brad's simple question, "And then what?"

Gareth's vague reply was simple enough. It was the guarded tone of his voice that set off warning alarms in Mary's head. But she couldn't be wrong. Everything *was* just as perfect as it seemed. The moment Gareth had burst through that door and swept her into his arms was the beginning of "happily ever after." She was certain of it.

Then Sharon jumped to her feet—as quickly as someone in her advanced state of pregnancy could jump. "Help me with the dishes, Brad, Davie."

As soon as they were alone, Mary might have run straight at repeating Brad's "And then what?" but Gareth forestalled her. "So what's the news from your side of the Atlantic?"

She hesitated. America seemed so far away. Had it really been only yesterday she left? With the time changes, she was never sure. "Well, let's see . . . I hear Michael has a new girlfriend." She laughed, recalling the man whose ring she had been wearing the last time she came to Scotland. Her eyes rested briefly on the amethyst thistle she wore on the lapel of her blue jacket, Gareth's gift that meant so much to her.

"Oh, aye?" Gareth moved her back to the conversation.

"Yes." She nodded. "A New York model, I'm told. Should be perfect for him."

"Mary." He looked at her very straight. "No regrets?"

"Over Michael? No way. It would never have worked. Even if I hadn't found you." She thought that might move the conversation to something more personal.

But he resisted. "And how was your teaching?"

Mary talked for some time about her end-of-the-year project with her class of lively high school students. Going back to Dartmouth for her education degree had been the perfect thing to do. It had given her a focus for her new life and opened the door to a field she really loved. Earning an earlier degree in drama had been fun but not very practical. Now she knew that whatever she did—and wherever she did it—she wanted to be involved in some kind of teaching or working with young people.

"You really love your teaching, don't you?" He looked up at her with his head bent forward.

21

Yes, she did. She loved the students, the teaching itself, the school . . . but . . . Mary took a deep breath, unsure whether this was the right time or not. Gareth seemed determined not to bring up the subject of their future, so perhaps she would have to. She had always been the rasher of the two of them anyway. "I didn't sign a contract for next year, Gareth." There it was. He could make of it what he would.

He didn't say anything, so she rushed on, filling the uncomfortable silence and holding off the moment when he might be forced to say something negative. "It's so wonderful to be back in Scotland. I'd forgotten how much I love it. I'm so excited to see more—all the places we didn't have time for before."

She warmed to her topic. "I want to go right to the top—to the Orkneys and the Shetlands. Or the Outer Hebrides. Or Ayshire—Rabbie Burns's home and all that." She looked right at him then. "I don't ever want to leave."

He nodded but didn't reply beyond a little "Yep" that let her know he had heard. Why was he so determined not to talk about the future?

She suddenly realized how vague were her own ideas of what the future would hold. All her thoughts had been focused on coming back, on being with Gareth. Well, here she was. So, as Brad had asked, what now? She realized she didn't know anything about being a preacher—minister—vicar—whatever Gareth would be. She had had such a struggle even coming to terms with the fact that he was studying divinity. Then she had so gloriously found the place of truth and faith in her own life that she had really given no thought to the practical application of a divinity degree. It struck her that it could be considerably less practical than a degree in drama.

As usual, she ran straight at the problem. "Gareth, what are you going to do now—preach, teach, write? What do people *do* with divinity degrees?"

During the past four years in New Jersey she had found a small church she loved. The pastor always preached a good message, and she had enjoyed participating in a drama group for Christmas and Easter, but she was really very new to structured Christianity.

Gareth ran long fingers through his hair. "Well, I can't do anything really permanent until I'm ordained. And I have to do my field experience first."

"What's that? Something liken an internship?" When he nodded but didn't say anything, she continued. "So what are you going to do? Where will you go? Do you get to choose? Wouldn't some place like the Highlands be fun? Or right here in Edinburgh—it's so beautiful . . ."

Why on earth did he seem so reluctant? What was it he didn't want to tell her?

"Well, actually, I'm leaving right after graduation."

"I don't understand."

He clasped her hand. "Ah, Mary, I didn't know how to tell you. I would delay going if there was any way. I know how much you want to see Scotland, and I want to take you more than I can tell you, but the job is there to do."

"What job? Where?"

"In a compassionate ministry center in Belfast."

Mary dropped back against the sofa. Northern Ireland? The newspaper headlines she had seen that afternoon swirled in her mind along with all the years of newsreels she had watched of riots and bombings: armored soldiers holding back angry mobs while being pelted with bricks and petrol bombs; pubs and fish-and-chips shops lying in rubble while reporters droned out the numbers of killed and wounded; a busload of schoolchildren bombed.

To her the most awful were the pictures of children, faces streaked with blood or looks of terror in their eyes as they clung to their mothers. The one that most stood out in her mind was of a small boy in striped T-shirt and shorts, nonchalantly riding his bicycle between burning bomb sites.

And now the pitifully short, fragile cease-fire had been shattered. And Gareth was going to *Belfast?*

"How long will you be there?"

"All summer. Maybe longer. I'm sorry, Mary. I would have written, but the opportunity just opened up. And it's so exciting—the Center is doing brilliant work. This is a chance for me to make a real difference."

The sparkle in his eyes spoke louder than his words. She wouldn't ask him to change his plans, even if she thought her asking would persuade him.

So what was she to do? Pack her bags and fly home as her father had suggested? What did she have to go home to? She had no job. Her belongings were all packed for shipping. Her sister Becca would have moved into her bedroom by now, leaving Julie to spread out in the room the twins had always shared.

Well, she could stay here in Brad and Sharon's nursery until "Angus" arrived. Doing what? Or . . .

She forced the most enthusiastic smile she could manage. "Gareth, I want to go, too. I came here to be with you, no matter where." She stifled an impulse to put a hand to her smile to keep it from wavering. "I've always wanted to go to Ireland—forty shades of green, penny whistles, soda bread . . ."

And then he kissed her. Was it just her dizziness from jet lag, or were his kisses that much better even than she had remembered?

It was a while later before either of them returned to sensible conversation. Gareth put a hand on each of her shoulders and pushed her back gently. "Mary, we've got to be serious about this. Your response was so beautiful. So like you to be so generous. I'm sure someone in the church that sponsors the center would put you up. But I don't want to presserize you."

He looked her straight in the eyes. "It won't be all penny whistles and soda bread. The Center is in the middle of the worst part of Belfast—what they call the killing fields. Twenty percent of all the violence in Northern Ireland has taken place within two miles of where I'll be working."

Mary bit her lip. In all the years she'd heard reports of bombings and assassinations, she had never in her wildest imaginings thought of facing such a situation herself.

He put an arm around her and drew her to him. "Don't decide anything now. We both need to give this careful thought."

"Nonsense." Mary's characteristic impulsiveness took over. If Gareth was going, so was she. "I'm going. Why shouldn't I?" She tried to sound sure of herself.

If this was to be Gareth's life, she would do her best. She had had some rather vague visions of being a vicar's wife in a charming village, serving tea to parishioners and arranging flowers on the altar of an old stone church dating from Norman times. Those visions faded as she wondered what the bad part of Belfast was like. She had seen the ghettos of New York.

Mary closed her eyes. Jet lag bore down on her, and she knew she couldn't cope with this right now. Through the haze one thing seemed perfectly clear to her, though. If she loved Gareth, she had to be ready to share his whole life.

As the weight of gravity pulled her eyelids down, her mind filled with old newsreels of bombs exploding, fires burning on rubble heaps, gas-masked army officers patrolling in armored vehicles. It wasn't like that anymore. It wasn't. It couldn't be.

2

"But this is absolutely beautiful!" Mary looked out the car window in amazement. "I thought Belfast would look like the news shots I've seen. It's all shiny and green!"

The sun shone on well-preserved older buildings and well-designed newer ones. And whenever they turned so that she could see to the end of a street, which happened regularly in that hilly city, Mary was surprised anew to be looking out to green fields with gentle hills in the distance. "There's no urban sprawl, is there? It's city, then country, just like that."

Sheila, who had begun the Cross Community Centre with her husband, Philip, met Mary and Gareth at the ferry and was giving them a quick introduction to the city. Her smile showed her perfect white teeth and made her small, sharp features come alive. "*I* think it's lovely, but then it's my wee home. Of course, so much of it is new since the troubles. So much that was destroyed had to be rebuilt."

They drove past a glass-fronted hotel with pillars several stories tall. "That's the Europa—it has the somewhat dubious distinction of being the most-bombed hotel in Europe. Beautiful now, isn't it?"

A few streets on, she pointed out tree-bordered Donegall Square, the hub of the city. "That's our city hall. A bit ponderous, I'm afraid, but the Renaissance style was all the thing when it was built at the turn of the century."

Mary thought the building of gleaming white stone, capped with an enormous turquoise copper dome, looked grand but didn't dispute their hostess's pronouncement. Gareth had just been telling her what an outstanding artist Sheila was and how she used her talents at the CCC.

Then, a few blocks farther along, Mary was confronted with quite another kind of art. Murals. The entire end of a large brick building was painted as a garish political poster. It was not graffiti; the paint was shiny, the lines sharp, the images precise. The green, white, and orange flag of the Irish Republic was depicted waving above a soldier wielding a machine gun. On one side of him the words declared:

ARMED STRUGGLE. The other side read: PEOPLES' POLITICS. Across the bottom ran a silhouette of a mob brandishing weapons, and above them, in letters five feet high was the word REVOLUTION.

Mary shuddered. Then she looked down the street to another building where, against a white background, the red fist of Ulster rose between the British Union Jack and Ulster's St. George's Cross. This mural proclaimed: NO SURRENDER.

The hard-line precision of the murals' execution seemed to symbolize the rock-hard attitudes that spawned them. They were far more obscene, she thought, than any vulgarity sprayed on with a pressure can. IRA . . . UVF . . . BRITS GO HOME . . . FREE IRELAND. And there seemed to be about an equal number for each side. It was militant propaganda reminiscent of Communist Russia or Nazi Germany.

"But how do they get there? I mean, do the people who own the buildings do them?" Mary noted that most were electrified to be brilliantly floodlit at night as well. "Or do they pay rent?"

Sheila gave a sardonic laugh and arched one eyebrow. "Hardly. They just come in and take over. Wire into the electricity of the building, too. The owner is stuck with the bill."

"But that's sheer vandalism. Why don't the owners just paint over them?"

"There's a barn near us. A Loyalist family. IRA put up a mural. Owner painted it out. They broke his back. He's in a wheelchair. It takes only a few smashed kneecaps to send the message."

"But that's mob rule!"

No one even bothered to respond to Mary's statement of the obvious.

Sheila changed the subject. "Now, shall we get you settled in, or would you like to go on to the Centre for a wee while?"

Mary hadn't slept well, and the ferry crossing had been rough. She was aching to get to her room and let both head and stomach "settle in." But she could sense Gareth's impatience to get to his new work. "Oh, let's go to the Centre," she said.

Sheila turned up Donegall Place toward North Belfast. "Actually, it comes to the same thing, since you'll be staying at the Centre, Gareth. Philip and I want you to stay with us, Mary. Our daughter Ann is looking forward to meeting you. Jeffrey—our son—is stopping with a friend at university so you can have his room." A few minutes later Sheila parked her little gray car in front of a remodeled warehouse just off the Shankill road.

Mary looked around warily, remembering the bombings that had occurred in this area. But today all looked peaceful. A few businesses clustered at the bottom of the street near the Centre. Beyond that, rows of red brick, two-storied terrace houses stretched up the hill on both sides of the road. It all had a scrubbed-clean look. No litter. No ramshackle buildings. No bomb sites.

Mary relaxed a little as Sheila led them inside.

The Centre was a hive of activity. Their hostess took them from room to room, introducing workers and clients who happened to be there and explaining the function of each area.

"This is our Braille transcription area." She opened the door to a room where several neatly dressed young men sat at computers.

Tommy, whose gentle smile made Mary feel welcome, explained that he was putting a study guide to the gospel of John into Braille. Explaining how the process worked, he typed on the screen the words of a Bible verse and pushed a button. A moment later he pulled a piece of heavy paper out of his printer and handed it to her.

She ran her finger over the raised bumps.

"There you are, a wee reminder of your visit—John 3:16 in Braille. That verse really got ahold of me in prison—changed my life."

Mary thanked him. Prison? She hurried after Sheila and Gareth, who were moving on to the print shop.

"And upstairs is our woodworking room," Sheila said. "These are all traditional prison industries. Our goal is to help the ex-prisoners in their transition to everyday life by learning to make their skills marketable."

Mary felt as if she had fallen overboard from the ferry. She was definitely in over her head. "Ex-prisoners?"

Sheila nodded. "For paramilitary activities. Thousands are imprisoned. Working with the men and their families is a major part of what we do."

Mary followed slowly as Sheila led them up a flight of cement stairs marked with bright blue handrails. Paramilitary—a polite word for terrorist, she thought. People who threw bombs and shot people in the kneecaps. But Tommy—he'd looked so . . . well . . . so sweet. What had she gotten herself into?

Looking back, Sheila must have read the expression on her face. "You know that's why we started the Centre, don't you? Philip was in prison on a life sentence."

Mary was too stunned to react. That must mean he had killed someone—and she was going to stay in his house?

Sheila's musical voice flowed on. "He started reading philosophy and theology in prison and became a Christian. He'll tell you all about it himself. But basically, when he got paroled out he wanted to do something to help other prisoners and prevent young people from going into crime and paramilitarism."

27

Mary gripped the handrail. She was as much overwhelmed by the matter-of-fact way Sheila said such things as by the information itself. She stumbled as she missed a step.

Gareth grabbed her shoulder and put an arm around her waist. "Steady there. You'll be all right."

Sheila moved ahead and opened a door. "Come in here. We always have fresh tea and coffee in the canteen. I insist on its being fresh—can't stand it when it's stewed."

Mary took the closest chair and accepted a cup. "Thanks. I'm fine, really. Just . . . er . . ." She had no idea what a sheltered life she'd led. This was like being dropped into a new world. "I guess I feel a little like Alice falling down the rabbit hole."

Sheila laughed, and her bright blue eyes, so surprising with her shiny black hair, danced. "What a perfect way to put it. A great deal of Ireland makes as much sense as Wonderland. You'll find all the beauty, adventure, and craziness Alice did, I'm sure."

Gareth began asking their guide more about the work of the Centre.

There were community activities for youth, art exhibits, drama workshops, writers' groups. Sheila explained how important it was for at-risk young people and reintegrating prisoners and their families to be able to express themselves and the important role sports and arts activities played in this.

Mary found it all fascinating, but she needed to sort out her feelings. She was determined not to be a drag on Gareth's work. She had hoped to be a great help. But she had to get a grip on her own reactions. She hadn't realized how little she knew about this country and about what these people had gone through.

Ireland had always existed in her imagination as a romantic, misty land of shamrocks and leprechauns—the home of St. Patrick. But everything was topsy-turvy. Her most romantic fantasies were wrong. Her worst fears were wrong. Somewhere in the middle was the truth. But where? The city she had expected to look like London after the Blitz was beautiful. And Sheila, so petite and sparkle-quick with her smart haircut and rich jewel-tone dress—this talented artist and gracious hostess was the wife of a man who had . . .

"Oh, Philip," Sheila's cry greeted the man who had entered the canteen. "Here are our wee recruits."

As Sheila made the introductions, Mary sized up the perplexing man before her. Philip Armstrong was tall and thin, very trim in a black shirt and gray slacks, but his was a muscular thinness. The square lines of his face were accented by dark-rimmed glasses over brown eyes that didn't seem to miss anything. His thinning hair had perhaps once been blond, but now both hair and skin were . . . Was it only her imagination that prompted her to describe his coloring as prison pallor?

Philip took a chair. "So, you've seen our operation here? What do you think of it?"

That was exactly what Mary was asking herself, so she was glad Gareth answered.

"It's brilliant!" he said. "We've only seen a bit of it, but it's impressive. I can't wait to get started."

Philip nodded. "I'm glad you feel that way. There's so much to do. Most days it seems it's two steps backward for every step forward. We're trying to get the communities on both sides of the road to cooperate for their mutual development, but it's so slow. There's so much in-bred suspicion and just plain pigheadedness."

Philip took a quick gulp of coffee, then turned back to Gareth. "I'm glad you're here. We have a meeting with a group of Unionists from the Shankill tonight. If we can get them to agree to meet with a group of Nationalists from The Falls, they might be able to get funding for a center for their youth. They need one desperately. These young people don't even have a place to play Ping-Pong. And now with the cease-fire broken—"

"Yes, I'd like to come." Gareth leaned forward. "I want to see how this works—what you do to bring people together."

"Good." Philip was on his feet. "I'm late for a committee meeting right now, but—" he looked around and pulled a sheaf of stapled papers from a stack on a nearby shelf "—here. This explains our conflict mediation process. We'll be working on the first stage tonight." As Gareth took the manuscript, he said, "Our live-in rooms here are on the top floor. Have you been up yet?"

Gareth shook his head.

"I'll pick you up here about half six. We can get some fish and chips on the way." And he was gone.

"Do you want to come out to the house with us, Gareth?" Sheila asked.

He looked up from the papers he had already started reading. "Oh . . . uh . . . no, thanks. I think I'll get stuck into this so I can understand what's going on tonight." He looked at Mary. "You'll be all right, won't you? Sheila will make you comfortable."

Mary bristled. She didn't want to be taken to the suburbs and coddled. If this was to be Gareth's work, she needed to get used to it. She wanted to work, to learn, to help. But she forced a smile. "Yeah, sure. I'll be fine. I'll have an early night. You can tell me all about the meeting tomorrow."

"Right. That's good. I'll ring in the morning." He brushed her cheek with a kiss.

Mary felt certain his first thought was to sit right down and read Philip's paper, but the innate good manners that had first attracted her to him quickly came to the surface. He walked her down the stairs and out to the car, held the door for her, and waved her away. Then, she was sure, he turned straight to his papers without giving her a second thought.

That was Gareth. Jump in with both feet and full steam ahead. Complete dedication to his work. Fine. But what about her? What about *them*?

The next morning, Mary sat in the Armstrong's small dining room while Sheila, who had refused her help, sang softly from a kitchen that emitted joyful sizzling sounds and tantalizing bacon and fresh bread smells.

She looked out on the green fields surrounding the housing estate and, over the laundry fluttering on Sheila's clothesline, admired the gentle hill in the distance. She could almost smell the clean freshness of the white linen as the sun sparkled on it.

Then the phone, sitting on its little brown table in the hall, gave three sharp rings, and Mary jumped at the sound she had been waiting to hear. She couldn't wait to learn how Gareth's meeting had gone last night. Would the young people get their community center?

What did Gareth—Mary sat back. She would have to wait a while longer for her answers. She could tell from Sheila's end of the conversation that this was Ann, ringing to say she would be staying late at school.

Mary had glimpsed the Armstrongs' daughter only long enough to be introduced to her last night, but was sure she would like the trim, shy girl when she had a chance to get acquainted. Ann was small and sharp-featured like her mother, but she had shiny, bouncing, honey-blonde hair like Philip's must have been before prison took the shine off.

Sheila came in with glasses of orange juice and a brown pot of tea on a green tray. "Ann said to wish you a good day from her. She won't come home until the library closes. The poor wee girl never takes a break. I don't know if she can keep up this pace for another six months. Sometimes I wish she weren't quite so intense." Sheila disappeared again into her kitchen.

Mary shook her head. Apparently the stress of study required to prepare for A levels—exams that would determine the fate of the rest of one's academic career—was something quite beyond the comprehension of American teenagers. And Ann hoped to take hers in five subjects, an unusually heavy load. Mary was glad she hadn't had to face anything so life-determining when she was seventeen.

"There now." Sheila returned, holding a blue-rimmed plate. She set the heaped platter before Mary.

"My goodness! That's beautiful." Mary's eyes grew wide at the colorful presentation.

"Ulster Fry. The only way to start your first morning in Ireland." Sheila pointed out the components of the dish: soda bread, potato bread, fried bread, eggs, bacon, sausage, mushrooms and onions, tomatoes.

Mary burst out laughing. "This is incredible! But shouldn't you be at the Centre rather than here spoiling me? I don't want to keep you from your work."

Sheila sat down and spooned marmalade on her own slice of soda bread. "No, I'd be working at home today anyway. I'm getting our next wee exhibit organized. This one will be a bit different because it's to be the work of current prisoners, rather than ex-prisoners and their families like we usually do."

Mary concentrated on arranging a bit of fried bread, egg, and bacon on the back of her fork. She was determined to eat continental style as everyone here did, but learning how to handle a fork upside down in her left hand was a challenge. When the bite was successfully accomplished, she looked at her hostess. "Sheila, I hope you don't mind my asking, but don't you ever worry? I mean, about being safe?"

Sheila set down her cup. "Not much for myself, but for Ann and Jeffrey. Especially when they were wee. I'm sure I overprotected them. I think now that's probably why Ann is so shy. But she was only five and Jeffrey nine when Philip went to prison. I had the total responsibility for seven years."

Mary couldn't imagine what life must have been like for this petite woman, alone in a violence-racked country with two small children, trying to keep their home together on the salary of a community art teacher. "It must have been awful." She took a gulp of orange juice. "But that's not what I meant. That is, I meant . . . er . . . working with prisoners . . ." How could she phrase it when Sheila's own husband was an ex-prisoner?

"I know this will be hard for you to understand, Mary. Impossible, maybe. But there's a sharp distinction here between paramilitaries who are fighting for a cause and criminals who mug and rape and murder for their own gain."

Mary didn't say anything, but everything she had seen in the news made her think that the paramilitaries had mugged and murdered plenty of people.

Sheila must have read her mind. "Yes, the paramilitaries are violent. And it's wrong. But, of course, on our side of the road we would say that the UVF was some different because they were responding in defense against the IRA."

Sheila didn't seem the least bit reluctant to talk, so Mary persisted. "How did you feel at the time?"

"About Philip's involvement, you mean? I had no idea he was involved—beyond a strong commitment to Unionist politics. The families of the men almost never do. Until they're arrested or shot."

For the first time Mary glimpsed the emotional scars left by the horrors this lovely woman had lived through.

Her hostess took a deep drink of tea. "And now with the cease-fire broken—when that bomb went off in London, we were devastated. It was like a bereavement. People were physically sick. The thought of going back to that after these months of blessed peace!"

Sheila lowered her head, one hand pressing between her eyebrows as if she had a headache. "We can't go back. I don't think I could take it. And Ann and Jeffrey—they had never known what it was to go to the cinema or any of the things young people do without fear hanging over them."

Silence hung in the room, and Mary thought of her study of the Thirty Years War. It had always seemed unthinkably awful. She could never imagine what it would have been like to live through thirty years of war. But that was exactly what these people had experienced.

Then Sheila gave a little shake of her shoulders and looked up. "As for working with the men now, that's one of the differences in working with former paramilitaries rather than criminals. There's very little recidivism. When the men get out, they just want to get back to their wee families and make something of their lives. A large percentage go into community work.

"Prison does that—gives them time to educate themselves, to think and sort things out. It's so easy to get caught up in the fervor of defending your way of life. We lose our perspective."

Mary was amazed to see that she had cleaned her plate while struggling to make sense of everything. She was just finishing her tea when Philip came in, and she jumped to her feet when she saw Gareth behind him. He could never look anything but wonderful to her, yet she noticed he was pale and drawn. She resisted the urge to fling herself into his arms.

When she crossed the room to him, he held out his arms and enfolded her. For just a moment she rested her head on his shoulder, drinking in the comfort of being with him. "How was the meeting?"

"Hard to tell. Philip said we made progress. I found it pretty confusing."

She smiled. "You too? I've been talking to Sheila. I'm not sure I've ever seen anything like the courage these people must have to carry on with it all."

As the four of them went down the hall, Mary noticed that Gareth's limp was back. It was just a small dragging of his foot that occurred when he was tired—a reminder of the severely broken leg he had been convalescing from when they first met.

Sheila opened the door into a cozy living room with green carpet and soft mauve upholstered furniture arranged in front of a window that offered a panoramic view of the farming valley.

"So did the two sides agree to build a community hall?" Mary asked Philip as soon as they sat down.

Philip's lopsided smile, accompanied by one raised eyebrow, was ironic almost to the point of cynicism. "They might in six or seven months, if things go well."

"Why, that's wonderful! They'll have their leisure center by next winter!"

Now the smile was decidedly cynical. "I've heard of American impatience." He shook his head. "I meant they might be *talking* to each other before Christmas."

"Oh." Mary blinked. "But I thought they'd already decided they wanted the facility."

"They decided that years ago. Each side decided for themselves. But the only funding available is for cross-community development. That means it has to be for both sides of the road. Which means they have to talk to each other first."

Mary's impulse was to accuse Philip of kidding her, but his expression told her this was not a joking situation. The divisions were so deep here that just getting people to talk to each other was a major challenge. She was beginning to understand the headlines that for years had topped news reports of the hassles surrounding political and diplomatic talks over the Irish question.

"How do you go about getting them to talk?"

"Our constituents come to me; the other group goes to my Nationalist friend Padraic, who runs a center similar to the CCC about a mile up the road. We start with three questions: What do you want the other community to think about you? What do you think the others think about you? What do you think about them? When they deal openly with those questions, they always see that the fears and perceptions of each side are exactly the same."

Mary was amazed. How many times she could have put a similar process to good use when dealing with obstreperous students. "And *then* they'll work together?"

"Not so fast." He held up a hand. "That's the first step. The community leaders each go back to their groups with the identified areas of common interest and common complaint. That's when they put the question to them: Would you be willing to meet together?"

She caught the implication. The question was *meet* together—still a long way from *work* together. "And if they will?"

"If both sides will sit down with a trained mediator, they have a good chance of developing the mutual respect we hope will result from the process. Once they feel they can trust their neighbors, they can work together for parallel development."

Mary felt dazed. All that, before young people could have a place to play Ping-Pong. How wonderful to have kids throwing balls rather than bricks and petrol bombs. If they could just get them together. "What a wonderful thing you're doing, bringing together people who have been battling far more than a quarter of a century."

Philip's shout of laughter was so harsh with irony it hardly sounded like laughter. He slid down in his chair and ran his hands through his thin, pale hair, the veins standing out on his sinewy arms. "You're right to say *more* than a quarter century. Actually, it's more like four centuries."

Mary gaped. "People have been fighting with each other here for four hundred years?" A clock on the mantel beside her struck the hour. For a moment she left thoughts of conflict to note the ornate scrollwork on the iron and gilt case. "What an unusual clock."

Philip nodded. "That's been in my family for about four hundred years, too. And in Ireland almost as long. I guess you could say that clock has seen it all."

"But I had no idea the trouble went back so far. What started it all?"

He hunched his shoulders inside his polo shirt. "Of course, there had always been trouble—squabbles between the various Gaelic lords. And it wasn't unusual for them to look across the water for support for their various causes. The entire Norman and Elizabethan periods are full of such stories. But most people date the beginning of the troubles from the Plantations."

Mary's mind briefly filled with visions of wide-skirted Southern belles walking on the pillared veranda of an antebellum home while slaves sang a spiritual in the cotton fields. Those certainly weren't the plantations Philip referred to.

"Ulster was left essentially leaderless by the Flight of the Earls, so James the First—"

"Wait!"

Philip must have seen the consternation on her face. "Yes, it is a confusing story—a tangled tale of noble sacrifice and greedy violence with plenty of right and wrong on both sides. I'm not sure anyone understands it completely."

Mary frowned. "But if we don't understand the past, how can we understand the present or make plans for the future?"

"Right." Philip gave her one of his fleeting smiles. "As they say, we need to know where we've been to know where we're going."

She looked at Gareth. If his work was to be in Ireland, even for a short time, she was determined to understand what she could of this country. Supreme was her desire to work out her relationship with Gareth. But perhaps before she could do that, she needed to find her own place in the larger scheme of things. And central to that, as long as they were in this mystifying land, would be to make sense out of Ireland.

Philip, never still for long—as if he had to prove to himself that he was no longer held in by locked doors—jumped to his feet. "Tell you what—I have a meeting in Londonderry tomorrow afternoon—the All-Ulster Reconciliation Union. We're searching for a new approach to bringing people together—something beyond peace rallies and interfaith hymn sings. But anyway, we can make an early start, and I'll take you around Lough Swilly to Rathmullen first. There's a wee heritage center there that makes sense out of the Flight of the Earls—as much as anything can, I expect."

Mary agreed readily. If this did make sense, it would be the first thing to do so since she fell down the rabbit hole.

3

The cry of a gull swooping over the silvery-blue surface of misty water welcomed Mary to Lough Swilly.

She hadn't realized that Philip's early start would mean half past five in the morning. But almost two hours ago, as they sped westward on the motorway at the rapid pace at which Philip seemed to do everything, she had suddenly jerked awake. "Uh-oh. I didn't bring my passport. I didn't think about the fact we'd be crossing the border."

"No problem." Philip looked over his shoulder at her. "You won't know you've crossed. Not until you notice the difference in the roads and hedgerows. Thank goodness they haven't reactivated the checkpoints. God willing, they'll never have to. It was such a nuisance—checkpoints crossing the border, checkpoints entering cities . . ." He pointed to a concrete tower with massive electronic equipment standing inside a heavy chain-link fence. It was as deserted as a medieval castle—or a concentration camp.

Mary shivered.

They were several miles inside County Donegal in Eire before the motorway came to an end. Philip turned north onto a small road winding between dewy green banks and untrimmed hedgerows. For a while they followed a small burn until it ran under a stone bridge and went gurgling toward the sea. Mary rolled down her window, and the car filled with fresh air glowing with morning sunshine.

The tide was out when they reached Lough Swilly. The wide mud flats, the gleam of water beyond, and the softly rounded mountains rising through the haze had a magical look. The whole scene was as gentle as a watercolor.

Mary slipped her hand into Gareth's. They had come to learn history, but maybe here in this peaceful spot, as a gull's cry called her toward the silvery mist-shrouded scene, she thought they could really talk about their future.

She leaned her head against his shoulder. "Gareth—"

"A great deal of Ireland's history has happened here." Mary jumped at Philip's brisk voice. He had stopped only to make a phone call. "This is where Lord Mountbatten was fishing when the IRA blew up his boat in 1979."

Mary sighed and moved away from Gareth. So much for the peace and beauty of this spot. She had read of the terrorist attack that killed the queen's favorite uncle. Mary decided that she would have been about eight years old at the time.

"It's also the lough Saint Columcille sailed from with his band of monks when they left Ireland to take Christianity to Scotland. Columcille—you may know him better as Columba—was born about fifteen miles southwest of here."

"Oh!" Mary smiled and relaxed. With St. Columba she was on familiar ground. She moved closer to Gareth again. A squeeze from his hand told her that he too was thinking of those enchanted days they had spent in the Highlands following Columba's steps.

But Philip was indefatigable. "And Wolfe Tone was taken prisoner here after the failure of the French expedition in support of eighteenth-century separatism." He grinned at Mary's baffled look. "Ah, lost you there, did I? Not to worry. We'll save that for another day."

Before Mary and Gareth had turned from the lough, Philip was halfway up the stairs leading from the beach to the gray stone Martello tower that was home to the exhibition.

With a continuing narrative, he hurried them forward, through the gate in the stone wall surrounding the courtyard and on up the outside stairs leading to the second story. "This battery fort is one of six fortifications on the lough built by the British around 1810 as a defense against a Napoleonic invasion of England through Ireland—which, of course, never happened."

Gareth stopped in embarrassment at the ticket barrier. "Um—I forgot about changing my money."

But Philip was ahead of them. He thrust tickets and a guidebook into Gareth's hands. "Absolutely no problem. No problem at all. I always carry both kinds of currency. You two go on. I've arranged to meet my colleague here so we can go to the meeting together—present a united front." He glanced at his watch. "No hurry. We've got plenty of time. Enjoy the exhibit." He dashed off.

Gareth grinned at her. "Right. Well, since we're here . . ." He opened the guidebook and read aloud:

> "On 14th September, 1607, a ship pulled up anchor and set sail for Spain, carrying into exile the last great Gaelic Chieftains. This exhibition focuses attention on the period leading up to the Flight of the Earls and the subsequent plantation of Ulster which rendered the extinction of the ancient Gaelic Order and saw Ire-

land enter a new phase in her history—that of a kingdom united under the English monarchy."

Mary shook her head. "Wish me luck. I feel lost already." She gazed up at a life-size wax figure wearing a green and gold velvet suit in the style she thought of Sir Walter Raleigh wearing. "'Red Hugh O'Donnell,'" she read, "'went to Spain for aid after the battle of Kinsale and was poisoned there by a spy.'"

She moved on to a figure in a saffron, red, and green plaid cloak and brown felt hat with an enormous eighteen-inch brim, which, the notice said, was worn by the ordinary foot soldiers of the day. At the moment Mary felt much in need of a teacher to take her by the hand and explain it all to her in simple words.

On the other hand, she and Gareth could dash back down the stairs and onto the beach. "Don't hurry," Philip had said. She could still get her chance to talk to Gareth before Philip took him off to that council meeting.

But already Gareth was in the next room, studying the illustrated story boards that covered the walls.

She started to skip ahead to catch up with him, then stopped. She had pulled herself out of a cozy bed at an unearthly hour because she truly wanted to learn about this. She was having a terrible time concentrating, but one thing seemed clear: from the beginning of time, the kings of the Four Provinces of Ireland—Ulster, Munster, Leinster, and Connacht—had fought among themselves for the high kingship.

Focus on this. Just read the words, Mary, she told herself.

In the middle of the 12th century the kings of Leinster and Connacht struggled over control of Dublin, which even then was the power centre of Ireland. The king of Connacht was winning when King Dermot of Leinster took the action that changed the course of Irish history.

He appealed to Henry II of England for help. And the Irish king swore fealty to the English. With that act Ireland was brought into the feudal world and began the struggles with England that have lasted until this day.

Mary was standing before a picture of Elizabeth I in all her jeweled splendor when Gareth returned. Her hand naturally slid into his.

"So it seems England had already ruled Ireland about four hundred years when Elizabeth came to the throne," he said.

Mary smiled and nodded, but she was thinking about him. He had finished touring the exhibit. Now he was going around again with her. The thought warmed her as she realized anew the patience and thoughtfulness of this man beside her—the man she wanted beside her for the rest of her life.

She pulled herself back to Elizabethan Ireland:

When Elizabeth came to the throne the English ruled The Pale—a 40-mile area around Dublin. The rest of the country was ruled by lords of ancient Celtic clans, with The O'Neill the head of the whole network.

The accompanying picture panel showed an enormous man in green kilt and jerkin. A scarlet cloak was held around his shoulders with a brooch the size of a man's hand. The long-haired, russet-bearded O'Neill stood proudly atop a rocky outcrop, gripping a huge broadsword. Two dirks hung from his wide leather belt. He was backed by a group of equally fierce-looking clansmen. Seventy-five years after the Reformation began on the Continent, Sir Hugh O'Neill led the Counter-Reformation in Ireland.

The next exhibit explained that Queen Elizabeth passed the Acts of Supremacy, establishing the Anglican church in Ireland. But she was lenient in the enforcement of the Acts because she feared driving the old English inhabitants of The Pale, mostly Catholic, into alliance with the Gaelic Irish and Spanish.

In an effort to establish control, the Crown began a concerted effort to encourage the settlement of English communities on Irish land. Ulster, which had always been the most unruly of the provinces, resisted.

In the 1590s, Hugh O'Nell, the earl of Tyrone, undertook to expel all English officials from Ulster.

Mary became so engrossed in the story that, when she stepped out on the balcony overlooking the lough, events four hundred years past were still vivid in her mind.

***

The dawn mist swirled, then lifted. The red-bearded man drew his green cloak tighter about him as he watched the tall-masted ship rocking gently in the lough like a great white bird. A shift of the breeze drew the vaporous curtain, shutting out the solitary picture of serenity. Sir Hugh O'Neill, earl of Tyrone, came back to the chaos around him.

His wife clutched his hand with both of hers and tugged urgently. "Hugh, Hugh. Why do you stand there so? They tell me there will not be room enough even for these few items we brought with us. What are we to do? How can we make life in a new land with *nothing?*" She started to sob.

Hugh put his arm around her in an awkward attempt to offer comfort. "Here, here, wife. Don't carry on. We'll be welcomed aplenty in Spain. There's naught left for us here."

"Yes, yes. We'll have our lives, but—" She looked around wildly, then gave a sudden shriek. "Conn! Where is Conn?" She dropped her husband's arm and darted off through the throng crowding the sandy beach, shouting for her son, who was nowhere in sight.

Horses snorted and stamped, tossing their heads in the crisp air. Babies cried. Gentle waves lapped the shore of Lough Swilly. Hugh had replied with hearty confidence to his wife, but his mind swirled with misgivings more chilling than the fog around them.

He had been so certain of the rightness of his actions when he had undertaken to drive the English from Ulster. It had been easy enough to gather support. He styled himself champion of the Counter-Reformation, and Catholic Philip of Spain rushed to his aid, sending four thousand Spanish soldiers to join the small band of Irish Hugh O'Neill led.

Aye, they had marched proudly, the Spanish in their dark armor on their fine, high-stepping horses, lances and pikes gleaming in the sun. And just as proudly marched the common Irish foot soldiers, wearing their Kilcommon cloaks and broad-brimmed felt hats with as much dignity as if clad in breastplates and helms.

They had marched to Kinsale with spirits high. Each Ulster lord led his men: Hugh O'Neill himself at the very fore, then the Red Hugh O'Donnell of Tyrconnell and his brother Rory, and Cuchonnacht Maguire, lord of Fermanagh. Who could stop them? Sure and was not God Almighty on their side? It was His church they were fighting for, to rid their land of the vile Reformers. Never before had the English in Ireland been challenged by so mighty a force.

So they had arrived at near the southernmost tip of Ireland. And there they were met by twenty thousand of Elizabeth's finest troops, commanded by Lord Mountjoy.

The Battle of Kinsale was bloody, brief, and decisive. The Irish-Spanish coalition that had threatened the very survival of English rule in Ireland was crushed with unquestionable finality. Never again would the old Gaelic lords rise to challenge English rule.

Winter of 1601, that was. Six years ago. The war itself had dragged on for another year, while Mountjoy completed the subjugation of Ireland.

But even then, O'Neill had entertained no thought of flight. Maguire was the one who had planned and schemed that for more than a year. Military service to King Philip of Spain would be far preferable to a life of poverty in Ireland, the lord of Fermanagh argued.

O'Neill, however, had returned to his vast earldom and worked to strengthen his control over his subchieftains and tenants. Indeed, he had been in Meath, helping the Crown's lord deputy in court sessions when a messenger arrived from Lough Swilly.

All was ready. A Breton fishing vessel awaited them, carrying silver and gold from King Philip. He would welcome the lords of Ulster to his service. O'Donnell and Maguire with wives, children, soldiers, and principal gentlemen were already en route.

O'Neill was caught between devil and sea. If the others fled and he remained behind, he would be accused of staying to rouse the country against the Crown. If he went to London for help, he would be thrown in the Tower as a rebel. The Spanish ambassador had already warned him of a plot by the English to poison him.

Yet, this was his native land. These were his people. It was his job as chieftain to protect and care for them. To fly to his own safety would be to leave his people leaderless, his lands unguarded. Still, they would be equally leaderless if he remained and was imprisoned or killed.

So he had hurried home to Dungannon and hastily gathered his household. They had fled by night to this desperate gathering at Rathmullen on the shore of the Swilly.

"Hugh!" His wife was back, her red hair wilder, the dark circles under her eyes blacker than before. "Conn is not to be found. No one has seen him since we left Dungannon! Where is our son?"

Hugh had no idea, but he could not feed his wife's hysteria by saying so. "He is well, wife. Like as not he took the tender to the ship with O'Donnell's men. Hush, now. You will find him safe on board."

A splashing of oars told him that the rowboat had returned from the larger vessel. O'Neill's men began hauling the most necessary of their baggage toward the water. This was the last load. Twenty strides and he would leave Irish soil forever.

"Come. It will be well." He grasped his wife's hand and led her forward. It would be well. It had to be.

Behind them were the stamp and jingle of horses left without anyone to hold their bridles. Ahead of them, the plash and roll of the waves. Overhead, the cry of seagulls.

The mist closed down, and Ireland was gone.

Mary turned back inside to view the last room. This told about the Plantations. Ah, here they were—not Old South cotton plantations but settlements more like Jamestown on the Virginia coast. The picture showed men and women in seventeenth-century clothes building a stockaded community and tilling fields beyond. "In 1603 James VI of Scotland had become James I of England and Ireland," the story board explained. "After the earls' flight, the lands of the Gaelic lords were seized by the Crown."

"'The undutiful departure of the Earls of Tyrone, Tirconnell, and Maguire offers good occasion for a plantation,'" an official of the Crown wrote to his sovereign. "'The whole realm, and especially the fugitives' lands, are more utterly depopulated and poor than ever before for many hundred years.'"

The king liked his officer's advice. He set about with vigor to establish a colonization process in Ireland—especially in "Ulster the Difficult."

Mary read about how the new order established towns and how, under James's plantation system, Ireland's medieval economy—in which cattle were the prime indicator of wealth—gave way to a modern market economy.

She was startled by Philip's voice behind her. "And that's how it came about that my ancestors came across the water."

"Oh, were they planters?" Mary asked.

"Well, no, not strictly speaking. They came to County Down, and Down and Antrim weren't 'planted'—they were settled. But they became part of the whole process that pulled Ulster from the medieval to the modern world in one generation.

"Planting to civilize the land and persuade the native population to the monarch's point of view was nothing new to Ireland. Mary Tudor had tried it fifty years earlier as a means of making her Irish subjects more governable. But James was particularly fortunate. Of all such attempts, his Ulster Plantation was the most successful."

"Or most devastating—depending on your wee point of view."

Mary turned to meet a pair of laughing green eyes in a freckled face framed with rusty red hair and a russet beard a few shades darker.

Philip put an arm around the shoulder of the short, stocky man. "This heathen Irish here is Padraic O'Reilley—the man who works with the communities on the other side of the street, as we like to say. You can see from his attitude what a cross I have to bear. But he's Dublin-born, so he can't be held responsible."

"And don't I have to struggle to do the best I can for my poor wee people living in occupied Ireland?" The lilt in Padraic's voice, even more than his mischievous grin, told Mary that the banter was a healthy outlet for these men from very differing backgrounds who worked together for the good of their communities.

Philip explained that Paddy's organization was called "Peace." It was a sort of pun, because sharing the peace is a part of the Mass where everyone turns and says, "Peace," to each other.

"I'm delighted to meet you, Padraic." Mary held out her hand.

To her surprise, Padraic bowed over her hand rather than shaking it. "And wouldn't it be just like this canny fellow to be introducing me to a fair colleen to distract me from the council meeting?"

"Give over, Paddy," Philip said. "I was the one who said we needed to be getting on to Londonderry."

"Right." Padraic dropped her hand. "Time to be getting on to *Derry*." His emphasis underscored the political significance of what one chose to call the second largest city in Northern Ireland.

Mary shook her head, smiling.

Gareth grinned and shrugged. "He probably supports Celtics, too." Even which football team was supported had political and religious meaning.

They were almost to the car when she said, "I'd like to hear more about your family sometime, Philip."

"Ah, would you? Well, then . . ." He veered from the car door he was about to open. "I just happen to have something here in the boot that might interest you. I had thought you could amuse yourself shopping this afternoon, but you might like to take a look at this. It's something I put together while I was a guest of Her Majesty. We'd kept boxes of old letters and journals in our family for hundreds of years. I doubt anything would ever have been done with them if I hadn't had enforced time to put it all together." He handed her a spiral notebook from the top of a stack of six similar books.

"Hope you can read my chicken scratches. My Auntie Joan in Newtownards has been asking to read the lot of them. Had them with me because I thought I'd be getting over there soon."

By the time they drove back across the border, Mary couldn't wait to read the manuscript she held in her hand. Perhaps this would be a key to the understanding she had come for.

Philip parked in a lot outside the medieval walls of Londonderry, still standing in perfect repair. "Only completely walled city in the British Isles," he said. "Best place to read would probably be in the gardens of Saint Columba's Cathedral." He pointed to twin towers rising above the stone wall. "We'll walk you there. Our meeting's close by."

Philip set out at a long-legged pace that Mary had to run to keep up with. She would have loved to have had a chance to take in all the historic architecture and charming, winding side streets, but she needed to focus all her attention on Philip's explanation.

"Appropriate setting for the story, too. One of the major actors was George Montgomery, who became Bishop of Derry."

Padraic gave a crow of triumph.

"Well, that's what it was called then, Paddy." Philip grinned at him. "Before modern civilization." He turned back to Mary. "Anyway, George and his brother, Hugh, were spies for King James.

"Conn O'Neill, lord of the Gaelic kingdom of Clandeboye, was a prisoner in Carrickfergus Castle. O'Neill agreed to divide his estate with the Montgomery brothers if they could get him a pardon from King James. They did, and that's how the Montgomery family got vast tracts of land in County Down, and—"

"Enough with you," Padraic interrupted. "Let the lady read it for herself. She'll do better without your editorializing."

Mary settled herself on a wooden park bench in the shade of a beech tree with a pansy and marigold bed at her feet. She looked up just in time to wave to Gareth before the men turned a corner at the foot of the cathedral grounds. Then she sat back and gave all her attention to the story Philip's pages told.

4

Calum Lanark's round breeches, padded stiff with bombast, chafed above his knees. His footsteps rang hollowly on the tiles of the great room of Dunlop Hall, a substantial merchant's home in the center of Glasgow. He ascended the black oak staircase, arguing his fate on each step.

"My Calum—" in his mind, Alisdair Dunlop offered his hand across the marquetry top of his walnut table "—you have lived a son in this house for fifteen years. I know your worth well."

But then, on the next step, Calum saw Deirdre's father jump up so fast the ball-and-claw feet of his chair skittered across the plank flooring. "So, this is the way you repay my generosity for giving you a home after your father died?"

Calum gripped the bannister and forced himself upward. A few more steps, and the scene in his mind shifted again. This time he saw Dunlop's sharp-pointed brown beard broaden as the face of the wool merchant who held the key to all Calum's future broke into a smile. "Do ye think me blind, man, that I've not seen the fondness between you and my Deirdre grow these many years? I'd no' say nay to my daughter's happiness."

He walked along the tapestry-hung gallery to Alisdair Dunlop's private sitting room, trying not to recall the man's jutting, furrowed brow, which gave the impression of a perennial scowl.

"Never! Are ye daft? Do ye think I'd marry my only daughter to a man who owns nothing more than the clothes he stands up in?" Dunlop grew an alarming shade of red, matching the enamel frame of the mirror behind him.

Calum had played the scene so often in his mind that it took him a moment to realize this was his answer. There was not another step to climb, another answer to imagine. He stood before the breathing man.

"And I'll not have ye in my house harboring such ambitions. Fifteen years I've fed and educated a viper in my nest." Dunlop paced to where a vigorous fire burned on the grate but failed to warm the February night. "I'll not throw you out in the black of night—but be ye gone by midday tomorrow."

Calum took a step backward. This was worse than anything he had imagined. One could not have lived in this household without knowing both Alisdair Dunlop's temper and the doting fondness he held for his one daughter among three married sons. Indeed, it was this fondness they had counted on. Deirdre had been certain her father would indulge her anything.

His back against the door, Calum tried again. "Sir, your daughter's happiness . . . Deirdre and I—"

Dunlop thundered so that a Delft bowl atop the spiral-legged cabinet rattled. "*Deirdre!* I'll not have you speak my daughter's name. Deirdre is to be betrothed to Fergus Ingram."

Calum tried to absorb what he heard. Ingram. The tobacco lord. The one with the fine mansion on Queen Street. He was double Deirdre's age. And fat. "But—but his wife just died. Only two months past—"

"All in good time, man. When it's decent."

Decent? It would never be decent. The idea was obscene. Calum groped for the door handle.

"Noon tomorrow—be ye gone. And see ye take nothing but what was your father's, or I'll have the sheriff after ye."

All the way down the stairs, Calum saw Alisdair Dunlop's black eyes glaring from under his jutting brows, and his words rang in Calum's head.

His feet hadn't touched the woven mat at the foot before a slim figure shot from the shadows under the gallery and grabbed his hand.

Deirdre, her soft leather slippers barely brushing the clay floor tiles, pulled him into the small porter's lodge beside the front door. It was long past the hour when the porter kept a check on visitors through the narrow squint window, and the room was deserted.

"I heard. I heard it all. Fergus Ingram!" She threw herself into Calum's arms. "We'll go now. I'll not stay here another night. Come."

She started to pull away, but Calum caught her shoulders and steadied her. "Deirdre. Deirdre, my love." She relaxed under his touch and laid her head on his chest as he stroked her back. "Do you think I'd take you out in a winter's night? With no place to go? I love you, Deirdre. I want to take care of you."

She stiffened, and he felt her hysteria rising again. "There must be someplace we can go. I must get away. I won't marry fat Fergus!"

"Now, now." He cuddled her in his arms and rocked gently. "Of course, you won't. But we've some time. Ingram's wife died in November. We've eight months till he's out of mourning. Be patient, Deirdre. Trust me. I'll find us a place."

46

His chest grew warm where her head rested against it. The tiny room was filled with only their breathing.

At last she asked, "Where will you go?"

"I'll find a place. I'm strong. I'm educated. I could be clerk to another merchant, work on a ship, a farm. I don't know. But trust me, my Deirdre."

In the dim light he more felt than saw the nod of her golden curls. He allowed himself only one kiss. But he did not hurry, for that kiss needs must last for many months.

"I must pack now." He turned toward the hall.

"Calum—"

He stopped at her urgent whisper.

"Send me word where you've gone."

He paused, trying to think how he would accomplish that.

"I must know how to pray for you."

And that was the answer. "The kirk yard. The big oak. Come early to prayers."

Calum wasted little time on sleep that night. He had few enough possessions to pack, but it was not an experience to be rushed. One leather satchel of clothes and personal items and two wicker baskets of belongings held his whole life. He had been ten years old when his father, Dunlop's clerk, died of a fever.

Gordon Lanark, who had raised his only child after his young wife died in childbirth, had been a father to be proud of. After long days of bargaining or record keeping for his master, after purchasing bales of wool at market or the weekly selling of cloth at Merchants' Hall, he had devoted time to teaching his son to read, write, and do sums.

Calum rubbed his hand over the leather cover of his most prized possession—the Bible recording the marriage of Gordon Lanark and Isobel Wishaw, and the birth of their son Calum on 15 August 1581. He wrapped the Bible in a doeskin bag and placed it in the Bible box his father had always kept chained to the foot of his bed.

By precept and example Gordon Lanark had taught his son the value of diligence, honesty, and industry. Now those teachings were to be sorely tried. Calum took his mother's ring-pattern quilt off his bed and folded it in the bottom of his last rush basket. Then he looked at the two household items that his mother had brought to their marriage from her father's house—a pair of brass candlesticks and a small clock in an iron and gilt case.

He hesitated. His fine linen shirts and padded doublet had been paid for by Alisdair Dunlop. He did not want to give the man any excuse for labeling him thief. But surely his long hours of keeping books for the merchant justified considering his clothes as wages? He used the clothes to wrap the candlesticks and clock. Then he looked at the pitiful huddle of baggage on the bare floorboards. After twenty-five years, could a man's life amount to so little?

Calum looked longingly at the small shelf of books near his bed: slim, leather-bound volumes of Sir Francis Bacon's *Essays*, Sir Thomas More's *Utopia*, and a collection of poetry by William Shakespeare, Sir Philip Sidney, Ben Jonson, and Sir Walter Raleigh. Only the More was old enough to have been his father's, and it wasn't. These dear friends he would miss sorely. But someday he would buy more—not a mere shelf but a whole library—for his sons. His and Deirdre's.

But first he must make his way in the world. He sat down to await daylight. He would go to the market at Glasgow Cross where Salt Market and High Streets crossed Trongate and Gallowgate. There he would buy a wheelbarrow to pile his belongings in, and then—well, then he would not stop searching until he found a place to make a home.

As soon as he heard stirring on the back stairs, he went down to the kitchen. He would not leave without bidding Cook and the servants farewell. He wished he had enough in the small leather pouch he carried inside his doublet to give them each a coin for the care they had taken of him all these years. But that was not possible. He had little enough, and dear only knew how long it must last him until he found a position.

Calum had just reached the first landing when the sound of angry voices stopped him. Surely Alisdair wasn't berating Deirdre in such harsh tones? But as he listened, he realized it was Cailean, the oldest Dunlop son, who was receiving the full force of Alisdair's temper this early morning.

Calum shook his head. Cailean was Deirdre's favorite brother. He had a rich wife and three beautiful children. He was the perfect son and heir, one would think. But Cailean Dunlop was never reliable.

His heir's unreliability seemed to be the theme of today's castigation. "The business in Gourock port did not require you to go so far afield . . ."

Calum moved quietly on to the kitchen. He didn't have his words of farewell out of his mouth before Cook shoved him to a seat at the end of the well-scrubbed table in the center of the room.

"Well, ye'll not be leaving wi'out your porridge, and that's final." She ladled a mound of oatmeal into a pottery bowl from the iron pot suspended in the massive stone fireplace, then poured on a layer of thick cream before setting it in front of Calum. A generous slice of ham and two slabs of fresh brown bread followed with a mug of ale.

Calum eyed Alisdair Dunlop's merchant mark carved on the right-hand side of the oak fireplace beam. Master Dunlop had given him until midday to be gone. He was entitled to break his fast first. He squared his shoulders and enjoyed his meal without any feelings of guilt.

Nor would Cook hear of his leaving her kitchen without taking a thick wedge of cheese, half a roast chicken, and a supply of oatcakes wrapped in a linen napkin.

Calum shook his head. "I might justify the food, but not the master's linen." He produced his own cotton kerchief to wrap the food.

It took him some time to locate a seller of carts and barrows at the bustling market. Indeed, it struck him that he had never seen the market so a-buzz, especially midweek in a winter month. But it was not long before the nub of the matter began to come clear. News was always the liveliest commodity at market.

The cart seller conducted his business almost offhandedly, allowing Calum a price of several merks less than he normally would have done had he been willing to extend the bargaining. But it was obvious he was anxious to turn again to the tale that had come up the Clyde with the morning's fishing boats.

"Ye say Montgomery's leaving Eglinton lands and taking his fine household to *Ireland?*" Jesse Carter slapped his leather breeches and gave a hoot of laughter. "Now that's as fine a tale as ever I heard!" The carter held his sides. "And all because some wild Irish got out of prison in a cheese?"

"No, man. Will ye listen or no?" The fisher gave him a cuff on the shoulder. The ensuing scuffle brought an increased audience, until a fair number stood around the market stall to hear the tale and to add to the confusion by contributing their own bits of information.

Apparently the hero of the hour wasn't the earl of Eglinton but a cousin of his who also owned lands in Ayrshire. The younger Montgomery was known to desire lands in Ulster. So when the Gaelic lord Con O'Neill wound up in Carrickfergus Castle at the end of the recent Irish wars, Con's wife approached Hugh Montgomery for help.

Calum drew closer to the news-bringer. It was even possible to temporarily forget his own troubles as he listened to the improbable tale that the fishmonger swore was true. It seemed that in exchange for O'Neill's promise to sell a goodly portion of his lands to him, Montgomery had arranged for O'Neill's escape and pardon. He began with sending an agent to court the gaoler's daughter.

"The resourceful lad plied his oar so well that in a few nights he'd won the maiden's love."

Here the listeners broke out in hoots of approval.

The fishmonger's wares lay forgotten on their beds of wet seaweed while he told how Con's wife, on one of her visits to the prison, smuggled in a rope to her husband, concealed in a great cheese that had had its core carefully hollowed out and the top replaced.

It only remained for the gaoler's love-smitten daughter to open the door of his cell and Con to let himself down the castle wall into a boat. Montgomery was rewarded with a third of the Clandeboye.

A short, fiery-haired man to Calum's left gave a shout and struck the air with his fist. "Aye, and there it is! The Irish and English war for nine years over that land, and the Scots finish with the prize. Aye, there's a fine thing. A fine thing!"

Calum piled his belongings in his newly acquired barrow and turned away from the noisy crowd. It was all very well to be rejoicing over a Scot's victory, but he would not feel very victorious sleeping in a field tonight, which is what he would be doing if he didn't locate some employment quickly.

He thought of going to Merchants' Hall, where he had so often worked for Dunlop. Many there knew him. Surely someone would be in need of a clerk who wrote a neat hand and could add columns of figures in his head. But he had gone only a few steps along Clyde Street when he realized that no colleague of Alisdair Dunlop would hire a man driven out by a fellow merchant. For the first time, Calum realized how truly bleak his prospects were. He had no reference, no one to vouch for him.

Which way should he go? He was about to turn south to the waterfront in hopes of seeking work on one of the small boats that came up the Clyde, when the bells from St. Mary's steeple chimed the hour. That comforting sound armed him. The kirk. He would go there. The Rev. Mr. Irving would be a sympathetic listener, even though he was unlikely to know of a situation. Still, there was little the parson didn't know.

Only by a shifting of his thin shoulders under his black jacket did Parson Irving betray his amazement at finding Calum Lanark with all his worldly possessions in a wheelbarrow on the doorstep of the manse. "Come ye in, lad, come ye in." His thinning hair emphasized the roundness of the head above his white Geneva bands, which proclaimed him a minister of the Reformed faith.

Calum made quick work of his story. Master Dunlop had thrown him out for daring to seek the hand of his daughter, and now he must find a new place to build his life.

Irving crossed his spindly legs and leaned back against the settle. "Aye, and have you heard of the opportunities across the water?"

Calum wrinkled his forehead. "In America? I don't think I'd much like to be going so far away."

"Nay, lad, the narrower water. I mean the new settlement in Ireland."

Calum smiled for the first time since he had made his fateful advance up the staircase at Dunlop Hall. "Oh, aye. You mean Montgomery's new lands in Ulster? The market's a-buzz with stories of rope in a cheese and the Gaelic lord a-hiding in a church steeple. Fine tale, but it's hard to make sense of it."

Irving crossed to where light from a small window fell on a table against the whitewashed wall. He ruffled through several papers, then triumphantly produced a small pamphlet. "Just give this a wee looking at."

Calum held out his hand. It took him only moments to grasp the import of the document. Sir Hugh Montgomery, ready to tenant his newly acquired lands with trusted people from his Ayrshire estates, was seeking undertenants to complete the settlement.

> Fayre Scotland, thy flourishing sister, brave Hibernia commandeth unto thy due consideration her youngest daughter, depopulated Ulster. Dispoyled, she presents herself in a ragged, sad robe. There remaineth nothing but ruins and desolation, with very little show of humanity; while of herself she aboundeth with many of the best blessings of God.
>
> Goodly Ulster, wasted by rebellion, for want of people her pleasant fields and rich grounds remain desolate . . .

There followed a list of the divers artificers such as smiths, masons, and carpenters, who would be most welcomed for the building of cottages and booths. The notice also provided the terms for undertenants. They would be provided passage and allotted grazing land if they could supply cows and sheep.

"'Make speede, get thee to Ulster, serve God, be sober.'" Calum read the closing exhortation aloud and looked up into Parson Irving's lively eyes.

"It doesn't mention a need for clerks," Calum said.

"And is that all ye'd care to be doing?"

"No. No, beggars canna choose. But I've no carpentry skills, and I own no cattle."

"And what would you, if ye could choose?"

"I'd own land." The words were out of Calum's mouth before he realized how farfetched such ambition was. Or how deep his desire. Orphaned since the age of ten, he had ever lived on the sufferance of another. Until he heard it from his own mouth, he had not known the strength of his longing for a place of his own.

But now that he spoke it, he realized that always, when he had pictured the future with Deirdre, it had not been living on as a clerk in Dunlop Hall but in their own home. He also realized the impossibility of it.

Parson Irving didn't laugh. He did shake his round head, though. "Well then, lad, ye'd best be learning to work the land, hadn't ye? There's a wee bit of the story ye may not have picked up in the market but that, I'm thinking, will make Montgomery o'eranxious for good settlers. The quiet word is that another third of the O'Neill land has gone to Montgomery's fellow adventurer James Hamilton. And that there's no love between the two. Some are saying there'll be a fierce competition between them to establish the most vigorous settlement. Such might work in the interest of a hardworking lad such as yourself."

Still overwhelmed by the whole concept, Calum looked back at the pamphlet in his hand. "It doesn't mention references, but . . ."

Irving smiled. "I'm thinking a warm, breathing body with reasonably sound limbs is all the recommendation you'll be needing. But as you've been a lad in my parish these many years, *I* can give you a character."

A short time later, Calum thrust Parson Irving's recommendation inside his tightfitting doublet, took his leave of the manse, and wheeled his barrow toward Bridgegate, where, the pamphlet stated, Montgomery's agent could be found.

As the iron wheel rattled over the cobbles, a plan formed in his mind. The required cattle were the main stumbling block. He felt the leather pouch inside his doublet and mentally counted the small supply of placks, merks, and groats. Perhaps enough to buy a few chickens. Certainly not sufficient for what he hoped would become the sires and dams of a fine herd of cattle and flock of sheep.

He was making his way back through the square when he decided what he must do—and not in the busy, bustling market but in one of the small shops in Glassford Street.

The clockmaker squinted at him over his high-bridged nose. "Eh, it's fine enough workmanship, but how do I know it isn't stolen?"

Not until he had handed his mother's marriage clock across the counter had Calum realized how hard it would be to part with this family heirloom. But at least he could assuage the clockmaker's suspicions. He drew out Parson Irving's recommendation of his character.

"Oh, aye. I know the parson." The clockmaker named a sum far less than Calum figured he would need.

Reluctantly, Calum added the finely wrought brass candlesticks to the bargain. It took considerable moaning and haggling from the wizened clockmaker and even more tenacity from Calum, but in the end they reached an acceptable agreement.

He turned northward then toward Cowcaddens Common, where cattle could be bought and then grazed until he sailed to a new life.

The sky clouded over, and a gentle rain began to fall, but Calum's spirits rose. It had been less than twenty-four hours since his world fell apart, and already he had made his plans. He would be an under-tenant, but in a land underpopulated and open to opportunity there would be a chance to advance. That was all he asked—a chance.

5

Less than two weeks later, Calum stood at the rail as the wind took the sails above his head and the *Dalriada* sailed out into the Firth of Clyde. As the ship rolled, he gave thought to his cattle in the hold. He had been disappointed that the best bargain he could drive resulted in only one cow and three sheep, but by the time he had driven them the twenty-five miles from Glasgow to the port of Gourock, he was thankful he had no more to manage. He hoped his inexperience with animals hadn't been too obvious to the others taking ship with him. Some would be his neighbors in this new venture.

As a thickening mist shrouded the steep, forested hills banking the Clyde, Calum gave a last look at the ancient standing stone above the village. Kemprock Stone, in olden times used by fishermen in rites to ensure good weather, was today used by couples about to be married, who circled it for good luck. The thought of holding Deirdre's hand in his and walking around the rock brought a cramp to his heart so sharp he caught his breath.

Closing his eyes, he saw her again as she had been a week ago when he had taken leave of her under the old oak beside St. Mary's kirk. Parson Irving had given Calum a pallet by the fire until he set out for Gourock, and Calum felt sure he had known of the secret meeting. The parson had never given St. Mary's bell a longer, more insistent ring, ensuring that any in the vicinity would hurry into the kirk rather than into the churchyard to disturb the couple.

The rail Calum gripped was hard and cold, but the memory of Deirdre's warm, soft hands was vivid.

"Aye, I'm to Ireland with Sir Hugh Montgomery's settlers. It's all arranged—land to lease for crops and grazing. I'll work hard, Deirdre. And I'll build you a fine house."

But instead of the enthusiastic response he had expected, her round blue eyes grew even wider. "Ireland? But it's a *savage* place. I've heard tales of wolves that eat orphans. And woodkerne—lawless men who set out on innocent people."

"My Deirdre, you are named for an Irish princess who fled to

Scotland with the man she loved in the days when *Scotland* was a savage place. Will ye not do it now, the other way round?"

Yes, of course, she would—anywhere with him, she had declared, clinging to him. And he had renewed his vow to return for her before eight months were out.

Her face, framed by her stiff white ruff, looked pale and drawn. "But, Calum, do beware the wolves."

"Isn't this a grand adventure!" A chiming feminine voice at his elbow jerked Calum from his memories.

He turned and looked straight into the brightest emerald eyes he had ever seen. Copper curls danced in the wind from under a white linen cap, and the young woman's cheeks glowed from the salt air. As a matter of fact, it seemed that everything about her glowed. The most surprising thing was that she almost matched Calum's considerable height.

"Er . . . Miss . . ." Calum pulled off his high, feathered hat. He was glad now that, hoping to make the best impression possible on his future neighbors, he had chosen to set sail in his best blue wool quilted doublet and padded breeches. It was obvious that his companion was noting his starched white collar and lace-lined cuffs.

"Ailsa Seaton." She sketched a curtsy, holding out skirts already widened by her fashionable farthingale, and laughed. "My brother Fulke is somewhere about. I should let him make the introductions for our family, as Papa will never stir himself. But it does seem silly to stand on ceremony when we're all off to start a new life together."

"Er . . . yes. Of a certain you're right, Miss Seaton. Are you from Glasgow, then?"

"No, no. From Braidstone"—Sir Hugh Montgomery's estate in Ayrshire. "Papa is to have the largest land lease because he's Sir Hugh's chief tenant."

"Oh, aye? What a fine thing." Calum had hoped his fellow settlers wouldn't be standoffish, but he wasn't prepared for such openness.

"And Papa and Fulke will build the finest house in the settlement—other than his lordship's, of course."

"Of course," Calum murmured.

"The Adairs and the Bracklies and Cathcarts are on this ship. The Harveys and Logans will sail next week. Simply everyone is going to Ulster. In two years we'll have a more fashionable establishment than any in Ayrshire." She smiled at his blank look. "Oh, but of course, you wouldn't know any of them, would you? You're not from Braidstone."

"No, from Glasgow."

"Oh, well, I'm certain you'll get on very well. And many will be coming. It's the only way for advancement. Everyone says so. My broth-

55

er talks incessantly about the rising population and soaring rent and food costs at home. Fulke says there's no scope for investment in Scotland." She looked at Calum's well-cut circular cloak. "But then, I expect that's why you've come, too."

Calum was feeling distinctly uncomfortable. He wanted to make a good impression but not a false one. All he owned in the world was a cow and three sheep and the contents of three containers piled in a wooden barrow.

His vivacious companion chattered on of the opportunities for advancement in a place offering cheap and fertile land with woods and fishing close at hand.

Just then they entered the wider waters round the Isle of Arran, and the *Dalriada* was tossed by a high swell. Ailsa, who had been standing up-deck of Calum, was thrown off balance.

Calum caught her just before she hit the high, wooden side of the ship. "Whoa, steady there. Are you all right?"

To his surprise, she did not pull away but nestled in his arms. She looked up and batted her eyes at him. Then, with a gurgle of laughter, she drew back. "Oh—Fulke—" She reached out to a man who appeared to be only a year or two Calum's senior. "Fulke, this kind gentleman is to be one of our neighbors. And I'm persuaded we could do no better. He's already saved my life, and I don't even know his name."

Calum introduced himself to Fulke Seaton, and Fulke presented his trim, dark wife, Effie, whose thick plaid cloak failed to hide her just rounding pregnancy.

"And where is your lease to be?" Fulke asked Calum.

"Er . . . I don't know exactly. The agent was somewhat vague."

Fulke looked surprised but answered smoothly, "Well, never mind. There's plenty for everyone, I'm told. Mind you get the largest lease you can, though, if you're going to be about making eyes at my sister."

"No!" Then Calum realized how ungallant his response was. "That is, yes. I thank you for your advice."

Further conversation stopped as a long-faced man dressed in black and gray ushered his wife, son, and daughter along the deck. "And a good day to you, Mistress Johnstone," Ailsa called out.

The woman gave a tight-lipped nod and continued her progress.

Mumbling an excuse about checking on his cattle below deck, Calum took leave of his fellow settlers. What had he gotten himself into? he wondered. He did wish he could be as optimistic as Ailsa Seaton.

Many hours later, he was still wondering. The *Dalriada* was sailing along the mouth of Belfast Lough as the first rays of the sun struck the stone walls of Carrickfergus Castle. They did not, however, take port beneath the crenelated gold and brown stones, but sailed on south across the lough to the fine new harbor Montgomery was building at Donaghadee.

The bustle of disembarking was unbelievable. Amid the mooing, squawking, and crying, Calum's head rang.

The worst came when he was finally ashore and sorting through the cattle pens that had been hastily erected on the sandy beach. He grasped the handles of his wheelbarrow. Somehow he must herd his beasts along the miles of rutted road leading southward across the top of the narrow peninsula.

Just beyond Donaghadee, Calum fell in line with the stream of other settlers from the ship. The well-to-do had brought horse-drawn wagons and carts and so could ride the seven miles to their new home. Some, like the Seatons, had servants to see to the cattle herding and baggage carting. Calum found himself walking to the rear with the servants and others who had come, like himself, seeking an undertenancy. At first he wondered why he was receiving so many odd looks from his fellow herders.

Then a saucy-looking girl who was herding geese with a long pole fell in step beside him. "And aren't you a fine-looking fellow to be driving your beasts with a barrow!"

Unsure how to answer, he looked at her rough homespun kirtle, her apron, and the plain white kerchief around her hair. Then his gaze shifted to his own mud-spattered but well-fitting hose and breeches. He realized that his clothes, appropriate for the household of a Glasgow merchant and mingling with gentry aboard ship, were hardly appropriate to his new state in life. He tried to stammer an explanation, but the girl merely laughed and urged her honking geese on along the dirt track.

The land they crossed was green and rolling. As the sun climbed toward midday, the morning haze cleared, and the air took on a special quality—the soft clarity of rain-washed, windswept air under a pale sun and gentle blue sky. Calum filled his lungs with a deep breath. The land, the very air, were as unlike anything he had known in his busy market city as his clothes were unlike those of his farm-bred companions.

In the gentle landscape there rose in the distance, a bit off to his right, one steep hill. That must be Scrabo, the ancient hill fort the agent had mentioned when he described the area. And straight ahead, whenever the road came to the top of a rise, he could see the gleam of the sun on water. The town Montgomery was building—or rather, rebuilding—was said to be at the top of Strangford Lough, so that sheen of silvery water must be the place.

Then his attention turned to his obstinate sheep. He shouldn't be looking at the countryside, no matter how pleasant. Moving his beasts forward required all his effort.

He waved his stick with a warning shout at his placid red cow. She had stopped her plodding pace to nibble a bit of the spring grass and bright yellow and purple wild flowers that lined the road. "Get on wi' ye, ye stupid coo."

She lifted her head, looking around at him with liquid brown eyes, then returned to her grazing.

"Go on, ye wee Besum!" He abandoned his pushcart and increased the fervor of his threats. Besum continued her midday meal. With the halt of their small band, Calum's sheep had wandered into the green field to the left. "Now, come back here, ye!" He started across the field after them.

A hoot of laughter stopped him, and Calum jerked around. Matthew Johnstone, son of the unsmiling couple he had seen aboard ship, stood holding his sides. "Have ye never herded a coo in your life?"

Calum started defending himself, then thought better of it and turned his back on the youth. He'd show him. But as he tramped angrily forward, the sheep increased their pace.

"Nay, man. Let us help." Matthew was still laughing, but his words were kindly spoken. He whistled to the black and white dog at his heels. In a matter of minutes, the wayward sheep were trotting back toward the road.

Calum gave Matt Johnstone a rather embarrassed nod, seeing that he had misjudged the boy. Though the youth, probably five or six years younger than Calum, was tall and thin and as soberly dressed as the senior Johnstone, his brown eyes held a mischievous twinkle that must have often put him at odds with his dour father. "I thank'ee," Calum said.

Matthew nodded. "Glad I could help. After all, we're to be neighbors. Tell you what—why don't I take these in with my lot? You don't seem to have anyone to help you, and I've got Coll and Anna—the dog and my sister." He gestured toward the small, white-faced girl in black dress and white cap whom Calum had seen holding to her mother's skirts on the deck. "Course, Coll's worth a lot more than Anna!" The lad laughed and took off at a long-legged lope.

Coll directed Calum's wayward sheep forward.

In an effort to make up for lost time, Calum pushed on at an energetic pace to which Besum, having had her graze, now made no objection. As the road wound through one of the thick woods that appeared to cover much of the peninsula, Calum overtook the party ahead of him and discovered that the man on horseback overseeing the work of his servants was Fulke Seaton.

Calum greeted his shipboard acquaintance.

Fulke returned the hello and, in his direct manner, spoke the thought that was on his mind as if they had been in conversation the past mile. "Oak, ash, elm, alder—do you have any idea what that represents in terms of barrel staves, ship timber, rafters?"

Although his experience had been with the wool merchants, Calum did, indeed, have an idea what quick profit one could turn by felling such woodlands.

Fulke spread his arms and took a deep breath. "We've come to the land of milk and honey, man. The Promised Land."

Calum supposed their trek did seem to bear some similarity to the Exodus. "Are you suggesting we're to take the place for God?"

Fulke tossed back his head, making his dark, pointed beard jut forward, and gave a shout of laughter. "Well, we're His people, aren't we? So I reckon using the land for ourselves comes to the same thing."

Calum was still trying to decide whether Fulke was being callous, practical, or blasphemous when the road curved past what appeared to be the remains of a burned-out abbey, and they arrived at last at the "Promised Land" of Newtownards.

Calum could only hope that the Promised Land description would prove more accurate than the name of Newtown, for this was a very old place, indeed. Old and dilapidated. He could see no more than thirty buildings, and none of them had stone walls or complete roofs.

The community huddled around a former Dominican priory, probably abandoned at the time of the dissolution seventy years earlier. The priory walls were stone, but like the smaller cabins around it, the building stood roofless. The remains of a tower house—perhaps once the home of an O'Neill lord—stood in the priory grounds.

The masons, carpenters, and smiths that Sir Hugh had had the foresight to bring with him were hard at work. They appeared to be supervising the work of both settlers and native Irish to make the tower house habitable for the Montgomery family and build cabins and booths all along the High Street.

Already a temporary market cross had been erected where Movilla and Castle Streets formed a Y with High Street. Calum, with his merchant's background, smiled. Apparently, Sir Hugh well understood that the establishment of an urban community would be more profitable than the letting of agricultural holdings. Besides, the fate of any new colony depended on the establishment of successful towns.

In spite of his background, however, Calum had no desire to spend his days in a merchants' hall or clerk's office. He wanted his own land in this new Canaan. A place to build for Deirdre and their children. Always it was the picture of Deirdre he held in his mind, urging him forward. Every Sunday, Parson Irving had admonished his flock at St. Mary's that the one doing the urging on must be God, who had predestined and called them. God was to motivate them. But it was Deirdre who motivated *him*. He could only pray that God had ordained that he and Deirdre be together.

With such thoughts as these, Calum approached the newly established office where leases, tenancies, and rents were settled.

Behind a long table sat a man with a well-trimmed beard and full, red cheeks. He wore a long velvet coat with fur-trimmed sleeves of the kind Glasgow merchants wore. Surrounding him were clerks busily penning documents and sorting papers. Calum joined the queue for an audience with Montgomery's chief agent.

The sharp tone of the man at the head of the line caught Calum's attention, and he recognized Calvin Johnstone.

"I will have no wild Irish on my land. And no incoming undertenants—either from Scotland or England. The scum of both nations, that's who'll come, I can tell ye. Debtors, breaking and fleeing the law, seeking shelter beyond the reach of man's justice in a land that knows little yet of the fear of God."

He half turned and scrutinized the settlers behind him with a hard eye. "No, I'll have none of it. And if ye're wise, ye'll none, either."

Johnstone turned back to the table and with a flourish of the quill pen signed his lease grant. The agent poured a blob of red wax onto the document and stamped it with Montgomery's seal.

Johnstone marched out, and the queue moved forward.

Calum looked over the shoulder of the man in front of him to see the large map of the Montgomery lands spread out on the table. As each lease was assigned, the agent carefully penned in the tenant's name. For all the apparent activity in the settlement, only a few of the leases were as yet allocated.

Calum remembered the optimistic, if vague, assurances of the agent in Glasgow: "Yes, yes, man. Land and enough for all to farm. Must have one's own cattle, of course." And then he had gone into a glowing account of the land, the woods, the fisheries, all of which appeared to have been true. Calum had been so glad to learn of a place where he could build a home that he hadn't asked much. And there had been nothing signed. Now he began to wonder how he could have been so rash.

The man before him completed his business and left, smiling.

Calum approached the agent.

Name? Assets? Experience? The agent barked his questions and frowned at Calum's answers. Not from Braidstone? Not a Montgomery tenant?

"No, I read the pamphlet you circulated. The agent in Glasgow said . . . " Calum stumbled to a halt. What had he said? What a fool he had been to come so far with no assurances.

The agent was speaking in a bored voice. ". . . leases granted only to tenants of proven worth and experience . . . only the most valued retainers . . ."

"But the man in Glasgow said you need able-bodied, hardworking men to farm!"

"Ah." The agent's cheeks puffed even wider when he smiled. "Your business is not with me, then. I'm certain any of our established tenants would rent you an acre or two in return for your labor." Then he apparently recalled Johnstone's words, because he added, "That is, most would be likely to."

Calum walked blindly into High Street. No lease? No tenancy? Just rent land on a hand-to-mouth basis? How could he build a life for Deirdre on such terms?

He kicked at a clod and turned toward the common. No matter what, Besum must be milked and the dim-witted sheep looked to.

6

Dawn came early in September, and the rooster who lorded over the hens scratching around Calum's cottage never failed to herald the first gleam. Calum groaned and rolled off his straw pallet. He could not get used to the feel of bare feet on a beaten earth floor. He sloshed water from a clay jug into a bowl on the table and sluiced his face. A brisk rub with a coarse linen towel helped get his circulation going.

He dunked a rocklike oatcake in a mug of ale to get it soft enough to eat. He could cook porridge, but it didn't seem worth unbanking the fire, when he would be out all day.

In the mote-filled light coming in the tiny window by the door, Calum surveyed his one-room house: the nook beside the fireplace where the bed would go, table and dresser on the opposite wall, cobble hearth set in the earth floor. He had a chimney—not just a smoke hole in the roof as most cottiers had. And soon Seamus O'Brien would help him build a proper bed. And Seamus's wife, Una, would make a ticking mattress for him to spread his mother's quilt on. There was so much—so hopelessly much—he wanted to do before he brought Deirdre here. But at least he would have a marriage bed.

He must make another chair. A proper one with turned legs. And when the barley was harvested, he would buy a copper kettle to hang from the chain in the fireplace so they could always have hot water. How he wished he could have a proper floor of wooden planks or stone flags for Deirdre. But that was unlikely, even as good as the harvest promised to be.

The past six months had been unimaginably hard. Yet they had been good, because every morning he woke with the knowledge that he was one day closer to the time when he would be able to go for her.

The blow of learning he wouldn't be allowed to lease land had been staggering, but Fulke Seaton had agreed to rent him two acres on the vast Seaton holding south of Newtown. Two acres for the rent of one boll of barley per acre. A fair price, especially when the harvest promised to be so good.

It didn't belong to him, he only rented from Seaton, but it was a start—a roof over his head. Someday he would have a real home for establishing a family—his own house on his own land—freehold, with goodly acres on a long-term lease. That was what he wanted. But for now he must be satisfied with the roof over his head. It was thatch, not slate, but it was a roof.

He could never have accomplished even such a meager start without his nearest neighbors, Seamus and Una. Only a few years older than Calum and with five bairns, the O'Briens were determined to stay on the land where their families had lived for generations. Fortunately, Montgomery did not clear the settlement of native Irish, and Seaton was glad enough to make use of the native Gaels for cutting timber and constructing buildings. Most of them, like the O'Briens, spoke this harsh-sounding Irish gabble among themselves but knew enough of the king's English to communicate with the settlers when it suited them to do so.

Calum had wondered at Fulke's quickness to offer land to one so inexperienced as himself. But Seaton had proved to be an excellent landlord. Ailsa came several times a week, bringing oatcakes or soda bread from the bake house she supervised at the fine manor they were building. Last week it had been a jug of her fresh-brewed ale.

Milking stool and pail in hand, Calum tramped through the dew-fresh grass to the pasture Besum and the sheep shared. He didn't mind the milking, now that he'd got the way of it. But today he was anxious and more to be done with it so he could go into Newtownards. This was the day that the trader would be over from Scotland.

Rabbie MacKinnon sailed the twenty-one miles across the Irish Sea every fortnight bringing welcome supplies to sell at the market cross. And he was always obliging about carrying letters back to the settlers' kinfolk.

Making soothing noises to Besum, who was anything but the disagreeable female her named implied, Calum looped a rope around her nose to make a halter and tied her to the rail fence. He had learned the wisdom of this precaution the day she wandered off after a tender clump of grass right in the middle of the milking and knocked the pale of warm, sticky milk all over Calum.

As the spurts of milk spattered into the wooden bucket, Calum thought of the letter lying folded and sealed on the windowsill in his hut. It was the first he had allowed himself to write to Deirdre, for the danger of their communication's being discovered by her father was great. But this one time he must dare—in care of the excellent Parson Irving—because it was to tell her he was coming for her. Surely the sweetest words ever penned. Even sweeter than the writing of "I love you," much as he had longed to send her those words.

Besum stamped a leg and swished her tail at a fly, nearly hitting Calum in the face. He patted her flank reassuringly, almost without breaking the alternating rhythm of squirts and without losing his train of thought.

He had first been attracted to Deirdre by her beauty, sweetness, and high spirits. Then he grew to love her most for her faith and courage. He would almost say stubbornness. He smiled at the memory of her sharp, jutting little chin and her snapping blue eyes when she was determined on a course of action.

But as the weary months apart dragged on, he had discovered that the thing he missed most was being able to tell her he loved her. He had played the night of their parting over and over in his mind, and always ended with an ache to be able to say those words to her again. Now he had done so. On paper, at least.

Grasping the half-full bucket more firmly between his knees, Calum shifted to the second set of teats and continued his pattern of stripping the milk down. But telling Deirdre he loved her was a small accomplishment next to the news he had to impart that he would come for her in October. Just a few more weeks. The thought was so astounding he almost lost his coordination.

Rabbie MacKinnon said mid-October was the latest he could count on sailing without fear of a quick-rising storm stranding him on one shore or the other, and Rabbie never liked to be away from his family in Scotland for more than one night. So Calum had set the date, giving himself as long as he could to get everything in order here—the best order he could, anyway. It would never be really good enough for Deirdre, he thought with a sinking heart. And yet he must not wait so long that there would be danger of her being left in Glasgow through the winter to be forced into betrothal to Fergus Ingram.

The plans were all set with Rabbie MacKinnon. "Aye, Besum," he told the cow, "only a few more weeks and ye'll have the fairest mistress in Ireland." He laughed aloud at the sheer joy of the thought. He could almost feel Deirdre in his arms, almost hear her lilting voice.

"Ah, Besum, wait till you see her. Just so tall—her head comes just above my shoulder, with golden curls that spring around her face. Wide round eyes—so blue—and a sharp little chin that juts out when she's in one of her stubborn turns.

"Yes, Besum, things will be different around here when my Deirdre comes. You'll have a thing better to listen to than those silly sheep bleating. Your mistress sings like a lark. Yep, Parson Irving should have my letter day after tomorrow, so Deirdre will know all the plans soon. I even told her about you, ye old Besum."

He went on, half deliriously telling the cow all about how he would sail from Donaghadee to Portpatrick on Rabbie's last trading circuit of the season and hire horses to ride to Glasgow, meet Deirdre at Parson Irving's, and bring her back to be married at Newtownards.

Still giddy, he walked back to his house in the deepening twilight. Just beyond the pasture he stopped and admired his two acres of barley blowing silver in the pale light. If this fine weather held, it would be ready to harvest next week. His first crop, grown with his own labor. The growing from seed to tender green sprout to full corn had been a delight to one who had spent all his days in a clerk's office. He would have to say that Alisdair Dunlop did him a favor when he threw him out. The Scripture crossed his mind, "Ye thought evil against me; but God meant it unto good."

Aye, less than a year in this land, and he could definitely say it was good—and going to get a great deal better when Deirdre came.

He looked at the house he had built for her. Its white walls glowed in the falling dark. It was sturdily built of sod between a double row of basketwork woven over rods set deep in the ground, then daubed with clay and whitewashed inside and out. He had Seamus to thank for that. The Scots builders were all busy on Montgomery's town, and the tenanted landlords hired all the available local workers. But O'Brien, seeing Calum's need, had helped him after long hours spent felling trees for the Seatons.

Calum smiled. He never ceased to be amazed at Seamus's charming, contrary nature. No matter how hard life seemed, O'Brien could always find something to joke about. And no matter how fond he was of his Una, he could always find something to fight with her about. Calum knew his life here would lack much without Seamus O'Brien's light-hearted sparkle—even when he'd had a wee bit too much o' the *uisce beatha.*

Only Calvin Johnstone had cleared his land of the native inhabitants. It was an act that Calum had spoken out against and thereby earned no love from his austere neighbor. He remembered the day, four months earlier, when Hugh and Cassie, the two oldest of the O'Brien brood, had been rolling with their new puppy near Calum's door. Johnstone, who held the next lease to the south, halted his carriage on the drive to town and admonished Calum to beware of allowing children of the wild Irish to play around his house. "They'll steal anything that moves, man."

At that moment the children's father was up on Calum's trussed roof beams, laying the light branches that would carry the under-thatch of sod. It was a process that wasn't absolutely necessary, Seamus had explained, but would result in a much tighter roof, so he would be glad to do it for Calum.

Calum had been so embarrassed by Johnstone's words that he spoke more harshly to the man than he might have otherwise. He had no desire to make an enemy of any person on the settlement. But as Calvin Johnstone drove off that day, he feared he had done so.

He turned to carry a load of sod up the ladder. "I'm fair glad of your help, man." He wanted to ask Seamus why he was willing to help a settler when most Gaels seemed to withdraw or behave in a surly manner toward the newcomers. Calum, though, couldn't figure out how to phrase the question.

Seamus nodded as he took a sod square. He settled it in place and answered Calum's unspoken question. "I'm not responsible for what others do—my people or the newcomers. I just want to live in peace and raise my family."

Tonight, however, Calum was in no mood to think on past disagreements. His mind was full of the future. He looked again at the thick thatch of his roof, securely roped in place. Someday he would have a slate roof. Slates were fireproof and provided no nesting places for vermin. But first, if he could only put in a wooden floor before he brought his bride here! Well, if the harvest was good enough . . .

7

Now that his letter was on its way, it seemed that, even more than before, everything Calum did was in preparation for Deirdre. And a few days later came the day he would make arrangements with the minister for their marriage.

Banns must be proclaimed on three successive Sundays in order to give time for any who might know of an impediment to the marriage to come forth. That meant the announcement must begin next Sunday.

Calum caught his breath at the thought. He could hardly imagine the fine feeling of sitting in the congregation and hearing his own banns announced—his and Deirdre's.

As today was the Sabbath, he rose even before the rooster crowed, made quick work of his chores, and took longer than usual over his washing. It was pleasant one day a week to get back into the fashionable hose and full breeches he had worn in his city life. Homespun, straight breeches, wool socks, and a heavy work shirt were his daily farmer's attire. But the Lord's Day was special. He took the Great Bible from its box on the shelf and set out to walk the two miles to town. He raised an eyebrow wryly at the thought of walking. He had always enjoyed riding to kirk in the Seaton carriage, but that would not be likely today. Calum had made no secret of the upcoming announcements

He was passing the O'Brien cabin tucked back in the woods when the colorful O'Brien brood emerged wearing their Sunday best. Little Cassie, the oldest daughter, pulled her finger from her mouth and gave him a bright grin. *"Beannacht."*

"And greetings to you as well, Mistress O'Brien."

The six-year-old giggled, then ran on at the insistent call of her brother Hugh.

Calum turned at the sound of an approaching horse.

"Papists!" he heard. "I don't see why Sir Hugh allows them to continue their mumbo-jumbo on good Christian land."

Calvin Johnstone clicked his horse to a faster clip as they passed.

But Matt, riding behind the pony cart that carried his parents and sister, gave Calum a friendly wave.

Calum had covered less than half a mile when he urged himself to increase his speed. The Rev. Mr. Robert Montgomery, a kinsman of Sir Hugh, did not look kindly on those who came late to kirk. And of all Sundays, Calum wanted to be in the parson's good graces today. Around the next bend he moved to the side of the road at the sound of another carriage.

Much to his surprise, this carriage stopped, and Ailsa Seaton called out, "Good day!"

As Mrs. Seaton was the one to offer him a seat, Calum could hardly refuse. And it was fortunate he had the ride, because they arrived none too soon. The congregation was just beginning the chanting of the first psalm when Calum slipped onto a rough-hewn bench next to the back wall of the old priory.

Although Sir Hugh had set his masons to work and hired Irish workers to fell timber, and although many of the settlers were contributing money, skill, and labor to build a proper church from the rubble of the old chancel, it would be a year or longer before the building was sound. The disrepair of the walls and the rough furniture, however, were no impediment to the black-robed Parson Montgomery, who stood at the reading desk and proclaimed from the Scots Confession.

"We call on God to record that from our hearts we abhor all heretical sects and all teachers of false doctrine, and that with all humility we embrace the purity of Christ's gospel, which is the one food of our souls and therefore so precious to us that we are determined to suffer the greatest of worldly dangers, rather than let our souls be defrauded of it."

Although this was technically an Episcopal church, the Bishop of Down made no objection to having the pulpit filled with a minister of the Reformed faith. He even allowed Montgomery a share of the tithes paid to the established church.

Calum joined the rest of the congregation in reciting the first Order. "We confess and acknowledge one God alone, to whom alone we must cleave, whom alone we must serve, whom only we must worship, and in whom alone we put our trust. Who is eternal, infinite, immeasurable, incomprehensible, omnipotent, invisible . . . by whom we believe . . . to be ruled and guided by His inscrutable providence for such end as His eternal wisdom, goodness, and justice have appointed, and to the manifestation of His own glory."

The third Order was Original Sin. Calum knew the words well, but these he repeated with less fervor. "The image of God was utterly defaced in man, and he and his children became by nature hostile to God, slaves to Satan, and servants to sin. And thus everlasting death has had, and shall have, power and dominion over all who have not been, are not, or shall not be reborn from above. This rebirth is wrought by the power of the Holy Ghost creating in the hearts of God's chosen ones . . ."

The service continued, but Calum shifted uncomfortably on his bench. He had been four years old when the Reformed church and the Scots Confession, establishing the doctrines of John Calvin, was established by the Reformation Parliament. Although his son was of tender years, Gordon Lanark had no one else to talk to of an evening. So Calum had been treated to long evenings of theological dialogue until he was ten and the elder Lanark died. But those early talks had done their work, and although Calum was a sober communicant of the kirk, he secretly harbored the questions raised by his father's theology, carried over from the old faith, whose patristic fathers had enunciated a doctrine of free will.

He certainly believed in the doctrine of original sin. It was the statement of predestination that he always mumbled in the Confession. For Gordon Lanark had declared on many a winter's evening that it would be true enough that everlasting death would have dominion over all men except God's chosen elect, were it not for God's prevenient grace, which enabled "whosoever will," not just a predestined few, to come to God.

Calum looked a few rows ahead to where Calvin Johnstone was continuing the recitation in his sanctimonious manner. Was it the man's unshakable conviction that he was one of the elect that made his company like the wearing of a hair shirt? Or would Johnstone have been self-righteous no matter what his beliefs? Certainly most of the settlers, including Johnstone's own son, were staunch enough in their theology without exhibiting such self-righteousness.

By the end of his two-hour sermon on the Unprofitable Servant, however, the Rev. Mr. Montgomery left no doubt in his hearers' minds that many in that very room were in danger of the curse of God. It was with some trepidation of falling afoul of such brimstone as he had been warned of that Calum approached the parson to arrange for the banns to be cried for the marriage of Calum Lanark and Deirdre Dunlop.

Parson Montgomery questioned him carefully about all the arrangements, and Calum answered honestly as to his desire to be married by his own parson in the land that would be their new home. He did not volunteer, however, the fact that the bride would be leaving her father's home without parental consent. Fortunately, Montgomery did not ask.

The afternoon sermon was only an hour and a half, so Calum was back home in good time. After his evening care of his animals—an activity that was allowed on Sunday because even Jesus taught that it was acceptable to pull an ox out of a ditch on the Sabbath—Calum would have much liked to begin work making Deirdre's chair. But woodworking was not an ox in the ditch. So he lit a small peat fire and sat before the hearth, reading some from the Bible but mostly thinking of the future. A smile played at the corners of his mouth.

Several hours later, he awakened to frantic barkings and shouts. Sleep-dazed, he stumbled out the door. Seamus O'Brien grabbed him by the arm and yanked him away from the house, pointing upward in the reflection of an unnatural light in the black sky.

Calum turned and gave an anguished cry. The thatch of his roof was on fire, and a stiff wind was blowing sparks toward the barley. He grabbed the milking pail and ran toward the stream behind the house. Seamus dashed off for his ladder.

Coll's barking brought Matt Johnstone and his father, who helped form a bucket brigade with Una. It was some time later before the Seatons became aware of the emergency and rallied with buckets, blankets, and pitchforks to beat at the blaze catching the edges of the barley field.

Most of the roof and one wall was burned before Calum turned his attention to his fields. The sight made him so sick he doubled over with a sob. More than half of his crop had burned, and the wind continued to whip the hungry flames away from the firefighters. He grabbed a shovel and charged across the ground. He must save two bolls just to break even on his rent.

He flailed in every direction, but for every spark he stifled, he sent three more flying to be carried by the wind. He burned his hands and feet but hardly noticed.

Matt Johnstone suddenly lunged at him with a wool brychan. He pushed the boy away, and the two of them rolled on the charred earth.

"What are ye doin', lad?"

"Your breeks were afire."

Then Calum felt the searing pain in his thigh where his pants had burned through. But he stumbled to his feet to fight on.

The morning sky was streaking red when Fulke Seaton halted his frenzied battle. "It's over, Calum. I'm that sorry."

Calum looked around at his blackened acres. There was no more to fight. The fire had consumed it all.

Una and Ailsa approached the fatigued men with jugs of ale and milk and a basket of bannocks. Fulke and the Johnstones ate and drank hungrily, but Calum was too sick and exhausted to eat, too numb to think. And it hurt too much to be still. So he turned toward the pasture.

Anna Johnstone and her mother stopped him. They had come with bandages and salves for the men's burns.

Calum started to refuse. "Almost milking time, Bes—"

Mrs. Johnstone set her prim mouth in a manner that would brook no argument. "Those hands'll do no milking for many days." She began bandaging.

"I can milk." Anna picked up a bucket abandoned by the fire-fighters and headed toward the pasture.

Mrs. Johnstone had just finished salving Calum's burned thigh when Anna came running back. "Pasture's empty. The fence is down."

She had no sooner spoken than several head of Johnstone cattle came wandering down the road. Matt dashed after them, shouting orders to Coll.

It was hours later before the straying cattle were rounded up—those that could be found. The Johnstones reported five missing sheep, the Seatons three cows. And all three of Calum's ewes were gone. Matt came back from seeking strays as far afield as Newtown with the news that Besum was in the pound. Good news except for the fine that must now be paid for her release.

A fine Calum could little afford to pay.

With promises to return later and help with the rebuilding, the neighbors left. Calum sat with his head in his bandaged hands amidst the debris of charred thatch and broken walls that had been his home only a few hours earlier. If Seamus hadn't insisted on building the roof with a sod under-thatch, he would have lost everything.

As it was, there was little enough left.

Afternoon sun coming through the broken roof highlighted the blackened remains of his belongings. It was impossible to tell if anything was still usable under the rubble. He looked at what had been his straw pallet and wool brychan in the bed space. One wall was broken away. He was glad now that he hadn't had time to build a real bed and cover it with his mother's quilt. That was safe in a heavy chest.

But then Calum fell to his knees and began shoving debris away from the bench where he had sat the evening before. He had lost so much—home, crop, cattle—that he didn't think anything was left to hurt as much as this sight did. The charred, curled pages of his father's Bible broke in his hands.

He got up and stumbled out of the ruined building. He sat on a stump of a felled tree with questions going around and around in his mind. *Why? Why? How? How did it happen?*

True, he had fallen asleep with the fire on his hearth unbanked.

But it had been such a small blaze, only enough to take the chill off the night air. It didn't seem possible that a spark from those few peats could have made its way up the chimney to cause such disaster.

It was windy, but the night was clear. There had been no lightning. Could the fire have been started by human hands? But who? Any name he thought of seemed impossible.

Calvin Johnstone because Calum had befriended the O'Briens? Or in hopes the O'Briens would be blamed?

He refused to entertain any idea that Seamus could have set a light to thatch he himself had laid. But what of another of the native Irish, retaliating randomly on the settlers? Perhaps one driven from his home by Johnstone?

Or, unlikely as it seemed, Fulke Seaton, assuaging his family's pride because Calum had chosen another than Ailsa? Then coming around to battle the blaze so that no one would suspect him—or out of fear that the blaze might spread to his own fields.

No, it must have been the woodkerne. One heard so many tales of soldiers from either side of the Nine Years War living by vandalism and plunder. And that would explain the missing cattle. They had probably set the blaze to distract attention from their cattle thieving.

An unsatisfactory answer, but Calum could think of no other. The creak of wood against leather penetrated his thoughts. He looked. Of his neighbors, only Mrs. Seaton possessed such a well-sprung carriage. He looked for something to wipe the soot off his hands and face, but he had not even a clean rag left to him.

Grime covered him from head to foot as he stepped around the corner of the hut, scattering the clutch of chickens scratching there. He blinked at the coat of arms on the carriage door. Not Mrs. Seaton but Lady Elizabeth Montgomery herself had come to call.

A servant helped her alight. Her starched ruff lay in precise folds around her neck, and three ostrich feathers fluttered atop her high-crowned hat. Her dark green damask skirt was held out at the sides with a stiffened frame underneath. In spite of his disheveled condition, Calum bowed as deeply as any courtier. "Your ladyship, forgive, uh . . ."

"Mr. Lanark." Calum was surprised she knew his name, but it was said she was a very careful mistress. Had she come then to evict him personally since he would be unable to pay his rent? Surely she would merely have sent an agent for that.

She took a step forward, then stopped when she observed the charred grass. "I am so sorry for your losses, Mr. Lanark. And Sir Hugh joins me in his concern."

"I thank your ladyship and my lord." Calum bowed again. It would have saved time if she had simply sent an agent.

"Sir Hugh and I are concerned that you will now be unable to pay your rent."

"I am hoping Mr. Seaton will be patient."

"Patient, yes." She lifted her head and observed the scene carefully.

Calum did not have to follow the gaze of her wide brown eyes to see the empty pasture, the blackened barley fields, the remains of the cottage.

"Yes, certainly patience is required in settling a new land. But surely you have no hope of paying before next year's harvest. You have no private fortune, I think?"

"Nothing, my lady." He had not realized how hopeless it would sound until the words echoed against his charred house.

"As I thought. It will be much the best then for you to leave—"

Calum opened his mouth to protest.

"—farming for the time being. I have need of a clerk to keep accounts of the grinding at my mill. I am told you have experience of accounts."

Calum let his breath out slowly. He had heard that little passed Lady Montgomery unnoticed. But that she should know so much about one of the poorest of their undertenants . . . "Yes, your ladyship. I thank you."

"Perhaps Seaton will extend you time for the land your cottage occupies, but you cannot expect him to grant you the use of an acreage, unpaid."

Calum shook his head in agreement.

"You will begin tomorrow." She extended her hand to the servant, who helped her back into the carriage.

A moment later Calum stood blinking as the conveyance turned out of sight around a bend in the road. Had that really happened?

He had come to Ireland hoping to lease land. He had been able only to rent. Now he had lost even that. He had found sheep to be silly and troublesome; all the same he had hoped to build a flock from them. Now they were gone. The cottage had been a poor affair, not nearly good enough for Deirdre, but it had provided shelter. Now it was a shambles.

Yet he would survive. Lady Montgomery had offered him a job—demanded his services, really. So he would survive. He could sleep in the shelter of the angle of two unburned walls that still had some of the under-thatch overhead. But what would he survive for? He could not bring Deirdre to this.

He had thought it would be a near thing to have time to complete the chair and bed he must have for his bride. Now, with every hand turned to the harvest and his to milling for the coming weeks, there would be no time to build a new cottage. He could hope to have some sort of shelter put up for himself before winter storms began, but he would not have a place to which he could bring Deirdre.

It was not until the next Sunday, sitting in his usual seat at the back of the kirk, that the full impact hit him. After the second reading from the Scripture, Parson Montgomery, solemn in black robe and white bands, cleared his throat. "I publish the banns of marriage between Miss Deirdre Dunlop of Glasgow and Mr. Calum Lanark of Newtownards. If any of you know cause, or just impediment, why these two persons should not be joined together in holy matrimony, ye are to declare it. This is the first time of asking."

It was like a blow to the stomach. Calum knew the impediment to this marriage. He had no home for his bride. And no prospects of gaining land where they could establish a family. He had to face the fact. Deirdre would be better off marrying Fergus Ingram.

Rabbie MacKinnon was due in Newtownards tomorrow. It would be his last trip before the one on which Calum had planned to accompany him to Scotland. Calum set his jaw and clenched his teeth. He must do the right thing. He must write to Deirdre, telling her of the disaster. He must explain it to her as clearly as possible. He could not marry her.

She would be waiting at the kirk, just as Calum's earlier letter had instructed. His mind filled with a picture of her, alone in her room, bending near the candle glow that made a halo of her golden hair, her eyes alight with anticipation.

Then he clenched his fists against his own pain as he saw her brightness turn to dismay when she read the letter he must send. A letter telling her he would never see her again. A letter telling her she must marry another.

8

The second Thursday in October was the worst day of Calum's life. It was even worse than the day he had bade farewell to his father in St. Mary's kirk yard as the shovelsful of dirt hit the casket.

From the many who had come with business at the mill that morning he had heard that Rabbie MacKinnon had returned on schedule. On this, his last visit of the year, he had brought many fine wares to see them through the winter. And as the harvest had been so fine, he was doing a brisk business, indeed.

Calum's informants no doubt thought his dejection at their news was due to their reference to the bumper harvest when Calum's own had been destroyed. Only Calum knew that Rabbie's return was the final dashing of his hopes.

When Ninian Barclay, the first to bring in a load of oats for grinding, told him of the trader's arrival, Calum realized that all along he had still harbored the tiniest hope. It had been a dim flicker, but it had persisted in his inmost heart. It was the hope that something would turn up, that somehow he would be able to send for Deirdre yet.

Now Rabbie MacKinnon was here, and Deirdre was not. It had not happened.

By midafternoon he had overseen the grinding of three loads of oats and one of barley. Each had gone carefully into the hopper to be milled between the large quern stones as the rushing stream waters turned the waterwheel outside. Calum saw to the bagging and weighing of the flour, and all was entered neatly in his meticulous ledger. Then the Montgomery portion was set aside as payment to the landlord—profitable business since all tenants were required to use the mill. Lady Montgomery's industry was talked of far and wide, and certainly her indefatigable attention to the welfare of the settlement was often contrasted to that of the languid wife of James Hamilton. The neighboring settlements were not making such rapid progress as the Montgomerys'.

So Calum, looking up from his account books, was not surprised to see Lady Montgomery's closed carriage stop in Mill Street. He was surprised, however, at how thorough she was in inspecting the operation he had been supervising for her. She scrutinized his bookkeeping. She looked at the room nearly full of Montgomery grain he had collected as the price for milling, and Calum sensed she was counting the value of every bag. She looked over the hopper, the quern stones, the bagging spout. Calum felt an urge to apologize for the thick layer of flour dust covering every surface, including himself, but in truth there was no avoiding it.

He rubbed his nose to avoid a sneeze.

"Yes, the mill has done well. As I expected. I am determined to build one in every parish."

"Aye. That'll prove profitable, your ladyship. And a fine convenience for your tenants, as well," he added hurriedly.

"As you say. I shall begin one in Comber immediately."

He wondered why she was telling him that, but all that was required was that he nod and mutter, "Yes, my lady."

"Good. I find all here most satisfactory. You may proceed." She turned, and Calum sprang to open the door for her.

Calum returned to his ledgers, shaking his head. Proceed with what? Impossible to know what she was talking about half the time. The lady was a whirlwind—but a whirlwind bound on the success of the Montgomery Settlement.

He dipped his quill. The door flew open. Calum looked up and blotted his book.

Deirdre took one look at him and ran across the room with a cry. He rose to meet her with a scuffle of paper and scraping of chair legs. He engulfed her in his strong arms. Then he lifted her off the floor and whirled her around the room. "Deirdre, Deirdre. It canna be." He kissed her soundly. "It canna be, but it is! Oh, Deirdre, how comes this miracle?"

She pulled away from him and assumed what severity she could. "No miracle at all, Calum Lanark. Just good Scots common sense. Fueled with a good dose of anger, I must say."

"Anger?"

She waved her finger at him. "How dare you tell me to marry fat Fergus Ingram so I'd have a comfortable house? As if I'd do such a thing. I've never been so insulted."

He backed away from her admonishing finger, then sat in his chair and pulled her onto his lap. "Oh, Deirdre, I canna tell you how glad I am that you disobeyed me. But you have no idea—I do not even have a roof over my head to offer you."

"But we will build new. Lady Montgomery said—"

"What do you know of Lady Montgomery?"

"I know she is a kind lady who is a wise judge of her tenants. Rabbie had a special order for her. Something from England that no one was to know about, so it had to be delivered first. Sacks and sacks of something very heavy—delivered directly to her.

"As soon as she heard my name, she knew I was to be your bride." She paused and considered. "How came she to know that?"

Calum nodded. "The banns. She heard at church."

"Oh, of course. Well, anyway, she kept me with her for hours, asking questions that would be most impertinent in anyone else."

Calum laughed. "Aye, her ladyship's a termagant, but a well-meaning termagant, I'm thinking. So that was what her visit was all about, inspecting my work to be certain she needn't forbid the banns." And then his lighthearted mood faded.

Slowly but very firmly, as if the moving apart was a ripping of their skins, Calum set her on the floor and moved to the far side of the room. He pulled a round, brown woolen cap off the peg by the door and a heavy iron key from the ring beside it. Then he turned back to Deirdre. "I'm thinking I'm the one that should be forbidding the banns. As ye've come this far, ye'd best see the worst of it."

He locked the door of the mill behind them.

As they started down Pound Street he told her in detail about the fire and the apparent theft of the sheep—for none of them had been found. And scattered reports of similar losses continued in the settlement. She seemed to find great comfort in the part about the safe impounding of Besum—most in the fact that Calum's long-faced neighbor had advanced him the money to redeem his cow.

"Aye, it was kind of him. I've been glad enough of the milk to drink. It's just that I dislike being more in debt. Oh, Deirdre, you don't know what you've come to."

Dusk was deepening and the air was chilly by the time they accomplished the two-mile trek to the remains of Calum's burned-out cottage. Deirdre looked around wordlessly as he lit a peat fire on the hearth. The smoke appeared to sting her eyes, and she coughed.

"I'm sorry." He stood and looked at her but did not move closer. "I had a chimney. Most cottiers don't—just a smoke hole in the roof like you see now—" He pointed to the space in the roof where the smoke was meant to be making an exit. "Seamus helped me weave a fine chimney canopy of rods, like basketwork, then we clay-daubed it and whitewashed it over."

He made a helpless gesture toward the blackened remains of what had been the best fireplace he could build. He tried to explain how, working from sunup to sundown at the mill, he had had time to achieve only the most minimal rebuilding of the roof and walls. Nothing had been newly whitewashed. But he had cleaned out the single room the best he could. Una had made him a new pallet. And that was all. He shook his head.

Deirdre saw it all. But her eyes would not stay on the shambles around her. She obediently looked wherever he pointed, but always she was drawn back to look at him. She was hungry just for the sight of him.

"Deirdre, now that you've come—now that I've seen you again— it would be death to me to lose you. But it would be better that you return to your father than to stay here and suffer. Without land, one has no prospects here. There is no hope of my ever being more than a cottier. At the moment I'm not even that. In time you'd come to hate this—and me. Rabbie returns to Scotland in the morning."

She shook her head and took a step closer. She allowed the fire-light to fall on her face so that he could see her sincerity. "And do you think I could leave, having seen you again? We'll manage, Calum. You have friends. Lady Montgomery is pleased with your work. This is a good land, a land of opportunity. We'll survive." She thrust out her chin. "No, we'll not just survive. We'll succeed. Together, we can."

His throat worked as he drew her to him and engulfed her in his arms.

Crushed against his doublet, she smelled oat millings and peat smoke, and her words rang in her head. She didn't know how she could make good on her declaration. But she was determined. She would find a way to help Calum. It looked more hopeless than she would admit even to herself. But somehow they would build a home in this land where, at the moment, everything seemed so desolate.

She knew that if she allowed the hovering despair to overwhelm her for even a moment, she would be lost. But she could fight harder than any threat. *It's hopeless.* No! This is my home. *Home?* Calum's here. It's home! *It's strange. Barren. Dangerous.* It's home. I'll make it home.

Still, what could she do? If only she had had money of her own to bring. As it was, arriving as she did with nothing except the small bag she could carry unnoticed from her father's house, she saw that she would only be an added financial burden to Calum.

She looked once more around the bare, dark room. The bleakness mocked her brave words. It was as clean as he could make it— except for one small charred pile in the far corner. Strange that he would have missed that. She looked closer and saw what it was.

"Oh, Calum!" She knelt beside it and touched a sheet of singed vellum. "Your father's Bible."

The flame from the rush light flickered, highlighting the strong, flat bones of his cheeks and square jaw. "I dinna have the heart to throw it out."

And then she remembered the one thing she had been able to bring him. How glad she was to have something. She dug in her bag. "Calum, look! I know it won't take the place of the Bible, but—" She held up the small iron and gilt clock that had been his mother's.

"Deirdre, how can this be? I canna believe it."

"Parson Irving told me. He knew you sold a clock to buy cattle. He didn't know which shop, but I found it."

He held it in both hands. "This makes it a wedding present for us too. Someday—I promise you—we'll have a fine mantel to put this on." He looked around, at a loss. "But for now . . ."

He set the clock on the table, placed both hands on her shoulders, and looked at her from under a deeply furrowed brow. "But what am I to do wi' ye now, lass? Ye canna stay here. Even if I had the accommodation, it wouldna be right."

She saw the truth of that. But she had no more time to think on it, for this was to be a day of hurried arrivals. They both started at the sound of sharp knocking on the door.

Calum opened it to a small servant boy.

"Master Seaton bids ye come drink the health of his first grandchild. 'Tis only a girl, but a lusty one." The lad tugged respectfully at his forelock and dashed on to take the news to the Johnstones.

Fulke Seaton himself met them at the door, fair chuffed over the beauty of his three-hour-old daughter, Judith, and the bravery of his dear Effie.

Ailsa emerged from her sister-in-law's room, and Deirdre gave Calum a questioning look. On their walk out from town he had told her of this tall, attractive woman's attentions to him, and she was indeed strikingly beautiful. Deirdre wondered if this woman's presence had played a part in Calum's resolve that she stay in Scotland. But the thought was unworthy. And when Ailsa herself suggested that Deirdre should stay at the Seatons' until the wedding could take place, there seemed to be little alternative.

In the following days, Deirdre divided her time between setting things to rights at Calum's cottage, trying to be helpful at Seatons', and puzzling over what she could do to help improve Calum's situation. Calum was not the only settler in similar straits, though his were the most severe because of the fire.

And across the settlement, cattle still continued to disappear. One afternoon Deirdre was thinking about the latest incident—they had just heard that three more cows had gone missing from another farm the night before—when Ailsa came in and asked her to sit with Effie while she attended to matters in the dairy.

Deirdre was more than happy to be of help, especially when it meant being near the delightful baby, Judith. Today, however, both mother and child were restless and fussy. Deirdre's attempts to soothe the baby by walking the floor with her failed to produce much effect.

Effie sat up against her pillows and held out her arms. "Oh, give her to me. It's not time for her to be eating again, but I cannot abide the whimpers."

The tiny bairn snuggled to her mother's breast, and the relaxation in the room was as if the very air changed color. Deirdre sank onto a stool by the window. For a while the mother's croonings and the infant's gurgling noises filled the space. But when they quieted, the silence became awkward.

"Would you like me to read to you?" Deirdre offered.

Effie raised her dark brows, which stood in such contrast to the small white oval of her face. "Read? Can you?"

"Yes, my father thought it a needful skill for my brothers if they were to carry on his merchant's trade. He allowed me to sit in on their lessons." She grinned. "Well, he didn't so much allow it as fail to forbid it. But it came to the same thing. Have you a Bible?"

"How lucky you are to read. We have a Bible, but my father-in-law keeps it locked." Effie smiled wistfully. "What I should like is some poetry, but Master Seaton is unlikely to have anything but sermons, so I suppose we must make do." She gestured to the next room. "There is a shelf next to his writing table."

Deirdre hesitated. "He will not mind if I help myself?"

Effie smiled. "Master Seaton will be most gratified. He is much concerned that his good daughter's mind is not on weighty enough matters."

Indeed, Master Seaton's shelf offered a wealth of weighty material. Deirdre found no fewer than five volumes of sermons to choose from. She picked up one and turned through it, hoping to find a message that ran on something other than judgment and punishment for those who broke God's laws.

She was thumbing through a third volume when a small sheet of tightly written paper slipped from the pages. Thinking it must be notes someone had made on a sermon he was reading, she picked it up with interest. She quickly saw, however, that it was a letter on some matter of business, so she stuck it hurriedly back into the book. As she did so, she noticed the strange mark that stood in place of a signature.

Instead of the usual X that indicated the signatory was unable to write his name, this was a complicated cipher. She sensed it did not indicate the illiteracy of the writer but rather his desire for secrecy. She smiled. Having grown up in a merchant's household, she well understood the need to keep certain business transactions quiet until the proper time. Little wonder that the Seaton household was so prosperous.

9

Then, at last, Deirdre and Calum's wedding day arrived. Lady Montgomery honored the occasion by loaning the bride her best pearl headdress and lace ruff. The pearls looked exquisite nestled in Deirdre's springy golden curls, and the ruff made a perfect frame for her pert features.

Her only regret was that her father was not there to see her married. But she put the thought quickly out of her mind as she looked at Calum in his starched, lace-edged collar and cuffs. His thick reddish hair trimmed to his jawline emphasized the strength of his face. She also noticed how well his brown hose showed off his muscled calves.

Parson Montgomery, however, made clear to all that *his* mind was not on such worldly external matters. His wedding sermon dealt on the perfection of the law and the imperfection of man.

"The law of God is most just, equal, holy, and perfect. But our nature is so corrupt, weak, and imperfect that we are never able perfectly to fulfill the works of the law. If we say that we have no sin, we deceive ourselves and the truth of God is not in us. It is therefore essential for us to lay hold on Christ Jesus, in His righteousness and His atonement, that the curse of God may not fall upon us."

Deirdre would have preferred a sermon on love rather than on judgment, but she kept wide eyes fixed on the preacher while she allowed her mind to wander. It had plenty of time to wander. The sermon lasted nearly an hour.

Finally, when Deirdre thought she could sit still no longer, the sermon came to an end with an adjuration against putting one's trust in "damnable idolatry," and the bride and groom stood together before the altar.

"The Lord sanctify and bless you. The Lord pour the riches of His grace upon you, that ye may please Him and live together in holy love to your lives' end. So be it."

Deirdre's heart repeated a fervent Amen to that pronouncement, and the congregation sang Psalm 128:

"Blessed is every one that feareth the Lord; that walketh in his ways.

For thou shalt eat the labour of thine hands: happy shalt thou be, and it shall be well with thee.

Thy wife shall be as a fruitful vine by the sides of thine house: thy children like olive plants round about thy table.

Behold, that thus shall the man be blessed that feareth the Lord."

Lady Montgomery had attended this, the first wedding in New-townards, wearing a white silk dress with a lace collar that extended beyond her shoulders and a farthingale that held her skirt out even farther. It was a copy of one Queen Anne had worn in Edinburgh.

Deirdre made her first curtsy as a married woman to her ladyship. "I thank you for your kind attentions to our wedding. I was most honored to wear your ladyship's pearls."

"I am very glad you enjoyed them, my dear. It is my duty and privilege to be of service to our people. You must let me know whenever I can help you."

Deirdre hesitated. In spite of the stiffness of the phrasing, she was sure Lady Montgomery was sincere. But would she think Calum ungrateful for the job at the mill if Deirdre mentioned their dearest dream to their landlady? She took a deep breath.

"Well, your ladyship, there is one thing. We wouldn't want you to think us ungrateful for all you've done already, but . . ." Deirdre found the words tumbling out as she spoke in the rapid way she always did when she was nervous. She told Lady Montgomery of their desire to lease their own land.

Lady Montgomery gave a decided flick of the double rope of pearls that hung past her waist. "Yes, it had occurred to me that you might be the right ones to begin my new project. Bring your husband to me."

Deirdre smiled. *Husband.* How good that sounded. She crossed the priory garden. "My love, her ladyship would have a word with you."

He seemed none too reluctant to leave his conversation with Calvin Johnstone and Ninian Barclay.

Lady Montgomery made her announcement in her usual direct manner. "I have decided to grow potatoes."

Calum stared.

"A most successful crop in the New World, I understand. Queen Elizabeth was quite taken with the ones Walter Raleigh brought her. Although that man's cleverness has not kept him from being thrown in the Tower by King James."

"God save the king," Calum replied.

"Indeed. And my potatoes." Lady Montgomery never veered from her chosen path for long.

"Will they grow in Ireland?" Calum asked.

"I don't see why not. I have been assured the soil and climate are most favorable. I believe, however, I shall be the first to plant them here."

Calum bowed. It was unnecessary for either of them to state the fact that Lady Montgomery very much liked being the first at whatever she undertook.

It was quickly agreed on both sides. Calum would be granted land in the parish of Comber—freehold for the house, the arable land leased —and he would begin Lady Montgomery's grand experiment.

The next day, they drove out in a pony cart borrowed from Calvin Johnstone to inspect the site of their new home. "I am glad we're still to be so near your old neighbors." Deirdre squeezed her husband's arm.

The land was just a mile south of Calum's cottage, on the gentle slope leading up to Scrabo, which loomed over the landscape. Strangford Lough lay to their left, and Deirdre could catch glimpses of it wherever there was a field that had been cleared of trees.

Calum carefully studied the land grant description the agent had given him, then pulled the pony to a halt. "Here we are, Mistress Lanark. Your new home."

She looked in the direction he indicated with a sweep of his right arm. The land was covered solid with a thick stand of timber. "But, Calum, this can't be right. You're to farm. There's no place to grow anything here. And we'll have so many expenses. How will we pay? It'll be almost a whole year before we've a crop to harvest—and we've a house to build . . ." She had meant to help when she spoke to Lady Montgomery. Had she landed them in a worse fix than ever by her meddling?

Calum laughed, and it was a joy to her to see the relaxed, open look in his gentle blue eyes. It was the first time he had been so since she came.

"Bless you, my careful good wife. We shall begin our first harvest tomorrow. Have ye any notion of the value of these sissel oaks that stand in the way of my nice, neat potato hills?"

It was the hardest winter of her life. Calum hired Seamus O'Brien and his brother Patrick, who had been cleared from his home in Bangor, to help with cutting the trees. The men worked from sunup to sundown during the short winter days, felling timber and grubbing roots from the sandy loam. And then they turned to work on the house

Deirdre planned. At least Seamus's merry, lighthearted ways were a good counter to the hardships of life in this foreign land. And, as always, as soon as the thought crossed her mind, Deirdre corrected it: it was home.

Still, there had been a cook and servants at Dunlop Hall—amenities she had always taken for granted. She had given no thought to what life might be like without them. Now, as she attempted to stir the stew pot hanging over the fire while her eyes stung from the smoke, she thought of the house they were to build. When that was done, then Ireland would truly be home. She swallowed a lump in her throat. No, she would not think of Scotland—of how lovely it was when the mist hung over the mountains.

She returned to the house plans. With an eye to the future, she insisted on two rooms. And the coziness of the bed outshot next to the fireplace was to be enhanced by a small wall jutting into the kitchen. She also wanted almost the entire kitchen lofted over to serve as storage space.

Deirdre could see that Calum worried over the fact that it was far from the grandeur she had left behind in Glasgow, but she would admit to nothing but excitement over her plans. Anything was better than marrying Fergus Ingram. She had no regrets over her choice. There was just so much to do—so hopelessly much.

Seamus looked askance at her plans for the loft. "Weel, ye must see that ye leave the space above the hearth uncovered so the warm air can rise freely into the roof space to keep your under-thatch dry. You'll not be wanting your sods to rot."

And she could tell he was equally skeptical about putting the byre on the downhill side under the bedrooms, rather than simply keeping the animals in a room open to the rest of the house as had always been the Irish way.

But no matter how skeptical others might be, Deirdre was not the least worried about the rightness of her plans—she never was, once her mind was made up—even when she sat shivering in the damaged cottage. Snow sifted through the patched roof, and it was impossible to stuff rags into the cracks of the walls tightly enough to keep out the winter wind that howled off the icy lough.

No matter how worrisome the continued pilfering or pressing the work, they always set aside the Sabbath for God and kirk. The partially rebuilt church offered no more protection from the winter weather than the patched-up cottage, however, and Parson Montgomery's sermons were scarcely warming.

"And so, destined to sin daily, we cry with the apostle, 'Who will deliver me from this body of death?'"

Deirdre wrapped her cloak more tightly around her shoulders.

Montgomery leaned over the pulpit, drawing every eye. "God the Father looks down on each of us—miserable sinners that we are—and beholds us in the body of His Son Christ Jesus. He accepts our imperfect obedience as if it were perfect. He covers our works, which are defiled with many stains, with the righteousness of His Son. When we have done all things, we must fall down and unfeignedly confess that we are unprofitable servants."

Deirdre had quickly realized that the Unprofitable Servant was the parson's favorite theme, and every Sunday she felt the weight more. Today she could repress it no longer. The wooden spoon moved more and more slowly as she stirred the pot of stew.

"Calum, what did you think of the sermon?" she began gently enough.

With the fond chuckle that was always music to her ears, he moved her away from the fire, sat on the chair, and pulled her into his lap—a normal expedient for them, as they still owned only one chair, and their single stool wobbled. "Oh, Deirdre, ye've no idea how good it is to have someone—to have you—to talk to! I use to talk to Besum."

"Really?" She leaned against his shoulder. "What did you talk about?"

"About you. I told her all about how beautiful you are, and how much I missed you. Besum is a good listener, but she was no good at talking theology."

Deirdre smiled. "I suppose it just proves my unprofitability to question the parson, but are all men such miserable creatures as he says? I know I make mistakes aplenty—like the oatcakes I burned yesterday—and worse." She shied from coming closer to the cause of her distress. "But I cannot think of you as so contemptible, and I cannot think God does either."

He shook his head. "Ah, my Deirdre, it's certain I'm a much worse sinner than ye. And I'm no theologian. But my father was, and he used to talk freely of such things. It comes to this: If ye define sin as *any* falling short of God's perfection—burning oatcakes, for example—then, yes, we are miserable worms. My father, though, was fond of reading the early church Fathers. They taught that sin is rebellion against a known law of God."

She stifled a sob against his shoulder.

He continued, "But with the help of God, such a spirit of rebellion can be forgiven, removed, not just covered over—"

She could no longer hold back her sobs. "Oh, Calum, that's worse! Don't you see?"

He looked at her in total confusion. "See what?"

"Rebellion against a law of God!" She had tried so often to push it out of her mind. She hadn't wanted to speak of it to Calum, lest he think she carried regret toward him. But she had come to wonder if part of the weight inside her, which she had put down to a natural homesickness, might be something deeper. After all, she *had* broken a commandment. Burning oatcakes was one thing. One could debate God's attitude toward such failure to reach perfection. But the Ten Commandments were not debatable. Not what she had done.

"Children, obey your parents," she whispered on a shaky breath.

It was little wonder she couldn't find the tranquility she had sought here when she had broken a commandment in the coming.

10

They talked long that night. Should they write Deirdre's father? Should they go back to Glasgow when passage was possible? The marriage agreements had been signed between Alisdair Dunlop and Fergus Ingram. What if Ingram claimed a prior contract and sought to have their marriage set aside?

"Don't fash yourself, love. We'll let the matter rest awhile," Calum said.

And although Deirdre continued to fret, that seemed the best they could do.

Then, at the end of February, bright flowers filled the meadows, birds sang, and Calum and Deirdre moved into their fine new house having two rooms, a proper bed, and a chimney that drew the smoke straight up.

The first evening in the house, Deirdre placed Calum's parents' wedding clock on the mantel and proclaimed that they were home. For a moment all worries about vandalism in the settlement and homesickness for Scotland fled. She found herself singing—albeit a Scottish song—"On the Banks of Helicon."

Besum was in her cozy byre under the spare room when her calf was born. Deirdre had just emerged from her morning visit to the mother and two-weeks-old calf when a large farm cart came rattling up the Scrabo Road and stopped at their house.

The cart was loaded with the mysterious sacks Rabbie MacKinnon had delivered to Lady Montgomery last October. Seed potatoes. It was time to prepare them for planting according to Lady Montgomery's precise directions.

Deirdre picked up one of the small, firm, brown vegetables and considered it as the man explained.

"Those pits in the sides are what you call 'eyes.'" He pulled a knife from his belt to demonstrate. "You cut each potato in 'alf, makin' sure there's eyes in each 'alf, because that's what sprouts the new plant. See?"

Calum nodded. "And that's what we plant?"

"Not so fast, mate. You can't plant it all wet and raw like. It'll spoil. Needs time to dry out a bit. Spread the cut tatties out and cover 'em with straw, that's the ticket."

Now Deirdre nodded. It looked as if this was going to be a bigger job than she had realized. As a child she had loved to hang around old Tom, who took care of the kitchen garden behind their house. But she had never seen anything like this.

What have we gotten into? she wondered as the man began hauling sacks off the cart. She'd had no idea there would be so many. The cart was piled high, but she had assumed he was visiting several farms, as Lady Montgomery had granted similar leases to others who agreed to grow potatoes in Comber. But he showed no signs of stopping.

"Er—are these all for us?"

The man nodded. "I'll 'ave the next load tomorry."

"Next load?"

He nodded. "A ton an acre, that's the rule."

When the empty cart rattled off, she looked at Calum. He appeared as dazed as she felt. "Well, we'd best make a start. How many acres do we have to do?"

"We only got three cleared this winter. Should have it doubled by next year."

By the end of the day, Deirdre's back was aching and her fingers blistered after hours of potato cutting. She looked at how few sacks she had finished and at how many were left. And another load was coming tomorrow.

In April the planting began. Lady Montgomery's overseer, who finally told them his name was Cedric, a man as small and brown as the potatoes he knew so well, carefully demonstrated the process.

Calum had hired Seamus and Patrick O'Brien to help. They were glad for the work. Like many of the Irish, they had found of late that less and less casual labor was being offered them as the Scots tenants completed clearing their land and building their homes.

"'Ere now, watch careful and do as I shows you." Cedric stood at the top of a long field with his left foot on the platform of a long-handled, narrow-bladed implement he called a loy. With successive quick jabs of his foot on the spade and turns of the sod onto the uncut ground beside it, he cut a strip ten inches wide, fourteen inches long, and three inches deep. He pointed to the freshly turned sod. "There now, you've a fine bed for the tatties, and a nice deep drain—that's what tatties like—good drainage. Let's us see you do it now."

Seamus and Patrick picked up the loys they had brought with them. Deirdre noticed that their turf-cutting spades had platforms on the opposite side of Cedric's. The O'Brien brothers dug with their *right* feet.

"'Ere, now. What's this? That's not right." Cedric stopped them. "You've gotta dig with the other foot. This'll turn your sod the wrong way." He frowned at the puzzling development and shook his head. "Never saw such a country. Don't even know which foot to dig with."

Deirdre saw the spark of defiance in the O'Briens' eyes. She knew their volatile humor could quickly flare to anger, and she stepped forward hurriedly. "I'm certain we can sort that out, Cedric. Suppose you show us what to do next."

Still frowning, he picked up a basket of the potatoes Deirdre and Calum had so carefully prepared. He examined them, then grunted his satisfaction. "They'll do." He eyed Deirdre. "Plantin's woman's work. I'll show you how to do it, so mind."

Deirdre gulped. Planting three acres of potatoes at a ton an acre was woman's work?

Calum caught her eye and winked.

Cedric dropped the potatoes on the ridge in three rows, forming a diamond pattern. "Now, soon's the shoots appear, cover 'em with three inches of soil from the furrow." He measured out about an inch between thumb and forefinger. "Little white sprouts. Grow from the eyes. You'll see 'em soon enow. Day or two of warm rain, that's all it takes." He picked up his discarded loy. "Just that and good manuring. Plenty of manure. Sea wrack's the best."

Then he tugged at his cloth cap, climbed onto the seat of his rattling wagon, and drove off to explain the mysteries of potato growing to the next of Lady Montgomery's pioneers.

Calum grinned at Seamus. "Suppose you and Paddy begin at the other end of the field with those right-footed loys of yours. That way we'll be turning our ridges in the same direction."

Deirdre turned to her woman's work. She had to admit that dropping the potatoes in the argyle design Cedric demonstrated, although back-straining, was far easier than cutting and turning sod.

It also gave her time to think. Standing for a moment with a hand easing her back, she looked around. She never tired of the beauty of her new home. Scrabo, probably the hill fort home of some ancient Gaelic chieftain, rose a brilliant green behind her. She turned to the east and smiled at the serenity of Strangford Lough.

And as love for her new land filled her, it heightened the ache for the old. Especially for the father she had fled. Would she ever be free of the longing? Would this never truly be home? She sometimes thought of her three married brothers, especially her favorite, the roguish Cailean. But that was more with curiosity to know how their families were growing than with any of the pain and separation she felt for her father.

In a rush she placed her next set of triangles in order to catch up to Calum. They could talk if she worked right behind him.

"Calum . . ."

He paused to wipe the sweat from his brow and smiled at her. "Is it too much for you, Deirdre? I've some money left from the last sale of timber. Even after I pay for the potatoes and the manure. I could hire—"

"No!" She stopped and looked at the size of the field. "Well, no, I don't mind the work. Although if the tatties are to be planted before summer, perhaps Una and her older bairns could help, too."

They worked on to the end of the row before she returned to the subject that was never far from her mind. "Calum, I've been thinking . . ."

"About yer father, lass?" He nodded. "Aye, and I as well. He was nae a bad man, Alisdair Dunlop." He turned two more spadefuls of sod. "He had his tempers, mind you, but he was very kind to his clerk's orphan. And how did I repay him?"

"You repaid him by making his daughter happy." She sighed. "If only he would see it that way. Calum, he was such a good father, so careful for my every comfort. And we were such good friends—especially after mother died and the boys were married. He always gave me everything I asked for." She planted another group of eight potatoes. "That's what I can't understand. He said yes to everything I ever wanted. Except to the one thing I most cared about."

At the end of the field now, Calum took a handful of potatoes from the basket and placed them on the ridge so they could walk to the top of the field to start a new row together. "I've asked myself over and over if I should have tried again—gone back and reasoned with him."

Deirdre shook her head. "You know what a temper he had and how determined he was when he was set on something. I begged him over and over to change his mind, but he was absolutely set on my marrying Fergus."

"And that'll just make it all the harder for him to forgive me for stealing you away."

Her chin jutted out. "If Rabbie hadn't come for me, I'd have left on my own. Father had Fergus as a guest for dinner at least once a week." She shuddered. "The way that man looked at me across the table. It was all I could do to keep from chucking farl-cakes at him."

She made a face. "He gorged himself on farl-cakes. Cook always made a whole batch for him. He'd have butter dripping off his fingers and oat crumbs sticking to his mustache."

Calum paused in his digging to look at her. "Deirdre, we've talked on this long enough. I'm going to write to your father. It will be a kindness to let him know his daughter's not dead."

She bit her lip. "That might be best. Let's think on it just a wee bit longer, though. Everything is so beautiful here—I don't want to spoil it."

She turned to her work, lest Calum should be able to read her thoughts on her face. If he delayed just a few weeks longer, they might have a somewhat different letter to write to her father. A few weeks, and she would know.

There was little enough time in the coming days for letter writing, anyway. Although well on her way toward delivering her sixth child, Una was happy for the opportunity to plant potatoes, and Cassie and Hugh, short enough so that they needn't stoop for the ridges, were efficient at the job.

All worked with very few breaks through the daylight hours of the lengthening days, even when the rain slowed everything by making the soil cling to loys and shoes. Of course, Una and her children wore no shoes, so it was less of a hindrance to them. She showed Deirdre how to kilt her skirt by tucking the back hem into the front of her apron, and Deirdre was happy for the freedom of movement.

Once the fields were planted, there was the manuring. Calum arranged for the carting of several loads of the seaweed that wrackers living along the Strangford shores gathered and dried. And then all hands were busy spreading it over the field.

"Next year, we'll manure the fields *before* we prepare the ridges. It'll make richer soil for the sprouts to grow in," Calum said.

Deirdre, rubbing her tired back, remembered what Cedric had said. As soon as the shoots started growing, the ridges must be covered with soil. Did the work never end?

That evening she sat at the table, too tired to turn to the dishwashing that awaited her.

Calum looked at her in that strange way she had seem him do of late.

"What is it, my love?" she asked. "Do I displease you?"

"Nae, never. I fear it's the other way."

"What makes you say that?"

"I've no' heard you sing months since. Ye sang so often before." He came over and put his arms around her. "Deirdre, I'd not have you be unhappy."

"No, I'm not unhappy." She made the proper assurances. "I've been much occupied with all there is to learn here. My mind has been full."

And she told herself that she must sing—even if it came from her head rather than her heart. She must not let Calum guess her homesickness or her worry over the continuing bedevilment that plagued the settlers. Last week it had been Ninian Barclay's haystack that went up in flames. The week before, three of Seatons' best milk cows disappeared.

It was nearing late summer, in the pause when the weeds slowed their growing and before the potato harvest began, that Calum and Deirdre sat down to write to Alisdair Dunlop. And by then there was no doubt about Deirdre's message to her father—he was to become a grandfather sometime near Christmas. Of course, Alisdair was already a grandfather several times, as his sons had children, but Deirdre hoped that the fact that his daughter was to bear a child would soften Master Dunlop sufficiently that he would return a conciliatory answer.

Thinking on Parson Montgomery's sermons, she added a prayer for God's forgiveness as she wrote her petition for her father's.

"And would ye like to be taking a ride into town in our fine new carriage to see to the sending of this?" Calum, quill in hand, looked at her across the candle glow.

The "fine new carriage" was the heavy farm cart he had purchased for hauling manure and potatoes. It offered convenience on days when the roads were clogged with mud, although the jolting of the iron wheels sometimes brought on Deirdre's nausea. The cart pony, which they had named Corbie because he was as black as a crow, had become a good companion for Besum in the byre.

Whatever the conveyance, however, she was delighted with the prospect of a trip to Newtownards. "Oh, yes, Calum. And we'll stop at all our friends' houses on the way and tell them our fine news." She clapped her hands. "Oh, it'll be fine to see Ailsa again. How much Effie's baby must have grown by now! Oh, and Lady Montgomery. I've heard their new house is complete—and very grand, too. Her ladyship is certain to want to hear how the potatoes are growing."

Calum crossed the room and put an arm around her, placing one hand on her rounded abdomen. "Aye, potatoes and other things we're growing."

The next morning they stopped first at Johnstones'. Deirdre knew better than to make any direct reference to her condition in front of Calvin, but the shape under her loose jacket told its own story. The girl Anna looked as pale and sallow as she had when Deirdre had last talked to her in the spring, but she was more than once aware of the girl's regarding her wistfully with a soft look in her eyes.

Matt was pleasant and friendly as always, though Deirdre was sorry to find him less exuberant. She could certainly understand how difficult it would be to hold onto a sense of humor in such a household.

They were taking their leave, something Deirdre was not sorry to do, when Calvin Johnstone looked down his long, sharp nose and said, "I expect you've heard that I was right. I must say that's some comfort to me, even though my losses have been as great as the rest."

Calum furrowed his forehead. "What are ye talking about, man?"

"The wild Irish. Never would have them on my land. But they sneak in at night and steal just the same. Finally convinced Seaton. They're all to go. And high time too."

Deirdre's hand flew to her mouth. Una's baby had been born just three weeks ago. She knew Seamus was worried about both mother and child. And now they were to be evicted?

She turned to Calum as soon as they were back on the road. "Calum, that's terrible! Where will they go? Can't you talk to Fulke?"

Calum urged Corbie forward with a jog of the reins. "I don't know. Fulke's a reasonable fellow, but I wouldn't hold out much hope for his father. For all he sits back looking indolent, William Seaton has his finger in every pie."

"But you'll try?"

"Oh, aye, I'll try. Might as well lose two causes as one." He sighed and patted the leather pouch carrying their letter to Alisdair Dunlop.

A short time later, Deirdre was hoping Calum's pronouncement wasn't an omen as to the success of their approach to her father, for the senior Seaton was as obdurate as Calum had predicted.

"Any settler who doesn't clear his land is a fool—deserves to have his cattle stolen and crops burnt. Hamilton handled it much better. Moved them all off soon as he got there. No such trouble at Bangor."

"But their families have lived here for hundreds of years!" She might as well have saved her breath.

"I've given them two weeks' notice. Generous, I know. Few give more than five days. But with the new bairn . . ." He shrugged.

"Mr. Seaton, surely you don't suspect Seamus O'Brien of stealing your cattle?"

"It little matters which one does the act—it all comes to the same thing."

"But Seamus and Una," Deirdre began, "they're our friends—"

William Seaton scowled. "Friends? I hardly think you mean that. Friends with a *papist?*"

Deirdre was in a storming fury by the time they got to Newtownards. As happy as she was to see Rabbie MacKinnon and to send the letter on its way to her father, she urged Calum to hurry.

"Don't ye want to take a bit of time to look at my wares?" Rabbie offered. "I have a fine soft bolt of flannel. Just the thing for wee garments."

"Oh, yes—no." She shook her head. "No, we'll wait till your next trip, Rabbie, when you bring my father's reply. We've urgent business with her ladyship now."

The trader nodded. "Oh, aye. I called at Newton House first thing, and a fine lot her ladyship bought. Aye, it's a grand place. Naething like it outside The Pale, I'm thinking. Oh, and did ye hear? Lord Chichester's building an inn in Belfast. As fine as any in Dublin, they say." As ever, a trader's stock was as much in the news he carried as in his wares.

But today Deirdre couldn't be tempted.

"I'm certain Lady Montgomery will do something for the O'Briens," she told Calum as they left the market square and turned up Castle Street toward the laird's newly completed great house. "After all, look how she helped you when your cottage burned, giving you a job at the mill." Deirdre stopped and gripped the wagon seat. She still was subject to attacks of nausea, and the day's proceedings had offered little concession to her condition. Her head swam. She took a deep breath and steadied herself.

Calum put his arm around her. "Deirdre, shall we go home? Shall I find a place for you to rest? A cool drink?"

"A glass of punch, perhaps, if Lady Montgomery offers. But I'll be fine as soon as I talk to her. It just upsets me thinking of Una and all those children being turned out of their home. As if they would ever set fire to anything but the peats on their hearth."

Calum lifted his head and sniffed. "*Something's* afire." He steadied Corbie, who caught the acrid scent at the same moment.

Then the church bell began an urgent ringing, and people came hurrying from every house and shop along the street.

"Oh, hurry, Calum. Someone needs help."

The added jouncing when Calum urged the black pony to a trot was no help to Deirdre, but she would not have him slow down. Even so, it was several minutes before she knew the cause for the alarm.

They passed a clump of trees, and she saw smoke pouring from the upper windows of Newton House, the Montgomery's grand new home. There would be no petitioning Lady Montgomery for help today or for many days to come.

Calum tied the horse to a post, and as soon as Deirdre assured him she would be all right, he rushed to help carry water buckets from the well.

Deirdre's brave words had been overly optimistic, however. The smoke, the alarms, and the confusion on top of the discomfort she had already been feeling made it impossible to continue sitting in the wagon. A quiet green park stretched behind the house. Turning her back on the bedlam, she walked into the welcome shelter of the woods.

She was sure that the nausea would soon pass if she could just rest. Beyond the soft dirt path, a clump of bushes circled a patch of inviting grass. She patted her abdomen. "We'll just have a wee nap, you and I. Then we'll be right as rain."

She didn't know how long her eyes had been closed when she heard voices.

"Ye took a desperate chance, man. What were ye about—setting it in the middle of the day? Why did ye no' wait till dark?"

"What are ye talking of?"

"Don't be daft with me. I was sent to help ye."

"I need no help. Who are ye?"

Deirdre had only to turn her head to see through the hedge to the path where two men stood. She held her breath as the taller of the two squatted down. Was he looking to see if anyone was behind the hedge, listening? What would he do to her if he saw her?

But the man merely reached for a twig and drew something in the dirt. He stood and pointed to it.

The other man laughed. "*Och*, and why didn't ye say so in the first place?" He put his foot over the drawing, apparently to rub it out. "Well, now, yon stramash's done." He jerked his head back toward Newton House. "What next?"

"The discoverers'll do the rest."

The two men continued on into the woods.

They had been gone for several minutes before Deirdre dared move from her shelter. She did not want them doubling back on the path and finding her. But at last she deemed it safe to creep around the edge of the bushes.

As she had hoped, the impression made on the soft path, though dimmed by the man's boot, had not been obliterated. She studied it carefully. Where had she seen that design before? A line with a triangle on one side and a square on the other? She was sure it meant something, but she couldn't think what.

11

Deirdre was waiting composedly for her husband when he returned to the cart more than an hour later. He had streaks of soot on his face and in his beard. His best doublet was singed, and he'd torn a hole in his hose, but he was triumphant.

"Aye, we got it out." In spite of his brave words, though, he shook his head. "Ah, but it's a poor sight. None so bad they can't repair it, but still a poor sight."

"Were you inside?"

"Aye. I helped carry out some of the fine furnishings. It was the slate roof saved it. As soon as I can, Deirdre, I'm going to send to Scotland for slates. Someday I'll build you a house with a slate roof. And floors timbered with oak and laid with Norway fir. And fine glazed windows." He took her hands. "I've ached at the hard work ye've had to do this year, Deirdre, but I'll see ye no' regret it."

"Calum, I don't regret it now. When we've made it all up with father, there'll be not the least thing to regret." She was certain that would soon be as true as she made it sound. When the babe was born, this would be home. The old longing would fade. She was so certain that she began gently humming "The Flowers of the Forest."

He shook his head as if to clear it. "Ah, Deirdre, I think the smoke got to my brain. It was the fire. It was like reliving that terrible night when I thought I'd lost everything—thought I'd lost you."

She squeezed his arm. "We've been so very fortunate, Calum. Blessed, I should say."

The cart started up High Street, where already some had built in stone from the quarry on Scrabo. A solid row of merchants' houses and shops spread toward the pound, punctuated by archways between every four buildings, giving access to the rear for the farm vehicles and animals used in the town's parks beyond. Some buildings were even roofed with the slate Calum so admired.

It was the talk of their own happiness and the sight of these prosperous buildings that brought a contrasting image to Deirdre's mind. "Calum, turn around."

"What?"

"Go up Movilla and out Back Street."

He frowned. "But why should I do such a daft thing? It's naething but a hovel."

"I know." She bit her lip. "That's why I need to see it."

He shook his head. "Ah, well. Never argue with a woman when she's in calf."

As Deirdre suspected, Back Street, the quarter allotted to the laborers and servants, mostly native Irish, was a single row of clay and thatched huts. There were no chimneys. There were no glazed windows. Children, puppies, and chickens tumbled around doorways that opened into beaten dirt floors. She had lived for many months in similar circumstances. She knew how it felt.

"Calum, we must do something for the O'Briens."

"Aye, but it will be a time before we can talk to her ladyship. And I don't know that she'll be too ready to help. There's many that blame the fire on the native Irish."

"Calum, it wasn't Irish."

He listened to her account, wide-eyed. "You mean the fire was set by someone who identified himself with some strange cipher?"

"What do you think it means?" she asked.

"I've no idea. What did you say the mark was like?"

With the tip of her finger, she traced the pattern of angles on the palm of his hand. "I've seen it before, but I can't remember where." She paused. "And there was something else they said. Calum, what are 'discoverers'?"

His lip curled in a sneer such as she had never seen on his kind face. "A pack o' ferrets, that's what they are. 'Gentlemen' who make it their business to search for technical flaws in the titles of lands granted by the Crown."

"But why would anybody do that?"

"Oh, it's a very profitable business. Grants like those given to Hamilton and Montgomery are vast and imperfectly surveyed—sure to be full of minor errors."

"But doesn't it make the king mad to be told he's made a mistake?

Calum shook his head. "On the contrary. The Crown encourages it—rewards the discoverers with money or land."

"Why?"

"It makes it possible to force the landholders to accept new grants at advanced rents. The increased rents fall on the undertenants —many lose their land."

Deirdre moved closer to him on the wagon seat. Everything was so insecure. Clearances, discoverers, fires. What if they lost *their* land?

A few days later Calum came in from the field with a basket piled high with fine brown potatoes.

"Oh, Calum," she cried. "They're much better than the ones we planted." She picked up the largest. "This one is twice the size of any I cut for seed."

"Aye, they're fine. I thought we could have them cooked for supper. If they cook right, we'll begin harvesting tomorrow."

"How?" All cooking had been a new experience to her, but at least she had thus far worked with ingredients she had seen their cook use in Glasgow.

Calum shrugged. "Boil in a pot, like carrots, maybe? Ask Una. Cedric said something about fancying his roasted. Just put them in the coals of the fire, he said."

"Well—" she took the basket from his hand "—I'll try."

An hour later she fished boiled potatoes out of the pot hanging over the hearth, then dug in the coals with a poker to retrieve her experiment. She placed them on the table with considerable skepticism.

Calum gave thanks, somewhat optimistically, she thought, for what they were about to eat and put one of the black balls on his plate. "I think you'd better peel it," she suggested and took one of the boiled ones as a more hopeful option.

Calum cut open the charred object. They both smiled to find the inside white and mealy. He took a forkful. "Not bad."

Deirdre had also churned that day, so there was a mound of fresh, sweet butter on the table. She pushed it toward him. "Try some of this on it." It was advice she found herself using a minute later on her boiled potato, which made a rather waterlogged lump on her plate.

"I can do better next time," she promised. "It's the cook's fault, not the farmer's. I think the potatoes will be fine. Really." She tried to keep any note of doubt out of her voice.

Calum laughed. "Aye, they'd better be. It's our only crop. If we can't pay for the lease land, we lose the freehold the house is on, too."

"Calum!"

He reached for her hand. "Sorry, lass. I shouldna have spoken so. It was a poor jest. We've a fine crop. And next year, when the rest of the land's cleared, we'll double it."

"Aye, that's grand." But her forehead was still knit in worry. "What about the O'Briens? They've only a few days left."

Calum nodded. "Aye. I talked to Seamus today. He was that worried. I told him I'd hire him for the harvest."

"And how is Una?"

"Not much improved, I fear."

She leaned forward and gripped her husband's arm. "Calum, we must do something. Where else can they go?

"Strangford. Work at wracking?" He sounded doubtful.

Deirdre shuddered. The wrackers, who lived along Strangford Lough, gathering seaweed and drying it for crop manure, existed in even more miserable conditions than those along Back Street in Newtown.

"Calum, that's awful. Why can't we lease them some land?"

He shook his head. "We would lose our own lease if we did."

"But we have to do *something*." She patted her swelling abdomen. "*Six* bairns they have." She thought for a moment. "Couldn't you loan them some land in exchange for their labor?"

Calum came to her side of the table and bent to kiss her forehead. "Aye, I could, perhaps—"

"Well, then, it's settled. You said it yourself."

"Said what?"

"Never argue with a woman when she's in calf."

As Calum predicted, it was a bumper harvest. And as Deirdre promised, she quickly became skilled at preparing this strange new food in palatable ways. Seamus was unspeakably grateful for Calum's offer to allow him three acres of uncleared land and set about doing the work of two men to earn the keep.

The first Monday in December, a skiff of snow fell on the top of Scrabo, but it wasn't enough to keep Calum and Seamus from continuing with the land clearing.

Deirdre felt unaccountably restless. She scrubbed the floor, churned the week's cream into butter, and baked a batch of oatcakes, leaving them by the hearth so they would be warm for Calum when he came in at the end of the workday. And all the while, she sang softly to the babe inside her.

If only Father could see me now, could know how happy I am, he would forgive me for leaving him. I know he would.

The theme was a familiar one for her thoughts. Although it had been three months since they had written, they had received no reply from Alisdair Dunlop, nor were they likely to now that the weather was so unstable for crossing the Irish Sea.

She did not want to stay inside with such thoughts. She took her hooded cloak from the peg inside the door. There were still two hours of daylight left, and Calum would work until the last streak faded, although there did seem to be some dark clouds brooding in the west.

The walk to Una's cabin invigorated her, and she was delighted to see Una and wee Sean much improved. The two talked for some time in the way of women about the birthing and rearing of bairns, while the five little O'Briens played around the cow, pig, and chickens stabled at the far end of the cottage.

Deirdre couldn't imagine living that way, but the O'Brien family seemed very much at home. She remarked on what a sturdy building job Seamus had done on their cottage.

Una smiled. "Sure and it's coming to seem like home. It was a wrench to leave the land my family had been on since the time of Saint Patrick, but we are glad to have this place." She looked at the baby sleeping in her arms.

Moving had been a "wrench" to Una, and she had moved only a little over a mile? Deirdre suddenly found herself telling about fleeing her own home, how much she missed it sometimes—no matter how happy she was here—and how she worried about her father.

"And you've not heard from him even though you wrote? Was he a hard man, your father?"

"No, he had a fiery temper, but he wasn't hard. Oh, I expect he could be in a business matter but never with his daughter."

Una nodded. "Then I'm thinking there must be something else. Something you do not understand that makes him so unforgiving. I will ask the Holy Mother to help you. She understands a mother's heart. She will know."

Deirdre stood abruptly. "Oh, it's gotten so dark. I must go." She could see at once by the confused look on Una's face that the woman had taken her action as a rebuff. But Deirdre was uncomfortable around papist talk. She couldn't imagine what the other settlers would say if they had heard that.

She opened the door and was almost blown off her feet by the wind that had come up while she'd been sitting by Una's warm hearth. She hesitated, peering out. How had she let the time get away from her so?

"Hugh, you must go with Mistress Lanark," Una called to the six-year-old who emerged from the cow stall with straw sticking to the back of his homespun shirt.

Deirdre started to protest that she would be fine. Then a sharp pain in her back told her she'd be glad for the escort. It had been foolish to stay so long.

They were well into the woods when a second pain all but knocked her to her knees. "Oh, Hugh, hold my hand. I almost stumbled."

She wished she could walk faster, but hurrying in the dim light could be counterproductive. Why hadn't Calum come for her? she wondered. Because he didn't know where she was. But surely he could have guessed. Where *else* could she have gone? He would have quit work long ago. He must be worried sick. Why had she been so foolish?

What if he had guessed wrong—thought she had gone to Johnstones' or Seatons'? Or even into the village? No, she was being silly. She would find him sitting by the hearth, eating one of the oatcakes she left for him with a mug of milk still warm from Besum.

"Can you walk faster, Hugh?" She longed to feel Calum's arms around her, warm and protective. "Oh!" She grasped a tree growing by the path and clung to it until the wave of pain passed. She had never had such a backache.

"Can you walk, mistress? Across the field would be quickest, but it's rough."

The ridges and trenches of the potato hills striped the field. It would be difficult walking. "Hugh, you run across the field, but be careful. Don't turn your ankle. You tell Master Lanark I'm coming around the road and to come meet me." She gasped at another twinge. "Hurry."

Afraid to hurry herself, yet desperate to be home, she turned toward the path that skirted the field to the main road. It would feel so good to have Calum's shoulder to lean on. Everything would be all right when he was here. Forcing herself to breathe evenly, she walked on.

It seemed ages later when she heard feet running toward her. "Calum!" It came out on a sob.

But it wasn't Calum. It was only the slight figure of a six-year-old boy.

"Hugh. Where is Master Lanark? Why didn't he come?"

"I don't know, mistress. He wasn't there. No one was there."

"That can't be. Did you look everywhere? In the spare bedroom?" That was it. Hugh wasn't used to houses with two rooms. He hadn't looked, and Calum was in there—fallen asleep.

"No, mistress. I mean, yes, I looked. He wasn't there."

"Well, the cow byre, then. You know—under the house. The door's around back." She should have been more explicit in her instructions to the child.

"I looked there, mistress."

"Well, he must be somewhere. Did you call out? He would have been at the peat stack, that's all." She hid her rising fear under irritation at the child. "Never mind, we're at the road now. Help me home."

By now Deirdre had a good idea what her pains were. Both Effie Seaton and Una had told her about the pains of childbearing. But she had not heard it said that they could come in the back. She had always imagined in the front, where the child was. She gripped the small of her back with both hands and hung on. This one lasted longer, and they were coming more often now.

Still, there would be plenty of time. Time for Calum to finish whatever he was doing and go for the midwife. Una had said it took hours and hours. Especially with your first. *Oh, Calum, where are you?*

Her unspoken cry rang hollowly when they finally made it to the house. The room that had seemed so clean and cozy when she left hours before was now dark and empty. She lit a candle and put another peat on the fire.

"Hugh, you must fetch your mother. Tell her the babe is coming and that—that Master Lanark is not here."

Even as she said the words, she could not believe them. Calum had always been there. When she was little and got scolded by her brothers for being a nuisance, she could always turn to Calum's gentle smile. When she fell down and skinned her knees playing ring a ring of roses, Calum carried her into the house. When her father was going to marry her to that odious man, Calum rescued her. But where was he now?

The warmth of the fire crept to her in the cozy bed, and for a time she slept.

She woke to the sound of an efficient voice. "That's right, put more water in the kettle. Then bring some clean linen from the chest."

But it wasn't Calum's voice.

"Una. Where's Calum?"

"Don't you be thinking about him. This is for women."

"But where is he? Why wasn't he here when I came home? Had he gone out to look for me?"

Una crossed herself, a gesture Deirdre was certain she wasn't meant to see. "Yes. Yes, that's right. He was out looking for you. I brought Cassie to help me."

"Has he gone for the midwife?"

"Newtown is a long ways. We'll be fine. I know what to do."

Another contraction ended the conversation. It was all she needed to know, anyway. Calum was all right. So everything would be all right. It had always been so in her world.

Una wrung out a rag dipped in sweet-smelling herbal water and put it on her forehead. "It's a pity to have back labor with your first. I had it once—in the early stages before the babe shifted. But it's terrible. Would you like me to sing you a wee song? It'll help the time pass."

Deirdre nodded. She had heard Una singing to her children before, but she had no idea how tender the Gaelic songs could sound even when she didn't understand the words.

Throughout the night she drifted in and out of restless sleep between contractions. Once she dreamed Calum had come back, but when she woke, the midwife wasn't there.

"What can be taking him so long?"

"I expect the midwife was out. Babes have a way of coming in batches."

And then, just when the first streaks of red were lighting the house through the eastern window, Deirdre didn't have time even to think of Calum. Every ounce of her attention and energy was focused on bringing their son into the world.

The room was filled with strong winter sunlight when Una placed a tiny, red-faced, swaddled bundle in Deirdre's arms and helped put him to her breast. "Encourage him to suckle all he will. It'll help your milk flow strong."

Deirdre looked at her wee son snuggling to her breast and felt such a rush of love she could hardly breathe. "Oh, he's wonderful. Oh, thank you, Una. You were wonderful, too. Does Calum know? Have you told him? Can't he come in now?" She looked around and started to call out to her husband.

Una drew a stool next to the bed and put a hand on her arm. "Deirdre, we must believe Calum knows. I told him. I'm certain he understood."

"Well, why doesn't he come in? I want to show him his son."

The hand on her right arm tightened. "You must be brave, Deirdre. Calum's in the other room. Seamus brought him in when you were asleep. It was their last tree of the day. A wind came up just as it fell—Seamus isn't sure what happened—but it hit Calum."

Deirdre stifled a cry. "I must see him. Here, take the babe. Help me up."

Una pushed her back against the pillows. "He's sleeping now. It's the best for him. And you need to rest, too. Seamus has gone to Carrickfergus. There should be an army doctor at the castle. We must hope for the best. And I will pray to—" She stopped.

At last Seamus arrived with the army physician from the fort.

Deirdre could hear little from the other room. She lay tense, trying to pray, trying to think. He had to be all right. Life without Calum was unimaginable. She closed her eyes, trying to block out the worries, but it seemed that just closed them in.

When she opened her eyes, Dr. Willson sat on the stool beside the bed where Una had been moments before. Deirdre didn't say anything, just looked at him wide-eyed.

"He sleeps. He may sleep for some days. Weeks, perhaps. Or more."

She tried to focus on the doctor's white hair and beard. "Do you mean he's . . ." She could not form the word her mind refused to think.

Dr. Willson shook his head. "He breathes. But it is a sleep he cannot be waked from by our efforts. It is in God's hands."

"But will he waken?"

"He may. I have seen it so with men who receive head wounds in battle. We must hope for the best."

"But *when* will he wake up?"

"Hope for the best," he repeated and turned to Una. "Keep him warm. Try spooning drops of broth or ale onto his tongue. If he swallows them, do more." He observed the babe in Deirdre's arms. "A fine wane."

"It is his son." She made the statement with fierce determination. The words were a defiance of anything that would keep Calum from knowing his son, of anything that would keep them from building their life together.

Having come so far, they would not allow this to defeat them. As on her first night in Ireland, when she stood in the ruins of the burned-out cabin, she renewed her resolution. They would survive. And they would succeed. This would be home.

12

His smile returned first. It was early in the new year as the wind blew icily off the lough and howled around the corners of the house. Deirdre almost wished she had the cattle in the house with her as the O'Briens did. At least Besum would provide warmth and companionship. But she had companionship. She had her son and her husband.

She took the swaddled babe from the cradle Calum had made months ago. "Here, Calum, this is your son. I named him Gordon Rory after your father. But I find myself calling him Rory, as it looks like he'll have red hair." She pronounced it Roo-ree.

As she talked, she sat on the bed and placed the babe in Calum's arms, folding her husband's arms—which moved only in restless twitching, if at all—around the baby.

And then Calum smiled. His eyes fluttered, and she felt a twinge of voluntary movement in his arms. That was all. But it was enough to go on with.

Through all the weary, frightening days past, she had fed Calum spoonfuls of the strong herbal broth that Una taught her to make from boiled sheep's liver—a recipe from Una's granny. She sang to him, talked to him, quoted every psalm she could remember. If only the Bible hadn't been burned. What a comfort it would be to be able to read aloud from it now. She renewed her determination that someday they would have a Bible of their own.

But for all her care, Calum had made no response. All she had to carry her was faith and determination. And love for these two helpless beings in her care.

Then that morning she felt overcome with desire that Calum should know the joy of holding such a precious life in his arms. And he had responded.

Calum's recovery was so slow that sometimes Deirdre despaired almost as much as during those darkest nights in the depth of the winter when he lay unmoving and unseeing. But he did progress. Once he was fully awake, there was a terrible weakness to overcome, uncoordinated movement, and slurred speech. Dr. Willson called in whenever he made a journey to Dublin. And each time, he assured them that Calum's condition was similar to others he had seen and that they could hope for continued improvement.

But at night the worries crowded close. Her courage held during the daytime. What would they do if Calum couldn't resume farming? If they couldn't pay the rent? If they lost the freehold to the property their house was built on? And what if she didn't hear from her father? Although spring again brought frequent crossings of traders from Scotland, no letter had arrived from Alisdair Dunlop.

Seamus, with all the help Deirdre, Una, and the O'Brien bairns could provide, had managed to plant the new crop of potatoes. But there had been no more land cleared. And Calum had counted on doubling his crop this year. She tried to talk to him about it without worrying him. But when she suggested they rent land to Patrick O'Brien so that he could work with Seamus, Calum was adamant. "There's nae land enough for three families. Invite him here to starve? No favor."

Talking tired Calum, and his frustration over the difficult task of forming words was so great that she sometimes thought she saw tears in his eyes. So she did not press the matter. But she must find a way. Ireland offered unbounded opportunities. Everyone said so.

But then she put aside such thoughts. Mrs. Johnstone along with Anna came to call, and a call from that formidable lady required all of one's attention. Deirdre was happy to have visitors. She had fewer now as the situation dragged on, and she enjoyed Anna's delight in amusing baby Rory. But she had considerable difficulty conversing with this woman who sat with her back straight and her hands folded in her lap.

"Please tell me all the news, Mrs. Johnstone. I've seen almost no one for a while."

Senga Johnstone's mouth was set in a prim line. "I never gossip."

"Of course. I only meant to ask what is happening in the wider world."

Senga sniffed. "William Seaton is building bigger barns and an addition to his house. I told him he should look to the Scripture to see what happened to the man who pulled down his barns to build bigger ones. But he only laughed at me. 'It's all right laughing at me, William Seaton,' I said. 'It's fine enough laughing at a poor woman. But there's a reckoning for us all. There'll come a reckoning.'"

Deirdre wanted to argue that building a bigger barn wasn't necessarily sinful, but she bit her tongue. "What are the barns for?" She hoped that was a safe enough question.

"Wool. Lady Montgomery's new scheme, you know."

Deirdre looked blank.

"Oh, of course, you wouldn't know, would you? Now, if you'd been coming to kirk regularly . . ."

Deirdre held her breath. She didn't need a lecture on Sabbath observance. The Lord knew there was nothing she wanted more than to be able to attend services with her husband as they had always done before.

"Or if you didn't hire papists for laborers. My Calvin says your troubles are a warning from Providence against harboring those that are lost in superstition."

Deirdre wasn't going to sit and listen to this. She was about to get to her feet, when Mrs. Johnstone hurried on.

"But I said I wasn't going to let the fact that some pray to idols keep me from doing my Christian duty. And it's clear enough we're to visit the sick and fatherless." She glanced at Rory reaching for the carved wooden lamb Anna held out to him. "Of course, your bairn's not exactly fatherless, but as good as, from what I hear of goings on at Seaton Court."

Seaton Court? What does she mean?

"Lady Montgomery's new scheme, Mrs. Johnstone?" She didn't try to keep the sharpness out of her voice.

"Cloth. Wool and linen, she says. The idea is to make the settlement self-sufficient. When she gets two more mills built, we'll not have to rely on Scotland for any milling. Next thing will be our cloth. Raise more sheep, spin and weave the wool right here."

Deirdre lost her irritation. She was interested. Spinning she could do. If only she could get a spinning wheel. And she was certain she could learn to weave. She knew a great deal about fibers and cloth quality. After all, her father had been a cloth merchant. Then she sighed. But they had no sheep. Calum really disliked them, and he had never replaced the ones that had been stolen.

"But we know our duty. We will make linen. Anna and I are going to start spinning as soon as the first batch of flax arrives. It's the Christian thing to do, I said."

Deirdre bit her lip. Apparently linen making wouldn't require the building of new barns.

But now she knew what *she* was going to do. She wouldn't tell Calum yet, because she didn't want to worry him, and it would spare him disappointment if it didn't work. But that night she wrote again to her father. The first time, Calum had written, begging Alisdair's forgiveness. Now she wrote, begging her father's love. For his new grandson, if he could no longer love his daughter.

And knowing her father's fondness for doing business, she proposed a bargain. She told him of Lady Montgomery's scheme to start a linen industry in Ulster. If Alisdair would send her a spinning wheel and loom, she would send him cloth to sell in the Merchants' Hall in Glasgow. The next day she asked Seamus to take the letter into Newtownards and to find a trader to carry it—she almost said "home." She had to remind herself sternly that Ireland was home.

As spring turned to summer, it began to feel more like home again, and although he often seemed withdrawn and silent, Calum's strength grew. He was able to work very little, but they took long, slow walks around their land in the golden evenings when the sun dipped behind Scrabo, leaving the world green and sweet. He still used a stick to aid his balance, and sometimes, if they walked too far, he would need to lean on her before they were back to the house. But it seemed that his vitality gained even as the potato leaves spread over the brown earth and as Rory grew.

They stood one day, arm in arm, looking at the slope rising behind their house. "Next year—" Calum began, then stopped and shook his head. "I've lost a whole year."

Her hand tightened on his arm. "But we didn't lose you, and that's the important thing." It was the only thing that really mattered. She could go on without anything—except Calum.

"Aye, we must be thankful. Next spring, if—" He stopped and started again as he did so often these days. "We'll plant fruit trees."

"Yes!" She caught the vision. "What a fine idea! Sweet with blossoms in the spring and heavy with fruit in the autumn."

"Aye, and when wee Rory's grown enough, he can climb the branches for all the fruit a lad can eat."

His delight in the plan made him seem more like the old Calum than anything she'd seen since the accident. Her mind filled with the picture of Calum lifting his son and tossing him in the air. Then she knew an ache because she understood just how much Calum longed to do such things. They turned toward the house, his hand heavy on her shoulder.

She almost told him then of her plan. But what if her father said no or simply maintained his silence? If the whole thing were to fail, it would just be another disappointment for Calum to deal with. And if he knew she had told Seamus to ask Patrick to help him, and promised that she would pay him, and that she had already arranged to purchase several bundles of flax from Lady Montgomery's first shipment, certainly Calum would worry. She was worried herself.

She told herself there was no reason to worry. Even if her father refused, she and Una could process the flax. She had made inquiries and understood that treating the fibers would require considerable work, which would not yield much profit without the spinning and weaving, but a little. Perhaps she should have just opted for that and saved to buy her own loom. Well, she could still do it that way if it came to it. No, then there wouldn't be enough to pay Patrick. Oh, dear, what had she gotten herself into?

It seemed she was soon to know. A cart came rattling up the road toward them, piled so high with bundles of flax stalks that it looked as if the wagon had a thatched roof. And, as a matter of fact, the driver's name was Thatcher.

As soon as he began throwing the four-foot-long bundles into a stack beside the house, Deirdre realized her mistake in trying to shield Calum from worry.

He looked at her in confused astonishment.

"It's flax," she said.

"I know what it is. I may seem daft at times, but I'm not that simple. But what's it for?"

"Linen." She knew she had said the wrong thing even before he started for the house. "Calum, let me explain!" She started after him, then turned back to Thatcher.

He jerked his head toward the house. "Go on, then. It's too late to start the rettin' tonight. I'll come back in the morning."

She ran to the house, undid the halter that kept Rory slung tightly to her left side, and placed him in the cradle before turning to Calum, who sat with his head in his hands.

"Calum, I'm sorry. I was going to tell you as soon as I knew if my idea would work. I—"

It would have been far better if he'd raged at her. As it was, she felt paralyzed by his icy bitterness.

"So that's what it's come to, is it? That's all I'm good for? You'll tell me about it when it's done?"

"No, Calum. I wanted to spare you the worry. All I want is for you to get well."

"But in the meantime you'll go ahead and run things very well your own way. And then if I don't recover, it won't make all that much difference, will it?"

"No, no!"

Now he did raise his voice. "Well, what else is there I don't know? Tell me now, woman. I'll not be a kept man in my own home." He slammed a fist against the table so hard that a wail rose from the cradle.

Deirdre drew back in alarm. Calum had told her he was capable of rage, but she had never seen it. Always he had been so calm, so patient. Una had remarked on it often. Hot-tempered as her Seamus was, she was amazed at Calum's gentleness. And that was the Calum

Deirdre had always known. Rory wailed louder, and her milk rushed painfully to her breasts. She didn't know what to do.

Then suddenly Calum slumped back in the chair, his hands gripping his head. "Or is this what I've to expect? Did the doctor tell you I won't recover?" He returned to the iciness that was worse than anger.

"Please listen, Calum." The telling sounded worse than she could have imagined. And the hardest was telling him about Patrick.

Calum turned away at that point. He did not look at her again as she went through the whole plan: how she had written to her father, arranged for the flax . . .

"Aye. Well, it seems ye have it all perfectly well in hand." He got up. His left foot dragged when he was tired, and now he stumbled and almost fell.

"Calum, would ye not bide in here tonight?" She patted the out-shot bed where she had slept alone since his accident.

He did not even answer.

And that was the moment the worst fear of all struck her. Ailsa Seaton. She could not imagine Calum being disloyal. And yet, had the tall, red-haired woman not grown more beautiful with the years? And she had remained unmarried. Ailsa had never made a secret of the fact that she admired Calum. And Calum admired her accomplishments. And Seaton Court stood so near, so welcoming. . . .

13

Deirdre took a deep breath and thrust out her chin. There was nothing to do but to carry on. Thatcher had taught her that the preparation of flax was a four-step process that must be overseen with care. First was the retting—soaking the bundles in water to dissolve the gummy substance around the fiber. This took about a week and must be judged carefully.

"Under-retting makes it hard to separate the fibers." Thatcher probed at a stiff stalk with his thumb nail. "This lot needs about two more days."

When Thatcher returned, Calum went out to meet him, and Deirdre watched tensely. Calum had been withdrawn and sullen for days. Was he going to order the agent off his land? Forbid her new venture?

Then her heart leaped as she saw Thatcher hand Calum a folded square of ivory paper. A letter? The long-awaited reply from her father? Calum merely looked at it, stuck it in his doublet, and went on to milk Besum. Fear flooded Deirdre. Could the letter have come from much nearer? From Seaton Court?

Clenching her fists to keep fear at bay, she turned to the retted flax in the slime-covered pond. She had no idea the rotting fibers could stink so. And it would be necessary to wade into it to retrieve all the flax. *Give me strength.* Strength to deal with the flax, strength to cope with Calum—whatever the situation.

Thatcher shook his head as the flax stalk he drew from the water shredded in his hand. "Over-retting weakens the fiber." He examined several more before he gave a jerky nod. "Aye, that's better. See here, soak it just until the outer layer of stems swell and burst."

Deirdre nodded. Now that she knew what to look for, she had a chance of doing it right.

"Then you lay them out to dry. Must be well cured before the scrutching."

Scrutching. "How long is that?" She still hadn't heard from her father. She hoped every day to receive word that a loom was on its way.

Thatcher took a long look at the gathering clouds and shrugged. "Depends. A few months unless the rain sets in good."

"Months?" She had thought a few weeks at most. She'd no idea it was such a slow process. Why hadn't she asked more questions? Why had she just rushed into all this? She had no way to pay Patrick, no way to pay for the flax, no assurance of a loom. And she was so tired. She could hear Rory crying in his cradle. She turned toward the house. It was all she could do to put one foot in front of the other.

Wearily she picked up her bairn and loosened the front of her dress. She didn't know where Calum was. Since that dreadful night weeks ago, they had spoken only when necessary. He went out every day after breakfast and came in for supper. She did not know if he was able to work, but she dared not ask. She assumed he was with Seamus, seeing to the potatoes. She hoped he wasn't—she shook her head at the unworthy thought, but it wouldn't stay back—she hoped he wasn't drinking. The charming, handsome Seamus was a good man, but she was well aware of his habits. Una never seemed to worry about it. "Ah, he has a fierce head the next day—and serves him right. But he never hits me or the bairns."

Deirdre knew *she* wouldn't be so philosophical if Calum were to come reeling home. It was almost worse than the thought that he might be seeing Ailsa Seaton. And once or twice she thought she had smelled it on him. She felt the tears spill hot on her cheeks and made no attempt to stop them. Still cuddling Rory, she crossed to the bed and lay down.

When she wakened, the room was dark, and she was aware of someone moving around. "Calum?"

"Aye."

"Oh, I'm sorry. There's no supper. I fell asleep."

"So I see."

She jumped up and lit a candle from the few live embers left on the hearth. There was cheese on the shelf and bread left from breakfast. She could fry some bacon. "I won't be long."

"Don't fash yourself. I'm not hungry." He went out. To Seaton Court? To Ailsa's arms, while he spurned hers? She ran to the door. "Calum, please."

He turned to her.

She couldn't reveal her deepest fears. She talked of the problem at hand. "I can't do it. I thought I could, but I can't. Not alone. Please don't go. Please help me."

He stood there.

She had thought—hoped—he would come to her. At least open his arms. But he just stood there.

"What do you need?"

He was polite enough, but she might have been a stranger.

So she answered him in kind, explaining the flax processing and the time needed for drying.

"But if ye had a warm, sheltered place, it would be faster?"

"Yes, of course. But—"

He looked upwards where her loft covered most of the room. She had directed the building of it, thinking to use it for storage. But she had nothing to store yet.

"*Yes*, Calum! That's it!" She ran and threw her arms around him. For just a moment, she felt his arms close around her. Then he withdrew.

Pulling away from Deirdre was perhaps the hardest thing Calum had ever had to do—even harder than the night he refused her invitation to return to their marriage bed. He would never have reacted so sharply then had it not been for the headache. But now he could see that perhaps it was best. He had to work this out on his own, just as she'd had to work out her problems on her own all these months he'd been sick.

If he gave in now and clasped her to him as he longed to do, if he began sharing everything with her again, she would be in a worse fix when—*if*, he amended firmly—if these blinding headaches kept returning. If they got worse. If she had to carry on alone.

No. It was no good borrowing trouble. He would get everything secured for her. Her linen industry was a godsend of an idea. He would see her established. And then, if it came to the worst . . .

He took one glance at their sleeping nook, where Rory still lay on the bed. No. He turned away. He must stay in his own room. He would not take the chance of leaving her with another child.

He reached under his mattress and brought out two items. He unfolded the paper first. He looked at his name so carefully penned on the outside and the word "Confidential" underlined in dark ink. He must deal with this matter. If only he knew what to do.

Then the words of the letter blurred as the pain that had been only a dull ache at the base of his skull gripped him like fierce tentacles. In a moment he would be lost in a blackness of agony. He reached for the other item from his mattress—the bottle Seamus had given him. One swig burned like fire all the way down, but it dulled the headache enough that he could sleep. And he must sleep, because every day was important.

By the time the potato harvest started, the flax was dry. Thatcher came back with his cart and demonstrated scrutching, the final step in extracting the fibers from the stalks.

"For a proper scrutchin' like, ye'd roll the flax between logs to break the woody stems. But as ye've nae such, we'll make do." He spread the dried stalks in the road and drove over them with the wide wheels of his cart.

Likewise, as they had no proper threshing floor, Una and Deirdre had to beat the bundles of stalks on a stony path to remove the final bits of hard straw. Now the fibers were ready for Una to spin.

"I thought to have heard from father by now. I had hoped to have a wheel so I could spin, too."

The disappointment in Deirdre's voice tore at Calum. He would have to tell her soon. If he could just be ready by the time Una finished the spinning. "It'll do for now, lass. Ye've done a good job." The glow in her eyes at his gentle words wrenched at him. If only it could be between them as before.

Perhaps, if all went well tomorrow . . . Thatcher had brought the letter from Montgomery's clerk. He would see him. If he could just get this matter settled before . . .

The next morning Calum hitched Corbie to the wagon while Una and her children spread the flax stems on the road. He drove over them repeatedly to do the breaking, then left the women to get on with the beating. He saw Deirdre's questioning look as he drove off. But he couldn't tell her yet. When the matter was settled would be time and enough. Hurting her now could do no good. Still, he argued with himself, she was so self-sufficient. Perhaps she would not be as upset as he imagined. If only he could get it all sorted out.

But that evening as Corbie plodded toward home, Calum's mind was full of more questions than answers. When he drove up the lane, he saw that the broken flax stems were cleared off the road—evidence of how hard Deirdre had worked. He hoped her flax-beating had been more successful than his errand. Perhaps the best would be to tell all, admit his failure, and prepare her for the worst.

But what would she say? What could they do? The smell of roast chicken told him he was home. And starving. The first sight that greeted him when he opened the door was a bowl piled high with snowy boiled potatoes. Deirdre had indeed learned how to cook them to perfection since her first disastrous attempt.

"Ah, lass, that's grand. I can't tell ye what an appetite I've on me." He washed at the basin on the sideboard.

"Eat you then."

He looked at her sitting by the fire holding Rory. He was not surprised that she sounded tired. But the hollow, bitter note in her voice made him wonder. "Deirdre? Will ye not eat with me?"

"I'm not hungry."

He was too hungry to hold back, even though his own chewing was the only sound in the room.

When he had finished, she rose and placed Rory in his cradle. She cleared the dishes from the table, then turned to the cupboard. She drew two objects from behind a large post and placed them on the table in front of Calum. "Your mattress needed turning. I asked Una to help me, since she was here."

He didn't know where to start. "I had been thinking it was time to tell you—"

She sat across the table from him. "Time and past, I would say."

"Did you read the letter?"

She shook her head. "It says confidential."

"Then you understand why I didn't show it to you."

"I don't understand anything. Especially that." She pointed to the bottle.

"The *uisce beatha*, water of life." He sighed. "If only it could be." She would have to know sooner or later. "Seamus gave it to me. For headaches. When I canna sleep."

"*Headaches?*" Now all her coldness was gone. "Calum, I've often seen you rubbing your head. But I did not know. Why didn't you tell me?"

He shrugged. "I didna want to worry ye." He could not speak of the worst he feared. "My father had such headaches before he—"

But he could see by the wideness of her blue eyes and the sudden tears that filled their corners that he need not say the words.

"Oh, Calum. No. No. It canna be." She left her chair and came to him. "You're getting better. You are."

She had not sat on his lap for almost a year. Now he held her as she clung to him and sobbed. At last her shaking subsided. She looked up and kissed the scar behind his ear where the tree had hit the hardest. "It's no' for certain, love? No' for certain?"

He shook his head. "Only God knows what's certain."

She gripped his shoulders. "Calum, that's true. We none of us know. We must make every day—every minute—count. Oh, Calum, please, please don't shut me out anymore. And I'll not rush ahead on things without you. Please. Whatever comes, we must face it together."

He couldn't believe how good those words sounded. "Aye. Together." And he couldn't believe how good she felt in his arms. How could he have forgotten? How could he have lived so long without holding her?

14

Deirdre awoke smiling. She was warm. She was happy. How long had it been since she had wakened so? She snuggled into Calum's arms. And then reality broke in with a chill.

The letter. Calum hadn't explained the letter. Had it come from Ailsa? Had he held another as he held her now?

She grabbed her shawl and stumbled from the bed.

Calum awoke to find her huddled in the corner. "Deirdre? What is it? Why are ye looking at me like that?"

Fear so choked her that she wasn't sure she could find her voice. And yet she must. She didn't want to know. Yet she must. "The letter, Calum."

"Aye." He crossed the room to pick it up from where they had dropped it the night before. He put it in her hand. "Read it."

She could tell from the look on his face that it was bad news. She held it as if it were a snake. Was this the end to all the happiness she had known? She forced herself to look closely at the handwriting. Then she gasped. "It's from Father!"

"Aye."

"Has he forgiven us?"

Calum shook his head. "He says nothing personal. It's all business."

She read. But she did not understand. "What does he mean? Discoverers have found fault with Montgomery's lease? We are to lose our lands! Calum, can it be so?"

He shook his head. "I dona know. I spent the day yesterday with Montgomery's clerk—"

"Montgomery's clerk! You were at Newtown House?"

"Aye. Where did ye think me?"

"I—I didn't know what to think. You . . . you just drove off and left me. I was so afraid."

"Oh, my poor lass." He lifted her to her feet and cuddled her in his arms. "Can you forgive me? I've been so worried, so confused. I thought to spare you."

She leaned into the delicious comfort of his arms, then drew away. "Now tell me everything. What of the clerk's office?"

"Well, as you read in your father's letter, the gossip in the Merchants' Hall is that discoverers have found a major flaw in the land grant of the Ards. Much of the land is to be Crown property again—to be resettled under the new Plantation scheme King James is beginning."

"And you wanted to see a copy of the grant for yourself?"

"Aye, I've had good training as a clerk. There's many a contract I've studied and drawn up in those days in Glasgow. I thought it just possible I might spot something useful. But—" He shook his head.

"You didn't find anything?"

"Nothing in the grant. It was when I was putting the papers back. They stuck halfway in. I kept pushing, then discovered a portfolio had fallen across the back. It had a strange cipher on it." He dipped a pen in the inkwell on the writing table and traced the mark.

Deirdre frowned, looking at the design. "Calum—those men in the woods. The day Newtown House burned. The man drew it in the dirt. I told you—remember? Something about someone ordering the fire. Do you think we should have told Sir Hugh? I didn't think—it was all so vague."

"It's still vague. But I read the letters in the portfolio. They were the correspondence between Hugh Montgomery and a fellow spy in the days of their adventuring for the Crown."

"You mean those old stories about Montgomery sending an agent up to Carrickfergus Castle and freeing Conn O'Neill—"

"Who came down the castle walls on a rope his wife had smuggled to him inside a cheese! That's exactly the story I mean."

"But that was so long ago. What difference could it make now?"

"Montgomery freed O'Neill all right, but he had to enlist the help of Hamilton, his former fellow spy, to secure O'Neill's pardon. Hamilton talked the king into granting him the Clandeboye lands promised to Montgomery. But King James said Hamilton must divide the land with Montgomery and O'Neill, leaving no one happy."

Deirdre nodded. "And with the Montgomery settlement being so prosperous now—largely due to Lady Montgomery's enterprise—Hamilton is jealous." She paused. "So was the cipher Hamilton's? Does that mean Hamilton's men set the fire?"

They stared at each other for several heartbeats.

"But I don't see how that helps clear Montgomery's land grant."

Calum put his hands to his temples, and Deirdre knew his head was aching again. "I'm afraid it doesn't. It all just seems to muddy the waters more."

"And is that all you found?"

He hesitated.

"Calum, your holding back worries me more than the truth ever could."

"Aye. Well. I may be imagining things. Or have them muddled. I do that when the pains are bad." He turned away from her as if to hide his weakness.

She reached out and began gently massaging his temples.

"Well, there was a letter from someone who signed himself Farl. He claimed that the agent who had wooed the gaoler's daughter in order to enlist her help—the agent had been obliged to actually marry the girl so that she would do as he asked. He wanted money from Montgomery to keep the story quiet."

Deirdre laughed. "Ah, a smart girl. Did Montgomery pay?"

"I don't know, but—" Calum took her hands in his "—Deirdre, the agent who married the girl was Cailean."

"My brother? That's not possible. Cailean had been married years before all that." Then she stopped. "Oh, dear. Charming, unruly Cailean. And gone from home so often. I suppose it was just the sort of thing he *would* do. I remember what terrible fights he and Father had in those days. Do you think Father knew?"

"I think it likely. And I think we should tell him we know. Even though the tone of your father's letter is so formal, I think it's his gesture toward a reconciliation. I think we should reply with complete openness."

"So do I." Deirdre reached for the quill. As she did so, she saw again the paper with the cipher Calum had sketched. She hesitated, quill suspended over the paper while a drop of ink formed on the tip. "Oh!" The black blob dropped onto the paper. "That mark—now I know where I saw it before!"

"In the woods. You said."

"No, I mean *before* that. We hadn't been here very long . . ." She shut her eyes with the effort of recall. "Yes, I do remember. When Effie had her baby. I was reading to her from a book of William Seaton's. A letter fell out. It bore that cipher." She grasped at the implication. "Could that mean that *William Seaton* was a spy for Hamilton?"

Calum considered. "All the problems that plagued the settlement—the fires, the stolen cattle, the missing tools—"

"And all blamed on the native Irish! Could Hamilton have been behind it all? And Seaton—William Seaton sneaking around stealing tools and cattle? That isn't possible."

"No, more likely he was directing a trusted servant." Calum was quiet for a long time, thinking. Suddenly he grabbed his wife's hands.

"Deirdre! That's it! If Montgomery can get proof of Hamilton's misdeeds (and we can tell him where to start—with William Seaton!), then Hamilton can be forced to call off his discoverers."

"But why would Seaton cooperate?"

"To save disgrace to his family. In exchange for a few acres of Montgomery land back in Ayrshire, perhaps." Calum bounded to his feet as lightly as he had moved before the accident. "I'll go to his lordship today. I think we may have heard the last of all this faulty title business."

"I'll go with you. Oh, Calum, do you realize how long it's been since we've gone anywhere together?" She picked up Rory and walked out at her husband's side.

When they drove by Seaton Court, she smiled and held tightly to Calum's arm. Her own happiness was such that she could almost feel sorry for William Seaton in spite of all the unhappiness he had caused. She savored the moment, for she had lived long enough to know that such moments of bliss were all too fleeting.

In spite of her worries over Calum's health, Deirdre's bliss held until the traders' return journey brought a reply to the letter she and Calum wrote to her father. And even then, the new worries the letter revealed were not unrelieved, because, for the first time since her flight from his house, her father had written to her.

Even as a frown wrinkled her brow, she clasped the letter to her breast. Tears filled her eyes. "Father! Oh, Calum, I hadn't realized I missed him so much. And he's suffered so much, too. I had no idea—" She held out the letter for him to read.

Calum had been right in saying they should be completely open in telling her father all they knew about Cailean. Their openness had prompted a surprising openness in Alisdair's reply, though written in a labored hand that showed how hard such confession was for him.

Deirdre waited until Calum finished reading before she spoke. "So Father knew about Cailean all along. And *that* was why he was forcing me to marry fat Fergus Ingram."

Calum nodded. "Because Ingram was the agent. When Montgomery refused to pay to keep Ingram's knowledge secret, Ingram blackmailed your father."

"I should have figured that out when you told me one of those letters was signed 'Farl,' The dinners I suffered through watching him stuff himself on oatcake triangles!" She shivered. "But Calum, the rest of it's so dreadful. Father doesn't exactly say, but he must be nearly destitute. All his apology for being unable to send me the spinning wheel and loom I asked for—could he be that strapped because of paying Fergus?"

Then her hand flew to her mouth. "Oh, Calum, that's terrible. That means *we're* the cause of Father's ruin. Our happiness at his expense."

"Aye."

She saw the deep lines at the sides of his mouth and knew that his headache was back. She stood behind his chair, massaging his neck and back, and after several minutes felt his scalp relax under her touch.

He reached up for her hand and kissed her fingers. "I'm thinking, Deirdre, that we should invite your father to come to Ireland."

"Oh, what a splendid idea!" She threw her arms around his neck. Then a second thought made her draw away. "But have we enough land? Oh, Calum, you'd not clear off the O'Briens? Not after they've been such help."

Calum smiled, but his eyes looked hurt. "Do ye not know me better than that, lass? No, I'm thinking that Alisdair Dunlop has paid dearly to keep the ignoble part of Hugh Montgomery's plot a secret. To my mind it seems it's his lordship that should do a bit of rewarding for such loyalty to the cause."

"But Father was paying for Cailean's reputation, not for Montgomery's. And Montgomery gave *you* no reward for giving him the tool to make Hamilton withdraw his troublemakers."

"I asked for none for myself. But I would ask for your father."

By the time of the third potato harvest at Comber, Calum had all his land cleared, so that by the next spring he could help his father-in-law with his land, which marched along the Lanark holding. Perhaps it was poetic justice that Alisdair Dunlop's holding was carved from Seaton Court. But Fulke Seaton made no objection. Ailsa had returned to Scotland with her father, and Effie Seaton, never vigorous after Judith's birth, had borne Fulke no sons to require land.

Deirdre held the hand of two-year-old Rory and patted her rounding abdomen as she watched the men go to the fields. God was so good. Only the slightest finger of fear touched her heart. Calum never spoke of his headaches, but she could often see the pain lines around his mouth, and his eyes, which had always been laughing, were now frequently strained and dark.

Of course, the headaches couldn't be really serious. It was unthinkable that anything . . . final . . . could happen to Calum.

Seeing his pain and courage made her love him so much that at times her heart ached with the tenderness of it. She prayed that life could go on and on like this. She prayed that life could always be so good for their son and for the new bairn she carried and for this Ireland that she at times loved as much as her home across the water.

No, Ireland *was* her home. She looked at the glimmer of Strangford Lough in the distance and smiled. Her family, her life, her heart were all here. And someday, perhaps soon, her head would no longer have to lecture her heart on the matter.

Let it be always so good, God. And help me to be truly grateful. Help me to love the new home You've given me.

She started back toward the house. Birds were singing and wild crocus bloomed along the path. Yes, surely life here would continue to be as beautiful as the land itself. The peace and gentleness of the land, the industry and organization of the new settlers, the kindness and rambunctious joy of the native people—it could do naught but increase.

Deirdre's glow of golden optimism held through the coming months. Dougal Alisdair Lanark arrived in the world that autumn with far greater ease than had her first bairn. From the beginning he was a more demanding babe than his brother, wailing lustily for his feeding every two hours, nursing so furiously that her nipples were ever sore, and then demanding to be put down. He was not a babe that could abide cuddling.

It was the arrival of the first ship at Donaghadee port after the winter storms that brought an inkling that life in Ulster was about to change. Alisdair had gone in to Newtownards for a new cart wheel that day and came home full of news.

Since her father had begun telling Calum while they saw to the evening chores in the byre, it took Deirdre some struggling to catch up with what they were talking about. She held a steaming platter of crisp, brown, spit-roasted mutton just out of their reach as they sat deep in conversation at the table. "Here, now. You two will tell me what your blethering about, or ye'll go to your beds with empty bellies."

Calum blinked in surprise, then laughed and held out his hands for the platter. "Give over, woman, or we'll nae have the strength to tell ye."

She lowered the plate of juicy meat toward him but kept a firm grip on it, her chin high.

Alisdair smiled at his daughter. "As fiery as I remember your mother, lass. I could ne'er keep anything from her either. The heart of the matter is that the Crown has published a comprehensive plan for settling the territory confiscated from the lords of Ulster. No one is talking of aught else."

Frowning, Deirdre placed the meat on the table and took her chair. "Surely *confiscated* is too strong a word, Father. Did not Tyrone and Tyrconnell flee and willingly leave their lands ungoverned and their people unprotected?"

"Oh, aye. True enough. They opened the door to it all." Alisdair reached for a slab of mutton. "But our Jamie was ne'er a king to let minor hairsplitting stand in his way. That only *some* were disloyal has not prevented a complete taking of the lords' territory—Tyrconnell and Tyrone to be sure, but Coleraine, Armagh, Fermanagh, and Cavan as well. All adjudged by the assizes to be Crown property."

Deirdre smiled at her father's dour head-shaking. He was high-handed enough himself that it was amusing to see him deprecate high-handedness in another. "So what will the king do with the lands now?"

Calum answered. "It seems he seeks to duplicate the success of his Virginia Plantation closer to home."

"Aye, and a fine thing that would be. But can he no' see he's going about it wrong?" Alisdair thumped the table, and baby Dougal stirred in his cradle across the room.

Deirdre turned her attention to helping Rory cut his meat and sop up the juices with a crust of barley bannock while the conversation continued around her.

Calum was less impassioned than her father, but she could hear the note of worry under his words. "Requiring the planters to build stone houses, defensive works, schools, and churches canna be a bad thing."

"But have ye seen the figures, man? Or have ye been too long away from your clerking to take note of the numbers?" Alisdair drew an imaginary circle on the scrubbed boards of the table. "The under-takers, who are to hold more than a quarter of the land, are required to clear it of native Irish and to plant it with Protestant English and Scots. A 'civilizing enterprise to establish the true religion of Christ among men lost in superstition,' the order says. But how are they to teach this true religion if they clear the land of those they are to teach? The thing will no' work."

Calum nodded. "Aye, I do see that. And I see another problem. There's only fifty of the next lot—the servitors, as they're calling the ex-army officers to be rewarded with property. They are to be responsible for a fifth of the land." He drew a quartering line across Alisdair's circle. "There'll nae be enough of them for the defenses they're expected to build. I know something about the difficulties of clearing and building, even if those advising King James don't."

Alisdair drew a final quarter. "And that much is left to the Deserving Irish who can prove their loyalty to the Crown." He wagged his head. "It's too harsh. Build a large class of anglicized, contented land-holders among the Irish—that's the way to have secure peace here. Give them schools and churches. That's what Chichester wanted to do—and he's no one to coddle the Irish. But he's a canny man. He knows how to build a stable country. James is going about it all wrong. Mark my words."

Deirdre had not felt such an icy grip on her heart since those terrible days after Calum's accident. She looked around the warm room. Her husband and father were here, her two sons were fine and healthy, the harvests were good. Why must these two forecast doom? Besides, the plantations were to be in the counties to the west. They wouldn't bother Down.

Calum looked at her as if he read her thoughts. "There will be trouble."

She felt an almost overpowering urge to gather her small family into her arms to protect them. *Let them be safe,* she thought. *Safe.*

15

Two years passed, and the trouble did not come. Deirdre, busy with her family and her flourishing linen-making business, paid little attention to the affairs of the outside world, though occasional reports reached her of the growth of the Ulster migration. Scottish nobles, younger sons of gentlemen, army officers who had helped conquer the province, rack-rented and evicted Lowland Scots farmers—all eager for lands to call their own—made their way across the water to claim their part of the cheap land offered there.

The next spring, relieved that Calum and her father had been wrong in their bleak predictions, Deirdre asked Calum if they could purchase some of the flax seed from Holland now being offered in Newtown and grow their own plants for linen making. He readily agreed, as he disliked relying on a single crop—even such a prosperous one as potatoes.

Alisdair made the trip to town and returned with both seed and news. "All the talk is of the new Bible King James has had translated."

"New Bible?" Calum asked. "And what was wrong with the old ones?"

Deirdre joined in. "Why do we need another? There's the Great and the Geneva and the Bishops—"

Alisdair grunted. "They say the Great is nae used much anymore, the Bishops was ne'er a good translation, and the king objects to the Geneva because of the Calvinist doctrine in the marginal notes. King James's Bible is no' to have margin notes—that way it can be the Bible of all the people."

Deirdre had once thought to buy a Bible but somehow, in the busyness of the days, had never done so. "What an enormous task that must be to translate the Bible. How do they do it?" She was overwhelmed at the thought.

"Much might be said against King James, not the least of which was his leaving his own realm of Scotland to take the throne in England, but there's not many that will fault his scholarship," Alisdair said.

"Father, you can't mean the king did the translating?"

He laughed. "Nae, daughter. But he did organize it. Six groups of translators—fifty men—working in London, Cambridge, and Oxford. Each group did a certain number of books, then circulated their work to the others for comments."

Calum shook his head. "It sounds a fair stramash."

"Aye, it well could have been a mess, but they say it's a right noble work."

And with that Deirdre renewed her neglected determination to buy a Bible. How wonderful it would be to have one of their very own, so that Calum could read to them every morning instead of relying only on the lessons they heard read in kirk on Sundays.

She would have to discuss the matter with Rabbie MacKinnon. In Glasgow, finding a Bible for sale would have been easy enough, once she'd saved the money. Glasgow boasted several fine stationers, some with hundreds, even thousands of volumes in stock. But there were none such here closer than Dublin. And if the itinerate chapmen at Newtownards market carried Bibles from the king's printer in London, she would be surprised. Once again she had to stifle a wave of longing for the life she had known.

But even with the new focus on the Holy Scriptures, Calum and Alisdair did not judge themselves to have been wrong in their prediction that, soon or late, there would be trouble in Ulster. And often the conversation around the fire in the evening would turn to matters of defense if conflict would come.

One evening Calum brought out a sheet of paper with a sketch on it.

Deirdre looked at the strange structure her husband had drawn. "What is it?"

"A bawn. A fortified enclosure. Every undertaker on the plantations is required to build one to protect his family, tenants, and cattle."

Deirdre frowned. The bawn was a huge building, one hundred thirty-three feet long and one hundred feet wide with a four-story round tower in each corner. "I don't understand. Is it a barn or a castle?"

Calum laughed and put his arm around her. "Both." With a stick of charcoal he sketched the site of their house inside the bawn walls. "A fine strong place for living and for sheltering cattle when needed. Do ye not think it a grand idea?"

She had difficulty summoning the degree of enthusiasm she knew he expected. "If it's walls you'd be building, Calum Lanark, what about more walls on your house? We need more space."

"I thought you'd say so. The lads will soon be needing their own room." With a few quick marks of the charcoal, he sketched additional rooms at the side and back of the house. "We'll roof it all with slate.

And put a room for a servant girl along this side. A girl who can help with the spinning and looming before our daughter is born."

"And what makes you so sure ye'll have a daughter this time, Calum Lanark?"

"It's that her mother's so feisty of late. She'll breed a fair female like herself."

The building of Belfast under the direction of Lord Chichester, King James's lord deputy for Ireland, attracted stonecutters, masons, and builders aplenty to the island, so Calum had no trouble securing the services of a highly qualified stonemason. Stephan Millar and his apprentice, Noll, saw to the cutting of stone from the quarry atop Scrabo, aided by Seamus and Patrick O'Brien. And now young Hugh was old enough to work with the men, as well.

Deirdre had reconciled herself to the project, but she was dismayed to learn that Calum meant to build the bawn first and then the addition to the house.

"But, Calum, can we no' have the rooms first? This monster wall of yours will take months to build! Our babe will not wait so long." She looked at the fine field of green where the flax seed sprouted. "And the room for the looming. We'll have need of it—" But she saw that her arguing was only making his head worse. Besides, she would not say what she truly felt—that this great stone structure of walls and towers would be so—so permanent. Although she never gave it words, even to herself, she knew that in her heart of hearts the small longing remained.

"Forgive me." She would have put her hands on his head and kissed him had not the workers been within sight. "I'd no' choose to worry you."

"Canna ye see, Deirdre? I want you safe."

She bit her tongue and would not argue, no matter how unnecessary all the wall building and defense work seemed in that summer of soft rains and gentle sunshine. Fields of dark green potato leaves grew close to the brown earth, and stalks of blue flowers rose in the flax field four feet high, where they caught the warm breezes.

And so the enclosure grew. Stephan Millar shaped an elegant, wide-arched entrance in the center of the wall that edged the road. The facing stones of the heading were of sandstone, neatly and accurately cut, testifying to Millar's craftsmanship. Deirdre watched as day after day the large, well-formed stones grew in their courses. Mortar held them in place, and the small spaces between the quarried rock were pinned by smaller stones. The south front tower had already risen above the second story with a window and two arrow slits on each floor.

Deirdre shivered as she looked at it. She could not imagine having to use the bawn for its defensive purpose. She tried to think of Calum and her father crouching at one of those long thin openings with drawn bows. Who would they be shooting at?

The bairn moved with a thump inside her. She must not think of such matters. It might mark the babe. Far better it would be that Calum should use his skill with bow and arrow to keep grouse and quail in her stew pots. She took a pitcher of ale and several cups from the larder and walked across the courtyard toward the men.

Stephan Miller saw her first. "Aye, there's a fine sight on a thirsty day. Thankee, Mistress Lanark." He drank deeply of the cup she offered.

He turned to his work, but Deirdre did not move on. She was caught by the mason's smooth movements: troweling the mortar that Noll carried to him from the mixing trough, settling each stone firmly in place, wiping the excess mortar with the edge of his trowel, then repeating the process. There was a steadiness almost like the waves of the sea.

"I hear Lord Chichester is rebuilding the castle at Belfast. Did you work on that?"

"No, mistress. I was master builder on the inn. And a fine one, too. A comfort it is now to travelers. Good lodgings." He talked with the same steadiness and rhythm as he worked. "Fine town, Belfast. That is, it will be. Plotted out all in good form. Streets on both sides of the River Farset, all the way down to the Lagan. Bridges across Farset. Quay at Lagan." He took a fresh hod of mortar from Noll, handed his apprentice the empty, and continued his work all without a break in the pattern.

"Fine town, Belfast." He repeated, beginning a new course of stone. "Many families already established. English, Scottish, some Manx. Good timber houses with chimneys. Fine as any in the English Pale."

Deirdre smiled and moved on. She would have listened longer, but her Rory and Sean O'Brien were chasing the chickens again. She gave each boy a basket and set them to hunting for eggs. "And see that you don't drop any, or you'll have naught but bread and milk for supper. If you find some nice ones, Sean, you may take them to your mother. She needs plenty of eggs and milk as she's so near her time."

Sean gave her a gap-toothed grin and wrinkled his freckled nose. He seldom spoke. He had little need to. He expressed himself so well with his countenance.

Deirdre smiled as the lads scampered toward the bushes searching for hidden nests. How had they grown so quickly? Rory already was filling out broad-shouldered and strong like his father. So steady and reliable. Next year he should begin school. She sighed. She had mentioned the problem to Calum, but they had come to no solution.

She had begun teaching Rory his ABC's from the book Calum's father had used to teach him. But there was so much more she would have her sons learn. She wanted them to be gentlemen. They would need Latin, logic, music, Greek. It would be a fine thing if they could go to a real school like the ones they had for the sons of gentlemen in Glasgow.

She looked at Dougal tumbling with a puppy. The sun was golden on curls the same shade as her own. Energetic from birth that one had been. He would run with the dogs until they tired, then move on to something else and not want to stop even long after dark. Could she bear to send her boys away to school? But Millar had made no mention of a *school* in Belfast. Besides, she'd not have them go so far away as that if she could help it.

As she worried over her sons' education, she renewed her plans for buying a Bible. She had asked Rabbie about the price of one of the new Authorized Bibles and learned that they were sold in London for twelve shillings. Twelve shillings sterling. That meant seventy-two shillings Scots. And in Ireland a shilling would pay a year's rent on an acre of land. Was she being silly, with their having the expense of the building and improving the fields?

But she recalled the night Calum had first told her about the loss of his father's Bible. It all seemed so long ago now—that dark, cold night with the rain dripping through their hastily patched roof. Then it was she had first determined that someday they would have a fine new Bible. She had had no notion that so many years would pass so quickly. Surely it was time now—no matter how much seed, cattle, housewares, or rent might cost.

They heard two lessons read every Sunday in kirk, but if their children were to grow up in the fear and admonition of the Lord, they would need more than that. It was a pity her father had left all his books with Cailean. No, perhaps not. Her brother seemed to have settled a bit—if his twice yearly letters were to be believed. She wondered briefly how Cailean had handled things with Fergus Ingram once he had to accept responsibility for his own actions. Having their father come to Ireland, so that Cailean had to manage affairs on his own, had probably been the best thing for her brother.

But what was the matter with her? All these long thoughts today, and she still had the butter to churn.

She turned to her work, determined to discuss the matter of schools and books with Calum that very night. But when he came in after a long day divided between the fields and the quarry, she saw his weariness. She would not add to his burden with her worries over the future.

Again she questioned the wisdom of this fortress building. She knew that similar structures were being built all over Ulster. But what of schools? And she was not at all sure that she should like living surrounded by walls thirty feet high and three feet thick. Were they a protection or a prison? Would danger be walled out, or would she be walled in?

But soon she had more immediate concerns on her hands, for their tiny, perfect Isobel was born two weeks early. Even the rambunctious Dougal hovered over the delicate infant and remembered to walk softly across the floorboards when she was sleeping. Deirdre found great joy in lying beside her daughter, stroking the downy-soft dark fuzz on the top of her head and feeling again, as she had at the birth of each of her sons, the amazement of new life.

Yet, as Parson Montgomery so often reminded them, pointing a long, thin finger from the pulpit, "in the midst of life we are in the midst of death." Why that came to her mind she did not know, but the image was sharp one evening when she saw Calum standing in the doorway, seeming hesitant to come in.

"Calum!" She felt a coldness that had nothing to do with the misty air that entered with him. "Your head—is it worse?" She left Isobel and hurried to him. He couldn't be worse. He had seemed so well of late, satisfied over the healthy crops and his building—tired but well within himself.

He folded her in his arms and rocked back and forth, making a soft crooning sound in her ear. "Nae, nae, Deirdre, my love. It's not me."

"Rory? Dougal?" She strained to look over Calum's shoulder. When had she last seen the boys?

"No, they're fine." His arm around her, he guided her to a chair. "It's Una, love. And her bairn. It was a hard birth. Too hard."

Deirdre was stunned. "It can't be. She had six—all healthy. I saw her yesterday! She and Cassie came to see Isobel." And then Deirdre felt guilty. Guilty at her relief that it was none of her own family. Una was her closest neighbor, had been her greatest help through all the hard times, and her loss would be devastating to her family. And yet Deirdre could not deny the relief that her own were spared.

"How is Seamus? Have you spoken to him?"

"No. I passed their cottage coming home. The priest was just leaving."

Deirdre flinched at the word. What dark rites had he performed over Una and the babe? She had heard Romish ways denounced, but she really had no idea what they did. And now, what of Una's soul? Was she burning in hell even now for her papist idolatry? The Rev. Mr. Montgomery would say so. She tried to blot out memories of Una's crossing herself and praying to the holy virgin. And yet Una had truly loved God.

Deirdre did not realize her face was wet until Calum took a large cotton square from his pocket and wiped her cheeks.

As Deirdre did what she could for the O'Briens, her pain for them made her all the more determined to love her own family better, as if in giving to her own children she could somehow make up to the motherless children in the world.

When Deirdre's tiny daughter was just one month old, the family crowded into the wagon, which Calum had swept clean of soil from the newly harvested potato crop and bits of straw from the flax now soaking in the retting pond, and drove into Newtownards for a Sunday that would include Isobel's baptism.

The once-broken chancel of the old priory now rose again. The work had been completed with solid stonework and polished timbers. A pulpit of uncarved wood stood centered toward a high-arched, glazed window of clear glass. The Reformers would have no stained glass to lead worshipers into idolatry. The only ornamentation that had been allowed was the magnificent arched doorway Hugh Montgomery had ordered. The stone was carved with ornamental fruit, birds, and geometric designs. The heavy oak door hung with massive wrought-iron hinges.

At the conclusion of the regular service of common prayer and preaching, Calum and Alisdair presented Isobel Deirdre Lanark to Parson Montgomery.

"Do you present this child and in her name renounce the Devil and all his works?"

"We do."

"And will you instruct this child in the way of godliness, teaching her to put off the pomp and glory of the world and all carnal desires of the flesh?"

"We will."

Lord and Lady Montgomery had kindly attended the baptism, as well as the Seatons and the Johnstones. Deirdre noted with surprise that Effie's Judith was a head taller than Rory, and realized what a young lady the Seaton girl was becoming. Then she smiled as she noticed Matt Johnstone's eyes following the saucy, plump Meg Barclay. Poor Anna was as pale as ever.

And as fond of babies. It seemed an infant was the one thing that brought a spark to the girl's eyes. As soon as they were in the churchyard, Anna came to her. "She's so lovely, Mrs. Lanark. Do you think I might hold her?"

Deirdre put the tiny bundle into Anna's arms.

Smiling and cooing, Anna walked across the soft carpet of grass beside the church. She was just under the lowest branch of the ancient oak that grew in the center of the yard when a shower of leaves and acorns fell on the girl and infant. She gave a startled cry. Isobel wailed.

Deirdre rushed forward and reached them just as Sir Hugh arrived from the other side.

"She's not hurt. I'm sure she's not hurt," Anna sobbed, clutching the still-wailing Isobel.

By then, everyone who had been at the service was converging on them, led by Rev. Mr. Montgomery, his surplice billowing behind him.

"What is this unseemly stramash on the Lord's Day?" He looked down the sides of his long, thin nose at Deirdre.

"I—I'm sorry," she faltered.

"It is not to me you should apologize, but to our Lord. It is His day, and you have mocked Him with this wailing."

But it was Sir Hugh who got to the root of the problem. "You are quite safe to jump," he called up into the tree. "I will catch you,"

With a fluttering of leaves and thudding of acorns, a small, blond boy hurled himself into Lord Montgomery's arms. The perpetrator of this unholy commotion made it out of the tree unscathed but not to the ground.

Parson Montgomery had Dougal by the ear before he was out of his lordship's grasp. "And what is to become of this settlement if this is the next generation we are rearing?"

No one but the parson could think to use such a tone with Lord Hugh Montgomery. One would have thought it was his lordship himself who had climbed a tree on the Sabbath and caused a disturbance in the churchyard. It was clear that the question was a continuing round in an ongoing discussion between the Montgomery cousins.

"John Knox prescribed a school for every community to teach children to read the Scriptures for themselves and become profitable instruments of the commonwealth!"

"Your point is well taken, Robert, but unnecessary. I have already made all the arrangements for the Newtownards school to open next autumn. You may hold chapel daily." His lordship turned to the guilty child still in the parson's grip. "And you will attend everyday, young man, without fail. And *you*"—he included Rory, who had crept closer to his brother during the fracas.

Deirdre closed her eyes and breathed a prayer of thanks. This was, indeed, a good land that the Lord had led them to. The school she desired for her children was to be right here in Newtownards.

Now she would quit worrying. Life would be complete.

16

For all Deirdre's desire that her sons be educated in Sir Hugh's fine new school, when the leaves turned October gold and the time neared to send away eight-year-old Rory and Dougal, not yet six, she felt a wrench as deep as her homesickness for Scotland.

All her efforts for weeks had been directed to seeing that everything was ready for the boys to go. They must have the finest linen shirts—four apiece—so she sat long hours over her loom, passing the shuttle back and forth between the warp fibers so carefully wrapped on the pegs of the frame and thought of the change this school was to bring to their lives.

Although they would be only a few miles away, she couldn't imagine life without Rory and Dougal bringing noise and confusion and smiles to her day. She passed the shuttle from right to left across the frame, shifted the foot pedal to move the upper and lower frames to alternate the warp threads, tossed the shuttle from left to right, pressed the foot pedal again, sent the shuttle skimming across the fibers once more. It would be nice when Calum finished the building of his bawn and she could have a new room for her looming and a girl to help.

She repeatedly skimmed the shuttle from right to left, left to right. Her foot moved on the petal without thought. Perhaps she would offer the position to Maeve O'Brien. The girl was well grown for her age and seemed bright. Cassie would have been her first choice, but, as the eldest, Cassandra had become mother to her five brothers and sisters.

She was still thinking on the matter when Calum came in with a bucket of milk. "Calum, I was just thinking, wouldn't it be a fine thing if Hugh O'Brien could go to school with Rory and Dougal? I know he will be needed to help at home, but—" She stopped short at the look of consternation on her husband's face.

"What would ye be stirring up now, woman? Or have ye no thought? A papist in our Reformed school?"

"Oh. No, I hadn't thought." She continued with her weaving automatically. "But what will become of them? Are they to have no schooling?"

Calum shrugged. "Their priests will teach them."

She nodded. That was probably best.

Before the leaves had fallen, John Maclellan arrived from Scotland to assume his duties as headmaster and to teach Latin, Greek, and logic. In addition, he hired a local academic to teach English and arithmetic and secured the services of the church choirmaster to teach music. Of course, all this was under the watchful eye of Parson Montgomery, who was concerned that young minds be instructed to be sober, practical in their behavior, careful in their management, thrifty with their money, ascetic in their tastes, and rejecting of all forms of hedonism.

Deirdre folded the nightshirts she had just finished stitching and put them in the boys' small trunk. Then she turned to plying her best boar bristle brush to removing all the dog hairs from Rory's jerkin. After that, she picked up Dougal's. He was already as tall as his brother, though not so sturdily built.

"Now try not to put holes in your hose. These must last you through the term." She tried to give Dougal a severe look. It would not do to break down and run her fingers through the blond curls turned into an aureole by the firelight behind her younger son. Tomorrow they would be gone. *Less than three miles*, she reminded herself, but gone from her home.

"And see that you keep your shoes dry. And wear your vests— both of you." She raised her voice to include Rory across the room, repairing a broken harness with his father. How did children survive school? Who would see that they were warm enough? That they ate right? "And that you wash your hands. Before every meal, mind."

"I dona think the Reverend Mr. Montgomery will be letting us forget, Mither." Dougal gave a final flourish of sheepskin to the boots she had set him to polish.

Deirdre had to laugh. No, that was one thing she would not have to worry about.

"I dona see why we must be making all this bother." Rory chucked the leather halter to the floor with a thud. "I dona want to go to school. We can learn far more useful things here."

"What nonsense, Rory."

Deirdre was thankful for the firmness in Calum's voice. She was not certain she could have managed it at the moment.

"You must learn how to become a gentleman. Someday all this will be yours. A landed gentleman must have the manners and education to go with his position."

"I could learn from you and Grandfather. I dona want to go away."

Deirdre was touched by the reticence of her firstborn. She saw no such reluctance in Dougal, who had been chatting for days about all he'd heard about the fine playing field for golf, football, and archery that Lord Montgomery had provided for the school. But Rory had ever been the more cautious one. She stifled the thought that if they were in Glasgow, she would not have to send her sons to board at school.

"You will make us very proud of you, Rory. Both of you will. Remember, we shall see you every Sunday in kirk. The pupils will have a special seat in the gallery, right behind Lord Montgomery and the burgesses. And you will be taught to sing in parts, so that in harmony you can praise God with the psalms." Deirdre hoped her enthusiasm didn't sound too forced.

The next morning she stood by the wagon. "Work you extra hard at your reading. We'll have a fine surprise for you when you can read." She followed the wagon across the courtyard and out the sweeping semicircular driveway onto the road, then waved them out of sight.

She turned to her loom. Now that she had her family clothed in fine linen, she could save for a Bible. As her hands and feet worked, her mind filled with the picture of the family gathered around the hearth in the evening, reading the Holy Scriptures aloud. Sometimes the scene would shift in her mind, and it was the great oak fireplace in Dunlop Hall reflecting light on her husband and children. She threw her shuttle so hard it overshot and landed on the floor. Would she ever be free of homesickness? *This* was home.

Alisdair heard that the best prices for bleached linen could be had at Merchants' Hall in Dublin, so he proposed to make a trip there as soon as Deirdre had enough bolts ready to make the journey worthwhile. She was glad to have a goal to work for, as it seemed so quiet inside the sheltered bawn now. It would not always remain so quiet. She suspected that within the year there would be another bairn to keep Isobel company.

In the coming days, which quickly melted into weeks and months, Deirdre found herself often alone for almost the first time in her life. Most of the time, Calum was out in the byres and sheds the bawn enclosed, and Isobel, who loved animals, chose to toddle after her papa. Often Deirdre found herself at her spinning wheel or loom, singing songs of Scotland. And then she would switch tunes quickly, for she did not want anyone to know.

She now could give full attention to her linen industry, for she had help with the daily work. "See to the oatcakes, Maeve. Don't let them burn," she said, turning toward her looming room. Eleven-year-old Maeve O'Brien came up every morning, and Deirdre couldn't imagine what she would do without the help of the capable girl.

A gust of wind whirled a handful of snow against the window, and

Deirdre smiled, glad her family all had warm cloaks. Then her thoughts turned to the less fortunate family in the cottier's hut down the road. The light had never returned to Seamus's eyes after the death of his Una. And Deirdre suspected he often took recourse to his *usice beatha*. She hoped they had clothing warm enough for this weather. She must ask Maeve.

She looked at the stack of linen bolts on the shelf and smiled in triumph. Even with saving one out to make clothes for the new babe, there should be enough to finish paying the seed, wrack, and lease for this year and enough left over at last for a Bible. She would have her wonderful gift for Calum. He worked so hard, never mentioning the headaches that she knew still plagued him, never complaining over the expenses of improving and developing the land he loved. To Calum this was the land of his heart. This was truly home.

She looked up at Maeve's entrance. "Anna Johnstone has come calling, mistress. Shall I bring her in here?"

Deirdre set her shuttle aside. "Anna has driven all this way in such weather? She must have interesting news indeed. Or be in dire need of a visit, poor girl. I'll come into the parlor." The former spare bedroom had been turned into a parlor, and where the outshot had once sheltered a cozy bed, a stairway now led to upstairs bedrooms.

Anna Johnstone was one of Deirdre's most regular visitors. In spite of her colorless appearance, she always managed to bring entertaining stories of the flourishing community. Still, Deirdre suspected that the girl—nearly a woman now—came more to see Isobel than herself. Her heart went out to Anna as she saw the longing expression in the pale eyes taking in Deirdre's once-again-expanding abdomen.

Deirdre had guessed right, however, that Anna had news. "It's been two years and more. But he's just now telling us. He feared Father would forbid it."

"You mean Matt has been courting Meg Barclay all that time, and you've all just now learned about it?" But Deirdre understood. She could well imagine the terror of facing Calvin Johnstone's disapproval. "I remember seeing them together at Isobel's baptism. Meg seems such a merry girl. But I had no idea—"

Maeve entered with a plate of fresh oatcakes. But before Deirdre could offer one to her guest, an insistent pounding came at the door. Maeve opened it.

Eight-year-old Sean, the smallest, most freckled O'Brien, tumbled in, out of breath. His rounded cheeks were streaked with dirt, and his bare toes dug into the woven doormat as if they would burrow into it for warmth. Deirdre started to protest at his going out barefoot in such weather, then saw his urgency.

His sister bent down to his level, the better to interpret the waving hands and facial contortions that accompanied the few words the child spoke. "Cassie sent you to fetch me?"

Sean bounced his whole body up and down rather than merely nodding. "Da is . . . sick." A string of Gaelic followed.

Maeve turned to Deirdre, her face white, her lips tight. "I must go, Mistress Lanark. Da is—" Her control crumpled. "He burned their clothes and bedding. He says they have the evil in them. Now he's gone off somewhere, and Cassie can't find Uncle Paddy."

Deirdre had never been happier to see Calum walk in than she was at that moment. It took her only moments to dig out an old pair of Dougal's boots for Sean, and then Calum left with the two O'Briens.

Even before the door closed, she knew what she must do. She had worked so hard, was so near her goal. But she didn't need a Bible in the house to know the commandment to feed and clothe the needy. "Anna, you must help me. It won't be far out of your way to stop by the cottage. Cassie and Maeve will need to start tonight sewing new clothes." She turned toward the weaving room beyond the parlor. "What a fine thing that I have so much made up."

She would not let Maeve know how much it hurt as she wrapped lengths of fine linen in canvas to protect them against the weather.

In a few months it would be time to plant a new crop of flax, and then the process could begin all over again. She would not give up.

Maeve O'Brien returned to her duties the next morning with many expressions of gratitude for the cloth. Calum had found Seamus at the cottage of a wracker by Strangford Lough. Patrick would sober him up. Deirdre shook her head. It was hard to recall the charming, high-spirited man Seamus had once been—the carefree smile, the twinkling eyes.

The snows melted, revealing beds of snowdrops and crocus in the meadow. The days grew longer and warmer. The promise of spring was just ushering in the fulfillment of summer when Deirdre walked along the field with Isobel dancing beside her and lovely, wee Katrina snuggled in her arms. She had stopped to admire the tender flax sprouts greening the fields when Anna Johnstone drove up the road in her pony cart. Deirdre was surprised to see Sean O'Brien and his sister Mairi with Anna, but she was glad to note the good job the older O'Brien girls had done in clothing the bairns with the cloth she had sent them.

The next thing she noted was the color in Anna's face and the light in her eyes. "You're looking well, Anna." Deirdre wondered why such good circumstance should make her feel apprehensive.

It was some time before she discovered the reason for Anna's shine. "I've come to ask if I could borrow the ABC you taught Rory and Dougal their letters with. I'll return it before Isobel has need."

Deirdre looked at the O'Brien children playing with a nest of kittens in the straw of the cart. She had no need to ask what Anna wanted the hornbook for. "Anna, does your father know what you're doing?"

Anna swallowed, but she did not back down. "Mother does."

"Anna—"

"Six motherless children, and Cassie little more than a child. There's so much I can do." But then she caught her breath and bit her thin lip. "You won't tell, will you? I've never been so happy. Besides," she added hastily as if she'd memorized the argument, "it's my Christian duty. How will they learn God's truth if they can't read the Scriptures?"

Deirdre smiled. "No, I won't tell." But she continued to worry in the coming days. Anna was happy. Cassie needed help. The children were receiving an education. Why was she so anxious?

Deirdre decided that she was just being silly. She waved to Calum working with Seamus and Patrick in a near potato field. Life was good. She must be getting old to be stewing so. She smiled as Isobel trotted off to her papa, and Deirdre turned to nurse her precious new daughter.

17

And then, with the swift turning of days, Deirdre found herself stifling her tears when Rory and Dougal came home for vacation grown seemingly half to manhood. She looked at Rory's face and saw bones beginning to form the face of a man. How could it have happened so soon? But any yearning she felt to have her little boys back was more than made up for by the pride Calum evidenced in his fine sons.

"Is it time, lass?"

She clapped her hands at Calum's question. "Yes! Now! Oh, I've waited so long for this—I promised you boys when you first went to school." It had seemed such a simple promise, and yet it had taken her three years. But she had done it.

Calum turned to a large oak box chained to a table by the parlor window and lifted out a heavy volume. "The Holy Bible, by His Majesty's special command, the Authorized King James Version." He ran his hand over the soft leather, and the gilt lettering gleamed.

Deirdre blinked back her tears. Surely this was the answer to her long seeking. Now, with the Word of God in their house as well as in their hearts, this would truly be home. She looked at the clock ticking on the mantle. It had been Calum's parents'; now it was theirs; someday it would be Rory's. *One generation unto another.* She smiled.

Calum opened to the first page and looked at his eldest son. "Start with the Preface. We'll no' miss a word."

Rory cleared his throat, then began in his carefully precise voice:

> "To the most high and mighty Prince, James, by the grace of God, King of Great Britain, France, and Ireland, Defender of the faith, etc. The Translators of the Bible wish Grace, Mercy, and Peace through Jesus Christ our Lord . . . .
>
> "The Lord of heaven and earth bless Your Majesty with many and happy days . . . to the honour of that great God and the good of his Church, through Jesus Christ our Lord and only Savior."

Thus began the time that forever lived in Deirdre's memory as the golden age. Their third daughter was born the next summer as potatoes and flax ripened in the fields. Across Down, the settlement flourished as everyone minded his trade and continued building. In fields, gardens, and orchards the settlers went about plowing, ditching, and setting fruit trees. The corn mills, potato crops, and woolen and linen industries prospered. It seemed that in every home the girls spun and the women wove, while the men saw to their cattle and crops.

Deirdre even became accustomed to living behind stone walls, and with every rainstorm she was thankful for their slate roof. Calum and Alisdair's dire prophecies of trouble made only the faintest echo in the back of her mind. After years of struggle, it seemed her only goal now was that the goodness should last. She knew that nothing lasted forever, and yet, "Let it be so for a space yet," she prayed.

It was seldom now that Deirdre looked at Strangford and wished it the Clyde. Seldom did she go to Newtownards and wish it Glasgow. She went for months—perhaps a year or more—without once waking with her face wet after dreaming she was back in Scotland.

Perhaps it had finally happened. Perhaps in the peace of the settlement she had found her own peace. Perhaps.

However, no life could be without worry, no matter how staunchly Calum strove to hide his headaches from her. And whenever she saw Anna Johnstone driving down Scrabo Road toward the O'Briens', she wondered. As she did when she saw Seamus's jaunty smile return.

Every vacation it seemed the boys had leaped further toward manhood under the tutelage of their schoolmasters, while Deirdre taught Isobel, Katrina, and Aileen at home. Proud as she was of the accomplishments of their sons, she was glad that the last three were girls and that she needn't send them off. Always after the boys were home for a vacation, she and Calum would discuss the changes they saw in them.

Calum worried less than she did. "It's a fine thing that Sir Hugh has taken such note of our Rory. Being invited so often to Newton House will open doors to grand acquaintances for him."

Deirdre thought of the doors that had been opened for her brother through his association with Hugh Montgomery. To be sure, there was no suggestion that Viscount Montgomery of the Great Ards, as Sir Hugh had recently been created, still undertook any of the shenanigans of his youth. Still, she expressed her concern to her husband.

"It's Dougal I'm fearing for," he said. "I heard little of his quick laughter this vacation." Then Calum smiled. "Ah, lass, our firstborn was ever so serious. Perhaps a wee bit of levity would not be amiss in his case."

"Parson Montgomery would suspect you of lacking in the virtue of asceticism."

"I canna think a God who made such beauty in the world would think all pleasure sinful.

Deirdre rested a hand on his arm. "It's a good thing, I'm thinking, that you left Scotland. Hearsay of such as that would not be smiled on there." She said it lightly, but there was truth to the matter. Cailean had written of the growing strength of the Covenanters. Perhaps it was better for all of them to be here. Perhaps she wouldn't go back now if the opportunity offered. But it little mattered, because, of course, such a contingency would never arise.

Another concern crossed her mind.

She did not often ask now, "How is your head?"

"Ah, it's grand," he would always answer.

But she knew from the tightness she felt as she massaged the back of his neck that it was less than grand. She trusted that the never-mentioned pains were better, but she knew he was never completely free from them.

Deirdre glanced across the room to where five-year-old Katrina, her only child with brown eyes and hair, was rocking six-month-old Aileen in the cradle that had slept all her babes. Aye, a God who created such goodness could not be as dour as Parson Montgomery presented Him.

"Walk out with me." Calum took her hand and helped her to her feet.

She hated to admit that after the birth of five children she did not spring up as readily as she once had. "Watch the girls, Maeve. We're just going out for a bit walk." She took a soft-brimmed hat off the peg in the entranceway.

"Yes, mistress. Sean said he'd come up after milking. He has some kittens he thought the girls would like to see. He said Miss Isobel could keep the black one if you approve. He chose it for her because it matches her hair."

Deirdre smiled at her oldest daughter's love of animals. "I'm sure I don't mind. We can always use another mouser. But is it sickly?"

"No, mistress."

Deirdre laughed. "Then I doubt she'll be interested if it isn't in need of nursing." She put her arm in her husband's and went out into the evening air, heavy with the sweet scent of the blossoming fruit trees that grew all along the south and east walls of the bawn.

They walked across the courtyard. Behind them the cattle lowed and munched in the byre as Hugh saw to the milking. An evening lark sang in a tree.

Calum laid his hand on the wall, where the stones still held the warmth of the sun, and quoted a verse from the passage he had read at prayers that morning, "The Lord is good, a strong hold in the day of trouble: and he knoweth them that trust in him."

And Deirdre shivered. The verse was meant to be comforting, an assurance of God's goodness and the security surrounding their lives. But to Deirdre it gave recognition to the tiny voice inside that said this was too good to last.

They turned at the sound of a high-stepping horse and carriage entering the courtyard through the arched entry of the bawn. Neighborly visits from Fulke Seaton were not a common occurrence. Although the families enjoyed friendly conversation after kirk and met occasionally on market days, it seemed that growing responsibilities kept each settler more sharply focused on his own lands than in the early days, when they had all worked together for survival.

As she greeted Fulke and asked after his family, Deirdre felt an ache of nostalgia for those early days. In spite of the hardships, there had been a comradery and sense of adventure that she sometimes missed.

They were settled comfortably in the parlor, and Fulke was telling about his recent visit to Belfast, when he took a long draw on his pipe and made an almost offhand comment. "Settlers in Antrim are astir. Sir Thomas Phillips is circulating a petition to send to the Crown. Says he fears the Irish will rise upon a sudden and cut the throats of the poor, despised British."

Inadvertently, Deirdre's hand flew to her throat. It was all she could do to keep from rushing to the bedroom upstairs to be certain her girls were asleep in their beds.

But Fulke laughed and crossed his legs, his fashionable yellow hose bright in the firelight. "Fellow asked me to sign the petition. I told him it couldn't happen here."

A banging at the door came so sharp and sudden that Deirdre sloshed the red wine she was pouring into Seaton's goblet. Had it happened? The Irish rising to cut their throats?

The door burst open, and Calvin Johnstone stood there, white with anger, brandishing a sword. "Where is she? If ye're sheltering the hoor, I'll kill ye."

Calum rose to his full height before the slighter man. "Sheathe your sword, man. I'll have no violence in my parlor. Now what's all this stushie?"

"Anna. My wife tells me this has been going on for years. O'Brien's your cottier. Ye're responsible, man. I told ye to clear your land. This comes of consorting wi' heathen." His hand was back on his sword hilt.

"Your daughter is not here, Johnstone. You have my word."

"Aye, but ye knew of her stravaigin' about!" He was trembling with rage.

Deirdre crossed the room to him. "I only know that Anna has seen to her Christian duty to visit the motherless and help the unfortunate, Mr. Johnstone. You should be proud of her."

"Proud of her? She's a hoor! I'll kill her."

Deirdre got a whiff of the drink on Johnstone's breath before he turned and slammed the door behind him. She looked at her servant, who cowered by the fireplace. "Maeve, what do you know of this? Has Anna been to your home a great deal lately?"

Maeve looked at the large buckles on her rough shoes. "She and Da were married by Father O'Callaghan yesterday."

Deirdre turned to Calum and Fulke. "Johnstone will kill them."

The men rushed to Seaton's carriage in the courtyard. Deirdre ran after them.

From half a field away she could hear angry shouts from the open door of the O'Brien cottage. Male voices yelling, a woman screaming, children crying all sounded above the squawking and barking of the animals. As Calum and Fulke leaped from the carriage, she saw Anna, standing by the fire in her white shift. The light behind her revealed what her heavier, fuller day dress concealed.

Calvin Johnstone lunged at his daughter. "I'll have ye bearin' no papist bastards!"

Calum threw himself at Johnstone. He grabbed the man's shoulders to pull him off the girl.

Johnstone spun, knocking Calum off balance. The two men fell heavily. The crack of Calum's head hitting a wooden chest sounded like the explosion of gunpowder.

The room froze.

"No!" Deirdre fell to her knees and cradled her husband's head. "No! Calum!" She ran her fingers through the crisp, gleaming hair so little streaked with gray. He was warm, his flesh soft. And yet Calum was not there.

All those years ago when he had fled to Ireland and they were apart so many months, still Calum had been her strength, her refuge. When the tree fell on him, and he lay helpless for so long, still his presence had been with her. But now he was gone.

She clutched him to her in a final embrace, then rose. The ice in her suddenly turned to flame. "Murderers!" she cried. "You killed him.

Both of you. Your rigid God!" she flung at Johnstone. "Your careless ways," she screamed at Seamus and stumbled toward the door.

The sunset sky was red and gold. Green fields tumbled down to the distant sea in a promise of fruitfulness. She shook her fist at it all. She was no longer screaming. Her speech came with a deadly evenness, broken only by sobbing gasps for breath. "You killed him. You— Ireland! You suck people in with your beauty, your softness. You make people love you when they don't want to. And then you take everything they ever care about!"

Fulke Seaton took her home. Effie came in to take care of her and the children. Fulke saw to the burial orders. Alisdair sat by her bed.

"Father, make the arrangements. As soon as the funeral is over, I want to go back to Scotland."

"Rest you, daughter. We'll talk on it later."

She grabbed his hand and felt her nails grip. "Cailean will make room for us. Anyplace. I don't care. I want to go home."

Alisdair nodded. "Aye. It's a sair loss. A sair loss."

She sat upright, tossing off the vinegar cloth Effie had put on her forehead. "It's this *land*, Father. Ireland. We thought it was our refuge. But it's a scourge. The people we thought our friends all these years— they're enemies." She slumped in his arms. "Take me home, Father."

Two days later Calum Lanark, beloved husband and father, was laid to rest under the great oak tree in the Newtownards kirk yard. Then the community went into the church for Parson Montgomery's "comfortable exhortation to the people, touching on death and resurrection," as prescribed in The Book of Common Order.

Deirdre did not feel comforted by the exhortation. Death was not comforting. Resurrection was too distant. The promises of Scripture rang hollowly in her ears, hardly reaching her mind, not coming near her heart.

"I am the Lord your God . . . I will bring you in unto the land . . . I will give it you for an heritage. I am the Lord," Parson Montgomery intoned, then closed with prayer.

She moved, puppetlike, when those around her moved. She got into the carriage when her father told her to. It didn't make any difference. Calum was gone. She would have to get used to that. Somehow. Maybe in Scotland. Maybe it would be easier there.

That evening she wandered aimlessly across the courtyard. Was it possible that she and Calum had walked here together only a few days ago? She looked at the branches, heavy with blossoms, and could not believe they were the same trees, that this was the same world. She and Calum had planted these trees together shortly after Isobel's birth.

She touched the wall. The stones still held the heat of the day's sun. A little of the warmth sank into her. She heard again Calum's voice when they stood together on this very spot. *The Lord is good, a strong hold in the day of trouble; and he knoweth them that trust in Him.*

"I want ye safe," Calum had said, and he had built this bawn for her refuge.

I will bring you in unto the land . . . I will give it you for an heritage. She didn't want this land. She wanted Calum. She wanted to go home.

She walked toward the archway and looked out across the sweep of green. *I will bring you in unto the land . . . . The Lord is a strong hold . . .* Slowly her heart opened to the words. Was not God her true fortress? He would not leave her, even in this contrary land.

She heard a call from the fields then and looked out where her sons were walking with their sisters. Isobel carried a puppy, Katrina held to Rory's hand, and Dougal had little Aileen on his shoulders. Calum's children walking in Calum's fields. Calum was gone, but they were still here.

And this *was* home. This was the success she had struggled for all these years. The home she sought was not on the other side of the Irish Sea.

Calling their greetings, her children ran across the field to her. She turned and, with them around her, she walked back into the place of refuge Calum had built for them. She had come home.

18

"Well, what do you think of it?"

Mary started at Philip's words, then looked questioningly at him, unsure what to say. She had been so wrapped up in the lives of those people of the past that she had forgotten she wasn't just reading a novel. She had read all the way back in the car yesterday and had fallen asleep over Philip's notebook last night. Now she sat in the Armstrongs' living room with her tea and toast cooling as she turned the final pages.

"It's great reading." Then she stopped. She wasn't supposed to be just having a good read. She was meant to be finding the roots of the trouble she saw everywhere around her today. "And I can see why there was so much resentment of the colonists. I mean, the idea of clearing the Irish off their land was terrible. But then, the in-comers did improve agriculture and education." She paused. "I guess if everyone had been as nice as Calum and Deirdre . . ."

Philip shook his head. "I don't know. Even the 'nice ones' weren't considered real Irish even after they'd been here for several generations, although the Old English—those from Norman times—were well tolerated. And of course, it's a simplification to start with the plantations. There had been conflicts for hundreds of years before that. Usually between two sets of Gaelic lords, with one or the other of them backed by English or Scots."

"Yes, and that really makes it harder, because no one can say, 'They started it.' And the Gaelic lords had every right to apply across the water for allies. That's what I'm really trying to work out—not just what happened, but who's right. Who's morally right?"

Philip laughed. "You do ask the hard questions, don't you? I wish more people would. If more people would ask, 'What's morally right?' instead of, 'How can I get more of what I want?' my job of reconciliation would be a lot easier."

He ran a hand through his thin pale hair and sat down, his long legs sticking halfway across the space between the chairs. "Well, for starters, I'd suggest that it's not morally wrong to migrate. It does have biblical precedence—not to mention the example of your own American history. So the fact of people moving from one country to another isn't immoral."

Mary nodded. "It's easy enough now, hundreds of years later, to say that the Elizabethans and Stuarts shouldn't have planted Ireland. Some might say the same thing about those who settled the States. But I'm glad our pioneers did."

Philip gave her one of his small, fleeting smiles. "I think there are a lot of similarities to stories I've read of your pioneers: following a dream, struggling for survival, building for the future."

"And mistreating the native people," she added for him.

They were silent for a moment, then Philip continued. "And the fact of the matter is that the Flight of the Earls did create a vacuum. If James of England hadn't promoted settlement, Louis of France or Philip of Spain probably would have."

"So your point is, it's not a question of people's *emigrating* being right or wrong—it's how they act after they get there."

Philip shrugged. "How they act and how they're treated. The wrong can be on either side—and it's usually on both."

Mary started to answer, then lost all track of the conversation for Gareth entered the room. Apparently he had stayed the night. She knew the men had worked late. She wondered if she would ever get over having her heart leap every time she looked at him.

He nodded with a small smile, then sat in the chair next to Philip rather than on the sofa next to her. Of course, the space beside her was covered with Philip's manuscripts. But she would gladly have moved them.

She wanted to include Gareth in the conversation, so she shifted to his area of expertise. "Something else I wondered about—Reverend Montgomery's idea of any mistake being a sin—isn't that pretty harsh?"

Even though she was turned to Gareth, Philip answered. "I think so. The thing is, you see, if you don't somehow distinguish between a nonmoral mistake—burning the biscuits—and a bad intention, you put them on the same level and remove the moral content from intentional wrongs."

"I guess that's what I was asking. It's just that, well, the way you wrote this—Calum seemed to think . . ." She didn't want to sound as if she was criticizing, and she knew so little about the subject. "I mean, can theology really be all that important? It's just ideas."

"Just ideas?" She hadn't seen Gareth's eyes spark like that since she'd arrived. "But it's ideas that govern peoples' actions. Ideas have consequences. 'Just ideas' have been behind at least half of the wars the world has seen."

"Theology and greed—the two great movers of armies. And wars fought over theology are the most dangerous." Philip jumped to his feet. "On the other hand, sitting here talking about ideas will never get that youth center built. The kids from the youth councils are coming in this morning. Hopefully, getting the young people themselves involved in the process will encourage the adults to cooperate." He picked up his briefcase. "Ready, Gareth?"

"I'm ready." Mary moved to the doorway. It was time to take her stand. She wasn't just a tourist.

"Er . . ." Philip frowned.

"Surely you have something I can do—dusting, filing, making tea?"

Philip threw up his hands. "Anything but the tea. The canteen kitchen is the only room in the center that's off limits. Dorinda's organization would put a Swiss clock factory to shame. But come if you want to."

Mary gave a satisfied nod and strode, head up, to the car. She stood at the right front door, waiting for Philip to unlock it.

He came around, slipped his key in the lock, and held the door open for her.

Moving a jacket that had been left on the seat, Mary started to sit down—and jumped out again. "Oh! You're awful! Why did you let me do that?" She had marched to the driver's side.

Philip shrugged, allowing only the slightest hint of a smile. "I thought maybe you wanted to drive."

Mary seldom minded a joke at her own expense, but the small incident did serve to remind her how much she had to learn, how careful she needed to be when pushing her way into this new environment. And how much she had to overcome before she could be of any real use to Gareth.

Still, she would never make progress sitting at home drinking tea. She would show them—and herself—that she could help. She would find something.

She turned to Philip. "Tell me about these kids that are coming this morning."

"The council only funds projects where cross-community cooperation has already been demonstrated. Too many good-sounding ideas out there. They have to see results first."

"Isn't that rather the cart before the horse? How can you demonstrate results before you have the program in place?" Green fields edged with well-trimmed hedgerows slipped past outside her window.

"That's why our Gareth here"—Philip nodded toward the backseat —"suggested having the presidents and representatives of the youth councils come to the Centre."

"What will you do?" She turned to direct her question to Gareth.

"That's what the kids need to decide—what they want to work together on. Of course, there's always football."

"One of Sheila's art exhibits might be safer—if what I've heard about emotions getting out of hand at your football matches is true."

"Yes, but just think what it would prove if we could keep it friendly." Gareth grinned. "One step at a time. Today, just get acquainted."

"That's right," Philip added. "These kids have lived within a few blocks of each other all their lives but probably have never seen each other. Certainly never spoken to each other, unless you count the possibility of a shouted obscenity."

"Yep," Gareth agreed. "A nice, quiet chat with a few giggles would be a major step forward."

Philip laughed. "You'd be lucky. It's always the same. They sit across the room from each other in tight, silent groups. They'll hardly mutter to their own mates as long as the other group is in the room. I've got some ice-breaker techniques. Just pray that they'll work. Getting them to talk—talk honestly—is the biggest challenge."

When they pulled up in front of the Centre, Mary could see through the large window that they were late. The lounge was full of teenagers. She thought of her first day as a schoolteacher. She wasn't sorry she wasn't going back to that. She just hoped this wouldn't be worse.

Philip opened the door, and Mary drew back momentarily at the shouting.

"I say good enough—serves him right!"

"Yeh! Got what 'e meant to give, didn't 'e?"

"You would say that! He was somebody's son. How do you think his family feels?"

"How would the families of his victims be feeling if—"

Baffled, Mary walked in. These were the young people Philip had been afraid wouldn't open their mouths? What had happened to rouse their emotions to the boiling?

A tall girl with streaky brown hair dashed tears from her eyes with an angry gesture. "Beastly IRA. I wish they'd all get blown up with their own bombs."

A thin boy with long dark hair and intense eyes propelled himself up from the corner where he had been sheltering. "And I suppose the IRA are the only ones who kill people? Shows how stupid you are." He returned to his crouching position, arms hugging his drawn-up knees.

The girl strode across the room toward him, legs long and white in denim shorts. She stood over the boy. "How dare you? How dare you call me stupid? I know. I know how it feels—" She dabbed at her eyes with clenched fists as her voice broke.

Mary turned to Philip. "Well, they're talking."

Philip turned to the woman at the receptionist's desk. "What started this? What happened?"

"Haven't you heard the news?" She handed Philip a newspaper.

Mary realized she hadn't seen the paper that morning, nor had they turned on the car radio. As the angry shouts continued from the room behind her, she leaned over Philip's arm to get a look.

The top half of the paper displayed a colored photo of a shattered, burning bus and what was left of the man who had carried the bomb.

She quickly scanned the story. Yet another bomb in London. The only victim a young man on a bus. Apparently he'd been the bomber en route to deliver his deadly load. Something had gone terribly wrong for him and terribly right for his intended victims. Now she understood the emotional accusations.

"Right. That's it. You've all had your say."

Mary turned in amazement as the room quieted in response to the calm, commanding voice of the speaker who walked between the impassioned antagonists. He held out his hand to the boy huddled in the corner. "Hullo. I'm Gareth."

The boy didn't move, just looked up at him with his burning, black eyes.

Gareth stooped and grasped his hand.

The boy let Gareth help him to his feet. "Liam. Liam O'Connor."

"I'm that pleased to meet you, Liam. You're president of the Falls Road Council, right? Can I ask you to help me with this rowdy lot here? Worse than a football match."

Liam ducked a kind of half nod.

Gareth turned to the girl who had accosted Liam. "Hi, I'd like you to meet a friend of mine." Mary caught her cue and hurried forward. "This is Mary. From the States. Mary Hamilton."

"Hi, I'm Debbie Downing." It seemed that Debbie was the leader of the Protestant group.

"Terrible—what happened." Mary sounded sympathetic.

Debbie tossed her head. Her silver earrings dangled. "Served him right. Got a bit of his own back."

Mary was shocked into silence. The girl couldn't have been more than fifteen. And so fragile-looking—long-lashed blue eyes, little turned-up nose, streaky brown hair falling around her face. Everything so at odds with the bitterness in her voice and words.

"Uh—I think they're about ready to start the meeting." Mary indicated that they should take seats. "All right if I sit with you?"

"Sure." Debbie shrugged and turned to her friends.

With the shouting match silenced, the groups re-formed into their traditional polarized positions.

Philip was still occupied at the desk, so Gareth carried on. "Um . . . hi." He gave a jerky little half wave, then grinned as he stuck his hand in his pocket in an almost shy gesture. "I'm Gareth." Even with his reticence, his latent energy and concern were riveting. His approach seemed to work. Most of the teens muttered a greeting.

An enormous boy sitting next to Liam spoke out. "Hi. I'm Gerry."

Gareth nodded at him. "Footballer, are you?"

"Gaelic football. Only sport worth playing."

"Maybe you'd teach me?"

Gerry hunched his broad shoulders. "No chance. Ye have to be born Irish."

Gareth grinned. "Yep. I know that's what they say. But I'd like to try." He turned to a girl with green eyes, wearing a copper-colored sweater that exactly matched her hair. "You don't play Gaelic football, now do you?"

Several giggled.

"Fiona step dances." Gerry answered for her.

"Ah, that's brilliant." Gareth turned to the other side of the room.

No one said anything, and Mary took Gareth's nodded hint. "This is Debbie. And I'm Mary." She turned to the boy sitting next to her.

"Martin." He was chubby with short brown hair.

"Syd." Syd's heavily freckled face split in a grin that could only be described as cute.

"Sarah." The girl on the end of the row answered in such a soft voice it was almost impossible to hear her. She seemed to withdraw inside her mane of curly blonde hair. It was impossible to believe that a few minutes earlier these near-silent young people had been yelling at one another.

Philip put down the phone on the receptionist's desk and joined the group. He stood before them, shaking his head. "Dreadful to think there's been more violence." He held his hand up at the muttered undercurrent and looked at them fiercely. "No matter which side did what—it's disastrous. You all know that."

The murmuring subsided.

"That's why your community leaders asked you to come here today—to see if we could sort out something to help bring peace."

Gerry raised his hand but didn't wait to be called on. "Easy. Send the Brits home."

The silence echoed in the room as Philip held Gerry's gaze until the boy's mocking grin faded. "Let's get something straight. We're not here to focus on the Brits. We're here to focus on us. This is your home. This is my home. And we all want to live in peace. The only way we can do it is together."

But Gerry wasn't backing down. "We'd have a better chance of it without the Brit soldiers sticking their guns in our faces."

"Sure, leave us to the mercy of your IRA terrorists," Martin shouted back. "We'd all be shot in our beds. Then you'd be happy!"

Mary held her breath. Would the whole room erupt again?

But even more dismaying than the shouters were those who withdrew into themselves. Liam hunched his shoulders and crouched in his chair as if Gerry's gunman were standing over him. On the other side of the room, Debbie ducked her head, her streaky blonde-brown hair covering her thin face. Sarah put an arm around her friend in a protective gesture.

"This isn't working," Mary whispered to Gareth.

Just then the phone rang in the side room. "He's in a meeting, but I'll see." The receptionist made a helpless gesture toward Philip.

All of a sudden Mary saw what needed to be done. Nothing could be accomplished in this explosive atmosphere. "We need to get them out of here, Gareth. Somewhere peaceful and quiet. Somewhere non-political."

Philip returned from his hasty phone conversation. "Look, I'm sorry. The mayor's trying to get a group together—people from both sides to see what we can do to calm this situation down." He ran a hand over his face. "People have got to stay cool. If the Loyalists get involved I don't know what we'll do. We could lose everything." He looked unspeakably haggard.

"Sure. Go to your meeting. No problem." Gareth put an encouraging hand on his arm. "Mary and I'll take care of this." He gestured toward the young people, now all sitting in sullen silence. "Is the mini available? Mary had a great idea. We'll take them out of town—get a little fresh air on the situation."

Philip nodded. "Good idea. See if you can get them to talk to each other—come up with something they can work on together. If they won't, they haven't got a hope of getting their leisure center." He picked up his briefcase and headed toward the door. "God help us all."

19

A short time later Mary found herself in the back of a minibus, sitting between Liam O'Connor and Debbie Downing while the beautiful green slopes of the Glens of Antrim rolled past.

"Oh, put your windows down and let some of that *green* in!"

The responsive laughter and the fresh air that flooded in at her request told her that this trip had been an inspired idea. The beauty of the gentle countryside, pastures dotted with grazing cattle, flowers and berries studding the hedgerows—all seeped into her spirit, bringing a peacefulness the latest bomb explosion had shattered.

Surely they could find a basis for cooperation in such a setting. She turned to the girl beside her. "What do you like to do, Debbie?"

"I don't know. Not much." The breeze from the window made her dangling silver earrings sway.

Mary noticed there were music notes on the ends of the tiny silver chains. "Do you like music?"

"Yeah, I like music."

"So do I. What groups do you like?"

Debbie was so slow to answer that Mary feared the conversation was over. Finally the girl said, "I like U-2."

Much to Mary's surprise, Liam, who had been gazing fixedly out the window to her left, spoke up. "Yeah. They're brilliant! I've got all their stuff. Do you have 'Unforgettable Fire'? That's classic."

Mary was amazed when Debbie almost smiled. "I don't have it, but I like it."

Then they fell silent, and Mary looked about for something else to keep the conversation going. She noticed Liam's hands. "And you must play the guitar."

"Yeah." His dark eyes were beautiful when he looked up. "How'd you know?"

"Nails. Long on the right hand, short on the left."

He gave a nod that was more a ducking of his head.

Silence again.

"Er. . . you guys like movies?" This was going to be a very long day. Mary felt like a fourteen-year-old on her first date.

Liam and Debbie each mentioned a couple of movies they liked. Then silence again.

They came to a small town where buildings of gray stone and painted stucco lined both sides of a wide street. The doors and window frames were painted various colors, but the curbs were all red, white, and blue. A Unionist town. A white wooden Victorian bandstand stood on the grassy diamond in the town center.

Gareth pulled the mini to the curb. "I've heard a rumor they make the best ice cream on the coast here. Anyone want to check it out?"

Everyone piled out, and their group filled a small shop that sported yellow and white striped awnings over the windows.

"Order what you want. My treat," Gareth said.

Calls for Pooh Bear Delight, Cadbury Flake, and Irish Cream rang out.

"Liam? What are you having?" Mary asked.

"I'm not hungry."

"Don't you like ice cream?"

Liam shrugged.

"How about a Coke or something?"

"No. Thanks."

What a strange boy. Mary licked her scoop of Honeycomb thoughtfully. With his strong features, thick black hair, and intense dark eyes he would be very good-looking if he weren't quite so pale and thin. But it was mostly his manner. He was not exactly hostile—just unassailable. The wall he had placed around himself reminded her of the massive peace walls that divided parts of Belfast to prevent sectarian conflict. Could anything bring such barriers down?

It was certain that if either the physical or the metaphorical walls were to be removed, one would first have to understand why they were erected. She wondered about Liam. Was he so obdurate now just because he was thrown in with a group that was more than half Unionist? Was he staging a personal demonstration against curbs painted the colors of the Union Jack? Or was he always like this?

She could imagine him as a little boy, running and laughing, riding his bike and climbing trees. Then she thought of what she knew about Belfast's recent history. She saw that little boy in her imagination as the one riding his bike past a still-burning bomb site. There were no trees to climb, just broken walls and rubble heaps.

And yet she had glimpsed flashes of charm and humor. She sensed that the trauma he withdrew from was more than the general disruption he had lived with all his life. And if so, what had caused it? How long had he been like this? The spark in his eyes made her believe he was bright. He liked music and played the guitar, so he wasn't without talent. She wondered about his family.

He left the shop and ambled out toward the bandstand. Mary followed and stood quietly to one side, watching two little girls skipping rope. One, with long dark hair, must have been about seven. " . . . sixty-nine . . . seven—*Ooo!*" She tangled in her rope and sat down hard. Tears formed in her blue eyes.

Liam lifted her to her feet. "Oh dear, oh dear, oh dear." He dusted off her skirt and handed back her rope. "You don't want to be crying now. You did fine."

Her eyes squinted as she smiled up at him.

"Off you go now." He waved her away, and the two girls skipped off across the grass. He seemed embarrassed when he turned back and saw Mary watching him. "I have a kid sister about that age."

"You were very good with her."

He shrugged.

"Tell me about your family. Do you have other brothers and sisters?"

"I had a brother."

Fortunately, the others emerged from the sweet shop just then, because the harshness in his voice told Mary she wasn't to intrude further on that topic.

This time she sat next to freckle-faced Syd, whose open, welcoming smile was a pleasant change. They chatted as the road wound northward to the coast. Now she glimpsed occasional snatches of ocean beyond the green fields.

Syd asked her about America, and she told him about her twin sisters who were about his age. "They're into everything—drama, music, debate, soccer, boys."

He raised a sandy eyebrow. "Hey, they should come over here. We've got all that. I'd show 'em around."

She laughed. "They'd love it."

"Look!" He pointed out the window to the ruins of a magnificent castle on a rocky promontory overlooking the sea. "That's Dunluce Castle." Corbles and gables rose crazily, clinging to the very edge of a cliff attached to the mainland by only a narrow bridge. "It's haunted."

"Oh, tell me!"

"The lord of the castle was giving a feast for his daughter's marriage to some prince. She didn't want to marry the guy, and her father was dancing with her out on the terrace right over the ocean while they argued about it. A terrible storm came up and washed away the

155

whole side of the castle right while the girl and her faither were dancing. She still walks there when it's stormy."

"Oh, that's a great story. Is it true?"

Martin, sitting in the front next to Gareth, turned around. "It's true enough. At least, a whole section of the castle did crumble away during a party."

Gareth added over his shoulder, "Dunluce was Richard de Burgh's castle. Remember? He was Robert the Bruce's father-in-law."

"I remember." Mary had forgotten very little of her Scottish tour with Gareth. It pleased her immensely when he referred to it.

"Just off there a bit—" he gestured past the green cliffs and craggy boulders lining the coast out toward the hazy silver sea "—is Rathlin Island. You'll see it soon."

"I remember! Where Robert the Bruce's cave is. Where he watched the spider!"

"Yep." Gareth shot her a quick, warm smile. For just that instant they were the only two in the minibus.

She turned to the scenery outside the window. The coastline became increasingly more rugged and dramatic. They passed great green heads jutting out into the ocean and sheer basalt cliffs dropped into the foaming waves.

Then Gareth pulled into a car park at the top of a cliff. "Here we are, folks. All out for the Giant's Causeway."

The young people tumbled out into the sunshine and fresh breeze. Here everything was shining green hillside and silvery rolling water with a gentle blue dome overhead. They were on a different planet, away from any hostility or violence.

Swept with the joy of the moment, Mary spread her arms and ran toward the long, steep walkway leading down the side of the cliff to the causeway. Wind tossed her hair. Below her, waves crashed and swirled beyond the jutting green hillocks. Seabirds swooped and called from jagged cliffs on her right.

She gave a little leap and a gurgle of laughter as Gareth caught up with her.

"The tradition is that if you run down, you have to run back up too."

She stopped, gasping. "No way. I'd die." She looked back to the precipitous path she had just plunged down.

"Well, then, we've a wee bit problem. Tradition is sacred in this country, you know."

Before she could protest, he moved on, pointing out a castellated rock structure looming on the cliff edge. "Chimney Point. The Spanish Armada fired on it, thinking they were attacking Dunluce Castle."

"That's amazing. How do you know so much about all this?"

He gave her a wicked grin. "Been here before, haven't I? This is a famous curtin' place."

"Curtain place?"

He put an arm around her shoulder. "Gaelic corruption of courting."

"Oh." She snuggled closer and put an arm around his waist as they continued downward. Then she stopped. "Wait a minute! Just who did you come curtin' with here?"

His eyes danced mischievously. "Can't remember. But it's the one I'm with now that counts."

She leaned her head on his shoulder. "Oh, Gareth. We've had so little time to talk—"

They looked around at the sound of laughter behind them. Sarah had picked up a long branch of seaweed and was using it as a skipping rope while Martin and Syd clapped and kept time on either side of her. Debbie followed more quietly, kicking at chunks of golden stone along the grassy verge.

Lagging a considerable distance behind, in a tight little group, came Gerry, Fiona, and Liam.

"Oh, Gareth. It isn't working at all. We'll never get them together."

And then they were at a sight the best calendar and postcard picture could never have prepared her for. As if all the organ pipes in the world had been gathered here, thousands upon thousands of ochre-colored columns formed great ridges and upright piles running out into the water. As Mary's eye followed the formation out into the sea, she understood. "It really *is* a causeway!"

Behind her Martin laughed. "It goes all the way to Skye. Finn McCool built it to bring his bride over from Scotland."

Gerry leaped lightly from the top of one hexagonal column to another, in demonstration of his athletic skill. "And what soppy story is it you're telling? It was to fight the giants in Scotland he was building it. And he beat them, too. Finn McCool was the greatest hero of all."

Gareth sprang onto a column near Gerry. "Race you to the water." He pointed across the vast mound of stone pillars to where the sea foamed like whipped cream and the causeway slipped beneath its surface. "Come on, Liam, Syd, Martin . . ."

Mary supposed she should be organizing the girls, but maybe, left on their own, the three of them would gravitate to each other. Besides, the pull of the incredible scenery about her was irresistible. She wandered along, jumping from column to column, sometimes examining each amazing shape, sometimes looking so intently at the larger scene around her that she thought her eyes would hurt from her desire to drink it all in. Indeed, it was one of the natural wonders of the world.

At last she sat down on a tall pillar. To her right, sheer green cliffs jutted into the sea. To her left, the water churned against rugged black rocks thrusting into the swirling waves as far down the coastline as she could see. A fishing ship moved slowly along the horizon. Overhead, the sun was a blinding glory above a pocket of clouds into which it would soon slip.

A shout from one of their young charges reminded Mary of her reason for being there. How could people live in all this peace and beauty, yet be so out of harmony with its Creator?

This land was so suited for the ancient saints by its beauty and its isolation: Patrick, who had lit the flame here and rekindled it across the water in Glastonbury; Columba, who had taken the faith to Scotland. Who would bring the peace of Christ back to Ireland?

A bouncing pebble made Mary turn. "Oh, Debbie. Come join me." She gestured to a rocky seat next to hers.

"I didn't want to disturb you. You were so quiet."

Mary smiled. "I'm glad you came. Actually, I was just thinking about Ireland. I want so much to do something to help, but . . ."

Debbie nodded. "Hopeless, isn't it?"

"No, it can't be hopeless. Nobody wants to go back to all the violence. There has to be something we can do." But in spite of her confident words, Mary sighed. "Do you have any ideas? That's what we're supposed to be talking about today."

The sea breeze blowing the girl's hair and dangling earrings made the only motion.

Abruptly, Mary recalled Philip's three questions for bringing opposing sides together. Why not try them? She had nothing to lose. "Debbie, what do you think of the others?"

"Others?" She shrugged. "You mean that Nationalist lot? I don't know."

"Not as a group. I mean, how about individuals? Liam, for example. What do you think of him?"

"They're all the same." Silence.

Well, that didn't work. Try something else. "Tell me about your family."

"There's just me. And my mom."

"What does she do?"

"She works for Courage."

"What's that?"

"They work with families and victims of violence. Help women get jobs when their husbands get killed—stuff like that."

Again Mary's mind boggled. The girl was so matter-of-fact. People simply took violence as a way of life. "That sounds like wonderful work. How did she get into that?"

"She started it when Da was killed."

Mary made a small noise in her throat. She hoped it sounded more like commiseration than shock. "How long ago was that?"

"Five years. He was a policeman."

"Was it in a riot?"

"No." Debbie told it in the same flat voice she might have used to list the subjects she was studying at school. "He was off duty. A Sunday. We were walking to church. He was right in front of me. A car drove by close to the curb. Three shots. My dress was all splashed with blood."

It was too horrible to react to, but Mary had to say something. Get onto a different topic. All she could think of was Philip's prescribed questions. "What do you think the others—Liam, for example—think of you?"

Debbie looked surprised that anyone would ask such a question. "He hates me. He doesn't know anything about what I've been through. His kind caused all the trouble. If he isn't IRA, he probably will be."

Fighting the feeling that maybe it *was* hopeless, Mary pushed on to the third question. "Well, what do you want Liam—or the others—to think of you?"

Debbie thought for a while. "I'd like it better if they didn't hate us."

Mary wanted to encourage the image. "Yes. Wouldn't it be nice if they didn't have those dreadful peace walls everywhere."

"And the murals. Everybody hates those. They're so garish."

"You know, don't you, that if you kids can find some way to work together, you've got a good chance of getting your community hall."

"Yeah. A leisure center would be brilliant." Her brief smile faded. "But I don't know what we can do. They'll never cooperate with us."

"Would you be willing to work with them on a project—if the others would?"

Debbie shrugged her thin shoulders. "Why not?"

Mary looked around and saw that Gareth had gathered the others into a group. They were sitting on a knoll just beyond the rocky causeway. By the time she and Debbie joined them, the fellows were deep into discussing project ideas.

"How about football?" Gareth asked.

"Yeh. Great. Gaelic football. We'll take 'em on anytime." Gerry gestured toward Syd and Martin. "Get your mates together."

"Right you are. We'll take ya. Association rules, though." Martin gave his mop of brown hair a defiant toss.

Gareth held up his hands. "No, no. You've missed the point, lads. We're to work together. On the *same* team."

Gerry and Martin glared at each other.

Syd shrugged. "Not enough of us for a team, anyway."

A trill of laughter behind them on the path turned everyone around. Sarah clapped as Fiona ended a step dance. "Oh, that's wonderful. Do you think you could teach me to do that?"

"Sure. It's not hard. It's just all step patterns—mostly jigs and reels. Keep your upper body still but relaxed. Not stiff. Arms at your side. Bow. Then point your toes out, heels facing in, one foot crossed in front of the other." The late afternoon sun gleamed off Fiona's copper hair as her feet skimmed over the tarmacked path. "Shuffle, hop back on right leg. Shuffle, hop back on left leg." She demonstrated. "Got that? Right—together now."

Sarah, trying to follow her, tangled her feet and sat down, laughing. "I'll never get it."

"Yes, you will. Come on, now. I'll go slower."

Mary jumped to her feet."Oh, I love step dancing. Can you teach me too?"

Fiona assured her that she could.

Within three sequences of Fiona's "Shuffle, hop back, stamp, stamp," however, Mary collided with Sarah and dissolved in laughter. "I feel like a chicken hopping. Riverdance is the most brilliant thing I've ever seen. I'd love to be able to do that."

Fiona continued with a delicate leaping, tapping, and turning while the others discussed the popular Irish dance troupe that had gained international acclaim.

"I love the way they use the traditional dances but make them look modern," Debbie said.

"I've got their music," Liam said. "I wish I had my guitar here." He turned to Mary. "You could dance a lot easier if you had the music. It's all in the rhythm."

Syd jumped onto the path, grabbed Fiona's hands, and spun her around at arms' length, then gave a heel-clicking leap.

And Mary realized the miracle had happened.

She wanted to shout, "That's it! Music, dance—we'll do a whole program. Sell tickets to raise money for the center!" She wanted to make plans. Set rehearsal schedules. Book a hall. But she'd been warned enough about her rashness. This moment of cooperation was a delicate thing. She held her breath, suddenly afraid the magic would explode in front of her.

She caught Gareth's eye across the circle and guessed that he was thinking in a similar vein.

When the dancers stopped for breath, he was ready. "Aye, that's grand. You must bring your guitar to our next meeting, Liam. And we need drums—" He looked at Martin, who nodded. "Aye. Grand. Saturday it'll be, then." He glanced over his shoulder at the sun dipping to the west where banks of silver clouds rimmed the horizon. "Just time for one song before we head back."

They followed him back to the grassy knoll where they had been sitting earlier. Gareth sat on a mossy rock, the others at his feet. "I think you all know this one. You can follow along if you don't."

He hummed a few measures for them to pick up the key. Then they began, more or less together: "Bind us together, Lord. Bind us together with cords that cannot be broken . . ."

Oh, yes. Mary's heart leaped. That was it. She joined her voice with the others. "Bind us together, Lord. Bind us together, Lord. Bind us together in love."

Yes, there was hope.

20

"It will work. I know it will." Mary ran her fingers through her long hair and flung herself back against the sofa cushions, almost knocking the teacup out of Sheila's hand. "We have to do something concrete to build on the start we made today. Get everyone involved with a role."

"I agree it could work." Sheila steadied her cup. "You'd have to pick just the right play, though."

Philip nodded. "I don't think we'd have much trouble selling tickets. And the development council would certainly be impressed if the young people raised some of their own money. What play did you have in mind?"

Mary hadn't really thought that far. "Well, I don't know. Shakespeare is universal."

"And English."

"Oh. Right. An Irish playwright, then. Synge, O'Casey, Yeats . . . I don't know. *Riders to the Sea* is pretty depressing. *In the Shadow of the Gunman* is about violence—probably not the right tone."

"Might do something by Tomelty," Sheila suggested.

"I've never heard of him," Mary said.

"Comedies. *Right Again, Barnam* does a good job of poking fun at both sides in their orange and green sashes."

"I'll have to give it some careful thought. Maybe I could spend some time at the library tomorrow."

Ann came in from the dining room where she had been studying. "We did *Juno and the Paycock* at school. I've got some books you can borrow. How about *Cathleen ni Hoolihan*? It shows how stupid it is to be marching off to battle all the time. I think Yeats means it to be glorious —I've never been sure—but I think it's stupid."

"Thanks. I'd like to borrow your books."

Ann left to find them. The phone rang, and Philip sprang to answer it in the hall. Sheila gathered their teacups and closed the door behind her. Mary and Gareth were alone.

She turned to him. "You were absolutely brilliant with those kids today."

"You didn't do so badly yourself, lass."

"Oh, I don't know, Gareth. I tried to talk to Debbie. Actually, I tried Philip's conciliation questions. But I certainly didn't achieve anything conciliatory." She shivered, remembering. "Her father was shot by the IRA, right in front of her eyes. I can hardly blame her for hating the other side. And fearing them. And she's convinced they hate her, too."

"Oh, but that's amazing." Gareth sat forward, his brilliant eyes shining. "That's exactly how Philip said it works. Liam said almost the same things to me."

"You got *Liam* to talk?"

"Not really. He just said he hates the Prods because they hate him."

"And Debbie said the other side hated her side, but she thought it would be nice if they didn't."

No wonder everyone was so confused that even the combatants hardly knew which side was which, she thought. If only they could see how they mirrored one another.

"Oh, Gareth, what are we doing here? They need more help than we can give them. And even if we could do something here—think of the hundreds—thousands—of others. It really is hopeless."

"It would be if it were all up to us. But there are far more out there working to put things together than there are those who want to tear things apart. We have to believe that good is stronger than evil. Where would any of us be if we didn't believe that right could win?"

Mary lowered her head. "And where would I be without you? You're so right. So strong. And I'm so afraid of letting you down."

Gareth brushed away her frown with a kiss. "Don't worry about those kids. You were grand today."

She relaxed in his embrace. "I'll see you tomorrow."

Two hours later Mary let Ann's collection of *Great Irish Plays* fall to the floor. She couldn't take any more. The trials of the characters too closely paralleled the conflicts in the daily newspapers and the lives of the very people she knew here. Maybe doing a play wasn't such a good idea. Maybe the conflict in the play would just bring their problems more to the fore.

On the other hand, there was Aristotle's theory of dramatic catharsis —that people could work out their aggressions and distance themselves from their problems through drama. Or was that too academic— something Dartmouth professors enjoyed expounding on but that didn't really work out in real life?

Again and again, however, in school and church groups she had experienced the incredible closeness that working together on a production could bring about in a cast and crew. Though surely even Aristotle had never faced such a challenge as her resentful, belligerent, traumatized group.

Her eye fell on the photo of her family sitting on her nightstand. Her sisters, Becca and Julie. Just the age of those young people today. She looked at their open smiles: Becca, short brown hair, shining bright eyes, wide smile; Julie, blonde hair the mass of natural curls that always drove her crazy, blue eyes sparkling, dimples dancing even in a photo. The whole look was so carefree. Of course they had problems. But problems were one thing. Emotional scars were quite another.

She wondered how her twin sisters would go about helping Debbie and Liam and the others. Would these youngsters react more easily to someone their own age? At least the twins could play football with them. She didn't think girls played football over here, but her sisters played on a mixed soccer team. They could stand up to some pretty tough males.

Hardly realizing what she was doing, Mary picked up the pen and paper she had intended for making notes on the plays.

Dear Becca and Julie,

About that special birthday present Grams promised you—do you think she had anything as extravagant as airplane tickets in mind? I think Dad has some frequent flyer freebies he could contribute, too. Anyway, how does a trip to Ireland sound to you? I'm a wee bit over my head here—actually a great big bit, but I like trying to sound like a native. That is to say, I miss you and could sure use your help. If you can work anything out, be sure to bring your soccer shoes and pads.

She wrote on until she all but fell asleep, telling them about what she'd encountered in Ireland. She tried to be honest—about both the good and the bad. If they were to come, she wanted them to know what they'd be getting into.

I don't know what Mom will say about the idea now that the cease-fire's broken. But you wouldn't be in London, and that's where all the trouble is. So far. Tell everyone I love them and miss them but not to worry. We're fine.

Love,
Mary

She was still thinking of her family the next morning as Philip let her off at the Linen Hall Library. She suddenly found herself missing

164

them terribly. She had been so excited to get back to the UK, back to Gareth, back to all she had left behind here four years ago, that she had never considered the possibility of homesickness. But being with those Irish young people, so unlike yet so like her former students; and writing to her sisters last night; and her increased caring for Gareth as they worked together; plus the fact that it was drizzling rain today . . .

"Good luck with your research. We'll pop round to pick you up after our meeting."

"Great. Thanks." She slammed the door and darted across the sidewalk, not taking time to put up her umbrella. She hurried into the historic building. Inside, all was dark walls and creaking wood floors.

A smiling, bald-headed man sat behind a narrow table. Behind him a flight of stairs led steeply upward.

"Sorry to bother you, but if you wouldn't mind just opening your bag."

She returned his smile and plunked her brown leather shoulder bag on the table for inspection. She was becoming accustomed to the routine search of bags, parcels, and coat pockets at the entry of most public buildings.

"Pity the weather's so nasty today," the little man commented as he gave her purse the once-over.

"It was lovely yesterday. We went to the Giant's Causeway."

"Ah, now that's a fine thing. Enjoy your stay." He waved her up the stairs with the same courteous friendliness she'd found everywhere in this land.

Two young women, one tiny and dark in a crisp white blouse and black skirt, the other lanky and awkward in an askew dusty-rose jumper, explained the cataloging system and scurried around bringing her the volumes she requested. Mary had heard of the Belfast harp festival, and it occurred to her that they might attempt some historical tie-in to promote their proposed evening of music and drama. She also needed all the interpretive help she could get if she was to tackle directing a Yeats play.

Yet she found her mind wandering to the people around her. What were their lives like—these helpful, friendly librarians? How had the troubles affected them? It seemed an oxymoron that someone who spent her days among leather-bound volumes, helping people and preserving knowledge, should have to face armed guards and possible violence on the streets.

Then she wondered—the old man, these two women, how did they feel about their country? Were they Unionist or Nationalist?

And then she felt hot with shame. She was falling into the same pattern of thinking that had divided Ireland for centuries. What difference did it make? They were all charming people, obviously good at their jobs. Back home, in library, restaurant, or shop had she ever once tried to figure out what political party or church the person helping her belonged to? It seemed that everything here followed that deeply ingrained pattern.

She turned to the stack of books in front of her.

The more Mary read, the firmer became her decision that William Butler Yeats was the playwright she wanted to work with. He had been at the heart of the Celtic Renaissance, the first to catch the vision of a national theater for Ireland. And his message was the message Mary wanted to convey to her students.

She smiled. The teacher mode was so ingrained in her that she already thought of the youngsters as her students. But, yes, Yeats's motivation was an excellent thing for those on both sides of the road to understand. An Anglo-Irish Protestant, his motivation as an artist sprang from his love of Ireland for her romantic beauty, her poetic speech, her passionate, spirited people.

Perhaps *The Land of Heart's Desire* would be a better play to express this theme than *Cathleen ni Hoolihan,* whose patriotic statement could certainly bear political interpretation. She began reading and immediately lost track of time. If the little dark-haired librarian hadn't brought her another book on the history of the Belfast harp festival, she would probably have read on to the end without ever thinking of the time. Luckily, she glanced at her watch before returning to the world in her head.

One fifteen. How could it possibly be so late? Had Philip forgotten to come back? Surely their meeting couldn't have gone on so long. She began gathering her notes and books. There were several pages she needed to photocopy. She would do those, then call the Centre.

She had just finished paying for her copies when Gareth bounded up the stairs. "Sorry we're so late. Had a spot of bother. Can I carry those for you?"

"Oh, it'll all fit in my bag, thanks." She jammed the papers into her pack and handed the books to the librarian.

Outside it was still wet and gray. She jumped into the backseat of Philip's car and busied herself arranging her papers. They had driven a few blocks through busy traffic when she looked up. Her heart stopped.

One of the little armored trucks that patrolled the streets like overgrown metal turtles slowed the traffic in front of them while policemen urged vehicles and pedestrians to keep moving. Garlands of yellow barricade ribbon surrounded the buildings to her right. Behind the barricade stood soldiers in battledress. Long, black automatic weapons were in their hands.

"What is it?"

Philip looked at her over his shoulder. "Bomb scare at the Europa."

"That's why we're late," Gareth explained. "Our meeting was in that building." He pointed to a modern brick office structure across the street from the hotel. "We had to evacuate, then find another place to meet. What a morning."

Gareth had been in a building evacuated in a bomb scare? What if it hadn't been just a scare? What if a warning hadn't been given? What if the Europa had been blown up as it had been so many times before? What if Gareth's building had been damaged—flying glass, falling bricks, fire? She felt hysteria rise in her throat as the images filled her mind.

Then she felt Gareth's hand clasp hers, and she opened her eyes.

"Mary."

He was turned around in his seat, looking back at her. He was so close. So infinitely dear. And he was safe. But it might have been different. She clutched his hand with both of hers.

"It's all right, Mary. It was nae bomb. Just a wee scare."

"But it might have been."

She shook her head, trying to clear the dire images. Bombs, blood, and fire mixed with the romantic poetry of the sensitive Yeats. Hatred, violence, and strife warred with the love, peace, and understanding so many were working for. In this tiny microcosm, this emerald speck on the edge of a vast ocean, raged all the forces of good and evil that had moved mankind through the ages. The struggle was cosmic, and yet it was on her own doorstep.

"But this can't go on! How can people *do* these things?"

"The roots are deep—" Philip started.

"I accept that. I know the settlers and planters took Irish land four hundred years ago. And they treated the Irish as inferiors. And it was wrong. But this is today. Surely those people don't think they can right the wrongs of centuries by blowing people up today. That can't be what it's all about."

"Not all. But it's part of it. A deep-seated part. You've read the beginning. My notebooks are in that box behind my seat if you're ready for more of the story."

She wasn't at all sure that she was. She didn't want to read of more violence and conflict. What she really wanted was a nice romantic picnic with Gareth. Or a party with singing and dancing. Or a movie—a really funny comedy.

With a forced smile she reached for the next notebook in the stack.

GENERATION TWO

CROMWELLIAN ULSTER
1625–1688

Hear ye, O mountains . . .
   and ye strong foundations of the earth:
For the Lord hath a controversy
   with his people. . . .
But thou, O Lord, shalt endure for ever;
   and thy remembrance unto all generations.
                          Micah 6:2
                          Psalm 102:12

21

"The Black Oath?"

Katrina shivered at the very sound of the words. She pictured a heavy black cloud hanging low above their bawn, blocking out all sun and warmth, threatening to rain destruction.

She looked from one to the other of her brothers seated around the carved oak table in the parlor of the Lanark farmhouse. Katrina knew there had been trouble in Ulster ever since King Charles appointed the autocratic Thomas Wentworth lord deputy. But she had not expected her brothers to return from their trip to Belfast with news that would change their lives.

Broad-shouldered, russet-haired Rory, who at thirty was the head of their family, spoke in his quiet, determined way. "Aye, we knew this king held little of the love his faither bore for the Plantations. But none would have guessed he'd actually make war on us."

Twenty-seven-year-old Dougal looked grim. It had only been the past few months that Dougal's smile had ceased to be as permanent a part of his countenance as his blond hair and blue eyes. "They say Wentworth has an army of three thousand." He made a scoffing sound. "It could be three million for all I care. *I'll* not sign his murderous oath." He added an oath of his own.

Aileen, youngest of the family, clapped a hand over her mouth, and her green eyes widened. Cursing was not tolerated in the Lanark household.

Dougal, however, was in no mood to stifle his outrage. "Do what ye want to, Rory, but I'll none of it. And I know Grandfather will no' sign either."

At the mention of their mother's father, who still managed the farm next to theirs in spite of nearing his seventieth birthday, Rory smiled. "I'd like to see the commissioner that dared approach Alisdair Dunlop with an oath requiring him to swear abjuration of the Covenant. Grandfather was one of the first in Ulster to sign."

Katrina groaned. Last October, Scotland's noblemen, ministers, and lairds had assembled in Greyfriars Kirk in Edinburgh to sign the

171

Confession of Faith that had since been often referred to as Scotland's "Marriage with God." Since then, copies of the document had been dispatched to garner the signatures of Scots everywhere.

After signing the Covenant, Alisdair had set out to insure that his grandsons signed as well. Nor were the granddaughters exempt, for although women did not normally sign, a few did. And scarce an evening had passed since then that the Lanark parlor had not rung with Covenanting debate. None of the younger Lanarks had yet decided on their action. And now there was the added confusion of this counteroath.

The disputations had borne in most heavily on Katrina, who hated controversy above all things. Her older sister, Isobel, simply absented herself from such discussions, as she had at the present moment, by slipping out to the byre to attend the animals that she loved so well. And plump, pretty Aileen had the happy faculty of being able to flip her golden curls at all contention as others would shoo away a housefly. Katrina looked at her little sister now, sitting where the early summer sunshine fell through the leaded window onto her embroidery.

But Katrina's only escape was to her imagination, where she could live in a world of peace and beauty, as night after night, Grandfather had read through the tedious catalogue of Catholic errors denounced in the Covenant and the list of the acts of the Scottish Parliament the Scots would uphold.

Whenever Rory or Dougal would protest over the idea of rebelling against their king, Grandfather would thunder at him. "This is nae a revolutionary thing but the revival of an old and respected document—the Confession of Faith of 1581—which was signed by the king's own faither, Jamie the Sixth." The Covenanters, he said, were countering a Catholic threat to their faith. This was not an attack on the rightful authority of the Crown.

And so the debates had raged for near to a year and a half. But now the prospects before them made those evenings that had been so painful to Katrina seem by contrast like the singing of birds in the garden. Every Scot in Ulster more than sixteen years old was to swear to the king's new oath—a countercovenant that, in essence, pledged their allegiance to the Episcopal church.

Professed Roman Catholics were exempt, but Presbyterians must swear the oath under the threat of fines, imprisonment, or death. And Wentworth was bringing an army of three thousand to see that none escaped. The oath was to be taken kneeling, in public.

Katrina could not imagine her brothers doing such a thing. So what would happen to them? She shook the soft brown ringlets that just brushed the top of her white, lace-trimmed collar and looked at the older brother she adored.

172

Rory seemed to read her thoughts. "I don't know, Catriona." He often gave her name its soft Gaelic pronunciation when he was being tender with her. "I don't know what any of us will do." He rose to his feet, handsome in his russet jacket and dark green breeches tied at the knee with yellow ribbon. Lace-topped hose frothed like sea foam above his wide boots. "I shall call on our neighbors. We will be stronger if we can act in concert."

Dougal laughed. "You'll be lucky if you can get this hard-headed lot to *talk* to each other, let alone act together. Calvin Johnstone hasn't said a civil word since Matt ran off somewhere south. What you mean is that you want to know Judith Seaton's opinion on the matter."

Rory simply raised an eyebrow and left the room. It was no secret that Rory and Judith were fond of each other. Indeed, Katrina was sure they would have been betrothed long ago were it not for Judith's loyalty to her widowed father. Judith had served as mistress of Seaton Court for the past ten years, ever since the death of her mother, Effie.

Judith had inherited more than her Aunt Ailsa's stunning red hair and green eyes. She was also as capable as Ailsa, who now held complete control of the Seaton lands in Ayrshire. The romantic Katrina longed for the day that would bring Rory and Judith's marriage. But now that Fulke Seaton was ailing, it seemed that they must delay their happiness even longer. This new trouble in Ulster was sure to delay that longer yet.

At least Katrina could take comfort, if somewhat selfishly, in the fact that the postponement would delay any change in her family. And change was something Katrina dreaded almost as much as she hated controversy.

She followed Rory out of the house and across the lawn to the stable. "I've finished the length of linen Judith bespoke. If you're going to Seaton Court, you might like to take it with you."

Rory's worried expression changed abruptly, causing her even more fear—he did not want her to see how troubled he was. But he wasn't too troubled to understand her unspoken offer. "Bless you, Catty. You knew I'd like company, didn't you? Aye, fetch your linen, and I'll hitch the carriage."

They had just driven out of the bawn and turned onto Scrabo Road when Katrina cried, "Oh, there's Mama!"

Deirdre returned Katrina's wave. She had been walking, as she did every day, no matter what the weather, around the land she loved so much. Today she had apparently been along the shores of Strangford Lough, for her arms were full of the long-stemmed white flowers that grew in such profusion above its banks.

"Where are you off to, my darlings?" she gave them a soft smile.

"Driving to the Seatons."

"I've the linen for Judith."

"Well, have a pleasant visit."

As they drove off, neither Rory nor Katrina expressed relief that she had not asked to join them. Much as they would have enjoyed their mother's company, they did not want to confront her with the distressing news of the Black Oath and Wentworth's army. Hopefully, they could delay telling Deirdre of any unpleasantness until they knew what could be done about it.

More than any of the others, Rory and Katrina shared the goal of saving their mother from upset. Rory was so much like his father, whose first care had always been for his Deirdre. And Katrina so hated being upset herself that she felt the least she could do was to spare her mother when she could not avoid her own agitation.

A short time later, when they arrived at the Seatons' imposing house set in carefully ordered gardens, she was very glad that her mother did not have to face the commotion they found there. Even from the front hall into which the servant ushered them, they could hear the thundering of Fulke Seaton's voice and Judith's pleas that he be reasonable.

When the girl greeted them, Katrina was shocked at her friend's distraught appearance. Her normally alabaster skin was splotched with red, her brilliant green eyes were red-rimmed and watery, coppery wisps of hair escaped the smooth bun on the back of her head, and the fringe of ringlets over her forehead was brushed awry.

"You've heard," Rory said.

Judith nodded and gestured toward the bench beneath the Flemish tapestry on the north wall. Brother and sister sat there while their hostess seated herself in a high-backed armchair. She gripped the chair arms so hard that her knuckles showed white.

"Your faither is much upset over the oath?" Katrina ventured.

"No. He is not upset at all. It seems he has known for some time that such was to come upon us. That or some similar abomination."

"But how could he? It was just made public this morning in Belfast by that overweening Bishop Leslie," Rory said.

"Something like this has been expected for some time by the Scots at court. They all believe Wentworth to be an emissary from Rome. Six months ago and more, my faither was warned to take precautions." Judith jumped to her feet and began pacing the clay tiles. "He has sold Seaton Court and made all arrangements necessary for our removal back to Ayrshire."

"*When?*" Rory's single word sounded strangled.

174

"At the next available sailing. It may take a week or two to get passage as so many are leaving."

Rory jumped to his feet and clasped Judith's hands. "No. You cannot be gone from me sae fast."

"Faither says we must. Before the constables arrive with the oath. Women are to swear, too—as I'm sure you know. He says I would be imprisoned as well, for I will not pledge myself to apostasy."

"Judith, stay here and marry me. I will protect you." He threw his arms around her.

Katrina was certain her brother had quite forgotten her presence.

Judith drew back and looked at him, her lips parted in amazement. "Stay here? Face ruinous fines and imprisonment, when we have a comfortable place in Scotland?"

"Yes, stay with me."

She shook her head as if to clarify her understanding. "You mean you plan to take the oath? And you would have me do so as well? Abandon all that the Scottish people believe in?"

"No, no. I don't mean that. I . . . I haven't decided what I'll do. But Judith, you can't go. It's clear you don't want to. I can see how upset you are at your faither's plan."

Judith's laughter was so high-pitched that Katrina at first thought she was hysterical. Then she realized that, though under enormous strain, Judith was quite in control of herself.

"Rory, you don't understand at all. I'm not upset to be going to Scotland. I'm delighted to be getting away from all this controversy."

"Then why—"

"I was—am—upset with my faither because he didn't tell you or any of our friends here. He says if his information had become widely known, he might not have been able to sell the farm—or get a good price for it, at any rate. But I say such very valued friends as your family shouldn't be left to the mercy of King Charles's henchmen." She put her hand fleetingly on his chest. "Rory, if you'd known sooner, you might have been able to sell, too. I'm not at all sad to be taking the lifeboat, but I do hate to think I'm deserting my friends. And that my faither failed to warn you to secure against losses."

"Losses? Deserting *friends*?" Rory seemed as confused as if she were speaking a foreign language. "But Judith, what of *us*? I mean, I always thought . . . hoped . . . Judith, I want to marry you!"

Judith kissed him lightly on the cheek. "I know. You're a dear, Rory—easily the finest man in all Ulster. Perhaps if things had been different . . ."

Then she turned and saw Katrina, who had pushed herself into the farthest corner of the bench, trying to become invisible. "Oh, Katy, what a love you are. Thank you for remembering my linen. I'm certain there won't be any half so fine to be had in Ayrshire. I'll send your money over with Dawson. He'll stay to take care of things until the buyers come—if they do come, now that this Black Oath thing has been made public."

Katrina could think of no possible answer to such a speech. It was just as well. She wouldn't have trusted her voice anyway. Her head high, not even looking at the woman who could so easily toss aside Rory's offer of his heart and life, Katrina gripped her brother's arm and led him from the room.

She sat close to Rory in the carriage but remained silent on the drive home. Judith Seaton was clearly unworthy of him. But Katrina knew this was not the time to express such sentiments. She felt battered by the events of the day. How could the world have shattered so suddenly?

In the copper light of the warm June evening, the land looked happy and rich. No one would guess the turmoil seething around the edges. Surely the Scots farmers were overreacting. They were loyal subjects. They wouldn't be forced to swear to a statement abhorrent to their faith. No mounted army could be gathering against them at this moment. Shadows of the trees stretched across the dirt road. Birds twittered in their branches. How could people be so hard when God's creation was so gentle?

All Katrina had ever wanted in life was to live quietly with her family. Just to go on living happily, securely, together behind their great stone bawn. Why would anyone want to interfere with that? They had harmed no one, meddled with no one else's conscience. She simply couldn't understand why anyone should choose to do such things to them.

She knew Rory was reeling from his abrupt dismissal by the woman he had for so many years considered to be his betrothed. Katrina didn't want to bother him with her own confusion, so she waited.

When they were home, she located Dougal in the cart shed, repairing a cracked shaft on the wagon. As usual of late, she was struck by the deep seriousness—she would almost say austerity—that had come over the brother who had always been the most lighthearted of the family. But at least his earnestness made him easier to approach on such a heavy subject as the one now weighing on her.

She perched on a sack of grain stored against the stone wall of the shed, which was a continuation of the house, and began without preamble. "Why do people always have to fuss at each other?"

Dougal put down the long thin bar to which harnesses were fastened in order to draw the cart. "What do you mean?"

"Why do the king and Wentworth hate us? Why does anyone hate us? I don't hate anybody." Schooled in strict honesty, Katrina paused to evaluate her statement. No, she didn't hate Judith Seaton; she was just very angry with her. That settled, she looked at Dougal for his answer.

He shrugged. "The king wants everyone to be Anglican. We're Presbyterian."

"So Anglicans and Presbyterians will kill each other? Why should everyone have to go to the same church?"

To her surprise, Dougal lashed out irritably. "Don't be an eejit. It's obvious. There's right and wrong. All people should worship the right way."

"And there can't be two right ways?"

"You *are* an idiot. Think. Can there be two kings?"

"Well, no."

"Of course not. Only one king. Only one church. Everybody knows that."

"Well, if you say so. But I wish they could settle it without all this fighting."

"Someday you'll understand that these things are worth fighting for." He looked at her in a way that made her feel that her twenty years were a very small accomplishment.

She might be a silly girl, but she wasn't giving in so easily. "If people worship wrong will they go to hell?"

"Of course, eejit."

It wasn't being called an idiot that made her eyes sting. It was this hardness in Dougal. "Then if people kill people for worshiping wrong, they are sending them to hell. Isn't that wrong?"

He shrugged again. "The heathen haven't been elected to salvation."

"Then what difference does it make how they worship?"

Dougal gave a final tug to the wire he was wrapping around the reglued shaft. "Lots of times in the Old Testament, God told His people to kill the heathen."

"Did God tell King Charles to kill Presbyterians? We aren't heathen."

"No, no, no. Don't you understand anything? The Anglican church is popery in disguise. *They're* the heathen. We must not submit. We must fight them."

Once again Katrina felt the black cloud of destruction descending on them.

22

Katrina soon discovered that it was not necessary for the king's army to march on them to have the sheltered peace behind the Lanark bawn destroyed. Rory and Dougal did that themselves with their raised voices and clenched fists.

"Compromise?" Dougal slammed a fist on the table. "There can be no compromise with the Devil. All free will preaching must be rooted out. Preaching the possibility of salvation for all flies in the face of God's sovereignty. He elects those on whom He will bestow His grace. All notions of free will are pernicious heresy."

Rory's normally blue eyes glowered like black coals. "So go ahead—sign your holier-than-thou Covenant. Don't think I didn't see the look on your face Sunday when we sat through the parson's two-hour harangue on upholding the Covenant. Don't think I didn't realize how near you came to joining Calvin Johnstone in signing that rebellious document afterwards."

"Rebellious, am I? I'd far rather be a rebel against King Charles than a traitor to my heavenly King."

"And how do ye propose to achieve that?" Rory leaned across the table toward him. "Rebellion against our earthly king *is* rebellion against the heavenly King, who set him on his throne."

Rory's temper hardened into stony logic. "I'm no traitor. I can be Royalist *and* Presbyterian. Montgomery is both."

The first viscount, Hugh Montgomery, who had established New-townards and the surrounding settlements, had died three years earlier. His son, the second viscount, remained a loyal subject of King Charles in spite of the fact that the Crown had increased his rents by more than 300 percent. He even maintained his support of the kirk despite the fact that the local Episcopal bishop had forced the Presbyterian clergy out of several parishes.

"Am I to understand you're thinking of joining the Black Apostate and swearing to his abominable oath?" Dougal made it a challenge.

"Montgomery took the oath. If our laird lost his lands, where would any of us be? He had no choice."

Dougal scoffed. "A free man always has a choice. A choice for right or for wrong. And it can no' be right to reject Scotland's marriage with God."

Now it was Rory's turn to scoff. "Your Covenant's no' a marriage with God—it's marriage with a theological position. And not even the way John Calvin stated it. It's not salvation based on the inscrutable will of God. It's salvation based on racial superiority."

"That's unfair!"

Rory grinned. "That's right. It's mighty unfair."

Dougal was in no mood for humor. "You twisted my words, and you know you did. We're nae talking about race—we're talking about understanding God right."

Rory was still grinning. "And *you're* right. You've got God all figured out."

Dougal banged a fist against the table. "Scripture says—"

Rory pushed his stool back with a harsh scraping. He rose and walked out.

Even if Rory hadn't ended the altercation by marching from the room, Katrina would have left. She could take no more. She had promised her mother she would have this pile of flax fiber spun in order to begin the weaving tomorrow, but she could stay there and listen no longer. She went in search of her sister.

Isobel was right to spend all her time with her animals. The gentle creatures took no sides in politics or theology. They ate and cared for their young and gave freely of their milk or eggs or strength—whatever was demanded of them.

In spite of the beauty of the summer day, which would normally have found Isobel in the paddock beyond the bawn feeding her lambs or simply enjoying the daisies that bloomed in such profusion along the fences, Katrina knew that today she would be in the byre. Ballycoo, her favorite cow, was late in calving.

As she approached the sturdy, whitewashed building, Katrina could hear her sister crooning encouragingly. "You're doing fine. It won't be much longer now. Just keep steady. You know how dear ye are to me. I don't know what I would do without you."

The rusty hinges on the byre door squeaked as Katrina entered. For a moment she could see only a hurried movement in the straw across the byre. "Isobel? Hasn't Bally calved yet?"

"Oh, Katrina, you startled me. Yes, yes. She calved fine. Here's the wee Gamhain."

Katrina's eyes adjusted to the dimness. She saw the wee wet creature in the straw at Isobel's feet. "Gamhain?"

"A fine name, is it not?"

Katrina started as the answer to her question came from a lilting male voice in the corner behind her.

"Ye'd no' do better than to be naming it with the Gaelic for calf."

"Oh, Sean. I didn't realize you were here."

"Of course, he's here," Isobel answered lightly. "It was a breech birth. I couldn't be dealing with it by myself."

"Our brothers would have helped you."

Isobel made a scoffing noise. "Those two. Last thing I'd want would be to have Ballycoo upset with their bickering."

Katrina had to agree with that. Besides, Sean O'Brien was as fine a hired man as everyone said his brother Hugh had been. Hugh had fled south when their father married Anna Johnstone. That had been almost seventeen years ago. As far as anyone knew, Johnstone had never spoken to his daughter since that day. There was gossip that he had beaten his wife for visiting her.

Katrina smiled. "Well, then, it's a good thing you were here, Sean." But for some reason she felt like an intruder here. Was there no place she could be at peace?

A week later the Seatons had their passage to leave Ireland. After the painful scene with Judith, Katrina had thought she would be glad of their going, but she had not realized it would be the occasion for yet another controversy within her family.

Alisdair Dunlop had come to supper. In former times, that frequent occurrence was an event Katrina delighted in. But that night she had sat on her mother's left at the end of the long table, holding her breath in dread of the moment the debate would start.

Surprisingly, everyone kept to innocuous topics—the weather, the crops, the condition of the roads—until after dessert had been enjoyed by all. Aileen had put much care into scalding the cream to just the right temperature to make it clot for topping the apple tarts. It was a delicious treat that deserved their full concentration.

When the last spoonful disappeared, the men pushed their stools back from the table and filled their pipes with tobacco. Alisdair took a small white clay pipe, pulled on it to start it drawing properly, and handed it to Deirdre.

He lit one with a longer stem for himself and leaned back in his chair. As the honored guest, Alisdair occupied the only chair at the table. "Ah, a fine meal that was, as fine as any I've had for many a day. A fine thing it is to enjoy God's goodness in the bosom of one's family." He looked around the table and smiled on each one. "Aye, it's my hope that we'll be enjoying many more such times for years to come."

A cold finger touched Katrina's spine. As much as she agreed with his sentiment, she preferred not to think about the future. Things were fine for the moment—if one didn't look too deeply. Best to leave them alone.

But Alisdair had never been a man to tread carefully when he knew his way. And he always knew his way. "The ship sails from Donaghadee next week. I've booked passage for us all."

Isobel's gasp was almost drowned out by Aileen's cry. The youngest Lanark turned to her grandfather and flung her plump arms around his neck. "Grandfather, you'd not leave us?"

He gave Aileen a fond smile and unclasped her hands. "Ye misheard me, poppet. I said I booked for us all. We shall *all* be on board. This notion of an Irish settlement was well enough in the time of the old king. We've done a good job improving the agriculture here. Aye, we can be proud of all we've accomplished. But times are moving on, and we're Scots, not Irish. Time we went back to the land of the Covenant." He looked at Deirdre. "Right, daughter? Ye'd like fine to see your brothers and the old place in Glasgow, would ye not?"

Deirdre smiled, as unperturbed as if her father had asked her to stroll in the garden with him. "Indeed I would, Faither. But this is my home."

Alisdair blew a cloud from his pipe. "There's hard times coming. There's no need our sharing it. Our job here's done."

"This is my home, Faither. Calum always knew the bad times would come. That was why he insisted on building the bawn for our protection. I'll bide here."

She would say no more on the matter.

Alisdair turned to his grandsons. "Can ye no' talk sense to your mither? This bawn will no' protect her from the Black Oath."

Dougal jumped to his feet and flung his pipe on the table. "Naught will protect us from the ungodly but God Himself. And it's time we made it clear we're on His side. I've decided. I'll sign the Covenant."

Alisdair rose and clapped his grandson on the shoulder. At seventy, Dunlop was still fine-looking, broad-shouldered, and square-jawed. His mane of gray hair was worn fashionably long. "Aye, ye've the blood of the Dunlops in ye. It's time ye made your place in Scotland."

"No, Grandfather. I'll no' run away. Because I've the blood of the Dunlops, I'll stay and fight. Our work's barely begun in Ireland. As long as the grip of popery keeps the land in darkness and superstition there's work for God-fearing men."

Alisdair turned to his older grandson. "Rory, ye'll listen to sense, man. Every week a boatload of settlers makes way back across the water. They know where the fair land is. Cailean reports the business is flourishing. But if ye've no taste to join your uncle in the merchant trade, we'll lease a nice piece of land in Ayrshire. I've a buyer for my house here who'll take over my lease as well. Ye can start new."

Katrina's heart thumped in her throat. She had been merely three years old when her father died. She had only the vaguest memories of him. But her grandfather had always been there. And now he was going back to Scotland? This was the first breaking of the unit she prized so much. But it would be far worse if Rory, the brother she idolized, were to go, too. If he went and the others stayed here, what would she do?

Rory gave a scoffing laugh. "Me? And why would I be running off to Scotland? I'm no Covenanter." He glowered at his brother. "Like some."

And then Katrina realized that even if they all stayed in Comber, the bond was breaking.

The following Sunday, Katrina gasped as she entered the kirk. Only the first three rows of pews were occupied. Even in the middle of the summer, the stark white walls reflected chill air, and the sun falling through the white-glassed, arched windows added no warmth. Even if the coals in the iron stove had been lighted, Katrina would have been cold with apprehension. Where *was* everybody?

A few months ago every seat had been filled. As the migration back to Scotland increased, there had been more empty spaces of late. But was it possible that the settlement was now all but deserted? Dougal opened the waist-high door of their pew and held it for Katrina, her sisters, and their mother. Dougal sat on the end. The door clicked shut. Rory sat across the aisle.

Parson Pym led the congregation in the confession:

> "O Lord God, which art mighty and dreadful, Thou that keepest covenant and shewest mercy to them that love Thee and do Thy commandments. We have sinned, we have offended, we have wickedly and stubbornly gone back from Thy laws and precepts . . ."

A sweetly musical voice reciting in front of her drew Katrina's mind from the catalogue of her derelictions. She had been so shocked by the sight of so many empty seats that she had scarcely looked at the ones that were filled. How could she have failed to notice the newcomers sitting in front of her?

As best Katrina could tell from the back, the daughter of the family, she of the melodious voice, seemed to be about her own age. The girl had soft brown hair under her white linen cap and a neat figure in her black dress. Her brother standing beside her was tall and thin and blonder than Dougal. This must be the Price family who had taken over Alisdair Dunlop's lease. That meant that these people were the Lanark's nearest neighbors. Katrina's spirits rose.

But the lifting of her depression was not sufficient to prevent her dreading the end of the service. Usually the Reverend Mr. Pym's two-hour sermon seemed interminable—a reaction she kept strictly to herself. But today it was all too short for her.

She knew the unlikelihood of Dougal's changing his mind. And yet she continued to hope. She would have prayed—were she not afraid it would be a sin to pray against the Covenant—that her brother would not add his name to the list of those opposing the king. Wentworth's threatened army had not marched upon them. Yet. The Oath commissioners had not made their way to Comber. Yet. But they would. And Dougal Lanark's signature on the document Mr. Pym was now urging his congregation to sign could bring disaster on them all.

"Do ye this now, before God and your neighbors, that our posterity may have this monument of God's mercy, this testimony of our fidelity in a corrupt time, this tie to bind them to the maintenance of the purity of God's worship in all time."

Dougal was the first to rise and walk toward the table where the parchment rested. But he had not yet seized the quill beside it before the young man sitting in front of Katrina rose also. Katrina could tell by the approving smile on the face of the senior Mr. Price that he had already signed. And she could see by the scowl on Rory's face that her brothers were as divided as ever.

But then her gaze was drawn back to the flaxen-haired young man who signed the Covenant after her brother. The newcomer was taller and more fashionably dressed than Dougal. His blue breeches were in the new, longer length, the sleeves of his doublet deeply slashed to reveal a pale yellow shirt.

Katrina shifted in her seat to get a better look, but when he turned she lowered her gaze modestly. Not, however, before she saw the blueness of his eyes.

23

Dougal's signing of the Covenant changed everything.

The very next morning, Katrina took a deep breath and tried to figure out what was different as she cooked the breakfast porridge. Then she knew. It was so quiet. As Dougal and Rory ate their bacon and brown bread, their chewing was the only sound. Could she hope that peace had at last been restored to Lanarks' Bawn?

She set the steaming bowls before her brothers and saw that Dougal's face still shone as it had yesterday when he turned from the signing, quill in hand. She could see yet the light from the window falling across his golden locks. But the real light had come from inside him. The difficult course taken, Dougal was at last free to be his true self. Katrina could hope that she would now have again the lighthearted brother who bounced and smiled and made few sounds that were not accompanied by laughter.

The other factor in the calm was more ominous, however. Rory's silence was heavy—a fact made more obvious by Dougal's lightness. Rory finished his meal and shoved back his stool, scraping the floorboards. "I'll be in the south field."

It was the first he'd spoken that morning. Desiring to encourage him, Katrina asked, "How are the tatties?"

Then she was sorry she had asked.

"If we don't get some rain soon, there won't be a harvest." And then he left.

And then Katrina decided to do something she had never before thought of doing. Leaving the breakfast dishes to Aileen, she removed her apron and took one of the last pots of apple preserves from the pantry shelf. "I am going to the Prices'," she told her mother, whose hands and feet worked rhythmically at her loom. "They should be officially welcomed."

"Yes, dear. What a good idea. Greet them for me as well. Since they've taken your grandfather's lease, that makes them almost family."

Katrina soon was hurrying along a lane bordered high on each side by wild berry bushes. She thought that the sentiment expressed by her mother was not displeasing.

The minute she entered the courtyard between the Price house and byre, Katrina sensed a different atmosphere from the comfortable former days when she had come here to visit Grandfather Dunlop. The place where the old merchant had established such staid routine now had been turned into a hive of activity by the newcomers.

The daughter, Margaret, was just approaching the dairy. "Oh, how lovely to have a visitor." Her blue eyes shone. "Come see. Robert is so clever. Just see what he has devised for Mother."

Margaret led her into the dairy, which bore a new coat of whitewash. Mrs. Price stood before a large churn. Its dasher was attached to the ceiling with a rope. She pushed downward with an easy sweep, but to Katrina's surprise, instead of then having to pull the plunger back up—always the most tiring part of the churning process—Mrs. Price simply loosened her grip on the long handle, and it sprang upward by itself.

"Oh," Katrina cried. "How does it do that?" Then she saw that a heavy coiled spring held the rope to the ceiling.

Margaret beamed. "Didn't I tell you Robert was clever? It reduces the work by half. And he has fitted the butcher shed with a row of tenterhooks for hanging the meat to cure. It's much more efficient. I think the meat even tastes better."

Just then the much-praised Robert entered, dressed far less finely than he had been at kirk but looking no less striking with his unusual height and his shoulder-length, cotton-white hair.

Katrina turned to him. "Your churn is wonderful! Could you show my brothers how to arrange one for us?"

"Aye, it's naething. Just a bit of coiled wire. I'll do it for ye myself."

Katrina caught her breath. Margaret Price wasn't the only one in the family with a beautiful voice. "I—I brought you some preserves." Then she blushed as she realized how forward that sounded. "For the family. From my mother. She sends her welcome. She would have come herself but she needed to finish her length of linen."

"Oh, aye, I'm that glad ye've come. I was hoping to talk to you."

Katrina was speechless. He had *noticed* her?

"About the linen. I've heard you make the finest in Comber. I'd like to know more about it. You see, a stone of flax is only two and sixpence. But if spun and woven into the best quality threads, I'm told it can fetch up to four pounds an ounce."

Katrina's heart sank even as she laughed at herself. It was not her person Robert Price was interested in but her knowledge of spinning

185

and weaving. "You really must come to the bawn and talk to my mother. She'd be happy to have you anytime, and the linen making is all hers. There's little she doesn't know about it."

"Robert!" Margaret, helping her mother take the paddle from the churn in order to remove the butter, laughed at him. "Is that how you greet our guest—with talk of linen prices? Sure and she'll never come back." She took Katrina's arm. "I've some fresh pancakes. Your preserves will be lovely on them. Come." She led the way into the house.

It was strange being in the house that was no longer her grandfather's. Alisdair had kept everything in perfect order, but now there was also new beeswax on the furniture, a pot of fresh flowers on the window sill, a woven rug by the hearth.

"How did you come to find this property?" Katrina asked as she took the chair by the window.

Margaret offered her a pewter plate of pancakes. "Faither saw an agent's advertisement. Our lease in Paisley was small, and with so many leaving their holdings in Ireland, Faither thought it would be a good opportunity. He had long wanted to lease more land in order to have enough for Robert's family as well."

Katrina almost choked. "Family?"

"Oh, aye. Jean will be joining us as soon as her wee bairn is old enough to travel. Oh, I canna wait. He's the dearest thing you can ever imagine."

Katrina swallowed her bit of pancake and forced a smile as Margaret went on describing the wonders of her new nephew, who was still across the water in Scotland.

"But aren't you worried to bring a wee'un here when things are so unsettled? Especially since you signed the Covenant? Did you not know about the Black Oath when you came?"

Robert nodded. "Aye, we knew. But I've noticed ye no" fled yourself. There's times when a man must stand for his faith. And God will stand with him. That's why I signed the Covenant. That document is Scotland's rededication to God. My signing it was *my* dedication to God and my country."

A short time later Katrina slowly walked home, thinking hard. She had heard too many of Rory's objections to feel comfortable with all the political implications of the Covenant, but she fully admired Robert Price's personal devotion. Perhaps it would help bring healing to the rift in the Lanark family if they could all hear more of Robert's ideas.

And perhaps an increase in their fortunes as well, for he had mentioned that well-churned butter sold for twenty-two shillings sixpence a tub in the country. If they installed three spring churns, she and her sisters could each churn a tub a day. Their cows didn't produce that much cream, but when the new family came to Seaton Court, perhaps they would have cream to sell.

In the coming weeks, Katrina found an excuse to call on the Price family every three or four days. After all, with their community so reduced, it was important to make close ties with the few neighbors they had.

One afternoon in late August, she was walking along the lane, now a-buzz with bees, thinking on the great joy these new friends had brought into her life. Suddenly her smile froze on her lips, and she stopped still in the road. Just ahead, Robert Price drove along the road from Donaghadee. And beside him on the seat was a woman in a yellow gown, holding a small, blanket-wrapped bundle to her breast.

The intensity of the pain in Katrina's chest made her catch her breath. She had not realized the large place these new friends occupied in her thoughts. No, not just friends in general, but Robert Price. He was the finest man she knew. He combined Dougal's devotion and Rory's gentleness. He had a readiness to work hard and a good head for business. And he had a wife and child.

She fled back up the road, hoping no one had seen her. She wanted to sob out her hurt. But even more, she wanted to shout out her anger. Anger at Robert? No. Anger at God? No. Anger at herself. She had known from the day she met him. It was no one's fault but her own that she had let herself go on fostering daydreams.

She ran to the apple orchard, her favorite place beyond the bawn. Today she scarcely noticed the undersized, shriveled apples the thirsty trees were struggling to produce. As soon as her feet touched the dry grass beneath the trees, her steps slowed, her breathing calmed. But her emotions still seethed. She must get control of herself before she faced her family.

Too late she realized she was not alone. Rory was just beyond the next row of trees, mending the fence.

He glanced her way but did not speak.

And because she knew of his own brokenheartedness over Judith Seaton, she knew that he was the one person she could talk to. Suddenly she understood his glumness of the past weeks. How could she have been so insensitive as not to have offered him more sympathy? It was his inner hurt and turmoil that made him seem so severe.

Now that she knew, now that they shared similar pain, she could talk to him. She ran forward. "Rory, I'm so sorry. I should have spoken sooner. We thought you were angry. You seemed so glum and long-faced like you were mad at us—" She paused to catch her breath.

Rory looked astounded. He ran fingers through his coppery hair. "What are you saying, Catriona? I'm not mad—not even at Dougal. He did right as he saw it. But now I must act as *I* see fit. I just fear my actions will cause pain to those I hold ever sae dear. That's why I've been sae much in thought of late."

Whatever could he be talking about? Had she once more jumped to the wrong conclusion, as was her wont? Did Rory mean to take the Black Oath? The cloud that had hung over them all summer lowered again. Every week they heard of more Presbyterians being sent to prison in Dublin Castle for refusing to swear. It was only a matter of time until the commissioners reached Lanarks' Bawn.

Yet, that did not seem to be what was on Rory's mind. He put both hands on Katrina's shoulders and looked intently down at her for several seconds. At last he took a deep breath. "Come with me, Catriona. There is someone I want you to meet."

The pony cart, loaded with his fence-mending equipment, was nearby. He helped her into it. At the foot of the lane they turned toward Prices' farm, and Katrina guessed his secret. "Rory!" She turned and gripped his arm. "I know what it is! You have a new *cailín*." She squeezed his arm as he gave a telltale grin. "And you thought we would think you fickle to have forgotten Judith so soon!"

Katrina laughed, carried along with her story. "But you must know we'll all be delighted for you. We want you to be happy, Rory. Of course, I'll be the happiest of all, I'm sure, because Margaret Price is a dear friend." For Rory's happiness she would put aside her own distress over seeing Robert with his wife. "She's a lovely lass, Rory."

But her speech of encouragement seemed to confuse her brother. He didn't say anything for a moment.

Katrina looked beyond the carriage to the roadside. "Rory? Where are you going? Here's the turn-in to Grandfather's lane—er, I mean to the Prices'."

His expression, which had been so relaxed and smiling while she talked of his happiness with a new girlfriend, was shuttered again. "You were part right, Catty. I have met a quite lovely woman. But it is not Margaret Price."

Katrina frowned. "But then who could it be? There's no one else new in the Ards. Oh, Rory, we aren't going clear to Belfast, are we? I should have put on a better dress—"

"We're not going to Belfast. Only to Seaton Court."

"But there's no one *there*. Only the old servant. The new people couldn't have come yet, or we'd have seen them at kirk."

"They came the week after Seatons left."

"But—"

How could such a thing be? That would be almost three months now. Missing kirk was unthinkable.

"The Guilfords are Old English."

Katrina's jaw went slack. Old English. Families who had come to Ireland before Elizabethan times. People who had adopted Irish ways —some said they had become more Irish than the Irish. People of English descent who had become Catholic.

Katrina was silent the rest of the way.

Minutes later they were being warmly received by Celia Guilford.

Still in shock at her brother's announcement, Katrina curtsied and surveyed the woman who held her brother's heart. Celia Guilford was all golden ringlets and blue taffeta. Her French lace collar was far finer than the English lace Katrina had purchased for a penny a yard from a traveling chapman. And Celia's collar didn't fall from high on her neck, as was the Scots fashion, but from a rounded neckline that showed her white throat. Her puffed sleeves ended below her elbows, revealing slender white arms.

"Er . . . welcome to Ulster, Miss Guilford."

Celia ushered them into the sitting room and poured small glasses of sweet red wine from a decanter as she explained her family's coming. "Of course it was a wrench for *athair* to leave the lands in Tyrone where our family had lived for so long, but he is the younger brother, and since he has three sons and my *uncail* has five sons, the land could not be divided among so many." She spread her hands and shrugged, a very pretty gesture.

The girl's voice was pronouncedly Irish, both in its lilt and in the heavy sprinkling of Gaelic she used. Yet, with her fair coloring and small, sharp features, she looked decidedly English. Katrina could imagine her fitting in perfectly at Charles's court, especially after Celia explained that her dress was a copy of one worn by Queen Henrietta Maria.

"I'm glad you're happy here." Katrina struggled to make polite conversation. "But I fear you've come at an unfortunate time—with the Black Oath hanging over all our heads."

Celia nodded, and her ringlets bounced. "Yes, it is a worrying time for all. But it's a mercy we will be exempt from the oath."

Katrina remembered that King Charles had married a French princess, and one condition of the marriage was that he would enforce no laws against Catholics. It was all so complicated. Katrina was relieved when Celia's older brother Henry joined them and the conversation turned from religion and politics to concerns for the approaching harvest.

They had had little rain in the past month. The fields that earlier had promised bumper crops were shriveling in the unseasonably dry weather. In some areas, Henry said, the crop failure would be total. And it was going to be difficult to harvest what produce there was, because the heavy emigration had so emptied the land of workers. The plantations and settlements had never been threatened with such disaster.

Katrina bit her lip. What would they do? Her life, which had been so secure, was suddenly endangered from every direction.

As they drove home, she strove to come to some understanding of what seemed utter madness on her brother's part. "Rory, how could you?"

"How could I love Celia? I should think it would be quite obvious even on the first visit. It was to me. I went to Seaton Court to arrange a matter of business with Dawson, and there she was—all sweetness and womanly charms. I'll admit it took me a few more visits to appreciate her beautiful spirit and her lively intellect."

Katrina believed that was a true description of the woman she had met. Yet the fact remained unalterable. Celia Guilford was Catholic. English, but Catholic. Katrina's mind balked at the very idea.

A few days later, she at least had the activity of heavy labor to keep her mind off such problems as Rory's inconceivable attachment and her own aching heart. Across Ulster, the few crops that hadn't shriveled from lack of water were rotting for lack of harvesters. The Lanarks refused to let that happen. They were determined to save what they could.

The apples ripened first. Indeed, many were already falling from the trees and rotting before Katrina, her sisters, and Sean O'Brien could gather them in. Rory and Dougal, their differences put aside for the moment, worked day and night in the potato fields, often with one of their sisters holding a torch to enable them to continue work long after the sun went down.

After three days, their mother was the only one not bent low with the stress of the situation. Deirdre returned smiling from her flax field. "This is so like the old days. Then, there was only your faither and Seamus O'Brien for all the work. And the flax fields were mine." She looked at her younger children. "And I would come in from the field and nurse my bairns." Her soft smile told Katrina that her mother was living much in the past. She was glad for the happy memories that sustained her, but she was concerned for her mother's health. Deirdre no longer had the strength she had in those fondly remembered long-gone days.

The next day Katrina and Isobel worked alone in the orchard, hoping to rescue the best of the apples from the encroaching birds and then get on quickly to the field where Aileen was cutting flax with their mother. As she worked, she worried. What would they eat? How would they pay for their lease? And worst of all—what would they do next year if they couldn't save enough potatoes to seed the new crop? If only they had more help, at least they could rescue the little they had.

Katrina passed a sadly shriveled apple to the basket her sister held. "I cannot believe that Sean would desert us. After all I've heard of the kindnesses our faither showed his family, you'd think at least he could help us when we need help so desperately."

Isobel flared. "Of course, he hasn't abandoned us. Sean is the kindest, most reliable person I know. He—"

"Yes, yes. Of course he is—when it pleases him to be so. All the wild Irish are. When they aren't drunk or angry or off worshiping idols. But where is this great reliability now?"

Isobel missed the apple Katrina tossed to her. It thudded to the ground.

The girls moved to another tree, and silence hung between them. Katrina looked up to pluck an apple from a branch above her, and sweat ran into her eyes. "Oh! Maybe we should have gone to Scotland with Grandfather. Then someone else could be worrying about this harvest."

Even as she spoke, a cloud of dust moving up the road caught her attention. "There's someone coming. Who could it be?" She slid down the tree so fast she ripped her skirt and scraped skin off her wrist. Such minor discomforts, however, added only little to her general misery. Surely it was not Wentworth's army. They had heard nothing for weeks. Was this the final destruction come upon them?

Isobel was running ahead, holding her skirts high, her black hair streaming. At the edge of the orchard she called over her shoulder. "What did I tell you? It's Sean! I knew he wouldn't let us down." She rushed to meet him.

It wasn't just Sean. It was a small army of perhaps twenty roughly dressed men carrying pitchforks, shovels, and scythes over their shoulders. There had been rumors of a native uprising. Was this it? Were they all to be slaughtered in the midst of their dying fields?

The laughter and enthusiastic chatter that came from Sean's band didn't sound like a rebellion, though. And a moment later when, at Sean's direction, several trooped toward the orchard, Katrina understood what was happening. Sean had gathered all his brothers and sisters and their native Irish friends into a harvest crew.

"Isn't it wonderful!" Isobel dashed back and hugged her sister. "I'll fetch Mother, and we'll bring them some ale. We're saved!"

With relief the Lanark women turned to their normal autumn tasks: packing the best apples in barrels of sawdust in the storage shed, setting aside the culls for cider, sorting potatoes into those to be stored for eating and those to be saved for seed, laying out the flax to dry, feeding the workers, and keeping them refreshed with ale. The stores were far less than in a normal year, but they would be enough to make it through the winter. Especially if God would send an early spring.

On the day the last field was harvested, Katrina saw to the boiling of vast kettles of potatoes while a sheep roasted on the spit, and Isobel and Aileen set trestle tables in the courtyard between the house and barn. By mid-afternoon the last load was in. The workers could feast before going on to the next farm where, hopefully, the unseasonable heat had left something yet to harvest.

Katrina had started toward the tables with a big platter of oatcakes when Aileen, her red-gold coloring glowing with the excitement of the harvest feast, ran to her with an empty pewter pitcher. "Here, I'll take the cakes around. You take this to Isobel and tell her she must open another keg of ale. She won't listen to me."

Katrina frowned. "Where is she?"

"In the byre with her animals! Where else?"

Irritated at being ordered to see to another's duties, Katrina crossed the yard to the barn. She must hurry. The last kettle of potatoes would be ready to take off the fire in a minute. She shoved the door open. "Isobel, come help us. Your coos can wait till the feast's over."

Then her eyes adjusted to the darkness. Isobel hadn't even heard her. She was lost in Sean O'Brien's embrace.

But Sean heard. He gently pushed Isobel away. "Aye, *Muirneach*, we must not be forgetting our work."

Katrina stiffened. "I'm sure we're all very grateful to you, Sean. But it seems my sister has an extravagant way of showing it." She thrust the pitcher at Isobel and returned to her potatoes.

It was a good thing she had been the one to find them, Katrina thought. The Puritan in Dougal would have ruled his good humor. He would likely have beaten Sean—and maybe Isobel. And she couldn't imagine how their mother would have responded. At least Rory couldn't have objected on the grounds of Sean's religion. She shook her head. What a tangle things were in.

It was a good thing Dougal didn't know Rory's secret. That would have set things off. At that thought she looked around, blinking. Where *was* Rory? He had left for the fields with the others this morning. Hadn't he? She couldn't remember seeing him when they took mid-morning refreshments to the field. She looked around the tables of talking, eating men. Rory was not there.

192

She was just thinking of looking in the carriage shed to see if he had driven out in a vehicle, when she heard the clatter of iron wheels and horse's hooves racing up the road and through the arch of the bawn.

"Rory!" she cried. But then she saw that it was not Rory.

At the same time, Sean O'Brien looked up from the table where he was sitting amid his brothers and friends. *"Anna!"* His shout was loud enough to quiet the feasters and get the attention of the distraught woman driving the pony cart.

Calvin Johnstone's daughter, who years ago had defied her father to marry the widowed Seamus O'Brien and mother his young children, jumped from the cart and ran to her stepson. "It's Faither. The commissioners arrived at noon. He will no' swear their oath. They have taken him to prison. Mother is levied a fine of thirteen thousand pounds!"

Katrina had never been fond of the long-faced Calvin Johnstone, but she could not bear to think of the proud old man being borne off in manacles. And how would Senga Johnstone ever raise such a sum—especially in a year of bad harvests? Would they imprison the tiny, bent old woman as well?

But then the full impact of the news struck her. If the commissioners were at Johnstones' today, they would be at Lanarks' tomorrow. This was one disaster not even the strong walls of the bawn could protect them against.

24

"On your knees, man. Swear it before God and this company with your hand upraised."

The morning sunshine glinted off the dew on the vines greening the bawn, cows mooed in the byre, hens cackled in the yard, but the proceedings in the center of the courtyard were out of kilter with all of God's creation.

Dougal stood tall and fair in his homespun work breeches and jerkin before two crimson-sashed soldiers and a black-suited magistrate.

"Kneel!" the magistrate repeated.

A soldier gestured with his pike to a spot in the gravel.

Katrina held her breath. If her brother refused, would the soldiers strike him down right there?

Dougal's only movement was a slight lifting of his chin, making his square jaw more prominent.

"You will swear to obey without protest every command of your sovereign, King Charles. Likewise you will renounce all covenants not ordered by him."

"I am no traitor to King Charles. But I serve One higher than he. The Covenant I uphold is based on Holy Scripture. I take my stand on Scripture alone."

Katrina's heart so swelled with pride that for a moment she forgot her fear and the certain destruction facing them all.

At a flick of the magistrate's hand, a soldier seized Dougal's wrists and clamped them in heavy iron chains. The magistrate smiled; his pointed black goatee adding to the leering effect. He nodded to Deirdre standing quietly beside a honeysuckle bush. "And now, madam, you may have the honor of declaring loyalty to your sovereign king. Kneel, woman."

Deirdre had voiced no personal allegiance to the Covenant. She had even once said that, if her Calum were alive, she doubted that he would have signed it. He'd always thought somewhat differently than most. But she was the daughter and the mother of staunch Covenanters. Katrina knew her mother would never swear to the Black Apostate's countercovenant.

Deirdre stood serene and silent as a light breeze blew her soft skirt. She looked directly at Wentworth's man, regarding him with interest but no defiance. Yet her very stillness made it apparent that she had no intention of falling to her knees with upraised hands.

What would Katrina do when her own turn came? *God give me strength,* she prayed. Even with eyes closed, she could see her mother. She dared not open them. Would the guards pull their swords on a woman?

But then Katrina did open her eyes for the sound of a carriage rolling into the courtyard jerked her to attention. This time it was Rory. Rory and Celia Guilford.

Rory helped her from the carriage and turned to his mother, eloquently ignoring the glowering armed men. "Mother, embrace your new daughter. We were married yesterday."

Isobel and Aileen gasped and cried out, but Deirdre opened her arms to Celia.

Then Rory drew a sealed document from his doublet and presented it to the commissioner. "Apparently we have arrived at an opportune moment to spare you from making a most awkward mistake. As you will see, you have no business here. Father Sebastian's signature should be sufficient to satisfy you that this household is not required to swear your oath."

The magistrate licked his lips, gave a curt nod toward Rory's certificate, and gestured to the soldier who still held Dougal. The man started to undo the chains.

"No!" Dougal all but spit at his brother. "I'll hide behind no papist's skirts. I'd far rather rot in prison than burn in the bottomless perdition God has prepared for the followers of popery." Then he flung at Rory, "And you a born Scot!"

Rory spoke so quietly that only those nearest him heard. "I'm Irish. I'm proud of my Scots heritage, but I was born here. Ireland is my home. I cast my lot with the land of my birth."

Little Aileen, the pink bloom drained from her cheeks, ran to him. "But Rory, you're a Protestant. You couldn't—didn't—" She choked on her sobs. "Rory, how could you marry a Catholic to avoid taking the oath?"

Rory put both hands on her shoulders to steady her. "No, dearling, I married Celia because I love her. It is a happy fortuity that our king also loved and married a Catholic and so granted them special graces."

Katrina shook her head in amazement. "I didn't think . . . I mean, I knew he was besotted over her . . ."

Dougal shook his fist, making his chains rattle. "*Bewitched* is more like."

Aileen's face blanched. "Celia is a *witch*?"

Rory cuddled his youngest sister. "Little goose brain, Celia is a wonderful, beautiful woman whom you will soon come to love as much as I do. Don't listen to narrow-minded people who would have you believe that God grants grace on the basis of racial superiority."

"God elects whom He will." Dougal shook his head. The defiant gesture showed that the manacles on his wrists had no hold on his spirit. His body, however, was obedient to the pike prod that marched him forward.

Katrina took a deep breath, trying to order her thoughts. But then she caught sight of Isobel embracing Celia. Isobel was transformed. There was a lightness, a radiance about her as if a hundredweight stone had suddenly slipped from her shoulders. A cheery whistle sounded from the paddock beyond the byre. Sean O'Brien was there, carrying oats to Isobel's favorite horse. Isobel heard, turned from Celia, and sped across the courtyard, her feet barely touching the stones.

Katrina staggered to a bench beside the house. Her head was reeling. The agony of seeing Dougal marched off between soldiers with drawn weapons, the sudden relief of having the rest of them spared similar treatment, the turmoil of Rory's marriage—and Isobel running to . . . to . . . At least Celia was English. But Katrina could hardly chide Isobel for choosing a native Irish. Her own sin was worse—she had fallen in love with a married man.

Robert. Why did she not think sooner? She jumped to her feet. The Prices lived right on the main road. The soldiers would have gone there first. She wasn't sure whether she was running toward the Prices' to offer what comfort she could or to see what solace they might be able to offer her. She only knew she had an instinctive urge to run. And she did.

Margaret Price met her halfway along the road.

"They've taken Dougal, Rory is married, and—" Katrina began, then stopped when she realized Margaret was sobbing.

"Help me. Oh, Katrina, help me. I've done the most awful thing. I was so frightened, but that can't excuse such a wrong." She buried her face in Katrina's shoulder, and the two women clung to each other.

"Margaret, what is it? Is it Robert? Have they taken him too?"

"No. No, he wasn't here. They'd all gone to Belfast for the day. I was alone. I didn't know what to do." She clapped both hands over her mouth, and her eyes grew even wider. "I didn't know what to do, so I just did what they told me. I thought they would run me through with their pikes if I didn't."

"The soldiers came, and you swore the oath."

Margaret nodded, seemingly overcome at the horror of her act.

"But if you didn't mean it, it means nothing. An oath taken under threat of life has no meaning." Did it? Katrina wanted to comfort her friend, but she wasn't sure.

Margaret shook her head. "I swore a falsehood. I have sinned."

Katrina thought of the horrors Dougal faced in prison. Could it be a sin to save one's family from that? "You did a brave thing, Margaret. I wish I could have saved my brother."

25

At least outwardly, the next several months settled down to a period of relative peace for those living at Lanarks' Bawn—a quiet that was the more amazing because of the turmoil that raged elsewhere.

At first it seemed that Wentworth's policy, however severe, had brought stability. The lord deputy, at the king's request, dispatched half of his army to Scotland to quell dissenters there. That left the few Presbyterians in Ulster who had neither fled to Scotland nor been imprisoned for refusing the oath free to continue their work. They carried on their worship the best they could.

The last of the Presbyterian ministers who had been allowed their churches by Episcopal bishops were now forced to flee. But many removed to southwest Scotland, from whence they could slip back across the narrow sea as often as possible to minister to hidden congregations. Others, such as Mr. Pym, remained in their parishes. Whereas an Episcopal priest now conducted the service from the Book of Common Prayer and received the tithes in the parish church, Parson Pym met the stalwart of his flock in hidden conventicles in barns and fields.

Katrina sighed as she set her curling iron aside and put on her high-crowned, broad-brimmed black hat. Going to kirk had once been the highlight of her week. The whole family, dressed in their best, had squeezed into the carriage, driven so sedately by one of her brothers. They would see all their friends and neighbors. Even when the church was cold and the sermons long, she loved it. But now, the March rain lashing the window of the room she shared with Isobel and Aileen seemed a fitting backdrop for the journey she and her sisters must make alone to an abandoned shed on the far side of Scrabo.

She went into Deirdre's room. "Are you certain you'll be all right alone, Mother? I wouldn't mind staying home." She smoothed the comforter over her bed.

"No, no, my dear. I'll be quite fine. It's just a little cold. If the weather were warmer, I'd go with you. But as it is, I think it best to stay inside. Margaret Price promised she'd come by with a bottle of her mother's recipe for the ague. I'm certain I'll be much recovered by the time you return."

Katrina hesitated. "Yes, I know, Mother. It's just so—so dismal with Dougal gone." Katrina refused to say "imprisoned" because of the horrors it conjured in her mind. "And Rory and Celia spending every Sunday at Seaton Court . . ."

Deirdre nodded. "I know, my dear. But we must carry on, no matter what the circumstances. If there's anything life has taught me it's that one must simply hold her head up and do what's right. Right doesn't change with circumstances, so our actions shouldn't either."

A knock at the door relieved Katrina of having to reply. She worried about Rory and Celia spending Sundays with the Guilfords. She suspected the family harbored a Jesuit priest at Seaton Court, and she wondered if Rory attended the Mass. The thought of his acquiescing to such idolatry was almost as terrible as the thought of Dougal in prison. And yet he seemed so happy . . . The knock sounded again.

Deirdre called, "Come," and Margaret Price entered.

As always, Margaret's sweet voice and gentle ways had a soothing effect on Katrina. And as she measured out a spoonful of her mother's elixir and gave it to Deirdre, it was clear that she had that effect on the older woman as well.

Katrina was happy enough to accept the ride Margaret offered the Lanark sisters in the Price carriage, crowded though it was. Robert drove at a leisurely pace. If an army officer should stop them, they would reply that they were calling on friends. That was true enough. They would, indeed, be seeing their friends. The necessity of worshiping in secret had much strengthened the bonds of fellowship.

After the others got out, Robert didn't go into the old sod shed but drove on to a clearing on the far rise. The men of the congregation took turns standing guard to sound an alert should soldiers approach. Today was Robert's turn.

Katrina went cold at the thought. They would not be the first if their conventicle should be broken in upon and the worshipers fined, beaten, or hauled off to prison. But she knew that neither were the Scots Presbyterians the first to be so persecuted. The early Christians had suffered similar treatment from the Romans. She prayed that she could be as strong as they.

When Katrina joined the hidden conventicle, she looked about. Surely it wasn't just the semidarkness and whispered talk that made it seem so much warmer in the unheated building. No, it wasn't just her imagination. There *were* more people in attendance. Something must have happened. Something that gave people a desire for comfort or for news.

Then the Reverend Mr. Pym announced his sermon topic, and she began to understand. "See how the mighty are fallen," he declared, his voice ringing off the stark walls. "The mighty are fallen, and the weapons of war perished! Rejoice, Babylon is suddenly fallen. The whore of Babylon is destroyed! Those who persecute God's chosen will come to utter destruction."

The preacher soon made his reference clear. "That handmaiden of Satan Thomas Wentworth has been called to account for his offenses against God's elect. He who less than a year ago was elevated to an earldom for the persecutions he had inflicted on God's holy church, is fallen." For the sake of the uninformed, Mr. Pym explained that Wentworth had been called to Westminster, but before he could work his evil scheme there, God Almighty saw fit to have him clapped in irons.

"We praise God for His goodness and His faithfulness. We praise Him for His justice. The Black Apostate has suffered the same fate he wreaked on so many of God's servants.

"Parliament has impeached Wentworth on grounds of his offering to take the Irish army to England to subdue the king's opponents there—as he sought to subdue us here."

Katrina's heart soared. Wentworth and his Black Oath were defeated! Then they were free of the awful threats that had hung over them for so long! She hugged her sisters to her.

Parson Pym continued in a vein similar to her own thinking. "God's elect have suffered the hottest piece of persecution our poor infant church has had to meet with. We have survived. By the grace of God, we have stood strong.

"And now we can say, 'Praise ye the Lord, praise the Lord, O my soul. Happy is he that hath the God of Jacob for his help, whose hope is in the Lord his God, who executeth judgment for the oppressed. The Lord looseth the prisoners. Praise ye the Lord.'"

Katrina's face was wet. It was the most joyful sermon she had ever heard. It meant that Dougal would be freed. Now life could return to the peaceful quiet she loved. Her heart soared as they stood to sing the closing psalm and Mr. Pym dismissed his congregation with prayer.

Two weeks later Dougal came home.

Katrina bit her lip as she pulled back from embracing him. "Dougal, you've—you've changed."

He had been gone eighteen months, but it could have been eight years for the changes she saw in him. He was thin, almost emaciated, though apparently not weakened. He was hardened, sharper. And the light in his eyes was now more a gleam of determination than of humor.

"Welcome home, brother." Rory stood in the doorway, his hand outstretched.

The pale, gaunt man regarded the broad, ruddy hand.

Katrina held her breath. *Please, God, don't let there be a fight on his first night home.*

Dougal nodded to Rory but did not take his hand.

Upset was averted by Aileen's bouncy entrance. "Come to the dining room, all of you. Mother and Isobel say you're much too thin, Dougal. Did they give you nothing but brown bread and ale? Isobel hardly spent any time with her animals all week—she was so busy baking and roasting for your homecoming."

Dougal's smile was the brightest Katrina had seen from him since he'd ridden into the bawn on a scrawny borrowed horse. He took a deep breath. "Aye, it smells grand."

They all trooped behind him to the table.

The tense moments were not all behind them, however. Dougal's seat was directly across from Celia's. He acknowledged her brief greeting with a curt nod.

Deirdre from her place at the foot of the table spoke quickly, "Dougal, our hearts are all so full of praise at your safe return. Won't you ask the blessing, please?"

Katrina was slow to close her eyes, and she looked at the strength of Dougal's firmly clasped hands and the radiance of his upturned face. This was a man who had experienced suffering and triumphed over it.

"Now, Lord, seeing that we enjoy comfort and quietness both in body and spirit, by reason Thy mercy granted unto us after our most desperate troubles, we ask that Thou will dissipate the councils of such as deceitfully work to stir the hearts of the inhabitants of England and Ireland against others. Let their malicious practices be their own confusion. Grant Thou of Thy mercy, that love, concord, and tranquility may continue and increase amongst the inhabitants of this isle, even to the coming of our Lord Jesus Christ. So be it."

Under her breath Katrina added her own thanks that Dougal did not open his eyes in time to see Celia bless herself at the end of his prayer.

As all concentrated on the platters of roast mutton, boiled potatoes with parsnips, and crisp oatcakes that went around the table, it almost seemed they had been transported back in time to the days before the Black Oath and its turmoil came into their lives.

Almost, but not quite. Aileen, always the irrepressible one, asked, "Dougal, tell us what it was like. Were you starved? Tortured? Were there rats?"

"Oh, yes, there were rats." He put down his knife and fork to measure a two-foot span with his hands. "Some of them longer than that. We made friends with them. I named my favorite Hubert." He grinned at his oldest sister. "I thought of naming it for you—knew you'd take it as an honor with your love for all creatures—but he seemed most definitely male."

Everyone showed appreciation of Dougal's attempt at lightness.

"And, no, we weren't starved, but I ken ye will all forgive me for eating like I'd been." He heaped an enormous mound of mutton and tatties on his plate and poured gravy over all. "We had food, but it nae tasted like this."

Talk then turned to matters of the farm and community. The hope was that now settlers would come back to Ulster and that by this autumn there would be adequate workers for the harvest.

It was much later, when Aileen and Deirdre were out of the room, that Katrina again raised the question. "You were right to put a good face on it, Dougal. But please tell us the truth."

His jaw tightened. "It was not exactly what you'd call torture. Not racked or beaten. Just locked in the cold and dark for months on end. Nothing but filthy straw to sit on and one blanket at night—for those who could afford to bribe the guards for such comforts. The young and healthy survived. The old and sick didn't."

Katrina was ashamed that she hadn't asked sooner. They had been so happy in their own good fortune that she hated to think of others for whom this was a time of sorrow. "Calvin Johnstone?" she asked.

"He died in my arms two months ago." Dougal scooted his stool back abruptly. "God forgive my selfishness in stopping here first. I must go tell his family."

"No!" Isobel jumped to her feet. "You're tired, Dougal. You've had enough on you. Stay here and visit with our mother. I'll go. I'll tell them you'll call tomorrow."

Dougal nodded. "Aye. I'd be that grateful."

"I'll go with you, Isobel." Katrina pulled her cloak off the hall peg. Sean was just finishing the evening milking when the girls went out. With intense breathlessness Isobel told him the news. Then both stood looking at each other. Not a word was spoken, but Katrina felt that volumes passed between them. At last Isobel shook her head. "I dona know. It will change things. But I dona know how."

"I'll drive ye," Sean said.

"We'll tell Anna first," Isobel decided. "Her grief may be the worse for all the years of estrangement that can never be healed now." She paused. "At least Senga Johnstone will be freed of that onerous fine."

They drove in silence to the small thatched cottage that had housed so many O'Briens. Here Sean had been born, here his mother had died in childbirth, here Calum Lanark had received a fatal blow while trying to make peace. The peat stack stood close to the door. Chickens scratched around it. In the field beyond, the potato rows stood ready for planting. But there was none of the liveliness that normally surrounded the house, no Anna energetically directing her three children and any stepchildren that happened to be around. The cattle made rustling noises from the end of the cottage that sheltered them. All else was quiet.

Sean said, "I've never seen it so deserted."

"Perhaps they've already heard. Maybe Anna went to her mother."

Isobel's words revealed the immense change Mr. Johnstone's death signaled. Anna Johnstone O'Brien had not been home since her father disowned her seventeen years ago.

A short time later they drove onto the Johnstone farm. Here were severely pruned bushes, clean white buildings, and straight-edged lanes. Daniel, Susan, and Neil O'Brien, Anna's children, came out to meet the visitors and usher them into the grandparents' house they had never before visited.

Senga sat in a corner of the parlor, so tiny she was almost invisible under her black shawl. Her eyes were red-rimmed, but she was calm. "I have lost my husband, God rest his soul, but I have gained my daughter back."

Anna came in then with a tray of oatcakes and small glasses of wine. It was clear that she too had cried but was finished with it for the time being. "It's all settled. We're going to move here and take care of the farm for Mother." She held out a hand to Sean. "I hope you won't mind. You know there'll be a place for you too."

Sean had always been a man of few words. He let his expressive features and fluid gestures do much of his talking. Now a rapid series of emotions flitted across his face before he spoke. "What does Da say?"

Anna's face lost some of its strained look. "And didn't you always know your da was the best of men? He's out now caring for the coos."

Seamus O'Brien was close to double Anna's age, but he had been a good husband to her these almost twenty years, seldom giving in to the bouts of drinking or temper he had sunk to after his first wife's death. And although gray-haired, he was still a strong, handsome man.

Sean, who possessed many of his father's strengths but without his volatility, turned to Isobel. "Da'll be needing help with the milking."

Isobel smiled her understanding, nodded, and went out with him.

Evening shadows were falling across the lane as they drove back to Lanarks' Bawn. This time Katrina sat alone, for Isobel rode beside Sean on the driver's seat. And Katrina was almost certain Isobel's arm was linked in his under the covering of her cape.

She wanted to cry out to them to stop. Hadn't their families had enough turmoil for a lifetime? Unless Dougal now raised a new fuss, Rory's marriage into an Old English family had achieved an uneasy acceptance. At least Celia's religion was simply ignored most of the time. But for Isobel to marry a native Irish . . . Katrina shook her head.

She had seen it coming for three years now. But Sean and Isobel had been patient this long. Surely they could wait a little longer. Please.

And perhaps Katrina's thoughts, which took the form of a prayer, were answered. Or perhaps Isobel and Sean saw the sense of the matter for themselves. Or perhaps Katrina had been wrong and their family would be spared the wrench she foresaw. But the summer of 1641 wore on quietly in their corner of Ulster. Again it seemed the walls of the bawn protected the Lanarks from the upheavals fulminating elsewhere.

Yet, all summer the rumors continued. Wherever people gathered—at market, at conventicles, whenever a traveling chapman passed and asked to exhibit his wares—the talk quickly turned to reports of unrest among the Gaelic lords. Riley Cavan, a red-bearded, round-bellied chapman who specialized in carrying ladies' dainties between the English Pale around Dublin and the Ulster settlements around Belfast, called at Lanarks' Bawn in mid-August.

Katrina, Isobel, and Celia admired his trays of ribbons, laces, and beads. Celia picked up a lovely triple strand of amber stones set in gold filigree.

"It's beautiful on you, Celia," Katrina said. "Perfect with your golden hair. But it must be incredibly dear."

Riley Cavan wiped his broad forehead and round cheeks with a large kerchief. "Aye, and doesn't the lady have a shrewd eye? This is the finest piece ever to honor my pack or likely the pack of any traveler. This belonged to the sister of Sir Phelim O'Neill, lord of Kinard. Ah, but hard times have fallen on that ancient house. That it should come to a descendant of the High O'Neills to be selling their geegaws . . ." He wagged his head again. "Hard times it is on us all."

"Oh." Celia gave the stones a gentle caress as she placed them back in the case. "I knew her ladyship. Our lands were near Kinard in south Tyrone." And Katrina heard the homesickness in her voice.

Celia continued. "It's a great pity. The British methods of estate management are so different from those of the old Gaelic families. I think they find it all but impossible to adapt to English ways. I don't know what will become of them."

Isobel selected a blue satin ribbon that just matched her eyes. "Sean said that Sir Con O'Neill has sold his last property in Clandeboye. His son is left to live by his wits at court."

And then Isobel did a surprising thing. She selected a length of ivory lace while Riley Cavan recounted a tale of the earl of Antrim's losing two thousand pounds at court during a single game of ninepins.

More disturbing than the financial ruin of the ancient lords, however, were rumors that Irish officers, returning from service in Spain with King Charles, were organizing an Irish army. But even that could be forgotten in the busyness of September's harvest.

The night before the potato harvest was to begin, Katrina had just swung a griddle dotted with circles of pancake batter over the fire and was waiting until their bubbling tops told her it was time to turn them, when she heard Isobel's footsteps clattering down the stairs.

She burst into the kitchen and grabbed Katrina's hand. "Oh, my dear, Mother has given us her blessing! At last! Sean and I are to be married. We will live in the O'Brien cottage. Mother says we may continue with the land Father allowed Seamus O'Brien. We shall raise horses."

The pancakes almost burned as Katrina stared at her sister.

"Hurry, finish those," Isobel urged. "Then join me. Sean is in the parlor now. We must tell our brothers."

Katrina would have chosen anything but to walk into that lions' den, but she knew her sister needed her support. She was slow removing the cakes, however, so the altercation had begun by the time she arrived.

"He's a fine man our sister has chosen. You'd no' deny that." Rory occupied the center of the floor.

Dougal faced him. "I would deny any such marriage. Scripture says, 'Be ye not unequally yoked together,' and there's an end to it. Marriage to a heathen is no marriage at all." Dougal's nose was only a few inches from Rory's. "But then I'd not expect you to realize that."

"Listen to me!" Isobel inserted herself between the brothers. "We're to be married by the Anglican priest. We're both joining the parish church."

The news brought enormous relief to Katrina, but not to Dougal. "Prelacy is naught but Protestant popery—it's all superstition and profaneness."

White-faced, Isobel turned back to Sean as Dougal continued.

"Without the blessing of the kirk, she'll be naught but a hoor." His voice bit like ice. "One in the family is enough."

Rory's fist slammed into Dougal's jaw. The crack sounded like a gunshot. Dougal reeled, but did not fall. The slam of the front door as he left accompanied Katrina's cry.

Rory turned to his wife, who sat white-faced with her hand on her swelling abdomen. He pulled her into his arms. "My dearling, I'm sae sorry ye had to witness that. He canna help it. His mind's that inflexible, and he believes God's is, too."

Across the room Isobel was likewise sheltering in her beloved's arms—and suddenly Katrina was overwhelmed by a sense of aloneness. In all the world *she* had no one to turn to for comfort. Even such conflict as they faced now might be bearable if she had a heart's companion to shelter her from the blows. But it was hard to imagine that there would ever be anyone for her.

Dougal did not return.

As in the past two years, the sparse population in that part of County Down banded together and went from farm to farm bringing in the crops. The process was slow, and many crops had passed their prime before the harvesters could reach them.

It was not until late October that Katrina and Deirdre could direct the setting of tables for the harvest feast in the open area inside Lanarks' Bawn. They had spent days baking, boiling, and roasting. This year would be special. It was to be Isobel and Sean's wedding feast as well.

So as to offer the least offense to either family, the couple was wed quietly by Parson Woodburn, who had been installed in the parish during the Wentworth-established Episcopal Ascendancy. But the feast was to be anything but quiet. The whole of the settlement had been invited.

Katrina draped the tables and even the low eaves of the byres with garlands of greenery and autumn flowers. She was determined that this occasion would mark not only her sister's wedding but also the end of the suffering and turbulence they had all known in past years. Sean and his brother had split and stacked wood for a magnificent bonfire, and any who played fiddle, drum, or pipe had been bidden to bring their instruments. Katrina had not even finished her work before guests began pouring into the walled enclosure.

"Oh, Isobel, you look radiant!" Katrina embraced her sister, admiring the raven ringlets circled with white flowers and framed by a high collar fashioned from the lace Isobel had purchased from Riley Cavan.

"I didn't know it was possible to be so happy!" Isobel spread her arms and twirled around, and her blue taffeta skirts rustled and swished. She stopped with a gurgle of laughter as her groom caught her in his arms.

"It's a grand sight ye are, my love. And I've a wee surprise for you here. We've a special guest come all the way from Armagh."

Isobel looked puzzled, obviously not recognizing the mature man with him.

He took her hand and bowed. "Aye, you'd not be knowing me. You were naught but a nipper when I left home. Perhaps you'll have heard of Matt Johnstone?"

"Anna's brother? Yes, I've heard of you, but—"

"Aye, I've been long in coming back—too long for some things I should have done." He looked toward his widowed mother, being offered a plate of black buns by Anna. "Ah, but the family is well, and this is no time to be harking on the past."

A fiddler started a lively tune, and Sean led his bride off in a dance.

Deirdre greeted the newcomer and begged him to give an account of what he had been doing. "You were a good friend to my Calum. I hope the years have been good to you."

"Aye, I knocked about a bit after I left home, working as hired man on the plantation in Armagh until I was able to lease my own land." He turned then to the handsome, dark-eyed youth standing quietly behind him. "Matter of fact, I've my landlord's grandson with me—thought the lad should see a bit more of this fair land. And I knew a harper would be a welcome guest at a wedding feast."

The young man smiled shyly as Matt pulled him forward and presented him to Deirdre, Aileen, and Katrina. "Eamon MacHenry."

Just then the fiddler came to the end of his tune.

"Oh," Aileen said, clapping. "Won't you play for us? I love harp music."

Eamon smiled again and drew an instrument of rich brown wood from the leather bag slung on his back. His long fingers slid over the strings in a smooth glissando, and then he plucked a sweet tune. Across the bawn even the rowdiest of revelers put down their cups and roast joints to listen.

When the melody ended, all was silent for several moments before the feast continued and fresh platters of meat were passed to the accompaniment of tin whistle and drum.

As Katrina moved among the guests, she noticed that Aileen never left the harper's company. Katrina wondered if she should say something to her sister. Then she shrugged. Matt would take Eamon MacHenry off to Armagh in a few days. What harm could it do for Aileen to have some fun? Katrina wanted this to be a grand time for all.

And as she surveyed the company eating, laughing, and dancing from one side of the bawn to the other, she knew it was. If only Dougal were here. They had not heard from him since the day he walked out. But no, she would not spoil the night with worry.

As soon as the evening chill came on, Rory set the bonfire ablaze, and that sparked a new round of singing and dancing. Senga Johnstone sat near the fire, clapping to the music of fiddle and pipe, her wrinkled face curved in a smile, her eyes never leaving the son who had been away so long. Across from her, however, Deirdre's smile showed behind it her sadness over the son who had not returned.

And then Eamon MacHenry played another harp tune. This one was so sweet that it brought tears to Katrina's eyes. It was the melody that made her cry, she insisted to herself, not the sight of all the happy couples: the bride and groom, Rory and his pregnant Celia, Robert and Jean Price, even Aileen sitting by the harper.

It was the fact that Aileen was also crying over the music that made Katrina determine to speak to her sister. Aileen mustn't do anything foolish. And giving her heart to a native Irish, especially one from another county—no matter how handsome his black eyes or how sweet his music—would definitely be foolish.

When the song ended and the harper turned to refresh himself, Katrina pulled her sister to the side. "Aileen, I've no wish to spoil your fun, but you must not spend your whole evening sitting at the feet of Eamon MacHenry. What will people say?"

Aileen's pink cheeks glowed. "Oh, it's all right, Katrina. His family is Deserving Irish. Dinna you hear Matt say he was the grandson of Henry Og O'Neill? The O'Neill was killed fighting for the Crown in some revolt when the plantations were new. That's why his family was left in possession of their estate." She sighed. "And have you ever heard more wonderful music?"

Aileen turned and called Eamon to join them. He was slightly built, barely taller than Aileen. His pale skin stretched tightly over the prominent bones of his face, giving him a sensitive, vulnerable look. "Eamon, I was telling Katrina about your family, but you can do it far better. Tell her about your fine home."

Long lashes lowered over his dark eyes in an engaging manner. "And haven't our people been there since the days when Brian Boru was High King?" He ran his fingers over the harp strings, making a sound like the flight of butterflies. "Aye, and it's said that it was Brian Boru himself who taught the first Henry Og to play the harp. And so it's been passed through our family. Someday I will have the teaching of my sons, the good God permitting."

Katrina had to agree that she had never heard more wonderful music. Nor had she met a more charming young man. But Deserving Irish or no, she still worried.

She had done all she could, though, so she turned to refill the empty ale pitchers. She was just returning from the kitchen when three horsemen rode through the entrance arch. It was late for guests to be arriving, she thought, but all were welcome. She hurried forward to greet them, then paused at the sight of their plumed hats, elaborate lace at wrists and boot tops, and swords hanging from scarlet sashes. Who could such elegant guests be?

Then she saw the badges—the Montgomery arms. The laird of the Ards had sent greetings to the wedding!

The horsemen dismounted, and one drew a rolled document from a pouch tied to his saddle.

Everyone drew near to listen.

Anticipation quickly turned to dismay, however, as the sense of the proclamation became clear. This was no lordly blessing on the wedding but the pronouncement of that which they most dreaded. The storm clouds that had been gathering for so long had finally burst upon them. The Gaelic lords had risen in a swift, violent rebellion.

Katrina gripped the edge of a trestle table as the tale of treachery and bloodshed poured out on the stunned assembly. All of central Ulster was in the hands of the rebel lords. Only two nights ago Sir Phelim O'Neill and his men had seized the fort at Charlemont, then galloped across country by moonlight. By midnight they had captured their second fort. Newry and Lurgan were in flames—even now were probably falling to the rebels.

Women's cries and men's angry shouts punctuated the announcement. But that was not all. The Crown was raising a Scottish army to defend Ulster. It would be weeks, perhaps months, however, before they could arrive. In the meantime the leading planters were charged to raise forces in the king's name.

"Viscount Montgomery—newly commissioned Colonel Montgomery"—the messenger raised his voice—"hereby issues a call for one thousand foot soldiers and five troop of horse. This to be raised from his own tenants." The messenger cleared his throat. "For which service and evidence of loyalty such tenants will be given an allowance off their rents."

The parchment rolled shut with a snap. The assembly burst into a hubbub of talking, shouting, and sobbing.

Katrina groped her way to a bench. The bonfire shot sparks and cast contorted shadows over the agitated crowd as if illustrating the battle scenes that had been reported to them.

And then she saw Rory turn from an intense discussion with the men around him. He approached the messengers.

The light of flaring torches glanced off the strong bones of Rory's face. "We have no weapons. Even our hunting rifles were confiscated by Wentworth, but we have hearts and bodies ready to defend our homes."

Robert Price and Matt Johnstone stood firm behind him.

Katrina wondered how the O'Briens, Eamon MacHenry, and the other native Irish present must be feeling. Surely these men who had been feasting and reveling together would not be soon fighting each other.

The recruiter bore on with his business. "Bring your scythes and pitchforks. They'll have to do for now. Montgomery will provide ye wi' muskets soon as may be."

And that seemed to be the most comfort anyone could offer.

26

By noon of the next day only the charred remains of the bonfire and a few garlands hanging limp and dead on the side of the byre gave the only evidence of the joyous occasion that had been.

Rory and the other recruits had ridden off with bold promises of putting a quick end to the rebellion. "Home before November's out," Rory called. His vow bore special significance because of Celia's expectant condition.

Now only the echo of their horses' hooves filled the silence, and Katrina discovered that the quiet she so often sought brought desolation rather than peace. How was it possible that savage battles could be raging twenty or thirty miles from them when all was so still here? She picked up a tankard and started toward the house. Then she stopped and listened.

Soft strains of music reached her from beyond the walls of the bawn. Eamon. She had not seen him since the devastation of last night's news. How was their young Irish guest feeling? Perhaps some of his own relatives were among the rebels. And he had been virtually abandoned here by Matt's enlistment.

She turned toward the orchard where russet and gold leaves covered both branches and ground.

As Katrina suspected, Aileen was there as well, sitting with her back against a tree trunk, her marigold colored skirt spread over the autumn leaves. The harper's fingers stilled on the strings at Katrina's approach.

She plopped down onto a pile of leaves. "This must be terrible for you, Eamon. What will you do?"

"I told him he is welcome to stay as long as he likes." Aileen's speech came in a breathless rush, as if begging her sister not to contradict her.

"Our door is closed to no one, sister. But I would like to know how Eamon feels—about everything."

He set his harp aside. His nose looked more prominent, his bones sharper than they had by firelight the night before. "And are

211

you thinking I've consorted with the rebels because my family is O'Neill? And aren't I as shocked as you by the events? You don't think I'd any part in such doings, do you?"

Katrina shook her head. Of course, she didn't.

"But I do think I've some understanding of the reasons," he continued.

Katrina sighed. "Well, yes, everyone knows of the terrible financial straits of the Gaelic lords, and the loss of their estates—"

"That's right. But it's more than that. The king was forced to grant religious independence in Scotland. Is it seeming too wild a hope to think he might be compelled to do the same in Ireland? And yet among my people there is a growing fear of the enormous Puritan power in Parliament. If they should gain control, would they not seek to root the Catholic religion out entirely? Sure and one of the reasons Parliament executed Wentworth was for his fairness to Catholics. It is a great fear among the Irish that we will lose what little is left of our ways."

In her own family Katrina had seen enough of the suffering religious persecution brought. "Yes, I see. Thank you for explaining. And, of course, you are welcome to stay for as long as you like."

And then there was another to welcome, for a few days later Dougal returned home.

"Oh, Dougal, I'm so glad you've come back. You know what's happened?"

"Aye. That's why I came back. That heretic brother of mine, joining the traitor's army, leaving his home and family unprotected."

Katrina stiffened her spine. No one could call her brother such things—not even another brother. "Rory answered Montgomery's call for a force to protect all of us. And Montgomery's no traitor—he's your laird."

"He's a Royalist! I didn't spend eighteen months in Dublin prison to support a Royalist army."

"Did you go to prison to see your family slaughtered in a native rebellion?"

"I went to prison to take my stand for God and His truth. No man will dictate to me of creed or conscience."

"Oh, Dougal." Katrina dropped her head in her hands. Would this argument never end? "Can you never soften? Must all be such hard black and white? Is there no gray?" She held her hand to his lips as he started to answer. "Nae, nae. I know what ye'll say." *No surrender, no compromise with the Devil—I've heard it often enough.* "But let it be. I'm ever so glad you're home. Come, greet our mother. I'm worried about her, Dougal."

Concern for Deirdre softened his features. "Is she ill?"

"No. And she seems in good spirits in spite of everything. But she hardly eats, and she's so frail." Katrina paused. "And there's another thing, I don't know, but it frightens me—she talks so much of Father. Especially since—" She started to say "Isobel's wedding" but didn't want to raise a controversial topic. "I think she's missing him more than ever. I—I think she wants to join him."

The homecoming of her son brightened Deirdre's spirits, however, as did encouraging news from the rebellion. The victorious Irish leader Sir Phelim issued a proclamation from Dungannon declaring that the rising was "in no way intended against our sovereign lord the king, nor to the hurt of any of his subjects, either of the English or Scottish nation, but only for the defense and liberty of ourselves and the Irish natives of this kingdom."

Soon others of the native Irish gentry issued similar statements, which the Scottish settlers repeated to one another with great relief. "I protest that no Scotsman should be touched," Sir Phelim's brother declared.

With a state of relative calm existing, Eamon chose to return to his home. Katrina suspected that it was as much Dougal's silent disapproval of him as his stated desire to be home before Christmas that spurred Eamon's decision. But, either way, she had to admit she was relieved to have him gone from Aileen, no matter how much she missed his music.

Katrina was deep in her chores, hurrying to set the bread dough so that she could get to the churning, when she heard an arrival in the yard. In spite of her determination, her heart leaped at the sight of Robert Price on the carriage seat beside Margaret. And then her greeting caught in her throat. "Robert! You've been wounded! Rory—"

"Nae, he's fine. He sends his love. 'Twas my own awkwardness that took a musket ball in the shoulder."

But his report of the battles was encouraging indeed. Montgomery's army had hurriedly marched to Lisburn at the pleas of Bishop Leslie, who was trying to hold the town against the insurgents. In an attempt to breech the walls, the Irish drove four hundred head of cattle against the gates. But Montgomery's reinforcements drove the rebels away.

In a few days, more good news followed. Carrickfergus and Belfast had likewise been saved for the Crown. Perhaps it was over, and Rory *could* be home for Christmas. The Lanarks still held with celebrating Christmas, although of recent years the influence of English Puritans, who declared such celebrations to be idolatrous, was making itself felt on the Presbyterians. Katrina wondered what Dougal would say when the time came.

But then she had more immediate worries. Almost overnight, the Catholic gentry who had issued such conciliatory statements lost control of the rebellion. Harvests had been poor in much of Ulster, and the peasantry began to feel the pangs of hunger as winter closed in. And worse, Sean O'Brien came to warn them, after he had rejected an Irish cousin's urging to join the rising, "There's aye wild rumors of a Puritan plot to massacre the Catholics. They'll nae listen to reason."

"Sean, you and Isobel must sleep here at nights. Bring your cattle too. We've plenty of room." Katrina gripped her sister's arm for emphasis.

"Don't be silly," Isobel said. "We're Irish."

Katrina was thankful Dougal did not hear that.

Now the heavy oak doors of the bawn were barred every evening at sundown. But they could not keep out the news of the terror that raged around them. County Down remained peaceful, as did Antrim. But across Ulster, county after county fell before the onslaught. Cavan was overwhelmed. Armagh capitulated. Fermanagh fell.

Near the end of November, Katrina went out one frosty morning to feed the chickens—just one of many of Isobel's former jobs she had taken over. Shivering with cold and fighting the bitter wind, she hurriedly flung the feed to the cackling flock. She had just turned to flee back to the kitchen when she heard loud and insistent pounding at the gate.

She ran for the house. "Dougal!" She grabbed a broom from behind the door, then exchanged it for a carving knife from the larder. "Dougal, they're here!"

"Who?"

"The rebels!" She looked at the knife in her hand and paused. "At least, there's someone pounding on the gate."

He shook his head. "It's not aye likely the rebels would be knocking for polite entrance, now is it?"

"Well, maybe not, but be careful. Take this." She held out the knife to him.

He gave her a disdainful look and went out the door. A few minutes later he returned with Celia's brother, Richard Guilford.

More than slightly chagrined, Katrina hurried to call Celia, then waited to hear what had occasioned Richard's singular call.

Wrong as Katrina had been about their danger, she was not wrong about the significance of the visit. Richard took Celia's hand and led her to a seat by the parlor window.

She moved slowly, as she was becoming increasingly heavy with child. "Is it the rebellion, Richard? Frank and Henry . . . are . . ."

"No, we're all well at Seaton Court. It's Guilford Hall."

"Aunt Edna, Uncle John, our cousins!" Her voice rose.

Richard shook his head. "Young Jack sent word. He made it out."

"The others?" It was a whisper.

"The rising is fierce in Tyrone. Thousands have been driven from their homes. Without even their cloaks."

"But it's so cold. It snowed last week, and—"

Richard spread his hands helplessly. "The suffering is terrible. Many have died from starvation and exposure."

"I—I should not say this when so many are distressed," Celia said. "But I do not understand. We are Catholic. I had heard that the Old English lords of The Pale considered joining the Ulster Irish lords." She stopped on a sob. "I don't understand. It's all so confusing. Who is fighting whom—and why? My husband fights to protect our government, but his brother calls him a traitor. The rebels say they fight to protect their faith, but they drive out their own. Nothing makes sense." Celia abandoned all attempt to talk and gave herself to weeping on her brother's shoulder.

"Celia, our mother bids you come home to Seaton Court. No one knows how long your husband will be gone. And we can offer you . . . comfort there."

Katrina, sitting in a far corner, wondered if the comfort Richard referred to was Father Sebastian's Masses. She thought Rory would want his wife to bide secure behind the strong wall of the bawn, but perhaps there were other securities more important at times like this. The only thing she knew was that Celia was right—none of it made sense. A war, if this was a war, should have two sides. This one had at least four. She didn't even know how to count the allegiances.

Celia chose to go to Seaton Court. And now Dougal kept the gate of the bawn barred day *and* night. As the days turned into weeks, Katrina had some idea of how he had felt all those months he spent locked in prison.

Deirdre had taken a chill, which settled in her chest. She didn't leave her room, and Katrina spent much of her time reading to her mother from the Bible that had always been Deirdre's prize possession. She had often told Katrina the story of how she saved and plotted to surprise Calum with that Bible. Now she lay quietly for hours, listening to the comfort of its words.

"Read about the fortress," her soft voice directed.

Katrina turned to Jeremiah 16. "O Lord, my strength, and my fortress, and my refuge in the day of affliction—"

But Deirdre had her own verse in mind. "I will say of the Lord, he is my refuge and my fortress; my God; in him will I trust. . . . Thou shalt not be afraid for the terror by night; nor for the arrow that flieth by day." She smiled at Katrina. "Your faither knew. All those years ago. He knew the trouble would come one day. He built the bawn to keep us safe. Thank you, Calum," she whispered. "The Lord is my rock, and my fortress, and my deliverer; my God, my strength, in whom I will trust . . ." Her mother's voice faded to silence, and her breathing slowed as sleep came over her.

Katrina tiptoed to the window and drew back the curtain. From the upstairs she could see over the bawn wall. All around them the fires burned, perhaps a mile away. Every night the rebels burned another barn, another haystack, another house. And every night the fires seemed a little closer. The bawn would protect them. But what of the others? Any who chose to were welcome to take refuge behind the bawn's protective walls. But failing a full-scale siege, none wished to leave their own homes unprotected.

Hugh Montgomery, nephew of the viscount, had organized the settlers into watches to guard their property, but they had accomplished little. The rebels struck always under the cover of darkness, always in an unguarded place, and always melted back into the woods where the defenders could not find them. Dougal had gone out on many such defensive forays, as had all the other men remaining in the neighborhood, including the now-recovered Robert Price. But always they encountered no insurgents, and they prevented no burnings.

The third week in January was the coldest anyone could remember. Snow covered the ground, and the icy winds blowing off Strangford Lough carried the chill inside even such well-built homes as the Lanarks'.

Katrina surveyed the dwindling stack of peat in the shed and worried. What would they do if they ran out? Still, she had no choice. The kitchen and parlor fireplaces must be kept blazing. There was no other hope for her mother, who shook with the ague even under multiple blankets. Katrina filled her basket with the earthy-smelling brown bricks and hurried back to the house.

She renewed the fuel on each fire, then slipped up to Deirdre's room with a bowl of soup. "It'll be warmer in a minute, Mother." She looked at the small square Dougal had cut in the floor so that the heat could rise directly from the kitchen. "Can you take a little broth?"

Katrina propped her mother to a sitting position with extra pillows, and Deirdre obediently opened her mouth. She was quaking so violently, however, that Katrina spilled more of each spoonful than she got into her mother's mouth. This was frightening.

She picked up Mrs. Price's bottle of elixir. "Perhaps you can eat more after a dose of this, Mother." The "black draught" was the only thing that seemed to ease Deirdre's shaking. Katrina had never attempted to make it. Thank God their neighbors kept her supplied.

She tipped the bottle. Only a few drops fell into the spoon. That was all. How could she have let the supply get so low? Perhaps Aileen had administered a dose without telling her. And then she spilled several drops of the precious liquid getting it past Deirdre's quivering lips.

There was only one thing to do. She tucked her mother in as cozily as possible and kissed her, then ran to her sister. "Aileen, you must sit with Mother. Read her a psalm. That calms her almost as much as the medicine. I have to go get more of the draught."

"You can't go now! It's dark. And Dougal has gone with the watch. What if something happened?"

Katrina closed her mind to Aileen's very sensible arguments and also to thoughts of the biting cold. "Don't be silly. What could happen? I'll be so quick you won't know I've gone. Just keep Mother comfortable." She glanced at the fireplace. "See, it's warming already. You'll be fine."

"But—"

Katrina grabbed her cloak and rushed out. Then she turned back. "Aileen, you must come with me to bar the gate. We can't leave it open even for so short a time." Fortunately, since Richard Guilford's visit, Dougal had arranged a bell rope outside the wall. She could signal when she needed the gate opened on her return.

In the lane the wind whipped at her far more viciously than when she had been protected by the walls of the bawn. But even more chilling than the icy air was the howl of wolves on Scrabo. More than anything else, that piercing wail made her realize how alone she was. Comber had become once again a frontier settlement, isolated on the edge of the wilds. She put down her head and ran.

"Katrina, come in out of the cold!" Margaret banged the door shut behind her, and Katrina almost collapsed as the warmth of the room enveloped her. "What could bring you out on such a night?"

"The ague medicine. We're all out."

"Oh, aye, we thought you'd be needing more. Mother's just finishing a batch now. But it'll have to cool before she can bottle it."

Mrs. Price was lifting a black cast iron pot from the fire. "Is your mother worse, dear?"

Katrina started to answer, but then fearful shouts and bangings sounded from outside. Even as she turned, a heavy log propelled by five men crashed through the door. Katrina and Margaret cringed and screamed. Mrs. Price, holding the kettle of boiling syrup, cried. "Dirty heathen rebels! Get you out of here!" She flung the pot.

The pot missed its mark and crashed against the far wall, but the scalding contents showered the intruders. The leader, his scraggly black hair and dirty leather jerkin dripping with the hot, sticky liquid, grabbed Mrs. Price. "Aye, like it rough, do ye? Well, happen so do I." Jerking harder with every scream, he pulled her toward the door.

The way was blocked. Kenneth Price, pitchfork in hand, straddled the entrance. Two other intruders attacked him, carrying the struggle outside. The sound of fist hitting bone was followed by the thud of a falling body. Terrified screams from Mrs. Price pierced the air.

The scraping of a shutter in the room behind them sent another rebel charging into the parlor. "Aye, fancy some fresh air, do ye?" He grabbed Jean Price around the waist and flung her away from the open window.

Jean lashed out with her nails. Red streaks appeared down both sides of the man's stubbly cheek. Behind her, three-year-old Michael emitted terrified shrieks.

"Wildcat, are ye?" Jean's attacker held both of her wrists and jerked her across the room. "Well, then, why don't you just see how you like it out there with the wolves!" He shoved her through the broken door. She landed on her knees.

"Mummy!" Michael wailed.

"And take your cub wi' ye!" With one hand the intruder flung the screaming child after his mother. Then, seizing the cattle goad strapped to his back, he drove them off into the darkness.

The two marauders left in the house now turned to emptying drawers and cupboards, obviously searching for valuables. Michael's silver christening cup was flung into a pile beside Mrs. Price's wedding candlesticks and silver teaspoons.

Watching things tumble from the kitchen shelf, Katrina spotted something that was more valuable than silver to her. One bottle of black draught was left. She nodded to Margaret. "Hide that. It's precious."

Margaret began working her way slowly toward the cupboard.

"Here now, what's this?" A cadaverously thin man with foul breath brandished a lethally pointed stick at Margaret's throat. "Hidin' valuables, are ye? Valuables stole from our people, most like. Ye've no right—comin' here and takin' our land. Now you'll see how it feels to be driven outta *your* homes. Filthy English!"

"But we're not—" Katrina began, then stopped, knowing it was useless to protest. The men were crazed from years of hunger and deprivation.

Margaret's attacker repeatedly jabbed the point of his pike at her

218

throat, drawing drops of blood. "Where is it? Where's your booty? More than like stole from a Catholic church. Huh? Huh? Dig a hole under the snow and bury it, did ye?'

"No, no! There's nothing. Nothing." Margaret backed against the wall. Blood stained her collar.

"Leave her alone!" Katrina grabbed at the man's arm. "They have nothing! Let her go!"

The man whirled, flinging out his arm. His heavy stick caught Katrina full on the side of her head. She slumped to the floor with a moan.

Minutes or hours later Katrina fought her way up through thick blackness. The pain was overwhelming. With every throb of her head a jagged streak of lightning went down her entire right side. She tried to stifle a moan, but it couldn't be held in. Her eyelids fluttered open. One brief glimpse of the scene was terrible enough to take her mind off her own intense pain.

Sweet, gentle Margaret was bound to a chair in the middle of the room. The men were burning the soles of her feet. Margaret shrieked. "No. No. I've told you!"

"Want it hotter, do ye?" He raked the candle flame up her bare foot from heel to toes.

Margaret's voice came out strangled with sobs. "There is no treasure. Nothing. We've nothing."

Katrina struggled to go to her friend's aid, but dizziness overwhelmed her. She fell back. Again Margaret's cries broke through the blackness. Now she saw that the soles of both feet were blistered and charred. The room stank of burned flesh. Margaret could protest no more. She was incoherent.

"Ah, ye'll get nothing." The younger of the two men turned to pick up the spoils he had gathered. "Leave 'em."

Katrina heard their booted feet thud toward the door. She relaxed. At last it was over. She might be dying, but it was quiet. The terror was gone.

And then she smelled smoke. The flaming oil from a fallen lantern had spread over the splinters of the broken door. Bits of dry wood crackled as the flames took hold. They would be burned alive. She must get up. She must rescue Margaret. But she could not move. She tried to cry out but managed only a moan.

Shouts and stomping. They were coming back. What for? It would be a mercy if the men killed them. But that was too much to hope for.

"Inside! Hurry!"

Dougal's voice! Was it possible?

In a moment her brother was leaning over her. The burning wall behind him highlighted his golden hair. "She's alive! They're both alive." Dougal lifted her in his arms and turned to the man behind him. "Here, take her out."

She felt herself being shifted to other arms and saw Dougal grasp Margaret, chair and all, and dash through the flames.

Then the blackness closed in again.

27

Katrina woke in her own bed to find Aileen bathing her head with vinegar water.

"Here, take this. Anna brought some poppy syrup."

She swallowed.

When she woke again it was night. Margaret lay beside her, moaning gently in her sleep. Aileen was asleep on the trundle near the window.

The next morning or the morning after—it was all a blur—she woke to find Anna and Isobel slathering Margaret's feet with goose grease and binding them in clean strips of cotton.

Katrina struggled to sit up. "The rebels. They burned—"

Isobel flew to her side of the bed. "*Shh*, we know, darling. Don't try to talk. You'll be all right."

"Margaret?"

Isobel stroked Katrina's brow soothingly. "Some of the burns were very deep. But she will heal if there's no infection."

"Tell me . . ." There were so many: her mother, Dougal, Mr. and Mrs. Price, Jean and the child—Katrina wanted to ask about them all, but she hadn't strength.

Isobel's news, however, was not of the people nearest Katrina but of the wider happenings. "The real attack began last night. Not just rabble like assaulted you, but a whole force. About a mile from Comber. Montgomery's army met them. Dougal went to fight with them."

Katrina almost smiled. If any good could be found in this terrible ordeal, it had to be the fact that Rory and Dougal were at last fighting on the same side. "And?"

"We've no word yet. We must pray and hope for the best. We're safe here. There are scorch marks on the gates—they tried to burn their way in. But the bawn held."

Aye, a fortress in time of trouble. Katrina accepted another dose of poppy juice. She could take in no more of horror and violence for the moment.

Several weeks later both brothers came home. The rebels had been repulsed. An army of ten thousand Scots under the leadership of Major General Munro had landed at Carrickfergus. One regiment would be stationed at Newtownards. Fighting still raged to the south, but they were secure here. Reports reached them from all over Ulster, each, it seemed, trying to outdo the last as to the enormity of the rebellion. Perhaps twelve thousand English and Scots had perished. The majority, robbed and stripped and driven from their homes, had died from the severe weather.

But the survivors of the families clinging together behind Lanarks' Bawn were too shocked by their own losses to grieve sufficiently for their countrymen.

Robert's grief had been the hardest for Katrina to bear. She was so shocked by the desolation in his eyes and the gauntness that aged him twenty years that she could find no words to speak to him. She held out her hand as he stood stoop-shouldered by her bedside. He clasped it for a moment, then turned and left the room with dragging step. He had not spoken a word.

Dougal later told her, when they were out of Margaret's hearing, of the morning after the attack on the Price farm. "I dona like to tell you this. It's not for woman's ear." He ran a hand across his eyes. "It's no' fit for any ears. But I think ye should know."

Katrina was glad she had not been told until she was stronger. As the picture grew in her mind she knew she would never be truly free of the specter. That night, after Dougal and Robert had raced, cold and stumbling, across the frozen fields to take Margaret and Katrina to refuge behind the bawn, they returned to the Price farm.

"By then the snow had started. It was our ally in putting out the blazing thatch of the butcher shed." Again Dougal covered his eyes. "Perhaps it would have been better if we'd let it burn. As it was—" It was several moments before he could continue.

"As it was, they were still hanging there. Robert went in first. I shouldna have let him, but I didn't think. I could have prepared him some—"

"Dougal, tell me." Katrina kept her voice soft and steady.

He shook himself. "The tenterhooks. They had hung them on the tenterhooks. Miriam and Kenneth Price—hanging like sides of beef in their own butcher shed—the hooks through their bodies, blood on the burned thatch fallen around them."

Katrina took him awkwardly in her arms, and they wept together. Wept for the dead and the living. Wept for themselves and their poor country.

At last Katrina pulled away. "Jean? Michael?"

"Frank Guilford found her two days later. Frozen under a snow-bank in his farthest field. There's nae sign of the lad."

Robert spent days tramping every field and path, searching for his son. But at last there was nothing for him but to sit hollow-eyed beside the bed where Margaret lay. Brother and sister tried to comfort each other but found few words.

Katrina was able to be up some now, although she was given to bouts of dizziness and her right foot dragged. She moved slowly about the house, leaning on a stick, which she gripped in her left hand because her right did not work well. But her greatest concern was for Robert. He could not forgive himself for the tragedy that had befallen his family. The one service Katrina could offer was a listening ear.

"I should have been there. I should have protected them," he would say over and over.

Katrina brushed his arm awkwardly. "It would likely have made no difference. You would probably have been killed, too. You did the best you could. You went out with the watch to protect your family."

"Aye. I thought I did right. But it couldna have been. My parents were hung on the very tenterhooks I put in place. It was my pride. A judgment on my pride. Like Job. I thought to build bigger barns, and the Lord required my soul."

Katrina suspected he was mixing his Scripture references, but she let him talk. Any talk, no matter how rambling, was preferable to the morose silences he lapsed into.

Dougal had told her of the small, sad burial service when Robert's wife and parents had been committed to the frozen earth. But neither man would speak more of it, and it seemed to Katrina that Robert became more withdrawn as the days dragged on.

Gradually, with the coming of spring, the burned and bloodied land began to recover, and with the gentling changes Katrina hoped for similar reconciliations in the family. The day Rory returned to the bawn, bringing Celia and their babe from Seaton Court, her heart soared. It would be like old times. The whole family together. Now they could put the past behind them and live together in peace.

At Rory's request they all assembled in Deirdre's room. It was so crowded that Katrina felt she could hardly breathe, but that was little matter. They were together. Rory placed his infant son in Deirdre's frail arms. "We've named him Calum, Mother."

Deirdre's faded blue eyes filled with tears as she drew a gnarled finger over the babe's soft cheek. "Aye, a bonny lad. Ye've a fine grand-son named after ye, Calum. A bonny lad."

Katrina hugged her brother. "Oh, Rory, it'll be so wonderful to have you living here! A baby is just what we all need—"

The look on his face silenced her more than his upraised hand. "No. Ye mistook."

"Rory?" She was always one to jump to wrong conclusions. Now, as fear gripped her, Katrina wished she could be wrong this time. "Rory, you aren't leaving the bawn? Celia only left because of the trouble—because you were gone. It's all over now."

He shook his head. "The toll of the rising was much greater in other areas. Tyrone was one of the hardest hit."

Katrina looked at Celia. Tyrone—her family's home.

"Only one cousin left." Celia's golden curls shook, but she steadied her voice. "Both of my faither's brothers, all their sons but one, and he not much more than a bairn."

Rory put an arm around his wife. "So Celia's brothers are moving back to Guilford Hall. Celia and I will take over Seaton Court."

Deirdre reached for her eldest son's hand. "And so you must leave us permanently, Rory?"

His attempted laugh rang hollowly. "It's only the next farm over, bar one. Nae so far, Mother."

"Not as the feet measure, but I fear the distance as the heart measures." She lay silent a moment, her breathing labored. She turned to Aileen who was closest to the door. "Bring me the clock."

"It's just after two o'clock, Mother."

"No. On the mantel. Bring me Calum's clock."

In a moment Aileen returned with that object ticking noisily in its iron and gilt case. She held it out to her mother.

But Deirdre gestured to her oldest son. "Give it to Rory." She looked at him. "If you must go, then I'd have you take Calum's clock with you."

Rory shook his head. "I couldn't. It's part of the bawn."

"That's why I'd have you take it—so part of Calum's bawn will go with you. So you'll not be forgetting your roots."

Katrina recalled her mother's stories of that clock, her grandparents' wedding gift. How much it had seen as it kept the hours of the lives of three generations of Lanarks. And how much would it yet see? She could only hope that it might mark many generations of peace.

Rory bent to thank his mother, but the moment was shattered by the slamming door of Dougal's exit.

Katrina shivered. Was this something more to divide their family? Couldn't they be at peace yet?

That night Deirdre went to sleep with a smile on her face. When Katrina went in the next morning, the smile was still there, but Deirdre was not breathing.

Katrina sat quietly on the edge of her mother's bed, holding her hand. She was so thankful for this time alone to tell her mother good-bye. But even as she thanked God for the quiet of these precious moments, she worried. What would they do about the burial? There was no question but that Deirdre must be buried beside Calum in the kirk yard. But it was now an Episcopal church. And the Reverend Mr. Woodburn would use the Book of Common Prayer, which prescribed a full order for the burial of the dead. That was unlike Knox's Book of Common Order, which instructed that the corpse should be reverently brought to the grave without any further ceremonies. Would the hardness of Dougal's creed extend even to his mother's funeral? She couldn't think how dreadful it would be if he refused to come.

She was still sitting, weeping, at the bedside when Aileen found her later.

Anna and Isobel, who in recent months had become such good friends that they were more like sisters than stepmother and step-daughter-in-law, saw to the laying out. It was a sorrow to Katrina that she was not able to perform that service for her mother, but her right side was still lame. She wondered if she would ever be strong again.

And so she sat by another who had not yet recovered from that night of horrors and told Robert about her fears over Dougal. "You signed the Covenant with him, so perhaps you know better than anyone how he feels. Will you talk to him?"

"Aye, I'll do what I can."

"And will you come to Mother's service, Robert? It would mean much to me."

"I'll come." Then he looked at Margaret, sitting across the room with her feet on a stool. "Perhaps there is one who can talk to your brother better than I. Will you, Margaret?"

Margaret smiled the sweet smile that had not been the least dimmed by all she had been through. She was lamed. The blisters on her feet had scabbed over, and the blackened skin had fallen away, giving place to rough, red scar tissue. She was able to walk only a few mincing steps. Even so, she stood gingerly. "Of course, I'll help. If I can."

But she made it only halfway across the room before she was overcome with pain and sank to her knees. And then—Katrina could never understand how he suddenly managed to be there—Dougal was lifting her in his strong arms.

"I will walk again. I will," Margaret said with quiet determination.

"Aye. Of course ye will, lass. Ye'll walk down the aisle o' the kirk to wed me. And if ye don't, I'll carry ye."

She laid her head against his shoulder. "Aye, you do that, Dougal Lanark. But first ye must carry me to your mother's funeral."

Dougal's jaw tightened, and his eyes glinted with the old hardness. Katrina could imagine that Margaret even felt his arms around her stiffen.

Margaret raised her hand and stroked his jutting jaw. "I'd take it as a great kindness."

And so Dougal carried Margaret to the kirk the next day for Deirdre to be laid to rest beside her Calum.

Katrina thought this was what all funerals should be—not an occasion of sorrow, but a celebration for one who had gone home. Mr. Woodburn, the wind blowing his vestments, met them at the entrance of the kirk yard and led the way to the gravesite, saying, "I am the resurrection, and the life: he that believeth in me, though he were dead, yet shall he live: and whosoever liveth and believeth in me shall never die."

They reached the place where a large beech tree was just showing a lacy frosting of green all along its branches and stopped before a newly dug grave. Then came the reading from the Psalms.

Katrina, knowing she would be slow, had elected to walk at the back of the procession. Even though she took her time, the walk across the yard had been a strain. Now she found herself leaning more and more heavily on her stick. She wished she had someone to hold her as Dougal held Margaret.

And then she felt a gentle nudge to her shoulder. Robert stood there, extending his bent elbow. She smiled her appreciation and linked her arm in his for support.

The priest turned to 1 Corinthians 15 for the reading of the lesson.

Out of the corner of her eye Katrina noted a small group of passers-by stopping beyond the low stone wall that circled the kirk yard—a shawled woman and a clutch of children of various ages, all with wild red hair flying in every direction. From the shabbiness of their dress she guessed they were wrackers from the shores of Strangford. She thought they would just pause and then go on, but they stood, observing the funeral.

Then the thud of the first clods of earth hit the wooden casket, and she turned back. Each family member cast in a handful of soil, the dark, rich soil of the land Deirdre had loved so much.

"Blessed are the dead which die in the Lord . . ." The Reverend Woodburn closed his prayer book.

Leaning heavily on Robert's arm, Katrina cast in her clod. "Amen," she whispered.

Robert put his arm around her for better support, and they started up the path. She was surprised to see that the group of observers was still there, as if waiting.

Just then a small, blond figure broke from the group beyond the wall and barreled toward them. "Faither, Faither!" the child cried.

Robert dropped to his knees. "Michael! Is it possible?" With a joyous shout he swung his son into the air.

Carrying the boy, Robert strode to the black-shawled woman. "How is this that you bring my son to me? I canna thank ye enough. I have no words. How? Where did you find him?"

With a wide smile the woman broke into a string of Gaelic. Katrina caught a few words: *buachaill . . . bheith ag falroid . . . fuar . . .* The woman hugged herself and pantomimed shivering against the cold.

"Wait. Please." Katrina held up a hand and turned to her sister-in-law. "Celia, can you help us?"

Celia was not a fluent Gaelic speaker but knew enough words that, with the help of the woman's pantomiming, she was able to explain. "One night when it was very cold, her pig got out. They live by Strangford. Kelp gatherers, I think. Anyway, she was afraid the animal would fall through the ice, so she searched up and down the shore. She found the pig. But she also found this wee boy wandering."

"Three months!" Robert almost shouted. "Three months I've thought my son dead! What has she been doing to him?"

Michael wound his arms around his father's neck and nestled against him.

"Apparently she has been feeding and clothing him," Katrina said. "He looks well, Robert. The kelpers keep entirely to themselves. I expect she was as fearful to come out until the rebellion was quelled. As we were."

After another outburst of Gaelic from the woman, Celia said, "They were taking him to Newton today to see if anyone knew him. When they saw the funeral, they thought the priest might know."

Robert's arms tightened around his son. "Aye, thank her for me. Find out where she lives. I'll send her a sack of potatoes and a side of bacon."

Robert settled Katrina on the seat along one side of the wagon and sat beside her. He was playing with Michael when suddenly he hit his own forehead with his open palm. "*Och,* I must be daft. What am I thinking? How could I forget? I *have* nae potatoes. And not even a rasher of bacon to call my own."

"We can loan you all you need until you've rebuilt." Katrina moved her hand through Michael's golden curls. The child did not seem to mind that her gesture was slow and awkward. "Now you have a reason to build."

She looked across the wagon bed to Celia holding wee Calum, and Dougal protectively guarding Margaret from the bumps of the ride. "Aye. There's always something to go on for. Mother taught me that." She just hoped there would be something for her. Someday.

28

"I don't understand, Auntie Katrina." Five-year-old Dereck, fair as his father, Dougal, but with his mother Margaret's musical voice, boosted himself up on the newly padded window seat.

Katrina liked to sit there for the frequent rests she required. She was only thirty but often felt like an old woman.

"What don't you understand, Dereck?"

"The celebration. Is it to be for my birthday or for the king's crowning?"

"Why, both, my darling. And for the Covenant. Now can you think of three grander things?"

Dereck sucked on a forefinger. Presumably he could imagine nothing more auspicious.

And neither could Katrina. For four years they had watched civil war rage in England between Royalists and Parliamentarians. After a series of Royalist defeats, King Charles had surrendered, was tried and convicted of treason. Just last month he had been beheaded.

His son had been proclaimed King Charles II in Scotland immediately after he signed the Covenant. At long last, king and kirk were united. No happier state of affairs could exist for Charles's Scottish subjects. The dreadful conflict was over. Ireland too could be at peace now. That was what everyone said. Katrina desperately hoped they were right.

Viscount Montgomery had at once drawn up a declaration stating support for the Covenant and assumed leadership of the Ulster Royalists. Dougal, however, held back for a time. Although Charles II was said to be a staunch Protestant, it was also said he had signed the Covenant with less than full-scale enthusiasm. Dougal did not want a monarch who was only halfheartedly for the right.

When the new Commonwealth regime declared complete toleration for most Protestant bodies, he had been outraged. "I'll have none of their *toleration*. Superstitious practices by Protestants are just as bad as superstitious practices by Catholics!" He struck a fist into the palm of his other hand and paced the floor. "Nae. Episcopal is worse. Does not Scripture give us warning? The Devil's servants go about in sheep's clothing."

But most forgave King Charles II his lukewarmness toward the Covenant, and, despite a few mutterings, the settlement was firmly united behind their new monarch. And tonight, which happened to be Dereck's fifth birthday as well, His Majesty Charles II was to be formally proclaimed in Newtownards.

"Now go see if your mother needs help getting Ruth ready to go. We don't want to be late." Katrina smiled at her chubby, brown-eyed nephew.

Dereck jumped off the seat. "Does Ruthie have to go? She's still a baby."

"That's why she'll need her big brother to take care of her. Now go." Katrina watched him trot happily off and smiled, thinking of the new beginning this celebration signaled for them all.

Before the Black Oath, there had been upwards of fifteen hundred Scots on Montgomery lands. That population had dwindled to near collapse even before the uprising. Afterward, in all of Comber parish there remained but four English or Scots families and three Irish. Newtown, the largest settlement, had only ten families of English or Scots descent and five of Irish. And so it went across Down. Celia's brothers wrote that it was much the same, or worse, in Tyrone, where the rebellion had been more thorough. But those who remained on the land put their hearts and their backs into rebuilding.

Tonight they were celebrating the fruits of their labors.

Dougal drove their best carriage. Margaret, holding two-year-old Ruthie, sat beside him. In the back, Katrina, the perennial maiden aunt, rode with her nephew. As they drove up High Street, Dereck grabbed her sleeve and pointed. "Look, Auntie Katrina. What are those people doing?"

"Celebrating, Dereck, celebrating." She laughed. Around each of the six sides of the massive stone market cross, men were shoving, shouting, and holding hats and bowls under the spouts. And it was little wonder that they were so merry. The fountains were flowing with red claret.

Just as the carriage reached the cross, six trumpeters sounded a flourish and, to the beat of the drums following, led a parade of revelers to the open field in front of the bawn that enclosed the church and Lord Montgomery's house.

Dougal parked to the side in a spot where the ladies could watch the proceedings from their seats. Both had recovered much from their injuries. But Katrina's right arm and leg remained weak, and Mar-

garet, who always padded her shoes with lamb's wool, still found pro-
longed standing painful.

He had provided them with a superb view. Across the green, soldiers drilled, giving a sharp right face salute to Colonel Montgomery,
who watched the proceedings from a reviewing stand. Hearing of
Montgomery's loyalty, Charles II had sent an envoy to confirm his lordship as commander-in-chief of the Royalist forces in Ulster.

Now the soldiers came to the end of their drill. Three volleys of
gunfire accompanied a toast to the king, and the crowd cheered. Formalities over, dancing, footraces, and games began.

"What say ye, lad? Shall we show them some real speed?"

Dereck jumped with delight at his father's suggestion. Margaret
said she would go with them in order to have a better view of such an
important event as the father-son relay.

"You'll prefer to stay here, Katrina?" Dougal asked.

She didn't, but it was easier to say yes. She sat and watched the
merrymakers.

Isobel and Sean O'Brien passed at a distance and waved. Aileen
was helping them with their three little ones, who seemed to be growing up wild as puppies.

Isobel left her charges and ran to the carriage. "Isn't this grand!
And aren't we lucky to have such good weather! Did you hear there's
to be an illumination tonight?" Hardly waiting for Katrina to answer,
she started to dart away, then turned back. "Oh, and Anna got a letter
from Matt. He's coming to visit again." And then she was off with a
bounce of golden curls.

Katrina refused to sigh. Things couldn't be better, she told herself. They had a new king to celebrate, a king who had signed the
Covenant, so they would have no more persecution. Everyone was
happy. What more could she want? She craned her neck, searching the
vast field for a glimpse of the racers.

"Ah, Katrina, I was fair hoping we'd see ye here today."

She startled at the sound of Robert's voice.

After all these years, she still hadn't managed to keep her heart
from leaping to her throat at the sight of that tall, cotton-blond man.
When Jean had died at the hands of the rebels, Katrina had thought
that, in time, perhaps . . . But six years had been time and enough.
Robert had rebuilt his ravaged farm and hired native Irish to help with
his work. He showed no signs of needing anything else in his life.

"Hello, Michael!" She smiled at the fine young lad beside Robert.
"How you've grown. How do you like school?"

Michael was a student at the Newtownards school just as his
Uncle Dougal had once been. He shrugged. "I like the music and the

football. Maths and Latin are awfully dull." Just then he caught sight of another lad about his age. "Oh, aye—Willie!" He called and waved.

His friend trotted over to them, running a hand over his disheveled locks.

"Faither, Auntie Katrina, this is Willie—William Montgomery—the best footballer in school. But he has to pay attention in grammar too, because someday he's going to write a book all about our settlement."

"That's aye a fine ambition, Master Montgomery." Robert smiled at the boy. "Will you include today's celebrations?"

"Oh, aye. Grand, aren't they? And there'll be bonfires as soon as it gets dark."

Robert drew out his purse. "Well, while you're waiting, mayhap ye'd care for some gingerbread." He gave each boy a penny. "I saw a seller in the High Street."

The boys ran off, and Robert turned to Katrina. "Would ye care for a stroll?"

Katrina gave him her hand, and he helped her from the carriage. Ever since he had supported her at her mother's funeral, Katrina felt more comfortable walking with Robert than with anyone else. He never seemed to notice her faulty coordination.

Even though the day was fine for February, the evening air grew chill. The mug of hot cider Robert procured from a vendor brought a welcome warmth, but it was no warmer than his smile. After so long, was it still possible to hope? To avert disappointment, she tried to tell herself this was just his usual thoughtfulness. But she couldn't stop hoping. Thirty was very old. But perhaps not *too* old.

As darkness fell, the trumpeters stood at the market cross and played reveille. Then, when the notes had died on the air, the owners of every house lining both sides of High Street lit candles in all the home and shop windows. The golden flickers began at the cross end, then spread the length of the street until all was a-twinkle as if the stars had come down to join the celebration. When bonfires were lit at each end of the street and beyond, it was as if sun, moon, and planets were joining in as well.

It wasn't until Robert looked at her with concern that Katrina realized her cheeks were wet.

"Have I tired you? Do ye want to go back?"

"No, no. I never want to go. Oh, Robert, it's so beautiful! Why can't it always be like this? Everyone in the whole Ards is here tonight—Irish, English, Scots; Presbyterian, Episcopal, Catholic. And everyone is happy and laughing. Why can't people always get along?"

He opened his mouth to answer, but she stopped him. "No, don't

231

say it. I know. Dougal talks all the time about punishing evildoers and never surrendering. And he's such a fine person—he must be right." She sighed and held tighter to Robert's arm. "But I do like it better this way."

"Aye. That's what we're celebrating, isn't it—king and Covenant, kingdom and kirk. I just heard some grand news. Montgomery wrote to the Scottish General Assembly asking them to send us a good Presbyterian minister. He's going to grant the kirk its own land and establish a stipend for the minister. No more conventicles in Ireland. And we'll no longer be at the mercy of an Episcopal bishop to turn a blind eye to the fact that half their vicars were of the Reformed faith."

Katrina bit her lip. Would this work? She recalled Dougal's fierce arguments that there could be only *one* church and that to allow false faith to be practiced was to compromise with the Devil. But she did not want to think on such things tonight. "Yes, that is good news." It *was* good—for them. What it meant for those such as Isobel and Sean, who were Episcopal, or for Rory and Celia, who were Catholic, she did not know.

A sharp wind began to blow. Robert put an arm around her, and she nestled into the warmth.

"I've somewhat else I'd speak to ye of, Katrina." The lights from the candles reflected in his eyes. "When the new minister comes, would it not be a fine thing if he were to wed us?"

It was the question she had dreamed of hearing for so many years.

"Ah, but I should not have spoken. Ye'd rather continue as we are." The desolation in his gentle voice jolted her to action.

"No, no!" She flung her arms around his neck. "I'd ever sae much rather marry you."

And just as he embraced her, the fireworks began on Fair Green behind them.

Katrina would have happily married Robert that night. Well, next week. It would take a month for the banns to be properly published. And so she waited, no matter how impatiently.

She no longer felt old and lame and awkward. Her heart was lighter and her smile brighter than any eighteen-year-old's. And while her movements were not as graceful as she wished, she was far less tired than she had been for years.

"Oh, Margaret, I didn't know it was possible to be so happy!"

Margaret laughed. "I'm so happy for you. And for Robert. I thought he'd never smile again after Jean and our parents—" she cleared her throat "—that is, since you're both so happy, why wait? Reverend Woodburn could marry you."

Katrina nodded. "I know. I agree. It doesn't matter to me, just so long as we're married. But it matters to Robert. And to Dougal. I have the feeling that hearing of the new minister's coming was one of the things that spurred Robert to ask me."

"Oh, surely not. I think he was waiting for things to get really settled. You know. King and kirk—all that. I don't think he wanted to take any chances of something horrible like the rebellion happening once more. I'm not sure any of us could live through such a thing again."

"Well, whatever prompted him, I'm so glad it did. But I do know how important it is to Robert to be wed with the Presbyterian service. He doesn't go on as much about it as Dougal does, but he's just as firm a Covenanter. I'm not sure he'd think us wed in the sight of God any other way."

She stopped to take the spool off her spinning wheel. Since her injury, she had not been able to weave high quality cloth because she couldn't throw the shuttle evenly with her right hand, but she had taught herself to spin left-handed, and they had hired a girl to help with the weaving.

"Anyway, I've waited all these years. I can wait a few more months."

Katrina was sitting in her favorite chair by the window, enjoying the warmth of the sun through the glass, when her younger sister came in. The care with which Aileen closed the door behind her and the speed with which she flew across the room told Katrina something was afoot, even before Aileen opened her mouth.

"Katrina, darling sister. I'm so happy! Wish me joy!"

"Of course I do. But why?"

"Matt Johnstone is returning to Armagh, and I'm going with him."

Katrina frowned. Matt had been visiting his mother and the O'Briens the past week or more. But she had not been aware that Aileen and he had spent much time together. Besides, he must be near to double Aileen's age. "You're going off with Matt Johnstone?"

Aileen nodded, and her curls bounced. "Traveling with him, yes. It's the perfect chance. We've waited so long." She hugged herself with joy. "Oh, I'm so happy. I was so afraid it would never happen. And now we're going in just a few days."

"But you can't. There's no time to announce the banns!"

Aileen seemed confounded for a moment, then broke into a peal of laughter. "Oh, what a goose brain I am! Dougal always said so. You didn't think I was *marrying* Matt Johnstone, did you?"

"Of course. I hardly thought you'd go off with him on any other terms."

Aileen gave another chime of laughter. "No, no, no. Matt is taking me to Eamon. Rory gave his consent years ago. But then that horrid rising ruined everything. And I thought—feared—"

"Rory gave consent?" Katrina was too flabbergasted to take it in. Of course, Rory himself had married a Catholic. Perhaps he had even secretly converted—she didn't know—but to allow his sister to marry a native Irish, even from a Deserving family! Isobel had married an Irish, but Sean and Isobel were Episcopalian—which Dougal said was as bad as Catholic. It was so confusing. Perhaps Dougal was right—there *should* be only one church. It would certainly make things simpler.

There was one point she was clear on, however. She turned to Aileen. "Of course, I wish you happy. But you must send us word of you often." First Rory and Celia, now Aileen—their family was slipping through her fingers. "I couldn't bear to lose touch with you."

She embraced her sister, and then they rushed upstairs to begin packing.

Isobel, hurriedly summoned, brought the fine lace collar from her own wedding dress and insisted that her sister be married in it. "That way I'll feel I'm at least a little bit part of the wedding."

A few days later, Matt Johnstone, with a crunch of iron wheels on gravel, drove through the arched gateway of the bawn.

Aileen, wreathed in smiles and golden ringlets, ran down the stairs. "And you are to have joy, too, sister! I couldn't leave with such happiness if you were not to wed your Robert so soon." She embraced Katrina. "I would wait for your wedding if I could, but Matt says we must be off."

Katrina kissed her. "Joy go with you. Time is so fleeting. Spend all of it you can in happiness."

Apparently Dougal had been right to doubt Charles's devotion to the Covenant. Although he had signed it as a condition of being declared king in Scotland, Charles II was no Presbyterian. And Charles knew he would need the help of loyal Catholics as well as Protestants if he was to defeat the Commonwealth and gain the throne. But as soon as they realized Charles was wooing Catholics as well as themselves, the Presbyterians mutinied.

The union of king and kirk had been celebrated with fireworks and a fountain flowing with wine a few months earlier; now the situation deteriorated to angry threats on both sides. And then the threats turned to blows in the street. Newtown became identified as the center of Royalist loyalties in Ulster.

And Rory Lanark once again joined forces with his laird. Since Deirdre's passing, there had been little enough communication between Lanarks' Bawn and Seaton Court. Now there was none. Katrina tried to tell herself that silence was better than argument, but she sorely missed the brother who had always held a special place in her heart.

For weeks, Katrina had nervously listened to news of renewed upheaval while inside her sheltered home she bent over her sewing, preparing her wedding finery. It was bad enough that her stitches were so awkward from her injury. It was worse that they must be slowed by the worry that more political turmoil would postpone her happiness.

But at last the day came that would put all such doubts to rest. For this morning Dougal and Robert had gone with the delegation to welcome the new Presbyterian minister to the Ards. And his first official act would be performing their marriage. Katrina glanced out the window at the sun. It must be midafternoon. The men had to go all the way to Carrickfergus to meet the minister's boat, but surely they should be back by now.

At last she heard the carriage and set her sewing aside with relief. She smiled as Dougal strode into the room. "Welcome home. Was Reverend Robinson late?" She stopped at the look of cold rage on his face. "Dougal! What is it?"

Her brother began pacing, hitting fist into palm, talking more to himself than to her. "He canna do this. Laird or no laird, we will not tolerate it."

"Dougal, tell me! What's happened?"

"Montgomery has placed Belfast and Carrickfergus under the control of Royalist garrisons."

Katrina's mind boggled. "Montgomery *seized* Belfast and Carrickfergus?"

"Aye." Dougal spit out the word. "He says he canna be certain the Presbyterians in control of the towns are loyal to the Crown." He spun on his heel to pace the length of the room again, each step giving force to his words. "And I say we'll nae be loyal to a king who isn't loyal to us. We'll nae be ruled by a papist sympathizer."

"But Reverend Robinson?" She held her breath. Her wedding!

"We're meeting tonight. All who've signed the Covenant. We'll act! The Almighty did not elect us to be wishy-washy."

"Dougal!" She stood up and stamped her foot. "Did the minister *come?*"

"Of course not, woman. Are ye daft?"

That night the Presbytery of Ulster drafted its warning to Montgomery. Katrina, unable to sleep, was waiting up for Dougal's return, and he read his copy of the document to her. "'The Lord will visit your family with sudden ruin and irreparable desolation, for you have been so grand an instrument to destroy the work of God here.'"

She clapped her hand to her mouth. "Dougal, no. You say that to your *laird?*"

"Aye, and more." He continued.

"We exhort your lordship, in the name of the living God, to whom you must give an account, in haste to forsake that infamous and ungodly course you are now in, and adhere to your former professions. Otherwise all the calamities that will ensue will be laid at your door. The Lord himself and all the faithful will set themselves against you and we will testify of your unfaithfulness to all the world, so long as the Lord will give us strength."

Heartsick, Katrina dragged herself up the stairs to her room. It was not so much the hardness of the words. It was the zealous ring in her brother's voice, the glint of fanaticism in his eyes. There would be no compromise. No peace. And no wedding.

29

August 14 should have been Katrina and Robert's wedding day. Instead, it was the day Oliver Cromwell landed in Ireland at the head of the Commonwealth army.

Dougal was already in the saddle, waiting impatiently to ride south to join him. Margaret stood beside her husband with terror-filled eyes, clutching her children's hands. Little red-haired Ruthie sniffed.

Margaret was silent, but Katrina was not. "Dougal, I beg you. Don't do this!" She clung to her brother's stirrup. "Rory rode south with Montgomery. You will be fighting your own brother!"

"Anyone who fights against God's side is no brother of mine." He jerked the reins and galloped out through the arch.

Katrina turned to Robert, who had not yet mounted. "Robert, please—" She choked. She could say no more.

"Do ye think me less a man than your brother? Do you think I could ever look at Margaret or at you again—knowing what those animals did to you—if I didn't take this chance to avenge their savagery?"

"Robert, no. That's not for us to do. 'Vengeance is mine, *I* will repay, saith the Lord.'"

He grasped her twisted right hand and held it to his lips. "You say that? After what they did?"

"We must forgive—"

He made a harsh noise in his throat that frightened her. "Forgive! You did not see my parents hanging there—the iron hooks through their skin—the blood. But I saw them. And I see them again and again in my sleep and wake crying." He turned away. "Aye, ye didn't know. I never told. That was one reason I was so slow in asking ye to wed. I thought it would go away. But it hasn't."

He clenched his fists and closed his eyes as if to shut out the sight still. "To this day I don't know whether they died of the bleeding or the burning. But do you think—if I could catch the monsters that did that —do ye think I'd not avenge my parents' agony?" When he spoke again Katrina could hardly hear him. "And Jean. She was with child. We were sae happy." His shoulders slumped.

Katrina put her arms around him. "Oh, my love. I'm so glad you told me this."

"Aye. I had to make ye understand."

"Robert, I understand your grief, your pain. I even understand your hatred. I always did. But more killing is not the way to deal with it."

His eyes were bleak. "I cannot forgive."

"No, but God can. He can forgive you for hating them. And then you won't hate yourself any longer."

He tore himself out of her embrace.

"Robert, wait!" She clutched at his sleeve. "Think! Where will it end? They killed our people for old wrongs. Now we kill them in vengeance. Then they will kill to avenge those killings. Robert, it has to end somewhere."

"Aye. And I mean to end it here. With my sword."

He sprang into his saddle and rode off without looking back.

Robert's bold exit did not clear his mind of Katrina's words, any more than time had been able to clear his sleep of the pictures of the atrocities his family suffered. On the long ride south to Dublin he tried to talk to Dougal. Could Katrina be right? Was there another way?

"Have ye ever thought that fighting could be wrong?" Robert ventured as they stopped at noonday to eat the hard cheese and crusty loaves they carried in their knapsacks.

Dougal lowered his flask of ale and frowned. "What do ye mean, man?"

"Our Lord said they that take the sword shall perish with the sword. Perhaps He meant as Katrina said—that fighting is not the way."

Dougal scoffed, "And did He not also say, 'I came not to send peace, but a sword'? Would ye have us compromise with Rome—with the kingdom of darkness?"

Robert shook his head. "Nay, I'd not. The truths of our faith are precious to me."

"Aye, so toleration is deadly sin. We must do aught necessary to enforce compliance with the true creed. Papacy and prelacy are twin evils." He paused to chew a bite from his loaf. "We fight to save the work of the Reformers. Mayhap we shall perish by the sword—the same sword that killed those martyrs who died to free us of Rome. Do ye not see that all the glorious truths of the Reformation are at stake?"

Far from bringing comfort or clarity, his companion's arguments raised more confusion in Robert's mind. Was he fighting to avenge his family and others who had suffered at the hands of the Irish rebels? Or was he fighting to save his faith from the Counter-Reformation? He wished he could have Dougal's clear-sighted focus. The man's burning zeal to purge the church from all taint of Romanism made everything so simple for him.

Three days later, when they arrived at the outskirts of Dublin where Cromwell's New Model Army was camped, there was little time for introspection. No matter why they were fighting, it appeared clear that Cromwell's twelve thousand men were a disciplined, well-equipped, seasoned force, ready to fight to establish parliamentary republicanism in place of a monarchy that claimed to rule by divine right.

The parliamentary army, clad in new uniforms (red coats and some red breeches as well, and with red ribbons around their legs and hat bands), turned the fields alongside the River Liffey to a sea of scarlet. Robert thought uneasily of the Egyptian waters that turned to blood. But that was a ridiculous analogy, for these soldiers whom he had come to join were not a plague. They were God's tools to prevent the establishment of Charles II on the throne and to secure the purification of the church.

An officer wearing a broad-brimmed, plumed hat and carrying a steel-tipped pike approached them. "Come to join up?" He surveyed them dispassionately. "Think we need help, do you then?"

"Aye. We all need help. God's help." Dougal faced him squarely. "We have experience. We would use it to fight for our homes and our faith."

The officer nodded and pointed. "Recruiting officer's tent is by the river."

Robert and Dougal emerged from the tent with their newly issued lobster-tail helmets just as attention to orders was sounded.

Oliver Cromwell himself, head uncovered, brown hair hanging to his shoulders, dark armor crossed with a scarlet sash, sat his prancing chestnut horse and surveyed his hastily assembled troops. His heavy voice rang across the field and echoed from the slope behind the encampment.

"Tomorrow we march north to Drogheda. The Marquess of Ormonde, head of the Royalist forces, has garrisoned the flower of his army there under command of Sir Arthur Aston. They shall be some thirty-five hundred strong—foot and horse."

A mingling of snickers and cheers met this announcement.

"True. We vastly outnumber them, but our power is not in numbers. It is in the strength of right. We fight for God. And God will fight for us."

He was interrupted by shouts and pious murmurs.

A nearby foot soldier who, Robert had noticed, had earlier been reading his Bible, raised his voice in loud assent.

Cromwell continued, "We shall carry out our task with sober justice and with such mercy as is compatible with justice. Hear me! As we march, I will tolerate no looting or cruelties upon the country people. Peaceable folk must be protected in their work, and all supplies are to be duly paid for."

A babble of resigned grumbling met this announcement. Soldiers were accustomed to living off the land where they were quartered. But Cromwell would not have the country folk turned against him—a sharp contrast to the Royalist army, which had stripped much of the countryside in demanding provisions from the people.

"Further, profane swearing, cursing, and drunkenness will be punished with extreme rigor."

The Bible-reading soldier, who wore a green ribbon around his hat identifying him as a member of the Levellers, raised his voice in agreement to this stricture.

His commander went on. "The importance of this battle cannot be overstated. The immediate conquest of Ireland is of supreme importance for the future of Britain. For the past eight years, Ireland, with its unruly rebels and papist royalists, has been a perpetual menace to the work of God."

Cromwell warmed to his subject. He stood on his toes in his stirrups and raised one fist for emphasis. "The republic is on a knife edge. The forces of darkness mass against it. At any moment, he who would be king over us might land in Scotland and set that country aflame to establish again the curse of royalty from which we have been delivered. If Ireland should be unconquered, England would be between two fires. Speedily and once and for all we must stamp out the embers of revolt!"

Again he was interrupted by cheering.

"This is not so much a war as it is surgery. The sharper it is, the more merciful it is. We shall wield sword and musket as the surgeon would apply scalpel and leech."

Cromwell proceeded to inspire his troops with the vision of all they would be accomplishing by the defeat of the confederation of English Royalists and Irish Catholics.

Robert wondered what Katrina would say could she be hearing this speech. She was a true daughter of the faith. Surely she would see the sense of what Cromwell said. Robert could see by the rapt look on Dougal's face that his friend certainly agreed.

And then Cromwell talked about the Irish levies, the group that made up a good portion of the Royalist common soldiery. And now

Robert could not remain dispassionate. For Cromwell charged that these were the people who had committed monstrous atrocities.

"These it was who broke the union of England and Ireland. It was they who, unprovoked, put the English to the most unheard-of and most barbarous massacre without respect of sex or age that ever the sun beheld, and at a time when Ireland was in perfect peace and the land productive and flourishing at the hand of English industry. Sunk in brutish barbarism and blasphemous idolatries, they have put themselves outside the human pale. Against such, you can be certain, God will grant us victory."

Robert couldn't help but join in the cheering at the conclusion of Cromwell's speech. It had revived the memory of the suffering of his own loved ones and strengthened his determination for vengeance.

That night, as he lay rolled in his blanket beside the campfire, in his sleep he was running across a snowy field. Each step sank deeper in the snow as he struggled to lift his feet and push forward at the insistence of Frank Guilford. And even as his mind would hold him back and his eyes strove not to look, he reached the corner of the field where the snow drifted against the hedgerow.

And there he found what he knew he would find. What he found night after night in his nightmares. Jean, his gentle Jean, lay curled in the snow, her azure gown stiff with ice, her lips as blue as her dress. But tonight she did not stay in her frozen coffin. Tonight she rose, cracking the ice around her into sharp splinters. She came toward Robert with ghostly steps, her hands held out to him, imploring.

"No!" He wakened with a shout and sat bolt upright.

Dougal knelt beside him. "*Och,* ye were just dreaming, man. Dona fash yourself."

Robert looked across the field of dim campfires surrounded by sleeping figures. The only movement came from guards on the outskirts of the camp. The sky was still black. They had hours yet till marching time. But he knew he could not sleep again. He did not want to sleep again. Not ever if it meant reliving that horror once more.

"Do ye want to talk about it?"

Robert rubbed his hand through his tangle of flaxen hair and told Dougal in as dispassionate a manner as he could.

Dougal nodded. "Aye. She was imploring ye to avenge her death. Dona worry. By the end of the week, ye'll have done it. Then she'll rest, and you can, too."

But Katrina's words had done their work. Robert was no longer sure of the right of the matter. "But can killing be put right by more killing? Killing the whole garrison would not bring my family back, would not change what they suffered."

241

Dougal did not argue. He clasped Robert's arm and sat by him, offering silent companionship.

On September 3, the army reached Drogheda, one of the most strongly fortified cities in Ireland.

The town lay totally within a formidable wall, twenty feet high and six feet thick. The city was situated on both north and south sides of the wide River Boyne, and the southern portion of the city was especially well-fortified. St. Mary's church, in the extreme southeast corner, offered a lofty steeple from which defenders could rain an almost constant barrage of shot down on besiegers. Along the east side of the wall ran a precipitously deep ravine known as the Dale. Inside the wall on the west was an artificial hill fortified with a massive palisade. In addition, Dubleek Gate, the main southern entrance, was heavily guarded.

But Cromwell was undaunted by such fortifications. He ordered the siege to take place from the south.

Cromwell directed his men to put down their muskets and pikes, and he issued shovels and hammers. They spent the next week digging trenches and erecting batteries. His supply ships carrying guns and siege weapons arrived in the Boyne estuary. Still, everyone understood that Drogheda's fortifications could easily hold against a siege for a month.

On the morning of September 10, Cromwell had eleven siege guns installed on a hill south of the city—all pointing at the wall. He directed the strategic placement of his twelve field pieces to cover the action of his troops. He was ready.

But first, he returned to his quarters. "Raise the white flag," he barked to the aide standing at attention. In spite of the confused look on his face, the young man snapped to obey orders. In minutes the white banner was whipping in the wind, clearly in view of the Royalist soldiers watching the siege preparations from the tower of St. Mary's.

Cromwell emerged from his tent and unrolled a parchment. "I send this message to Aston." Then Cromwell read aloud his dispatch to Sir Arthur Aston, the brave, determined English Catholic who defended the garrison, a man whose artificial leg testified to his battle experience.

"Sir, we have brought the army belonging to the Parliament of England before this place to reduce it to obedience. To the end effusion of blood may be prevented I thought fit to summon you to deliver the same into my hands to their use."

Cromwell raised his gravelly voice on the last sentence. "If this be refused you will have no cause to blame me. I expect your answer and rest Your Servant, O. Cromwell."

The parchment was inserted in an official communication pouch, and a red-coated officer on a white horse galloped to the Dubleek Gate.

Robert and Dougal waited with the rest of their company. When the sun reached its apex, they divided a cold boiled chicken between them.

"Ye paid for that, did ye now?" A musketeer with a cartridge box suspended from his belt rested his fire lock against a supply wagon and grinned at them.

Robert wrenched a wing off the bird and handed it to the soldier. "Aye, I'd not like to end up at the wrong end of your musket."

The newcomer nodded. "When the commander-in-chief issues an order, he means it."

Robert nodded. He didn't want to talk about the two soldiers who had been executed two nights ago for stealing a hen.

The soldier, who now introduced himself as Farley from Sussex, was clearly fond of his leader. He lounged against a water barrel and began a narrative of his battle experience under the intrepid Cromwell, which went back to five years earlier.

As the sun continued across the sky, Robert, although not following Farley's account in any detail, was glad enough for it. It provided a distraction to the hardness he again felt growing inside him. He could not help hoping Aston would refuse to surrender. He had come all this way for rebel blood. This was his chance to lay his personal ghosts. He did not wish to be denied.

His thoughts were interrupted by a great cheer running in waves through the massed troops. The white flag was lowered. A red one flew in its place. Aston had refused surrender.

The first round of cannon boomed from the great siege guns. In spite of himself, Robert trembled as the earth shook under him. As the smoke cleared after each round, he expected to see the great wall reduced to rubble. But it was not to be so easy.

The steeple and tower of St. Mary's church crumbled under the barrage, but when night fell, the wall still held.

As the troops prepared to return to their cold, damp tents, Cromwell went among his men. "Hold your courage high, men! Tomorrow we shall do our utmost to make the breaches assaultable. And by the help of God we will storm them! Aston, that ally of Satan, is resolved to perish rather than to deliver up the city. God helping us, we will see that he keep his resolution."

The ghosts of his parents' memory walked again in Robert's sleep. He saw them twisting and turning on their tenterhooks. He heard his mother's scream as bits of burning thatch fell around her.

243

In the morning he was pale and drawn. Steely determination made every movement jerky. "Aye. This is the day," he said to Dougal, who sat on a folded sack reading his Bible.

Throughout the morning and into the afternoon, the siege cannon boomed, and Robert's tension mounted. Surely this would be the day. He could endure the inaction no longer. He could not face another night of haunted sleep.

Suddenly he heard a cheer. The wall was breached! Robert smiled. Aye. Now it was too late. The rules of siege warfare were clear. Once a breach was accomplished, no quarter would be given. It was too late for Aston to march out under a white flag. Robert would have the blood he came for.

He mounted and waited for the order for the horse troop to advance. Their captain had explained the battle plan. The foot would go first and storm the church. Once secured, that would provide a place from which they could successfully hold off Aston's foot and horse. Then the Parliamentary horse would enter.

Robert could not see the battle at the wall, but time and again he imagined he heard the order to advance. So strong was the image that more than once he had to rein his horse back after putting spurs to his flank. Still the order did not come. The Royalist defenders fought with ferocity and courage. Cromwell's troops were repulsed.

Robert could not believe the sight of the New Model Army in retreat, the red from their wounds mixing with the red of their uniforms. Col. James Castle, commander of a regiment of foot, had been killed, a sore loss. Incredulous, Robert turned from the sight.

But he turned again at a shouted command from the wall. Cromwell himself was rushing into the breach. Soldiers around him fought fiercely to hold their position. Colonel Ewer signaled the command for reinforcements. In a mass of confusion, shouting, and fighting, thousands of Cromwellian soldiers poured through the wall. They seized the defended church and nearby fortified areas, and now surely Robert could at last spur forward.

But not yet. The breach was not wide enough for a horse regiment to enter. Only the foot soldiers advanced.

His impatience was long past the breaking point by the time the gate had been opened and the cavalry could charge.

Robert's company spurred into the town, past scenes of violent fighting. Battling for every step, the invaders pushed the Royalists back and back. Aston and his defenders withstood the attack from atop the palisade walls. The Parliamentary musketeers returned shot for shot, even with the difficulty of fighting uphill.

And then the shots quieted. Robert looked around, puzzled.

They had not taken the mount. Why had the attack halted? Could it be that Aston had surrendered? He could see no white flag.

Confusion spread through the ranks. Aston had refused to surrender when quarter was offered. Could he have changed his mind? Would Cromwell now grant it, against all rules of war? Robert was too far back to see what the defenders were doing. But there was no question that their musket fire had ceased.

Then there was movement in the ranks, and Robert could see. The unexpected had happened. Aston's men had put down their arms! Cromwell's officers were collecting swords and muskets from the defenders.

As the pale light glinted dully off his black armor, Cromwell rode to the head of his troops. He shouted a command that was repeated back through the ranks. *"No quarter! Put all to the sword!"*

Cromwell spun his horse around. "I warned them!"

Robert felt the surge of energy among the troops, heard the cries of bloodlust, felt his own blaze of white-hot emotion. Even as a small voice in the back of his mind rebelled at striking down unarmed men, the surge around him carried him forward. He thundered ahead, sword slashing right and left at the Royalist bluecoats and goldcoats. He had no idea how many he struck down—or if he did any damage. The rage inside him and about him simply drove him on.

"His leg!"

"Get his leg!"

"Gold! It's solid gold!"

Robert reined to the left where a surging, shouting mob surrounded Sir Arthur Aston. Those on one side pulled him from his horse while those on the other held to his artificial leg. A great shout arose when the leg detached.

"Gold! He keeps his fortune in it!"

The cries for gold changed to outrage when an ordinary wooden limb was passed from hand to hand. And then a soldier, taller and broader than his fellows, seized the leg and rushed at Aston with an angry bellow. The commander, held at sword point by his captors, fell under the blows from his own wooden leg.

Colonel Ewer, brandishing his sword for attention, shouted orders above the melee. "Attention! Present arms!"

Robert held his blade ready, although no armed enemy advanced.

"Run them through!"

Robert held his upraised sword, unmoving. The break in momentum, watching Aston being bludgeoned to death, had allowed his passion to subside. Run his sword through unarmed men? Men who had surrendered, apparently under the notion, no matter how illogically, that they were to receive quarter?

"You heard the order, trooper!" The captain pointed his iron-tipped staff at Robert's chest. "Put them to the sword. Your sword!"

Robert advanced. The face of a young Royalist just beyond his sword thrust filled his sight. But the bloodlust was gone now. The white-hot energy that had thrust him into battle yelling and hacking had cooled. This was a far different matter. He was to put his sword through an English foot soldier younger than himself. And if he didn't, he would be run through by his own officer.

Robert slashed his sword across the boy's shoulder. "Fall down, blast ye," he growled.

Whether from the pain of the cut or from amazement, the soldier fell. It would not work for long. Another Cromwellian would surely find the wounded lad and finish the job. But for the moment, Robert had spared his conscience.

And then reprieve came. The signal for his company, blown repeatedly, finally attracted the attention of even those most intent on carrying out the ordered slaughter.

"They're escaping over the bridge!" The captain pointed northward to where a single bridge spanned the Boyne. "After them. Hunt them down!"

Hundreds of weaponless Royalist soldiers fled toward the long bridge, as Cromwell's cavalry swooped down on their heels.

Robert spurred his horse, managing to reach the bridge, narrowed by the rows of houses on each side of it, before it could bottleneck with fleeing soldiers. Once across, he galloped onward, leaving the scene of slaughter behind him to approach the battles raging in the north of town.

By far the larger part of the town lay to the north. Here streets and lanes crisscrossed in a maze, and buildings crowded together. Robert pushed up the main street.

He tried to keep his eyes straight ahead, struggling to shut out the sights around him. Women shrieked. Babies cried. Children and animals darted everywhere. He gave a moment's thought to wonder where Dougal was. Somewhere behind him, he was sure. He hadn't seen him since he crossed the bridge, but he assumed Dougal had heard the order for their company to leave the Mill Mount.

Ahead of him the road branched. A tall-steepled wooden church stood in the Y. Several Royalist soldiers ran into the church. Before they slammed the door, Robert caught a glimpse of Mass in progress.

"Ah! We've got them!" a Cromwellian officer shouted and spurred ahead, almost running down three brown-robed clerics who were crossing the churchyard. A pair of dragoon officers swept around the corner from a side street and attacked the priests.

Robert was glad enough to follow a command that didn't involve use of his sword. Three men bearing battleaxes hacked through the church door, and the rest of the company was set to pulling out wooden benches and altars while the frightened women, children, and old men huddled in corners.

"Under the tower!" The captain shouted. "Higher. Bring more. Come on. Move!"

Robert obeyed without thought. But when the benches were stacked well above their heads, leaning against two sides of the church, he understood. Those who had taken refuge in the church—soldiers and civilians alike—were to meet their fate in a giant funeral pyre. Sparks flew from struck flint. In a matter of minutes, flames leaped up the side of the building, billowing smoke before them.

"There are women and children in there!" Robert cried. It wasn't so much a protest as a desire to understand what was happening. How could godly soldiers be burning women and children?

The officer in charge turned to Robert and shrugged. "Nits make lice."

Robert tried to close his ears against the shrieks.

"God confound me! I burn! I burn!"

All eyes turned upward to the arched opening of the tower. The screaming man gave a final shriek as flames swept up his body.

Sometime later, Robert found himself in a side street, unsure how he had arrived there. Three drunken soldiers staggered by, two of them with bloodied priest's vestments over their armor, laughing raucously. Just then a dark-haired young woman, fleeing a soldier behind her, rounded the corner. The mock-priests staggered toward her, shouting obscenities.

The girl backed away, holding out her arms, pleading. Robert saw that she was pregnant. And he saw Jean as she had been in his dream. She hadn't been pleading to be avenged. She was pleading for mercy. Mercy from him—to be granted to others.

In the seconds before either set of pursuers could reach the woman, Robert prayed, *Father, forgive. Forgive me!*

He sprang from his horse and clutched the woman in his arms, ignoring her screams. "My prize, I think."

The drunken men backed away from his steely glare. The soldier who gave chase first, however, was harder to dissuade.

But Robert put one hand to the hilt of his sword. "Shall we fight for her? A tasty prize, worth the effort, don't you think?"

The musketeer gave a lecherous laugh. "Enjoy your booty, then.

There's enough for all." He caught the struggling woman's hand and held it to his lips. "Have fun, me love. But don't forget me. I'll see you later." He went off, laughing.

Robert dragged the woman into the doorway of a building. "Easy, lass. I'll not hurt ye."

It took some doing to make the woman understand, especially since she spoke only a little English and Robert almost no Gaelic. At last, though, he was able to communicate to her that he meant to help her escape.

"*Buíochas le Dia! Buíochas le Dia!* Thank God!" The woman cried over and over, crossing herself repeatedly.

Robert evaluated his chances of getting her out the city gates, even in the quickly gathering dusk and with the argument that she was his prize. He did not like the odds. There was only one other exit from the town. The river.

He shouted to his horse to follow. Then, acting as if he were drunk and half dragging the woman, Robert staggered to the bank of the Boyne.

Then his heart sank. The tide was running away from the town, but there were no boats in sight. Of course, there wouldn't be. Others would have attempted a similar escape in any boat left on the quay. But he must hurry, for soon the army—those who weren't already too drunk—would think of this route and guard it.

The warehouse behind the wharf had been broken into. Its wide doors hung on broken hinges. And within was a small rowboat that had apparently been dragged in for caulking. Robert turned it over and shoved it to the water. He gestured to the woman to get in.

She stood as if frozen.

"Come, on, woman. You'll have no chance if you don't hurry."

Her eyes widening, she pointed behind him.

Robert turned and found himself looking down the long blade of a cavalry sword.

"What do ye think you're playing at, soldier?" his captor barked.

Robert knew the voice. He raised his head so that his face could be seen behind the guard of his helmet. "Do ye not ken your own mate, Dougal?"

The sword lowered but was not sheathed. "Ah, Robert. I didna ken ye. But I'd still be knowing what you're about."

Robert pointed to the woman, shivering with fear in the shadows. "I'm doing it for Jean. She'll have a chance in the river. More of a chance than Jean had in the snowstorm."

Dougal looked from the pregnant woman back to his friend's face. "Aye, I see ye are." He nodded briefly and turned his head away.

Robert waved the woman to the boat. "Lie down and let the boat drift until you are past the walls." He had to repeat it three times, accompanied by pantomime, to make her understand. She lay down, and he placed a sack and an empty crate from the shed over her. At the last moment he thought to pull out the bread and cheese he carried in a pouch and give them to her. It was all he could do.

The current had no more than taken the flimsy craft when an officer clattered down the street on a sweating horse. "What are you doing?" he shouted.

"Searching for escapees, sir!" Dougal brandished his sword.

The officer looked at Dougal's and Robert's blue lapels and red coats. "Captain Everet's company, aren't you?"

"Yes, sir."

"Then get back to your company. At the bridge!" The officer pointed, then rode off when they mounted in obedience to his orders.

They stopped short just before the bridge, and Robert saw what was happening. "Oh, my God!" It was a prayer. "I thought we were done with that. Can there be still more poor devils in need of slaughtering?"

Royalists fleeing from the fort were still being driven across the bridge to be cut down on the north side. As Robert and Dougal watched, a Royalist soldier reached the end of the houses lining the bridge and jumped into the river. He was shot before he hit the water.

But his action sparked his comrades. Undoubtedly knowing they were marching to their death anyway, the trapped men rushed toward the steep banks of the Boyne. Many were shot or run through before they left the bridge, but some reached the river and began swimming. New Model Army musketeers on the banks fired at the bobbing, splashing forms. Red streaks ran in the churning water.

Behind Robert, Dougal made a choking sound. Robert turned to see his friend being sick.

Dougal wiped his mouth. "The horror—it goes on and on."

Now the Parliamentary soldiers ran along the banks to give chase to the men still swimming.

"There's one! I'll get 'im!"

Robert recognized Farley, who had entertained them with his war stories that morning. It seemed a lifetime ago.

Farley detached himself from the others and rushed to the bank by Robert and Dougal. He aimed.

Just as Farley fired, Dougal shouted and lunged from his horse. "Rory!"

Robert looked at the form struggling in the water. Rory's russet hair and forehead were unmistakable.

Dougal dived into the river. At first it appeared he was trying to finish the work Farley had done in wounding the Royalist soldier. But when Dougal pulled his brother to shore and began struggling up the steep bank with him, his intention became clear.

Robert heard the click of Farley's flintlock. He whirled and drew his sword. "No!"

His shout was drowned out by exploding gunpowder. As Robert lunged forward, his sword found its mark and Farley fell. But he was too late. Dougal, shielding his brother's body, had taken the full impact of the blast.

The shouts and clatter of battle receded as the action moved farther downriver. Robert dismounted and stood in a pool of silence as the evening shadows covered them. Rory moaned.

Then Robert dragged the brothers up the embankment. Nothing could be done for Dougal. But Rory's shoulder wound could heal if he received care. Robert cut off Rory's Royalist uniform and stanched the flow of blood with wadded cloths. He tore his linen shirt in strips and tied the bandage tight.

Then he put Dougal's jacket and helmet on Rory. Farley's flask still contained some whiskey. He poured as much as he could down Rory's throat. "Can you ride?"

"I'll try. But—" Rory gestured toward his brother's form.

"Nay. There's nothing we can do—except escape for him. He saved you."

It was a fair trek across the bridge and out the Dubleek gate in the best of times. And these were the worst. Time and again they had to circle around fallen men and horses. Again and again drunken soldiers blocked the way. The smell of blood and burning made Robert so sick he had to stop more than once to heave. And Rory's strength was waning so fast that Robert feared he might fall from the saddle.

Upwards of three thousand of the enemy had been put to the sword. The population, those that had not met a similar fate, were in hiding. And Cromwell's New Model Army—the best-equipped, best-disciplined fighting force in Europe—abandoned itself to drunkenness, looting, and rape.

No one challenged them.

30

All the long, weary, slow trip home, Robert led Dougal's horse, which now carried the older brother. He stopped, sometimes for whole days, while Rory's fevered mind wandered. He tried to forage food from a terrified populace. He tried to make sense out of what had happened.

Well into the second week of their journey, they stopped for the night to shelter in a haystack. Robert had spent his last pennies buying fresh-baked buns and a pot of milk, still foamy and warm from the cow, for their supper. Now Rory seemed to be sleeping. At least his breathing was rhythmic between the soft moans he made when he tried to shift his shoulder. Robert lay with his hands behind his head, looking at the stars in the black sky. And again he wondered what it had all been for.

He had joined the battle with an idea of avenging the suffering and death of his family. But what was the chance that any of the garrison of Drogheda or its people had been the ones who attacked his family—or anyone else in Ulster?

Dougal had joined with elevated notions of defending the true faith and wiping out heresy. So what had all the destruction and bloodshed accomplished? Freedom for the Ulster Scots to worship? Perhaps that. But converts to the faith? An effective Christian witness? He rolled to his side, not even able to look into the face of the sky with such a thought.

Still he sought an answer. It couldn't all have been for nothing. There must be something. Peace, perhaps. Had the near annihilation of the Royalist army ended the war? If so, maybe something of worth had been accomplished. No, there were certain to be more battles. But he could still hope peace would come. It would be a great boon to the land if the people could now live in peace and rebuild all that the past decade of struggle had destroyed.

Only time would tell if lasting peace had come to Ireland.

But Robert could answer for himself. He had seen more than enough bloodshed for several lifetimes. From this time onward, he would make it his aim to live at peace with all men. He felt a lightness such as he had not known since the rising—had thought never to know again. His resolution for peace had produced a great inward calm. He was filled with wonder that he could ever have been so full of hatred.

But he had. He shuddered to remember the bitterness, the ugliness, the unhappiness that had filled him. Katrina had been right to plead with him to forgive. Ah, Katrina. The very thought of her brought a soft smile to his lips and an ache to his arms. Tomorrow they should reach Comber. By this time tomorrow he could be holding her, feeling her small softness, smelling her clean, flowery hair...

And even as he thought of the goodness he had thought life could never hold for him again, he marveled once more that his prayer for forgiveness, brief as it had been in the heat of battle, had been answered. He knew God had forgiven him. And as Katrina had said He would, God had enabled him to forgive those he had seen as his enemies.

But remembering had been a mistake. Alongside the realization of the good, the scenes of horror also returned. And he realized that forgiving the Royalists he had been fighting wasn't enough. He must forgive all sides—even his own. He must forgive the rebels for the rising that took his family. He must forgive Cromwell for the horror of Drogheda that took his best friend and so many others. He must forgive Dougal and all like him who engaged in hardline thinking that left no room for peaceful compromise. He must forgive himself for the hatred he had borne for his fellow creatures.

For a time Robert's mind swirled again with scenes of blood and smoke. His ears rang with the tumult of shouts and cries. And again, above the mayhem, one word rang. *Forgive.* God forgive the rebels. God forgive Cromwell. God forgive his own hardness.

That night Robert's sleep was undisturbed by nightmares.

The next morning he rose and brushed the straw out of his hair. He went to a nearby stream and brought back a cup of clear water for Rory.

Kneeling beside his friend, he helped him to an upright position and was gratified to see that his eyes were brighter. "Get you up, man. We're going home."

31

Mary had known the history of Ireland was troubled and violent. But she had had no idea of the intensity of the violence. She could take no more. She put aside Philip's manuscript and headed to the kitchen. She needed a cup of tea. No more history for a while.

She clicked on the electric kettle and warmed a small teapot with hot tap water. It was late morning already. Last night she had announced she was going to stay home today and finish reading Philip's account. And she had done that, not even emerging from her room until she finished.

The fact that the reading had taken her almost two weeks was testimony to the increased level of activity she had undertaken with the young people at the Centre. *Land of Heart's Desire* was cast and in rehearsal. They held play practice in the crowded quarters at the CCC, but now Liam had found them a performance venue—a church on Skegoneill Avenue that ran the day care center his little sister attended. Because it was in a mixed area, both sides would be willing to attend.

Mary pushed away the conflicts of the history she had just read by going over the delightful program that was taking shape. Fiona was working out a brilliant step dancing routine, and the children from the daycare center were going to sing "Shine, Jesus, Shine." They had Martin's drums and Liam's guitar, and she was still hoping to find someone to play the Celtic harp. Tommy, the ex-prisoner working in Braille transcription, had volunteered to play the tin whistle.

The kettle clicked off. She reached for the canister of tea bags and looked around the kitchen. Where *was* everybody? She turned on the radio for company, then froze, unbelieving, as she heard the news report.

"More than two hundred people were injured in the explosion of a massive bomb in downtown Manchester just hours ago. The bomb in a parked van ripped out the side of a shopping mall, littering the streets with glass and sending scores of people screaming for cover. Police say the bomb that demolished the city center was planted by IRA guerrillas . . ."

Mary doubled over with a wave of nausea. *This can't be happening. The peace talks have started. They will have stable peace soon.* She ran outside.

In the back garden a soft breeze blew Sheila's white sheets. Flowers grew along the garden wall. A small brown bird chirped in the bushes.

It was a mistake. This was not a land at war. She had heard wrong. But even as she argued, she knew. Two bombs in London. A scare in Belfast. Now Manchester. The massacre of Drogheda—three hundred years ago—was still going on.

The door from the kitchen banged shut. If she had had any doubt about the truth of the news report, the look on Gareth's face would have eliminated it. She ran into his arms. "Gareth, I just heard." She buried her face in his shoulder. "Two hundred people. I just can't believe it."

He stroked her hair and held her while she sobbed. She cried for the victims of the rising, she cried for the victims of Drogheda, she cried for the victims of the Manchester bombing. And she cried for her own helplessness. What could anybody do?

"It's hopeless. It's just all so hopeless." She pulled away and dabbed at her eyes, and Gareth handed her a clean white handkerchief. "This is stupid, Gareth. Hopeless. Let's go back to Scotland and get on with our lives. This isn't our fight. Let's go before something worse happens."

His arm around her, he led her to the bench at the bottom of the garden. "It's a terrible, terrible thing. But it's not hopeless. Not with God. Not while people are still working for peace. We have to keep believing. We have to keep caring."

"But that's what was so terrible." She bit her lip. How could she admit this to Gareth? How could she even admit it to herself?

"What? Tell me."

"Well, I'd just read about the massacre of Drogheda. I've never been much of a fan of Cromwell—but that was unbelievable. And I kept thinking how he was supposed to be the great Christian leader. His men read their Bibles and sang psalms! And I kept thinking, *How? How could he do that?*

"And then I heard the news. And my first thought was—if that's the way these terrorists are going to act, they should bring in the army and let them have it. They don't deserve the protection of law." She looked at him, her eyes wide with horror at what she had said and at the fact that she had been capable of feeling that way.

Gareth dropped his head into his hands. "Aye. I know."

"You too?"

"It isn't right. It isn't Christian. But it is honest emotion."

"And do you still feel that way?" Her voice was barely a whisper.

He shook his head, looking at her with soft eyes.

"I know. You prayed." It was almost an accusation. She would never be as good as he was, nor did she want to be. She would have no part of surrendering herself to anything that meant she would have to stay here. She would make her own choices. And she chose to leave. She looked up to say that to Gareth and was caught by the intensity of his face. The energy that fired all he did held her to listen to him.

"Aye. I prayed for the strength to remember that all people— even people who commit terrible crimes—are human beings. Christ died for the terrorist and the pacifist alike. He loves them and is willing to forgive them. Even when I don't feel that way, I need to remember that God does."

She was silent, and he went on. "Like when that second bomb went off in London, with that young man holding it. And people said, 'Good enough. He got what he meant to give others.' But I had to think, that lad had a mother, he had a family who mourned him. Maybe he had someone he loved as much as I love you."

Her defenses crumbled. As much as she wanted to be away from here, she couldn't possibly turn her back on such love. With a sigh she nestled her head on his shoulder again. "It doesn't make much sense."

"It doesn't make any sense. We just have to keep believing that God is in control and keep working for peace."

"Oh! That reminds me, Gareth. How was your meeting? Your Committee for Reasonable Compromise."

He shook his head. "No meeting."

"What?"

"The bomb. Everyone on both sides is scared to death. Everyone has simply gone to ground."

"How's Philip?"

"Sick. Frantic. Trying to hold everything together even while it all unravels before his eyes."

Mary jumped to her feet still holding his hand. "Come on. Let's go to him. Maybe we can help."

The atmosphere at the CCC didn't seem frantic to Mary. It seemed frozen. All went mechanically about their work in the office, print shop, art room. But no one talked. No one smiled.

Mary sat in a chair across the desk from Philip.

He sat ashen-faced. The pen in his hand didn't move. He rubbed one hand over his face. "My life just flashed before my eyes. Everything I've ever worked for has just gone up in smoke."

"Not everything, Philip. It's a terrible setback. But the peace talks are continuing."

He nodded. "I tell myself I have to keep believing that He will reveal to them the abundance of peace and truth. There *is* an abundance of peace and truth for us. Somewhere. Somehow."

She smiled encouragingly. "That sounds like Rory. He must have seen even less peace after Drogheda than we do now. And it must have been even harder to sort out what was true. I just can't understand. Why did Cromwell *do* that? How could he as a Christian? He seemed to feel the rising justified it, but . . ." She found it impossible to put all her questions into words.

"Oh, aye. The rising was a terrible thing. The Cromwell massacre was a terrible thing. But two terrible things do not make a good thing. The killing must stop. The hatred must stop. Without peace and love what kind of life can anyone have here? It must stop some time. If not now—when?" He rubbed a hand across his face again—his characteristic gesture of frustration. "Well, there. You got the speech I was going to give at the meeting that got canceled. Now, what were you asking about Cromwell?"

"About the rising."

"Oh, yes. Well, it's hard to tell at this distance just what happened. Historians fight over the evidence. The key fact is that Cromwell believed the slaughter from the rising to have been terrible. Doesn't make his vengeance right, of course, but helps explain his motive. The bottom line is probably that he lost his temper. He was known to have a violent temper."

"And then it all seemed to be complicated by the fact that it was largely English fighting English."

"Right. And that's been true of most of the wars in Ireland—not really Irish versus English as one thinks, but Spanish, English, French, Scottish—all mixed in on one side or the other—or both." Philip was quiet for a moment, then quoted—mostly to himself, it seemed—"'Turn back, each of you, from your evil way and from your evil deeds, then you shall remain in the land which the Lord gave you and your fathers from of old. . . . But you would not listen to me, says the Lord . . . and the land is made desolate by the sweeping sword.'"

After a moment Mary asked, "But were the Puritans and Reformers really such awful people?"

Philip's eyebrows shot up. "Not at all. They loved God, worked hard, had strong family values, promoted education."

"And smashed more art than Hitler's bombs." Mary had her prejudices, too.

"You're not the first to draw a parallel between Cromwell and Hitler."

"Isn't it absolutely dire that the 'most Christian' land in the world has a history of holding to some of the least Christian attitudes?"

He gave her an ironic smile. "You mean killing and persecuting one another, when Christ said to love your enemies? And legalistic religion, when Christ taught salvation as a free gift?"

"I think that's what's the hardest for me to deal with—the fanaticism."

"Every movement has its fanatics—although I'll certainly grant the Puritans and Reformers an above-average percentage. But those who were mean, legalistic Puritans would probably have been mean, legalistic people in any other age as well."

Gareth, who had just joined them, spoke for the first time. "Perhaps, but I think you can make a good case for the idea that their theology set them up for it."

"What do you mean?" Mary asked.

"It's a recipe for disaster when one is completely convinced that only he is God's elect."

"Aye," Philip said. "People who are sure they are right—chosen to be right in the eyes of God—can easily take that as license to treat others as inferiors."

"Nits make lice," Mary suggested.

"That's right." Gareth said. "When someone like Cromwell thinks he has the mind of the omniscient God and gets into power, terrible things can result. Especially when he believes he's been specially elected by God to subdue people who haven't been chosen."

Philip's ironic half-smile returned. "And then, the English as a nation—God love them—are so certain they're right. And so you had the Royalists, who believed they were there by divine right, and the Covenanters, who believed they were married to God—" He threw up his hands. "As Gareth said—a recipe for disaster.

"Pain in the past can make a person or a family dysfunctional. It can do the same thing to a nation. Ireland is dysfunctional from all the pain in her past. But there comes a time to put these things behind you—whether it's an unhappy childhood or a troubled nationhood. Just as we cannot fight our children's battles for them, we cannot right the wrongs our grandparents suffered. We have to say, 'I learn from the past. I build for the future. But I do what is right for today.' We have to work with today's situation—not 1641 or 1690, but today.

"I want to do what's right to build a solid peace so my grandchildren won't have to refight 1690 or 1916. That's why I'm so committed to getting people together to talk.

"And I'm not one of these 'it's all right what you believe so long as you're sincere' types. Believing everything leads to believing nothing. I'm talking about differences of opinion among Christians, which, to our shame, have been among the most violent differences in the history of mankind."

Then he grinned. "Yes, I do believe Nationalists can be Christians —and not all Unionists are godly people. That was a lot of what I came to see when I studied it all in prison. And my own family story helped me see that."

The phone rang. A newspaper reporter was seeking Philip's comment.

"We're trying to hold it together. Our message is 'Stay cool.' If the UVF get involved, I hate to think what will happen. It's up to us to hold together, to give confidence."

He stiffened his back at the next question. "Absolutely. *All* killing is wrong. There's no such thing as a legitimate target. The very term dehumanizes people." He paused. "No, I'm not nonviolent. I'm anti-violent. Violence doesn't solve problems."

Another brief pause. "Where do we go now? The dialogue must continue. And the violence must stop before there's dialogue. The eighteen-month cease-fire wasn't long enough. It takes time to stabilize the situation."

The next question took him another direction. "Yes, we need closer north-south cooperation—agriculture, tourism, whatever. But we also need closer east-west cooperation with England and Scotland."

The sound of a slamming door and angry voices rang through the hushed room, and Mary ran to quiet them. "*Sh*—Philip's giving an interview—oh, Debbie, Liam . . ." She looked from one to the other, bewildered.

Debbie was flushed, Liam rigidly white.

"It was a stupid idea to think we could work together in the first place," Debbie flung at him.

"What do you mean, 'the families on your side of the road don't feel they can trust us'?" Liam gestured with a clenched fist.

"And why should they? It isn't our lot who's setting off bombs."

Liam dropped his head, and his shoulders sagged. He looked as if he could crumple into the corner. But he held his ground. "And it isn't our lot either. Don't you see? I feel just as awful about this as you do—worse, because I know we'll be blamed." He raised his head and his long hair fell back from his face. His dark eyes glowed. "Do you think I'm a terrorist? Do you think Fiona and Gerry go home from play practice every night and make bombs?"

Debbie made a groping gesture toward him. "Of course, I don't think any such thing."

"And don't you think I'm just as upset as you are to have our whole project come to nothing?" He turned away.

The hallway rang with hopeless silence.

"What do you mean, *nothing?*" Mary's voice echoed in the gloom. "You aren't quitting?"

Debbie shrugged. "It's our parents. They've been on the phone all morning. They don't think it's safe—working with the other side of the road just now."

"It's called the fortress mentality," Liam replied to Mary's baffled look.

"But we were just proving everyone *could* work together . . ." Mary started, then nodded as the reply rang in her own head. *And that bomb just proved they can't.* "But we can't let the terrorists win. That's what they want—for everyone to pull back from all the cross-community cooperation. If everyone works together peacefully, then they'll have lost their power base." She was working it out as she spoke, but she knew she was right.

"This is important," she said. "There's more at stake here than just an amateur drama or a leisure center. We have to prove to our own community that peace works better than violence. And demonstrate that neither side needs terrorism to protect their rights."

She wanted to rage. The dark was winning. They were slipping back down into the hopeless slough of violence everyone in this land had wallowed in for centuries. And she didn't have a lifeline to throw to them. "We have to try *something.*"

32

Mary pushed down her disappointment and anger as she looked at the two young people. She sensed that Debbie and Liam had come to the Cross Community Centre for more than just delivering their news that the play would have to be canceled. The Centre was a place of reconciliation. It offered hope, comfort, and practical approaches to the problems around them. And Liam and Debbie were in dire need of precisely that. She couldn't just let them walk out now. Funny, an hour ago she herself had been ready to leave on the next ferry.

"Um, how about a cup of tea?" She fell back on the one unfailing, all-purpose cure-all.

"Sure."

"Why not?"

She led the way up to the canteen.

Sheila was there, hanging a series of floral watercolors. "Aren't these lovely? They're done by a friend of mine, Nimah. Her husband died in prison, and her son was crippled in a knee-capping. I'm hoping I can help her find a market for her work."

Debbie admired the paintings while Liam helped Mary carry the teacups to a table.

Sheila joined them, chatting easily. "I think I know your mother, Debbie. The friend who did these paintings works with her at Courage. What a good name they've chosen. It does require courage to face a shattered life."

Debbie nodded, and Sheila continued. "They do a wonderful work—I think she said they have worked with more than four hundred families of victims who've been bereaved, disabled, or traumatized."

Liam raised his head and looked at Debbie.

Sheila went on. "Nimah told me about a ten-year-old boy she's working with. He chased the men who had just shot his father—hurled a trash can at them but missed. He tried to commit suicide because he blamed himself for not doing more."

Liam withdrew again, head down, shoulders hunched.

Mary was amazed to hear of the work Debbie's mother did. In

260

spite of such commitment, she would make her daughter withdraw from their project? Or maybe it was *because* of her work. Perhaps seeing all this made her more protective of her daughter, who had also been through so much. Mary could think of nothing to say, other than commenting on the delicate coloring of the paintings.

The whole conversation ground to an uncomfortable silence.

Then the canteen door swung open, and Gareth burst through. As always, the room came alive in response to his electrifying energy. "The YP from the church are having a wee outing to Carrickfergus. Shall we join them?"

Debbie and Liam looked at each other distrustfully.

Sheila answered, "Sure, that's a grand idea. It'll be good crack for you. Ann is even taking time off her studying. She'd love to see you there."

Mary turned to Debbie. "Go on—call your mother. I know she won't want you out late, but we could take you home so you wouldn't have to ride the bus after dark."

Debbie went to the phone.

"Do you want to call home?" Gareth looked at Liam.

Liam shrugged. "Ma's at work. Da won't care."

Mary knew his mother worked long hours as a waitress and that his father was unemployed. She suspected Mr. O'Connor would be in the pub.

They were heading out of town when they stopped at a red light and Mary noticed the building by her window. "My word! That's amazing!"

She was looking almost straight up the front of a large, stone structure with rows of tall, arched windows. But the astounding thing was the several-times-life-size statue of a sword-brandishing man on a horse prancing atop the building. The gigantic sculpture loomed against the silver-blue sky, as loudly energetic as if horse and rider would leap upon passers-by with a triumphal shout.

It wasn't so much the sense of exultant victory that made Mary recoil. It was the in-your-face arrogance of the statue. The light changed, and they drove on. "What *was* that?" She turned around in her seat, looking back at the statue.

"That's King Billy," Gareth said.

"Who?" Mary's simple question was met with gasps of disbelief from the backseat.

"Sorry. Should I know him? I'm new here, you know."

"The 'Glorious Twelfth' and all that." It had been some time since she'd heard that note of bitter sarcasm in Liam's voice.

"And have you not heard of the war of the two kings and the Battle of the Boyne, then?" Debbie asked.

Mary shook her head, more bewildered than ever.

Gareth came to her rescue. "King Billy—as in William of Orange. You've heard of William and Mary?"

"Oh, *that* William." The pieces fell into place. "William of Orange. The Orange Order."

"Yep. That's it. Another tangled tale. Seems they all are. After Cromwell, Charles II was restored to his throne. Next came his brother, James II. He was Catholic and a pretty weak king. Parliament drove him into abdication and set his Protestant daughter, Mary, and her husband, William of Orange, on the throne."

"OK. I'm with you. I had that in some history class somewhere in the murky past. William and Mary are probably best known in the States for the college named after them."

Now they were on the motorway. Green hedgerows and fields lay on their left and glimpses of Belfast Lough on their right.

"Well, over here, William—King Billy—is best known for establishing the Protestant Ascendancy by defeating King James at the Boyne in 1690."

"But why would they put a statue on top of a building like that?"

"That wasn't a 'building.' That was an Orange Hall." Liam had withdrawn farther into the corner of the backseat, his arms crossed over his chest.

"Looked brown to me." Mary attempted a mild joke, but no one laughed. "I guess I said something wrong?"

"No, no. It's just too near marching season to be a laughing matter. The Orange Orders all march through Catholic areas to celebrate the Protestant victory. Orange sashes fluttering, drums booming; a lot of beer and militant songs. Sort of a 'Ha, ha, our lot beat your lot' thing. Then, of course, the Catholics march. Hibernian Lodges with *green* sashes."

Mary had the picture. "And the Catholics throw petrol bombs at the orange sashes, and the Protestants throw petrol bombs at the green sashes."

"Something like that," Gareth said.

"My mother says it didn't use to be like that," Debbie chimed in wistfully. "She said it used to just be a holiday for everybody. Both sides of the street would go watch the parades, then end up at the park with games and food. It was good crack." She took a deep breath and gave a sideways glance at Liam before continuing. "My da took me once before . . ." She swallowed. "My uncle is an Orangeman."

Mary wasn't sure whether the final statement was a challenge or an apology. But she did know this wasn't the result she had hoped to achieve on this outing. She wanted to say something conciliatory but was afraid anything she might say would make the situation worse.

"There it is."

Mary looked in the direction Gareth pointed. Before them a great, gray stone castle spread out over the rocky promontory thrusting into the lough. The high, square keep rose solidly above its walls, on the very spot it had stood for more than eight hundred years since King Henry II granted Ulster to the Norman knight John de Courcy.

"That's the castle Philip's ancestor helped that Gaelic lord escape from."

She looked at the drop from the sheer rock walls. "That's amazing."

Gareth pulled into the car park below the castle walls and glanced at his watch. "Ah, that's grand. We've time before the castle closes." He locked the car and set the alarm, as Mary had noted everyone always took care to do.

Just as she started up the stone steps leading to the castle, Mary noted the round blue plaque on a stone pillar. "To commemorate the landing of King William III at this pier on 14th June 1690." On the other side of the walkway a statue of King Billy stood atop a similar stone column. Neither monument was anything more than a straightforward marking of an historical event, but after the uncomfortable conversation in the car, Mary was glad everyone hurried through the gatehouse, across the outer ward, and up to the keep.

"Oh, look!" Debbie pointed to the center of the hall where a carpet formed a giant game board. "Snakes and Ladders! Come on, Liam." She bounded across the floor and picked up a die the size of a box. She gave it a toss. "Three. Ha! A ladder on my first roll." She moved her marker, and Liam reached for the die.

Mary was on her third roll when a chattering, laughing group entered the great hall. It was Ann, Jeffrey, and their friends. Mary introduced Liam and Debbie, and in moments the young people were all giggling as their markers climbed ladders only to be eaten by snakes.

"We're going to the Knight Ride next. Want to come with us?" Jeffrey offered a general invitation.

Mary started to ask what that was, but Gareth said to the young people, "Brilliant. You go on. I want to show Mary more of the castle. We'll meet you later."

"Sure. After the ride we'll go to the wee coffee house right across the street." Jeffrey waved, and the young people started for the door.

The room was suddenly quiet.

Gareth looked around, an enormous grin on his face. "There're great views from the next floor." He grabbed her hand and led the way to a spiral staircase.

They stood on a narrow balcony looking out over the harbor. Gareth put his arm comfortably around Mary's shoulder. "Carrickfergus—the rock of Fergus. King Fergus MacErc was shipwrecked here on his way across the water. Remember Fergus MacErc, who led the Scots to Scotland and founded Dalriada?"

"Sure do." A breeze blew her hair, and for a moment Mary pictured herself once again standing atop DunAdd—the spot where Scotland was born. "Gareth . . ."

She wanted to ask if he would be going back to Scotland when the summer was over. If she would be going back with him. He had said more than once that he loved her—beautiful words. But he had made no attempt to settle their futures.

"The *Titanic* sailed right past here on her way to her maiden voyage. She was built in Belfast."

"Mm." Mary made interested sounds, but she didn't want to talk about anything sinking. She felt as if that was exactly what everything around her was doing.

Gareth put a finger under her chin and lifted her face to look straight at him—a sight she never tired of. "Mary, I know this is all wrong. I wanted a nice dinner with roses and violins, but it seems there's never any time and—" He stuck his hand in his pocket and pulled out a small box. "And the fact of the matter is, I've carried this in my pocket for three days now, and I just canna wait any longer. Mary, will ye marry me?"

For weeks she had tried to arrange a time for them to talk, to sort out all the uncertainties. And now, suddenly, there were no uncertainties. All the trouble and violence around them seemed to dissolve in the mists. There, high on the edge of a centuries-old castle, as the sun sank toward the west behind them, tinging sky and water peach and gold, her questions and doubts dropped away.

Will you marry me? For four years there had never been a doubt but that that was exactly what she wanted to do.

Somewhere in the castle, musicians began playing a Celtic tune on panpipes and flute. Across the lough the evening mist rose, and lights came on around the harbor.

"Yes, Gareth. Yes. With all my heart."

He opened the box and took out the most beautiful cloddagh ring Mary had ever seen. In traditional style, two hands held a heart topped by a crown. But this one was handcrafted of heavy gold. Inside the band were the deeply engraved initials MH and GL. And a row of tiny emeralds encircled the band.

"Gareth, it's beautiful. I've never seen anything like it."

"I had it made special. Rings banded with stones are called Eternity Rings here."

She smiled. Yes. Eternity. She would cherish Gareth's love forever.

He took her left hand and slipped it on her fourth finger. "To have and to hold, as long as we both shall live."

She wasn't sure how long they stood clasped in one another's arms, encircled with gentle mist and lilting music, but when they turned to go in, their arms still around each other, the red had faded from the sky, and silver lights encircled the water.

"I expect we'd better catch up with the YP."

Mary had forgotten everything but the wonder of their love and the beauty round about. But now duty awaited them.

The coffee house rang with lively conversation and rock music. Mary squinted against the bright lights. Liam waved to them from the counter where he and Debbie were waiting to order.

Debbie surveyed the menu. "Hey, they have sticky toffee pudding!" She clapped her hands.

"Mm. My favorite." Liam grinned.

"Is it really? Really your favorite?"

"Yeah, it is."

"Brilliant. It's mine too."

A few minutes later they were giggling over thick squares of rich brown pudding, slathered with gooey toffee sauce. Mary couldn't believe these were the same two young people who had been at loggerheads a few hours earlier.

Mary's own pudding sat untouched after her first bite. She was too happy to eat. And in this mercurial land she wanted to savor every moment of beauty and peace. Gareth had been holding her left hand, but now she pulled it out of his grasp and placed it on the table so nonchalantly that every eye turned to it.

Debbie squealed. Ann hugged her. Jeffrey went to the front of the room and called for attention. "We've got an engagement to announce!" He held out his hand, and Mary and Gareth stood to applause and cheers. The guitarist struck up a familiar tune, and soon everyone in the room was singing "When Irish Eyes Are Smiling."

The joy and good will lasted until they took Debbie home. She directed them to a quiet street of brick row houses just off Skegoneill Avenue. Here the curbs were painted red, white, and blue, and all the murals featured Union Jacks, the red hand of Ulster, and such slogans as Who Will Defend Ulster?

A man was approaching the door as Debbie got out.

She thanked Gareth and Mary. "I had a great time. It was really good crack. Bye, Liam." Then she called to the dark-suited man in the bowler hat. "Hi, Uncle Billy!"

When he turned, Mary saw the Orange sash.

Liam's punching the back of her seat didn't hit Mary nearly as hard as the wave of anger she felt behind her. They drove past one of the overweening walls, taller than the buildings it separated, known as a "peace wall"—although it was a symbol of anything but peace. Then they turned along Falls Road and drove through neighborhoods that looked almost exactly like Debbie's except that the curbs were orange and green and slogans urged Free Ulster and Brits Go Home.

"Here. This corner."

They stopped. Liam got out and started to walk away.

Mary couldn't let him just leave without another word, not when things had been so good for a while. "Liam."

He stopped.

"Thanks for coming."

He shrugged and walked off.

"Oh, Gareth. Do you think he'll come back to the Centre? Why was he so angry?"

"I'm sure there are lots of reasons for the anger. But seeing Debbie's uncle in his Orange Lodge outfit seemed to trigger it."

Mary sighed. Just when she thought they were making some progress. Just when she thought she was beginning to understand. Well, at least she now knew who King Billy was. Tonight she would start Philip's story about him.

She would rather just sit and daydream about the future with Gareth. But he was meeting Philip to go over a report. She might as well try to do something constructive.

GENERATION THREE

THE ASCENDANCY
1689–1788

Thy name, O Lord, endureth for ever;
and thy memorial, O Lord,
throughout all generations. . . .
And this day shall be unto you
for a memorial;
And ye shall keep it a feast to the Lord
throughout your generations.

Psalm 135:13
Exodus 12:14

33

"'Then Christian was afraid, and thought also himself to go back.'" David paused and cleared his throat. No matter how beautiful the truths of *The Pilgrim's Progress* were, this was a topic toward which he did not wish to turn Janet's thoughts.

"Do go on, husband. It is a wonderful story." She turned her head toward him. Her cheeks were as pale as the fine linen pillowcase.

"Indeed, it is." He lowered his eyes to the thick ivory paper. "'He thought nothing but death was before him.'"

Janet sighed and smiled softly as Christian, trembling for fear of the lions, approached the Porter.

"'I am come from the City of Destruction, and am going to Mount Zion . . .'" David read on, the steady timbre of his voice apparently soothing to his wife, whose restless movements stilled. But it did not calm his own worries.

As if it wasn't enough to have his beloved Janet in such pain, Graham—their only son—had just announced he was not going to university. Instead, he would remain at home and run the farm with Uncle Malcolm—David's older brother, who had inherited Lanarks' Bawn and its considerable leases from their father.

"'This house was built by the Lord of the hill, and He built it for the relief and security of pilgrims.'" The Porter answered Christian's questions, but no one could answer David's questions about his worries that extended far beyond Lanarks' Bawn.

Indeed, all Ulster held their breath as they looked across the water and beyond. Their troubles came not, as they were accustomed to, merely from England. Now all Europe was ready to ignite in the flame of war. William of Orange, Stadtholder of Holland, prepared to invade England. James II had raised an army of Irish Catholics to protect his throne. Louis XIV of France was invading William's Holland. Germany rallied to Holland's defense.

And now word had come that King James had fled to France. The English aristocracy, unable to defend themselves, had offered the throne of England to William, who was married to James's daughter.

David struggled to put such concerns out of his mind and to focus on his reading.

> "The Lord of the hill had been a great warrior, and had fought with and slain him that had the power of death, but not without great danger to Himself. . . . 'I believe,' said Christian, 'He did it with the loss of much blood. But that which puts the glory of grace into all He did was that He did it out of pure love.'"

So, with all Europe up in arms, what of Ireland? With Catholic James uniting with French Louis and looking to the Catholic Irish for support, what would that mean to Ulster Protestants? Was the peace they had known for almost forty years to be torn in bloody conflict?

Janet's thin hand moved across the covers in search of David's. The feel of what seemed little more than a few twigs brought a wrench to his heart. What need had he to worry about struggles of life and death further afield?

> "Thus they discoursed together till late at night; and, after they had committed themselves to their Lord for protection, they betook themselves to rest. The Pilgrim slept in a large upper chamber, whose window opened toward the sunrising. The name of the chamber was Peace . . ."

David turned at an insistent knocking at the door. "Come."

The stocky form of his man, Miles, filled the doorway. His round, ruddy face was more flushed than usual. "Sir . . . er . . . Mr. David. It's important, sir."

David brushed Janet's cheek with the back of his finger as he stood. "Send for Fanny to sit with her mistress." He strode into the hall and closed the door behind him. "What is it, man?"

The servant, his boots caked with mud and the wide cuff of his plain brown coat freshly stained with sweat from his horse, held out a rumpled sheet of paper. "I've been in Comber, sir. The whole town is astir."

David took the document but looked over his shoulder toward Janet's door as a caution to Miles to say nothing that might be overheard. From long practice he was able to descend the scrubbed wooden stairs almost silently in spite of his haste.

In the security of the front parlor he gave his full attention to the paper his servant had brought to him in such a pelter. It bore yesterday's date, 3 December 1688, and was addressed to Lord Mount-Alexander:

Good my Lord, I have written to you to let you know that all our Irishmen through Ireland are sworn that on the ninth day of this month they are to fall on to kill and murder man, wife, and child; and I desire your Lordship to take care of yourself.

David's first instinct was to crumple the paper and throw it across the room. This was ridiculous. An illiterate hoax. "Where did this come from?"

"Found in Comber, sir. Lyin' in the High Street where the villain dropped it."

"Who found it?"

"I couldn't rightly say, Mr. David. Copies like this are circulating everywhere."

"Do people believe it's authentic?"

"There's some as say yea and some as say nay. But the Reverend Mr. Houston has called the gentry to a meeting tonight, sir. Knew you'd want to attend. That is, unless Mr. Malcolm—"

David made a scoffing noise. "You know the answer to that, Miles. My brother cares so desperately for the land that he wouldn't lift a finger to protect it. If I catch any of those pacifist Quakers hanging around here, I'll give them what for."

"Aye. But they're mighty fine linen weavers, sir."

"And a fat lot of good it'll do them when the Catholics rise up in the middle of the night to strangle the whole pacifistic lot. Throttle us all with thread from their own looms most likely." David ran a hand abruptly through his sandy hair. "God forgive my lack of charity. They are good people. May they long have the privilege of being so, even if at the expense of others defending them."

He looked again at the paper he had crumpled. Was this a poor joke? An attempt to inflame Protestant feelings against the Irish? Or an honest warning? Apparently Mr. Houston, the forceful Scots minister of Newtownards, was taking it seriously. And one did not dismiss lightly what the leader of the Covenanters decreed to be important in any area of life.

"I shall attend this meeting, Miles. But do not speak a word of this to anyone. Do you hear me?"

"Master Graham, sir—"

"I shall see to informing my son. But I will not have this matter talked about. I do not want word of it to reach my wife. I will not have her worried. Do you understand?"

"Aye, sir. But I fancy she worries anyway—"

"Of course, she worries. There's aught all to worry about!" David strode from the room and slammed the door behind him. Then he regretted his hasty action. The noise would disturb Janet.

He approached the top of the stairs, treading softly, just as the door was flung open and Fanny charged out carrying a bowl of vinegar water. She stopped so abruptly the water sloshed down the front of her white apron. The blonde curls escaping around the edges of her white cap were at odds with the plainness of her bucktoothed face. Her thin, large-boned frame delineated a woman that would have made a good farmer's wife—should any farmer have spoken for her. Perhaps there would be someone when her work here was done.

"Is your mistress still awake?"

"Aye, sir. And just as sweet as always. A saint she is. My mistress and me was just talking of the old days in Derry. If I may say so, sir, she'd never ask it, but I fancy a visit from her mother would come a comfort for her."

"Yes, thank you, Fanny. We'll see what can be done." Whatever next? Still, he might be able to arrange something. Unless the Irish rose and slaughtered them all in their beds first.

He entered the hushed room, and, as always, the smile on Janet's thin lips spoke only of her love, never of complaint for the pain that he knew tore at her stomach. "I must be gone this evening. There is a meeting of the gentry about affairs of the county."

"Aye, husband. You must do your duty. Never think to be detained by me. I have all I need."

And he knew she meant it.

The door clicked shut, and Janet closed her eyes. Consciousness of the room around her faded immediately. Even awareness of the burning in her stomach paled as she focused her thoughts upward.

When she had been forced to take to her bed more than a year ago, she at first thought she would go crazy. All knew Janet Lanark as the hardest worker in the parish. Her chickens laid the largest eggs, her rabbits were the fattest, her household the best run. One would never find weak ale, stale bread, or a speck of dust anywhere in Lanarks' Bawn. Many said Malcolm had not bothered to take a wife, because he could never find a match for his brother's. And then there were those who said that any woman Malcolm might have looked at would have been scared off at the thought of coming under the scrutiny of Janet Lanark's sharp eye. But perhaps that was unfair. People will talk so.

In the past months, however, increased weakness had forced Janet first to give over care of her hares and poultry and then her household duties to her cousin Hannah, who had come from Belfast to help out. Janet could keep going against the pain, but the weakness defeated her. And it was a kindness to the maiden Hannah, who had lived on suffrage in the home of her elder brother. Knowing that Hannah was happier here helped Janet accept the inevitable.

The greatest blow to her pride was having to accept the well-meaning but awkward ministrations of Fanny. That she who had always been the first up, her soft hair smoothed under a crisp cap, a clean white apron covering the skirt of her fine linen dress, and well into her work before even the servants stirred—that she should now be reduced to having another bathe her and change her linen . . .

Janet turned her head on the pillow and rejected the thought. *Father, forgive me. I would not question. I would not complain. Help me not to sin by wishing Your will for me were otherwise. Help me to submit more fully to Your sovereign will. Help me to draw closer to You in my state of enforced quiet. Help me to use my time more profitably by praying ever better for my husband and my son.*

Janet was only dimly aware of Fanny's reentering the room and adjusting the window shade. Her whole being was now focused on her sovereign Lord and God, whose will for His creatures was perfect and whose perfect will for her David and Graham was all she asked.

She spent many hours a day praying for her loved ones. And she perceived that in doing so she accomplished far more for them than she had when her time was consumed in cooking and spinning and sewing for them.

Yet, in spite of her fervent prayers, she was aware of the tensions between father and son. She did not understand why it was so. What could be the cause of such friction? She might never know, but she knew that she would die happy if all could be well with David and Graham.

In the courtyard below Janet's window, David sprang into the saddle of the horse Miles had readied for him. They were just exiting the gateway of the bawn when they encountered Malcolm and Graham coming up the road with a wagon stacked high with bricks of peat.

Graham pulled the team to a halt. "Oh, Father, we've just been to the high field." He tipped his head toward the rising slopes of Scrabo. "Uncle Malcolm's new tup is doing his work grand. We'll have a fine time of lambing next season."

"Aye." David's older brother nodded with satisfaction. "Wool. That's where the profit is. Won't be long before we can build a fine new house beyond the bawn. No need to be living in a fortress these days."

David ground his teeth and bit back the hot answer he would like to make. How anyone so good in matters of land and animals could be as dense in the ways of the world as his brother never ceased to anger him beyond expression. And that his own son should choose to follow Malcolm rather than himself! He ground his tooth.

Knowing the futility of exploding at Malcolm, David rounded on the boy. "Aye. It's a fine thing ye'll have your sheep. That's all you'll have." Even as his anger rose, Graham's blue-eyed fairness, so like his mother's, tore at David's heart.

"Must we go over that again, Father? University would be a waste of three years that I might spend learning all I need to know here."

David eyed the wagon. "Aye. Cutting turf like a peasant."

"Father, you know I just have no desire to follow you in Parliament or the military—"

"Enough." The note of pleading in Graham's voice irritated David even more than his words. "We'll none of us have any lands or careers to worry about if there's another rising."

Malcolm guffawed. "Rising? What alarmist talk is this, brother? Surely you jest."

"The Reverend Houston is taking it seriously, so it behooves all Christians to do the same." David informed his brother of the Comber letter and the meeting he was going to. Then he jerked his head toward the farm of their nearest neighbor along Scrabo Road. "I shall leave it to you to inform the Prices, if you'd be so good."

Michael Price was little over half a century old but seemed a full hundred. His small, wizened appearance gave credence to the stories of his having been stolen by gypsies in his infancy. He had kept to himself ever since the smallpox carried off both of his sons, the oldest son's wife, and Michael's only daughter in the space of two months. He'd been left with a brood of rowdy grandchildren who seemed to be growing up with less discipline than the wild Irish.

"He'll take little enough notice of the warning, but he should be told. It's only fair to Sheila."

Michael's half sister kept house for him with some help from the oldest child, Molly, and exercised what little control existed over her great-nieces and nephews. Keeping that house was all Sheila had known her entire life. Her mother, Katrina, had died at Sheila's birth. All said it was due to injuries she had suffered in the '41 rising. It seemed a mighty hardness on Robert Price—who was a good man—as his first wife, Michael's mother, had been killed in the rising as well.

"Aye." Malcolm nodded his broad-brimmed hat. "They can take shelter inside the bawn if it comes to it." He jumped from the wagon, the skirts of his long coat flapping. "I'll walk across the field. Take the peat on in and stack it against the north wall of the bawn, lad."

David watched Malcolm set out across the field with as placid an air as if they had no more than exchanged pleasantries. The man was a fool. And Graham wanted to be just like him.

He looked at his son. "Take care of your mother. I'll return as soon as I may—but these things can drag on."

"Yes, Father. I will." The boy's clear blue eyes met his openly. "You can count on me." He hesitated and shifted on the wagon seat. "I would make you proud of me, Father. If I could." Again, there was a note of pleading in his voice.

"Aye." David nodded his farewell.

Graham clucked to his horses, and the wagon rattled on up the lane.

David dug his heels into Trapper's flanks. Graham was a good lad. He would take good care of his mother. He would be a good help to Malcolm. But he would not prepare to join the militia. He would not prepare to take his father's seat in Parliament. He would not go to university. He would throw it all away—all David's dreams for his only child, his son and heir—throw it all away to cut peat and scrutch flax and raise lambs. Yet he was a good lad.

The horses' hooves thudded hollowly on the frozen earth of the road to Newtownards. Their steady rhythm calmed him. The horses' warm, moist breath made puffs of white as it met the chill air. The land lay low and green beneath an iron gray sky.

They were some way along the road before his servant broke the silence. "Er, Mr. David, sir, do you reckon we ought to tell *them*? Er, that is . . . what I mean is . . ."

David looked at the faded splendor of Seaton Court, which they were nearing. "What you mean, Miles, is that my distant cousin Gavin is a Lanark—at least in name. Even if he is now serving in James's Catholic army." He rode steadily past the deeply rutted turnoff to the house and continued on past the overgrown hedgerows. "Ye'd be suggesting that I should tell him of the rising so he could be first in line to slit our throats?"

"Sir, you don't think—"

"Of course, I do. Murdering, thieving lot. Never met a Seaton Court Lanark I'd trust at my back. And don't you start on like that milksop son of mine—thinks I should take steps to mend the feud. He'll think it's mended when he feels their steel between his ribs."

David prodded Trapper to a brisk trot.

It all started when Rory Lanark took a papist bride and went to Seaton Court—taking with him that which rightfully belonged to the bawn. And then Rory's grandson Gavin had been bewitched by a pair of dark eyes in a pretty face and married a connection of the Tyrone Guilford's—a connection that was Old English and Catholic. David scowled. To think that, of the three Catholic families in the vicinity, one of them should be his own second cousin—a fact not overlooked by David's enemies when he stood for Parliament. But he had won over his opponent from Donaghadee anyway, because all knew of David Lanark's strict Presbyterian uprightness.

He heard the sound of laughing voices on the other side of the hedgerow and turned to see three of the Seaton Court brood gallop across the field on a motley assortment of ponies. How many children did they have? It was little wonder that Seaton Court had gone to rack and ruin, what with Gavin's careless ways and so many mouths to feed. And yet whenever he encountered any of them, they always seemed to be laughing.

God had promised to inflict punishment on the children of those who hate Him down to the third and fourth generation. So why were these larcenous papists so happy—and so numerous—while he, who kept all the Law and the Prophets and saw that his household did the same, had one disappointing son and a dying wife?

Riding on past his cousin's weedy field dotted with gently grazing sheep, David thought on the passage Mr. Stevenson had expounded on just last Sunday. The minister had carried the service into its third hour on the words from Jeremiah:

> And hast given them this land, which thou didst swear to their fathers to give them, a land flowing with milk and honey; and they came in, and possessed it; but they obeyed not thy voice, neither walked in thy law; they have done nothing of all that thou commandedst them to do: therefore thou hast caused all this evil to come upon them.

The first part was clear enough to David—an obvious parallel to Ulster, a land given by God to their fathers, a land they—the Presbyterians—had possessed. It was the second part that puzzled him. How could it be charged that these sturdy Ulster Scots had failed to obey God's voice? They had obeyed all the commandments. They were good churchmen. They were good Protestants.

And yet it did seem that evil was about to come upon them. How could that be? What could God possibly find wanting in a people so upright?

It was late afternoon before they reached the low, thatched building situated between Greenwell and Movilla Streets that housed the Presbyterian congregation. Miles took Trapper's reins and went off to find stabling.

Discussion was already under way when David took his place on one of the front pews. He quickly caught the drift of the debate:

Should Sir Robert Colville be invited to join their public safety committee?

A small, black-clad man was speaking. "Aye, 'tis true enough that Captain Colville owns the land we all of us takes our livelihood from. None would slight him in matters of wealth and power. But, gentlemen, he is not one of us. I have it on the best authority that he comes from low origins. *And* he worships with the prelacy."

David sat back in his seat with a groan. He had hoped that the plans for defense could be drawn quickly. He had hoped to return home this evening. But he could see that debate over the makeup of the committee could go on indefinitely. Ownership of the vast Montgomery lands had passed to the Colvilles a generation ago when the young earl of Mount-Alexander had fallen hopelessly in debt and sold the land to Robert Colville. The community looked askance at their parvenu landlord.

Apparently Mr. Houston shared David's frustration over the pace of the deliberation. He thudded his fist sharply on the table at which he sat.

The droning speaker jumped, gave a curt nod, and sat down.

"Thank you, gentlemen," Houston said. "So I believe we are agreed then, that, in spite of the reservations of some"—he gave the recent speaker a sharp look—"the serious nature of the present exigency behooves us to set aside our differences and work together for the safety of our families."

"Hear, hear." David led the assenting voices.

"Hearing no objection, then . . ." Houston glared at the solemn faces of the ten men in the room, daring anyone to object. "Good. We are in agreement that Sir Robert is to be invited to our meeting." He appointed a committee of three to take word to Sir Robert Colville. While they were about that duty, the rest of the committee would retire to the inn across from the Market House for hearty mutton pie. It would be long into the early hours of the following morning before the final decisions were made.

Colville more than justified the wisdom of his inclusion in the defensive plans by pledging to raise a regiment from his tenants. They would join the confederate forces of Antrim and Down under the overall command of the earl of Mount-Alexander. "And I can promise you, gentlemen, we'll give that lying Dick Talbot what for." Colville slapped his buff-breeched thighs and flipped the tails of his green coat. He sat down to cheers from the committee.

Richard Talbot, head of the Catholic forces in Ireland, was doing his best in Dublin to pursue King James's policy of de-Protestantizing Ireland. Colville, who was conservative enough in his religion in spite of his ties with the established church, pursued an independent political line. He had served for some time, attempting to mediate between the Dublin government and the Protestant gentry of the north. The situation now, however, had gone beyond the bounds of mediation. Now men would be sharpening their swords and cleaning their firearms.

Then they moved on to the wider matter of raising all Ulster, for the threat was not just to County Down. Even as they spoke, the clerk for the proceedings dipped his freshly sharpened quill in the inkpot and began making another copy of the infamous Comber letter. As soon as there was enough light to make the roads passable, copies would be taken to Belfast, to Garvagh, to Limavady, and to Derry. These must be warned. It was now the early hours of 5 December. The letter had set 9 December as the day when the Irish were "to fall on to kill and murder man, wife, and child."

The extreme urgency meant that the message should be carried by no mere postboy but by committee members themselves. Houston's orders were clear. The situation must be taken seriously, but not *too* seriously. They must take action without causing panic. And they must act together.

David moved his legs restlessly. If they would just settle this matter, he could be out of here and on his way home. Never mind that the roads were as black as the sky. He would rouse Miles from his bed at the inn and order him to light a torch. He could be home in time to greet Janet when she woke—always her best time, if the doctor's poppy syrup had produced a night of sleep. Then he could oversee the Bible reading and prayers, which Malcolm would be inclined to let slide without the firm hand of the younger brother.

And he must see to securing the bawn. Its stone walls would count for little if the gates were not kept locked, a practice that had fallen into disuse of late. The hinges must be oiled, every speck of rust rubbed from lock and key, sentinels set to watch from each of the corner towers.

He grimaced at the thought of Janet's chickens and rabbits occupying the south tower—and Malcolm's dogs, kenneled in the east. Such laxness really would not do. Kirk discipline for parents who allowed their children to play on the Sabbath or for men who beat their wives on the Sabbath was all very well. People must be kept to the straight and narrow path. But such strictures were not enough. Military precautions were necessary as well.

"Right, then." Mr. Houston thumped the table again. Several nodding heads jerked upright. "Right. All's settled except a volunteer to carry the warning to Derry." Houston's piercing eyes rested on David.

"Aye, sir. I'd not be one to shirk my duty. All in this room know that. But my wife is that sick. And—"

Even as he voiced his protest, Fanny's words came to him—*A visit from her mother would be a fair comfort.* Was this the voice of God directing him to go to Derry? He could accomplish two goods at once.

He cleared his throat. "That is, yes. I'll go."

34

David entered Londonderry late in the evening two days later, almost dead in his saddle from endless hours of riding over eighty miles of frozen earth. He had broken his journey for only a few hours of sleep and a hot meal after rounding the top of Lough Neagh the night before. This day he had spent urging the indefatigable Trapper forward and reminding Miles to keep a sharp lookout over each shoulder.

The thousands of woodkerne that had plagued this area with daily robberies and murders in earlier generations had been brought under control when Derry was handed over to the Corporation of London in 1613, renamed Londonderry, and planted with a large colony of Protestants. Since then, Londonderry had been repeatedly fortified as the chief place of refuge for the colonists of the Ulster plantation.

So it was not for fear of Gaelic outlaws that David had armed his servant, carefully polished his own sidearm, and refilled the powder box that he wore strapped to his chest. The Comber letter had warned against a rising of native Irish, but David felt far more concern for an attack from the duly sworn forces of King James II. All garrisons had been ordered to surrender to His Majesty. All but two had complied: Enniskillen and Londonderry. Neither James nor his chief deputy were likely to take such defiance lightly.

David and Miles took the ferry across the River Foyle and entered Ferryquay Gate. At the portal, David looked up, noting the heavy black iron portcullis held up by a rope wound around a wheel so that it could be dropped at a moment's notice. Inside, he looked as well at the thickness of the stone wall surrounding the city and the thick, iron-mounted timbers of the gate itself. Londonderry well deserved its fame as the best-fortified city in Ireland.

Trapper's footsteps clopped steadily but with a slowness that proclaimed the animal's fatigue. Just before they reached the diamond, David turned along one of the rabbit warren tracks leading off the main street. He stopped before the third in a row of narrow front doors in houses whose top stories overhung the street. A thin line of light escaped beneath the tightly shuttered windows. He handed Trapper's reins to Miles and mounted the steps.

At last a candle-bearing old woman wrapped in a thick shawl opened the door a crack but did not say a word.

"Please inform Mistress Cole that her good-son is arrived."

The door flew open, and the candle wobbled dangerously in the gnarled hand. "Oh, sir—sir, you've not come to tell us . . . oh, lackaday, lackaday!"

"No, no, woman." David pushed his way into the narrow entrance hall. "My wife lives. At least she did when I left home two days ago. But whether I shall survive such wailing is another matter. Please be so good as to show me to your mistress."

"Oh, yes, by all means. Oh, it is good that you've come, Master Lanark. We have been so worried—with Miss Janet taken so poorly and that papist Tyrconnell vowing to drive all God-fearing Christians out of Ireland, and . . . oh dear, oh dear, oh dear."

When a sharp breeze all but extinguished the candle, David closed the door with the heel of his boot, and the slam interrupted the woman's woeful recitation. "It is precisely such difficulties I have come about, Esther. But we shall accomplish little nattering on here. Where is Mistress Cole?"

"Oh, yes sir. Forgive a foolish old woman. I do take on so. It's just that—"

"Yes, yes. Quite. This way, is it?" David started for the staircase.

"Yes sir. Yes, my mistress is in her sitting room. Here now, whatever am I thinking of? Let me light the way." Esther held her candle aloft, dripping tallow on the stairs as she clambered stiffly upward.

In contrast to the considerably older Esther, Margaret Cole sat plump and calm before a small peat fire, her feet on a round stool and her brown terrier, Peedie, on her knees. She calmly bade him sit before the fire and ordered Esther to bring them refreshment. David had never appreciated his wife's mother's tranquil good sense more than at that moment.

The cake crumbs remaining on a tray on the side table told David that these would not be Margaret Cole's first fortification of the evening. "Thank you, ma'am. But I left my servant in the street. If Esther could just show him where to stable the horses and provide a bite of supper for him too?"

The order was given with a wave of Margaret's hand. "Now tell me of my daughter and grandson, Mr. Lanark."

He gave as objective a report as he could.

"It is a great pity. I do not believe my daughter will recover in this life. But her spirit is at peace?"

"Very much at peace. It seems that her serenity grows daily. If only it could infuse the rest of us."

"That will come." She selected the largest cake crumb and fed it to Peedie. "But, glad as I am of your visit, I do not think you have come all this way in tearing haste—two days, did you say?—to give me a report of my daughter."

David dipped his head in assent. "As you guess, I have business. It will take me a day or two. When that is executed, I would have you return to Comber with me. My Janet would be much comforted to see her mother."

"As I to see her. You are a good man, David Lanark." Margaret Cole's dark eyes snapped in her round face. Her quick assent to setting out on such a journey in the middle of winter showed that she was not so indolent as she appeared.

"Fine. I will instruct my man to secure a carriage and help with any arrangements you require while I am at my business. Could you be ready to travel in three days' time?"

Esther entered with a tray of cold meat and cheese as he spoke. At hearing his question, she shook the tray with such alarm that David jumped to his feet to rescue his supper from certain disaster.

"Oh, you can't mean it, sir. You'd not have my mistress travel when there's papists about! We'll be slaughtered in our beds, we will. I well remember the winter of '41. More than a hundred thousand Christians slaughtered in one night, they was. And I was just a girl, but I knew my commandments and my psalms and the Lord's Prayer and—"

"I'm sure you were very properly instructed, Esther." David heaped a pewter plate with bread, meat, and pickle, then leaned forward to thrust a poker into the red coals in the fireplace. After a moment, he put the glowing end of the stick into his mug of cider, then sat back in his chair to enjoy the warm drink.

"I believe you have little to fear at the moment." It was well that she had no notion of the letter he would tomorrow present to the Derry city council. "The roads are quite passable—evidence my having just passed over them myself. And as a captain of the militia, I am quite qualified to protect you from bandits should you be so good as to accompany your mistress." He considered whether pulling back his coat and revealing his firearms would comfort or upset her.

But there was no need to make the decision. Esther all but threw herself on her mistress's bosom. "Oh, Mistress Cole, you know I'd never leave you. I have no fears for myself. I was thinking only of your comfort. I'd not see you set off to the other side of Ulster without me. I pride myself that I always know my duty."

Margaret moved her a pace backward while protecting Peedie from being knocked from her lap. "Indeed, Esther, I do appreciate that. Your presence will be a great comfort to me. Now you must go see to the comfort of Captain Lanark's man."

David smiled as he chewed a bite of thick, crusty brown bread and propped his feet on the fire irons. His Janet had inherited her perfectionist energy from her father, who had been killed in defending Londonderry against the 1649 siege by Royalist forces. The town held out for twenty weeks. Troops loyal to Cromwell finally broke the siege, but Captain Cole had been killed in the last battle. Yes, Janet's forcefulness had come from Edward Cole, but her calm good sense, which lasted when her physical strength was gone, had come from her mother. He would be glad indeed for Margaret Cole's presence at Lanarks' Bawn.

All would be well if he could, as he had so blithely promised, get these women from the city before there should be a rising and then secure their journey across three counties. He feared, though, that Esther Randall had more of the truth of the matter than he cared to admit. And tomorrow he must somehow convince the aldermen of Londonderry of the danger they faced—without causing panic in the citizenry.

He shuddered at the thought of what his failure could produce: Women such as Margaret Cole slaughtered in their parlors. Women such as Esther Randall running hysterically in the streets. He must use all his skills as a parliamentary and military strategist tomorrow, or the results could be dire indeed.

The next day as he faced the hastily assembled political and religious leaders of the city, David's feeling that his task was not to be an easy one was reinforced. He recalled Houston's directive that, whatever they did, the leaders must act together. The prospect of getting these authorities to act together—indeed, to act at all—seemed dimmer and dimmer the longer they debated.

John Campsie, who had been removed from his office of mayor as part of the policy to drive all English and Scottish out of Ireland and to replace Protestantism with the old faith, sat beside Ezekiel Hopkins, Bishop of Derry. David immediately sized them both up as weak men. He cast a disgusted glance at the red heels of Campsie's shoes and wanted to bark at the man to quit running his fingers along the edge of his shoulder-length black wig.

"I tell you, gentlemen"—David tried again to push his hearers to action—"I would not have ridden pell-mell across the breadth of Ulster if I did not believe the threat to be serious. The Comber committee has taken precautions for the defense of our property in Down. I beg you to do likewise."

Bishop Hopkins, whose seat was in the cathedral where they met and so must be afforded a place in the proceedings, adjusted his lawn and lace cravat and cleared his throat. "I'm sure we all appreciate the efforts you have taken on our behalf, but I can see no cause for alarm. I'm sure that, even new come to our city as you are, you have noticed the excellence of our city walls. Indeed, no other such fortifications exist in all Ireland. Tyrconnell and his rebels have plenty to do without attempting our defenses."

Several bewigged heads nodded sagely.

"No!" The Reverend Mr. George Walker, in a black coat with unadorned white bands at the neck, jumped up from his pew. "No! We must not rely on brick and stone to do our work. No man ever accomplished more with stone and mortar than did King Solomon. And yet it was counted as evil against him that he failed to stop the idolatry of his day. We must never consider surrendering to superstitious idolaters."

Alderman Alexander Tomkins was next. "Gentlemen, we must consider our families. I think of my own wife and newborn daughter and of my three sons, the oldest of whom has just taken his apprenticeship. I would not have my family threatened. I say we must take precautions."

Again the sedate wagging of heads.

"Aye, take your precautions, man." Bishop Hopkins smoothed the white shirt sleeve extending below the cuff of his coat. "I also have a wife and family, and I'd not have them disturbed by wild rumor."

Campsie followed. "And how much will your son's fine new apprenticeship be worth, Mr. Tomkins, if all our commercial efforts are diverted?"

Rather than having his frustration build at the dragging debate, David allowed his attention to wander. This was the first Protestant cathedral to be built in Europe since the Reformation. He could not suppress his sense of satisfaction at the thought of such distinction belonging to Ulster.

But then he glowered at the high altar, at the reading stand to one side and the pulpit to the other. Such was not right. His ancestors did not fight the Reformation to retain a style of worship that led straight back to idolatry and superstition. Let all who would avoid such heathen practices place their pulpits in the center front of the congregation where all could focus on the preaching of the Word. Scripture only was what pleased God, not the prancing and bowing over sacraments such as went on with prelacy and popery.

The next speaker's words jolted David from his reverie on church architecture and theology. "Mr. Chairman, several of us are scheduled to attend a dinner of the Corporation tonight. I move that we adjourn until tomorrow morning."

Could the worthy alderman not see that, unless measures were taken, there might be no Corporation left with which to dine in the future?

"Gentlemen"—David was on his feet again—"the letter clearly states that the rising is plotted to take place two days from now. Would you be caught fiddling while Rome burns?"

But he might as well have saved his breath to use in blowing out any such fires. The meeting was adjourned. And the next day there was even less progress, if that could be possible. The same feeble arguments were repeated and examined from every side. Fear and apathy alternately drove the discussion.

Very well. Let them natter on until the day of doom and past. David had done all he could do. He had carried the warning posthaste. He had urged defense. But still the aldermen counted the cost to the city of added defenses, while Mr. Walker punctuated the proceedings with Old Testament passages pronounced with apostolic fervor and Bishop Hopkins counseled compromise.

Shadows falling through the round western window of the cathedral warned of the shortening of the hours of another day. Simpson, the fat alderman, was on his feet, surely intending to propose another adjournment for yet another dinner.

Decide what they might, David had determined that tomorrow he would set forth homeward with Margaret Cole. If the warning in the letter proved true, he did not want to be caught with the responsibility of protecting two elderly women inside the walls of one of the two cities that had defied James's order to turn their garrisons over to Tyrconnell. But while there yet remained time to make a difference, he would make one more attempt.

"Gentlemen"—he began even as Simpson took breath to speak—"hear me. Let you do just two things—and let me remind you that if the city is taken unawares and your friends and families slain due to your inaction, it will be on your heads."

Several of his hearers blanched and looked over their shoulders uneasily.

"Let you send word to the governor of Derry, begging him to secure the passes against James's army so that they may not cross the fords to attack us. And let you send to the commander of the garrison to have every bastion at every corner of the wall double-manned and the cannon made ready."

At first light that morning, frustrated beyond any possibility of sleep, David had walked the entire circle of the city wall, built in 1618 to protect the English settlers. The walls had done their work in the '41 rising, providing refuge for some four thousand people. And David saw that they could so serve again—if they were properly prepared and manned.

John Campsie rose to respond to David's request, but the assembly never learned what his response was to be.

There was a thud of heavy doors at the back, and a young voice rang out. "Right this way, Sir George. My father and the others are meeting in here. You can address them all at once. They'll be right glad of your news."

"Thomas?" Alexander Tomkins turned in shock. "What are you doing here, son?" he muttered. "If you're shirking your apprenticeship, you'll deserve the beating you'll get."

Spur-clad boots sounded on the floor tiles. A newcomer followed the lad down the aisle of the cathedral. "It's Sir George Phillips, Father. I was making a delivery by the gate when I heard him asking directions, so I offered to show him the way."

"Yes, yes. That's fine, son. Welcome, Sir George. Now get back to your work, boy." Tomkins's head turned like a swivel as he addressed one and then the other.

Sir George Phillips shook Tomkins's hand. "That's a fine boy you have there. Bright, decisive. Takes initiative. He'll go far. You must be proud of him."

"Rash, that's what he is. Needs to learn to consider before he acts. But I'm glad he could be of service to you, sir."

Tomkins introduced the newcomer, but all there recognized the grandson of Sir Thomas Phillips, who had played a key role in the establishing of Londonderry Plantation.

Phillips brought word that twelve hundred Catholic Redshanks marched toward Londonderry. The Jacobite regiment commanded by Lord Antrim had been ordered to replace the Protestant garrison that controlled the town.

Dire though the news, David smiled. There. That would do the trick. This was more than vaguely threatening words on paper. This was a solid number of marching, uniformed, *armed* men bearing down on the city. Now they would act.

First on his feet was Bishop Hopkins. "Gentlemen, Lord Antrim's troops must be admitted. They represent the law and order of our rightful King James. We cannot resist our crowned monarch without being guilty of treason."

He had not closed his mouth before Parson Walker was on his feet. "Hear the word of the Lord. 'He shall not come into this city, saith the Lord God of Israel. For I will defend this city, to save it, for mine own sake, and for my servant David's sake.'"

"If we cooperate, it may be that King James will restore . . ." It was obvious that top priority in John Campsie's mind was having his mayoralty returned to him.

David rose and walked from St. Columba's Cathedral. He would wait no longer. Tomorrow he would stop in to bid farewell to this municipal debating society, so that he could report to his committee that he had done his best to discharge his duty. Already he had stayed too long.

What if the defenses he had established at the bawn weren't enough? What if the easygoing Malcolm failed to bar the gate properly? What if . . . But he was eighty miles from home. There was nothing he could do. He must do his work here and hope for the best.

At least all was in readiness at Margaret Cole's house. Miles had secured the hire of a fine closed carriage and team that would transport the ladies in comfort. Even Esther had put her flutters aside to see to packing her mistress's trunks. The day girl, who came in to help, was given notice. The elderly man who cared for the garden at the back of the house would still come once a week, and Cook would continue in her downstairs rooms and see that all remained in dust-sheeted order above stairs. They would be well beyond the walls of Derry before any attack could come, whether from wild Irish or from the king's troops.

But on the following morning all did not go as planned. For all her good sense, Margaret Cole overfed Peedie. The smoked trout made him sick. Traveling in a closed carriage with a sick dog was impossible, so they must wait until the attack passed.

And then Esther, who had hardly been outside the city walls since 1641, was overcome with jitters. "My dear papa said God gave us these walls for a defense, and we could trust in them as we trusted in Him. I would not defy God or Papa's memory. If anything should go wrong . . ."

David controlled his impulse to raise his voice. "Nothing will go wrong, Esther. Get your cape on. Please."

But his restraint counted for little, because in the next instant every head in the house was raised as a crash and a series of bump, bump, bumps told him that Miles had dropped a trunk at the top of the first floor stairs. There was little damage done beyond scratching the treads and rail, but in lunging to retrieve the trunk, Miles had sprained his wrist.

David forced his own frustrations aside as Cook bound the swelling wrist. "Take care of that, Miles. I hope you realize how highly I value your work." He meant more than just the excellent effort the fellow put into everything he did. Miles was like a part of David's family.

"No serious harm done. I shall drive the carriage myself, and you can serve as outrider." He did not add, "Thank God it was the left wrist." Miles could be called upon to shoot with his right hand.

But they would leave town a few hours behind schedule. David walked to the door. "I'll be back from the livery stable within the hour. I'll ask them to lend me a boy to help with the loading. Rest that arm, Miles."

The carriage stood in front of Pilcher's livery barn. A fine vehicle it was, just right for their purposes. Except that it sat on only three wheels. The fourth corner was propped on a block of wood.

The stable owner met him, wringing his hands. "I don't know how to explain it, sir. Franklin here's a new apprentice." He boxed the ears of a broad-shouldered lad of thirteen or fourteen. "Said he could handle a team." He shook his fist at the boy. "You lie to me once more, and I'll break your apprenticeship, you young hooligan."

The boy shifted his shoulders and now David saw welts under his homespun shirt.

But young Franklin did not cower. "I am sorry, sir. I've driven many teams on the farm, but these spooked, and I misjudged the height of the kerb stone." He turned to David. "It's my fault, sir. I am sorry."

"Here now, that's enough answering back." Pilcher raised his hand again.

But David intervened. "When will the wheel be fixed? I would like to start as soon as possible. Is there another carriage I can hire?"

"Only others are those two open ones." Pilcher gestured to the back wall. "I'd lend you my own if I had such a thing."

Stuffing down his frustration, David went to the cathedral, where the council debate continued.

Alderman Simpson was on his feet. "See, gentlemen, you can believe what we've been telling you. You can put your faith in the voice of reason. This is the dreaded ninth of December. Where is the rising? Have any of you been threatened? Have any of you seen a single Redshank?" He paused dramatically. "Does not this tell you that we have spent the past days dueling with shadows as the butt of a prankster's joke?"

And then the indefatigable Walker countered, "Deliver me from mine enemies, O my God; defend me from them that rise up against me. Deliver me from the workers of iniquity, for, lo, they lie in wait. The mighty are gathered against me."

Shaking his head, David left. He would call in at the wheelwright and learn the progress of matters there.

The workshop, in a narrow lane near the gate, was an efficient establishment run by Wallings, the master wheelwright, who oversaw the work of two journeymen and three apprentices.

David recognized Tom Tomkins. His long blond hair was tied out of his way with a leather thong. A sweat-stained leather apron covered his woolen breeches.

Tom greeted the prospective customer. When he learned what David wanted, he showed him the wheel over which two journeymen and an apprentice labored, replacing a broken spoke and reshaping the iron rim.

Master Wallings assured him that the wheel would be stronger than ever and securely back on the carriage early tomorrow morning.

There was nothing for David to do but return to his mother-in-law's home and pray that the rising did not occur.

That evening when they had finished their stew and oatcakes, David suggested that Margaret gather her household for evening prayers. He read to them from the prophet Zechariah, "'The Lord of hosts shall defend them. . . . And the Lord their God shall save them in that day as the flock of his people: for they shall be as the stones of a crown, lifted up as an ensign upon his land. For how great is his goodness, and how great is his beauty!'"

David took heart from the words. Surely, the Lord would defend them, for were not the Ulster Presbyterians His people, the jewels in His crown? God would show His goodness and beauty through those loyal to the kirk because they honored Him.

He must have been right in his conclusion, because the city slept peacefully that night without a single alarm. The next morning David bade everyone to eat heartily—except Peedie, who was to be kept strictly to a small piece of boiled chicken and a hard biscuit. Although Miles was still unable to do any heavy lifting, the swelling in his wrist was much reduced. Esther had regained such composure as she was capable of. And, with the deadline of 9 December passed, David's heart was much lightened.

He would call at the wheelwright's himself to see that all was going according to schedule. Perhaps Wallings would loan him the services of that bright Tomkins lad to help with the loading. And *then*, at last, they could be off.

Walking in long strides to stretch his legs, he reached Ferryquay Street and was just turning right toward the wheelwright's when he heard a commotion. He would go to see what the ado was.

City Hall stood in the center of the open green of Londonderry, where the four main streets, each running from one of the city gates, intersected. As he approached, he realized that some sort of impromptu meeting was being held on the hall steps.

The speaker was Alexander Tomkins, splendid in his crimson alderman's robe. He was backed by Bishop Hopkins, Mr. Walker, and the other aldermen. Had they, then, decided to take action?

When David drew within range of Tomkins's voice, he almost laughed aloud. How typical of government. Now that 9 December was passed, the town council had voted to inform the public. Alexander Tomkins was reading the Comber letter to the citizens of Derry. "'They are to fall on to kill and murder . . .'"

There was a shout.

At first David thought the shout that interrupted the speaker was in outrage at the horrors the letter described. But as he turned to look down the street, he saw that it was quite another matter.

"They're coming! The Redshanks! They're at the ferry!" Tom Tomkins ran at the head of ten or so other apprentice lads. "Father!" the boy hailed. "A thousand. More. They've crossed the Waterside. Many are already on the ferry!"

John Campsie stood on one foot and then the other. "The garrison. Where is Captain Ash? Why isn't he about?"

"We don't need the garrison." Bishop Hopkins held out his arms. "Let them come. We will negotiate with them. We are all civilized men."

But Parson Walker had no intention of welcoming the enemy. "No!" His single cry riveted the crowd. He thrust a clenched fist upward. "No surrender! No surrender!"

"Now, now, I'm sure we can be reasonable—"

"No surrender!"

"But surely, we must discuss this."

"No surrender!"

The yelling on both sides of the issue increased in volume and fervor. But no one did anything.

David, at the back of the crowd, heard Tom Tomkins shout, "The gate!" and saw the contingent of apprentice boys running down Ferryquay toward the gate that stood open to the whole Waterside valley.

Tom was the first to reach the open archway. He sprang up to the gatekeeper's unattended platform and cranked the wheel holding the rope that suspended the heavy iron portcullis over the entrance. The wheel creaked. The mechanism made a groaning sound. The rope lowered half a foot. And stuck.

"Come on, Tom, you can do it!" Franklin yelled.

"Steady on, Tomkins!" a tall, green-capped lad cheered.

"Kick it loose!" The other boys shouted encouragement while two apprentices put their shoulders to the iron-hinged gates.

Tom tried kicking the wheel. And pulling. And pushing. Finally, he grasped the rough rope and briefly swung out over the cobbled paving, pulling with his whole weight against the jammed wheel. The mechanism would not budge.

Now people on the wall began shouting. The first ferryload of troops was across. Another boat right behind them. Now Redshanks were marching up the steep Foyle banks.

Perhaps the wooden gate that Tom's friends were struggling to close would hold against the soldiers. But if the city was to be secure, they needed the added protection of the portcullis.

From the platform, Tom looked around desperately. "Aye, Joseph!" the boy shouted to one of the apprentices putting his shoulder to the gate. "Your knife, man. Throw me your knife."

A flash of silver streaked through the air. Tom caught it and set to work. The rope was an inch thick, perhaps two, but he was determined. And as the feathered hat of the first Jacobite soldier appeared over the crest of the hill, the portcullis clanked into place. Tom leaped from the keeper's platform just as his mates thudded the gates closed and thrust the heavy iron bar into place.

A great cheer went up from the citizens of Londonderry. The city was secure from King James's troops. Derry would not capitulate before tyranny.

"No surrender! No surrender!" The cry rang against the stone walls.

David raised his voice with the others. The apprentice boys had saved the city.

The troops turned away, but David knew that James would not give up this easily. The Jacobite army would be back and in greater strength. But next time the city would be ready. While their elders debated, thirteen boys had shown the way.

35

The days moved with slow, steady rhythm at Lanarks' Bawn. Janet kept abreast of as much news as she could persuade her household to divulge. She knew they sheltered her from anything worrying. They did not understand that she was beyond worrying over earthly matters except as they touched her family. For her family to do right, be safe, and please God was her all-consuming prayer. But, still, she was interested in wider affairs. The snippets of news each brought to her quiet corner relieved the tedium of the day.

"Is there any news of Captain Lanark, Fanny?"

"No, mistress, not as I've heard. But there's been snow. News travels slower on white feet—that's what my maither always said."

Janet sighed. "Fanny, don't take the slop bowl out without a cover."

"Yes, ma'am. Sorry, ma'am."

Janet closed her eyes against the sight of Fanny's energetic curtsy while holding the slops. She did try to let loose of housekeeping details, but some things were too deeply ingrained. "When Master Graham comes in from the milking, please tell him I'd be pleased of a visit. But go slowly, Fanny."

Fanny bobbed another curtsy and clattered from the room.

It was mid-morning before a firm, booted tread outside her door told Janet that her son was coming. No one, not even her beloved David, could light her eyes like that strong-boned, clear-eyed boy/man with cheeks flushed from cold air that now filled her room with freshness. "Graham, I think spring cannot be far off with you so glowing."

"*Och*, 'tis nae spring that makes my nose so chill." He brushed her cheek with his cold nose as he kissed her.

"Is all well, Graham? No one will tell me any news."

He looked uncomfortable.

"Tell me, son. Whatever it might be, I am perfectly capable of imagining worse—which I promise you I will do if you will no' tell me the facts."

He shook his shining head, a gesture that made Janet think of her favorite horse when she was a girl. Romero had been all golden and of a high spirit as well. Like Graham, his firmness had not been readily apparent to every observer.

His mother's remark seemed to relax Graham, for he smiled. "That's just it, Mother. There are no facts. Only conjecture. It is said, though, that Tyrconnell is much outraged that Londonderry and Enniskillen stand out against him. The talk is all of James's troops mounting a siege on Derry. The people of Coleraine are preparing to evacuate to Derry as it is said that they lack sufficient arms and food to withstand a siege."

Janet nodded. "I thank you. You have helped me greatly, Graham."

"I have?"

"Certainly. My sole occupation is to spend my time in prayer. I can pray far better for situations I understand." She smiled. "I expect it matters little to God. *He* knows all and will do as pleases His sovereign power. But it is a great aid to me to know what I pray for." She paused. "But there is no news of your father?"

"I'm sure he will come soon."

The flat tone in which the words were spoken told Janet much. She took her son's hand. "Try to get along with him, Graham. I know he is not always easy. But he is a good man. He wants naught but the best for us all."

Graham's generous mouth tightened. "Aye. The best. *His* idea of the best. Father has no concept of my love for the land. Every morning I go into the fields it's like the world made new. Whatever the weather, whatever the stage of the crops, whatever the need of the animals, it's always new. I mean no disrespect, Mother, but I feel a co-creator with God . . . well, at least a gardener for Him." His voice faded, and he lowered his eyes, obviously embarrassed that he had revealed so much of himself.

Janet squeezed the hand she held—the hand that was so broad and firm, just like his father's. She determined that she must pray harder.

It seemed he would say more.

"There is perhaps another matter on your mind?"

"No." He paused. "That is, nothing of much consequence. It is just that I happened to see my cousin Molly Price in the lane a few days ago. It was snowing, and I had the wagon, so I gave her a ride."

"That was thoughtful of you."

"Yes, well, she said something that set me to thinking. She had been to Seaton Court—visiting their Bridie. At Seaton Court they light candles for Christmas—enormous red candles in every window and set up a replica of the Christ child's manger in their parlor."

"Aye. I know, son. It is a great heaviness to us all that those of the Lanark name should be papist. Such a burden to your father that his own flesh and blood . . ."

"Yes, I know that having figures of the holy family about and burning candles to them is idolatry. It's just that Molly told me Uncle Michael said they would have a special dinner on Christmas Day at Price farm. It sounded rather pleasant. I was wondering . . ."

"Graham, don't you dare breathe such a thing in your father's presence. It might be we could roast a special joint to mark his home-coming, but there will be nothing of superstitious rites at Lanarks' Bawn."

Nodding resignedly, Graham squeezed her hand and left.

Janet tried to turn her thoughts to prayer but was dismayed at how her mind wandered. The safety of the province troubled her, the safety of her mother and husband traveling over snow-packed roads patrolled by Jacobite soldiers, the lack of understanding between her husband and her son . . . And now Graham was having his head filled with dangerous notions by one of Michael Price's unruly brood.

Oh, why did she have to lie confined here, so useless day after day, when her family needed her energies? There was nothing she could do except take it to the One who could do all.

It was a few days before Christmas when Janet finally heard the sound for which she had been listening. The crunching of carriage wheels on the courtyard beneath her window told her that David had arrived. He had sent only one message, but it told her that he was bringing her mother and Esther, so she well understood the slowness of his return journey. And now she smiled at his impatient rush as he ascended the stairs two at a time.

"Quickly, Fanny, my lace-edged cap. And put another pillow behind my head. Oh, if only I could walk to him!"

Then the door flew open, and her David, with snowflakes on his cape, gathered her into his arms. "Aye, good it is to be home, wife." He drew back and regarded her at arms' length. "Faith, I don't find ye too poorly, lass?"

"No, David. And much stronger for your being here."

"Aye, and I've brought a dear comfort for ye. Your mother will greet you as soon as she sees to Esther." He shook his head. "That's a fine state of affairs—the mistress that must care for the servant."

Janet smiled. "Esther seemed ancient when I was a child. I think she helped raise my mother. She certainly helped raise me."

"Janet, you'll forgive me. I've not even time to change my boots. I must bear reports to Houston and the burgesses."

She nodded, determined not to let him see her disappointment. "I know you're a man of affairs, David Lanark. See you to them."

He clasped her hand. "I'd not fret ye, Janet, but you must know, these are dangerous times. We must take precautions."

"You needn't worry, David. Malcolm sees to the locking of the bawn every night. And our God is a mighty fortress."

"Aye." He paused at the door. "I'll take Miles with me. Don't worry if we're not home tonight. I can endure the discomforts of an inn one more night well enough if required."

"You protect us all in defending the county, my David."

As much as she hated to entertain the thought, Janet had to admit that the more fully David was occupied, the more easily conflicts between father and son could be avoided. Then she smiled at the swishing sound of her mother's dress as she approached. There was no situation that could not be eased by Margaret Cole's presence.

And so the days continued, alternating between added comforts and added tensions. The household conflicts were always silenced outside Janet's room. But the stress that arose over now having two housekeepers living under one roof—and Esther and Hannah's both being of very insecure natures—seeped under her door.

David did not return from his burgesses meeting until almost the new year, so the roast mutton and extra honey in the oat cakes that Janet requested Hannah to prepare for 25 December went unnoted by him. The fact that Esther added cinnamon and nutmeg to the stewed apples, however, did not escape Hannah's notice. Nor did Janet miss the fact that, although Graham expressed much appreciation for the fine meal, he left quickly and did not return until well after dark.

When Malcolm made a brief appearance at her door to pay his respects, she asked if aught was amiss with the sheep or if any of the cattle were ill.

"Nae, nae. Why do ye ask that, lass? All as tidy as a Christian could hope. And don't you be fretting about your hens and rabbits. They're happier in their new shelters than ever they were in the south tower. Can't say my hounds like their new kennel half so well, but there it is. We must keep the watch." And he had gone out.

So Graham wasn't spending his hours on animal husbandry. Janet had not seen Molly Price for almost two years, when last she was able to attend services in the meetinghouse. But she well remembered the brown eyes and soft cheeks framed by dark brown curls under Molly's white cap. It was an odd thing to remember, but Janet had especially noted that the edge of her cap had been adorned with a chain stitch of exquisitely delicate blue flowers. Even then, she had approved Molly's sweetness and her skill with a needle. She wondered what else Graham had found to approve.

Then David returned, and it seemed that the house sprang to life. He was so full of plans that for once even he forgot to shield Janet from outside affairs. She missed the quiet times he used to spend sitting beside her bed reading to her, but she much appreciated being made a party to all that was in his mind.

The earl of Mount-Alexander was taking command of the confederated forces of Antrim and Down. A council of Protestant gentlemen from the four northeastern counties were meeting to organize resistance to Tyrconnell. Colville was raising a regiment from his tenants around Newtown. Many fathers and sons were joining.

David stopped, his mouth tightening at the corners. "But not my son. The heroic apprentice boys that saved Londonderry from invasion and roused all the city to resistance were younger than Graham! Yet he still spends his time in the pastures."

"I understand that the lambing is going well. We shall soon have a fine flock." Janet tried to turn the conversation. She met with little success.

"Wool. A new madness. The wool trade will not make Ulster's fortune. Linen built Lanarks' Bawn, and it will build Ulster. But any excuse serves as well as another for one intent on shirking his duty."

Janet refused to admit even to herself that it was a relief when David went to his meeting. Even though the pain increased, it seemed easier to pray.

At least Esther and Hannah had settled a truce whereby Hannah reigned supreme in all kitchen matters except those pertaining solely to Janet's mother, who liked her morning coffee to be of a particular rich flavor. Esther saw to the upstairs rooms, thereby keeping her mistress's chamber and that of Janet Lanark to a much higher standard than Hannah had managed.

In the late afternoon, Graham snatched a few minutes from the lambing to look in on his mother. Janet wondered if the sparkle in his eyes was solely over his satisfaction with another safely delivered ewe. Then a wave of pain and nausea that she could not hide swept over her, and she was thankful that Esther had so carefully instructed Fanny in the proper drawing of the blinds against the sunlight.

That night Janet took an extra dose of poppy syrup, a measure her doctor had warned her to resist in all but the most extreme need. The elixir proved a shield against both the pain of the burning in her body and the pain of David's hasty departure for battle the next morning. He would never have intentionally revealed so much to her, but, in the heat of the moment, even David failed to think how clearly conversations funneled up a staircase.

"Those fools!"

She heard a muffled question that must have come from Malcolm. Then David continued. "Mount-Alexander assaulted Carrickfergus last night. Can you believe it? One of the strongest castles in all of Ireland and fully garrisoned with Redshanks. At least he could have called Colville's regiment. Left us sleeping in our beds while he set about his half-baked plans. His men were for the most part without arms! The ones they had were unfit for service."

A voice lower and slower than her husband's interrupted.

"Of course, they were cut to ribbons. And now we must do what we can to make the best of it. Hamilton and his Jacobites are sweeping northward. Perhaps we can cut him off at Dromore." There was a pause and a scraping of chairs. "Ready, Miles? We must off. I canna think what I'd do without ye, man. At least my servant will fill the place my son should."

She heard the clank of his spurs cross the hall toward the door. The sound stopped at a mumbled question.

"Oh, *och,* to think I forgot. Sure, I'll bid the lass farewell." He came clanking up the stairs.

"Fanny, tell my husband I sleep. Tell him it's the poppy syrup."

And, of truth, it must have been. Nothing else could account for the fact that she, who never knew if that day's sunrise would be her last, should send her husband to battle without a "God attend thee." She had not thought she could ever be so weakened that she would not face any dissension for David.

Even to protect her son. When the door thudded closed she turned to Graham, sitting beside her. But he did not return her weak smile.

"Thank you, Mother. I know you did that for me. I did not need to hear my father call me coward again." He stood and gazed out the window. "*Am* I a coward, Mother, that I shelter here when my father goes off to battle?"

"There is more than one kind of valor, my son. Continue your reading."

He was silent for a moment, then sat and took the book in his lap.

"Christian had gone but a little way before he espied a foul fiend named Apollyon coming over the field to meet him. Then did Christian begin to be afraid, and to cast in his mind whether to go back or to stand his ground. But he considered that he had no armor for his back . . . so he went on."

In the next few days Janet gave much thought to Christian's fight with Apollyon and puzzled over its application to their lives. It did seem that the struggle of the prince of this world for the service of those who had chosen to follow another King was particularly appropriate at that moment. Could James really be the Devil incarnate, as some claimed?

And if so, what did Christian's battle teach them? Was not Christian's victory the result of his disputing with the fiend? And was not his final victory with the sword really a symbol of using the Word of God? But how should this lesson be applied?

She sighed and shifted to a more comfortable position. The notion of resisting earthly powers with other than force of arms seemed impractical. It was a good thing that such matters were left to men of affairs such as David. But whatever the right of the matter, she was glad her son was at home. And she prayed for her husband's safety.

David had been gone barely a week when Janet was jarred from her meditations early one morning by a wailing below stairs. She went so numb she thought that perhaps this was the release she had so long awaited. Indeed, she went so numb she could perceive only shrieks and sobs so shrill they would surely rend the floorboards.

If she'd possessed the strength, Janet would have raised her voice with Esther's. There could be only one thing that would produce such an outcry. David was dead. There was no other explanation. The irony—that she whose death had been imminent should be preceded to the Celestial City by one so vigorous!

Oh, Lord, forgive me. I should have bade him Godspeed. I should have prayed harder. I should have . . . She was interrupted by her door's being flung open.

"*David!* Oh, David, is it you? I thought—"

And then she stopped, for she saw that, although he stood before her living, he had not escaped unscathed. Even now, blood soaked through the white bandage that bound his left shoulder.

He knelt by her bed. "Forgive me for coming to you in such a state, Janet. I'd not have, but with the fuss that fool woman is making, I knew you'd not believe I had breath in me unless ye felt me warm."

"Your shoulder?"

"Aye, I took a musket ball. But I'll recover. I was blessed."

"And the others?"

He shook his head. "Miles. He was beside me. The musket fire . . . when the smoke cleared . . . nay, I'll tell ye of it later, lass. I'll have—I'll see to this first." Clasping his shoulder, he backed from the room.

She did not protest. She knew he would not tell her the worst of it. But the fact that he would not tell meant that the news was dire indeed. And she grieved for Miles. Always he had been the faithful servant, but he was more than a servant to David. He had almost been a younger brother—replacing Alexander, who had slept in the churchyard these many years now. Miles's earthly body could not rest in a peaceful churchyard but, rather, in a torn and scarred battlefield.

She turned her face to the wall. How many more lives would end so before it was settled? And with her prayers for the families of the fallen, she added a word of thankfulness that it had not been Graham riding beside David at that moment.

Over the next several days, word of events filtered upward by bits and pieces, and she was able to fit them into a more or less coherent picture. And she knew how much she had to thank God for. Hamilton's Jacobites had overwhelmed the defenders at Dromore, but her David had escaped.

And then the victorious army swept on northward to Derry to mount its long-expected siege.

On the very eve of the Jacobite victory, King James himself had landed at the southernmost tip of Ireland and made a triumphal march to Dublin. Now the news raged so hot that even David made no attempt to keep it from Janet's room. Her mother proved to be her best informant. Margaret Cole had no patience with the king who had made such a cowardly flight to France—England's longest-standing enemy.

"Think, Grandmother. I'd not defend James, but his action was maybe nae sae daft," her grandson reminded her. "France is Scotland's old alliance."

But she tossed her white-capped head. "And what is that to me? You Scots are of fine blood, or I'd not have let my daughter marry one, but the Coles are English—descended from that Old King Cole so often sung of in nurseries."

Margaret Cole's sensitivities were further heightened by the accounts that reached them a few days later.

"What did I tell you? The man is no king. Entered Dublin on a nag, they said. Dressed in a plain cloth suit and a black slouch hat. And that Mad Jack Tyrconnell rode in front of him, bearing the Sword of State. Can you imagine? Four bishops, bearing the Host, greeted James at the city gate, they say. And the king dismounted and fell to his knees. But what can you expect of a papist?"

The news got worse. A few days later, James left Dublin at the head of twenty thousand troops to take command of the Irish army quartered near Londonderry. It was unclear whether Janet's mother was more outraged by James's treatment of her beloved city or by the increased hysteria that his actions produced in her maid. Esther took to her bed. So now there were two who must be nursed.

Those inside the walls of Derry, however, were not taking to their beds. General Hamilton had fired a single cannonball into the city. The ball had been bored out and a parchment roll put inside. The parchment listed the terms for the city's capitulation.

The citizens of Derry had not changed their minds. "No surrender!"

King James, sitting his horse in the pouring rain had been so disgusted at such obstinance that he returned to Dublin, leaving his Irish troops, which he castigated as being a poor-hearted lot indeed, to besiege the town.

But for all the Protestants' brave words, the prospects were bleak. The banner flying from Dublin Castle answered Ulster with the cry of the Irish Catholics, "Now or never! Now and for ever!" And it was to Dublin Castle, flying that brave banner, that James summoned his Irish Parliament.

Janet fought against the discouragement that threatened to overwhelm her. She had not always been so useless. Why, why must she be so now? She tried to pray, but now she prayed more against the darkness of despair threatening to overwhelm her than for protection of family and country.

"But, David, you cannot go to Dublin Castle. You are wounded." In spite of her weakness, Janet's voice held a strong note of exasperation over the irrationality that could make such demands.

To her surprise, David smiled. "Aye, and a fine thing it would be if I appeared at James's Parliament wearing wounds received fighting his troops." He shifted on his chair to ease his shoulder. It had been nearly two months now, but he still carried his arm in a sling.

"What will James do if you fail to obey his summons?"

"No more than he will do to any of my fellows. Few enough Protestants will kowtow to him."

"But, David"—now her irritation turned to fear—"to defy your king—"

"James is nae my king."

She knew. It had been almost three months since the English Parliament had declared William of Orange and his wife, Mary—James's eldest daughter—joint sovereigns of England, Scotland, and Ireland. "Yes, but William and Mary . . ."

She could not argue with what David said. She knew no good would come of this defiance, and yet she would not have him go to Dublin. It was a relief when he picked up the book and began reading again. His reassuring, clear, strong voice never failed to soothe her.

Until today. Perhaps it was just that they were at such a disturbing part of the pilgrimage:

"When Christian was got to the borders of the Shadow of Death, there met him two men. . . . "Back, back! If either life or peace is prized by you." . . . "Why, what's the matter?" said Christian. . . . "The valley itself, which is as dark as pitch. . . . We heard also in that valley a continual howling and yelling, as of a people under unutterable misery."

And it seemed in the coming days, as they awaited news of James's Parliament, that Janet could not wrench her mind from the echoes of those miserable people. Often in her poppy sleep she would imagine that it was her own voice.

Not even the coming of May with its sweet breezes, birdsong-filled air, and fresh scents could lift the depression the news brought when it finally came. Of the hundred-odd Irish peers who formed James's House of Lords, only fourteen obeyed his call. Ten were Catholic. James had hurriedly created seventeen more peers to fill the vacant seats. The House of Commons should have been more obedient. Of its 250 members, only six were Protestant.

David ran his hand roughly through his sandy hair and paced the floor beside Janet's bed. "They'll come round to James in the end. He'll get what he wants. And then God help us all."

"But what does he want, David?"

"War. James leads a formidable French army. James would conquer Ireland, then England. This is not to be an Irish war; it is to be a French war."

"And the *Irish Parliament* will vote him support?"

"Nothing else seems likely. Perhaps I should have gone. Obeying James's summons would have looked like support—but if I had been there I could have voted against him. Did I do wrong, now, wife?"

Janet had no answer. She had found no comfort. She had none to give to another.

A few days later she had an unusual pair of visitors. One was Graham. At first she thought his hesitancy was due to the fact that his father was with her. Then she saw that he had left the door open for a purpose. "Mother, are you verra weary? That is, one has called with news for father. I thought, perhaps—"

"Yes, son, of course. Bring him in." It would be refreshing to hear the word firsthand, although she doubted that the news could be good. Yet, how odd that Graham would bring the minister to her room to give his information.

A gentle swish of petticoats on the floorboards told Janet that her caller was not the Reverend Mr. Stevenson.

"Molly, child." Janet held out her hand. "How long it has been since I've seen you. And how lovely you look." She wanted to ask after the health of all in the Price household, but she could see by the deep furrows in Molly's brow that she had something of immediate concern to impart.

The girl bobbed a curtsy. "Thank you. Uncle Michael said I should come. He said that Captain Lanark should be warned." She turned to David, her soft brown eyes wide with alarm. "Uncle Michael was in Belfast . . . the news has just arrived there—"

"Get on with it, girl!"

"Go on, Molly," Graham murmured encouragingly from behind her.

"The Irish Parliament. They have abolished the supremacy of the English Parliament over Ireland."

David sprang to his feet with a whoop. "They have *what?* They passed no resolution to help James regain his English throne?" He slapped his buff breeches. "What a wily lot! James meant to use them for his purposes. Instead, they use him to deliver them from the English!"

"It is said James was so upset that his nosebleeds started again."

Molly's words brought a burst of mutual laughter from David and Graham. But their happy reaction seemed to increase her discomfort.

"What is it, my dear?" Janet asked quietly as the men enjoyed their rare moment of levity. "The Parliament did more, I think."

Molly looked at the tips of her shoes protruding from under her skirt.

A knock at the door below and the sound of Hannah's footsteps relieved Molly of having to speak.

This time the caller was indeed the Reverend Mr. Stevenson. At the sound of his voice, David hurried from the room, closing the door carefully behind him.

Janet shook her head at the futility of his attempt to keep unpleasantness from her. But as the full impact of the news nevertheless echoed up the stairway, she was thankful that Graham and Molly were with her.

"What do you mean, repealed the Act of Settlement? James's own grandfather James I secured those land grants to Scottish immigrants. That's our land. They can't—"

"Aye. But it seems they have. Dispossessed the English landlords as well. Protestant church property handed over to Catholic clergy. Aye, they can. They did."

At that, David apparently bethought himself of the invalid upstairs. The sound of thudding boots and a slammed door cut off further conversation.

And so Janet was forced to wait two more hours, fretting and guessing what disasters were to come upon them. She heard David ride off—whether to a meeting of the burgesses, or of the Committee of Safety, or to the militia, she did not know. She only knew he was gone.

When Graham returned from seeing Molly home, Janet's mother was with her, sitting with her sewing by the fading light of the western window. He sat heavily by the side of her bed and took her hand. "Mother, it cannot be kept from you. And we need your prayers."

"Tell me, Graham. You know I rely on you."

"Yes, I know. I have come to tell you. Yet—" He pushed to his feet again and faced the wall.

Margaret Cole's needle stilled. It was as if no one breathed, waiting to hear the worst. Graham swallowed. "The Irish Parliament passed an Act of Attainder. It lists three thousand people, including half the peerage and most of the Protestant gentry. They are to be hanged, drawn, and quartered without trial. Father's name is on the list."

36

"The pathway was here so dark that ofttimes, when he lifted up his foot to go forward, Christian knew not where or upon what he would set it next. About the midst of this valley the mouth of hell stood hard by the wayside. . . . Flame and smoke would come out in such abundance with sparks and hideous noises . . . that he cried, 'O Lord, I beseech Thee, deliver my soul.' Thus he went on a great while, yet still the flames would be reaching towards him."

"Do I tire you, Mistress Lanark?" Molly put down the book.

"Perhaps I should rest now, Molly. You are a dear girl to come to me. A comfort."

"Oh, Mistress Lanark, *you* comfort me. That is, no one else understands . . ." Molly looked around in embarrassment. "I mean . . ."

"You mean that it helps just knowing that I love Graham as much as you do."

The girl's smile was dazzling. "Oh, yes. Yes. Thank you for saying it for me. I knew you understood." She lowered her eyes again. "And you know . . . know . . ."

"How little enthusiasm Graham has for military matters."

Molly nodded. "He does not want to kill. He wants to produce life—the land, the animals." She squeezed Janet's hand and tiptoed to the door.

Janet closed her eyes. This past year, living under the terrible weight of the Attainder, the one bright spot in her life had been the warming relationship between Graham and this lovely girl—that and the fact that the threatened disaster had not yet been carried out.

The officers of the Irish Parliament had other matters to keep them busy. Before they could act, King William's General Schomberg arrived in Carrickfergus at the head of ten thousand troops. The French councilor had reportedly suggested to James that he retaliate by massacring all the Protestants in Ireland, thereby separating Ireland and England forever. To his credit, James had reacted with horror.

Beyond preventing the carrying out of the Bill of Attainder, however, the eighty-year-old Schomberg was able to accomplish little for the English cause. And the matter still hung over their heads, a constant threat, which King William's army was able only to delay.

The army was undisciplined, untrained, and unsupplied. All winter, reports reached Lanarks' Bawn of pikes so rotten they broke in the soldiers' hands, uneatable food, no shoes.

When seventeen hundred Williamite soldiers died at the battle of Dundalk and another thousand died of fever, Graham announced, "I have enlisted in Colville's regiment."

"But, Graham, the land!"

"Don't you see? It is precisely because I love the land that I must fight for it, Mother. The Attainder must be defeated. James must be defeated. If we lose and our land is taken from us, I would never forgive myself for not adding my strength to the effort. Always I would think that perhaps I could have made a difference. And if we win, I could not live happy here on the fruits of other men's struggles."

Janet understood. "Have you told Molly?"

"Aye." His voice told her the difficulty of that telling, and yet, the light in his eyes said that the parting had not been entirely unsatisfactory.

And so Graham marched away. Janet could only hope that he and his father might be reconciled now that David had the soldier son he had always wanted. But it was little comfort to the wife and mother, who could only think that those she cared for most slept throughout that severe winter in tents pitched by a marsh while fever raged in the camp and Tyrconnell's Jacobite army burned their forage.

And even if they survived the ravages of fever and battle, Janet's hopes that she would see either of them again grew dimmer daily. Throughout winter, her pain increased. The sense grew with increasing urgency that her time was short. And now, when she needed it most, her spiritual comfort failed her. No matter what the daily fears and conflicts, she had always been able to close her eyes and be in the presence of all Comfort. But now she closed her eyes on blackness.

Had she failed somehow? Not prayed enough? Not been good enough?

It should have been a warming June day, but cold rain lashed against her window. It was so dark that she kept a candle beside her even in the afternoon. All she could think of was David and Graham out somewhere in such weather. And she could not pray for them. She could say the words—with great effort—but she could make no contact with the Hearer.

Hannah bustled in, and the draft from the door all but extinguished Janet's candle. "Would you be liking a visitor, ma'am? It's the parson. I told him I'd just see if you're awake."

Janet clutched the edge of her blanket. "Mr. Stevenson? Has he brought news? Has there been a battle?"

"No, ma'am, I don't think so. He said as how he was just passing. He don't look fretted."

"Thank you, Hannah. Please show him up." Had God sent him? Had He heard after all and sent one to speak words of comfort? For a moment Janet's heart warmed with hope.

The thin features in the man's kindly face were an easing sight. They exchanged pleasantries, and then Janet, keenly aware of how little time she had, got quickly to what was on her heart.

Mr. Stevenson clasped his Bible to his chest, seemingly aghast at Janet's question. "*Good* enough! Oh, my dear Mistress Lanark, could I have been so remiss in leading my flock? Could my sermons have so led you astray?"

Janet wondered if he was about to reprimand her for having been absent from meeting for so long, but then he went on.

"Oh dear, oh dear, oh dear. Of course, you haven't been good enough. None of us has. '*All* we like sheep have gone astray.' There is none worthy. There is no goodness in any of us. Only He is good. Only He is worthy. Our depravity is total. It is all of grace. In His grace He has chosen you, elected you to His glorious salvation. All of grace, all of grace irresistible."

With those beautiful words, Janet's heart opened, and she slept without her poppy syrup.

It was the middle of the night when the wind howling at her windowpane woke her. Or *was* it the howl of the wind? Perhaps it was the howl of hell, of the creatures Christian had heard crying in the Valley of the Shadow of Death. For that was surely where she was now.

The minister's words had provided comfort at the time. But now, in the dark of night, an awful void opened. *What if she hadn't been chosen?* Not foreordained to receive God's grace? What if the door closed, and she was left on the outside?

How could she die without God? Where was He? He had been so close. She had been so assured of His presence. And Parson Stevenson had assured her over and over again that one could not lose her salvation. It was secure in the work of Christ. But what if one had never possessed the salvation she thought she had? What if she had only imagined His presence?

The pain of this emptiness was far sharper than the gnawing in her stomach.

David sat astride Trapper at the top of a small rise. Beneath him the River Boyne wound gently through a wide and peaceful valley. Five miles to his left was the town of Drogheda, still an open sore from the curse of Cromwell. Four miles to his right rose the Hill of Slane, where St. Patrick lit his Paschal fire. And straight ahead, across the river, across the green valley in the woods on the hill, was King James II and the Jacobite army, twenty five thousand strong.

David wiped the sweat from his brow. It was unusually hot for the last day of June—had been hot ever since that glorious day two weeks ago when King William III, affectionately called King Billy by his subjects, sailed into Belfast Lough with a fleet of three hundred ships and stepped ashore. It was strange here, the serene silence of this valley, while two great armies camped on its banks. But David could still hear in his head the thunderous cheering that had greeted King Billy as he rode into Belfast.

As a captain in the militia unit attached to the Enniskilleners, David was on the pier when the king was rowed ashore. His first sight of King William was disappointing at best. It was known that the king was not robust, that he suffered much from asthma. But David was little prepared for his first sight of the man he was to follow into battle.

The great wig under King Billy's broad, feathered hat seemed too cumbersome for his frail body. His face was pale and lined with pain. His hooked, slightly twisted nose looked enormous above narrow, hunched shoulders. This was the man who was to save Ireland?

Then King Billy mounted his great white horse, and a transformation took place. Now David could see the strength of the man. The same resolve that had led him to overcome illness could lead them to overcome their enemies. David cheered with the throng and rode behind the king's entourage the ten miles into Belfast. He had not known the region was so populous. The crowds that came out to cheer seemed numberless.

The Jacobite garrison had abandoned Belfast the summer before when Lord Donegall had written from Belfast Castle to assure William of Belfast's support. Now that support was made visible by the welcome of its people.

Sitting atop his fine stallion, King William addressed his loyal subjects. "We have observed the land we have ridden through. And we are pleased. This is a land highly worth fighting for." The king's English was halting, but the people understood and responded vociferously.

"We have come to see that the people of Ireland are settled in a lasting peace. But we are not come to let the grass grow under our feet."

King William did not, however, turn his hand first to military matters. The business class, largely Protestant English, had fled the country. Ordinary commerce was virtually at a standstill. Inflation soared. As silver coins disappeared into the coffers of hoarders, James replaced them with brass money made from melted-down guns. But William had brought chests of genuine money to pay his troops. As those coins began to circulate, King Billy's popularity rose to an even greater pitch.

Then William led the march south through twelve days of scorching heat, unrelieved by a single shower. The troops sweated across hills and valleys where no tree was to be seen to offer protection from the sun. At every place they expected to encounter the Jacobites, they found that James had moved on ahead of them. Dundalk they found mercilessly ravaged by James's army. Most of the adult population had been carried off as prisoners. Those left behind were starving.

Next was Ardee. Again, James had been there first and had plundered it before moving on. William's men found nothing but houses with bare walls and a few bedridden elderly, dying of hunger and misery.

David spared a few crusts to help those he could, but there was little anyone could do. William had brought provisions for only five days, expecting to buy supplies en route. The army had run out of flour for its own bread. Did James mean to retreat all the way to Dublin?

Then, at last, James stood. His French and Irish troops were encamped in tents over there across the Boyne. Here the future of Ireland, the English Crown, and the European balance of power was to be decided.

David turned at the sound of an approaching horse. "Aye, what would ye?"

Even as the words came from his mouth, David regretted their sharpness. Why should the sight of his fair-haired son cause irritation to rise in him? Had this not been the very thing he had desired for so long—that he and Graham should bear arms together? He worried much over how the boy would quit himself in battle. Yet, was this not a son of which any father should be proud? So why was the lad's presence an annoyance?

"I've come to report that I've returned, sir." Graham patted his horse's neck. "Easy, Hazel. Stand, boy."

"Aye, and none too soon. If James had stood at Dundalk, ye'd have missed the fun." And again David knew he was unfair. He was implying cowardice in the boy, when it was by David's own orders that Graham had turned aside to see that all was well at Lanarks' Bawn. He had had no word from Janet for three months. If he were to command his men with single-minded intensity, he needed to be at rest on the matter, one way or the other.

Now he realized that his irritation with Graham was really fear. What had the boy found at Lanarks' Bawn?

"My mother sends her love."

David let his breath out slowly. "She lives, then."

"Aye. She sends love and her gratitude for your kindheartedness toward her. She was much moved that you would think so softly of her when such great affairs press."

"And how was she within herself? How did she seem to you?"

"She said to tell you that she was as well as may be."

David nodded. He could see the brave smile with which she would have said it, no matter what the truth. David knew that Janet always protected him just as he strove to protect her.

Father and son talked on. Molly Price had called to sit with Janet while Graham was there. She had recently seen Bridie from Seaton Court, who said that her brother Charles had joined the Jacobites.

David scowled and clenched his jaw. "Our own kin, bearing the name of Lanark. My own cousin's son." He shook his head. "Our family suffered as greatly as any at the '41. And yet a Lanark could side with the papists!" He would have said more, but a small group of riders in the valley caught his attention.

He watched, frowning, as they approached the bank of the river and stood at loose rein, pointing each direction as if planning battle strategy.

Then the breeze fluttered the ends of a blue sash across the chest of the lead rider, and David said, "That's King Billy!" He looked uneasily across at the shrubbery along the opposite bank. The thought that Jacobite soldiers might shelter there was just taking shape in his mind when a cannon shot rang out.

One of William's officers fell to the ground, his horse shot dead under him.

King William turned to the fallen man. A second shot whistled across the silver ribbon of river. King William slumped forward onto the neck of his horse.

A shout of joy rang from the south bank as James's men ran to spread the news. "The king is dead!" "William of Orange—fallen!" "God has delivered us!" Their cries were muffled as they crashed through the brush.

Horror-stricken at what had taken place before his very eyes, David turned toward camp in shocked silence. The urge to rush forward with the dreadful news warred with a desire to go slowly, to deny what his own eyes had seen, his own ears had heard.

But the stunned hush and frozen figures that greeted him in

camp told David the news had preceded them. Here and there the ominous stillness was broken by an angry outburst or cry of anguish.

The Dutch Count Solms, one of William's friends, flung himself to the ground and sobbed with grief.

"What will happen now, Father? Will Schomberg command?" Graham asked.

David did not know, but surely it would not be the eighty-year-old marshal whose inept dithering had necessitated William's taking personal command in the first place. There must be someone better. But there would be no one as good as King William of Orange. In the few days he had followed the man, David had developed a profound respect for King Billy. There was no other who could command so well or whom the men would so readily follow.

He turned at the pounding of horse's hooves and recognized Lord Selkirk's dappled gray. Selkirk had been with the king by the river. He might have saved himself the trouble, David thought. Couldn't he see that they already knew the worst?

"Up man. Up!" Selkirk shouted at Solms. "Your sorrow is mistaken!"

Solms looked up, but refused to stand. "Sir, you mock my grief."

"Believe me. It is true. The ball merely ripped the king's jacket and grazed his shoulder. It drew half a spoonful of blood. That is all."

Solms shook his head. "I cannot believe it. I dare not give way to such hope." But then he leaped to his feet.

David and Graham joined in the shouting. For King Billy was riding into camp on his pale stallion, waving his right arm to show that all was well.

Tuesday, 1 July 1690, dawned bright and clear. David emerged from his tent to see that it would be another hot, glorious summer day.

The order went round that the Williamite soldiers were to cut small green boughs to wear in their hats to distinguish them from the Jacobites, who wore white feathers in their bonnets. Very few of these troops were uniformed regiments as Cromwell's New Model Army had been, and a means of distinguishing their fellows was necessary.

Captain Lanark relayed the command to the men in his charge. "Aye, get ye to it, men, and we'll have no twigs. A fine green clump, mind you."

David felt the apprehension that reigned. None knew what the day would bring. William had been on horseback since six o'clock, riding among his troops, giving last-minute instructions and encouragement everywhere. But in spite of the king's spirit, which lent animation to all his men, David noted that he carried his sword in his left hand. He hoped not too many others noticed. That the king could not use his sword arm was not welcome news.

310

There was no flagging of the Williamite orders, however. At precisely nine of the clock, William ordered his Blue Guards across the Boyne. As soon as they reached the water, James's men opened fire from behind the bushes. A few fell, but the Guards pushed steadily through. For a time it looked to David, watching from amid his Enniskilleners, as if the entire river was crawling with blue-clad soldiers.

Then they were across and onto the other bank. And the guns silenced.

The Irish fled before William's advancing army, but James's French troops did not flee. Commanded by Tyrconnell and Hamilton, the best of the Jacobite leaders, their white feather badges gleamed in the sun as they advanced. On the north side of the river, William's Huguenots approached the crossing. The Huguenots hesitated, then fell back.

Old Marshal Schomberg thundered to the French Protestants in their native tongue, "On, men! There are your persecutors!" He thrust his sword toward the unit of French Catholic soldiers. It was his last order. As the Huguenots surged forward, they did not see Schomberg fall with a bullet in his neck.

But Capt. David Lanark, tensed to receive his own orders, did see. Now there was no second in command. And if the Jacobites should be able to finish what they had begun the day before in wounding William, the outcome could still be disastrous.

William would take no precautions to protect himself. It seemed that he was everywhere, easily identifiable on his white charger. James, however, did not appear on his side. It was said he directed from an old church, well behind the lines.

Now suddenly William appeared in the thick of battle on the *south* side of the river. He had made the dangerous crossing farther down the Boyne. At sight of their king, the troops surged forward, driving the French and Irish on up the hill.

The king turned then to those waiting to charge from the north side and raised his left arm, flourishing his sword. "Men of Enniskillen, what will you do for me?" The cry carried across the melee, hit the slope behind them, and echoed back. "Men of Enniskillen . . ."

David gave one fleeting thought for the son behind him, who had yet to be tested in battle, then spurred Trapper. "Forward, charge!" he shouted to his company.

"What will you do for me?" Graham never hesitated. He gathered his reins and followed. The river was churned to mud, but, even so, the drops that splashed on his face felt refreshing. It was a stirring moment, riding forward to answer the call of king and country. He would not have chosen to miss this.

And yet, his pistol remained in its holster, his sword in its sheath. He did not know if he would draw them. All those months ago when he had joined the regiment in a burst of patriotism, he had given the matter no thought. He had come to support his king, to defend his home, to defeat the Attainder, not to kill Jacobites. But now, as he rushed toward the enemy, the question had to be answered. No room remained for vacillation.

In a small part of his mind, as he urged his mount toward the other bank, Graham heard Molly's voice, *Come back to me, Graham. Come back.* If he must draw weapon to fulfill his pledge to Molly, he would do so. What he could accomplish was doubtful enough. The officers had held precious few drills. Truth, until William's supply ships arrived, there had been almost no weapons to practice with. Schomberg had spent more time castigating the men for swearing than in weapons practice.

And then Graham was in the thick of it. For several minutes—which seemed hours—the press was so thick that there was no question of drawing a weapon. Indeed, he would be more likely to do damage to his comrades than to the enemy if he did. Instead, he turned Hazel this way and that, urging the horse to strike out with her hooves, to move them forward, to press the enemy back farther. For a time it appeared they could simply drive the Jacobites from the field by force of numbers.

They had almost done it, too. The woods thickened just ahead of them, and Graham could see that, as the white feathers reached the shadowed cover, they continued to flee. There could be no more than three or four companies remaining to be swept from this portion of the field.

He looked to see how the battle went downriver. His father was just to his left, embroiled in a sword fight. And then, a rider bore down on David from behind. Graham saw the sunlight flash on the man's cutlass as it curved in an arc toward his father.

With a shout he whirled Hazel. Charged forward. The enemy soldier had fallen from his horse before Graham realized he had unsheathed his sword. He looked in amazement from the hilt in his hand to the red stream oozing from the man's head. He looked into the face of the fallen soldier. And the sword dropped from Graham's hand.

It was as if he looked into a mirror. The hair that was matting scarlet was the same shade of ripe flax as his own. The eyes that now glazed in death were the same blue as his. The broad forehead, the high cheekbones. Graham had seen his cousin Charles Lanark fewer than five times in his life, but he could not mistake him in death.

"Pursue them, men! Pursue!" Captain Lanark, unaware that his son had saved his life, led his unit surging up the hill.

Graham did not heed the order. He slipped from his saddle and knelt beside his cousin. There was nothing he could do for Charles. Dimly aware of the retreating battle sounds, he took the bloody head into his lap. Without the white feather on one cap and the green bough on the other, the two men were barely distinguishable. Except that one breathed and one did not.

Even as the soldiers disappeared from view, the women and the rabble who always followed armies appeared at the other end of the battlefield. Like the carrion they were, they set about systematically to strip every body—even those with breath still in them.

William had given strict orders that such desecration was not to take place. No one connected with the Williamite army was to molest the wounded or touch the dead. But William was not there. William was leading the pursuit of James's ragtag army.

Already bodies were stripped naked. In a short time the work would be done. Then the scavengers would set up a market, selling their bloodied goods right there on the battlefield.

Graham knew what he could do for Charles Lanark. He could defend him from this final indignity. Gently he put the head on the ground and rose stiffly to retrieve his sword, just before a half-naked, emaciated boy snatched it. "Sorry, lad, I've more use for this."

The child spit at him and shouted a string of Gaelic invective, but he backed off.

Graham turned back and saw that he was none too soon. "Stand back!" He brandished his sword at the young man who approached the body. "No one strips this man." The youth did not yield ground. Graham lunged at him, sword extended.

To his amazement, the youth fell to knees, sobbing, and buried his face in Charles Lanark's jacket. Was this some ruse to steal valuables from the body under the guise of mourning?

"Here now, what's this?" He pushed at the fellow's shoulder, turning his face upward. Then he saw that the tears were genuine. And he saw the white feather on the youth's cap.

"Please, sir, I'll be your prisoner, but let me bury this man first. He's my kin." The young man spoke heavily accented English, as if he would be more comfortable using the Gaelic.

Graham thrust the tip of his sword into the lad's jerkin far enough that he was surprised he didn't draw blood. "I'll not hear your lies. I know this man's family. You're no kin. What's your name?"

"Henry MacHenry. From Donegal."

"Lanark here is from Comber. The Lanarks have no kin in Connaught." This time he did prick a drop of blood.

But the lad held his ground. "Calum Lanark, the first of our family to come to Ireland, had three daughters. The youngest was named Aileen. She married my grandfather, Eamon MacHenry."

Graham lowered his sword. "Aye. I've heard of Aileen Lanark. But Calum Lanark would not have married his daughter to native Irish."

Henry MacHenry drew himself up, his blue eyes snapping under his mop of black hair. He was of a slight build, but he carried himself proudly. "The MacHenrys were Deserving Irish. We were allowed to keep our lands in Armagh when the English portioned it out for their plantations."

Graham half raised his sword again. Henry MacHenry's ragged breeches and homespun jerkin did not look like the clothing of one from a propertied family.

But the boy continued, "Cheats that the English are, they did not explain. We were allowed our lands for my great-grandfather's lifetime. When he died, we were evicted."

Graham sheathed his sword. The story rang true. He hated the thought of his own ancestress being driven from her home.

"Driven to Connaught, they were." MacHenry bit out the words. "They could afford a lease only in the poorest province."

Graham recalled Aileen Lanark. Old Michael Price had told tales of her—golden-haired and laughing, the darling of the family. So she had married this lad's ancestor and gone off in happiness to his estate, only to be turned out to cold and starvation. It didn't bear thinking on.

"But how did you come to know Lanark?"

"Didn't until I joined up." He shrugged. "Promised to pay us, didn't they? A Catholic king would be a fine thing, but food in our bellies would be finer. They didn't say we'd have to be about burning the land. And then there *was* no pay. And now there'll be no Catholic king."

Graham felt a warm rush of kinship for this boy who couldn't be above sixteen. "What of your family, lad?"

Long, dark lashes shaded the blue eyes. "*Máthair* died afore I joined. I'm the last."

The hollow silence following that statement was filled with cackling laughter and greedy shrieks as the body robbers worked around them. "And how did ye get to know Lanark?"

"He were our ensign. Heard his name, asked about his family . . ." MacHenry bit his lip.

"Right. Well, let's get on with it." Graham moved to lift Charles's shoulders. "Ensign, you say? I saw no flag."

The thought jarred MacHenry to action. It took a few moments of searching—the banner Ensign Lanark had carried had been ripped from its pole and so ground into the mud that it was hardly recognizable, which was probably what saved it from being snatched by one of the spoilers.

"Wait." The boy ran for the river. In a few moments he returned with the flag, ripped and dripping but washed free of mud. He spread it over the body of Ensign Charles Lanark. "There is a quiet spot in the woods." He pointed uphill.

Graham took the head and shoulders. It was his right and his duty. He would let no other carry the wound he had inflicted.

Swords and sticks made poor instruments for digging, and it had not rained for many days, so the soil above the river plain did not yield easily to their efforts. But at last the two kinsmen achieved a shallow grave.

Graham folded the flag and removed Lanark's belt and cap. What else should he take to the fallen man's family? He felt in the breeches pockets. A letter. From his sister Bridget. That Bridie who was such a friend to Molly. A great sense of loss washed over Graham. If matters had been different—if religion and family feuding hadn't kept them apart all these years—he and this man he had killed could have been friends.

And he wondered—had the fortunes of war been the other way round—if Charles would have done the same service for him that he now performed. Burying one's dead had been a right and duty of kinship from earliest times. He looked at the pale face surrounded by rich, dark Irish earth and felt certain that Charles Lanark was a man who had always done right as he saw it.

Henry MacHenry was on his knees at the foot of the grave, scooping soil over the body. Then he stopped and looked up. "It is not right. There should be a priest. This ground—it is not blessed." He crossed himself.

Graham shrank back as if the boy had made the sign of the Devil. "Well, it's the best we can do. A far sight better than leaving him for the vultures." He spoke brusquely. He did not want to be reminded of their differences at this moment.

Yet it seemed he should do something. He filled in the rest of the grave. Still on his knees, he looked at the brown mound scarring the green. And he knew what to say. "Our Father, who art in heaven . . ."

"Hallowed be thy name . . ." The Catholic boy joined him.

"Thy will be done on earth as it is in heaven . . ." Their voices blended.

"For thine is the kingdom and the power and the glory forever. Amen," Graham finished. Henry MacHenry had not added his voice to the final phrase. Graham was starting to rise when a new sound held him.

A gentle, hauntingly beautiful melody filled the air. Henry MacHenry stood at the foot of the grave, his head back, his eyes closed, singing.

Graham understood not a word, but he sensed it was a prayer. As the song winged its way upward, he felt compelled to remain on his knees, praying for his cousin and for their battle-torn land.

When the last notes had faded, he rose. "Aye. That was fine."

"Patrick's Breastplate, it was. Written by Saint Patrick himself." Henry looked at his hands as if he couldn't understand why they were empty. "I'd have liked best to play my *clairseach* for him. But I'd not bring it into battle."

Graham placed the folded ensign in the boy's hands. "His family would want you to have this."

Henry MacHenry sketched a salute toward the new-turned earth and walked slowly uphill in the direction James's men had fled.

The turmoil of battle raged in Graham's mind, while the memory of the song lingered to soften the tumult. Regret would have pulled him again to his knees, but he would not go back over that ground. If it was preordained, naught else could have happened. He must accept all as the sovereign will of God.

And he must look to the future. Just as he would put the battle behind him. Surely Ireland would do so as well now. If James was as soundly defeated as he appeared to be, they could all—Jacobite and Williamite—return to their crops and flocks. The burned, trodden land needed time to recover, as did the people from their wounds. Perhaps much time.

But healing *would* come. Life would spring anew.

37

"Would you hear the Scriptures, daughter?" Margaret Cole opened Janet's curtains only a few inches. "Ah, it's a fine, thick mist now, but morning will break."

Janet focused her strength to smile at her mother.

Perhaps more than any other person, this dear woman had sensed that Janet's spiritual troubles were far greater than her physical. And they each knew that little time remained before both would overwhelm her.

Janet nodded. Yes, she would gladly hear the Scripture.

Margaret seated herself and picked up the heavy volume that had been in the Lanark family since their earliest days in Comber. "The epistle first, perhaps?" She turned the pages without waiting for an answer.

"'He also himself likewise took part of the same; that through death He might destroy him that had the power of death, that is, the devil; and deliver them who through fear of death were all their lifetime subject to bondage.'"

Janet's breathing became less labored. Was it just the soothing tone of her mother's voice, or were the words actually reaching her heart?

"'For in that he himself hath suffered being tempted, he is able to succour them that are tempted.'"

Yes, Jesus.

Margaret paused. "A psalm now, I think." She turned to another reading. "'Who passing through the valley of Baca make it a well.'"

Yes. Baca. The desolate valley. Janet was too weak to give any outward sign beyond a faint smile, but her heart danced. She felt like Christian after he had gone through the Valley of the Shadow of Death and looked back to see that the hobgoblins and dragons were all afar off. With Christian she said, *He has turned the shadow of death into the morning.*

And then Hannah burst in, sloshing the coffee she carried. "Oh, Mistress Lanark. Oh, I daresay there's news. Miss Molly drove over in the trap. She's coming in now. Oh, my—" Hannah turned toward the partially draped window.

Margaret Cole intercepted the coffee and moved to give her daughter sips of the invigorating liquid. "Thank you, Hannah. Please send our visitor up."

In a few moments they heard Molly's light steps flying up the stairs. She knelt by the bed and took Janet's hand in both her own. Her cheeks were flushed, her eyes bright. "Oh, I've just heard. Oh, the best news in the world! Graham is well—survived the battle without a scratch. And Captain Lanark. Both are well. Please God they may be home soon." She squeezed Janet's hand.

"That is excellent news, indeed, Miss Price. And are we to take from that that our troops have been victorious?" Margaret Cole asked what her daughter didn't have strength to voice.

"Oh, yes, a great victory. Two thousand Jacobites killed, four hundred of our own. King William is in Dublin. And James fled back to Paris."

Margaret patted the girl's shoulder. "Good news, timely delivered, Miss Price. My daughter and I thank you. Now if you'll excuse me, I must go tell the others. Such happy tidings must not be kept back."

Molly bounced to her feet and smoothed the skirt of her gown. "Oh, Mistress Lanark, I am so happy. I cannot tell you." She went to the window and flung the drapes wide, then whirled back to Janet's bedside. "Would you have me read to you? We have nearly finished the book."

Janet's nod was barely perceptible, but it was enough.

Molly picked up the book and removed the white ribbon marking her place.

> "Behind them, they could just see, looking back, a shadow in the sky, which marked the place where Doubting Castle stood. But ahead, there was a perfect view of the Celestial City, a City founded higher than the clouds. Its walls and towers shown in the sun, so dazzling that pilgrims had to look at it through clouded glass."

The shining city took shape in Janet's mind as the words brought joy to her heart.

> "Now, behold, a company of the heavenly host came out to meet the pilgrims, and the two Shining Ones said, 'These are the men that have loved our Lord when in the world. . . . Now they may go in and look their Redeemer in the face with joy.'"

Molly paused and gazed toward the window. The clouds had cleared. Bright rays of sun streamed into the room and fell across Janet's bed.

"Then the heavenly host gave a great shout, saying, 'Blessed are they which are called to the marriage supper of the Lamb.' The King's trumpeters, clothed in white and shining raiment, made even the heavens echo with their sound."

The world around Janet seemed to be slipping away. She could not feel her bed or the covers. There was no pain in her body.

"The Shining Men bid them enter at the gate . . ."

It was beautiful. She was so happy. But she had not meant it to be yet. She had hoped to wait. She did want to see her David again. But then, there would always be the next world.

"Now I saw in my dream that those two men went in at the gate; and lo! as they entered, they were transfigured; and they had raiment put on that shone like gold. And they were given harps and crowns—the harps to praise with, and the crowns as tokens of honor. Then I heard in my dream that all the bells in the City rang again for joy. And it was said unto them, 'Enter ye into the joy of your Lord.' And the men themselves sang with a loud voice, saying, 'Blessing and honor and glory and power, be unto Him that sitteth upon the throne, and unto the lamb, forever and ever!'"

Graham stood beside her grave. He came weekly to this quiet corner of the churchyard under the widespread leafy branches. It had become a pattern that helped fill the void left now that he could no longer sit beside his mother's bed and draw from her gentle wisdom. As he stooped to place a handful of Michaelmas daisies on the green mound, the church bells rang above his head. They recalled the wild ringing of the bells that Sunday morning almost three months ago when King William made his entry into Dublin.

The heat had been oppressive, he well remembered, but the skies were overcast and gloomy. Nothing, however, could spoil the rejoicing of the city's Protestant citizens. Graham had crowded into St. Patrick's Cathedral with all the others, barely finding room to stand. The king, wearing his Crown of State, listened as the Church of Ireland bishop emphasized that the mightiest of earthly armies were but a faint shadow of the power of God.

During the following days, the army waited in wind-whipped tents outside the city while King Billy made an effort to settle Irish affairs by peaceful means. He promised mercy to all his Irish subjects in exchange for obedience. He promised amnesty to all rebels who submitted to him. "We abhor all manner of violence done to our loving subjects of what religion soever."

And then the army moved out to Limerick on the banks of the Shannon. Graham closed his eyes against that memory. Even in Ireland, no place had ever been so wet. Rain poured incessantly. The Williamite army camped in a swamp. And against all expectation, the Irish army, which had been so quick to run away at the Boyne, now resisted steadfastly. Even women and children defended their town with murderous courage. It was little wonder that Graham thought of the miry field as the Slough of Despond.

And far worse than the dismal living conditions was the deteriorating situation with his father. So much worse it was, coming as it had on top of the eased relations they had known before the battle. David and Graham were the enemies, not James and William. His father's remembered words ripped the quiet of the graveyard.

"Deserter! Insubordinate traitor! My son—my own son—refuses my command to pursue." The accusations repeated time and time again echoed as from the tombstones.

Graham's reply had been equally hot. "I was nae deserting. I followed William's orders. Our king would prevent the looting."

"Coward! Milksop coward. My son. A traitorous coward."

Time and again Graham had opened his mouth to explain, to speak the words he would rather forget. To save his father's life, he had killed his own cousin. And then he had given him burial—rather than follow orders. Was David right? Had he deserted?

"Nae, Father. I'm no defector, I—"

"Enough! No more, or I'll have ye shot yet." David stormed off, as such sessions always ended.

Graham felt relief. If his father had not stopped him, would he have told this time? Told of the pitiful funeral with three Lanark kin— full knowing it would the more enrage him? Told of the bag of Charles's effects he even now hoarded in his own kit—knowing David would forbid his carrying it back to Seaton Court?

And then it was that the messenger from Comber found them in their rain-soaked bog.

David had received the man's news stoically. "Aye. She were a good lass, a dear wife. She deserves her reward." He bit his lip. "But I would have liked to see her again."

Two days later King Billy lifted the siege of Limerick. It was his only defeat in Ireland. But escaping that mire-choked camp did not feel like a defeat. And the newly widowed Captain Lanark and his son were given leave to return to Lanarks' Bawn.

They had been home for almost two months now. The trees were October gold. A warm autumn haze hung over the world. But the home they returned to was cold. *Chill and silent as a tomb,* Graham thought. He'd known he would miss his gentle, loving mother. He had been prepared for the emptiness of her room. But he had no idea that the whole house, even all inside the bawn, would be so desolate. He had not realized her spirit had reached all of them so vibrantly even when she never left her bed.

And not only Janet was gone. Margaret Cole had requested David to escort her and Esther back to Derry soon after the men returned. The awkward, impetuous Fanny had gone to Belfast to seek new employment. So the house was occupied by three men who rubbed along uneasily at best, waited on by the aging Hannah. If Graham had joined the army to heal the breach with his father, the effort had been wasted.

David still did not know Graham had saved his life. And Graham did not choose to speak of it. The killing haunted him. Again and again in his sleep he would charge forward on Hazel—sometimes into battle, sometimes into a thick fog, sometimes down a steep incline. But always there would be a bloodied victim at the end of the charge. Sometimes it was his cousin, sometimes it was his mother, sometimes his father. And always he woke sweating and thrashing at his covers.

The dreams would fade, he assured himself. He was not the first to be haunted by the horrors of battle. It would fade.

"And then I'll be about it, Maither." When he was certain there was no one around, Graham sometimes spoke to Janet in an audible murmur. It helped him focus his thoughts. "It's a great comfort to me to know that you loved her as much as I do. And she you. When the dreams clear, I'll speak to Molly, Maither. But you see how it is. I canna speak as I am now. And I've aught else to do first. I've delayed overlong as it is."

He turned from the grave and paused briefly at the next tombstone: Alexander Calum Lanark, David and Malcolm's brother, thirteen when he died. Graham wished he could have known this other uncle.

Slowly he mounted his tall chestnut. As he did so, he kicked the bag strapped to the back of his saddle. The belt buckle clanked against the sword hilt in the pack, and Graham shivered.

Molly knew he had brought Charles's effects home to his family. He had told her he saw his cousin fall and that he buried him. Graham even told her about the amazing meeting with Henry MacHenry. Molly had been so pleased that Graham could do that service for the Seaton Court Lanarks. And she had urged him over and over to hasten in taking Charles's things to the family. Bridie would be so comforted—so happy to know Charles had received her last letter. Graham was so good—so thoughtful. Fortunately she did not ask how Graham knew Charles. Or how Charles fell.

Gavin Lanark, Charles's father, would ask, though. Or one of his brothers or sisters. Someone would ask. And Graham did not know what he would say. But he could delay no longer.

In spite of the slates missing from the roof and the peeling paint on doors and window frames, Seaton Court retained much of the elegance of past generations. A breeze had risen, and the elms lining the entrance lane showered Graham with bright leaves.

As he approached the door, Graham realized that not all his reluctance sprang from a guilty conscience. Part of it was chagrin that kin living no farther apart than this could have been separated for so long. Could it have been only the religious difference that caused so deep a rift? This was the first time in Graham's life to approach this door. When ill feelings had been allowed to go on into the second and third generation, it was far easier to turn one's back on the boil than to lance it—especially when the lance of truth Graham carried in his chest was so dreadful.

He tied Hazel to the hitching post, all the time his head prickling with the sensation that someone was watching. Or was that just his guilty conscience? At first Graham thought no one would answer the door. The house was unnaturally quiet. The younger children—three of them, weren't there?—were probably riding their ponies over the fields as he had so often seen them do. But someone must be about.

The door creaked open then, just enough to reveal a short, stocky man with a balding head and square jaw. Graham had seen Gavin Lanark only from a distance. Distance enough that he had not seen the bitter look in his eyes before.

The man's tongue was no less sharp. "David Lanark's boy, aren't ye?"

"Yes, sir. I—" Graham had to tell *this* man that he had killed his son? "Er . . . that is, I much regret the lack of discourse between our houses. I've come to—"

The door slammed in his face.

From the other side the harsh voice barked, "Ye can tell your father it stays here. He'll not have it."

Graham looked at the bag in his hand. He had come to take nothing away, rather to give something. "But, sir—" He knocked again. There was no reply.

He looked from the bag to the house and back to the bag. What should he do? If he left the things with no explanation, would they realize they were Charles's? Momentary relief washed over him. Yes. Leave it and go. He had tried to make a clean breast of the matter. Now he was free of obligation.

But even as he stooped to place the bag on the step, he knew this would not put things to right. Then he heard a light step behind him.

"Sir—" The girl was the image of Gavin Lanark, short and plump, but her expression was sweet, her voice soft. "Are you Graham? Molly has spoken of you so often, and I've seen you ride by on the road."

"Aye. I'm Graham. You'll be Bridie—er, Miss Bridget?"

"Sure. Everyone calls me Bridie." She looked toward the barred door. "You must forgive my father's harshness. He grieves much. My mother died less than a year ago. And now our Charles." She swallowed. "You'll know he was killed at the Boyne?"

"I know." Graham's discomfort grew. The girl's sweetness was harder to bear than the father's sharpness. "That's why I've come. I wanted to tell . . . That is, I wanted to give . . ."

They both turned at the sound of wheels on the gravel driveway. The carriage was old, the paneling much in need of fresh paint, the seat wanting new upholstery, but the bay coat of the well-bred horse pulling it shone with care.

Bridie ran to the driveway. "Oh, Finn, well come. Just when we've a visitor."

Graham saw a lad, perhaps five or six years younger than himself, darker and of slighter build but with a definite family resemblance to those Lanarks he had just met—and to the one he had buried. Bridie held out her hand to help her younger brother from the carriage. "Come meet our cousin, Graham Lanark."

When the boy moved toward him, Graham was surprised to see that it was with the heavy limp of one born with a clubfoot.

"This is my brother, Finlay," Bridie announced.

The boy's thin features lit with a welcoming smile, and he held out his hand to Graham. His grip was strong. "Will ye come in, cousin?"

"Um, thank you, no. Not into the house, at least. I'll gladly go to the barn wi' ye if ye'd be about unharnessing that fine creature."

"Ah—" Finlay's eyes lit with pride at mention of his horse "—he is a fine one, my Shandy. I'd be glad of your company."

Graham and Bridie matched their steps to Finn's slower pace. "And did you see Mr. Monaghan, brother?" Bridie asked.

"Aye, I did."

Inside the barn, chickens clucked and flapped while pigeons cooed from the rafters. Dust motes danced in shafts of sunlight from high windows.

Finlay set about the unhitching with precise, efficient movements, patting Shandy and murmuring to him even as he answered his sister. "He said he'd be fair happy to take me as apprentice when Father Joseph's finished cramming all he can into my head." The boy's smile gleamed in the dimness of the barn.

"That's fine!" Bridie turned to Graham, beaming proudly. "Our Finlay's a bright lad—brightest he's ever taught, Father Joseph says. And he has his heart set on being a barrister." She turned back to her brother. "Oh, Finn—apprentice to the best barrister in Belfast! You'll be in Parliament someday! That'll show father!"

Graham smiled. Were fathers never happy with the sons they got?

Shandy stabled, the three sat on a bench just outside the barn door. The peat stack a few feet beyond scented the air with its earthy, smoky tang. The late afternoon sun warmed Graham's head, bringing with it the thought of the merciless pounding of the heat last summer. This recalled him to the duty he was to perform.

"I . . . uh . . ." He cleared his throat. "I've come on more than a pleasure call—although I'd say making your acquaintances is a pleasure—a long overdue one." He picked up his sack and handed it to Bridie. "I thought you'd want these."

Bridie took the bag with a quizzical expression. She drew out the sword first. Her finger moved slowly over the hilt. When she looked up, her eyes shimmered. "This was Charlie's."

Graham nodded. She took out the black leather belt with its heavy brass buckle and handed it to Finlay. Next was the letter. A single tear rolled down her round cheek. She put the folded, soiled page to her lips, then tucked it in a pocket under her apron.

The girl reached into the sack one last time. Charles's black hat still had a bit of broken white feather clinging to the wide brim. Bridie said, "I fixed those feathers there for him. Plucked them from my prize goose—a whole handful. 'I'll not have a brother of mine mistaken for a traitor to our rightful king,' I said. I spent a whole evening sewing them on. Broke my best needle doing it." She choked and was silent.

"How came you by these, cousin?" Finlay's voice was pleasant, warm with interest, a lilt in the question.

Graham would have far preferred thundering accusations. "I was there."

"Did you see him fall?" Bridie's hand was warm on his arm.

Graham stared, unseeing, at the straw-littered ground. His mind filled with images of the body-strewn battlefield. And the one body he had caused to lie there. "Aye. I . . . I saw him fall. I didn't know . . ."

"Was it quick? I've so hoped he didn't suffer long."

Graham shook his head. "A single stroke. One slash of the cutlass." To his horror Graham realized he had slashed out with his arm, reenacting the hateful deed. He clasped his hands in his lap. "He felt nothing. I can give you that comfort," he finished in a whisper.

Bridie's soft sniffs were the only sound for several moments.

"I'd also have you know I buried him." He could see the girl's hunger for details so he recounted the scene exactly.

She looked up, her eyes shining, at the account of Henry MacHenry. "Another cousin? That is a richness indeed. That our dear Lord sent family members to do the offices those closer in blood could not do." Now she squeezed Graham's arm. "I shall be forever grateful. Forever grateful." She rose and started toward the house. "I shall tell Father. Perhaps it will soften him."

Finn accompanied Graham to where Hazel waited. He held out his hand. "It's good of you to come, sir. I hope you'll come again."

Graham took his hand. "I'd like to."

Finlay looked him fully in the eyes and held his gaze, the lad's face full of wisdom beyond his years. "Do come. But say no more on this subject. My sister is happy. That's enough."

Graham rode off, puzzled by that strange parting speech and by his own conflicting mood. He had accomplished far more than he had expected to: delivering Charles's things, comforting Bridie, making what he felt certain were new friends. So why did this heavy weight remain on his chest? Surely he had said enough. To say more would have been to destroy the comfort he had given.

Indeed, to have spoken more fully would have relieved his conscience but put the weight on the heart of those who had no duty to bear it. And would have widened the rift between their houses. The terrible, secret knowledge of what he had done was his alone to bear.

Even the sight of Molly waiting for him at Lanarks' Bawn did not raise his spirits. "I brought some pear preserves," she said. "We made them today. Sheila knows your Hannah has more than her hands full feeding you three great louts."

When his smile was only cursory, she became serious. "You went to Seaton Court."

"Aye."

"They received you?"

"Bridie and Finlay did. Their father slammed the door." He considered for a moment. "Strange, that. I'm thinking it must be more than the religion. Gavin Lanark admits his Price cousins to Seaton Court."

Molly nodded. "Yes. I've had no trouble with him. And Sheila has called with me more than once."

"He said something about not giving something back. I wonder what he meant."

"Perhaps he borrowed some money once upon a time?"

Graham considered. "My faither would no' loan to him. And Malcolm would like have mentioned it had he done."

An uncomfortable silence fell between them. He hoped he had steered the conversation far enough away from the outcome of his visit. But he did not know where to go from here. He'd thought that once he had made his pilgrimage to Seaton Court—once Charles Lanark was finally buried—he would be free to look to the future. Free to speak to Molly of that subject closest to his heart. But the guilty weight blocked words of love as well as words of confession.

And it was really all sae daft. One went into battle to kill the enemy. Graham had done no more than his duty. Actually, he had behaved heroically. If Charles Lanark were not filling that grave beside the Boyne, David Lanark would be. But no argument could clear his mind. And perhaps it was not the circumstances at all. Perhaps it was the simple fact that he had killed another human being. He, who had never wanted anything but to grow crops and nurture animals, to spend all his energies bringing forth new life, had killed. His hands were red, and they would not wash white.

And so the seasons turned. David returned to the regiment, for, even though neither king remained on Irish soil, the supporters of James and William battled on.

And Graham returned to the farming he loved. But there was less joy in it than formerly. He saw Molly every Sunday at meeting and occasionally between. Always her sweet looks and wide brown eyes made him catch his breath, for he could not believe that from one seeing to the next she could become more dear to him. And yet he would not, could not, speak.

It was the following July, just a few days before the anniversary of his mother's death, that Graham took the notion of carrying *The Pilgrim's Progress* with him when he visited her grave.

There, in the quiet of the churchyard, it seemed most natural to sit beside his mother's resting place, somewhat leaning on the stone of him who would have been his Uncle Alex, and read the book he had so often read to her in life.

He found little comfort in the story, but he felt a growing kinship with Christian, who was so weighted down by the great burden he carried. He read on until Christian fell into the Slough of Despond and "could not get out because of the burden that was upon his back." Graham closed the book, leaving himself and Bunyan's Pilgrim both in the slough.

Two weeks later, David returned with news of the victory the Williamite army had won at Aughrim. A great victory, but at great cost. Some said it was the bloodiest battle ever fought on Irish soil. Even David, the hardened soldier, shook his head as he recounted the toll: one general, three major-generals, seven brigadiers, twenty-two colonels. More than seven thousand of other ranks.

But the bloody tally did not prevent the Protestants of Ulster from celebrating. Bonfires blazed from one side of the province to the other. As the news of the victory of the Glorious Twelfth spread, beacons burned in every village and atop every hillock. After more than a year of struggle, the Jacobite rising had been put down. Ulster Protestants had survived the '41, and they had survived James. They intended to continue surviving.

But the next news that swept the land was not so welcome to the victors. The terms offered by William's general were generous to the point of giving away the victory. Fifteen thousand Irish soldiers were allowed to sail away to serve the French king. Those who stayed and swore allegiance to William and Mary could keep their land. Where were the massive land confiscations the victors so deserved? As a final affront, Catholics were to have freedom of worship.

Graham rejoiced at the lenient terms, thinking what gladness they would bring to his cousins and others like them. But the following Sunday, standing outside the meetinghouse, he discovered how alone he was in supporting the terms of the Treaty of Limerick.

David wagged his head, and the buckle on his high-crowned black hat gleamed in the sun. "He's given it all away! We fought our hearts out for King Billy—and I'd do it all again, for he's a fine, brave king—but he's given it all away! After all those months in choking mud and blazing heat—he's given away all we fought for."

Even Michael Price, leaning heavily on his stick, seemed uncharacteristically gloomy. "Aye. We'll lose our land yet. I remember well the tales of my grandparents' butchering in the '41. Might as well have given the heathen the land then if we're to give it to them now." The agitated old man began to teeter.

Sheila Price, his half-sister and faithful housekeeper for as long as either of them could remember, put a steadying arm around him. "We'll all be slaughtered in our beds yet. But there it is. Might as well enjoy a good meal afore it happens. Come along, Michael."

A group of young boys at the side of the church began chanting, "The conquerors lose, the conquered gain in their defeat. We fight like heroes, but like fools we treat." As it was the Sabbath, they did not go so far as to sing their rhyme or to dance to its rhythm, but no adult hushed their recitation.

"What now, Cap'n Lanark? What's to be done?" a man from the other side of Comber asked.

David squared his shoulders. "We're no' beaten yet. We must take action."

"Aye, aye."

"Make our victory secure."

"We'll no' surrender."

It seemed to Graham, standing quietly at the back of the circle, that the very walls of the meetinghouse echoed the sentiment. "No surrender!"

"But what's to do?" another asked.

Again it was David who replied. "The guns are silenced. We must fight with laws. If the Glorious Revolution means aught, it means that even the monarch must bow to Parliament. Billy will no' get his will in this matter of our land."

Graham turned away. Must they fight on even when they'd won? He heard the fear in their voices. He saw the insecure looks on their faces, even though they shouted, "No surrender." Could there not be peace even when the armies had disbanded? What strife would come next?

38

Sentiments had changed little, except to harden, by the following year when King William III summoned his first Irish Parliament.

David sat beneath the high ceiling of the Great Hall of Dublin Castle, listening to the angry debate reverberate between the stone walls. He gritted his teeth and squared his jaw. He was adamant, as were all the Commons. No matter how long it took, they would get their message across. This Parliament would not end until the matter of land ownership was settled in favor of the victors of the Battle of the Boyne.

He was determined. This was his chance. He had served in Commons for twelve years. Under James's attempt to de-Protestantize Ireland, he had borne the oppressive fear and stigma of Attainder. He had been forced to stand aside while the army and the law—the two activities that made up David's life—had been rapidly Catholicized by James. But now King Billy was triumphant. Now was David's chance. There was much to be accomplished in the matter of lawmaking, and he intended to be part of it.

The days of the London Parliament reigning supreme came to an end with the death of Cromwell and the restoration to the throne of King Charles II. But the power of British monarchs was still much constrained. Cromwell's Parliament had struck as firm a blow to absolutism as had the Magna Carta more than four hundred years earlier. And no monarch, even King Billy, could deny the ascendent rulers of Ireland the position they had earned.

"Gentlemen, gentlemen!" Lord Sidney, the king's viceroy, fought for control of the assembly. "It is His Majesty's wish that all his subjects—of whatsoever religion—be treated equitably."

"You call giving our land to papists an equitable act?" Philip Freeman's long black wig just brushed the tips of his thin mustache when he leaned forward. "I say there is but one hope for Ireland. We must be free of the yoke of England! I call upon this Parliament—"

He was drowned out by raucous cries of approval.

"Gentlemen, gentlemen!" Sweat formed on Lord Sidney's brow.

"Are you mad? Come, let us reason together. All in this room are Protestant landowners. We can be reasonable. We can support our good king and queen, William and Mary—"

David added his voice to the shouting that drowned out the viceroy. They were Protestant landowners, but they were not English— no matter where their ancestors hailed from. They were Irish. And they would be ruled from Dublin, not from London. And they would not surrender their property.

In the coming days David raised his voice with all his fellows to protect their land. "Aye, aye." King James's grants to his favorites were revoked. "Aye, aye." Jacobite land claims were denied. "Aye, aye." Half a million acres of good Irish earth were available for sale—to Protestants.

David heaved a huge sigh of relief. They had done what they came to do. He urged Trapper to a faster pace when the craggy shape of Scrabo appeared to his right. He turned toward Lanarks' Bawn with a satisfied smile on his face. Now they could rest secure on their own land. They had the victory for which they sought.

Of course, they had taken no action to separate from England. On reflection, perhaps that had been just wild talk. Yet, in substance that was what they had done. The Irish Parliament had the bit in their mouth, and not even King Billy could take it out.

David drew in his breath sharply as a flutter of blue fabric caught his attention. A young woman walked through the field ahead. The soft breeze was blowing her skirt. David jerked Trapper to a stop and rubbed a hand across his eyes.

He knew well enough it wasn't Janet. Even before he recalled the green mound in the corner of the churchyard, he did not think of Janet. In those dear, gone, happy days when Janet had walked in that same field, she had not moved so lightly. Always Janet had been focused, purposeful in her movements.

This woman moved as if propelled only by the breeze wafting the long-stemmed flax around her. How long had it been since he had taken pleasure in so simple a matter as seeing a woman in a blue dress walk through a field blue with blossoming flax? How long had it been since he had noticed a woman at all?

At first he thought she was coming toward him, and he started to raise his arm in a wave, although he still did not recognize her. But she turned and drifted down the hill toward Strangford Lough.

David rode on to Lanarks' Bawn. The house was dark and quiet when he entered. Malcolm and Graham were both in the fields.

Hannah came running at the sound of his step on the scrubbed boards of the entrance hall. "Oh, Captain Lanark, you're come home, and I've nothing but small beer and oatcakes to offer you." She dipped a curtsy.

From force of long habit, David was three steps up the stairway to Janet's room before he realized there was no one to go up to. "Thank you, Hannah, my throat is very dry after my ride."

He sat on the straight wooden chair by the cold fireplace, sipping his ale. Late afternoon shadows filled the low-ceilinged room, even though the shutters were opened wide. Surely it hadn't always been so silent here, so dismal. It couldn't be just the quiet after the tumult of war and parliamentary debate.

He thudded his tankard on the table with such force that its pale contents sloshed onto the polished wood. Then he jumped to his feet and began pacing. He was still vigorous, just turned forty. Always he had been a man of action, the person all turned to when danger threatened. Now there was no danger. The peace was established. But David felt less at peace than when he rode into battle.

"Ah, Father. I saw Trapper in the barn, or I'd not have known you were here."

Graham stood in the doorway, beams from the open window lighting the strong bones of his face, emphasizing the breadth of his shoulders. His son was a man grown. A man with his whole life ahead of him, while David's life was over.

"I'm here. Aye." There seemed to be nothing more to say.

"It went well, then? Parliament did?"

"Aye."

Father and son argued little now. They never referred to the soreness between them. But neither did they talk much.

The silence grew. At last David filled it by telling about the land that was available to new settlers now that Parliament had dealt with any question of its remaining in the hands of the Jacobites.

Graham nodded. "I hope it'll be for the best, Father."

"Of course it's best. It's the only thing. Ye'd not give the land to the papists so they could form another rising, would ye?" His old irritations flared again.

"No, I'd not. And it's as well there's land available—as many as have been coming across from Scotland of late."

"Oh, aye?"

"Our numbers have like to doubled at meeting in the time you've been in Dublin, Father."

"I'm not surprised. Now that we've settled the peace, we've such a promise of civil security as has never been known in this land. Now the settlers will flock here."

"Aye, that's some of it, Father. And they'll be welcome on the farms laid waste during the trouble. But it's a matter of push as much as pull. You'll have heard of the hardships the Scots leave behind?"

David frowned. "I'd a letter from some distant kin in Glasgow last year. He said the crops were poorly. But that happens. Most like this harvest will be better."

"Last year's harvest was the third failure in a row. And the winter severe. Many who hoped to hold on for the next harvest died of starvation. They say in some villages no more than two or three cottages are occupied with breathing bodies."

Then Malcolm entered in his quiet, stolid way, still wearing his muddy boots from the field, and the talk turned to matters closer to hand.

David thought little more of Scottish immigration until he entered the meetinghouse the next Sunday. Indeed, Graham had been right. The congregation was doubled and more. They stood to sing, and David's breast filled with pride as he sang Psalm 149:

> "Let the saints be joyful. . . . Let the high praises of God be in their mouth, and a two-edged sword in their hand; to execute vengeance upon the heathen, and punishments upon the people; to bind their kings with chains, and their nobles with fetters of iron; to execute upon them the judgment written: this honour have all his saints. Praise ye the Lord."

David gave two grim nods as he snapped the hymnbook shut. Aye, God *had* given them a two-edged sword. Aye, they *had* executed vengeance upon the heathen, and judgment was executed upon their king and nobles. Praise the Lord. Now David would enjoy the fruits of his labors. He would reap the benefits that he had helped win for his people and for his God.

He sat back on the wooden pew and folded his arms across his chest as Parson Stevenson began his sermon.

But David's mind was not on the preacher's words. His glance had strayed to the far side of the room where light from the clear leaded window fell on the whitewashed wall—and there she was. Her dark hair and eyes were framed by a crisp linen cap. She wore a soft blue-gray dress. It was the girl of the flax field.

David usually enjoyed every word of the Reverend Mr. Stevenson's sermons. He listened carefully to every point and discussed the message vigorously all week. But today he could not have told anyone the text should he be quizzed on the matter.

David could do no more than raise his hat in the young woman's direction on the Sabbath. A few days later, however, he saw her walking in the field again. This time he waited until she neared the road, almost holding his breath for fear she would vanish, so insubstantial did she appear. But she did not dissolve, and he dismounted and approached, introducing himself as her neighbor.

She replied in a soft voice that was more blown to him on the wind than by her own breath. Her name was Lorna Firth.

Up close, David was shocked to see that what from a distance appeared to be delicacy and grace was in truth emaciated frailty. Lorna had been starved. Her face was white, the bones barely covered by the thin skin. It was no wonder he had seen her eyes as large and dark— they were almost all that existed of her face. And now he saw that her dress was not a delicate pastel but, in fact, merely faded and threadbare.

And yet she smiled. The smile, more than anything else, told him of the suffering she had endured and the bravery required of such people to bring them across the water with the courage to start again. A great wave of protectiveness washed over him. He wanted to take care of Lorna Firth. He wanted to bring back the bloom to her cheek and the spring to her step. She looked as near death as he had ever seen Janet. But this one he would not surrender to the reaper. It did not matter that she was half his age.

"You . . . er . . . I believe you are new come from Scotland?" The girl had a great stillness about her that made David feel years her junior.

"Yes sir. From Muirkirk. Father was the pastor. He brought us over. The seven that were strong enough to make the trip, that is." Her gaze stretched northward, back toward Scotland. "We buried my mother and baby brother before we came. There are only my father and myself left now. The twins were aye weak; they went in the first hunger."

David had to stop himself from putting out a hand to support her. But even as he stifled the impulse, he sensed the latent strength of spirit beneath the skin-covered bones. "I am sorry." His words sounded so hollow. "Please tell your father I shall call with my condolences. My wife died last year as well."

The wide dark eyes turned full on him. "Oh, was there famine here too? I had understood—"

"No, no. It was a longstanding sickness."

There seemed to be nothing more to say. He asked the location of the cottage the newcomers had leased from Sir Robert Colville and learned it was a short distance to the south, nearer the lough. Only a short walk from Lanarks' Bawn. A short, pleasant walk and an even shorter, more pleasant, ride. One that David Lanark made almost daily.

"Dearly beloved brethren, we are gathered together in the sight of God and in the face of His congregation to join these parties together in the honorable estate of matrimony, which was instituted and authorized by God Himself in Paradise . . ."

In spite of the fact that the law recognized only marriages solemnized by the established church, Lorna would not hear to being married by any but her father. And David had held no love for the notion of being married in the Anglican church in Newtown. So, as duly prescribed by The Book of Common Order, the bride and groom came before the altar at the beginning of the sermon. The civil code could be no match for God's law.

It was not concern for legal requirements that made Graham avert his eyes from Capt. David Lanark and his new bride standing before the altar of the meetinghouse. Nor was it the fact that the bride could have been Graham's younger sister. The past summer marked the second year that David had spent as a widower, and there seemed to be no reason he should remain in that state any longer.

Through the summer months Graham had often watched his father in newly polished boots and smartly brushed coat ride down the lane in the direction of the Firth cottage. Graham did not begrudge his father his happiness. But he longed for the freedom to win his own.

That was the crux of the matter. To all appearances he had the freedom. He had just passed his twenty-first birthday so was an adult in the eyes of all. He shared equally in the work with Malcolm, and his uncle had made clear that Graham was to be his heir. And although Molly never pushed herself at him, her smile never failed to brighten when they met. Yet, he felt this constriction around his heart that blocked offering his tender feelings to another.

He looked at her now, sitting at the end of the pew, crowded with assorted members of the Price family, her eyes straight forward, her hands folded in her lap.

Mr. Firth's words sounded clearly. ". . . to have Lorna Mary Firth, here present, for your lawful wife and spouse, promising to keep her, to love and entreat her in all things according to the duty of a faithful husband . . ."

But even as Graham wished it were Molly and himself standing before the minister, the weight of his wrongs pressed on him. He thought of the advice of Worldly Wiseman to Christian to get rid of his burden for he would never be settled in his mind until then, nor could he enjoy the blessings that God had given him until it was gone.

And Graham would have responded as did Christian: "That is what I seek for, but I cannot get it off myself. Nor is there any man in our country that can take it off my shoulders. And so I am going on my way to be rid of my burden."

Late that afternoon he stopped briefly by his mother's grave, then continued down the road away from Lanarks' Bawn. The bridal couple would be sitting down to dinner soon. And although he wished them well, Graham preferred to be alone. He was almost at Seaton Court before he realized he had turned Hazel in that direction.

In the two years since his first call there, Graham had occasionally seen Finlay and Bridie, usually driving in the carriage behind the high-stepping Shandy. The brother and sister were always friendly, inviting him to call and interested in his family. But Graham's consciousness of his deed cast a dark shadow between them and prevented the growth of real friendship. Thankfully, he had seen Gavin not at all. He hoped that now there would be no such encounter.

His luck held, for Finlay was in the yard, brushing Shandy. He waved and limped toward Graham, smiling. "A fine thing it is to see you at Seaton Court, Graham Lanark."

"I was just passing and thought I'd inquire how you all are." He nodded toward the well-groomed horse. "I see Shandy's well."

"He's grand. It's lucky you've come just now. Next week I'll be in my lodgings in Belfast. I'm to start reading law with Mr. Monaghan." The lad beamed.

Graham could see that Finlay had a love for the law akin to what he himself felt for the land. Or at least like that he had known before the war unsettled his peace.

But then the cheerful Bridie joined them, anxious for details about David's new bride, and there was little time for reflection—although Graham thought that more than once she left a meaningful pause, should he wish to divulge anything about himself and her friend. She once even casually brought up Molly's name. But there was nothing he could say that would satisfy her or himself. And so the long day drew to a close.

That winter was one of the longest and coldest in anyone's memory, and the gray chill seemed to enter Graham's heart as well. And now the great divide that had so long existed between Graham and his father appeared to be developing between himself and Molly. He could not understand himself. It was as though seeing the happiness of the newlyweds sparked his irritability, which he would then take out on Molly when she called to see Lorna. Lorna, at least, was blossoming. Hannah's abundant cooking had put flesh on her bones and color in her cheeks.

In contrast, Molly seemed to wilt as Graham grew more distant.

Next time, he vowed as he mounted the slopes of Scrabo with his shepherd's crook, *next time I see Molly, I'll be different.*

Then "next time" became "this time," for from his elevated position on Scrabo, he saw Molly enter the bawn.

Graham decided, as he rubbed salve on a ewe's sore leg, that this was his chance. He hurried through his rounds of inspection, picturing Molly sitting by the fire with Lorna, talking comfortably in the spot he would have be her very own. He pictured himself entering. He would offer her a warm greeting as in former days. Her smile would be as warm.

His fingers, stiff with the cold, patted the ewe on her rump and moved on to the next one. The flock baaed and shifted, milling around him. The dogs kept the strays in order. This was what Graham had always loved doing. He'd never wanted anything else. This life and Molly.

As soon as he finished, he would leave the sheep to the care of Tag and Bob, his trusty sheepdogs, and he would go.

This was hardly the first time he had vowed to talk to Molly. Only last Sabbath he'd determined to speak kindly to her after meeting. The breach must be healed. An earlier generation had opened a divide between Lanarks' Bawn and Seaton Court. He could not be responsible for a similar chasm between the bawn and Prices' Farm. And the silence between him and Molly was leading to just that. He had gone to sleep Saturday night, planning to speak the following morning.

But that night he had had the dream again. He spurred furiously, and Hazel lunged into the swirling battle. He brandished his sword, slashed this way and that, drew it back red each time. Then he had made one final, terrible lunge. And the face at the end of his thrust had been Molly's.

The next day he avoided her entirely.

The sheep baaed and moved away, almost upsetting Graham. Only then did he realize how tightly he had entwined his fingers in the ewe's wooly coat. Aye, he had failed last time. But not now. He looked out over the broad backs of his flock, and a little of the satisfaction of former times returned. They were fine beasts. They had responded to the cold with a vigorous growth of winter coats. Aye, a fine flock. And Molly was sitting by the fire in Lanarks' Bawn. Graham whistled all the way down the hill.

He changed his boots, washed, and made his way to the front room with vigor born of anticipation. He opened the door—and stopped.

Quite a different visitor than he had expected sat by the fire with his father.

The minister, Mr. Houston, stood, took his hand, and launched immediately into his concern. "Ah, Graham, well come. I know we can count on your support in this. And we need every voice. Fewer than a dozen seats in both houses of Parliament are held by Presbyterians. All is ruled by the landed gentry of the established church. We have to present a united front."

Graham frowned. "But surely the issues are the same for all."

"For all Protestants, aye, although I'm not so sure those of the prelacy realize how much they need our support. Ulster may be a minority, but we'll no' be silent."

The men settled into their chairs, and Houston produced a sheaf of papers, which he thrust at Graham. "Here. Your father has often mentioned how he would have you take greater interest in the making of laws. This is to be voted on in the next Parliament. Let us hear your views."

Graham took the papers, still adjusting his mind from the scene he had expected to encounter. Although disappointing, perhaps this was best. He had thought to heal the breach with Molly, but perhaps making strides with his father was the more important. Pleasing his father in the matter of joining the army had brought disaster, but surely just reading a proposed parliamentary bill could offer no dangers.

He moved the candle closer to his chair and leaned over the paper headed "An Act for Banishing all Papists Exercising any Ecclesiastical Jurisdiction and all Regulars of the Popish Clergy out of this Kingdom."

> Whereas, it is Notoriously known, that the late Rebellions in this Kingdom have been contrived, promoted and carried on by popish archbishops, bishops, Jesuits and other Ecclesiastical Persons of the Romish Clergy. And forasmuch as the Peace and Publick Safety of this Kingdom is in Danger . . .

"What is this saying?" Graham spoke before he thought. "Peace and public safety in danger! What danger are we in from a handful of priests and papists? Are my lame, bookish cousin and his soft-spoken sister about to storm the bawn?"

His father was on his feet before Graham fully realized what he had said.

"To whom do you dare refer in this house? Have ye been consorting with that vile brood of Gavin Lanark's? In front of the very mantel his family deflowered?"

Graham sat completely baffled. "I have no idea what you're talking about, Father—but I doubt it bears much on the matter of this bill." He waved the sheets in his hand. "Look at this. 'They do move sedition and rebellion, to the great hazard of the ruin and desolation of this kingdom.' *What* sedition and rebellion? James's soldiers are gone. A few outlaws roam the woods, but—"

The minister slammed his fist on the table. "And have ye never heard of the merciless havoc and slaughter which laid desolate this kingdom in the year of our Lord 1641? It must ever be our duty to prevent the growth of popery by a hearty and zealous instigation of such laws as are necessary to keep the land free for the *true* faith."

Graham was silenced. He felt the eyes of both men on him as he returned to reading the document. The only sound in the room was the peat shifting on the grate.

He quickly saw that he held not just one such law but, indeed, a collection of such papers. If these were passed by the Irish Parliament, Catholics would be prevented from bearing arms, educating their children, or owning a horse above five pounds in value.

Graham looked up. "Does His Majesty support this? And how could such things be enforced?"

Houston shrugged. "King Billy does no' rule the Irish Parliament. Nor will he oppose us."

Graham shook his head. Catholics would not be able to buy land, vote, join the army, serve in public office . . . "These proposals—" he hit the stack with the back of his hand "—they will take years even for Parliament to *enact*. Such laws are nothing less than unmitigated disqualification of a large part of our population. They will create chaos!"

Mr. David Houston's square jaw jutted forward. "The law does not assume there to be any such person as an Irish Catholic."

Graham dropped the papers on the floor and began to pace the room, trying to sort out his thoughts. "I canna imagine inflicting such a Table of Proscription on a people. Taking away a man's vote is the taking away of his shield not only against oppressive power but the worst of all oppression—the persecution of private society and private manners. Common sense and common justice dictate—"

"Enough." His father was back on his feet, fists clenched. "I will not be spoken to like that by a son of mine." He turned his back on Graham. "You can count on my full support, Houston."

Graham exited the room, banging the door shut behind him. He had crossed the hall before he saw that someone stood in the shadows. "Molly. I thought you had gone."

"I was in the kitchen with Lorna. I didn't mean to eavesdrop, Graham. Lorna had asked me to inquire whether Parson Houston would be staying to supper." She looked hard at the floor. "I heard your speech, Graham. It was a fine thing."

"Aye. And sensible. But they'll no' listen. It may take months or years, but it will come. They'll pass those laws."

Molly voiced the thought uppermost in his mind. "Bridie? Finlay? The younger ones?"

He nodded. "Aye, that's it. It'd be a fine thing if the disenfranchising of their priests would make them turn Protestant. How such fine people can worship idols, I cannot—" He stopped and shook his head. "But no schools for the children, no buying of land, no holding office—every door closed to them. It is no' right. Not even able to own a decent horse—"

He had not thought of it until the words left his mouth. "Shandy. Finlay's Shandy."

Molly looked up at him. "What can we do? Could you no' persuade them to leave that one item off?"

"They'll not listen to me." He turned away. "It's the sheer pettiness of it. If they really fear a rising, then bar the papists from the army. Keep firearms, even sharp knives, from them. But this—refusing education to their children—will just make matters worse." He turned back to Molly. "But I'll think of something. There must be some way we can help Finlay, at least. I'll do what I can."

Molly's gesture was so quick he barely felt her hand on his arm. But the warmth of the touch remained long.

39

For all Graham's good intentions, one thing followed on the heels of another with such rapidity that, although he never entirely forgot his vow to Molly nor her warm reaction, the thing did not get done. A heavy snowfall a few days after Houston's visit necessitated his spending every daylight hour, and many dark ones as well, with his sheep. And then there was lambing—a triumphal season in that his flock was near to doubled with the bounty of small, wobbly lambs. But then, so was his work doubled. And there were the fields to prepare, and the planting, and it seemed Graham had barely blinked before the harvest was upon them.

It was said by some that near fifty thousand Scots had come across the narrow Irish Sea, as the harvests continued poorly there. But the fine harvest and improved fortune of so many of her countrymen was not Lorna's only reason for joy. It soon became obvious that Graham was to have a half brother—or sister—by the time lambing season arrived next year.

The uncertain sunshine of early March covered the green land, and white snowdrops and gold and purple crocus brightened every sheltered corner when David made his hurried return to Lanarks' Bawn from Dublin. The Commons and Lords were still debating at Dublin Castle, but not even the protection of the landed Protestant gentry could take importance over the birth of his son.

"Aye, a braw wee bairn." And as the proud father bent adoringly over the wooden cradle that had sheltered so many Lanark babes, Graham had to agree that wee Davey was a fine babe.

All the bawn had been brightened by his arrival. Hannah scoffed at the slightest suggestion that the extra laundry was anything but a delight. Malcolm, who was much attached to his vittles, seemed not to notice when meals were late or undercooked. And Graham would never have dreamed of speaking a word of objection against being wakened more than once during the night by high, thin wailing. After less than a fortnight's residence, Wee Davey was king of the bawn.

But now His Majesty screwed up his small red face and let his obedient subjects know that he wished to eat. Hannah bustled in, scooped the infant from the cradle, placed him in Lorna's arms, and shooed the men from the room.

They settled themselves around the fire, chatting about the planting of crops, the arrival of yet more Scots immigrants, and the liberal heresies of the New Light Presbyterians. The conversation continued so comfortably that Graham dared to hope that Wee Davey had accomplished that greatest of miracles and brought peace to Lanarks' Bawn.

Malcolm leaned forward, lit one end of a small stick in the fire, and stuck the glowing end into the bowl of his newly filled clay pipe. Then he leaned back in his chair, pulling intently to get the pipe to draw, and exhaled a sigh. "Aye, that's fine. Now, tell me, brither, what of these fine laws ye're making such a fuss over away down in Dublin?"

Graham tensed, knowing that his father's reply would signal the end of the peace they had enjoyed through all of David's absence and that Graham had been so foolishly optimistic as to hope could continue.

David nodded with a satisfied air. "Aye, brither. Fine work it is, indeed. And well worth making a stushie over." He took a deep drink from his tankard of ale, lowered it slowly, and wiped his mouth with the back of his hand. "Aye, fine work, but slow. We mean to make a thorough job of the matter. If it can be done by force of law—and I believe it can—we'll not have another rising. We mean to establish the peace for a hundred years."

"Aye? And how do you think to go about that?"

"As I said—by means of the law. Penal laws that will keep those insolent rapparees under control."

Graham bit his lip. Those Jacobite soldiers who had remained in Ireland, rather than going into exile and serving in the French army, were now dispossessed and discharged. They lived as outlaws, mostly along the southern borders of Ulster, terrorizing the country by holding up coaches, rustling cattle, and robbing the homes of the rich. Indeed, such needed to be dealt with.

But his nod was an expression of thinking, not of agreeing. Aye, rapparees must be controlled. But the same crushing economic laws that applied to Catholic outlaws would apply to such as Henry MacHenry and Finlay and Bridie Lanark as well. Besides, brigands were not the genuine focus of the punishing laws the Irish Parliament passed. The true objective was the land—to wrest all they could of that still remaining in Catholic hands. Land was the source of all wealth, security, and power.

At least Graham was pleased to hear that, although highly popular with some MPs, efforts to deny Catholics the right to vote were progressing so slowly that it might take twenty or thirty years before such a bill passed. He could only hope that his vehement speech supporting Catholic suffrage might have had at least a shred of influence with his father. Perhaps there was hope yet.

But David's next words brought Graham out of any such rosy daydream.

"Aye, economic pressure—that's the ticket, I say. Limit them to short leases with high rent, see that all public office holding is closed to them, and keep them out of the legal profession!"

Graham came upright in his chair. "The legal profession? Father, you'd not keep them from the protection of the law?"

David swirled the contents in his mug. "I'd deny that to no man or beast. You know that, son. It's the *profession* we've closed to papists. The law's a lucrative business and an important one. Can't let such matters be handled by . . ."

Finlay's friendly, open smile and dark, intelligent eyes filled Graham's mind. He had worried about what the boy, slow and awkward with his clubfoot, would do without his horse—Graham's conscience smote him that he had done nothing on that matter. But this was so much worse. Shandy was a convenience, a source of pride, and a great pleasure to Finn. His chosen profession would be his whole life. Graham could only imagine how he himself would feel if he were to be denied all access to the land and animals he so loved.

"Excuse me, Father . . . I . . . er . . . uh . . . I think there's a ewe . . . Tell Hannah not to wait supper." He strode from the room.

He would have galloped all the way to Seaton Court, but his need to think required a steady hand on Hazel's rein. He had no clear plan. He simply knew he needed to do *something* to stem the tide of injustice that was sweeping the country.

"And what are ye thinking to be doing on my property, I'd like to know? Have I not made myself clear that you're no' welcome?"

Graham had been so intent on the problem at hand that for once he had not thought to worry about Gavin Lanark and the incomprehensible feud between their families. Now the old man's sharp-toothed leer and the snap of a rifle's cocking brought the matter into sharp focus.

Graham dismounted and held his hands out, palms open. "Quite clear, Mr. Lanark, but if I could just see Finlay—"

The rifle prodded his ribs. He backed up a step.

"Come to gloat are ye? Did your *athair* send ye for it? You can tell him his fancy laws might keep my boy out of the law courts, but they won't get the Lanark treasure back inside your bawn."

Was the man mad? There was no Lanark treasure. He knew something of his ancestors. Good, careful farmers and linen merchants. Respectable, hardworking, God-fearing. That was all. No treasure.

But he focused on what Gavin said about Finlay. So word had reached Seaton Court. Had Mr. Monaghan sent his apprentice home? Had Monaghan himself been disbarred? Surely the enforcers were not out yet. But perhaps as soon as the courts knew of the bill's passing, they refused Monaghan's briefs? Graham was unsure about the process but not about its effects on this family.

"Go on—back on your fine horse and off my land!" The steel barrel jabbed him again.

"*Athair!* What are you doing?" Capless, her long hair flying around her face, Bridie came running from the side entrance of the house.

"I've warned him before. I'll have no descendant of Dougal Lanark on my land."

Graham groped for his saddle. One leap and he could be up and off. But not before the man could pull the trigger his finger was caressing. At that range there was no chance he would miss.

"For shame, *Athair.* Give me that gun. Would ye shoot the man who cared for our Charles in his last moments?"

The barrel wavered. "What are ye saying?"

"Aye. You heard me." Bridie wiped her hands on her long white apron and held them out to take the rifle. "That's what he came to tell you on his first visit, but you were too bullish to listen. He brought us Charlie's things."

"You said a soldier who fought in the same battle brought them."

"Aye. In the same battle. I ne'er said on the same side."

Gavin's face hardened. He raised the sight to his eye. "Go on wi' ye."

Bridie put a hand on her father's arm. "*Athair*, he gave Charlie burial. He said the Our Father over him."

Graham more sensed than saw the conflict within the man. His face fell. The long black barrel of the rifle lowered.

"Come ye in." Gavin turned toward the house.

Graham looked at the reins in his hand. He could still ride out. Facing Gavin's hatred was one thing. Accepting his welcome was quite another. It was far easier to face a loaded rifle than to take his guilty conscience into the Seaton Court parlor.

"I'll take Hazel to the barn." The hitching post was almost within reach, but stabling his horse would give him time to think.

Bridie nodded. "Finn's there as well."

He wasn't sure how welcome that news was, but at least it was a situation he had come expecting to face.

As Finn came to welcome him, Graham was struck with how

much his cousin had matured in the few years since he had first met him. The deep eyes that had formerly looked at him from a boy's face were now framed by a man's firmness. He also saw how much heavier was the drag of the clubfoot. This, he sensed, was a matter of spirit. And yet the clasp that took his hand was firm.

Now that he was dealing not with a boy but with a man, Graham knew how to proceed. This was not a matter of sympathy or of charity but of business.

"I've come on a market matter, Finn." He cleared his throat to sound more the man of affairs. "I hope I'm not too precipitous in this, but I'm thinking I'll soon be needing another horse, and I'd not care to see such a fine one as Shandy go to just anyone."

Finlay turned and looked at his horse. Even in the dim barn his coat gleamed. It was a gleam that could be accomplished only by the best breeding and the best care. He nodded his head slowly, his eyes lowered. "Ta. The restrictions."

"I'd not like to think of Shandy going to anyone who would mistreat him."

They settled a price—somewhat at the low end of fair—but then, money wasn't the issue. And the law provided that a Protestant could simply take such a mount from under a Catholic and leave him standing in the road with a five pound note in his hand.

"Now, if you wouldn't think it asking too much, I'd take kindly to another favor. What with some poorly lambs needing extra shelter and all, my barn's full at the moment. Perhaps you'd be so good as to stable my new horse for a time—for a consideration, of course. I'd no' ask you to feed another man's beast for naught."

Few things had ever given Graham such pleasure as watching Finn's face.

The downcast eyes flicked up, skeptical. When he saw Graham's meet his levelly, the look changed to puzzlement. It took a long moment of thought before Finlay's countenance split in amusement. He caught himself just short of bursting out laughing. Instead, he rubbed his hand vigorously over his coat, then solemnly offered his hand to seal the bargain.

"Done, then." Graham said. "And as fine a bargain as I've ever made."

"You're a good friend to this house, cousin."

Graham matched his stride to Finn's as they walked to the house. "I'll have an official document drawn up. We'll want it all legal. And you'll see to it that my horse is well exercised?"

"Ta, and I will."

In her best mother-hen fashion Bridie shooed the men into the parlor and brought them home-brewed ale and freshly baked baps.

Although Graham had undertaken the matter of Shandy out of desire to help Finn and to please Molly, he had hoped it might also ease his conscience somewhat. Buying a horse for one son could never compensate for killing another, but he had hoped. He glanced up to Charles's sword over the fireplace and his cap on the mantel next to a small iron and gilt clock. For a brief moment Graham considered confessing all right then. The relief would be enormous.

But then he would have to confront the looks of horror, consternation, and disgust on the three faces before him. Finlay and Bridie would conclude that Gavin had been right all along. Rather than healing the breach as he desired, such action would cement it forever.

The ticking of the clock made him realize how silent the room was. He saw Gavin's eyes on the sword and knew that at the next moment the father would ask about the details of his son's death. Graham leaped to fill the conversational lag but came up with a topic almost equally uncomfortable. "And have you given thought to what you'll do now, Finn?"

"Now that your lot has slammed the door in his face, you mean?" Gavin Lanark might have permitted Graham into his house, but that was not to indicate that a truce had been declared.

"It's not Graham's fault, *Athair.*"

"They're all the same. He's a Prod *and* a Lanark of the bawn."

"And your guest, *Athair,*" Bridie added.

Gavin stood. "Aye. I invited you in for Charlie's sake. Now I'm inviting you out for Finn's sake."

Both Bridie and Finlay started to argue, but Graham rose. "No, he's right. Thank you for the refreshment." He set the pewter tankard on the table.

He was halfway across the yard with Hazel when Finn met him. "I'm sorry." He shrugged his shoulders helplessly.

Graham shook his head. "I think I make matters worse every time I come here." He paused. "But what *will* you do now, Finn?"

"I don't know. Mr. Monaghan says commerce is the only door left to us. Textiles, he says. Linen and wool. I haven't much capital, but perhaps with careful investing—" He grinned. "I've the purchase price for Shandy. And my legal training might be put to some good use in commercial matters."

Graham would have liked to have been able to give him some good advice or to offer help, but he was a complete stranger to the commercial world. It sounded risky to him. The only solid security was in land, but he couldn't say that to his cousin, who was debarred from purchasing land or holding it on a long lease.

He opened his mouth to wish Finn well but got no further. At that moment the barnyard filled with shouting children, yapping dogs, and racing ponies. There were only three young Lanarks, but they made enough confusion for ten.

"Three o'clock, Finn. Tomorrow."

"We saw Mariad at market," one child announced. "She held up three fingers."

"And made her fist like a rock. That means the rock beyond Scrabo."

"And she sends her love." The youngest, a scrap of a girl on the tallest pony giggled and trotted just beyond Finn's reach.

"Get on with you, Cally. You didn't even speak to Mariad O'Brien."

"No, but she smiled. Big. So I knew she was thinking of you." The small round face stretched to imitate the smile.

The raucous scene did much to lift Graham's spirits. All the way back to the bawn, he enjoyed the information that Finlay Lanark was courting one of the ubiquitous O'Briens. In any case, that must have been what the coded message, delivered in such a helter-skelter manner, meant. Apparently Finn was to meet Mariad at Scrabo rock at three o'clock tomorrow afternoon. Well, he was glad Finn would still have Shandy to take him to meet his lady fair.

Graham was still smiling to himself the next day as he rode Hazel to the foot of the hill to check on his sheep pastured there. Whoever would have thought Finn was such a sly one? The lad seemed so intent and studious, it was hard to imagine his sneaking off to an assignation. Was Mariad the one with the brilliant red hair?

Graham knew several of the O'Briens by sight—Janet had thought of taking one on as a servant but then chose the older, quieter Hannah instead. And there seemed to be an unending number of healthy young O'Brien males that could be relied on as hired men at harvesttime. But he wasn't acquainted with any of them.

Well, it would probably be a suitable match, since they were both papist. There *was* one O'Brien family that went to the Anglican church in Newtownards—not that there was a ha'penny difference between the two, of course.

Tag and Bob came bounding toward him, yapping. Graham dismounted and knelt down to give them vigorous rubs behind their ears. "Good boys. Taking good care of the sheep, are ye?"

Just before Graham turned to his flock, he looked out over the green valley where his family had lived for a hundred years. A fresh breeze whipped the spring air. He wondered if Lanarks a hundred years from now would be tending sheep on this same slope.

Then a carriage moving along the road caught his eye. Was that Finn, driving to his rendevous? Graham smiled, allowing room for just the tiniest ache that he was not off likewise to meet Molly. He looked to the field beyond and saw two women. Farther over yet, a boy drove a gaggle of geese down a dirt lane. It seemed the fine day had brought out everyone.

But then Graham's whole attention was claimed by his sheep. He checked on the ewes, who were near their time. He watched those born within the past weeks to make certain they were getting plenty of suckle. He noted that none had wandered beyond the sharp eyes of Tag or Bob. He would make quick work of this, if he could, and get on to Malcolm, who was plowing in the south field, readying to set a new bed of potatoes. Graham knew his uncle would be glad of his help, although he had hired a boy to assist in the backbreaking task.

There. Perhaps an hour later, Graham stood and rubbed his hands together. *That should do them.* The finest flock anywhere around. And he'd built it with his own efforts.

Malcolm much preferred working the soil. And to Graham's mystification, it seemed that earlier Lanarks had kept only enough sheep to put roast mutton on the table. He shook his head, thinking of the pleasure they missed.

He was halfway down the slope to where he had tethered Hazel, when Bob raced toward him, barking insistently. "What is it, boy? One of the lambs wandered off? Well, don't tell me about it. Go get him. That's your job."

But the dog would not quit yelping.

"What is it? Something you can't handle?" He looked back over the flock. Could one of the ewes be in difficulty lambing? He was certain he had counted them all present when he first arrived.

Bob continued his din.

"All right, all right. I'm coming."

The dog bounded off, leading slightly uphill toward the back of Scrabo.

Graham wasn't surprised at that. The far side of the hill was seamed with steep gullies thick with trees and underbrush. If a lamb were to wander into trouble, that would indeed be the place to do it. He gazed at the crook on his staff. He hoped it would do the job. He didn't fancy having to crawl through some of the brambles he'd seen around there.

As he expected, Bob led him toward the edge of a gully, then sat down, looking ahead intently.

"That the place, is it?" Graham listened, expecting to hear the bleat of a trapped animal. Instead, he heard a soft murmuring. Was it a voice or merely the wind in the trees? He walked forward, hoping not to find a dead lamb.

The murmuring became louder. Definitely a human voice. Male.

But he didn't recognize the language. Then he thought of Finn and Mariad. He started to turn away, but Bob uttered a throaty growl. The next step took him over the lip of the draw, and he could see through the thinly leafed trees.

There before him was the appointed rendezvous. But Mariad had called Finlay to a place of worship, not to a romantic tryst! A Catholic priest was saying Mass. The breeze fluttered the ends of his long stole as he elevated the chalice. Perhaps ten or twelve people stood below the makeshift altar.

Graham had heard of Mass rocks. He knew that many priests, deprived of their churches, had taken to chanting their superstitious rites in the open air. But he had never thought to see such a thing. The law imposed a ten shilling fine on all caught attending the forbidden ritual—or public flogging in lieu of payment. And Graham knew that few of the devout gathered at the Scrabo rock could ever pay such a fine.

Bob made a guttural sound, and Graham backed away from the lip of the gully, putting a hand on the dog's head. "It's all right, boy. They'll no' bother your sheep."

He considered the matter as he rode slowly toward Malcolm's potato field. His father had reported the success they were having in preventing Catholic worship. Only last year, more than four hundred priests and monks had been exiled. Several bishoprics were empty. There had been no Catholic archbishop in Armagh for several years now. There were rumors of priests going about disguised as wandering bards, but the authorities had found none. Priests could say Mass as long as they registered with the authorities. But only a handful had taken the required oath abjuring the authority of the pope.

Yet, in the face of severest restrictions, the practices obviously continued. Was it not possible to extinguish a faith by legislation? If not, what was to be done? One had to fight ignorance, superstition, and error.

All agreed that anyone who thought his worship was right would naturally be zealous to make as many proselytes as he could. But if such undermining of the faith were allowed, a nation could have a hundred different sects, each with its own leader. Every sect's adherents would have an equal right to plead that they must obey God rather than man. The choice was clear: established religion or chaos.

However, he couldn't help wondering how he would feel if the shoe were on the other foot. What if Presbyterians were to find their chosen professions closed to them? What if they were required to hold their meetings on a hillside instead of in their meetinghouse?

That was silly conjecturing. Calvinism was the true faith. This would never happen to the Lord's elect.

40

Graham pulled young Davey to the carriage seat beside him. The lad adjusted his thick stack of books, securely strapped and slung over his shoulder.

Lorna held tightly to wee Helen's hand and waved with the other. "Now see you mind everything the Reverend Mr. Harris tells you to do. Your faither's like to be returned from Dublin when you come home end of the week. Make him proud of how well you can read your lessons." She cut her wave short to place a hand on her rounded abdomen.

"I will, Mother. Don't worry."

Graham smiled at the note of forced courage in the lad's voice. How well he remembered the day he had likewise been driven off to the school in Newtownards. In the very same carriage, even. How could so many years have passed? The century had turned the corner with the speed of a clod falling off the top of Scrabo. And now it was 1704.

The carriage rolled down the rutted road as Graham clucked the horse to a trot and Davey bounced on the seat, chatting about the excitement awaiting him. Graham wished he could remember what it had been like to be so full of expectant wonder. He had thought that by the time he reached the weighty age of thirty-two—as he would next month—he would have sons of his own like the one beside him. He and Molly.

He had long ago given up the notion of waiting until he found peace within himself before speaking to her. He'd decided that turmoil and struggle were the very nature of the human lot, so he had made up his mind to accept it and get on with things. The dreams hardly ever came to him anymore. He'd determined to ask Molly to be his bride.

Five years ago, that was. But then Michael Price had had a paralyzing stroke, and Sheila, in the midst of caring for him, had taken a chill. Molly had helped her aunt to bed that night, and when she took a bowl of gruel to her the next morning, Sheila was dead. Graham did what he could to see that the farm was cared for, but the full care of the five younger Prices all fell to Molly. And so the seasons had spun.

After depositing Davey in the school on Movilla Street, Graham had several matters of business to see to in Newton, and it was late evening when he returned to the bawn. He was surprised to find Trapper in the stable.

His father wasn't due to return home until the end of the week. Had Parliament completed their debating early? It seemed unlikely. It was his observation that they always ran long, never short.

Then from the doorway Graham heard Lorna's sobs. What could be wrong? Was it the babe she carried? It should not be due yet. He hurried in and found them both in the front room, David bending over Lorna.

"Do not be so upset, lass. Aye, it's an outrage. But we've weathered worse."

"But what can you do, David? If you've no seat in Parliament, you'll have no power to change things."

Graham strode into the room. "What's this, Father? You've resigned your seat?"

"Not precisely, son. But it'll come to that. London returned our latest bills to Prevent the Further Growth of Popery. The Privy Council added a clause."

Graham slammed a fist against the table. "What else have they thought to proscribe? What can be left to take away from these people?"

His father shook his head. "It's nae from the papists. It's from the Presbyterians."

Lorna was racked with a more violent onset of sobs. David thrust a large handkerchief toward her, and Graham shouted for Hannah to bring her mistress a cup of water. Helen, who trotted in behind Hannah, was terrified by the sight of her sobbing mother. She set up a howl of her own. At least that seemed to remind Lorna of the importance of self-control. Hannah took the child from the room. By the time Malcolm came in from milking, relative order had been established.

Lorna punctuated the conversation with only an occasional sniff as David made yet another attempt to explain matters. "The bill states that any person holding public office must produce a certificate proving that he has received the sacrament of the Lord's Supper according to the usage of the Church of Ireland."

"But that's ridiculous." Malcolm gestured impatiently. "The papists are already disqualified from holding public office. What purpose does this serve?"

"It disqualifies *us*, brother." David's voice was grim. "All dissenters who hold to their true faith are disqualified from any public office. *I* am disqualified."

Graham took a deep breath. "From your seat in Parliament."

David nodded.

"From your commission in the militia."

David nodded.

"Parliament! Militia! Who cares about that?" The men turned with a start as Lorna jumped to her feet. "Do you men think of nothing but laws and wars? You've not told them the worst, David."

He looked at her in confusion. "What do you mean, worst, woman? What could be worse?"

"Our marriage! Our children!"

"Oh, aye. But that's nae new, lass. The law has long been thus."

"Yes, but the appeal—to the Lord Lieutenant—you told me . . ." She sank back into her chair, clasping her abdomen.

"The appeal failed, Father?"

"Aye. We are required publicly to confess ourselves guilty of the sin of fornication."

"Our children are declared *bastards!*" Lorna spit out the word. It was still ringing in the room when she cried out again and doubled over, both arms encircling her belly. "Hannah! Quickly. Get me to bed. David, go for the midwife."

David went as instructed, returning in less than an hour with Mistress Goodall.

And so the evening dragged on into the night. The men ate the plates of stew that Hannah set in front of them, but their conversation was desultory. Their attention was divided between the dire news David had imparted and the intermittent cries from the overhead room.

At last David flung down his spoon and began pacing, his hands to the sides of his head. "What will I do if she dies? Am I cursed that two wives . . ."

"Nae, Father. It's a woman's part. Lorna has given you two fine children. This babe will be a third. Come, sit down."

"But it isn't her time yet. It was the news. I was so full of the matter. But I shouldn't have sprung it on her in her condition. I—"

"Father. Come sit. Ye can do nothing upstairs. Let us consider the matter of the proscription on dissenters."

David all but leaped to the table. "Aye. That's it! We'll no' take it quietly. I'll write a pamphlet. The Test Act is wrong. It is unfair, unrighteous. I'll fight it. Bring me a quill."

Graham found quill, ink, and paper, and David filled the room with the sound of pen scratches. By the time Graham had arranged the candles so that light from one on the table fell across the paper and one in a bracket shone across his shoulder, David had a full para-

351

graph composed to His Honor the Lord Lieutenant, Queen Anne's viceroy in Ireland.

David looked back over his words, shaking his head. "This would nae have come upon us were King Billy still alive. Anne will be run by her ministers, and they bear us no love."

"What have you written, Father?"

David cleared his throat.

"The Protestant dissenters of Ireland are known to be a body of people universally well affected to Her Majesty's person and government and inviolably attached to the true interest of their country. Of this they have given many signal proofs. We cannot therefore but think it hard to be laid under such legal disabilities as tend to deprive us of our birthright and to fix an undeserved brand of infamy upon us ranking us with the known enemies of the government against whom we have always heartily joined in defense."

A muffled call from above was quickly followed by the sound of feet running up the stairs.

Graham stepped into the hall.

Hannah was coming back down.

"Is there news? Can I be of help?" he asked.

"Oh, Mr. Graham. The kittle of water boiling on the cob. If you would just carry it up the stairs." She turned back to the labor room, appeared again to take the water, and firmly closed the door in his face.

His father looked up when he returned to the front room. "How does it go?"

"I don't know. They needed water." He paused, then gestured toward David's papers. "Have you finished?"

David rubbed a hand over his eyes. "Aye. I've finished." He moved the paper closer to the flickering candle. "'The Protestant dissenters think these hardships are an unkind return for the vigorous and successful stand we made at the late happy revolution against popery and arbitrary power . . .'"

The sharp wail of newborn life taking its first breath extinguished all further thought of pamphleteering. David rushed from the room and up the stairs. Graham watched from below.

Hannah opened the door above. "A fine son, a wee braw bairn, sir."

"And Lorna?"

"Aye, the lass is tired, as well she might be, but all's well."

The coming days flowed to the demanding and often conflicting requirements of a new babe in the house and harvest in the fields. As he had for the past several years, Graham, who was taking over more and more of the work from Malcolm, planned his harvesting to include the Price farm as well, although Molly's older brothers Rob and Josh were quickly becoming big enough to shoulder more of that responsibility. It was a great relief to Graham that all the flax, barley, and potatoes from both farms was safely in the barns before the autumn rains came.

And as a double thanksgiving, that Sunday was wee Dereck Calum Lanark's baptism. In spite of the penal laws now applying to Presbyterians, they were, for the time being at least, allowed to worship in their meetinghouse. How long the privilege would hold, no one knew.

But it was apparent that not even David was thinking of such gloomy matters. He stood before the congregation while Parson Stevenson read from the Book of Common Order.

"Therefore it is your duty, with all diligence, to provide that your children be instructed in all doctrine necessary for a true Christian, chiefly that they be taught to rest upon the justice of Christ Jesus alone and to abhor and flee all superstition, papistry, and idolatry . . ."

In a clear voice David repeated the articles of faith that he would instill in this child, and Graham was struck with some understanding of the awesome responsibility of being a father. It was little wonder he had never pleased his own father and that the elder Lanark had always hounded him to do better.

He thought of the minister's exhortation—the same exhortation that would have been given at Graham's own baptism: "To make you diligent and careful to nurture and instruct him in the true knowledge and fear of God."

Graham looked across the church to where Molly sat with her family. Would he ever stand before a minister making these formidable vows for a child of his and Molly's? He had waited so long—waited for peace in the land, for peace within himself—but the waiting had not made him more peaceful. It seemed that the land would always be in turmoil of some kind. If that were the case, he had far rather face turbulence with Molly than without her. Again he decided he would speak.

After the service, he made his way to her just in time to hand her into the wagon. "I'll call on you tomorrow evening, Molly. If it's convenient?"

She looked surprised at the formality of his request, accustomed as he was to dropping in at the Price farm at all hours. "Why, yes. That would be convenient."

The decision at last made, Graham had never known a day's work to be accomplished with such a light heart as it was that Monday. In the morning he had thought the hours would drag on endlessly. But when evening milking was over and he looked back, it seemed as though it couldn't possibly be later than noon. He took the milk pails into the dairy with such a spring in his step that he nearly sloshed their contents.

One of the young O'Briens, a green-eyed girl named Clare, was up to her elbows in sudsy water, scrubbing the separating tubs. "Ooo, careful, Mr. Lanark. Now aren't you the fine one to be spilling the milk?"

"And how's your family, Clare?"

"Have you heard? Our Mariad's marrying Finn Lanark." She paused in her vigorous scouring. "Will that make *us* relations, Mr. Lanark?" Her eyes got even wider at the thought.

He laughed. "Perhaps it will in a way, Clare. But you'll still churn my butter for me, won't you?"

"Don't you worry!" Her merry laughter followed him out of the dairy and buoyed his spirits even higher.

The mood in the house, however, was not in keeping with his own.

"The man is a fool! How can they print such blatant falsity!" David's voice thundered from the front room.

An infant's cry was followed by cooing and shushing sounds from Lorna. "Must ye bark so, David? You've frightened the poor wee bairn."

"And there's plenty to be frightened about if drivel like this is to be permitted to infest the popular reading."

Graham stepped into the room to see his father waving a pamphlet with a light brown cover. It bore the title *Dangerous Consequences of Repealing the Sacramental Test.*

"Sit down, man." David pointed at his son. "I'd have ye hear this."

Nothing could have suited Graham's mood less. He had thought it would take him less than fifteen minutes to be on his way to Molly. Wash up, put on a clean shirt, shine his boots—

"Sit." David would have no argument.

Graham suppressed a groan and perched on the edge of the closest chair.

"This—this man—J. Roberts, whoever he may think *he* is—has the effrontery, the audacity—"

"Just read it to me, Father." Graham knew he would be there all evening if he didn't cut the fuming short.

"Aye. I'll read. But ye'll not believe the ink would stick to such words.

> "By receiving this Sacramental Test, a man must be supposed to renounce all dishonesty, fraud, oppression, injustice and such like. This does not appear to be any burden to tender consciences."

He shook the pamphlet. "Does that mincing high-churcher think that only Anglican communicants are free of dishonesty, fraud, and injustice? Bah! It's more like only those who *don't* take to their incomprehensible rites can be renounced of such."

"Yes, I'm sure you're right, Father." Graham started to rise.

"Of course, I'm right. But that's not all he says. Just you sit back and listen."

This time Graham's groan was audible.

> "The two sects against which the rulers of this nation ought particularly to guard are the dissenters and the papists. Both equally zealous in a bad cause and the principles of both equally tending to the destruction of our present happy constitution. We must look to the past, however, to see that the dissenters have been more destructive to the public than the papists . . ."

Graham could see that the pamphlet went on for several pages. Could nothing but open defiance of his father get him out of there?

Lorna, cuddling wee Dereck, put a hand on David's arm. "Our supper is cooling, husband."

Graham prepared to hear his father declare that he couldn't eat while such impudence was being circulated.

That undoubtedly was what David intended when he waved the seditious pamphlet aloft and drew breath. At that moment, however, the infant Dereck turned his face full toward his animated father and gave him a wide, toothless grin.

"Ah, who's a good boy, now? Aye, there's a pretty boy." He dropped the pamphlet, took his son from his wife's arms, and turned to the table.

Graham slipped silently from the room.

It was a golden autumn evening. Dust from the harvest had added vibrance to the red and gold streaking the sky behind Scrabo. Graham loved the rich, fruity scent of the air.

Aye, he had waited long for this night. And now the time was right. The concerns and problems that had kept him waiting so long seemed now totally beyond recall. His future with Molly was all that filled his mind. He stopped Hazel and dismounted to pick a handful of purple and golden flowers.

Graham had just turned into the Price lane when he was met by a carriage coming out, a fine vehicle pulled by a pair of perfectly matched grays. He recognized it as the carriage of Sir Robert Colville.

Graham smiled at his fortunate timing. If the Prices had had business to conduct with their landlord, it was as well that he hadn't arrived earlier. Best to be here now and share the relaxed atmosphere of concluded affairs.

He was surprised that no one answered his knock, since Molly was expecting him. However, he felt free to let himself in. A jamb wall served as a screen between the front door and the kitchen. He stepped around it.

Molly sat at one end of the well-scrubbed white ash table flanked by a brother on each side. Rob and Josh were both flushed red, but Molly's pale cheeks looked ghostly. She sat so still she hardly seemed to be breathing.

Graham crossed to her. "Molly, are ye ill?"

The slight shaking of her head was his only indication that she had heard him. At last she took a deep breath that shook her whole body.

Rob spoke up. "It was Colville's agent. Happen you saw him leave?"

"Yes?"

"He was here for the rents. Our lease is up come November."

Graham did not understand. That was the normal procedure. The standard lease in Ulster was thirty-one years—far longer than any granted in Scotland and one of the inducements for settlers to come to Ireland. He thought back. This must be about the third renewal on this lease. But for such fine tenants as the Prices, it would be only a matter of routine. "So, what—"

"We've been rack-rented." Josh slammed a fist on the table.

"Oh." Graham dropped into the nearest chair. "Aye, I've heard of that. But I never thought . . ." The idea of a landlord raising the rent on a lease was unconscionable.

"'There are many applicants for the land,' he says. 'A careful property owner must make the best possible bargain,' he says." Rob ground out the words. "Our people have been here for four generations—longer. We've improved the land, brought wasteland into cultivation, applied new methods. *We've* made his land valuable by our sweat and toil. Now he wants to charge us for our own labor!"

"'Money is scarce in Ireland, even among landlords.'" Josh's voice was mincing high, mocking the agent. "'One can hardly blame them for wanting as much income as they can get from their estates.'" He dropped to his normal voice. "He's right. Money is scarce. So where does he think we'll get the money to pay his increases and feed ourselves?"

"His rents are impossible to meet?" Graham asked.

Rob answered. "Next to impossible. *And* it's the injustice. It's never been done this way before. Rents are fixed. God created the land—its value is stable. I'll not give in to this. I say we resist."

"But what will you do?" Graham turned then to Molly, who still sat as if frozen.

She turned her round, brown eyes on him, and it was all he could do to keep from sweeping her into his arms even in front of her brothers. Her silence struck a far deeper chord with him than he could have thought possible. Other women might rail and throw things or sob with hysteria, but Molly's brave, white face spoke far more vividly of the destruction of everything she had known and loved.

Suddenly he had the answer. He jumped to his feet, knocking over his chair. Yes, it was the solution to everything. All his happiness, her security. "Molly, marry me. Marry me and come live at Lanarks' Bawn!"

Molly's rigid composure broke. The small, stiff features crumpled. Her laughter filled the room. The shock was enormous. She had been so silent that Graham wasn't sure she retained the power to speak. Color flooded back into her face, her eyes glistened. The tears she would not shed for sorrow poured from her eyes in laughter.

Graham was at a complete loss. In all the years he had looked forward to this moment, of all the reactions he had imagined, he had never considered that she would laugh at him. Nor had he thought he would propose in front of her brothers.

Rob got up, grabbed his sister by the shoulders, and shook her roughly. "Stop it, Moll. Stop it! You're hysterical, lass. Quiet ye."

Graham understood. Molly wasn't reacting to his proposal but to all the problems around her. His words had merely broken the tension that held her so tightly. He turned to the bucket on the sideboard and dipped her a glass of water.

Three wide-eyed young girls stuck their heads around the corner.

"Get the wee'uns to bed, Nan. All's well here." Rob scooted his sisters ahead of him. Josh gave a satisfied nod and left the room. Rob stopped at the door and looked back. "Happen she'll be cold."

Graham did not need another hint. He pulled the trembling Molly into his arms. Eventually her shivering stilled.

"Graham, can you ever forgive me? What a weak, fitful creature you must think me."

"On the contrary." He tightened his sheltering hold. "I think you one of the bravest people I know. You've borne so much for so long, been the center stay for all your youngers. That's one reason I've nae spoken sooner. But now, I could hold it in no longer." Still holding her, he drew back enough to look in her eyes. "Marry me, Molly."

She looked down. "In all the years I've dreamed of hearing you say those words, in all the responses I've dreamed of making, I never once imagined such a thing as laughing at you. Of late, I've not imagined laughing at anything. Forgive me."

"Only if you say you'll marry me."

"But my family. I'm all they have. I can't abandon them." She spread her hands helplessly.

Graham grabbed her hands. They were cold. Rubbing them, he said, "Come to the bawn. All of you."

Now her laughter was the merry tinkling of bells he was accustomed to hearing from her. "Oh, Graham. My dear, dear sweet, impractical Graham. Can you imagine? Rob and Josh—awkward, overgrown colts that they are, and Nan, Betsy, and Lila. At least Nan's good in the kitchen, but the other two squabble from sunup to sunset. All that with David's bairns—and one of them a wee'un?"

Graham ran a hand through his already tousled hair. "I don't know. There has to be a way. I'll think of something. Just say you'll marry me."

"Oh, Graham." She came back into his arms. "Of course, I will. There's naught else I want in the whole world. When the way is open. We've waited so long. We want to do it right."

"Right? How could it be wrong?"

"Besides the matter of the lease and settling all the youngers, I'd not care to be married by any but a minister of the true faith—I'd not want our babes declared bastard."

Graham nodded. As much as he hated to admit it, she spoke sense. And the concern for legitimate heirs carried more consequences for him than for his father. David had no property to leave to his eldest son. Graham was Malcolm's heir. What would happen to Lanarks' Bawn if his own children were declared illegitimate?

No matter how reluctantly, Graham had to admit that Molly was right. How could she be so patient? Even as his mind formed the question, he realized the dichotomy. His having at last spoken—and Molly's having accepted—increased his urgency to wed but at the same time made him more resigned to waiting. Just so they didn't have to wait too long.

41

"Now. Are you fine gentlemen ready to start the bidding on this excellent piece of property?" Martins, Colville's agent, stood on a wagon bed parked near the front door of the Price farmhouse. "Sir Robert offers a generous thirty-one year lease for some of the most productive land in all the Ards."

The wind lashed rain in Graham's face, and he ducked his head. He was determined to do what he could, but that would be little enough.

A few years ago, when the wool business was at its peak, Graham could have outbid all comers. But the fine Irish wool had proved to be intolerable competition to English textile interests, so the prosperous woolen trade had been severely crippled by an act of Parliament prohibiting export to anywhere except England and Wales—where the prices were kept low.

Graham, like so many of his fellows, had discovered the loophole that allowed him to export *yarn*, but it was a depressed market. Only his fondness for the sheep prompted him to continue with his flock. There was no profit there to support taking on another lease, no matter how he longed to do so.

It was the linen that kept affairs at the bawn on an almost even keel. Across Ulster, linen had taken up the slack caused by the setback to the wool industry. The Huguenot colony planted near Lisburn by King Billy had set about with industrious ingenuity to stimulate the cultivation of flax. What had formerly been a small, domestic enterprise to provide employment for the women of a family was now being developed on a large scale. Although the flax harvest had been good this year, the long processing of the fibers was not yet completed. Graham would be hard put to come up with a sizeable amount of cash.

"You'll notice the good stonework of the outer walls." Martins gestured toward the sturdy, whitewashed house that had been home to generations of Prices. "I invite you to walk around back where you'll find a surprising feature in a house of this class—a backdoor. And don't fail to note the superior condition of the straw thatch. The roof was redone just two years ago. A thatching job like that will last for years."

"Aye," Rob growled, not quite under his breath. "And every hand-ful held secure by a scollop stuck in by my own hand. To hear that man, ye'd think Colville did it himself."

"Feel free to go right on inside." The agent gestured expansively.

Graham felt Molly, standing beside him, shrink from having her house invaded by the clutch of twelve or so muddy-booted men who had come to appraise the Price farm. They had already inspected the fields (cleared and drained by generations of Prices) and tramped through the barns (built by Price hands), so mud was the least objec-tionable of the properties clinging to their feet. Graham felt a moment of gratitude when Finlay Lanark, limping at the back of the group, paused to scrape his boots.

Martins called through the open door, "You'll note that the origi-nal two rooms have been expanded to five, and the earlier clay-plastered wickerwork chimney canopy has been replaced by fine brickwork."

"Aye, and wouldn't Michael Price be proud to know all his hard labor went to enrich Sir Robert Colville?" Josh did not restrain his comments to those nearby as Rob had.

Martins shot him a warning look, and Josh subsided under the implied threat of expulsion.

The agent returned to his job. "Don't overlook the half loft in the kitchen, my good sirs, and the hollow earthenware tiles on the kitchen floor—a most unusual feature in a farmhouse."

Graham thought how many times he had gone in and found Molly on her hands and knees scrubbing those tiles.

He went over the calculations in his mind for at least the fiftieth time. He had been doing so ever since that night last month when Martins informed the Prices of the rent they could not meet. But the immediacy of the situation today did nothing to increase the tally.

He felt Molly shiver and knew that the cold rain was little of the cause. He longed to put a comforting, warming arm around her but knew that any such public display of affection would be severely fined. A fine he could little afford to pay.

The men drifted back outside. Graham recognized most of them. Good, solid, Protestant gentry. Except Finlay, of course.

Graham had seen little of the Seaton Court Lanarks lately, but he had heard that Mariad had just given Finn a second lusty son. He must be thinking of buying an additional lease with an eye to the future. Colville was offering a thirty-one year lease, rather than the more secure named-lifetime contract. Therefore, a Catholic would be eligi-ble to bid under the Penal Laws. And he had heard that Finn's com-mercial interests had prospered. Well, Graham was glad enough for Finn, but it dimmed his own chances even further.

"If you'll just gather around now, gentlemen, in the name of Sir Robert Colville I now put up to auction the lease for this fine property. Who will open the bid?"

A man to Graham's right started at three shillings an acre. Ah, that was fine. Graham could beat that. No one spoke. Graham offered three shillings sixpence. Molly's grateful glance warmed him in the chill drizzle.

"Do I hear another offer? Come now, gentlemen. You've seen what a fine, prosperous property this is."

A man on the edge of the group made an offer Graham couldn't hear. Martins repeated it. Graham sucked in his breath. He could see that. Just. But if the bidding went on for long, he would soon be outdone. He had known that from the first, of course. But he had so hoped. Hoped for Molly, hoped for the younger Prices, hoped for himself.

The next offer came from behind him. Graham did not turn around. He knew the voice. A tall, crabbed man who drove a carriage pulled by a horse that looked as if it was beaten regularly. This farm that had been lovingly tended for so many years couldn't go to that man.

Graham made his top offer, four shillings sixpence per acre. It was really more than he could pay, but he would manage somehow.

"Six shillings."

In less time than it took to draw breath, the man who opened the bidding had topped Graham surely well beyond even Martins's avaricious expectations. And certainly beyond Graham's means. Drops of water flew in Graham's face from his hat brim as he shook his head.

"Well, now—" Martins's voice was thick with pleasure. He would undoubtedly get a generous bonus from Sir Robert for handling this matter so profitably. "If you're all done, gentlemen—"

"Seven and six." Even Martins almost gasped at the lilting voice that cut through the sound of dripping water.

"Done!" Martins was unable to keep a triumphant ring out of his voice. He banged his hand against the side of the wagon.

"Daftest *roup* I ever saw," a thickly Scottish voice muttered behind Graham. "A lease like this going to a native Irish. Nae Scot would bid sae wild."

The men drifted away.

Graham smiled. Finlay Lanark was no wild Irish, but the men would be equally outraged—perhaps more so—if they knew the lease was in the hands of a Catholic of Old English and Scots descent. Barring the Prices and himself, there was no one Graham would rather the land go to. Of course, it did nothing to move his marriage plans forward, but at least the land would be well cared for.

361

Molly looked resigned, if not happy. Together they turned to Finlay who had just finished shaking hands with the agent.

"You've a fine farm, Finn," Graham said.

The dark eyes sparkled. "Ta. And only one problem."

"Oh?"

"My business affairs leave little time for farming. I'll be needing a trustworthy subtenant. Happen you hear of one, you'll let me know?"

"Um . . ." Molly floundered for words.

But the rambunctious Rob didn't hesitate. "Mr. Lanark, my brother and I are young, but we're strong. And we know the land well. We'd work as hard for you as we did for ourselves."

Finn smiled. "I couldn't ask for a better offer. I'm sure we can come to terms. And as I still have the use of Shandy, I'll have no trouble keeping an eye on my investment." He gave Graham a half grin.

Graham's response was a weak reflection of the gratitude he felt. It could be nothing else with Molly's shining face before him.

Tears of joy mingled with the raindrops running down her cheeks. "Please, Finlay, won't you come in for a cup of ale?"

"Ta. The better to inspect my property," Finn said.

But as Graham watched them move toward the house, his gratitude turned to an increased weight of guilt. He had done little enough to make restitution for the wrong he had done that family. And now he had this magnanimous gesture of Finlay's to add to the burden.

He could not continue on forever under the encumbrance of unconfessed sin. He certainly could not take Molly to wife until he was free inside. Years of ignoring the great burden on his shoulders, of pretending it wasn't there, had taught him that one could, indeed, carry on under such pretense for a time. But when the burden resurfaced, it was heavier than ever.

Heavier, he thought, and more difficult to dislodge. Now, speaking to Gavin was more impossible than ever. Now, it was not only his own welfare and happiness at stake, but—far more important—that of Molly and her siblings as well.

As he walked slowly back to the bawn, he played out a scene in his mind: forcing his way into Seaton Court, blurting out the truth to Gavin Lanark, Gavin pulling Charles's sword from the mantel and settling the score. A son for a son.

Graham sighed. An act that was little less than suicide might still his conscience but would be no solution either for his soul or for his desire for a happy conclusion to matters with Molly.

Nor would it contribute to spanning the gulf between himself and his father.

Graham stabled Hazel with slow, mechanical movements. At this late date he didn't know what else could be attempted with either his father or Gavin. But he would try. He had learned that old wounds didn't just go away; they festered—sometimes for generations, even. Sometime, somewhere, the feud must be healed. He would try again for all their sakes.

He heard raised voices when he opened the door of the bawn house. He had vaguely noted the wagon in the yard but had given it little thought. Now he turned back and regarded it. Oh, yes. The Reverend Mr. Firth. Now he remembered hearing Lorna say that her father would fetch Davey home from school for the weekend. She was planning a pleasant family supper.

"It's intolerable! We can take no more!"

A wail from the parlor told Graham something had gone very wrong.

"I don't mind, Mother, really I don't." Young Davey had an arm around his mother's shoulder. "There are more of us. Six against four. And we always beat them at football."

"That's a fine spirit in ye, lad." David smiled at his eight-year-old son. "But it's no right for ye to bear such persecution. The arrogance of the established church!"

Graham stepped into the room just as Hannah exited with Helen and a toddling Dereck. He looked to the minister for an explanation.

"The schoolmaster rearranged the classroom. Legitimate sons to the front. Bastards sit in the rear."

"It's all right, really it is," Davey persisted. "This way Mr. Harris doesn't see when we draw pictures on our slates. Hamish drew Mr. Harris with horns. It was a fine laugh."

David slammed a hand on the table. "*Wheesht!* Enough. I do not send ye to school to be called bastard, and I do not send ye to school to laugh at daft pictures."

"Nor did we come to Ulster to be persecuted!" Lorna's father said. "Good Presbyterian ministers thrown out of their pulpits. Can't bury our dead without an Episcopalian reading his service over the body . . ."

"Aye, and the government is in shambles," David continued. "In Belfast the entire Corporation was swept out—esteemed, weighty citizens who knew how to run a city. And who did they put in their place? Mere callow youths, persons of little repute—whose only recommendation is that they go to the established church."

Firth nodded. "Aye, aye. That's the way of it, all right. And in the final analysis, the Test Act favors Roman Catholics."

Lorna looked up. "Surely not, Father?"

"Aye, it does. Those of the prelacy will contend that at least Catholic priests are lawfully ordained, whereas Dissenting ministers are mere sanctified upstarts. Not in the line of apostolic succession, they say."

"But that's terrible—" Lorna's protest was interrupted by a knock at the door.

A moment later Hannah ushered in Mr. Stevenson, his thread-bare black coat shiny with rain. David seated him close to the fire and took his hat.

The man looked so drained that it was amazing he could sit upright. He ran a thin hand over his bald head. "Thirty-two years. Thirty-two years, dispensing God's mysteries to my flock. Always I proclaimed faithfully the Word of God and ministered the sacraments sincerely." His thin, stooped shoulders shook. "Preaching the Word and ministering the sacraments."

Lorna went to him and put a hand on his shoulder. "What is it, Mr. Stevenson? What's happened?"

"The church is boarded up. I'm expelled from my pulpit. How will I shepherd my flock without a sheepfold? My people must have the Word and the sacraments, or we will perish. The Great Tribulation has come upon us."

"Aye." Firth nodded. "I remember in Scotland—many's the night I listened to my faither tell tales of the Covenanters worshiping in their hidden conventicles. But I never thought such times would fall on us."

The recitation of woes continued until Hannah informed her mistress that supper was ready.

The doleful group moved down the hall to the kitchen and, after Parson Stevenson's lengthy pronouncement of grace, interspersed a discussion of what should be done with taking bites of crusty brown bread and hot mutton stew.

Lorna urged the idea of going back to Scotland. Many Presbyterians were now doing that. But, her father pointed out, the conditions that led them to come to Ireland were unchanged there. Scottish harvests were still poor, land still scarce.

It was after the meal, when Lorna had gone upstairs to tuck the children in bed and the men were sitting around the table with their ale and pipes, that Lorna's father told of the letter he had received from a fellow minister. The man had gone to the American colonies ten years earlier.

Stevenson shook his head. "Ah, brave fellow to face the howling wilderness."

"Nay. The colonies are flourishing. New Jersey, Delaware, Virginia—Scots and Ulstermen prospering in all of them."

Stevenson scoffed. "I suppose next ye'll be proposing we should all set out to this New Jersey place. Those as didn't die of seasickness would be sure to be killed by red Indians."

Firth pulled on his pipe, then let the smoke out in a long, slow cloud. "A generous, fair government in a miraculously productive land. Stability. Prosperity. Hospitality. Might be worth taking a few risks for."

"Ah, you're daft. There's no place like that. Not this side of heaven. You've been listening to wild tales, man."

"Nae sae wild, it seems." Firth pulled a pamphlet from inside his vest and dropped it onto the table. "This William Penn's quite a fellow. A Quaker he is, with sincere religious convictions. And common sense."

Stevenson fingered the document but did not pick it up. "What's this, then?"

"Penn wrote it himself. Has made several trips to Europe encouraging settlers to come to his colony. Makes a man think. Why stay where we're not wanted when Penn's begging for settlers? Take it. Read for yourself."

Stevenson drew back as if he'd been bitten. "Nae."

But Graham picked it up. After a few moments of reading, he set down his mug and moved a candle closer. He read aloud:

> "Rich, virgin soil, healthy climate, advantageous geographical position in the midst of the English colonies in America. . . . All external circumstances offer promise of economic success for a man willing to work."

He lowered the pamphlet and looked about the room. No one spoke, but all eyes were on him.

"Beyond these material advantages, Penn guarantees in his charter a government based on almost universal male suffrage—"

Stevenson scoffed. "And you said he was a man of common sense, Firth! Whoever heard of such a thing as letting every Tom, Dick, and Hamish vote?"

"Next thing to anarchy, that is." Even Malcolm, who had hardly spoken all evening, was moved to comment on such a radical idea.

David chewed on his pipe stem thoughtfully. "Aye, unheard of, and likely dangerous to sound government. Still . . ." He returned to puffing on his pipe.

"Listen to this," Graham continued. "Penn guarantees in his charter complete freedom of conscience." He scanned the rest of the page. "The man appears to be an uncompromising defender of the cause of religious toleration. As a member of a faith that has suffered for their nonconformity, he feels profound sympathy for others now enduring religious disabilities." He dropped the pamphlet on the table. "Well, what do you think of that?"

"I think it sounds like heaven."

All eyes turned to Lorna, standing in the doorway, her eyes shining. "When we came here from Scotland I thought we'd found the Promised Land. But now I see it was just a testing ground." She came and knelt by David's chair. "Oh, husband, what a fine place for our children to grow up. Free from threats by papists or prelates. Free from the Test Act. Free from having our children declared illegitimate . . ."

"Get you up, wife." David put a hand under her elbow to raise her.

"But think, David."

"Aye, I'll think. And you think, too. This would be naething like crossing the Irish Sea. Three months on a small, crowded vessel, the children exposed to smallpox, cholera, storms . . ."

"Nae, don't be so gloomy, man." Firth refilled his tankard from the pitcher on the table. "It's a matter of organization. Charter a ship, hold consultations, organize a migration group. It would take time. Property must be sold—"

"You can nae organize the smallpox away, man." Stevenson pointed a finger as if he were in the pulpit.

"I've done it before."

"Aye, long before."

"You think I'm too old, is that it? Well, read your Bible, man. I'll have you know Moses was—"

Graham pushed back his chair and walked from the room. The pamphlet had indeed been persuasive. Penn was offering what every man wanted, freedom to worship God and prosper on his own land. And that was the crux of the matter. *This* land was his. It had been Lanark land for a hundred years. He had no desire to leave it for another—even better—place.

But if his father should choose to go in order to gain land for his young family, then the way would be open to bring Molly and her sisters to the bawn while Rob and Josh remained at the farm! The pleasure of that thought held only for moments before he realized that it could well take years before everything Mr. Firth outlined could be accomplished. He could not wait so long to wed Molly.

And he could not let his father sail off to the American colonies without true reconciliation. Reconciliation between father and son and between Lanarks' Bawn and Seaton Court. All Graham's life, it seemed, those had been his goals. Now time could be running out. If his father chose to emigrate it could be months—possibly years—but there would be a deadline.

42

Through the coming months, emigration talk was on every tongue, especially when the Presbyterians met in sheltered barns for their services. But talk was all it was.

And then talk changed to concerns closer to home. It was late in the following autumn when Graham, on his normal rounds of inspecting the cattle, met a grisly sight. Auld Glenny, his best milk cow, was on her side. Her top legs stuck far into the air. Her abdomen extended as far as the skin would stretch. Realizing nothing could be done for her, he knelt by her throat and drew the knife he wore at his belt. Before he could end her agony, however, Auld Glenny's labored breathing ceased.

He moved on. Hare Bell was still on her feet, but her head and throat were swollen. Graham frowned. He knew the signs of distemper only too well.

Malcolm was the best of cowmen. They brewed a strong elixir of coal tar, herbs, and rough ale. Together they worked long hours, forcing as much as possible down the throats of the suffering creatures. Still, thirty-four cows died before the first frost.

And the Lanarks were among the lucky ones. Many lost their entire herds. Rob and Josh would most certainly have been among those to lose all had Graham not taken them vast pots of Malcolm's elixir and instructed the Price brothers in administering it to their beasts—and to the Seaton Court cattle as well. Most of them were pastured at the farm now.

A hard winter followed. Many of the cows that died of distemper would have died a few months later of the cold. And many that might have otherwise survived the cold were so weakened by their brush with the disease that they succumbed anyhow. Potatoes in storage for spring seed and those set in clamps in the fields for winter sustenance were destroyed. Barley and oat seed, weakened by the frost, mildewed. And so it went.

By the following year, marks of hunger and want showed on every face Graham saw. Although the laboring Irish were hit hardest, all were affected. Little Helen lost the look of sturdiness that had always been such a comforting sight. And although Graham looked on Molly's dear face as fondly as ever, he saw it lose its roundness. Hannah, now stooped and wrinkled, coped valiantly with the little she had to work with in the kitchen of Lanarks' Bawn, but when the price of oatmeal doubled, Graham's own belly growled so constantly that he finally ceased to hear it.

That summer, the poor, whose winter sustenance was ever potatoes, were driven to eat the tatties out of the ground before they were fully developed. They would survive, only to die more painfully in the winter—unless there should be a mild winter. But even then, those who survived the winter would have nothing left with which to seed their potato hills come spring.

And it was not a mild winter. The hardest freeze anyone could remember lasted seven weeks. Potatoes were destroyed, cattle died in the fields, water-powered mills were stopped by ice.

David returned from a trip to Belfast so shocked that he was unable to eat the thin potato soup Hannah set before him. He waited until Lorna and the children were gone from the table before he said to Malcolm and Graham, "I had no notion. I knew the hunger was deep, but—" he paused "—three, maybe more, dead bodies by the roadside. God forgive me, I averted my eyes. There was nothing I could do. One poor soul was being buried right in the field where she fell. Her family looked too weak to have carried her to a graveyard, could they have afforded a plot.

"Just outside Belfast a military horse had stepped in a ditch and broken its leg. As I approached, the lieutenant drew his gun and ended the beast's suffering. Maybe twenty passers-by set upon the animal, hacking off pieces to take home to their family's stew pots."

"Aye, and worse will follow."

Graham started at Lorna's voice. He had assumed her to be out of hearing.

"When there's famine, the pestilence is always right behind. Just as it was in Scotland. If we don't die of hunger, we'll die of disease. Is that what ye'd have for your bairns, David Lanark?" Her voice had risen steadily throughout the speech. It was approaching hysterical pitch. "We came to Ireland to find a better life! To escape these very things—"

"Aye, lassie." David crossed the room to take her in his arms. "Aye, be calm and come see what I got in Belfast today."

He led her to a seat and drew a document from his pocket.

Lorna frowned in puzzlement as she examined the official-looking paper. "Husband, I—"

A knock at the door was followed by a stamping of boots in the hall. Mr. Firth entered. He took one look in his daughter's direction and swooped down on the paper she held. "Ah, well done, Lanark! The very thing. Now we can get matters rolling."

"But what is it?" Lorna asked.

"Our reply from William Penn himself." David's voice rang with triumph. "Your father petitioned him for a grant of land. We've been given three hundred acres for a settlement."

"Aye, that's a fine thing." Firth read the document and gave a satisfied nod. "Now we must gather our group. About a dozen good, solid families. I'll advertise."

"Oh, Father! David!" Lorna looked from one to another and jumped up, clapping her hands. "Land, food, our children declared legitimate, freedom to worship openly . . ." Her voice caught on a sob, and she sat down again. "It's a dream. It's too good to be true."

"Aye, it's good but not too good to be true," her father replied. "It's all of God's grace, who loves to give good gifts to His children. Let us thank Him now for His bounty towards us."

A hush fell over the room as all bowed in stillness before God, the giver of all good gifts.

"Eternal and ever-living God, Father of our Lord Jesus Christ, Thou who of Thine infinite goodness hast chosen to deliver us out of the land of the Egyptians and now to bring us up out of this land unto a land flowing with milk and honey, lead us that we may go out with praise and shouts of joy and be led forth in peace. Let the mountains and the hills break forth before us into singing, and all the trees of the fields clap their hands.

"Our Lord Jesus reigneth, to whom, with Thee and the Holy Spirit, be all honor, praise, and glory, now and ever. So be it."

Graham rose and walked quietly from the room. He had known that this time would come. He had even looked forward to it, had encouraged his father in it. Now the die was cast. He could no longer think all decision lay in the future. He would act now. It was only a short distance over the field to the Price farm, which retained its name no matter who owned the lease. He would walk.

Molly saw him coming and ran to meet him while he was still in the field. Her face was thin, but her brown eyes warmed like roasting chestnuts. "You look animated, my Graham. Has aught happened?"

"Aye." Much had happened. Which should he tell her first? "The emigration—it's settled. They're going." He paused. Best to settle one issue at a time. "Molly, it sounds like Beulah Land—free for the working. With no disabilities of law."

Molly's hand was on his arm. "Graham Lanark, are you saying you would choose to emigrate as well?"

He shook his head. "Never I. Not myself, Molly. But *we.* It would be a fine place for bairns."

"And would it be a fine place for you, my Graham? Would you be happy there?"

"I would try to be if it's what you want."

Her laughter was like bells on the evening air. "Everything I want is *here*, Graham. It seems we can save ourselves the trouble of making such a great journey to find what we already have."

"Aye. But the hunger—"

Molly put a hand to her hollow stomach. "I would be aye happy for one more tattie a day. But 'tis a wide ocean to cross for a tattie. Parson Firth led his people from Scotland for food. Now he leads them to Pennsylvania for food. Where will they go next?"

Graham nodded. "Such is part of the human condition. And I'd nae like to leave here. Especially were we wed." He paused, gathering his arguments. "Molly, I'd not wait longer for that. Yearly our ministers petition King George for relief from the Sacramental Test. His Majesty is more favorable to us than was Anne, and the Whigs in Parliament have made some modifications, but toleration could still be long in coming. Would you marry me now—soon—and face the consequences?"

"Aye. I would."

He was dumbfounded. No tears, no protests, no railings against the unfairness of the laws. A simple "Aye" from his Molly, and all the world was right.

But that thought had no more than crossed his mind than Graham knew that *still* all was not right. "Molly, I've aught to tell you, but I'd not have ye standing here in the middle of the flax field to hear it." His arm around her shoulder, he guided her back to the bawn. They found a bench along the wall beneath an apricot tree.

The night smells of damp stone and fresh grass, of shut-up rabbits and apricot blossoms mingled on the air. Graham drew a deep breath. "Molly, I'll not come to you unconfessed. I've a great weight that I would be free of if I but knew how."

Candles flickered in the windows of the old house. Graham fancied he saw them reflected in Molly's eyes as she waited for him to continue.

"I killed a man. My own kin."

Molly blinked, but her only sound was a sharply in-drawn breath. The hens fluttered in their roosts just beyond as if his words had startled them.

"Charles Lanark. I didn't know he was my cousin until . . . after." Graham closed his eyes, reliving the scene as if the bench beneath him were Hazel and the barking dogs in their kennel were the cacophony of battle.

"My father was just ahead of me, fighting two Jacobites at the same time. This other soldier came at Father's back. I lunged for him. I did not see his face." Graham did not know whether the moisture on his face was sweat or tears.

Molly took his hand. "Then you saved your faither's life. Surely you don't repent that."

"No. I don't. But I could have done it otherwise—knocked the man off his horse . . ." He shrugged. "I don't know. I've thought it over and over. Still I don't know."

"Does your father know?"

"I could not speak of it. I let him think I was a coward rather than tell what I'd done. I *was* a coward—afraid of my own act, afraid of my own words."

"And Gavin, Bridie, Finn?"

"I've tried. The first time I went to Seaton Court I meant to speak. Time and again I've played it in my mind." He gripped the edge of the stone bench. "Coward!"

"Nae!"

The fluttering of hens and barking of dogs increased.

Graham's father stepped from the darkness.

"Nae. No' coward—hero."

Graham sat stunned. "Father." He blinked into the darkness. "How—what—you were with the dogs?"

"Aye."

"And you heard all?"

"Aye. Why did ye never tell me you saved my life? Why let me think you a deserter all these years?"

"It was too painful to me that I'd killed my own cousin."

David gave a harsh laugh. "Aye, but that's the good of it. Saved my life and did in one of that turncoat lot all at one slash."

"Father, you canna mean that! You canna hate your own blood so. What can have caused such hostility between these houses for so many years?"

"The *clock*, of course."

Graham was astounded. David spoke as if he referred to Scrabo. Some object of enormous proportions that stood over all their lives. Some object that everyone knew of and took for granted everyone else knew.

"*What* clock?"

"The Lanark dowry clock! Our family's most prized possession from the auld home. It should have remained at the bawn. But when my great-grandfaither married a papist, he took it with him to Seaton Court. My faither went to the law over it. But they ruled against him—a Crown court left our dowry clock in a Catholic house!"

"And *that's* what this feud has been over for three generations? A *clock?*"

"It was our heritage. A symbol of the Lanark family. Our birthright."

"And for that you're pleased that I killed Charles? You would trade a man's life for a *clock?*"

"I did it to make my father proud of me." David's non sequitur was delivered in a strange voice. It took on a faraway sound, as if the David Lanark of many years ago spoke. "My father never liked me. I wasn't good with the cattle like Malcolm. I wasn't clever like Alex. As a lad I tried everything I could think of to please him, but he never noticed. The night he returned from the assizes so angered over losing the case, I knew what to do.

"I worked it all out with Alex. He was the bright one and just two years younger than me. He'd do anything I told him. I fired his imagination with tales of glorious vengeance. We waited, hid in the hedgerows until they drove off to Mass—the whole lot of them, family in a carriage, the servants spilling out of a wagon—all off to their superstitious rites. It should have been an easy thing. Most didn't bar their doors in the daytime. But that one was locked tight. So I told Alex to do it."

David took a gulp of air that shook his whole body. "He didn't want to. But I made him. Alex was small. I could always force my way with him. I made him break the window. 'Just give it one good whack with your fist,' I said.

"And he did." David put a hand over his eyes. "The blood spurted. A great red stripe on the whitewashed wall. I'd seen Malcolm care for a cut calf, so I knew what to do. I ripped my shirt and bound his wrist. I tried to make the blood stop. I tried everything I could. But he died just as I got him home."

The silence was so long that Graham thought he was finished.

Then David drew a shaky breath and continued. "My father never forgave me. I never forgave myself. I couldn't forgive you. And that clock is still at Seaton Court."

Graham was stunned.

He had paid little attention to the clock on the mantel at Seaton Court, but he recalled it now. A small object in an iron and gilt case, obviously very old. An interesting piece, that was all. Yet three generations of Lanarks had fought each other over it. Two young men had died for it. This was enough.

This one thing—and all the squabbles that had resulted from it—had poisoned the lives of two families for generations. But no more. He would put an end to it, no matter what the cost to himself. He couldn't be responsible for what his ancestors had done, but he was responsible for what he did. And he was going to clear the way for peace in the future.

He slept little that night. When he did, his sleep was filled with confused dreams. He was sitting in church listening to the reading of the lesson. Cain rose up against Abel, his brother, and slew him. Jealous because God had smiled on Abel's offering and not on his own . . .

Graham rolled over, and the scene shifted. "And Jacob said, Sell me this day thy birthright. And Esau said, Behold, I am at the point to die; and what profit shall this birthright do to me? . . . And he sold his birthright unto Jacob."

And then he was in battle, slashing at Abel—lunging at Esau—killing Charles.

The next morning he set out for Seaton Court without his usual ale and porridge. He would tell Finn. He could no longer hide behind the argument that confessing to Finn would likely result in the Prices losing their subtenancy. The good that came of truth and the evil of lies were more important issues than the lease of a farm. Graham would take his stand for the truth.

But not with both Finlay and Gavin at once. He was prepared to face the younger man first, then ask—beg, if necessary—his help in approaching the senior Lanark.

It was not to be, however, for both father and son stood beside the barn looking over a board fence down into a muddy pen where an enormous pink sow lay on her side suckling a dozen squirming piglets. Gavin held a long, thick stick, which he used to scratch the sow behind her ears. She responded with a grunt.

Finn turned at the sound of Hazel's hoofs on the graveled yard. His wave was welcoming. But when Graham dismounted and approached the sty, Finlay's warm smile faded. "*Dia Duit*. You have come on a serious matter, I think."

Gavin stood silent and frowning.

"Aye. I have come about the sin that has divided our families unto the third and fourth generations."

"Rantin' fanatic," Gavin growled at him. "No man calls the Roman faith sin on my land."

"No, no. You take me wrong. Covetousness, greed, selfishness—that's what I refer to. I knew nothing of the rights and wrongs of property settlement."

"Oh, so that's it!" Gavin brandished the stick and would have brought it down with a heavy blow on Graham's shoulder had Finlay not intervened. "We're as much Lanark as ye—more so—we're in the line of the eldest son. The bawn and all the property went to the second son. Rory got naught but his mother's clock." He spit in the gravel.

"I did no' come to argue ancient wrongs. 'Sufficient unto the day is the evil thereof,' and our day has enough evil of its own without dragging up that of our ancestors. It's my own sin I've come to confess—mine and my father's. He carries a great guilt—incurred when he tried to steal the clock—"

"Aye, after his *athair* failed in his attempt to steal it through the courts." Gavin raised the stick again.

"His little brother died as a result. His father carried rejection of his son—my father—to the grave. And so my father rejected me. In an attempt to earn his acceptance I joined the army, fought in the Battle of the Boyne, and killed my own cousin."

The words came out so easily that he hardly realized he had spoken them until he saw the look on Gavin's face. Now he would feel the stick. And deservedly too. The blows would almost feel good. The lashes of penance. He began to remove his jacket so the strokes could fall on his thin shirt.

But the heavy stick clattered to the gravel.

Gavin seemed frozen, so Graham turned to Finlay. "I did not know. Not until I had struck the blow. I meant to tell you the day I brought his things. But I couldna do it. The words would not come." He dropped his head. "Can you forgive? I don't deserve—"

Finn's hand clapped Graham's shoulder. "But I always knew. I thought you understood, when you took my hint that ye not tell Bridie."

The name brought more shame on Graham. "And I must tell her. I must be rid of my guilt if there's ever to be peace."

"She's away. She'll hear you later."

Graham turned back to Gavin, who still had not spoken. His cloth cap was awry. He looked pale and vulnerable in the morning light. His square jaw hung slack with amazement, emphasizing the wrinkles in his face. He suddenly looked an old, frail man.

"I'm sorry. I'm so sorry. About everything." Graham could think of nothing more to say, so he turned and mounted Hazel, barely able to lift the weight of his burden into the saddle.

It was well that he had planned earlier to stop by the graveyard of the boarded-up meetinghouse, for he was in no state to return home. In all the years he had wrestled with the burden of making his confession, he had never thought there could be such an outcome—that Gavin would be so deflated, so completely disarmed. That Finlay had already known and, knowing, had rescued the Prices from their dilemma. Finlay had always known and had always been a friend. That, perhaps, had been the thing Graham had dreaded most—losing Finlay's friendship.

The overwhelming defeat had not been in the reactions of those to whom he confessed but in himself. Always he had thought, *Someday*

I'll make a clean breast of the whole matter. Then I'll be free of this enormous weight I'm carrying around. Someday I'll take care of this. Someday had come. He had told everyone—Molly, David, Gavin, Finn—but there was no release. If anything, the burden was heavier than before, because now that he had done all he could, he could no longer look ahead to "someday."

Graham was so lost in thought that Hazel made his way to the church of his own accord. There he dismounted and walked to the far corner of the unkempt kirk yard. He gazed at the weather-battered stone marking the grave of Alexander Lanark. He had stood by it, unnoticing, many times, but now he felt he knew the lad who slept there —a fellow victim of the Lanark feud.

After a time he turned to his mother's grave and pulled a book from his pocket. How long had it been since he had read here in memory of old days? Not since 1690? His mind boggled at the thought. So much time wasted, consumed by the worms of fear, self-focus, and covetousness. He opened Bunyan's allegory.

And then he understood why he had put the book away for so long. Reading had been too painful. He had left off at the part where Christian was suffering under his burden.

> "Sir," he said to Mr. Worldly Wiseman, "this burden upon my back is more terrible to me than any other thing you could name. Nay, methinks I care not what I meet with in the way, if so be I can also meet with deliverance from my burden."

Graham paused. The words could be his own. Then he read on as the sun climbed toward noonday.

> And Christian ran on, but not without great difficulty because of the load on his back. He ran thus until he came to a place somewhat ascending, and upon that place stood a cross, and a little below, in the bottom, a sepulchre. And the shadow of the cross fell across him, and the burden loosed from off his shoulders, and fell from his back. It began to tumble, and so continued to do till it came to the mouth of the sepulchre. It tumbled into the mouth of the tomb. And was seen no more.
>
> And a Shining One came to Christian and saluted him. "Peace be to thee. Thy sins be forgiven thee."

Graham read of Christian standing, unburdened, before the cross with his cheeks streaming from the springs in his eyes. He put a hand to his own cheek. It was wet.

Then Christian began to leap for joy, and Graham felt his heart leaping and singing with him:

> Thus far did I come laden with my sin
> Nor could aught ease the grief that I was in,
> Blest cross! blest sepulchre! blest rather be
> The Man that was there put to shame for me!

And Graham went home. Unburdened.

43

"The Lord sanctify and bless you; the Lord pour the riches of His grace upon you that ye may please Him and live together in holy love to your lives' end. So be it."

Parson Stevenson raised his hand in blessing over the couple before him at the altar of the Presbyterian church in Comber.

They had taken something of a risk in unboarding and cleaning the meetinghouse for the wedding, but all across Ulster the enforcement of the Penal Laws was slacking. The government simply didn't have the manpower—or the will—to enforce such crushing laws on the vast majority of its population. Although the disabilities remained in the legal codes, more and more priests of the Romish faith had returned to say Mass at hidden rocks and in homes, and more and more Presbyterian ministers were holding services in the pulpits they had been ousted from.

Graham smiled down at Molly as they sang the closing psalm with the congregation, "Blessed is every one that feareth the Lord; that walketh in his ways. . . . Yea, thou shalt see thy children's children, and peace upon Israel."

The bride and groom had time to give their guests only a hurried greeting, then all the family, including Bridie and Finlay, who had attended the bride and groom, must be off.

But through all the formalities of the ceremony, the well-wishes of the guests, and the rush of leave-taking—along with being certain that all the Prices and the Lanarks from both bawn and court were accommodated in carriages and wagons—Graham had eyes for only one small woman in a summer-green gown. He reached for Molly's hand to lift her onto the carriage seat. Her white lawn puffed sleeve covered both their hands, and she squeezed his fingers tightly, not letting go when he was on the seat beside her.

"Will we be on time, do you think?"

"Oh, aye, love. They'll no sail without their leader." He motioned toward the ever-efficient Mr. Firth, who was still checking off a list of bags and trunks in the last of the wagons even as others in the caravan set out on the road north.

"Yes, but it's thirty miles to Larne, and they must catch the tide," Molly persisted. "I'd nae want anything to go wrong now. They've planned for years."

Graham longed to kiss away the slight furrow between her brows. But he knew he would be fined for such a public display, even though they were wed. "Aye, and so have we, my love."

She gave him a shy smile. "It was worth the wait."

"Worth every minute." He squeezed the warm hand sheltering under the full sleeve. "I'd have waited twice as long if I'd had to, but I'm verra glad I didn't have to."

The road to Belfast and on north to the port was bordered on each side with promising green fields, fresh from last week's June rains. If the drought of the past three years was broken, there would be potatoes in Irish stew pots this year. The world was a hopeful place once more.

Graham saw the billowing white sails of the *King Billy* as they approached the port. The quay was a hubbub of activity—milling people, crying children, squawking sailors carrying trunks and boxes to the tenders to be rowed out to the tall-masted ship. Five Presbyterian ministers and nearly two hundred members of their congregations were making the trek to the New World; Firth and his band among them.

It was amazing how quickly the confusion sorted itself out, a testimony to the orderliness and discipline of the travelers. The next three tenders would be for the Firth party and their luggage. It was time to say farewell.

As Graham looked at his family, it struck him how *much* he would miss them. What a gap would be left in his life with the absence of the demanding father whose expectations had dogged his boyhood and early manhood and whom he had come to understand in only the past three months.

Only three months of sympathetic relationship with the man who would now be going out of his life forever, he thought. But he was grateful he had had those three months.

And Lorna, the woman who had done such a fine job of filling the void in David's life after Janet's death. So unlike Graham's own mother but such a good mother to her brood. He looked at the nearly mature Davey. It likely wouldn't be long until they received a letter telling that Davey was taking a wife of his own. He looked at Helen, sturdy and sensible, born to brave the New World. And there was wee Dereck, who was already saying he wanted to be a minister just like his Grandfaither Firth.

Graham's throat closed at the thought that he would never see any of them again. He started to reach for his father's hand.

But Gavin Lanark preceded him. Wordlessly, Gavin pumped David's hand, nodding his bald head in the same up and down rhythm. Then he nodded to Finlay, who stepped forward and held out a small wooden box. "A gift for your departure. To remind you of your homeland and your family. To wish you God's hand on your journey."

David lifted the lid and took out a small clock in an iron and gilt case. His throat worked. He shook his head. He took Gavin's hand. "Brother."

Gavin nodded. "*Bráthair.*"

Behind them, Reverend Firth loaded his daughter and grandchildren into the tender. "David, we go!"

David looked from the package in his hands to his son. He started to say something, then hesitated.

"David! The tide!" Firth shouted.

David ran his hand over the object that had divided three generations of Lanarks. "So many times my father would tell the tale: our ancestor Calum pawned this in Scotland for passage to Ireland. His bride redeemed it and brought it to him when she crossed the water—her dowry. She set it on the mantel of the bawn house herself and bequeathed it to her eldest son. As a wedding gift. So I would bequeath it to my eldest son."

He put the clock in Graham's hands. "Put it on the mantel where it belongs, my son. It will give me pleasure to think of it there. When I look at the mantel I will build for a new family of Lanarks in a new land, I will think of the mantel in Ireland."

He turned away and strode to the tender.

Graham stood on the quay, holding Molly's hand, until the wind caught the sails. The *King Billy* set out for the New World.

44

"I don't believe it. This can't be happening. Listen."

The slam of a door and Gareth's agitated voice pulled Mary from her manuscript. "What is it? What happened? You look absolutely dire."

He flopped onto the sofa beside her and switched on the radio he carried. "Listen for yourself. It *is* dire." In spite of telling her to listen, he continued talking over the voice of the newscaster. "How can they do this? How can they be so pigheaded? They're throwing away all their support. Why do we try? Maybe we *should* just go home."

Mary had never heard him talk like that. It frightened her, even though it was exactly what she'd been wanting all along. Go back to Scotland with Gareth? Yes! Go back to Scotland and plan their wedding. She twisted the band on her finger. They hadn't talked about setting the date, but the sooner they got back across the Irish Sea, the sooner she could become Mrs. Gareth Lindsey.

Her smile faded, however, as Gareth turned up the volume on the radio, and they both listened. The scene took form in Mary's mind as the reporter's voice filled the room: Downtown Belfast in chaos. The worst street violence in Northern Ireland in a decade. Smoke rising from buildings. Unionists barricading streets. Orangemen threatening more disruption in response to a police order requiring them to reroute their march to avoid a Catholic neighborhood.

"We have the power. We can bring Northern Ireland to a standstill," an Orange leader declared to a cheering throng.

"Oh, that's awful. Turn it off. I was just reading about the celebrations of the Williamite victory three hundred years ago. To think it's come to this." She paused. "And the irony is, the first Twelfth of July bonfires were Episcopal celebrations of their victory over Presbyterians and Catholics. Now most of the marchers are Presbyterian."

"That's right."

At the sound of Philip's voice, Mary turned to see him standing in the doorway.

"The Penal Laws applied to Presbyterians and Catholics alike. The thing is, the Protestant dissenters didn't hold onto their resentments, so they healed faster." He crossed the room and sat in front of the picture window opening out onto the green valley beyond the garden.

"But what about all this Ascendancy business?" Mary persisted. "I can't decide whether it's something to celebrate or not. In the light of how things have turned out, that is."

"Who knows what might have happened if any of the Jacobite risings had turned out differently?" Philip said. "For a while there, in 1745, Bonnie Prince Charlie's victories made it look as though they would. Culloden put paid to that."

As so often before, Mary was amazed at how the Irish talked about events of hundreds of years ago as if they were in the morning's newspaper. But then, in a way they were.

"One thing's certain," Philip continued, "William was no Cromwell. When he had the entire Catholic army in his power after the Battle of the Boyne, he didn't execute the vengeance of the Lord upon them. He gave them their choice of sailing for France or swearing loyalty and retaining their property. The Battle of Aughrim—after the Battle of the Boyne—was the last decisive battle fought in Ireland, as well as the bloodiest. The Treaty of Limerick, which followed, granted freedom of worship to Catholics. William also did what he could to limit the scope of land confiscation. But his was a constitutional monarchy—he was obliged to bow to the wishes of Parliament."

"Oh dear, British rule again?"

"Funnily enough, it would probably have been better if it had been. The king's viceroy tried, but he found the Irish Parliament 'a company of madmen'—his term—because of their agitation to free themselves from England's yoke. You understand, the only people who could hold office in those days were the landed gentry of the established church. That meant that in the early eighteenth century it was Protestants who were shouting, 'Brits go home!'"

Mary laughed, but it was in exasperation rather than amusement.

"It's also important for today's Anglophobes to understand that the Penal Code—designed to protect the insecure Protestants from such near ruin as they had faced at the '41 Rising and James II's policy to de-Protestantize Ireland—came from the *Dublin* Parliament, not London. Irish MP's suspected the English government of being soft on protecting Protestant liberties. By Protestant, they meant, of course, the Episcopal church. The laws not allowing dissenters to own land, inherit, or vote were applied somewhat erratically to Catholics and Presbyterians alike."

Mary couldn't imagine living under such oppression. "How long did that go on?"

"The Ascendancy lasted throughout the eighteenth century—

381

until Union in 1801. But the Penal Laws weren't enforced nearly that long. They just faded out of practice because the government didn't have the stomach or the staff to enforce them."

Mary thought for a moment. "They simply had no concept of religious freedom, did they?"

"*No* religious group sought toleration. They sought victory. It doesn't seem to have entered anyone's head that a nation could have more than one church. Of course, in those days, *church* meant established church—and each one wanted to be established."

"I never realized what a totally new idea it was when our founders established freedom of religion." Mary struggled to recall her American history. "Each colony had its own established church before the Revolution. Then they saw that if they were going to form a unified nation, they had to make room for all faiths." She grinned ironically. "Ireland apparently still hasn't seen that."

The clock on the mantel that had kept the hours through so much of Ireland's turmoil chimed the time.

Gareth turned the radio back on. "Maybe they'll have a new report."

The horror of the situation became clear: a standoff was developing between police and thousands of Orange Order marchers. Unionist gangs were attacking the Royal Ulster Constabulary, who were 93 percent Unionist themselves. Unionist leaders adamantly asserted their right "to walk the Queen's Highway."

Mary got to her feet. She could take no more. "Why did it have to happen? Just when it looked as if things were cooling down again. Now Mother will never let Becca and Julie come. I was so looking forward to seeing them—and they were so excited." Just yesterday she had received a bubbling letter giving all their plans and schedules. Now everything would have to be canceled.

Philip rose, too. "Well, I'd better get down to the Centre. See what I can do. I wonder if anyone will listen to a voice of sanity in all that."

"Do you think you can get through to the Centre?"

"I don't know. The reports didn't say which streets were barricaded. But I'll try." He left the room.

Gareth picked up his jacket to go with him, and Mary grabbed his arm. "Gareth, don't go. It might be dangerous. They said shootings and petrol bombs . . ." She gripped him tighter.

He put his free arm around her. "I have to, Mary. It's my work. You'll be safe here."

She choked back hot, angry tears. It was the same argument they'd had before. They were on an interminable merry-go-round of attempts at peacemaking being torn apart by bombs and violence. "I don't want to be safe here. I want to be with you. Preferably, safe in Scotland."

"Mary, Mary." He cuddled her tight with a gentle rocking motion. "I'm sae sorry about all this. I know it's so hard on you."

She gave a loud sniff and straightened her back, pulling away. "Oh, forgive me. I'm being selfish. It seems I just can't help it. I'm just so upset about everything falling apart. I even thought we'd be able to start play practice again. Debbie's mom said she'd talk to Martin's and Sarah's mothers about letting them come back. I thought . . ."

She fought down her frustration angrily. "I really thought we could prove something here. I actually thought people could be sensible enough to get along so these kids could have their youth center. It seemed a reasonable thing. I didn't think I was asking too much. Silly, silly me!" Her voice rose hysterically.

She turned away, fighting for control. "I—I suppose I blew it out of proportion, but I had this idea that we were working in a sort of microcosm. That the youth center was a symbol for all Ireland. That if we could resolve the conflicts in that one little area, it would mean that ultimately it could all be solved. I just hate, hate, hate to fail!"

She turned to him again, flipping her long, bright hair out of her face.

Gareth stood quietly observing her. "Oh dear, oh dear, oh dear." He opened his arms, and she walked into their comforting security.

"Are you coming, Gareth?" Philip stuck his head in at the door.

Gareth raised one eyebrow and looked at Mary.

"Yes. We're coming." Her voice was firm and calm.

Amazingly, they had no trouble driving right to the CCC. When they rounded one corner, Mary thought perhaps she glimpsed a plume of smoke toward the Falls, but she wasn't sure. "I thought it was *all* burning."

"A few streets undoubtedly are," Philip replied. "But the media always exaggerates. I think they're to blame for a lot of the trouble."

"Because they blow it out of proportion?"

"Sure. They thrive on other people's troubles. The more trouble, the better their job is." He pulled into his usual parking spot and was occupied for a moment locking everything securely. "I'm probably being too harsh. But I do think a lot of the agitators are playing to the TV cameras. I always suspect that if the media would stay away, protests would die a lot sooner."

Inside, the receptionist was handing Philip a long list of phone calls he needed to return, when a cheery laugh sounded. "Aye, and may ye be in heaven half an hour before the Devil knows you're dead."

"Paddy! How good to see you!" Mary was delighted to see the red-bearded man with the crinkly, freckled face. "I was afraid we wouldn't be seeing you—with all the stuff going on."

"Ah, you've a lot to learn about the Irish. We're at our best when there's the least to be laughing about. Seriously, this is when our people need us most. I'd not be letting them down."

"But what can you do when people just go away and don't—or can't—come back?"

"You mean like your youth council?"

Mary nodded. "I understood why parents wouldn't let their kids come out after the Manchester bombing. But things were quiet for a while, so we thought we could start again. Now with all this—" She gestured hopelessly. "I don't know what to do."

"Mary—"

She turned to the receptionist, calling her.

"Trunk call. You might want to take it in Philip's office. It's not a very good connection."

"Oh. Thanks." She hurried down the hall. Even though she'd been expecting it, she didn't need this last piece of bad news. This would be her sisters, calling to explain why they weren't coming. As if she didn't understand. She certainly wondered often enough why *she* had come.

"Becca, Julie! It's so good to hear your voices." She had missed her vivacious twin sisters. "Where are you?"

"We're in Scotland."

"With Auntie Val and Brad and Sharon."

"Of course."

"Where did you think we were?"

"Didn't you get our letter with the schedule?"

"You should see Sharon—she looks like she's having twins!"

"Edinburgh is so great!"

"Wait! Wait!" Mary yelled into the receiver. She knew her sisters. This running dialogue could go on for hours. They were like hot and cold water faucets both turned on full blast—American mixer faucets. "Do you mean Mom let you come after the news?"

"What news?"

"We aren't anywhere near Manchester."

"Auntie Val says—"

Mary started laughing. "I get it. You must have left home before the riots started here. Oh, I am glad. I thought it would all be off. But you'll be perfectly safe. Don't worry."

"Worry about what?"

"We brought our soccer pads like you said."

"And Brad's taking us to the castle in a minute."

"We'll see you Saturday."

"Bye."

"Bye."

"Love you."

"Mom and Dad send love."

"And Brutus."

"He knows how much you miss his licks."

Mary returned to the reception lounge still laughing at her irrepressible sisters and shivering at the memory of being licked in the face by their enormous black Labrador.

"It must have been good news. It's fine to see the sparkle back in those blue eyes."

"It was good news, Paddy. My sisters are in Scotland. They'll be here this weekend. I didn't think they'd get to come. If their reservations had been for a day later, they wouldn't have." She told him about Becca and Julie.

"Ah, well now, that's grand. We must give them a proper Irish welcome. We'll have a *caidleagh*."

"They would love a party! That would be great. We can have Debbie and Liam and Fiona, Gerry, Sarah—" She broke off. In the excitement of her sisters' good news she had momentarily forgotten the realities.

"Oh." She sank into one of the deep blue chairs. "No one can come to a party. Not now."

"What's this, then? Throwing in the towel already? I thought Americans were the ones who held on till the last Alamo."

Mary laughed. "Paddy, you're great. Of course, I'm willing to carry on. I just don't have a clue what to do."

"Well, then, like I said, let's have a *caidleagh*. That's an Irish tradition: when there's nothing else to do, throw a party. Those kids you were naming, they're from the youth councils that are trying to get funding for the leisure center?"

"Yes. They were planning a play and a program to raise money and demonstrate cross-community cooperation. *A Night in Olde Belfast*, we called it. The bomb in Manchester ended that. And now—"

"Aye. I know the ones from my side of the street. I'll see what I can do. What about the others?"

"Well, Debbie Downing is the Protestant youth council president. Her mother runs an organization for victims of violence, so she's pretty approachable."

"Downing? That'd be Louise Downing with Courage?"

"That's right."

"Well, there you are, then. I was going to her office later this morning. I have a client for her—young woman who was baby-sitting for her sister so she and her husband could have a night out. Someone threw a petrol bomb through the window where the baby was sleeping. The girl was badly burned trying to save the child. Three years ago. She still can't face people well enough to hold a job."

"So you're taking this girl to Debbie's mom?"

"No, I'll tell Courage about her. Give them her address. They're proactive. Have to be—they deal with people who are too traumatized to go to them. They just go to people. Say, 'We're here to help.' Louise Downing will be a good ally for getting your group together again." He laughed. "Besides, a party is something no Irish person can refuse. Come along with me. See for yourself."

Paddy drove through a confusing maze of streets, all constituting neighborhoods of tall, neat, brick-terraced houses with lace curtains at the windows. It was a mixed community, without painted curbs.

Mary was surprised when Paddy pulled up in front of one in the center of a block. "I thought we were going to an office."

"It's Nimah's home—the woman Louise works with. Their clients feel more comfortable in a home. And Nimah had the space."

Mary saw the small yellow placard in the window. *Courage*, in red letters. "Oh, yes. I remember. She's Sheila's friend. Her husband killed, her son crippled."

"That's right. These are brave ladies. It's easier to live with what you're used to—even if it's violence—than to set to work changing things." He led the way to the door.

Louise Downing was tall and had a sturdiness that stopped just short of being plump. She wore a navy tailored suit with a red and gold silk scarf. Her smartly styled dark hair showed silver at both temples. She was gracious but lacked some of Paddy O'Reilley's devil-may-care optimism.

"I'm so glad you came to me about this, Mary. Of course I'll let Debbie go to a party for your sisters. I've always tried to keep everything as normal as possible for her—especially in times of crisis. We must do our best to make Julie and Becca welcome. What a shame they had to arrive at such an awkward time."

"And do you think you can talk to the other parents?"

Louise pushed some papers around on the table in front of her. "I can try. Certainly. But I don't know. Canary Wharf . . . Manchester . . . now riots in Belfast. It's brought it all back, everything we've been through, all our personal losses. So many of the people our counselors were working with have completely reverted. A young mother whose husband was shot a couple of years ago was just ready to go back to school. She'd wanted to for some time, but her two little girls couldn't be away from her. We'd just got them settled in a good daycare. That night they saw the Canary Wharf thing on the telly. Now they're so clingy again that their mother can't go to the loo."

The woman bobbed her head. "Fear is like a life force. Far stronger than any walls." She stood up. "But I'll try. We always keep trying. Maybe someday peace will win."

45

The canteen of the CCC was alive with teenage voices, mostly Irish, but the two American ones were easily identified. Garlands of red and green crepe paper—left over from Christmas, no doubt—looped around the walls. Popular music played from a tape player in the corner, and everyone laughed while Gareth organized a game of Twister. Julie, Martin, Gerry, and Debbie pulled their shoes off and stood by a large plastic mat with rows of plate-sized red, blue, green, and yellow spots.

"Right. I'll spin. Last one to fall over wins—and no pushing."

General hilarity reigned as the pointer spun around the card, then a shout of laughter when he announced, "Left foot, yellow," and the players leaped for the mat.

On the other side of the room, Jeff was leading a game of Christian Rock Group Trivia with Ann and her friend Gillian from church. Tommy, the ex-prisoner working in Braille transcription who shared upstairs quarters with Gareth, joined the trivia table and introduced his special guest—a beautiful girl with long chestnut hair named Lila.

Louise smiled across the small round table at Mary. "I'm delighted to admit that I was overly pessimistic. All the parents seemed to think it really important that we give the American young people a warm welcome."

Mary took a handful of popcorn and passed the bowl to her. Mary had insisted that Dorinda make it American style—with salt rather than sugar. "You know, that's one of the most charming things about Ireland. I think it must be one of the few places on earth where it's a decided asset to be American. They really *like* us here."

"Probably because there are more Irish living in America than in Ireland. You'd be hard put to find anyone here who doesn't have some family member that went to America at some time—or at least wanted to." She watched the game for a moment. "And your sisters fit in so well. They're so natural and uninhibited."

Mary laughed. "They've simply adopted Ann. She's more like a sister to them than I am. Sheila thought Ann would just abandon her room to them and sleep on the sofa. But they opted to bunk together. You should see them—just room for one girl on the floor on each side of Ann's single bed. I think they were up most of the night, giggling. I just hope this doesn't put Ann too far behind on her studying."

By now the mat was a mass of twisted bodies. Gareth whirled the spinner. "Right hand, blue." Julie was completely covered by Martin leaning across her to reach a spot. Debbie and Gerry lunged for the same blue circle, bumped heads, and fell down laughing.

"You've done a remarkable job with Debbie," Mary said to Louise. "She told me what she'd been through. I think it's amazing that people survive such things—let alone turn out so seemingly unscarred."

Louise licked the salt and butter off her fingers. "That's good—I never had popcorn that way before." Then she nodded. "Yes, I think Debbie is doing very well. I'm so thankful. She was completely withdrawn —frozen—until I got her into a bereavement program at Courage."

"What's that?"

"I think it's one of the most important things we do—our bereavement and support groups for teenagers. You see, medical help has been the only thing available to most people. They've had to cope with the rest on their own. So we focus on trauma recovery with special programs for children and teens."

"That's wonderful. How are you funded?"

"We're mostly volunteer. There's a community relations council that provides some funds for two licensed social workers. They oversee the therapy, train volunteers, refer cases to psychologists when necessary. We manage to scrimp along."

"How does your teen program work?"

"We do nine weeks of group sessions. The first step is getting the young people to talk about how their families have changed due to bereavement and disability. Once they face that openly and talk about it together, then we can get them to deal with the feelings of anger, revenge, fear, guilt. If those things stay stuffed down inside, sooner or later they're going to erupt in rage."

She shivered. "Sometimes I wake up at night thinking about all the traumatized people out there and worrying about how and where all the bottled up wrath will erupt. I worry about that a lot more than about petrol bombs." She gave a nervous laugh. "Oh dear. This is no conversation for a party."

Across the room another game of Twister was just breaking up. Liam, who had held aloof from the game, picked up Gareth's guitar and started playing "The Irish Washer Woman."

Mary was especially happy that he had come. After their last parting, she wasn't sure she'd ever see him again. While Louise was talking, she thought about the bursts of anger she had seen from Liam. At times, with his intense, burning eyes and gaunt features, he seemed like an unexploded bomb. And yet he could be so charming. She wished she knew what had caused the pain and rage he kept inside himself.

Liam had played only a few chords when Fiona skipped to the center of the room and began the step dance routine she had choreographed for *A Night in Olde Belfast*. Becca and Julie were fascinated with the marionettelike movements.

"That's incredible."

"I've never seen anything like it."

"Your feet don't even touch the floor."

"Could you teach us?" As usual, their words tumbled out on top of each other. Tall Becca with her short, nut-brown hair and wide brown eyes and Julie, golden curls bouncing and round cheeks dimpling, bounded forward.

Soon every chair in the room was pushed flat against the wall, and everyone was step dancing with varying degrees of skill. Martin got a wooden spoon and cutting board from the kitchen to use as an impromptu drum, providing a decided help to those whose sense of rhythm needed all the help it could get.

When they all collapsed, gasping for Cokes and lemonade, Gareth took the guitar. They'd barely had time to catch their breath before he had them singing, "Rejoice! Rejoice! Christ is in you, the hope of glory in our hearts. He lives! He lives! His breath is in you, arise—"

The song engendered all the enthusiasm in its singers that Graham Kendrick's music always did.

Then came singing and clapping through three verses of "Shine, Jesus, Shine," and finally, "Bind us together, Lord, bind us together . . . bind us together in love. . . . There is only one God, there is only one King; there is only one body." Why couldn't people understand that?

Mary saw shining, intent faces. Such beautiful young people, so full of energy and hope and, at the moment, love. This was what Mary had worked, hoped, and prayed for. There had been glimmers of cooperation before, tentative times of working together. But now she could feel the oneness in this room. "Bind us together with cords that cannot be broken."

They had achieved oneness. Now they could go on. Now they would produce their program. They would build their youth center. Tomorrow she would call all the parents and get their permission to start practice again. They had lost a lot of time, but with hard work they could still produce the program on schedule.

She fell asleep with designs for sets and costumes dancing through her head.

The shrilling phone jolted Mary awake sometime in the middle of the night. But its piercing sound was not as troubling as the urgency she sensed in Philip's dash down the hall and his tense replies to the call.

Every word carried in the night stillness. "Was anyone hurt? How bad? How much damage? I'll be right there."

Mary was already pulling on jeans under her gown. She went to her doorway, heart pounding in her throat. Not another bomb? *Dear God, not another bomb.*

Sheila, putting on a robe, hurried to Philip. Becca, Julie, and Ann, looking like tousled puppies, tumbled out of their tiny room.

Philip held up a hand for silence before the demands for information could start. "Break-in at the Centre. Back window broken, door smashed, computers stolen."

"Gareth?" Mary was terrified to ask, but she had to know. Had he heard the noise—gone down to investigate? She could think no further.

"The thieves would have gotten a lot more if Gareth and Tommy hadn't interrupted them. They are the only two in the dorm just now. Mary—" He started down the short hall to her door. "They've taken Gareth to hospital, but they don't think it's serious. He was hurt in the scuffle—kicked or something—but he'll be OK."

"Can you take me to him? Now?"

"Of course."

Mary sat frozen with tension as they sped through the dark to the Royal Victoria Hospital. She wanted to pray, but the only thing she could say was, *Please. Please, please, please.*

Finally Philip broke the silence. "They think it was straightforward vandalism, not sectarian violence. Hoodlums seizing their chance while all the constabulary are occupied with rioters."

She nodded. If Gareth was hurt, it didn't make much difference who did it. Gareth was all that mattered. Well, that did it. As soon as he could travel, they would be on that ferry. It was no good anyone's trying to persuade her otherwise. Gareth was OK this time. But it could have been . . .

They pulled into a well-lit lot, and Philip, directed by hospital staff, steered her through a maze of doorways and corridors.

Gareth lay propped against pillows, pale, the strong bones of his face more prominent than ever, his dark hair and eyes black pools in the sea of whiteness.

"Hey!" He held out a hand to her.

The next moment she was in his arms, trembling uncontrollably as the tension let go.

"Oh dear, oh dear, oh dear." Philip stood on the other side of the bed, shaking his head. "I forgot to mention that heroics weren't part of the job description."

Gareth smiled weakly. "That's a good thing. Afraid I wasn't very heroic."

"The *garda* seem to think differently. They say we'd have lost a lot more if you hadn't interrupted them."

"Tommy did most of it. He's a wildcat when he gets going. Is he all right?"

Philip nodded. "He's helping the police sort things out at the Centre. I need to go help them. Just wanted to be sure you were in one piece." He grinned. "Besides, we'd have had another casualty on our hands if I didn't get Mary here pronto." His eyes twinkled. "I suppose you're ready to go, now that you see he's breathing?"

"No way." Mary gripped Gareth's hand so hard she was afraid she might hurt him. "I've waited all summer for this one to stop long enough to have three words with him."

"Right. You'll be set till morning, then?" He indicated a large lounge chair in the corner, where Mary could take a nap if she were so inclined. "Matron said they'd keep the lad for the night if he didn't cause too much trouble." He grinned at Gareth, then closed the door behind him.

Mary settled on the edge of the bed. "What happened?"

"I'm a little muzzy. I heard a crash. Woke Tommy. Told him to call the police while I went down to investigate. There were two blokes, I think. I went for the one rifling the desk. I remember he had white hair. He brought a chair down on my leg. Then Tommy came in, shouting. They fled. Police came. End of story."

Mary looked at the mound under the covers running down the left side of his body. "Oh, no—the same one."

"Ah, it's nae so bad. Not like last time. Enough to put a crimp in that football game I promised your sisters, though."

"Silly, brave hero." She had to hold onto him just to be sure he was there. "Gareth, I—" She tried to swallow down the enormous lump in her throat. Fear and relief, love and worry all fought for expression.

Gareth held out his arms, and she settled into them, sitting crossways across the hospital bed. It was so wonderful just to be with him. No matter that it was in a hospital room. They were alone. Together. She could have remained so for the rest of the night without even moving.

He stroked her hair with his right hand, fanning the long, golden strands out over the sheet. "Mary, you know how dear you are to me—

how much I love you." And then he picked up her left hand and kissed the finger encircled with his ring. "For eternity. That's a grand sight—I should have put it there sooner." He paused. "To be honest, I've been afraid."

Mary raised herself on one elbow and put a hand on his cheek, tracing his strong jawline with a fingertip. "Afraid I'd give up and go home? And we'd never see each other again?"

He shook his head with a sad little half smile. "No. I was afraid you'd go home and I'd go with you." He took her hand in his, moved it to his lips, and kissed each finger. "As much as I love you, Mary, my commitment has to come first. But that's verra hard. So I have to be sure there's no conflict." Now he looked her right in the eyes, intensely. "I have to be sure, and you have to be sure."

She knew he was right. And that was why they hadn't set a wedding date yet. But now they could! Now that they'd be leaving Ireland, none of this would matter! She told him all that, words and laughter tumbling out together. "As soon as you're out of the hospital—tomorrow morning—we'll put all this behind us—"

He gripped her shoulders until her words ground to a stop. "Mary, do you still not understand? I can't leave. This is my—"

"Job. I know. And I know it's important. But there are other jobs."

"No, Mary. It's not just a job. It's a commitment—a calling. I'm where God wants me, and I can't leave."

Mary pulled away. She could argue with Gareth. He was reasonable and always ready to compromise. But she couldn't argue with Gareth's God. He asked that His followers put His will ahead of their own. Commitment, Gareth said. She shook her head. The cost was too high.

46

It was two days later before Mary caught up on the night of sleep she had missed and things were organized and ready for business again at the Centre. The burglary brought about one improvement in arrangements from Mary's perspective. Because the three flights of stairs were awkward for Gareth with his walking cast, he moved to the Armstrongs' and slept on their couch.

It was midafternoon. They were sitting around Sheila's dining room table devouring slabs of soda bread with marmalade, chocolate biscuits, and large cups of strong, sweet milky tea.

Sheila refilled Mary's cup and passed it back to her. "I'm so delighted Lila's parents agreed that Tommy could stay in their spare room. I don't know when we've worked with a young man I thought had more potential. Maybe this will give them a chance to get to know his fine qualities and not just see him as an ex-prisoner."

Becca and Julie hadn't been told that story.

"That darling guy at the party?"

"He was a prisoner?"

"Lila was the one with the long black hair?"

"She's gorgeous!"

"I knew they were in love!"

"They looked sillier than Mary and Gareth."

The twins lapsed into giggles, sighing and making eyes at each other.

Mary longed for something to throw at her sisters, but fortunately Ann came in just then to take the twins off for a hike up Knocka.

"Jeff said he and a friend might meet us afterwards, so don't worry if we're late," Ann told her mother.

Mary was amused to note how Julie's eyes lit up at Jeffrey's name.

Philip came in then with a sheaf of papers and sank into a chair, pulling off his glasses.

Sheila set a steaming cup in front of him and let him drink before she asked, "Well, how is it? Have they found anything yet?"

He shook his head. "Police took some fingerprints—not much

chance they'll turn anything up. I have the list of losses complete: two computers and the fax machine. One monitor was smashed. There was some cash in one desk—they got that. Then the cost of repairs—window, door, one file cabinet damaged." He ran his hands over his face. "What's the news today? I haven't had a minute." He reached for the radio sitting on the sideboard.

Mary wanted to stop him. Whatever the news was, it was always bad. Couldn't they just go on drinking tea for a little longer? She didn't want to hear that more Unionists were making more threats against the police. She didn't want to hear that the peace talks had bogged down. She didn't want to hear—

The clipped tones of the BBC reporter interrupted her mental protest.

"In a surprise speech to Parliament today, the Prime Minister announced that the rock called the Stone of Scone is to be returned from London to Scotland, seven hundred years after it was carried off as war booty by Edward I. Somewhat tardily, Major's gesture will make good on the 1328 Treaty of Northampton in which the English promised to return Scotland's historic coronation stone. Tradition holds the chunk of sandstone to have been the biblical Jacob's pillow.

"Response from Scotland has been mixed. The leader of the Scottish Nationalist Party—"

Philip snapped off the radio, drained his cup, and jumped to his feet. "Well now, that'll give them something to chew on for a while. What in the world will the Scots do with the thing?" The question was rhetorical, and he picked up his papers and left.

Mary sat with a dreamy smile on her face. She should go help Sheila with the dishes, but the sense of déjà vu was simply too delicious.

Gareth, his fiberglass cast propped on a stool, grinned at her. "Just like old times. Here's me hobbling around again and that old lump of sandstone getting all the attention."

"A pretty special lump of old sandstone. It brought the two of us together. Maybe we could use it for a kneeling bench at our wedding."

Gareth was quiet. She knew her desire to leave Ireland was a sore spot between them. But she was still here, wasn't she?

"Well—" she pushed her chair back "—I must get to work if *A Night in Olde Belfast* is to have another chance. I can't imagine anyone will let their kids come to the Centre now that it's been vandalized."

As Louise had said about the victims she worked with, there was a special fear connected with knowing someone had marked your place. People in Belfast lived with fear anyway, but when an incident happened, the fear was intensified. And suspicion increased. *Who fingered me? Who set me up? Was it my neighbor? Someone at work?*

They all seemed so certain it was just robbery, nothing paramilitary, nothing special about the Centre's being marked. She still felt uneasy. And she knew the parents would, too. She went into the hall and picked up the telephone.

Louise had already said Debbie could come back. Mary decided to start with Sarah's mother. She worked at an insurance office, and Mary was soon talking to a lady with a lovely, lilting voice.

Well now, she would think about letting Sarah come back if they would provide transportation home, that is. She didn't want Sarah on public transit after dark. If they could get a center in their own neighborhood, she wouldn't have to worry about that, would she? She was so sorry to hear about the break-in. She didn't know what things were coming to anymore. Did they lose much?

Mary told her the extent of the damage.

Insured?

Mary thought there was some but not nearly enough to cover the losses.

There was no answer at the number Martin had given her, so she tried Gerry's, aware that this time she was calling "the other side of the street." How would parents there be feeling now when the Unionists were making so much trouble?

"Hello, Gerry? This is Mary at the Centre. Is one of your parents there? I'd like to talk to either of them about starting up play practice again. Would you like to give it another try?"

"Sure. It was good crack. Hold on. Me da's here."

Gerry had told her his da was a meat cutter and Gaelic footballer. Mary had no trouble picturing the burly man on the other end of the line. Like Sarah's mother, he would consider letting his son come back to the CCC, and he wanted to talk about the break-in. "Do you have an alarm system?"

"No, we don't. But obviously it would be a good idea." Mary had noticed that most buildings there—homes and businesses both—had little brightly colored boxes somewhere near their front doors—burglar alarm systems. "It's always a matter of raising the money—and now with the losses—I don't know."

"Well, I'll tell you what. You've been good to my boy. I appreciate what you're trying to do for our young people, and here's me with some extra time. If you can see your way to buy an alarm, I'll come install it for you. I helped put in the one at the butcher shop. Be glad to give a hand."

Mary was almost breathless when she hung up. The fresh-mouthed Gerry had been one of her most difficult youngsters. She had never imagined such support from his family.

She went on through the list and, amazingly, met with no flat refusals. She was overwhelmed at the concern everyone expressed about the damage to the CCC. "You folks are doing good work. We need more like you," she heard over and over. Syd's mother even said she had told Syd he wasn't going anywhere until the disturbances stopped, but she would consider letting him come back to the Centre, seeing as they needed support after what had happened.

Just as she hung up from talking to Fiona, who said she would have her mother call, Sheila walked through the hall to the dining room, her hands full of mail. "One for you, Gareth."

Mary was busying herself with one more call when a gasp from Sheila sent her into the room around the corner.

Sheila sat staring at the contents of the first three letters she had opened. "I can't believe this!" She gestured to the letters. "Every one of these contains money or offers to help repair the Centre. A man who owns a glass shop says he'll replace our window." She picked up a sheet of pale blue paper. "This one says, 'We're not of your faith, but we're so sorry about what happened.' They sent a check for ten pounds. I just can't believe it."

"And that's just the sort of response I've been getting from the parents I've been talking to. It's wonderful. People really do want to rebuild their community." Mary felt breathless. The terrible setback of the break-in had actually produced good. Crisis had brought the community together—and brought the play back to life.

Mary and Sheila put their heads together over the rest of the letters, exclaiming over people's kindness and generosity.

"Come on." Sheila jumped up when the last one was opened. "I can't wait to show Philip. Let's go to the Centre now." She began gathering the scattered letters. "Do you feel like going with us, Gareth?"

He looked up at them from the other side of the table, still holding his letter.

Mary realized that he had not said one word about the marvelous contents of the post. "Gareth? Are you all right? Is your leg hurting?"

"No, no. Not much." He folded his letter and put it in a pocket. "Sure, I'll come. I'm fine." He rose so smoothly that Mary could see the walking cast wasn't going to slow him down at all.

They were well on their way when Mary remembered to tell Sheila about Mr. O'Rourke's offer to install an alarm system.

"Oh, that's grand! I expect the money we received in today's post might be enough for a down payment on a good system." She slowed as they approached a police blockade. "Oh dear, dear, dear. I hope there isn't more trouble ahead."

But they were simply asked for identification, then directed to take a route several blocks out of their way.

Sheila shrugged. "As long as we have to go around the long way, we might as well go just a bit farther and stop in at an electronics shop. I know the place Philip would want to get the security system. We could just pop in and get some information on prices."

The traffic got heavier, then slowed almost to a stop.

"The shop is just in the next street." Sheila pulled into a car park. "I think it'll be best to walk from here. Would you rather wait here, Gareth?"

"No, no. I'm fine." He even got out swiftly enough to open Mary's door.

They rounded the corner at the top of the street and came to a stop at a wall of people lining the sidewalk. Beyond the people, Mary saw a row of policemen keeping the street open.

"What is it?" she asked.

Before anyone could answer, she heard the booming of drums and trill of fifes. Down the street behind a fife-and-drum band marched an enclave of black-suited, bowler-hatted men, all with fringed orange sashes around their shoulders. A huge orange satin banner proclaimed the name of their lodge.

"I don't understand," Mary protested over the incessant boom of the enormous Lambeg drums. "I thought the marches had been prohibited. Isn't that what they've been rioting about—that they couldn't march?"

A man next to her in tweed jacket and cap shrugged. "Changed their minds, didn't they?"

"Who? The police?"

"Police and Brits."

"But why?"

The man shrugged again. "Who knows? That's the way it is."

Another Orange lodge passed in review, this one almost shouting their marching song. Mary couldn't get all the words, but the ones she did and the defiant tone in which they were delivered made her shudder:

> Here's to the lily, that dear Orange flower . . .
> The emblem of men who defied popish power . . .
> So let the march pass,
> Down with popery, priest, and the Mass.

The booming of another contingent of drums swallowed the next verse as the seemingly endless parade of orange sashes and banners snaked down the street.

Mary looked around nervously.

Suddenly an angry shout came from across the street. "Brits, go home!"

"No surrender!" The reply rang back.

A rock whizzed over Mary's head, and she ducked as a reflex.

Gareth tugged at her arm. "Let's get out of here." Holding Mary and Sheila close on each side, he began pushing his way through the crowd back toward the car.

A brick struck a young man to their right. Blood spurted from his forehead and ran into his eye. His mates began scrabbling for something to throw back.

Mary heard a window shatter, setting off an alarm. Just as they reached the car, there was an explosion. Then the wail of a siren.

"Oh, I had no idea!" Sheila cried when were all safely in the car with the doors locked. "There hadn't been any trouble on this side of town. I'd never have brought you here if I'd known." She was so white that Mary feared she might faint. But she started the car and drove without the slightest falter. Her knowledge of the back streets brought them quickly to the CCC.

Mary was still trembling, thinking of what they might have been caught in if Gareth hadn't thought quickly and used his footballer's skill to get them through that mob. But she was delighted to see Liam at the center. He was helping Tommy straighten up the last of the files that had been scattered when the cabinets were dumped over.

"Liam, I'm so pleased to see you. Have you heard? We're going to start rehearsals again Monday."

Liam looked up from where he sat on the floor, circled with papers, folders, and clippings. "Ah, that's brilliant. Aisling will be happy enough about that. The kids at the daycare have been practicing their songs—drives me crazy with them, she does."

As if on cue, Liam's little sister, who had come with him since Noah's Ark was closed on Saturdays, skipped into the room beside Julie, both singing "Shine, Jesus, Shine."

"Show them what you made, Aisling." Julie had learned to give the name its proper *Ashley* pronunciation.

The seven-year-old held up a bright watercolor painting of yellow and pink flowers splashed against a green background. Her bright hair cupped softly around her round face, and her wide blue eyes smiled up at Mary.

Sheila knelt for a closer look. "Why, that's very nice, Aisling. You know, Mary, I think we should do an art exhibit to go with your music and drama show."

Then Becca, rushing down from the canteen, shattered the convivial atmosphere. "Mary, are you all right?" She threw her arms around her big sister.

Julie was quick to catch the alarm in her twin's voice. "Why? What happened?"

Becca whirled. "There's a riot. It was just on the radio."

"We ran into the march, but—" Mary began.

Liam jerked up, and the strained intensity that was never far from him showed in the lines around his eyes and mouth. "What march?"

"The Orange Order. In south Belfast."

"No!" Anger grated in Liam's voice. "The police said there wouldn't be any. They promised."

Tommy looked up. "Maybe they compromised." He looked at Sheila. "What did happen? The Orangemen agree to change their route?"

Sheila shook her head. "No, the police backed down. Let them march."

The room was quiet with held breath for three seconds. Then the sound of an armful of files slathering across the floor dispersed the silence. The papers Liam had so patiently reorganized cascaded into a chaotic jumble where he had flung them.

He grabbed Aisling's hand so abruptly she cried in alarm. He strode toward the door, pulling his sister behind him. He yanked the door open, then turned back, white-faced. "Betrayed again. Always the same. Another double-cross. Why did I think it would be different this time? Stupid. That's what I've been. Stupid." The door slammed.

"Liam—" Mary started after him, but Liam was gone.

Becca looked from one face to another, bewildered. "What happened? Did I say something wrong?"

Julie stood beside her twin. "I don't understand."

"I'm not certain anyone understands," Sheila said.

"It's not your fault, Becca. You didn't do anything." Gareth was trying to reassure the worried girls when an exclamation burst from Tommy.

Tommy had picked up Liam's disordered file and begun to replace it in the drawer. Now he looked with concern from the labeled files in his hand to the drawer space. "Something's missing." He pointed to a gap in the cabinet.

Sheila looked over his shoulder. "Maybe you misfiled something, Tommy."

"I hope so, but I don't think so. I think some of our files have been stolen."

It took them nearly three hours to work through all the drawers, checking each file against its index list. But in the end, there was no mistake. Five files were missing, files containing personal information on ex-prisoners the CCC was working with. One of the missing files was Tommy's.

"What sort of information was in there?" Gareth asked.

Tommy sat down and dropped his head into his hands. "My record, my associations, family names and addresses." He came to his feet. "Lila! Her name and address. I've got to warn her family." He slammed a fist against the desk. "Stupid, stupid me. They were right not to want their daughter to date an ex-prisoner. Now I've endangered her!"

Philip came in just then with two men from the print shop. He listened stony-faced to the disastrous news. "I need the names from all the missing files." He turned to the computer on his desk. "At least they didn't get the right computer. Good thing you two interrupted them, or we'd have lost the master."

In a minute the computer was booted, and Philip and Tommy were reconstructing the stolen information and trying to work out who would have taken it. Which side would such information be valuable to? What would they do with it now?

What next? Mary wondered.

Gareth turned to her. "Come on, Mary. I'm taking you out of here. Now."

She followed without protest. She felt so insecure. She jumped every time a phone rang anymore. She looked around cautiously at every red light. She, who had always been one to rush into anything without thinking, was suddenly seeing a paramilitary in every shadow. No wonder the young people here were skittish.

Instead of driving straight to the Armstrong home, however, when they were well out of town, Gareth turned into an area of natural parkland along a small stream. Over to one side, several children kicked a ball around. Their voices rang happily. Here and there, people strolled along winding footpaths, most accompanied by large dogs. A narrow wooden bridge led over the tree-lined brook, and green fields stretched beyond to the gentle rise of a rounded hill. Shadows lengthened toward the east, and evening larks sang in the hedgerows.

Mary rolled down her window, took a deep breath, and felt the turmoil of the day fade. "It's a different world out here, isn't it?" It was impossible to believe that, only a few miles away, people were doing dreadful things to one another.

He took her hand in one of his. "It is, indeed." With his other hand he drew a brown envelope out of his pocket. "Read this."

The letter was from the program adviser who oversaw Gareth's field experience. She read it through twice to be sure she understood what he was proposing. "Gareth! This is wonderful! A job in Scotland, planting a new church. What would you be doing? Where is Crieff? When will you—we—go?"

He smiled at her. "I guess the answer is yes, then?"

"Well, of course. Is there any question?" No more riots, bombings, vandalism. No more dividing people by what church their ancestors went to. Back to the security, freedom, and rugged beauty of Scotland. They could take the twins to the Highlands. Then she looked at his face. "There *is* a question?"

"I don't know. I just want to do what's right. Right for us, right for people here—"

Mary rolled her eyes and groaned. She knew her Gareth. "I know—and right for God." She thought for a moment. How could she argue this in Gareth's terms? "Well, He wouldn't have opened up this opportunity if He didn't want you to do it, would He?"

Gareth was quiet.

"I know the people here need you. But you're needed in Scotland too." She held up the letter for emphasis.

They talked about the little town along the River Almond just at the beginning of the Highlands. About the people there who wanted to start a church. About how much fun it would be to help them. It sounded wonderful, exciting, peaceful, and yet a challenge, all at once. So why was Gareth so subdued? Why did she sense he was forcing his enthusiasm to match hers?

As he started the engine and drove slowly homeward, Mary examined her own feelings. Beyond the relief and excitement of looking forward, how did she feel about looking backward? What had she accomplished in Ireland? How would she feel about leaving these people?

She wasn't going to give in to a guilt trip over things unaccomplished. Nobody could have tried harder than she had. It wasn't her fault the Unionists chose to riot rather than change their march route. It wasn't her fault the police knuckled under and now the Nationalists were irate. She wasn't responsible for the break-in at the CCC and the risk to their clients. She certainly wasn't responsible for Liam's temper. Or the youth center that wouldn't get built now. If people were going to be pigheaded and refuse to work together, it wasn't her fault.

Gareth walked her to the door, then left to return to the center.

The phone rang as she stood waving good-bye, and Ann rushed from her room to pick it up.

"Oh, hello! Yes, she's right here!" She held the receiver out to Mary. "It's for you. Your mum!"

Mary clutched the telephone. "Oh, Mom, it's so good to hear your voice!" She had to hold onto herself to keep her own voice steady.

She had never imagined it could be so comforting just to hear her mother's voice. "Oh, no, no. We're all fine. Don't worry, Mom. You know how the media always overplay everything."

"We just heard the news about the shootings." Her mother sounded as if she were on the other side of town, not the other side of the ocean.

Shootings? Mary sank onto the small seat by the telephone table. What did her mother know that she didn't know? "Oh, don't worry, Mom. I think that was a long ways from here." She hoped.

"Well, I'm glad to hear that. But your father and I are not happy about you girls being over there. We'd never have let Becca and Julie go if we'd had any idea all this would happen. We think you should go to Auntie Val's."

"Mother, Gareth is doing important work. He can't just up and leave." *What am I saying?* "Listen, don't worry. Actually, we just got some news today. We'll be going back to Scotland very soon." She told her about Gareth's job offer. "So really, there's nothing to worry about."

"Oh, I'm so relieved, dear. That's wonderful. Your father will be so happy."

"Give him my love."

They talked for a few more minutes. Yes, Becca and Julie were having a great time. Yes, she'd tell the twins that Brutus sent his love, too.

She hadn't even replaced the receiver when the door flew open and the twins burst in, windblown and laughing, knee pads streaked with grass stains. Jeffrey and a couple of his university friends were with them. "Julie, Becca, that was Mom!"

"Oh, great!"

"Cool!"

"How is everyone?"

"Worried. The folks want you—us—to go back to Scotland."

"Scotland?"

"Why?"

"We've already been there."

"They're worried about us. All the troubles right now."

"What troubles?"

"That's silly."

"Besides, we can't leave."

"We're doing cross-community work."

Mary had to laugh at their earnestness. "You're what?"

"Soccer."

"Football, you mean."

"Football, right. The YP and the teens from the youth council—"

"They never saw girls play before. We said all the teams in our league are mixed."

"They thought we meant Catholic and Protestant!"

"So, anyway, we integrated them."

Julie broke into giggles. "But here that doesn't mean black and white. It means orange and green!"

Jeffrey intervened to explain that he and his mates at church played in a football league every Saturday. They always said anyone was welcome. They had just never thought about "anyone" meaning girls or Catholics. But there was really no reason it couldn't—except they were too rough for most girls.

When the boys had left, Becca held out an elbow bandaged with gauze and sticking plaster. "It doesn't hurt much. I made a goal—a brilliant headshot—you should have seen it!"

Julie had her share of scrapes as well. "But we won. Gerry was terrific. And Fiona's brother isn't a great footballer, but he's cute!" The girls turned toward their room, giggling.

"Wait." Mary called them back. "I told Mom you—we—were going." Well, sort of. Now she wasn't sure what she'd said.

"We can't. We've got a return match next week."

"Gerry said you're starting play practice again Monday."

"Call her back."

Mary's head was beginning to throb. "Go take a shower. You smell like a locker room."

The living room was blessedly deserted. Mary closed the door behind her, sank into the cushions of the plush sofa, and picked up the TV remote. She needed some escape. A music show. A cartoon. A rerun of an old comedy.

It was a rerun, all right, but no comedy. Smoke from a burning car billowed across the screen. Behind their riot shields, a line of helmeted police faced an angry crowd. Shouts and chants surged behind the reporter's voice.

"Protestants today were allowed to march through the Catholic area of south Belfast, ending five days of riots protesting a police ban on the annual marches. The marches now have set off Catholic riots protesting the marches. Two hundred Orangemen and four fife-and-drum bands marched the five-mile route, leaving a new outburst of sectarian violence in their wake."

The camera panned the scene: rioters overturning parked cars and setting them aflame; angry young men throwing bricks, stones, and petrol bombs; a large black dog, his hindquarters tucked under, limping across a pile of rubble.

"Two police officers have been wounded by gunfire. Hundreds of civilians are being treated for injuries. Soldiers and riot police are attempting to saturate the neighborhood with armored vehicles in an effort to bring order."

Three gray, metal-plated cars, yellow lights flashing, crept down the street, separating the rioters. A shower of bricks and stones rained down on them. The camera focused in on a clutch of youths hurling rocks and angry words toward the vehicles.

And Mary caught her breath. That slight boy to the side—the one with long black hair and intense dark eyes burning in his pale face. Liam. The camera moved on. It was only a flash impression. Yet she was certain it had been Liam.

Liam. Outraged by the police, who had vowed to protect his side of the street and then gave in to pressure, he'd allowed the anger he'd kept so tightly bottled up to boil over in the ugliness of riot.

Liam. Bright, caring, talented, with surprising flashes of wit. She had seen such progress. But now there was this terrible sliding backward toward the abyss of violence. Just like Ireland itself. Eighteen months of peace. Now the worst violence in a decade.

Liam. What terrible hurt had caused the pain that now spilled out in such rampage? He saw the police as having betrayed him. Abandoned him. How would he see Mary if—when—she left?

She turned away from the TV, seeking something else to focus on. Her eye lit on Philip's box of manuscripts on the floor beside the sofa. Reading was always a good escape. She picked up the top notebook.

Just before clicking off the TV, she took one last glance at the screen. The camera had moved to the end of a street where the green countryside opened out beyond. A crowd of rioters was chasing one man, shouting invectives, waving sticks, throwing stones.

Mary clicked off the remote and opened the notebook, shifting her attention from the story unfolding on the television screen to the account of events two hundred fifty years before, recorded on the pages on her lap. But the picture did not change.

***

The angry mob surged forward. A burly man lunged, wielding a meat cleaver. Behind him, a well-dressed magistrate held a flaming torch aloft, while a distracted woman dodged between them, intent on rescuing a child who had fallen under the feet of the mob. A black-bearded man flung a brown ale bottle, ignoring the protests of a woman in a white gown who held a baby in her arms. Angry shouts accompanied each lash of a cracking horsewhip. A man brandished a pitchfork.

The focus of the uproar was a youth with smooth, shoulder-length brown hair and clad in a plain black coat. He carried a large black Bible.

Thomas Walsh refused to give in to the terror he felt inside. The taunts of the mob rang in his ears, but he forced his feet to walk steadily along the rough cobbled street of Newtownards.

As a lad helping his father on the farm, he had once faced a mad bull. He had known then, as he knew now, that the most dangerous thing he could do would be to show fear. He tightened his grip on the Bible and continued to walk toward the edge of town. If he gave in to his instincts and let himself run, he would be overwhelmed. In his mind he felt the flame of the torch, the sting of the horsewhip, the thrust of the pitchfork, but his heart felt the comfort of God.

"We'll have no mincing Methodists here!"

"As soon papists as Arminians!"

"Methodstophilis! In league wi' the Devil!"

A stone clattered at his feet. A clod of mud struck his cheek. Whether it drew blood or merely left a trail of muck, he knew not, but he felt something oozing down the side of his face.

The crowd came no closer, but their threats increased, as did the hail of sticks and stones on his head. Just a few more yards. If he could just keep his pace to the end of the street, he could duck behind the last barn and disappear into the spinney beyond. Once clear of the town, he would give way and run. Ah, how good that would feel. He would run and run and run until he could run no more.

To steady himself, he looked at the high green hill beckoning beyond the barn. Scrabo. *I will lift up mine eyes unto the hills, from whence cometh my help. My help cometh from the Lord, which made heaven and earth.* Could he make it that far? Would the mob allow him the sanctuary of Scrabo? Or would they hunt him down with torches, pitchforks, and dogs?

"We'll hae none o' your enthusiasms."

"Get ye gone from us, Apollyon!"

"No surrender to Satan!"

A tomato struck the back of his head. An egg caught his sleeve as he darted around the barn. The air filled with a sulfurous smell as if billowing from the pit the mob accused Thomas of coming from. Now within the safety of the screening trees, he took to his heels.

The wind whistled in his ears. His breath came in tearing gasps. His sides heaved as if they would cave in on themselves. But in spite of the pain in his legs and the leaden weight of his arms that made him slow first to a trot, then to a walk, and now to hardly more than a crawl, he would not stop.

The last of the rioting mob had fallen back two fields behind. Most had not left the town. But he was determined to reach the top of the hill. There, like Moses on Mount Sinai, he would await a word from the Lord. The wind was chilly. The sky threatened rain. But he would spend the night there, as many nights as it took, until he could be clear what God desired of him. He would do anything his Lord asked. Thomas Walsh's life and soul were the complete property of Jesus Christ.

Minutes or hours later—he had lost track of time—Thomas reached the top of Scrabo and sank under the scanty shelter of a hawthorn bush. His breath came back slowly. Gradually his heartbeat steadied. When the pounding in his ears ceased, he could think.

It had begun ordinarily enough. Methodist field preachers thought nothing of facing angry crowds. Usually the troublemakers tired quickly and went to seek their pleasures in the public house or at a cockfight. If one began with a forceful proclamation of Scripture, the faithful would usually belt forth a lusty version of "O for a Thousand Tongues," the hymn that was quickly becoming the national anthem of Methodism, and then they would listen gladly to even a very lengthy sermon. One expected that some seed would fall on stony ground and some among the thorns. But the amount of fertile soil in Ireland, ready to receive the good news of God's free salvation, was far above enough to recompense all hazards.

Even so, tonight's brawl in Newtownards was not the first anti-Methodist riot Thomas Walsh had encountered. Thomas was a Limerick man, a former Roman Catholic who had been converted on one of John Wesley's first trips to Ireland. Wesley had been amazed at the heat the fire of faith had kindled in Walsh. Studying night and day, it was no time at all until he was thoroughly comfortable with the Scripture in both Hebrew and Greek. He became one of the most effective evangelists in Ireland—preaching either in Gaelic or English, as was most appropriate to his hearers.

Catholic peasants in the countryside would gather in groups by the crossroads and listen, rapt, as he preached in Irish. The Anglo-Irish in the towns were also often ready to listen in large numbers, and many Methodist societies had sprung up across the width of the country from Cork to Down. And yet many *Protestants* seemed to hate Christianity.

Cutthroats who murdered itinerate preachers as they rode along peaceful roads were a constant concern, as were riots in cities and towns. It was a common thing for Protestant magistrates to allow the riots, then accuse the Methodists of breaching the peace. And yet Thomas would willingly face worse than that for the joy of proclaiming the gospel and seeing the light of salvation dawn in the life of a sinner.

But not tonight. For the moment Thomas Walsh had taken all one man could endure. Pulling his coat about him and clutching his Bible to his breast, he lay his head on the root of the sheltering hawthorn and slept.

***

Mary looked up from the pages of Philip's manuscript. The television screen where she had earlier seen the news of today's rioting was black now, and yet her mind projected on it the scenes of the sectarian riots of two hundred fifty years ago. The two blurred in her mind. There were the same harsh, shouted threats and accusations, the same hurled stones and blazing fires, the same frightened, bleeding people. Did nothing change? She couldn't wait to get away.

GENERATION FOUR

THE UNION
1789–1844

One generation passeth away,
and another generation cometh:
but the earth abideth for ever.
Thy faithfulness
is unto all generations.
Ecclesiastes 1:4
Psalm 119:90

47

"Stupid cow! Can't you stand still?" Carolenn thrust out her lower lip. The charcoal pencil in her fingers hovered above the sketch pad.

But Bessie continued to shift her position.

"Be still! Do you think I *want* to draw your hindquarters, you witless beast?" With thirteen-year-old determination, Lenny stomped around the big red cow, plunked herself down on a large stone, and made a sweeping mark across the paper.

Bessie rolled her docile brown eyes, flicked her tail, and proceeded to turn around, hindquarters once again toward the young artist.

"All right then, have it your way. But I warn you, this is not your most flattering position." She sighed. "I suppose your mama failed to teach you to always put your best foot forward." Carolenn straightened instinctively in obedience to her own mother's careful teaching.

Bessie looked vacantly over her shoulder and chewed her cud.

An hour later, Carolenn left the field. Her sheet was smudged and a little frayed along the edge, but at least Mr. Wimborne couldn't fault her energetic effort.

Besides, there was little chance that the organist from Newtownards, who served as art and music master for the Price daughters and philosophy and Latin tutor to their brother, would give her work more than a perfunctory glance. Thorpe Wimborne's concern was all for Carolenn's sixteen-year-old sister, Sarah. Lenny rolled her eyes in imitation of the gawky teacher whose lovelorn glances at Sarah made Bessie seem astute by comparison. Still, Lenny loved dancing, and in spite of his long, thin legs and enormous feet, the earnest church musician was amazingly agile.

In her hurry to cross the field, she lifted the flounce on her cambric skirt and mounted the stile. Her choice to jump down, rather than descend the three steps, resulted in dislodging her straw bonnet and splashing mud generously over her half boots and the hem of her ivory dress. She ignored a faint ripping sound as she hurried homeward.

"There you are, Lenny. Whatever can you have been thinking of? Evan has almost finished his recitation. Mr. Wimborne will want us next." Sarah, standing in the doorway, tossed her carefully coifed head of golden curls and started for the drawing room, where her harpsichord lived, but then she turned back. "And wash your hands! Do you want him thinking us wild Irish?"

Lenny skipped to the kitchen, where a basin of water and a cake of lard soap always stood available on the dresser. Sarah's sharp words didn't bother her in the least, but she was sorry to be so late returning.

When she could manage it, she always chose to spend Evan's recitation time doing her required hour of embroidery. Sarah thought her terribly perverse to insist on sitting in the chair that gave the poorest light, but Lenny knew her stitches would be uneven no matter how good her light, and her object was to be able to hear her brother's philosophy lesson.

Evan had almost completed Aristotle, Augustine, and Aquinas—as well as the more enlightened eighteenth-century European thinkers—qualifications that boded well for his ambition to be admitted to Trinity College. But that meant that Lenny's lessons were numbered. She should have just sketched Bessie's hindquarters from the first, rather than wasting time trying to get the obstinate creature to pose.

Lenny's desire to learn unsuitable subjects was the despair of her mother and sister. Even Lenny herself had trouble understanding her insatiable curiosity. She supposed she would have been happy with art, music, and needlework if she were any good at them. She wouldn't even ask to be as good as Sarah—just proficient enough not to be an embarrassment would do.

But the matter was hopeless. Philosophy was what she liked. She wanted to know the truth about things—the right and wrong of every issue. She felt as bound by unanswered questions as a kitten tangled in yarn.

And there could be nothing less useful than a Latinized female. She couldn't enter the legal profession. She couldn't enter the church. She couldn't stand for Parliament. To a female, philosophy was of less use than the smudged sketches and tangled embroideries she produced.

"Well done, Mr. Evan. Well done, indeed."

Lenny could picture Mr. Wimborne's head bobbing as he praised Evan. Of course, everyone praised her studious brother, who was destined to make a brilliant career for himself in law and politics. After all, wasn't that why their father had declared for the established church when his son was born?

Lenny had no personal knowledge of the matter, as all that was five years before she made her appearance in the family. But she knew what their strict Presbyterian relatives said. Aquinas's theory of natural law wasn't the only thing one could learn by bending so intently over one's embroidery that others thought one oblivious to all else. Her needle stilled as her mind wandered.

Archibald Price was the family renegade—far more shocking than Guilford Lanark, whose Catholicism was taken for granted. And the Seaton Court Lanarks could simply be ignored. Catholic gentry were easily tolerated, especially now that all the legal disabilities except voting and holding seats in Parliament had been lifted. But for one descended from generations of good Presbyterian stock to have taken up with the established church!

"It's just a mercy that poor dear Mama never lived to see it. She couldn't have held her head up at meeting." Aunt Adelaide had been so nearly overcome at the thought that a slosh of amber Bohea tea escaped over the edge of her dish.

Lenny took another stitch. It was outside her pattern, but it didn't matter—the work would have to be redone anyway once Mama scrutinized it.

Aunt Marguerite had heaved a sigh that managed to shake her entire body. Aunt Marguerite always called with Aunt Adelaide. And since they inevitably came in the morning, the young Prices had dubbed them the Aunts AM.

"Leave it to Archibald to look out for the main chance." Lenny imagined she could see Aunt M's folds of flesh ripple as she gazed around the newly refurnished room. Her scrutiny had fastened on the fine Turkish carpet. "And I must say, he has done well enough by it."

Lenny wondered at the logic of the implication. After all, the new house Douglas Lanark had built on the high ground beyond the bawn was far grander than the comfortable Price home that had grown by higgledy-piggledy addition after addition through the generations.

The Lanark home was still called Lanarks' Bawn, although the bawn itself now served entirely as dairy barn and cattle shelter. While far smaller than the Palladian manors the Anglo-Irish landlords were building for themselves everywhere across the land, the new house still reflected that taste for elegance. Apparently such gentility was acceptable because Douglas Lanark remained staunchly Presbyterian, without even a whiff of the New Light apostasy into which so many of the faith were lamentably falling. And, of course, the new Lanark residence was appropriate because the Aunts AM resided with Douglas and his son Jay, ostensibly keeping house for them since the death of Douglas's wife.

Lenny remembered Aunt Adelaide's tossing her lace-capped red head. "Well, of course, the Prices aren't *real* Lanarks—just some connection by marriage which one can never quite sort out." She lowered her voice to a conspiratorial tone. "And what a mercy that is now, with Archie's new *enthusiasm*."

Marguerite gasped and clutched her ample bosom. "You don't mean to say it's *true*, do you? Oh, surely not. I mean, one hears rumors, but surely . . . one can't think even Archibald would go that far afield."

And so the two had gone on . . .

The door beside Lenny swung open, and the tall, thin master was standing before her, requesting her assigned artwork.

"And now, what do you have t–to show me?"

Lenny reoriented herself and produced the bovine sketch.

"Ah, yes. Well, Miss Carolenn, you have, as usual, attacked your s-subject with vigor and originality." Fortunately, Mr. Winborne didn't spend long on her daubed efforts before turning to Sarah's exquisite watercolor of a daisy-strewn pasture—with all the cows facing forward.

When even their tutor's supply of encomiums was exhausted over Sarah's painting, they moved on to the music lesson. His wrist extended a good three inches beyond his sleeve as he offered his hand to assist Sarah to the harpsichord bench. "And how are you coming with the Vivaldi divertimento, ladies?"

"I'm sure you'll be the best judge of our progress, sir. I trust we won't be too severe a disappointment." Sarah's dimples winked at the corners of her pink lips. The folds of her muslin dress, sprinkled with sprigs of blue flowers, fell about her as gracefully as her fingers coaxed sounds from the keyboard.

Lenny clutched her flute with sweating hands and bobbed her head in vigorous time to mark her entrance into the duet. One measure. She took a gulp of air and, pursing her lips, blew vigorously. Mr. Wimborne winced, but the next note was less shrill, and so they continued to the end of the blessedly short piece.

It was not a hot day, but Thorpe Wimborne drew a white handkerchief from his pocket and mopped his brow. "Lovely, Miss S-Sarah, lovely. Ah, Miss Carolenn, your interpretation was vigorous and original, as usual. Vivaldi, however, is best when approached with a certain lightness—delicacy, even. When playing the flute, if one could picture conversing with birds in the trees rather than . . . uh . . . perhaps leading troops into battle with bagpipes . . ."

Mr. Wimborne's artistic delicacies were spared having to suffer through the assigned Bach prelude by the entrance of Archibald Price.

Lenny smiled at the dark, curling locks, broad features, and laughing eyes of the parent from whom she had inherited her looks. "Oh, Papa, you missed our duet. What a pity." It was a joke between them. She well knew he had waited at a considerable distance until it was over. "Shall you have time to hear our Bach?"

The twinkle in his eye matched her own. "Alas, my poppets, as much as it would pleasure me, I'd not interrupt your lesson. I've come in search of your brother. I've just received word that Mr. Wesley is to preach in Newtownards this evening, and I would have Evan accompany me." He turned to the tutor. "And you too, Wimborne. Be most glad of your company."

Thorpe Wimborne assumed as much dignity as his gawky person was capable of achieving. But he failed to conquer the slight hesitation that was almost a stammer when he was overcome with strong feeling. "Sir. With all d–due respect. I'm s–sure you'll excuse me. The Reverend Mr. Cleland would not approve." A slight wobble to Wimborne's head implied that if Reverend Mr. Cleland did not approve, no right-thinking person could possibly approve. The Reverend Mr. John Cleland, for whom Thorpe Wimborne was organist, was the parish's Anglican minister and agent and adviser to Lord Londonderry.

At that moment Evan entered from the dining room where apparently he had been working on his Tacitus translation. Lenny smiled at the brother who was all perfection in her eyes. His pale buff trousers and cutaway jacket exhibited his perfect build—neither too broad nor too thin. A crisp, white linen cravat accented his strong jaw line and thick brown hair.

"You'll soon be done with that, Evan? I'd have you go to Newtownards with me." Archibald's address to his son stopped short of a command, but it was clearly more than a casual request.

Evan looked at his father levelly, his face expressionless. He always thought before he spoke, an exceeding rarity in an eighteen-year-old. "I will, of course, go if you say, Father. But I'll tell you now, I do not approve of Mr. Wesley."

Archibald's reply was equally civil. The men of Price Manor did not argue. It was understood from the outset that Evan would accompany his father as requested, but Archibald would hear his son's thoughts on the matter. "You quite amaze me, my son. I was not aware that you had heard the preacher. Surely Mr. Wimborne hasn't assigned you copies of his sermons as reading matter?"

Archibald winked at his younger daughter. They never failed to appreciate each other's humor.

Thorpe Wimborne, however, did not comprehend Archibald's humor. "Sir—Mr. Price, sir, I d–do a–assure you—"

"My father is hoaxing you, Wimborne." Evan placed a steadying hand on the tutor's arm. "One needn't read John Wesley's sermons to know that he is hardly a representative of the Enlightenment, Father."

Archibald smiled. "You shock me. I should think Rousseau would thoroughly approve of preaching in fields—it seems appropriately rustic for his natural tastes."

But Evan disregarded his father's remark. "It can be little wonder if Wesley's sermons are all of emotion, as would appeal to his bands of enthusiasts. I wonder that you would expose yourself to such a mob, devoid of the rational, Father."

"I will not argue the matter. It would be exceedingly irrational in me to discuss the absence or presence of reason or emotion with one who is informed only by tittle-tattle."

Evan's slow smile twinkled in his eyes. "Touché, Father."

Evan and Archibald left the room, both smiling.

Lenny watched their departing backs longingly, but Mr. Wimborne had not forgotten the Bach. He was unlikely to forget anything that would lengthen his time in Sarah's presence.

So it was considerably later that Lenny hurried down the hall to her father's office, all but praying that he wouldn't be too deeply engrossed with his overseer or, worse yet, have gone out to the fields. She had little enough time to accomplish her ends, and her only hope was to approach Father alone.

Now she understood that enigmatic conversation of the aunts on which she had eavesdropped. Archibald Price's shameful "enthusiasm" was not a matter of manuring his crops or improving his cattle in some way advocated by the agricultural revolutionary Jethro Tull, as she had supposed when she heard their remarks. Father was interested in the religious enthusiasms of the Reverend Mr. Wesley and his Methodist bands. And Lenny had long ago discovered that if a topic was considered worthy of scandal by the aunts, it was worth learning about.

She rounded the corner and breathed a sigh of relief before breaking into a skip. Her father's office door was open, and he was at his desk.

"Go to Newtownards with Evan and myself?" He looked at her with skepticism.

"If Mother approves, of course," she added hurriedly. She knew the drill.

Archibald leaned back, elbows on the chair arms, points of his fingers together. "Oh, well, of course. If your mother approves, certainly I'd be happy for your company."

Lenny skipped off. It was the oldest trick in the book. Funny her father hadn't cottoned onto it. Or maybe he had.

"Mother."

"Yes, dear?" Harriet Price looked up from her writing desk.

"Father says I may go into Newtownards with him if you don't mind."

Mrs. Price ran the soft white feather of her quill over her cheek. "No, my dear, of course, I don't mind if your father wants it so."

And there it was. Now it was merely a matter of keeping her plans a secret from Sarah so that her sister wouldn't upset the cart by lecturing their mother on how unsuitable it was for Carolenn to attend a Methodist meeting.

She tied the ribbons of her best straw bonnet under her chin and selected her warmest paisley shawl. Even though the sun had shown without wavering all day, they were only nine days into June—a month when the weather was often even less stable than usual in Ireland.

She slipped quietly out the side door and waited just beyond the barn until her father came with the carriage. It was unlikely anyone would interfere with her well-executed plans now, but experience had taught Lenny the expediency of staying out of the way once she had achieved her ends. It would be just as well to be down the road before Sarah discovered what she was about. Sarah could never understand her little sister's desire to *know* things.

And so she listened avidly to the discussion between Archibald Price and his son as they drove to Newtownards.

"No, I've not heard the man myself, either," Archibald admitted. "Although my friend Ramsey was most affected by Wesley's preaching in Lisburn."

"Undoubtedly, but one wonders how Hume or Rousseau would have been affected," Evan muttered.

Archibald recounted his friend's information. Mr. Wesley, now nearing his eighty-sixth year, had made forty-two visits to Ireland, eleven of which had included Newtownards in his itinerary. He often preached in the elegant Market House in the middle of town, but this time, his first visit in eleven years, he had been invited to speak in the Presbyterian meetinghouse.

Lenny wondered what the Aunts AM would think of that. Had Mr. Wesley become respectable? She hoped not. Respectability would lessen the interest.

She soon saw, however, that they were not going to the large First Presbyterian Church today nor to one of the fashionable but theologically suspect New Light churches. Instead, they drove farther down the road to the Non-Subscribing meetinghouse. Mr. Wesley was quite safe from achieving the stigma of the aunts' approval.

It was a good thing they had arrived early. It was only a little after eight—the preaching was scheduled to begin at nine—but already the street was choked with carriages, and a number of people milled around the churchyard.

Archibald's friend must have been watching for them, for they had no more than secured the carriage at a hitching post than they were approached by an effusive, sandy-haired man whose well-cut brown coat proclaimed his position as one of the leading linen drapers of Lisburn.

Lenny bobbed a curtsy when her father presented her and Evan, then looked up with surprise when Mr. Ramsey turned to introduce a slim, quiet lad who all this time had been standing on the far side of his father. It was a good thing she caught the pleasant tone in Sheldon Ramsey's voice when he was presented, because his "Your servant, sir" to her father were almost the only words to pass his lips the entire evening.

The party, however, did not lack for conversation. Lenny, with her voracious appetite for information, could not have been more auspiciously placed than in company with the effusive Baird Ramsey. He seemed to know everyone.

"Ah, Harry," he hailed a short, dapper man. "I want you good folks to meet my fellow linen draper Henry Munro. Just back from Dublin, eh, Harry? What's the news?"

The little man bowed. "Well now, and so you might ask. More news than you'd guess. Rumor going around that Pitt sent an agent to Ireland to assess opinion here regarding the notion of union."

"Union?" Consternation showed on every face.

"Union of Dublin and Westminster, you mean?" Archibald asked.

"*One* parliament?" Ramsey almost bellowed.

"Impossible." Evan shook his head.

"Apparently that's what the agent determined as well. 'The very idea would excite a rebellion,' he said."

The company was still reeling with Munro's news when their host pointed out Mr. Wesley.

Lenny was amazed. She could barely imagine one being so ancient as the preacher was reputed to be, and yet this man looked healthy and vigorous. His thick white hair curled to the shoulders of his black robe. His skin seemed as white and as thin as the fine lawn Geneva bands fluttering in the breeze below his chin. Yet his face was firm and almost wrinkle-free, his eyes piercing bright, and his carriage erect.

Mr. Ramsey explained that the preacher had recently held a conference of Methodist preachers in Dublin and was in the midst of a preaching circuit around the island. It was his habit to preach no less than three times a day. The first was usually at five o'clock in the morning so that field laborers could attend without being late for their work.

Lenny offered a ready audience, so Ramsey continued. "Aye, and a great reader he is, too. Used to read while traveling on horseback— up to fifty miles a day, summer and winter. Only trouble is, one can't be watching the book and the horse and the road all at the same time. So many a gorse bush was honored by having the Reverend Mr. Wesley plummet onto it. Finally his friends got concerned. They clubbed together to buy him a carriage. He loved it. First thing he did was have bookshelves built behind the carriage seat. And then it's said—" Ramsey swung around "—ah, but here's the man himself. Why should I be nattering on when you can hear it from the man's own lips?"

He stepped forward. "Mr. Wesley! Ah, now, sir, I'd be right honored to present some friends of mine. Their first Methodist meeting, this is, and there can't be a better introduction than meeting the man himself, I say." Baird Ramsey made presentations all around.

Lenny bobbed her best curtsy and smiled at the famous man. He had such kind, intelligent eyes, and she liked the way a smile played at the corners of his mouth when his face was at rest. "I was just telling the young lass here about your vigorous schedule. Mighty impressed she was, too."

The preacher inclined his head in a courtly manner. "I daresay I am living proof that nothing is too hard for God. It is now eleven years since I have felt any such thing as weariness. Many times I speak till I can speak no longer. Frequently I walk till I can walk no farther. Yet even then I feel no sensation of weariness but am perfectly easy from head to foot. I dare not impute this to natural causes. It is the will of God, and I fret at nothing."

"Aye, that's a grand testimony." The effusive Ramsey seemed to stop himself just short of giving the octogenarian a hearty slap on the shoulder that would surely have sent him reeling. "And what of the conference? Did you have a good group in Dublin?"

"Much satisfaction. Much. Between forty and fifty traveling preachers." Wesley's eyes sparkled. "I found such a body of men as I hardly believed could have been found together in Ireland. So sound experience, so deep piety, so strong understanding. I am convinced they are no way inferior to the English conference."

"Ah, that's a fine thing. You're not likely to find much here inferior to the English. Even our roads are far superior. Many travelers say they far prefer the Irish roads to all other."

Lenny would not have thought it possible for the fluent Mr. Wesley to be confounded, but Baird Ramsey's praise of Irish roads seemed to have accomplished the impossible.

At length the preacher found his voice and a tactful, if evasive, answer. "Indeed, I have more than once observed the prosperity of Ulster. The difference is easily observed as soon as one crosses into the province. The ground so well cultivated, the cottages not only neat but furnished with doors, chimney   s, and win

"Aye, and orderly. You'll find naught of contention here."

Wesley appeared to wonder if he had heard aright.

Ramsey pressed his point. "But then, you'll have experienced the peaceableness at your conference, no doubt."

"Ah!" Wesley brightened, as if greatly relieved to find a point of agreement. "Perfect unanimity among our preachers in their determination to give themselves up to God. There were other issues, I'll admit. The old consideration of leaving the Church." He bobbed his head. "I stand firm for the Anglican Church. In a course of fifty years, we have never willingly varied from it in one article either of doctrine or discipline."

A newcomer approached and introduced himself to the guest of honor. "Mr. Wesley, I have come expressly to invite you to attend meeting at our new meetinghouse in Belfast on Sunday next."

Wesley returned the man's bow. "I thank you for your invitation. But I never go to a meeting."

The man's face drained of color. "Do you mean to say you're a mere Church of England man?" He turned on his booted heel and left without waiting for an answer.

Wesley watched the departing back with sadness. "We are so. But we condemn none who have been brought up in another way. Though we cannot think alike, may we not love alike? May we not be of one heart, though we are not of one opinion?"

The chairman of the local society came then to take the preacher into the meetinghouse, and Ramsey ushered his group into the rapidly filling building.

Lenny soon found herself sitting on a backless bench between her brother and the hopelessly silent Sheldon Ramsey. She clasped her hands, almost bouncing on the bench. "Wasn't that famous! Our own interview with Mr. Wesley." She couldn't have imagined the evening getting off to a better start.

Sheldon, however, did not voice an opinion, and since Lenny had no patience with the stupid or the boring, she turned to Evan. "Now aren't you glad you've come, brother?"

"Hume would perhaps approve the man's tolerance for other views," Evan offered cautiously. "I will be amazed, however, if he doesn't lapse into vulgar feeling within twenty minutes of his sermon."

Lenny was just delighted with the experience of being there, whatever it offered. She stood readily for the first hymn and turned to the book a society member put into her hands: *Hymns for the Use of the People Called Methodists.* "O for a thousand tongues to sing . . ."

By the time they reached the eighth verse, Lenny imagined the rafters were ringing. She knew her head was.

When they went on to another vigorous song also penned by Mr. Wesley's brother Charles, she glanced up at her brother. The tight lines at the corners of Evan's mouth showed he believed himself to be proved right. And he was not amused.

Lenny had never heard such lusty singing in a church. And she rather thought the tune was one she had heard emanating from a public house when she had once been in town late with her parents. It was fun to sing, however.

Then John Wesley announced his text from First Corinthians: "'In understanding be men.'" Without prelude, he launched directly into his sermon. His voice was as steady as that of a man twenty years his junior.

"From earliest times there have been well-meaning men who imagined that reason was of no use in religion, yea, that it was a hindrance to it. And then there are those who, impressed with the absurdity of undervaluing reason, make it little less than divine—very near, if not quite, infallible. So much easier it is to run from east to west than to stop at the middle point!"

The preacher continued in orderly fashion, pointing out to the undervaluers of reason what it can do; then to the overvaluers of it, what reason cannot do.

But while she listened with half an ear, Lenny's agile mind continued exploring the preacher's opening metaphor. Even at her age she had observed what Mr. Wesley pointed out. People *were* wont to run from one extreme to the other; very few stopped at the middle point. Her mind filled with images of people running from one side of the Price cow field to another, where Bessie stood chewing her cud. When the conjured-up Bessie turned around, presenting her tail to the whole frenzied lot, Lenny almost embarrassed herself by laughing aloud in church.

"Reason can accomplish much in the affairs of common life. It can assist us in going through the whole circle of arts and sciences. But what of the things of another world? What can reason do here? It may do much in the affairs of men, but what can it do in the things of God?"

Lenny looked at Evan. His face showed little of the amazement she knew he must be feeling at hearing such cogent thinking. But she could tell he was listening.

"The foundation of true religion stands upon the oracles of God. And how are we to understand the essential truths contained therein? Is it not by reason, assisted by the Holy Ghost? Is it not by reason that we are enabled to understand the attributes of God—His eternity and immensity; His power, wisdom, and holiness?"

It almost seemed that Evan nodded. Lenny relaxed. Her brother's opinion was all in all to her. She liked the preacher, and she did so want him to receive Evan's all-important stamp of approval. If Evan approved, all the aunts in the kingdom might be withstood.

"Let us now coolly consider what reason cannot do."

Lenny sucked her lower lip. Evan would care less for this part. A disciple of Hume would not like to hear reason disparaged.

"First, reason cannot produce faith. Faith is always consistent with reason, yet reason cannot produce faith. Reason is a divine evidence, bringing a full conviction of an invisible eternal world. But reason cannot put all your doubts to flight. As a case in point I would cite that great admirer of reason, Mr. Thomas Hobbes."

Evan stirred at the mention of the philosopher who had characterized life as being "solitary, poor, nasty, brutish and short."

"None would deny Hobbes's strong understanding, but it gave him no assurance of the eternal. When he lay dying, his friend asked, 'Where are you going, sir?' Hobbes answered, 'I am taking a leap in the dark!'

"Reason alone cannot produce hope in any child of man whereby we 'rejoice in hope of the glory of God.' This hope can only spring from Christian faith."

Wesley advanced to the third failure of reason. It could not produce love, neither love for God nor love for neighbor, and thus could produce neither virtue nor happiness.

By now, Lenny was looking inside herself. The importance of balance was a new concept. Did she see such equilibrium around her? Perhaps in her father. Certainly he seemed to possess open-mindedness, discipline, and humor. As for others she knew, she could only see them running from east to west and coming to disaster in Bessie's cow field. She managed to keep her face straight.

"Suffer me now to add a few plain words. First to you who undervalue reason. Do not imagine you are doing God a service when you endeavor to exclude reason from religion. It lays the foundation of true religion and directs us in every point both of faith and practice.

"And to you, likewise, who overvalue reason. Why should you run from one extreme to another? Is not the middle way best? Let reason do all that reason can, while at the same time acknowledge it incapable of giving either faith or hope or love. Expect these from a higher source—even as the gift of God. So shall you be living witnesses that wisdom, holiness, and happiness are one and are, indeed, the beginning of that eternal life which God hath given us in His Son."

They were barely out the door of the meetinghouse before Baird Ramsey was extolling the fine sermon. "Aye, did I not tell you it would be so?"

Archibald Price nodded. "I'm not disappointed. I've read many of Mr. Wesley's printed sermons, but I see they're even more impressive in the living voice."

"Aye, a fair pity Mrs. Ramsey has taken one of her poorly spells. She loves a good sermon." Ramsey replaced his high-crowned felt hat as they walked toward their carriages. "Scripture, reason, experience, tradition —those are Mr. Wesley's measures for knowing truth. Remember those, and you won't lose your head."

They reached the Price carriage first, and Lenny extended her gloved hand for Evan to lift her to the seat.

She was surprised when it was not her brother but rather the reticent Sheldon Ramsey who provided the steadying boost. "Wicked of you to giggle in church." The corners of his mouth twitched. "But never fear, I'll not tell."

Just then her father hung a lighted lantern on the side of the carriage. She had not realized Sheldon Ramsey had such warm brown eyes.

All the homeward drive, Evan and Archibald discussed the remarkable sermon. As much as Lenny tried to follow the conversation, however, her mind kept drifting. That single sermon had opened to her a world the existence of which none of the lessons imparted by the earnest Mr. Wimborne had even hinted.

And even more powerful than his words was the man himself. "I fret at nothing," he had said. That struck the young girl who seemed to fret at everything. Cheerfulness, spirit, and those penetrating hazel eyes framed by silver-white hair. Lenny would long remember her encounter with John Wesley.

And she was determined. All others around her might spend their time running from east to west. But she would stand in the middle. Not all soppy emotion or all cold logic. A balance of Scripture, reason, experience, and tradition.

But where did one find that perfectly ordered territory? When achieved, how did one know? And hardest of all, how could one maintain such a position were one to attain her goal?

Lenny pulled her shawl around her shoulders and leaned into the corner of the carriage. She soon slipped from consciousness and saw herself in the pasture, surrounded by people seeking a place to stand as the ground under them tilted and swayed. Sarah sat on a boulder sketching while Mr. Wimborne effused. Then Bessie turned around and swished her tail across Sarah's sketch pad.

Lenny woke herself up giggling.

48

Lenny now found a new spark added to the philosophical discussions as she listened outside Evan's classroom door. Thorpe Wimborne was not a man who would take lightly the possibility that one of his pupils might be tainted with Methodism. Nor was Evan one to allow a man he had come to admire to be belittled.

"I despair, Mr. Evan, I truly do. After all I've taught you of the rational approach . . ."

"That is precisely my point, Wimborne. Much to my own surprise, I did not find Mr. Wesley to be irrational."

"I am much relieved to hear it. However, I fear your thinking has been diverted from the central issue of our study. To return to the Second Discourse, Jean Jacques Rousseau teaches us to think of primitive humanity—to rediscover our vigorous, naturally healthy, moral, compassionate state from which we have fallen through the corrupting influences of society."

Lenny pricked her finger and stuck it in her mouth. Needlework was certainly one of society's demands that she would be happy to throw off.

Apparently Evan was not so certain. "You quite amaze me, Wimborne. And you a churchman. And what of the teaching that it is not society but the Fall of man that has corrupted human nature?"

"Ah, yes. But suppose the inciting incident was not a bite from the symbolic apple but rather the claim to private property. Perhaps that first man who, after enclosing a piece of ground, took it into his head to say, 'This is mine,' was Adam. Would not that prove Jean Jacques correct?"

It was a mark of Thorpe Wimborne's enormous respect for the French philosopher that he never called him Rousseau but, rather, Jean Jacques, as if he were a dear friend or relative.

"An intriguing idea, Wimborne, but how is it then that the American Indians and other noble savages which Rousseau idolizes were apparently not affected by the Adamic Fall?"

As she listened, stitching doggedly away, Lenny held to her image of herself seated securely in the center while all around her ran back and forth, seeking ground on which to stand. The only trouble was that she didn't have much idea what she was in the center of.

"Right, Wimborne. It seems perfectly obvious Rousseau is correct that man has fallen from the perfect state in which God created him. But I simply do not see how we can achieve salvation through forming a social contract."

Wimborne took such a deep breath that it must have made his head wobble.

Lenny almost committed the fatal error of giving away her presence by giggling. But she needn't have worried.

The tutor's voice rang with the same level of fervency that his organ preludes preceded the Reverend Mr. Cleland's sermons. "We can improve our condition and strive to return to a state of nature by not surrendering our natural rights to any single sovereign but to society as a whole—which is our guarantee of freedom and equality."

Evan laughed. "Edmund Burke would find little comfort in having his freedoms held in the hand of the 'swinish multitude.'"

The mention of Archibald Price's favorite politician brought another outburst from Wimborne.

With a sigh, Lenny put her embroidery aside. Not that she had any reluctance to abandon the hateful piece, but if her mother did not hear her at flute practice, Lenny's forceful parent would come to see what she was about. And Harriet Price was one who could always see through Lenny's ruses.

Lenny walked to the far end of the long, pleasant drawing room. It was furnished in the best Georgian style. A bay window housed Sarah's harpsichord and served as the music alcove in which the daughters of the house were expected to perform whenever there were guests for dinner. Actually, Lenny liked music very much. That was why she hated practicing. She would have enjoyed it, could she have produced a musical sound. But to be required to murder "Sheep May Safely Graze"—surely one of the loveliest melodies ever written— was torture.

Lenny's lack of talent was not the only hindrance to her musical development. She also found it impossible to keep her mind glued to the sheet of music before her. Her thoughts wandered back over the discussion she had just heard, and she wished for the thousandth time that she had someone with whom she could discuss such things. Her father would be tolerant if she went to him with a question, as she sometimes did. But a succinct answer to a question was not what she longed for. She wanted a friend, a girl her own age who shared her interest in *ideas*.

That was silly, of course. All properly brought up young women cared only for music and fashion and the social graces that would stand them well in the marriage mart. Fortunately, Lenny had a few years before she had to worry seriously about such matters, and for the moment their mother's efforts in that direction were all focused on preparing Sarah. But Lenny knew her time would come.

A thin wail emanated from the instrument in her hands. Lenny looked at it as if trying to remember what it was, then turned her attention to the music on the stand before her. She had no idea where she was. Nothing for it but to start the piece over. And pay attention this time. Unfortunately, though, the long introductory passage was highly repetitive and not conducive to holding her attention. She began picturing where she would meet such a bosom friend as she longed for and what the girl would be like.

Lenny had tooted and wheezed her way through three more lines when the door at the far end of the room opened.

At the sight of her mother, Lenny instinctively straightened her back and made sure the gauze fichu filling the neckline of her pale green muslin gown was in acceptable order. She knew the ribbons attempting to curtail her unruly black locks were hopelessly askew. She would simply have to suffer her mother's rebuke on that score.

But for once Harriet failed to notice her younger daughter's shortcomings. As a matter of fact, her mother's own lace cap was a bit awry. "You must put that away, Carolenn. Go help Cook assemble a tray of cakes and cold meat and cheeses and—well—whatever she has to hand. Your Uncle Lanark has just arrived with the most shocking news. Your brother's lessons must be interrupted as well, I fear." She turned to the double doors leading to the dining room.

Lenny heard the news from the lips of Douglas Lanark when she returned to the room a short time later, bearing a tray of cakes and wine.

"Twenty thousand troops marching toward Paris. King Louis the Sixteenth has called them in from all the provinces."

Lenny set the tray on the sideboard, then fled to a chair in the dimmest corner. She did not want to be told to leave.

Trouble in France had been brewing for well over a year as Robespierre, Mirabeau, Lafayette, and other reformists worked against the feudal, privileged establishment. All spring the *Belfast News Letter* had been rife with reports of riots and attacks on convoys of grain throughout France as the price of bread rose to unmanageable heights. The matter seemed to be coming to a head, if the French king had called his army.

"And what do you think of this affair, cousin?" Archibald asked his guest.

Lenny awaited the answer. She knew her father and his politically active cousin agreed on few things.

"How could any member of the Dungannon Convention not support the right of his fellow creatures to a more representative government?" Douglas Lanark's presence seven years ago at the convention that had led to Ireland's securing the independence of her own legislature was one of her uncle's proudest claims to fame.

She looked at Evan. What would her brother say to this? Would a successful French reform prove Rousseau correct?

But apparently Evan was not so easily swayed. "But your 'free' Irish Parliament represents property, uncle, not the people. Only Protestant freeholders sit in the Dublin Parliament."

Now Archibald Price entered the debate. "What would you have, son? Surely you're not suggesting universal suffrage?"

Evan glanced at his tutor sitting quietly behind him, then cleared his throat. "Rousseau would. But I doubt anyone else would go so far. What say you, uncle? The Dublin Parliament has had much to say about a more equal representation of the people. Does 'more equal' mean extending the vote to Catholics?"

Douglas Lanark rubbed a hand along one dark sideburn. "At Dungannon we resolved that 'as men, as Irishmen, as Christians, we are rejoiced in the relaxation of the penal laws against our Roman Catholic fellow subjects.'"

Evan slapped his knee. "Well said, uncle. All Irishmen must work together. We must not be north or south, city or country, Catholic or Protestant. We must be Irish. We must unite."

An explosive silence filled the room, and it was several seconds before the elder Lanark spoke. "You quite mistake me, nephew. Nothing I said must be taken as allowing legal toleration of the popish religion. Popery is of a persecuting spirit and has always marked her steps with blood. We Protestants could expect no security for our own religious liberty were Rome to rule us."

Lenny's mother looked uneasily around the drawing room. No hostess wished for the atmosphere to become so charged. It was very bad form. With a bright smile she began handing around the cake tray.

It was Archibald, however, who shifted the focus from local politics. "I thank you for bringing us news of the situation in France, Douglas. But I fear for it. Edmund Burke, that most sensible of men, has warned that—if the king is overthrown—France will suffer a bloodbath. Fear and terror will follow the breakdown of the rule of law."

"Surely not, Father. Burke supported the American Revolution."

Evan paused mid-motion in slathering a thick slice of cold beef with a fine brown mustard.

"Burke upheld the American patriots because they were fighting for the rights Englishmen have always taken for granted. Magna Carta had been denied them. They could do no other than rise up in arms."

"But the French fight for rights, Father."

Archibald shook his head. "I fear law and order have broken down. The reformists appeal not to ancient rights but rather to the general will. We cannot accomplish a perfect state of harmony with the universe by tearing down all institutions of church, state, and society." He took a sip of wine. "The Jacobin ideal is a single elite guiding the state by that vaguest of whimsies, 'public opinion.' You watch. We shall see not democracy but anarchy. Once the reformists have cut down all the protective barriers, they will have no place to hide when the mob turns on them."

Lenny felt a chill of fear prickle her spine. She longed to be able to ask questions. But no one would talk about such things to a thirteen-year-old girl. She might as well be Bessie chewing her cud for all anyone expected her to know of politics. Was she the only female in all Ireland who cared about events in the wider world?

In the following days, Lenny took to slipping into her father's office when she knew him to be in the fields. She read the copies of the *Belfast News-Letter* that he always kept neatly piled on a corner table. She learned much of the struggles of the French peasants and the Parisian crowd. Even so, she was as amazed as everyone else when, in mid-July, her father called the family together to tell them of a momentous event.

Archibald began by holding out a newspaper so that all could see the headline for themselves: The Greatest Event in Human Annals.

"What can it be? Oh, do read it out, Father!" Lenny fairly bounced on her seat.

"I trust it won't take too long. I have an appointment at the dressmaker's." Sarah's voice held an impatient edge.

Archibald gave his elder daughter a subduing look and shook out the paper. "'Twenty-six millions of our fellow creatures bursting their chains and throwing off in an instant the degrading yoke of slavery—it is a scene so new, so sublime, that the heart which cannot participate in the triumph must either have been vitiated by illiberal politics or be naturally depraved.'"

"It sounds splendid, Father," Lenny cried. "But what *happened?*"

Through the coming days, little else was talked of. With the aid of local gossip and further accounts in the press, Lenny gradually formed a picture of what had happened—and was still happening in Paris. On

July 14, after pillaging an armory, a mob made its way to an old fortress called the Bastille. Apparently only seven people were actually imprisoned there—and two of them were mad—but it had long stood as a hated symbol of absolutist oppression. The crowd forced the governor to lower the drawbridge, and the people rushed in. It was a great victory for liberty, equality, and fraternity.

One afternoon after reading the latest account, Lenny found herself crying for joy at the thought of those seven poor beings who had been incarcerated so long in their dungeon, and those who had been equally starved outside its walls, now freed. Celebrating with the French citizens, she rushed out into the field, her bare arms spread to the free, fresh air and sunshine. She whirled and danced, singing the tune that was on every tongue in Ulster, "The Boyne Water," that great song of their own Glorious Revolution, with new words to it: "From France now see Liberty's Tree—its branches wide extending . . ."

And it seemed that all Ireland rejoiced with her. Douglas sent word from Lanarks' Bawn that the Volunteers, inactive since their 1782 victory at Dungannon, were re-forming. The reason for their resurrection was unclear, but the Lanark men were enthusiastic. Even Evan now abandoned all thought of theology and philosophy classes. He too was swept up in revolution fever.

Lenny's father said little, but he pointed out the reports hidden on back pages of the newspapers. Across the French countryside, peasants armed themselves and stormed castles and manors, burning and wrecking. He shook his head. "It will become something worse."

Lenny again felt a prickle at her spine. "What, Father? What will it be?"

"I do not know. But we have seen only the beginning. Burke is right. The glory of Europe is gone forever. You watch, my poppet. It will be so." He ruffled her dark curls as he left the room.

Lenny sighed. It was as close as anyone would come to discussing affairs with her. She buried her embroidery deep in the sofa cushions and went out. Bessie was as bad a conversationalist as she was an artist's model, but she was a good listener. And Lenny didn't have anyone else to talk to.

49

"Lenny, you can't possibly intend to wear that bonnet!"

Sarah stood in the doorway, striking-looking in her newest gown, taken from a French pattern card. The light fabric draped her form, the skirt falling smoothly from a wide linen belt. She somewhat resembled a painting Lenny had seen of Liberty leading the French people. It was appropriate for the day's celebration marking the second anniversary of the fall of the Bastille.

But Lenny, now fast approaching her sixteenth birthday, was not one to be dictated to in the matter of fashion. "I always wear this bonnet. It's my favorite." She held out the fine straw. She liked the yellow ribbons, and she thought the high-poke brim flattering in that it gave an oval illusion to her round face.

"*Always* is precisely the problem. On this day you must adopt a new style to reflect our sentiments—a bonnet of the populace." Sarah placed the article on Lenny's head. It was a white cap with a drape of gathered fabric covering her hair. The tricolor band and rosette, the red, white, and blue of the French flag, looked appropriately patriotic.

Lenny, however, frowned at the result.

"It's because your hair is all wrong." Sarah began pulling out pins, then grabbed a boar bristle brush and attacked her sister's hair. "You must wear it long, flowing free over your shoulders. It is the style of the people."

"But in *Belfast?*" Lenny pulled back. "We'll be laughed at."

"On the contrary, I assure you. Anything less would be unpatriotic. We must show our agreement with the Volunteers, who are going to such effort to mount a fine display of Irish support of French liberty, equality, and fraternity." Sarah clasped her hands. "Oh, that such splendid sentiment could rule in our beloved Ireland."

Lenny thought that perhaps it was more often Rousseauan splendid sentiment that ruled in Ireland rather than Burkean common sense. But she meekly submitted to wearing the really quite flattering bonnet of the populace.

A few hours later she wasn't sorry to be showing her support for liberty, equality, and fraternity. The Price Manor family had joined the throng standing before the Exchange, the Georgian market house that Lord Donegal had built to mark the birth of his first son. Today the arcaded front of the building was draped in red, white, and blue bunting, and a band played lively marches from under the arches.

Lenny positioned herself next to Evan. It was so good to have him home from Trinity College. She wasn't sure whether she had missed him or his overheard philosophy lessons more. But now that he was home for the summer, she had them both back, and she was enjoying every moment.

Mr. Wimborne, who continued at Price Manor as music and dancing master while his philosophy student was at university, was a member of the party today. Lenny felt certain that if the dignity of his office of church organist had not been at stake, he would have donned the red wool bonnet of the revolutionaries as so many others had. As it was, he contented himself with casting admiring glances at Sarah's flowing golden curls.

And since the men from Lanarks' Bawn were to be marching with the Volunteers, the Aunts AM were also part of the company. "Oh, what a grand thing, a grand thing! I allow I'm quite a-quiver." Aunt Marguerite's quivering was a notable sight.

Adelaide was not to be so easily taken in. *"Hmph!"* She sniffed and looked around her. "I daresay there'll be as many spies as supporters here."

"Spies!" Now Marguerite's quiver was more a tidal roll. "Addie, you can't mean it. *French* spies in Ireland?"

"French, indeed." The ostrich feather adorning Adelaide's bonnet bent in the breeze. "What need do you suppose we have of *French* spies, sister? Do you think us not capable of producing our own?"

"I can't imagine what you mean, Addie, but you excite me exceedingly. I vow you'll bring on my palpitations."

"Deep breathing. It's simply a matter of deep breathing. I never have palpitations. I refer to Lord Londonderry, of course. It's said he'll have none of this reform in County Down. And there's plenty who will inform on any turbulent persons about."

At her sister's alarming news, Marguerite took a step backward and all but flattened a young man standing quietly behind her.

"Oh!" Sheldon Ramsey threw his arms wide and braced himself. "Oh, madam, I do apologize." Only his quick response prevented his sprawling in the mud of Linen Hall Street.

The young man had actually behaved with grace and decorum, but the whole situation sent Lenny into a fit of giggles. And the more hotly Sheldon blushed, the more she giggled.

She had seen him no more than two or three times since the Methodist meeting. He had grown much taller, and his shoulders had broadened, but apparently he had managed little increase in his vocabulary. He bowed stiffly to her and turned to his father.

Baird Ramsey was, as always, immaculately attired. It was, however, the magnificent green cockade on his hat that drew all attention. He tipped the hat to the ladies of the Price party and introduced the man with him, who was likewise sporting an Irish green cockade. "And may I be granted the privilege of presenting Henry Joy McCracken, honorable secretary of the Belfast Whig Club."

"Servant, ladies." McCracken's vivacious intelligence showed in his lively face and energetic bow.

Lenny made her deepest curtsy, for once thankful for her mother's deportment lessons. The tall, athletic Henry Joy McCracken was one of the most handsome men she had ever seen.

He turned the full charm of his smile on her. "Miss Carolenn, I wonder if you would be so good as to indulge me in a favor?"

"Of course, sir." She swallowed and bobbed another curtsy.

Henry Joy glanced around. "Ah, splendid. There you are, Mary Ann! Look sharp now—here are some new friends. You can watch the proceedings with them."

A young woman with snapping black eyes and bouncing dark curls under a high-crowned felt hat was coming toward them through the crowd. Lenny thought she had never seen a young woman move with more freedom and self-assurance.

"Really, Henry, you needn't foist me off! I'm perfectly fine on my own."

Henry Joy McCracken introduced his sister, then went off with Ramsey to their places in the procession lining up in front of the Exchange.

Although Mary Ann was much closer to Sarah's age, Lenny felt drawn to this new acquaintance and liked her instantly. She would much like to get to know her better.

Just then the band struck up a rousing version of the "Marseillaise," and the procession began to the accompaniment of wild cheering on both sides of the street. A well-turned-out troop of light dragoons from the Belfast Volunteers led out.

"Oh, there they are! There, right there! Yoo-hoo! Dougie! Jay!" Aunt Marguerite, thoroughly recovered from her near fall, stood on tiptoe and waved a voluminous silk handkerchief.

Next came the artillery corps, trailing four brass cannons. Then came a tableaux. Two members of the Northern Whig Club held aloft portraits of those great revolutionary leaders Benjamin Franklin of

America and Honore-Gabriel Mirabeau of France, followed by a banner portraying the release of the prisoners from the Bastille.

A rousing cheer went up from the crowd, and many threw their hats in the air when they read aloud the motto—Fourteenth July, 1789 —Sacred to Liberty. But as the painting passed on up the street, the viewers suddenly became sober. The picture on the back of the banner was different, indeed. A large figure of Hibernia sat with hand and foot shackled while a Volunteer presented a figure of Liberty to her.

"It makes one think," Mary Ann commented to Lenny as they moved up Linen Hall Street with the crowd.

"Indeed, it does."

A volley from one of the brass cannons echoed against the walls of the buildings. The shot was answered with an artillery salvo and then wild cheering. The exercise was repeated twice more, the level of cheering increasing each time. The speaker, standing on a podium in front of the arching entrance to the Linen Hall, had considerable difficulty silencing the crowd in order to read the declaration of Volunteers and citizens to be sent to the national assembly of France that very day.

He held the parchment in both hands. The green cockade on his hat fluttered. "If we be asked, what is the French revolution to us? we answer, 'Much!'"

Cheers interrupted him. Several band members added trumpet blasts and drum rolls to the general cacophony.

"Much," the speaker repeated, when at last he could shout over the noise. "Much as men!" Again he was obliged to wait while his hearers vented their enthusiasm. "It is good for human nature that grass now grows where the Bastille once stood."

The bearers of the tableaux banner hoisted it aloft. Renewed cheers.

"And it means much to us as Irishmen."

Lenny expected an explosion of acclaim to greet that statement. Instead, the mall in front of the Linen Hall fell breathlessly silent. The air tingled expectantly as all assembled waited to hear what came next.

"As Irishmen, we too have a country we hold dear. So dear to us its freedom that we wish for nothing so much as a real representative of the national will—the surest guide and guardian of national happiness."

Men nodded. Ladies dabbed at their eyes. Aunt Marguerite sniffed loudly.

"Go on, then—great and gallant people! You, our French brothers, have shown us the way. You are, in very truth, the hope of this world!"

Now the cheers rose unabated. A fine white horse was led to the platform, and the speaker mounted. He held the rolled parchment aloft, and, escorted by drum and fife and followed by light dragoons, the proclamation began its journey to France. Many spectators followed along, while Volunteers not in the procession to the quay turned into the Linen Hall, where a banquet awaited them.

Lenny took a deep breath. At last there was quiet enough for conversation within their own party.

She turned to the intriguing Mary Ann McCracken.

But apparently she was not the only one to find Miss McCracken attractive. Evan was quick with a bow and the offer of his arm. "Miss McCracken, since your brother will be long at his banquet, might I have the pleasure of escorting you to your home?"

Mary Ann's smile produced dimples at the corners of her full mouth. "Thank you, sir. Our home is just here along Rosemary Lane, but I should be glad of your company." She placed her left hand gracefully on Evan's arm and reached for Lenny's hand with her right. "You'll stroll with us, won't you? I'm longing to get to know you all better."

Sarah did not refuse Mr. Wimborne's arm for a stroll, either, so it was agreed that Mr. and Mrs. Price would bring the carriage around after Archibald had seen the Aunts AM to their landau.

The McCracken home was a residence as suited one of Belfast's most prominent merchants. A servant saw them coming and opened the door, but they couldn't enter until three small dogs bounded out and each had his ears scratched by a laughing Mary Ann. "Our house is often called Noah's ark. No stray animal is ever turned away."

They went into a pleasant parlor, and Mary Ann asked the servant to bring wine and biscuits. The cool, orderly room was a blessed place of respite after the hubbub of the day.

Mary Ann's dogs and two cats followed her in. As soon as the cats were settled on her lap, she turned to animated discussion. "Well, wasn't that simply splendid! The French Revolution must be one of the most astounding events the world has ever seen—particularly to the inhabitants of Ireland."

Evan leaned back in his chair, thinking, as always, before he spoke. "One cannot deny its importance, Miss McCracken. But how do you see the French Revolution applying to us?"

Her eyes snapped. "Why, sir, it shows the way to reform, to liberty, to abolition of the abuses which have maimed and disfigured our laws. Surely you agree that we must have similar reform here?"

"Reform, certainly, but not revolution."

"You are quite wrong, sir. 'Man is born free but everywhere he is in chains.' It is only by revolution, I think, that such chains can be cast off."

A slow smile crossed Evan's face. "Ah, the lady quotes your eminent French philosopher, Wimborne."

The tutor, who had selected a chair in the farthest corner, nodded but did not answer.

Lenny wondered at Wimborne's behavior, but she had noticed before how silent he often became in company. Perhaps his slight stammer made him shy.

But she saw no reason for reticence on her part. Here, at last, she was in company where she might speak. "Mr. Burke would say that wrongs must be redressed gradually. When change is too violent, one breaks more than chains. Tradition, values, the spiritual resources of society are lost, and one is left to the unrestrained rule of mere numbers."

"Really, Carolenn! Where did you ever take such notions into your head? I quite blush for you."

Lenny had spoken without thinking of the presence of her older, very proper sister. She ducked her head.

But their hostess was not in the least put off. She matched Lenny's outburst. "But Rousseau argues we can only be free, moral, and good when we are governed by free and natural people."

Characteristically, Evan's reply was more cautious. "I see one of the most splendid hopes for the future of our island coming from the united efforts of our Volunteers—here in Belfast, where Catholic and Protestant march side by side. Whatever we do, we must act together."

There was a round of applause from the parlor door, and every head turned. A young lad stood there in buff trousers and a blue coat.

"John." Mary Ann held out her hand in greeting. "You must join us." She presented her younger brother and smiled at Evan. "You and my brother will find you have much in common."

The young men fell into instant dialogue, John quizzing Evan on the ideas he had just expressed and Evan responding with reasoned answers.

Mary Ann smiled at Lenny. "Would you care for a turn in the garden?"

As soon as they were alone in the enclosed yard, the young women turned to each other. "How do you know Burke?" "How do you know Rousseau?" they asked almost in tandem, then laughingly embraced.

"I listen at doors," Lenny said. "At least, I did until my brother went to university. And you?"

Mary Ann tucked Lenny's hand into her arm, and they began strolling along the banks of colorful flowers.

"Are you not familiar, then, with Mary Wollstonecraft's *Thoughts on the Education of Daughters?*"

"I'm afraid I've never heard of it."

"Well, you must. A remarkable work by a remarkable lady. Mrs. Wollstonecraft despairs at the fashionable young women today who spend their time 'going they scarcely care where for they cannot tell what.'" Mary Ann gave a small shudder at the thought of such a shallow existence.

Lenny nodded, thinking of her sister.

"Mary Wollstonecraft believes women should study politics, enter business, or take up the art of healing. My sister Margaret and I quite agree."

"And your family—father, mother, brothers—they do not disagree?"

"On the contrary, they encourage us. My mother has even entered into a small muslin business with my sister and myself."

"Oh, but this is too wonderful! I had hoped and prayed for a friend such a you, but I had not thought it possible." Lenny stopped and regarded the older girl—almost a woman. "That is—we *can* be friends, can we not, Miss McCracken? I should like it so much."

Mary Ann patted the hand on her arm and laughed. "And so should I. You must call me Mary Ann. None in my family ever tire of new friends with whom to discuss the affairs of the wider world. And my brothers are always happy to meet young men of just such sentiments as your brother expressed. We have a very forward-thinking friend coming in a month or two. You must come to Belfast then. You will find him most stimulating."

Lenny couldn't believe how fast the days sped through the rest of that summer and into the autumn. Mary Ann was a fine correspondent, and every letter from her new friend brought word of the much-anticipated arrival of the McCracken's enigmatic Dublin acquaintance. Lenny's impatience grew to meet the remarkable Theobald Wolfe Tone.

She soon discovered that writing letters could be nearly as good as conversation. Sometimes letters were better because, when Lenny was lonely or frustrated, she could always go to the carved wooden chest on the parlor writing desk and enjoy the written conversation all over again. And Mary Ann McCracken's letters were well worth multiple readings. They were full of ideas and events:

My Dear Miss Price,

I have been reading Bishop Berkeley's *Querist* papers. He is quite brilliant in both theology and economy. Although written 45 years ago, it seems he has much to say to today. "Whose fault is it if poor Ireland still continues poor?" he asks. "Would not it be more reasonable to mend our State than complain of it? But how much is in our power?" I often wonder, too, yet do not despair, my dear Carolenn, for surely much might be done—nay, *will* be done. It is, as your brother said, a matter of Irishmen putting less important matters aside and, united, working for the good of all. Henry continues to receive encouraging correspondence from our friends in Dublin, but we have no word yet of their so-anticipated arrival.

Remember me as usual and believe me to be

Yours affectionately,
Mary Ann McCracken

That evening at dinner Lenny ventured, "Father, who was Bishop Berkeley?"

Archibald paused with a spoonful of leek and mutton soup balanced above his plate. "Bishop of Cloyne. Eccentric but much-loved. Very sound in his defense of theism and Christianity and his attacks on deists and freethinkers."

"Carolenn, straighten your spine. A lady does not lean against the back of her chair at the table."

Lenny stiffened her lower back in obedience to her mother's directions. She would have liked to ask more about the Irish philosopher, but Sarah required her father's opinion on the relative merits of pulling her hair up with flowered ribbon or wearing it looped under with a concealed thong. Lenny turned her attention to her soup and determined to write to Mary Ann as soon as she could escape to her room after the evening musical hour.

Between snippets from Mary Ann's letters, surreptitious peeks at her father's newspaper, and the information she had garnered from overhearing Evan's conversations with Thorpe Wimborne, Lenny knew that matters in France were still unstable. King Louis had disguised himself as a valet and attempted to flee the palace with his family. They had been arrested and brought back between two files of soldiers. From all Lenny gathered, one thing seemed certain—war was inevitable.

She cringed. All the moving talk of rights and freedoms, the stirring parades with uniforms and bands, the vision of a happy, wealthy land to be gained—must it end in the horrors of war? War in their idealized France? War in her own dear Ireland?

If war came here, who would be caught up in it? Certainly her uncle and cousin. Douglas and Jay Lanark had already marched down Linen Hall Street in their fine green and black uniforms. As had Baird Ramsey and Mary Ann's brothers Henry Joy and Francis. What of others? What of the quiet young men such as John McCracken and Sheldon Ramsey? They were too young to take the Volunteers uniform—now.

437

And what of Evan and her father, who wanted reform but were opposed to revolution? Would they be drawn into it anyway? Or Thorpe
Wimborne, who so delighted in spouting radical theory? Would he
exchange his organist's robes for a uniform? If war came, would it swallow up everyone she knew?

Lenny shivered with the tingle of fear she had felt two summers
ago when she first heard of the French Revolution.

50

"No, no, no. I cannot say it more strongly. Ireland's abiding evil is not England. The root of all our troubles—the same today as it was two hundred years ago—is the fact that Ireland's people are disunited."

The speaker was a tall man with a high-bridged nose and heavy eyebrows accenting his fierce eyes. He held all attention in the McCracken drawing room.

He had finally come. Theobald Wolfe Tone. And Lenny was far from disappointed. The Dubliner who had composed the Resolution to France read at last summer's commemoration had all the brilliance and passion for reform that Mary Ann had led her to expect.

"Hear, hear!" Evan's was just one of many voices raised in support of Tone's call for unity. Although this was simply an evening's gathering of friends, it carried the atmosphere of a formal meeting of a political club. And it was all beyond Lenny's wildest dreams. Simply having such proceedings reported to her had been the height of her hopes heretofore. But now she was present, actually part of the company! She knew her excitement showed in the redness of her cheeks, but she didn't care.

"Furthermore," Tone continued, "when we resolve the one, the other will resolve itself naturally. So there it is, gentlemen—and ladies." He nodded toward Lenny and Mary Ann. "An Ireland of united Catholics and Protestants would have nothing to fear of England or anyone else. I ask you—why does Ireland remain corrupt, unfree, and unrepresented even though we've had an independent Parliament for almost ten years? I'll tell you—Ireland is not free because Ireland is not united."

"Precisely why we have asked you to come to Belfast, Tone." Henry Joy took up the conversation. "Your thoughts are well known, your pamphlets widely read. As a Protestant, yet a member of the Catholic Committee, you are the man who can show us how to unify."

The room erupted in general conversation while Mrs. McCracken and her older daughter, Margaret, passed among their guests offering glasses of sherry and stronger spirits. None appeared to be opposed to the goals expressed, but the practical barriers to achieving such ends were alarming.

Lenny was surprised at the animation shown by her usually reticent brother. Evan seemed much at home here and in little danger of arguing for Burkean caution. Once again, Thorpe Wimborne was the only one not entering fully into the discussion.

A rotund young man—not more than three or four years older than herself, Lenny guessed—wearing silver spectacles and a high-collared black coat, spoke up in a clear, musical voice. "You all seem to be thinking in terms of political unity, but might I suggest another force?"

The general hubbub quieted. "What do you suggest, Bunting?"

"That is Edward Bunting, my harp teacher," Mary Ann whispered to Lenny. "We call him Atty."

"I was thinking of the power of music to bring people together. Ireland is possessed of one of the world's richest traditions of music and poetry, and yet this great force that can move men's hearts and minds so palpably is so seldom thought of."

"Appeals to our romantic past can have their affect on some minds, but a more hardheaded approach is called for here." Theobald Wolfe Tone thus made it apparent that he had little time for Gaelic romanticism.

Thomas Russell, a blond, strikingly handsome man in the uniform of a British army officer, drew a pamphlet from his breast pocket and handed it to Henry Joy. "Here we are, fresh from the press and available for a shilling. Tone's latest."

"*Argument on Behalf of the Catholics of Ireland*," McCracken read. "Shall I continue?"

General acclamation urged him on.

"No reform can ever be obtained which shall not comprehensively embrace Irishmen of all denominations. Irishmen are now faced with two choices: We can remain oppressed, unknown in Europe—the prey to England. Or we can unite to secure a complete and radical emancipation of our country."

Everyone applauded.

Tone stood, tall, intensely grave. He raised his glass. "Gentlemen, I give you the Society of United Irishmen."

It was a moment before the import of the words struck his hearers. This was not just a toast to a sentiment. It was a formal proposal for the formation of a society—a society of far wider-ranging vision than any Whig or Volunteer club now so popular across the country.

Thomas Russell and Henry Joy McCracken jumped to their feet at the same moment. "The United Irishmen!"

Others followed, and the room rang. "United Irishmen! United

Irishmen!" No one was quite certain what it meant, but it sounded splendid. It spoke of a golden future when all Ireland would live free in liberty, equality, and fraternity.

Mary Ann's invitation had been open-ended. Lenny and Evan were to stay at the McCracken home for as long as they could be spared from Price Manor—and Mr. Wimborne for as long as he could be away from his Newtownards church duties. John Cleland seemed to be a most flexible man, for Wimborne had ample time.

The large home on Rosemary Lane always kept extra rooms ready, but Lenny was to share Mary Ann's room. It was late before the Dublin visitors retired and the young women could enjoy a quiet time together, wrapped in dressing gowns. Mary Ann began brushing her hair, but Lenny picked up a small shirt in need of hemming. Sewing for the poorhouse was a never-ending activity at Rosemary Lane, and even Lenny's uneven stitches were welcomed here.

"What a splendid gathering! I've never seen anything like it." Lenny was certain she would never be able to sleep. "What will happen next? It's all so brilliant, but how will they bring it about?"

Mary Ann's dark hair fell softly over her shoulders as the silver-backed brush moved in the glow of the candle on her dresser. "The resolutions must be written. Wolfe Tone will do that, I've no doubt. Then they must be approved by a formal committee of organizers. Then others can begin uniting." She smiled. "All across Ireland— Catholic, Protestant, farmer, merchant, all joining United Irishmen." The ornate brush stilled. "And United Irish *women* too. Why not?"

Lenny nodded. Indeed, why not? It was an inspiring thought. A bit nebulous, perhaps, because she wasn't quite clear what people would do once they had joined. But perhaps the joining would be enough. "I did feel just the least bit sorry for that poor Mr. Bunting. He seemed rather out of place. How did he come to be in a political meeting?"

"Oh, he lives here." Mary Ann shrugged. "He's like one of the family."

"Here?" Lenny knew of the McCrackens' open-door policy to guests and stray animals, but she didn't realize it extended to permanent lodgers.

"He came to Belfast seven years ago as assistant to the organist at St. Anne's. He has no family, so my mother took him in." Lenny was still staring in amazement when Mary Ann added, "He's wonderfully musical." That seemed a complete explanation for the unusual arrangement.

As her fingers mechanically stitched, Lenny's thoughts moved on to a more interesting topic, Theobald Wolfe Tone. She sighed as his melting, beautiful eyes swam before her. And Mary Ann had taken few pains to hide her admiration for Thomas Russell. How marvelous it would be if the four of them . . .

"Mr. Tone is very handsome."

Mary Ann paused again in her brush strokes. "Well, striking-looking, certainly."

"What does he do? Besides writing political pamphlets, I mean." She felt a great urge to talk about him. Just saying his name was pure joy.

"He's a lawyer. Although he has told Henry he hates it. He wanted a military career, but his father insisted he study law."

"Does he have any . . . any . . . er . . . attachments?" She prayed he wasn't betrothed.

"His first year at Trinity, he eloped with his Matilda." Mary Ann dropped the stunning words so calmly.

"Eloped!" Lenny was stunned indeed. In her darkest fears she hadn't imagined him married. She pressed a hand to her chest.

Mary Ann rushed on, unnoticing. "They were forgiven. Matilda was not yet sixteen and as lovely as an angel. And I've heard their daughter is as angelic as her mother. From all reports they're idyllically happy."

Daughter? He was husband *and* father? Her shattered dreams choked her. Yet she must know more. "How did you come to know them?"

"Through Mr. Tone's writings. Henry, as secretary of the Northern Whig Club, has corresponded with him for some time."

"And his friend—Captain Russell?"

Mary Ann's smile would have told Lenny that her hostess had, indeed, noticed the handsome army officer, even if she hadn't already noted Mary Ann's eyes following him all evening. "Captain Russell is here with his regiment. Henry and he became friends at the Whig Club, but it was Edward who brought him to the house."

"Edward Bunting?"

"Indeed. Mr. Russell is quite passionately fond of music. He and Edward get on famously."

"He is very handsome." Lenny left unspecified to which of their visitors she referred.

"Indeed. A model of manly beauty." It was clear Mary Ann's referral was to Thomas Russell, although she attempted to sound matter-of-fact.

"And is he married, too?" Were both she and her friend destined to hopeless love?

"No. But his affections are engaged." Mary Ann snuffed her candle and crawled under her thick down comforter.

Lenny put her sewing aside.

She lay long in that midway state between waking and dreaming, wondering why the knowledge that Wolfe Tone was married didn't stop her tender feelings for him. What was this infatuation that the very thought of him could make her heart leap? She ached likewise for her friend. How could Russell possibly prefer another to the captivating Mary Ann McCracken?

As her feelings threatened to overwhelm her, she rolled toward the wall. Was this love? This pain? Was it worth it? Surely it must be. It must be preferable to care grandly for someone—especially if he was as handsome as Wolfe Tone—than to find no one in the whole world to raise one's pulses. What if the entire population contained no one more interesting than . . .

She paused, trying to decide on her candidate for the most insipid male. Thorpe Wimborne. What if all the men in the world were Thorpe Wimbornes? She stifled a giggle. Her stiff cousin Jay Lanark. No. Sheldon Ramsey. What a truly dispiriting thought. One thing was clear: if she were ever to care for anyone he would have to be possessed of as brave a sentiment as Wolfe Tone.

Two days later, Lenny's enthusiasm for Tone's sensibilities found justification. The days in Belfast had been full of gaiety and gatherings. Whether meeting friends for parties or having company in, there were always people around, people talking of ideas literary or political— and laughing.

But nobody laughed one evening when Tone returned from the Donegal Arms with a sheaf of papers under his arm and announced that he had drafted the declaration and resolutions for the Society of United Irishmen of Belfast.

Lenny had not witnessed a more solemn, intent group in the McCracken drawing room. Even the dogs sat with their ears pricked as Tone read.

> "In the present great era of reform, when unjust governments are falling in every quarter of Europe; when religious persecution is compelled to abjure her tyranny over conscience; when the rights of man are ascertained in theory and substantiated by practice . . ."

Lenny had some trouble focusing on the glorious words, distracted as she was by the speaker. But she saw the intensity with which Evan and Wimborne were listening. How many times had she heard them discussing the theories of the rights of man? How amazing to think that now they were present where such rights would be put into practice.

Tone's fervency increased. "It is our duty as Irishmen to come forward and state our heavy grievance—that root of all afflictions: *We have no national government!*"

Here the room erupted in cheers, but Tone barely paused. "We are ruled by Englishmen and the servants of Englishmen, whose object is the interest of their own country. Such an extrinsic power can be resisted only by unanimity, decision, and spirit in the people!"

Tone paused for acclamation and received it. He smiled as he said, "I thought that would meet with approval. Next, I call for equal representation in Parliament of all the people."

"Right." "It must be so." Henry McCracken and Thomas Russell spoke at the same time.

Tone gave a sharp nod and returned to his reading. "Impressed with these sentiments, we have agreed to form an association to be called 'The Society of United Irishmen,' seeking a cordial union among all the people of Ireland."

Matilda had been only about Lenny's age when she had eloped with Wolfe Tone. Lenny wrenched her thoughts back from her daydreaming.

There followed the three resolutions of the Society: first, that a union of all the people was required as a balance to the great weight of English influence in Ireland; second, that a complete reform of the representation in Parliament was necessary to oppose the English; and third, that no reform would be practical, effective, or just that did not include Irishmen of every religious persuasion.

The next day the euphoria from Rosemary Lane carried to Peggy Barclay's tavern just off the Four Corners. Evan was the first to return to the McCracken home with a glowing report of the formal meeting of the committee. "It's official. The committee unanimously approved the declaration. Twenty-eight members sworn and plans under way to cover the country with societies. Dublin next, of course."

"Oh, Evan, that's splendid!" Lenny hugged him. "Did you join?"

"Not yet." Evan was cautious, as always. "I want to think further on the matter."

Lenny felt a bit of impatience with her brother's hesitation, but then Tone, Russell, and the McCracken brothers burst in upon them, and all began toasting the successful launch of their endeavor, amid much talk of sympathy for Catholics, antipathy to the scavengers in Parliament, and the difficulty of defining the newfangled doctrine of the Rights of Man.

Mary Ann said, seemingly out of the blue, "A symbol. We need a symbol for the Society."

It was like tossing a fresh bone among dogs—friendly dogs, but ones that would grapple with any bone presented, whether or not they were hungry. A figure of Liberty was too complicated, a Phrygian cap too revolutionary, a tricolor rosette too French, a green cockade too Whig, a red hand too limited to Ulster. They might never have hit on the answer had Edward Bunting not returned from organ practice at St. Anne's at that moment.

Bunting stood just inside the door listening to the cacophony of debate, his hands in his pockets, a small smile curling the corners of his mouth. At last there was a lull in the discussion.

"A harp," Edward Bunting said.

Mary Ann jumped. "Edward, you startled me. I didn't hear you come in. What did you say?"

"A harp. What could be a better symbol of Irish unity than a picture of the thing all Irishmen love—our music?"

Wolfe Tone frowned. "Music is well enough in its place. But this is a *political* society."

Thomas Russell, however, the music lover, caught the vision. "Ah, but my friend, this is *Irish* politics—as much music as debate. Our ideas, like our music, hark back to the days before we were divided, back to our ancient traditions from which the strength of our peoples come. Well spoke, Bunting!" He raised his glass toward the newcomer.

Tone started to object, but Mary Ann said quietly, "And what about a motto? It should be more than just a picture."

Once again, ideas, accolades, and objections flew.

While the others examined each new idea, Lenny picked up the sketch pad she had been working in earlier, attempting a picture of Mary Ann's favorite puppy. She turned to a clean page and began drawing a harp. The earlier suggestion of using a figure of Liberty as the symbol intrigued her. Maybe she could work in a similar form as a figurehead on the harp, which would also suggest a ship sailing into the future. For once she was glad of Mr. Wimborne's drawing lessons.

"Liberty, Equality, Fraternity" was proposed as their motto with support from Tone. Evan, however, questioned the wisdom of such overt alignment with the French revolutionaries. "We don't know what the future holds there. It seems that every side in France wants war. I do not think this is the image we would best promote."

"I would fight for Ireland's rights! Would not we all?" a young man Lenny did not know all but shouted.

Several concurred.

The debaters continued, at last agreeing that the concept of equality was central to their ideals.

Lenny added a waving banner over the harp bearing the word *Equality.*

"But we need a phrase to tie the music idea to reform." Russell ran his fingers through his wavy blond locks.

"The Voice of Ireland, the Voice of the Future."

Bunting's suggestion was the best she'd heard so far. Lenny drew a longer banner, curving around the bottom of the harp.

She had just started printing the words on the ribbon when Tone took the pad from her hand, looked intently at the harp she had drawn, and cried, "It's New Strung and Shall Be Heard!"

Debate stopped, and acclamation for the motto expanded to the new ideas their Irish harp should soon be singing.

Lenny put the words in the banner and framed the whole with an oval of laurel leaves.

Edward Bunting, looking over her shoulder, nodded in approval. His small, bright eyes shone behind his spectacles. "Well done, Miss Price. And what would you say to a great gathering of Irish harpists?"

"I think it would be brilliant. Will you propose it?"

"Indeed, soon. But I think our friends have quite enough on their minds this evening, don't you?"

Lenny grinned and nodded. Edward Bunting was a charming conspirator in his own quiet way, entirely as dedicated to his vision for Ireland as her politically radical friends were to theirs.

That was what made it all so bewildering. So many visions, so many theories, so many goals and notions of how to achieve them. And all these were entangled with her confused emotions. This was what Lenny had always longed for. And yet, could one live *always* at the center of upheaval?

She was aware of needing respite from conflict, and the concept of a harp gathering was inordinately soothing. Perhaps it was just because she wasn't accustomed to such a level of free disputation, but, in spite of its stimulation, the atmosphere raised a flag of concern within her. It was impossible to imagine a more cohesive group than that which she sat in. And yet they argued so hotly. Here, at the very birth of a society for unity, she had to admit to feeling unease about the practicality of unifying the land through political reform.

Perhaps Bunting was right. Perhaps the brightest future for Ireland lay in rediscovering her artistic past, which had been buried so deeply under the Ascendency fashion for English society. Lenny felt relaxation washing over her as if the warm sun shone on her head. The very idea of a festival focusing on music and poetry allayed her fear of war and conflict.

51

Apparently Lenny was not alone in catching the vision for a festival of Irish harpers, for a few months after her return to Price Manor, Mary Ann wrote:

> We are quite caught up in preparations for next summer's harp ball. Henry Joy and Atty are part of a committee who have declared themselves interested in everything which relates to the honor, as well as the prosperity, of our country, and so have opened a subscription for the cause of reviving and perpetuating the ancient music and poetry of Ireland. The plan is to assemble those descendants of our ancient bards, who possess all that remains of the music, poetry, and oral traditions of Ireland. You must plan now to be in Belfast for the great event. It is proposed to coincide with the Bastille commemoration next summer.

Lenny's friends appeared capable of operating on many fronts at once. It wasn't long until Mary Ann's letters were also informing her of the successful launch of a newspaper, the *Northern Star,* to promote the radical cause and the spread of United Irishmen throughout Antrim and Down as well as in Dublin.

Lenny was glad their plans seemed to be progressing well, but it was the harp ball and Irish music that focused her attention through the spring of 1792. When Thorpe Wimborne arrived one day for the inevitable music lesson, she called his attention to the advertisement in the *Northern Star* promising "a considerable sum in Premiums" to be distributed to the performers, according to their merits, and assuring that every performer would receive some award. "It does sound such a grand scheme, does it not?"

Wimborne smiled and arched one thin eyebrow. It was a stylish pose, the effect of which was much vitiated by his protruding ears and gangly person. "Thinking of contending for a prize, are you, Miss Carolenn?"

Lenny giggled the notion aside. "Oh, but I do wish I knew some old Gaelic tunes. Couldn't you teach us some?"

Sarah ran her fingers up a scale on her harpsichord. "Speak for yourself, sister. I have no notion of undertaking such coarse material."

Their tutor bowed. "I am certain your sister jests, Miss Price. No such music is published. Perhaps you would like to begin with your Vivaldi?"

But Lenny was not ready to lay aside the newspaper. "It says here that there have been three such harp balls in County Longford. They drew upwards of a thousand listeners, but only ten harpers. The last time there was such squabbling over the prizes that the sponsor refused to hold another." She put down the paper. "Must people squabble over *everything*? I do hope our festival won't be marred by such disputes. Surely musicians should be above that."

"Apparently you have more faith than the sponsoring committee," Wimborne said.

"What do you mean?"

"The object of promising prizes to all participants is obviously an attempt to stem discontent." Their teacher gave a nod to the harpsichordist to begin.

But before her sister could strike the first chord, Lenny said, "There were harpers in our own family—I've heard the Aunts AM talk about them. They moved out west. I don't suppose anyone knows where." She sighed. "Wouldn't it be *exciting* if one came to the festival?"

Sarah hit an impatient note. "What odd tastes you have, sister. I hope to goodness none of them is related to us."

"But don't you see, Sarah? It's the future of Ireland. Our future must be rooted in the traditions of our past."

Sarah's peal of laughter was a far more musical sound than anything Lenny was likely to produce on her flute. "You much relieve my mind, sister. I had feared for the radical notions you might take up with those reformist friends of yours. If a harp festival is to be their most revolutionary act, I believe we might all sleep easily in our beds."

Lenny opened her mouth to reply, but their tutor rapped sharply on his music stand, insistent that they begin.

The argument, though quelled at Price Manor, did not die. In an effort to quash counterrevolutionary efforts in France, the French Legislative Assembly declared war on Austria. Everywhere France's voteless citizens were donning the cap of liberty and arming themselves with pikes. French revolutionary sentiment was mounting to fever pitch. And the Belfast Harp Festival was to be held in celebration of this movement? As the fourteenth of July drew closer, Lenny was not even certain her father would allow her to attend the event.

"Celebrating the heritage of Irish music is one thing. Celebrating mayhem and mob rule in France—which they are now extending to their Austrian neighbors—is quite another." Archibald poked a fork at his fried sweetbreads without taking a bite.

Lenny looked at Thorpe Wimborne, who had been invited to stay to dinner. Surely her music master would support her desire to attend a music festival.

The tutor, however, took a quite different approach to the subject. "I would propose that any road leading to an earlier, s-simpler day is a proper way to travel. Does not all the turmoil we see prove Jean Jacque's thesis that society has removed man from the natural, perfect state in which God created him? If, through our own early music, we can return to the original world in which man was free and good and moral, would that not be a fine thing?"

"Bah! What nonsense you talk. All of you. Looking for political and moral salvation through music."

Lenny had seldom heard her father come so close to raising his voice.

Her time with the McCrackens had taught her the value of voicing her opinions, though. She needn't hide the fact that she possessed ideas of her own. Besides, focusing on the theoretical helped keep down the longings she still harbored for the leader of the movement in spite of her most sensible determinations.

She decided to mount her own defense. "Surely you'll grant it's less harmful than violent revolution, Father. And Mr. Burke would doubtless be most supportive of the ideals of the festival."

"Because he's an Irishman himself? You may be right. He has more than once landed himself in trouble with his constituents and been accused of papist leanings for the stands he's taken for Ireland."

"No, that's not what I meant." Lenny could see a softening in her father, and she was determined to press her full advantage. "Burke says that it's not merely the old social order that is being pulled down in France. He says the moral fervor of the revolution is causing a loss of inherited values—a destruction of the spiritual resources of society."

Archibald Price regarded his daughter openmouthed. "Indeed, he does. But where did you come by this?"

"Miss McCracken favors the thought of Rousseau, Father, but quite everything is read and discussed in that house."

Archibald took a long sip of wine before answering. "It is, indeed, the destruction of spiritual resources which concerns me. I have been reading a sermon published in commemoration of Wesley's death last year—he would agree with Rousseau to a point, Wimborne."

Archibald laid aside his white linen napkin and rose. In a moment he returned with an open volume in his hand. "'God made man upright, perfectly holy, and perfectly happy,' Wesley says. He does not, however lay the loss of this happy state to the building of cities. Man destroyed himself by rebelling against God. Man was created in the image of his Creator, but he lost that image by rebelling."

Her father laid down his book and gave her a solemn look. "I do not believe, daughter, and surely neither do you, that your harpers festival will succeed in restoring to man the lost image of God."

Lenny thought on her father's words as she prepared to attend the festival, for after that conversation he had given his consent. And truly, although she anticipated much pleasure, she could not say that she looked for Ireland's salvation in either the harp festival or the United Irishmen Society. Yet one must do something to work for the good, and she hadn't heard any better ideas proposed. Besides, Wolfe Tone would be there.

Thousands gathered in Belfast to celebrate the third anniversary of the fall of the Bastille. And by staying with her friends in Rosemary Lane, Lenny couldn't have been nearer the center of things.

She had not seen Mary Ann since the previous October, and she immediately noted a special shine on her friend's countenance. Before she could inquire as to the cause, however, Henry and Francis entered with Wolfe Tone. Lenny was struggling to control her emotions when she realized, from the light in Mary Ann's eyes, that Thomas Russell was with the company.

Their party went early to the opening of the three-day festival. The main assembly room was an elegant long hall, lined on one side with tall windows and on the other with walls decorated with round portraits and plaster garlands. The barrel ceiling was richly carved with floral bosses. A platform had been erected at the far end of the room.

Ten harpers, including one woman and a boy of fifteen, sat on the platform with their harps before them. As nearly all were from Ulster, Lenny's hopes of encountering a long-lost cousin from Connacht were dashed.

Also, she soon began to wonder whether Sarah had had a better estimate of the truth than she had with her romantic notions of the event. Six of the harpers were blind. Most were shabbily and carelessly dressed.

Mary Ann pointed out one very old man with flowing white hair. "That's Dennis Hempson. He's nearly a hundred, and the only one who plays with long, hooked nails."

Another blind man, well into his sixties, sat in the center of the group. He played a lilting, if somewhat thin, air on his harp.

"Arthur O'Neill," Mary Ann said.

Lenny noticed that, in contrast to the other performers, O'Neill was well dressed. As they drifted closer to the platform, she could see that the large silver buttons on his long coat bore the Hand of Ulster, the emblem of the High O'Neills of ancient time.

She raised a hand in greeting to Edward Bunting, who was sitting in a chair drawn up to the very edge of the stage.

He acknowledged her with a nod, then turned back immediately to an open notebook in which he was scribbling with great attention.

When, in a highly inflected Gaelic voice, Arthur O'Neill announced the name of his next tune, "An Chūilfhionn," Lenny was surprised to see Bunting taking down the title. "I didn't realize Mr. Bunting had the Irish."

Mary Ann smiled and shook her head. "He doesn't. The committee invited a specialist in the Irish language to attend and record the proceedings. He didn't come, so apparently Edward is attempting the task." She observed for a few moments, then laughed. "He seems quite consumed by the music, and certainly he's perfectly competent with musical notation. But I can't imagine attempting to record the titles in Gaelic. He must have devised some sort of phonetic code to work with."

The fashionable audience continued their conversations throughout the numbers, applauding sporadically for each performer and drifting in and out of the room. When O'Neill finished his first set of airs, he was led to a seat at the back of the platform by his attendant, and Charles Fanning of County Leitrim took the center seat. Fanning's playing was lively enough to attract the attention of some of the most vigorous conversationalists, and they paused to listen to his music.

The blind Rose Mooney was playing a sweet tune when Lenny happened to glance across the room. Her heart leaped to her throat. For a long moment she couldn't tear her gaze from Wolfe Tone, lounging against the fireplace, arms crossed, a bored look on his face.

Slowly Lenny turned back to the performer. The woman from County Meath plucked out a pleasant melody, which Bunting was recording note for note. It was a pity her cap and long white apron were so soiled. Surely the music would make more of a mark on society if the performers looked less disreputable. She turned to Mary Ann. "There is Mr. Tone. Shall we go see how he likes the music?"

Mary Ann laughed. "Indeed, let us go tease him."

They crossed to the aristocratic-appearing Tone.

"Really, sir, it won't do. It's much too bad of you to disparage our poor musicians."

Tone raised an eyebrow at her. "They're poor enough all right. Seven of them are downright execrable."

"Indeed, your opinion was quite plain to see from across the room."

He ignored her commentary on his behavior. "Fanning is far the best, of course." Tone yawned. "I wonder that they continue at this. There can be no musical discovery here. I believe all the good Irish airs are already written."

Thomas Russell joined them then, and Mary Ann smiled.

Whatever ideas some might have had for the unifying power of music and national heritage, it was clear that Wolfe Tone saw little to hope for in that direction. The next harper had played only a few chords when Tone shook his head. "Strum, strum, and be hanged." He made an abrupt bow to the ladies and strode from the room.

Russell's bow was more gallant, but he followed his friend.

Lenny watched Mary Ann's gaze follow the army officer from the room. She had never broached the subject before, but somehow the atmosphere seemed conducive today. "You mentioned once that Mr. Russell's affections were attached. Is it a lady of my acquaintance?"

"Alas." Mary Ann sighed. "I fear his heart is broken. His lady chose another."

"Ah!" Lenny could scarcely hide the fact that she considered this good news on her friend's account. "Poor Mr. Russell, indeed. But perhaps—in time—he might be consoled with another of far greater worth. And then he would count such misfortune a blessing."

Mary Ann smiled. "You are a dear friend. We shall see. In time." She gazed around the room absently. "I do declare, Mr. Tone might have been right. All these melodies are beginning to sound alike. My time could be better employed sewing for the poor!"

Lenny nodded to Evan and Thorpe Wimborne, who were seated near the back with some men she had seen at the McCrackens' last October. It would be pleasant to visit with them, especially with such agreeable melodies floating on the air—at least *she* found them agreeable—but she accompanied her friend.

The next day's weather was dismal, so the ladies waited indoors, sipping hot chocolate and nibbling biscuits by the fire until, finally, the rain seemed to be dashing itself against the window with less vigor and they might venture out on foot without encountering too much violence to their carefully coiffed hair. Lenny was thankful that she had been obedient to the urging of Sarah and her mother and had one of the fashionable new shawl dresses made. The warm silk and wool shawl stitched onto the dress was just the thing for such inclement weather.

Apparently few shared Wolfe Tone's poor opinion of the harpers. Today an even larger gathering filled the assembly rooms.

"*Casadh an tSugāin.*" Arthur O'Neill announced the piece he was to play next, and Edward Bunting, sitting just below the platform, as if he hadn't moved since the day before, bent over his notebook.

As Mary Ann chatted with acquaintances, Lenny gazed around the fashionable assembly. The waving plume on a beaded purple turban caught her eye. The wearer of the turban waved a plump gloved hand.

Lenny turned to Mary Ann. "Will you excuse me? I see my Lanark aunts. I must pay my respects."

Aunt Marguerite, wearing a flowing velvet cloak that matched the turban, made room for Lenny to perch on one of the two chairs she occupied. "Isn't this dear? Can you imagine anything more charming than the music of our brave, grand bards of old?" The ostrich feather swayed. "One can just imagine oneself riding into battle beside Brian Boru."

The image was indeed formidable. Lenny bit her lip. "I'm pleased to see you, Aunt Marguerite." She turned to the other side. "And Aunt Adelaide."

Adelaide sat pole-erect in her trim brown jacket and velvet beret. "Marguerite always was easily amused," she said, sniffing. "Should have a Lanark to show them how it's done. Well, actually our harpers were named MacHenry—but blood will out. Still, that Rose Mooney woman plays tolerably well, I'll allow. And one must do one's part to support civic efforts."

"Yes, indeed," Marguerite took up the idea with fervor. "Especially with our dear Jay making such an effort. It quite makes one shudder to think of the bravery of our dear, dear boys for our beloved homeland."

"Jay is here?" Lenny looked around for her cousin. He must have escorted the aunts. But what else he had done of valiant patriotism would be a surprise to Lenny. Joining the Belfast Volunteers was hardly a matter of extremist bravado.

"I wonder you haven't heard. Or that your Evan hasn't followed his example." The tassels on Marguerite's embroidered silk reticule quivered with the rest of her.

"I believe my brother will be here later. Perhaps you can ask him." Lenny had no notion as to what Auntie M was referring, but she did not care to have any aspersions cast on her brother's courage. "I have always known Evan to do the right thing."

"Oh, yes, my dear, quite so, quite so. Honor runs deep in our family—even in those less closely connected. How often have I felt the stirring in my own bosom whenever there is call to duty and country."

"Aunt Marguerite, please. What has Jay done?"

"Why, nothing less remarkable than joining the Bleary Boys!" She paused for effect. "Now, what do you think of that?"

Lenny thought very little of it. She had never heard of the Bleary Boys.

"Surely you know, my dear. You've heard of those fine, stalwart Peep o' Day Boys in Armagh?"

That she had. Nowhere had the tolerant spirit of the Dunganon Convention deteriorated faster than in Armagh, where sectarian gangs had been brawling for years. Recently the Catholics had been calling themselves the Defenders, whereas the Protestants chose the name Peep o' Day Boys. A year ago there had been a horrible affray when Defenders attacked a schoolmaster's home and cut out his tongue as well as that of his wife and her young brother. The affair had been brought on by competition over land and linen prices—and by desires for freedom fanned by the French Revolution.

"But what can all this have to do with Jay?"

"Why the Bleary Boys have the same high determination to defend their homes as the Peep o' Days." Auntie M dabbed at her eyes with a lace handkerchief. "Such noble sentiment."

"Yes, I'm sure." Actually, Lenny was sure of very little except her determination to learn something about this association her cousin had joined. In the meantime she sought about in her mind for a less controversial topic.

Aunt Adelaide was the one to curb her effusive sister. "Marguerite, I'd remind you to keep your tongue quiet in your head if you don't want to end up like that schoolmaster's wife."

Aunt M clapped a hand over her mouth. "Whatever can you mean, Addie?"

Aunt A looked over each shoulder before replying. "Spies."

Marguerite laughed loudly enough to cause several heads to turn with a quelling look, even though the tune coming from the platform at the other end of the room was a particularly scratchy one. "Oh, Addie, how unlike you to make such a jest. As if a *spy* could be interested in anything *I* would have to say."

Adelaide was not amused. "I assure you I make no jest. It is common knowledge that Lord Londonderry views anyone who differs with the government on any issue to be his personal enemy. The entire county is quite riddled with a network of informers."

Lenny found such idle tales too exasperating to be borne. "Oh, aunts, you must excuse me. I see my brother has just come in. I must greet him." She dipped a curtsy and fled.

Then Lenny recognized the young man with whom Evan was so

454

deep in conversation. She hadn't seen Sheldon Ramsey for more than a year now. His eyes bore a more intense sparkle than she had remembered, didn't they? And his soft brown hair more wavy.

Both men bowed, but she begged them to continue their conversation. She had caught enough to know they weren't discussing politics, and for once she welcomed a more soothing subject, especially as Charles Fanning was now performing.

A plaintive melody wafted down the room, a tune of yearning that made a listener feel homesick even in her native land. It created a sense of loss and longing that seemed a perfect background for Evan and Sheldon's discussion of spiritual matters.

"It is a pretty theory of yours, Ramsey, but I fear I see very little of the divine image in those around me. And even less in myself. Wesley was too optimistic about human nature."

"Indeed not. Wesley would say that it is precisely because of our human failures that we need God dwelling in us. Until our spirits are renewed, we can have no communion with the Almighty."

The reference to Wesley reminded Lenny of something she had wondered when she heard that the preacher had died. "Perhaps you can tell me, Sheldon—" Suddenly it seemed very forward to be calling this young man by his Christian name.

But he didn't seem to mind. He turned to her, all attention. "Yes, please. I should be so happy to help if I can."

"Well, it had occurred to me to wonder—that is, I recall Mr. Wesley's sermon in Newtownards—" She paused.

He smiled and nodded encouragingly.

"He recounted Hobbes's departure from this life as testimony to the unsatisfying nature of his philosophy. So I wondered, were *Wesley's* final words hopeful?"

Now Sheldon's smile was brilliant. Had she ever seen Sheldon Ramsey smile before? He had always been so painfully shy, it was hard to believe the transformation. "Indeed, yes. It was just a year ago. Knowing his life on this earth was near the end, Wesley calmly took to his bed. That evening a group of his friends gathered around him. Someone asked him what he would say. 'Nothing,' he replied, 'but that God is with us.' Then he repeated the thanksgiving that he had always used after meals, 'We thank Thee, O Lord, for these and all Thy mercies; bless the church and the king; and grant us truth and peace, through Jesus Christ our Lord, forever and ever.' Then he slept."

Lenny was amazed at how deeply the account touched her. She pictured it in her mind—the aged holy man with long white hair, propped on pillows, his friends and family around him, praising the

God he had loved and served all his life. "That's beautiful," she murmured. "When it comes down to it, what more could one ask?"

"Yes!"

Sheldon turned to her with such warmth that she thought he was going to grasp her hand. She took a step backward.

"Oh, forgive my enthusiasm, Miss Price. It's just that you so perfectly expressed my own thoughts when I heard of the event. As a matter of fact, that was when I decided."

"Decided?"

"To take holy orders. I go up to Oxford next term."

"But why would you do that? I mean, I thought you would go into the linen-draping business with your father."

"Yes, that is what I had always rather thought—but now I see how much more good I might do working for men's souls rather than to dress their bodies. I mean—when one grasps the vision that it is possible to restore the relationship that was lost at the Fall—well, nothing else seems very important."

"That's . . . er . . . amazing, Mr. Ramsey—Sheldon." She looked at the floor, then over his shoulder, then at her hands. "I'm very happy for you. Now I'm sure you'll excuse me. I must return to my friends."

Wolfe Tone, Thomas Russell, and Henry Joy McCracken had joined Mary Ann. Tone seemed even more bored with the music than he had been the day before. Lenny sat with them in one of the Sheraton chairs that offered conversation grouping at the side of the room.

"What remarkable ladies you were conversing with, Miss Price."

Lenny started and looked up at Wolfe Tone. "My Lanark aunts, sir." She felt suddenly so shy she could hardly get the words out.

"Lanark? I had no notion they were relations of yours, Miss Price."

"You know them?"

"Indeed. Guilford Lanark is a leading member of the Catholic Committee. I'm proud to be associated with him."

Lenny dropped her head. "Alas, sir. You refer to the Seaton Court Lanarks. I fear there is not much interchange with that family branch. The Lanarks' Bawn aunts are of a quite different viewpoint."

Tone smiled his understanding. "Ah, I see."

The warmth of his smile encouraged Lenny to continue. "I am glad of a chance to talk to you, Mr. Tone. I wanted to ask your opinion of these organizations people are talking about."

"And what organizations are those?"

"Peep o' Day Boys, Defenders, Bleary Boys . . ."

He made an impatient sound. "Do you really need to ask, Miss Price? There could hardly be anything to which I am more opposed than sectarian strife." He raised his fine nose and sniffed. "Protestant laborers, encouraged by their landlords, fomenting endless quarrels— and the Defenders just as bad. Only good that can come of it is that the more cottages they burn, crops they destroy, and cattle they maim, the more clearly they spell out the need for Irishmen to unite. What good can possibly come from brawling, evictions, and deaths? As things stand, what good would it be if England vanished from the face of the earth? It would make little difference. Irishmen would still be fighting each other!"

As they returned the next day for the final performance of the festival, Wolfe Tone's statement hung over Lenny like a small black cloud. He had tossed off the words like a man throwing a silk scarf over his shoulder, but the truth of the matter had left her feeling breathless.

What *did* it matter whether England, France, or Spain influenced Irish politics? Even if the unimaginable happened and no foreign power wielded influence over their small country, what would be accomplished if Irishmen continued to squabble among themselves? And what hope was there of changing anything so endemic to the Irish nature as bickering?

Even former harp festivals had ended in altercations over the awarding of prize money. Would it be so here? The Belfast Harp Ball had been a grand social event. But would anything of lasting value come from it?

When the festival closed a few hours later, it did seem unlikely that they had accomplished much beyond providing society a pleasant gathering place during three days of inclement weather. The top awards were made to Charles Fanning, Arthur O'Neill, and Rose Mooney, in that order—the same as at earlier festivals. Lenny believed the awards fair, but the prizes aroused little excitement even among the harpers.

It was Edward Bunting, who had spent the past three days sitting by the stage, recording every word spoken and note played, who emerged as triumphant as if he had been awarded all the prize money in a golden pot.

"And wasn't that just the grandest event you've ever witnessed?" Bunting's black suit was rumpled, his collar points limp, and his white cravat askew, but his cheeks were pink and his eyes bright.

If Lenny didn't know better, she would have thought the young man had fallen in love. "It was very pleasant," she replied with as much enthusiasm as she could muster. "I was very happy for a visit with many old friends."

"Yes, yes, I daresay. But the music! The music! Never before written down. In a few years it would have been lost." He patted his thick notebook, from which papers hung on every side. "But I have it all right here. Recorded for posterity. I shall publish a volume: *General Collection of Ancient Irish Music.*"

She smiled. "What a fine notion. I should be very happy of a copy, sir."

Bunting bowed. "You shall have a copy, Miss Price. And of all its successors too."

"How is that?"

"Indeed, I am most determined. These past days have shown me the way. A lifetime work it is, but, oh, so worthily spent. I shall travel Ireland from Derry to Kerry, from Dublin to Donegal. I'll search out all the authentic harpers. None shall escape me. The old bardic music shall become one of our great national treasures."

Henry Joy McCracken joined them just in time to hear the last sentence. "A fine thing, man, fine. The Belfast Reading Society will back you in it, I've no doubt. I shall put my name down as your first subscriber."

Lenny mentioned her family connection with a harper somewhere in Donegal. Bunting made a note, and the two men turned to matters of organizing such an undertaking.

Lenny was far quieter than usual when she returned home to Price Manor the following week. The music had been pleasant but not particularly memorable. The images that burned in her thoughts were of the young men afire with such diverse visions for the future: Sheldon Ramsey—who would take holy orders that he might change the country through turning men's souls to God; Jay Lanark—who would protect his land by fighting those who challenged his rights; Wolfe Tone—who would bring good to the nation by uniting Irishmen; Edward Bunting—who would build the future by preserving the heritage of the past. Each was so certain his path was best that he was willing to dedicate his life to his chosen course. But who was right?

She found her brother and Thorpe Wimborne talking in the drawing room. Wimborne showed intense curiosity about Jay Lanark's new allegiance, but with a wave of his wrist he dismissed Bunting's venturing across Ireland to collect old tunes. He yawned over her report of Sheldon Ramsey's religious zeal but then smiled indulgently. "Oh, yes, there were many s-such in my class in university. Put one in mind of Wesley's Holy Club." But the tutor's interest returned when she talked of the United Irishmen.

"I wonder you don't join them yourself, sir," Lenny suggested.

"Indeed, I would if Mr. Cleland thought it proper. The vicar says a man of the church can't be too careful about his associations."

Lenny wandered listlessly from the room. Everything seemed vague and purposeless. Perhaps it was just the contrast of being back in the quiet country after a week with the McCrackens, where all was so lively and everyone driving toward such elevated goals. But the more time she spent with zealous advocates for causes, the more confused she was. Why couldn't she just be like Sarah and think of nothing but fashions and beaus?

"And why that frown on your lovely brow, my daughter?" Archibald Price set aside the book he was reading.

Lenny's wanderings had taken her to her father's office. She knew that she had instinctively come to the one person who might understand her vague questions.

He smiled indulgently. "You are asking why mankind is selfish and confused, blown here and there by transitory whims?"

Lenny clapped her hands. "Oh, yes, Father. Thank you. Somehow just having my question put into words gives me hope of finding an answer."

"And you can take heart from the fact that you're not the first to ask it." Archibald leaned to a bookcase beside his desk and drew out a well-read volume. "I was visiting with an old friend just recently. That's what reading is, you know—exchanging ideas with the minds of great men."

Lenny groaned inwardly at the sight of the volume of sermons her father held. Still, the answers Wesley found had provided solid ground to the last. Perhaps he deserved listening to. She held out her hand for the volume and read where her father's finger pointed.

> By rebelling against the Divine, man destroyed himself, lost the favor and the image of God and entailed sin, with its attendant pain, on mankind and all his posterity.

She nodded. Indeed, everywhere she looked she saw people intent on destroying themselves even as they worked for freedom and fulfillment. Then she read on.

> Yet man's merciful Creator did not leave him in this helpless, hopeless state: He appointed His Son, His well-beloved Son, "who is the brightness of His glory, the express image of His person," to be the Savior of men; the great Physician who, by His almighty Spirit, should heal the sickness of their souls, and restore them not only to the favor but to "the image of God."

"Yes." She handed the volume back. "That's beautiful. I should be very happy to think it true."

One truth, certainly, was undeniable. Man had lost the image of his Creator. But was it because of sin, as Wesley believed, or because of society, as Rousseau believed? Was the solution to be found in reconciliation to God through faith or in return to nature through politics?

52

In the coming months Lenny enjoyed the achievement of her seventeenth year, the age at which carefully brought up young ladies were officially allowed into society and granted such privileges as a place at the adult table. Lenny, however, through her friendship with the McCrackens and because of her father's enjoyment of her company, had long known such freedoms. Being officially eligible for male attention now meant less than nothing to her. The only man her heart could care for was married and expecting his third child in Dublin.

The only accomplishment her age brought her was no longer being required to sew on hopeless samplers or to take music lessons. Her freedom from the schoolroom, however, did not mean that Price Manor saw any less of the gawky Mr. Wimborne. Rather the contrary, for as Sarah approached her twentieth year, the tutor increased his pursuit. Lenny couldn't understand why Sarah didn't send her ungainly suitor packing.

"He amuses me," Sarah would say offhandedly. "And he is an excellent dancer, for all that his feet are so enormous."

Lenny had to admit that she was glad enough of Thorpe Wimborne's presence when he and her father discussed affairs over their newspapers. And, indeed, one must read a newspaper or converse with those who did during 1793 and 1794. Affairs of great moment were taking place in France.

In January 1793, the revolutionaries brought King Louis XVI to trial. The American revolutionary leader Thomas Paine, who had been elected to a seat in the French National Convention, tried to save the king's life by arguing in favor of banishment. But the death sentence was handed down. One week later, King Louis was led to the Place de la Révolution and guillotined. Ten days later, France declared war on England.

Lenny wondered what effect this turn of events would have on her United Irishmen friends. And more specifically, what must Wolfe Tone be feeling, he who had shared so passionately in France's high ideals of liberty, equality, and fraternity?

Others wondered, too. It was the first question Wimborne asked Evan when he came home from university that summer.

Evan shrugged. "I've had little time for political meetings. But I've seen no lessening of activities. I've heard that even Tone doubts the wisdom of copying Irish Volunteer uniforms directly from that of the French army."

"I don't wonder that he would." Wimborne's nod always made Lenny choke back a giggle, because it did so look as if his head were loose. "It does rather look like flying in the t–teeth of the government."

But there was little to giggle about that autumn. The news became increasingly horrifying. The radical Robespierre, who ruled the Committee of Public Safety, decreed death for those he considered enemies of the Revolution. Thousands were arrested and guillotined—with or without trial. Thousands more languished in prison, where many died. The papers were calling it the Reign of Terror.

And Lenny's heart went out to her hero. What would he do now? Where could the United Irish look when their model was in such shambles?

Archibald lowered his *Belfast News Letter*, wagging his head. "What would they expect? Burke predicted it years ago. You can't tear down all the safeguards of church, state, and tradition and expect to maintain a civilized society. Reforms must be *gradual*. Wrongs must be redressed step by step. Killing the king, killing the nobles, killing all those who dispute within the party, then killing each other is what you would expect from people who have no respect for their traditions. Tradition and sentiment keep society together."

Lenny put her own paper aside. In the heat of such exciting events, it had become fashionable for ladies as well to read newspapers. In London society, women even took subscriptions to reading rooms, where they read newspapers in public. So now Lenny could do so openly without fearing reprimand from her mother.

"Poor Marie-Antoinette. She seemed a rather silly creature, but I can't believe she did anything deserving to be guillotined."

"Ah, but Burke would say that the guillotine is the logical outcome of insisting that political and moral duty come from pure reason rather than collective experience and traditions." Archibald leaned forward, and his eyes glowed. "The Terror is implicit in the French Revolution. Demands of immediate, complete change are not only unrealistic but also dangerous. The danger lies in adopting abstract theories that have no connections to historical experience.

"And now Robespierre has announced a new policy—de-Christianization." Archibald continued to hold the floor. "No religious ceremonies to be allowed outside churches. Some vague form of Deism is to replace Christianity. Pity Rousseau isn't alive now. I wonder what he would think of his handiwork."

"But J–Jean Jacques deplored revolution. Said so in his *Confessions*." The *Northern Star* crinkled in Wimborne's hands.

"Ideas have a way of taking on a life of their own. Even good ideas can have bad consequences if pushed too far," Archibald replied.

Throughout the autumn, Lenny thought many times about her father's comment. Was he right that even good ideas could cause harm? What about her Theobald's idea for Irish unity? Surely a good idea if ever there was one. Was it in danger of being pushed too far? Of causing harm? That November, her questions mounted, and she longed even more to discuss such ideas with someone. But her father had accompanied Evan when he returned to Dublin for his final year at university and would remain there for some time on a matter of business.

Although she continued corresponding with Mary Ann, replies sometimes took weeks, whereas news and questions mounted daily. A Festival of Liberty in Paris. People marching in the streets. All the churches in Paris closed. The former Cathedral of Notre-Dame stripped of all Christian symbols. The great building reconsecrated as a temple to Reason.

Was this, then, the culmination of the belief that Reason was leading mankind to all knowledge and happiness? How *reasonable* was the French Revolution?

"*Urrgh!*" Lenny hit the arm of her chair in frustration.

Her mother looked up from her delicate needlework. "Carolenn, dear. That really won't do. I've told you so many times not to make such unladylike noises. And your expression—you look quite out of sorts."

"I *am* out of sorts. There's nothing I despise more than illogic. Mob rule, anarchy, slaughter. How can they call this *reason?*"

"I really have no notion what you're talking about, Carolenn." Sarah lay aside a packet of pattern cards. "But I can't think it could be worth getting so worked up over."

Lenny made no pretense of a ladylike exit. She tossed the paper to the floor and stalked from the room. Bessie. She hadn't had a good conversation with Bessie for ages. And she was certain to get more sense out of her than from her sister.

Lenny plunked herself down on her favorite rock. "You don't know how lucky you are to be a cow, Bessie. I always thought reason was the very thing that kept us all from being beasts, but it seems reason has turned people into beasts in Paris." She hadn't thought to bring a shawl, nor had she realized that the November fog had settled quite so thickly. Still, the warmth of her thoughts carried her forward. "Burke, Hume—even Wesley—laud reason. But if reason leads to a reign of terror, what hope is there for any of us?"

"Reason is a useful guide. Not an end in all."

Lenny jumped to her feet. Bessie swished her tail, clearing away a strip of fog. But Bessie had not spoken. Lenny sat down again. "Oh, Sheldon. Where did you come from? Aren't you at Oxford?"

"My mother was ill. Father thought it advisable for me to come home. Fortunately the danger is past now. I'll be returning to university shortly. He asked me to bring this volume of sermons for your father."

"You've come all this way on foot?"

Sheldon looked at the ground, his former shyness seeming to return. "Forgive me, Carolenn. Or would you rather I call you Miss Price?"

"Some family members call me Lenny. I'm sure you're much like a brother—cousin, at least."

"Yes. Well, do forgive me. I'm rather afraid I followed you here when I saw you leaving the house."

"I'm glad you did. I've had no one sensible to talk to for days and days."

"So you took refuge in dialoguing with Bessie?"

"Precisely. Except it's more of a monologue. What was that you said when you materialized from the fog?"

"I said reason is a useful guide—not an end in all."

"And turning Notre-Dame Cathedral into a temple to Reason made reason an object of worship, rather than a tool." Lenny spoke slowly, working out her thoughts.

Sheldon nodded. "Reason can *lead* to faith—and the two of them to fulfillment—as Wesley taught. But pushed beyond its usefulness— made to stand alone—it can lead to the horrors of the Reign of Terror."

"But how do you know when you've pushed too far?" Lenny began to shiver uncontrollably.

Sheldon wrapped her in his long-skirted greatcoat. Its wide revers and high velvet collar were warm around her neck.

"That's why you need balance—Scripture, reason, tradition, experience. France threw out Scripture and tradition and opted for a system with which no one has had any experience. Is it any wonder things got out of balance?"

They began walking slowly back toward the house.

"But where will it all end? A hundred people guillotined every day, the paper said. Blood runs in the street. And they call it *reason*. What will happen next?"

Sheldon helped her over the stile. "Edmund Burke predicts the rise of a Caesar-like dictator—a despotic figure that will bring order out of this chaos—but at the price of any liberties that have been gained."

"Yes, that seems likely in France. But I mean *here*. In Ireland. So many are devoted to the principles of the French Revolution." The image of Wolfe Tone filled her mind. "Will we follow France's path? Will there be blood in the streets of Dublin?"

Part of Lenny's question was answered the next summer when France's Reign of Terror ended with the fall of the man who had started so much of it. On July 28, 1794, Maximilien François de Robespierre was led to the guillotine himself.

But France's troubles did not end with the life of one radical. Inflation soared. Despair engulfed the people, though the French army marched to victory.

At Westminster, Parliament took measures to secure Britain's survival. Political dissent was not to be tolerated at such a dangerous time. Security measures were rushed through the Irish House of Commons.

Lenny learned of it first in a hastily written letter from Mary Ann: "A perfect inquisition reigns. Leaders of the United Irishmen in Dublin have been arrested."

Lenny's eyes blurred, and she stifled a sob before she could read on. The next words, though, brought a sigh of relief.

> Thankfully, Tone is still free and is negotiating with France for support. But my brother fears many fine men will lie in prison without trial for who knows how long? Defenders have been publicly executed in Dublin with every display of cruelty and humiliation. I fear we have our own *Petite Terror*.

Lenny set the letter aside. She would reread it later.

Feeling enormously isolated from affairs in the great world, she began pestering her father daily to go into Newtownards to collect the post. The newspapers were all very fine for delivering news of Paris and London, but they achieved nothing like a personal letter when one worried ceaselessly about friends in Belfast and Dublin.

"I am sorry, Lenny, but I've far too much business to see to here today," Archibald said one morning. He looked up from his bookkeeping and rubbed his eyes.

Lenny understood. The invasion of Ireland loomed as a fearful possibility, and, with few troops to be spared from the Continent, the government had formed regiments of Yeomanry. That meant every sheepman and linen grower in Ulster was pressed to produce more and faster, for the Yeomen must be outfitted.

She nodded and turned away with slumping shoulders. Did she dare attempt going herself? She could easily ride that far and back, but how would she explain the letters she returned with?

"Miss C-Carolenn, I have not seen you pout so since you left the schoolroom."

She jerked her head up and sucked in her lower lip. Sarah had mentioned that Thorpe Wimborne was to come today because she had a new piece she wanted help with, but Lenny had paid little attention to the information.

"Might I hope to be of s-service?"

She could never understand how one so ill-proportioned could bow so gracefully. Lenny sighed. "It's of little moment when one considers the wider world. But I did hope to have received a letter from Mary Ann today. And I had one to post to her as well." She pulled a pale blue rectangle from her pocket.

Thorpe extended his long, thin hand. "I should be most honored to be of service."

"Were you going to Newtownards soon, then?"

"Indeed. As a matter of f-fact, I am to meet with Lord Londonderry this afternoon."

"In that case, I thank you for your service!" She dropped the letter into his hand.

It was the next morning, as Sarah plunked determinedly at the harpsichord, that Lenny received Mary Ann's letter. With the tip of a penknife she carefully lifted the wafer of wax and turned to her friend's news. If she was looking for comfort, however, she was to be disappointed.

Reform has been driven underground. It seems that now there are to be *secret* societies of United Irishmen. Henry says we must organize on a military basis. Indeed, street scuffles become quite common. Henry was involved in one just last night. It is become a common saying on careless lips that the country will never know peace till Belfast is in ashes. It is also said that, as the government has stifled moderate opinion all over Ireland, the extremists have gone underground and are centered in Belfast. My brother laments that the moderate men seem sound asleep.

There is much secret action. Our William's brave wife, Rose Ann, has joined the United Irishwomen. But I deplore mole work. It goes against my nature. I hope to have better news soon and long to see you. Will you come to Belfast? Henry has hopes of seeing your brother in May. I believe he hopes to interest him in a position. Do come with him then.

Lenny folded the letter carefully and placed it in the small locked chest on the writing desk, where she kept all her letters. She was just about to drop it in when she saw that the top letter was folded oddly. That was strange. She was so careful with her correspondence. She smoothed the ivory vellum and straightened the contents of the box, then went off to find her brother. Henry McCracken's news of a job would be welcome indeed.

Since completing his university work, Evan had applied for more than one government situation. He had interviewed with two or three Belfast lawyers, but no position had opened. Just last night he returned discouraged from Armagh. Since Catholics had won the right to enter the legal profession three years ago, positions were harder to obtain—although all the Price family who had opinions on such things were solidly behind Catholic emancipation.

Last year Catholics had been given the vote, largely due to the efforts of a young Dublin lawyer, Daniel O'Connell, whose gift for oratory enabled him to use the courts as a forum. Only one disability remained—the right to sit in Parliament. But not for long, surely. They expected good news on that subject daily.

She found Evan just finishing a late breakfast.

"McCracken might have a suitable job for me? Well, that is good news. I shall definitely go to Belfast in May."

"Evan?" Lenny folded her hands behind her and sucked in one corner of her mouth. It was a pose she had always found effective with her brother.

"Yes?"

"She invited me too."

Evan's brown eyes twinkled. "I can't think why. Nuisance that you are." His slow smile curled his lips. "Only fair to spare the family here, though, I suppose."

She skipped from the room. Would Wolfe Tone be in Belfast? Her mother had been at her to visit the dressmaker. Now Lenny had a reason to comply. Perhaps a gown of yellow damask?

A few days later, Lenny returned from the dressmaker, her head full of visions of the grand time she would have with her friends in Belfast —and the new, high-waisted dress with puffed sleeves that she would wear. At her mother's urging she had even ordered an embroidered shawl and satin slippers with ribbon lacings to complete the outfit.

She tripped lightly into her father's office. "Oh, Father, the new fabrics are . . ." Then she looked from his face to the newspaper in his hand. "What has happened? Is it the French? Have they attacked? Uncle Douglas in the Yeomanry, has he been shot?"

"No, it hasn't come to military action yet. But it may soon. And not from the French but from our own people, I fear. Pitt has drawn back."

"What? There is not to be complete emancipation?" Lenny sank into a chair. She knew what a blow this would be to her United Irish friends, who so strongly supported the Catholic Committee.

"King George is adamant against it. Pitt says the time is not yet." Archibald lowered his head.

"It's a grave mistake." Evan spoke from across the room. "They can have no notion in England of the unrest that will create here. Dashing moderate opinion will only allow the extremists on either side to have their way."

It had been long since Lenny had felt that chill of apprehension travel up her spine. She recalled the high hopes of recent times: the celebration of the fall of the Bastille, the formation of the United Irishmen, the Belfast Harp Festival. Was all they had gained to go for nothing? There would be more hopeful news soon.

But the next morning at a late breakfast, Lenny needed only one look at Evan to know that the news was not good. "You've heard from Dublin, brother?"

He nodded. "Wolfe Tone has been found out negotiating with the French for armaments."

The words were still ringing in her ears when it seemed they hit the pit of her stomach. "Found out? What does that mean? Is he taken up?" She felt she couldn't breathe.

"No one knows for sure. It is believed a spy reported on him and he had been watched for some time."

"Is he to be hanged?" The words nearly choked her. That handsome, vibrant man, so idealistic and energetic for the future of Ireland. This couldn't be. Lenny had thought herself much recovered from her schoolgirl crush, but now she knew her emotions were still strongly engaged.

Evan looked over his shoulder to be sure no servants were listening. "He has been given opportunity to escape. The government fears bringing him to justice for dread of making him into a martyr."

Her anxiety eased slightly, but her next thought was for the wider issue. "But, Evan . . . negotiating with *France?* We are at war with them!" She was not so befuddled that she couldn't see the moral question.

"The opinion seems to be that England is at war with France but Ireland is not—and may find her friends where she will."

"And what do you say?" She had always known her brother to be the most cautious of men.

"I am not prepared to take a position. It is a most tangled affair. And one that will lead to great danger if not handled with enormous delicacy."

Mary Ann's next letter reflected the accuracy of Evan's assessment. "Belfast grows sullen. Shopkeepers protested the failure of emancipation by closing their businesses. Harry goes about his work with greater intensity. Where it will lead I don't like to think."

In spite of, or perhaps because of, the tensions, Lenny wished even more ardently to see Mary Ann. Her older friend, living in the heart of affairs, would know so much more what was happening. Lenny felt herself divided. On one hand, she wanted to be at the center of events, knowing what was happening and playing a part. But another side of her dreaded the turmoil and danger. If Ireland were to be torn by revolution, she would not want to be here. For all her interest in politics, she would not have wanted to live in Paris during the Terror.

53

"Oh, yes, I'm quite convinced that the entire borough is simply crawling with turbulent persons." Aunt Marguerite looked over both shoulders, and Lenny was positive that if her corpulent aunt had been more agile she would have sunk to her knees to be certain there were no rebels under the sofa.

"Turbulent persons being defined as those who disagree with Lord Londonderry?" Lenny set her tea on the sideboard. While her head was turned, she winked at Evan.

He quite often disagreed with Lord Londonderry, who had succeeded to the vast estates once owned by the Montgomery family. As landlord of most of Newtown and the Ards, he controlled the borough.

"Indeed, I mean all those disaffected persons who give offense to the government and make it quite necessary for neighbor to keep watch on neighbor."

"I believe that's more generally called spying and rumormongering, Auntie M." Evan could be assured of being forgiven his cheekiness for he accompanied his words with passing to his aunt the tray of rich lemon cheesecakes.

She selected the one with the thickest pastry, then licked her fingers. "And now that odious liberal newspaper is printing these letters ridiculing poor Lord Londonderry and those who give him information. I should think the man quite derelict in his duty if he *didn't* keep informed on events."

Lenny was determined to stick up for her friend's newspaper. "Do you mean the stories of Lord Mountmumble, Squire Firebrand, and Billy Bluff? I find them quite humorous. And with so much unpleasantness to read about these days, I think we can all do with a chuckle when we can get it."

Aunt M brushed the crumbs from her bosom and leaned forward. "Yes, yes, but do tell me—all the world knows Mountmumble is Lord Londonderry, and some say Firebrand is Mr. Cleland. But *who* could Billy Bluff be? Oh, do say you have some idea!"

"Some poor farmer so desperate for a farthing that he would sell his neighbors' tattling." Evan was dismissive. "Most of which is in the newspapers anyway."

Marguerite turned quite pale. "No, you don't say! Reading newspapers is considered turbulent? Should Douglas cancel his subscription, do you think?"

"As a member of the Yeomanry, I should think our uncle's loyalties are above suspicion."

Evan's words soothed Aunt M, but Lenny couldn't help thinking that people had been guillotined in Paris for less than reading liberal papers. The idea of their quiet neighborhood's being riddled with informers made her distinctly uncomfortable.

She rose abruptly. "Well, we really must be on our way. Our friends are expecting us in Belfast this evening, but we did just want to call in and see how Aunt Adelaide is feeling."

"Oh, my poor, dear sister. So kind of you to call. I do know she'll be much affected by your attention. I fear it's her nerves. With the French preparing to attack our very homes at any minute, we might all do best to take to our beds."

"I wonder that you haven't moved back into the bawn, Auntie."

Evan's teasing only further distressed his aunt. "Oh, do you think we ought? I wonder that Douglas hasn't thought of it. And him off drilling with the Yeomen. I shall speak to Jay."

"Yes, do that. Cleaning out the cowshed could make a useful activity for his Bleary Boys. Pretend the straw piles are Defenders."

Marguerite looked out the curtained window of her drawing room to where the south tower of the bawn could just be seen beyond the orchard. "Perhaps you're right, but it would be most awfully uncomfortable."

Lenny gave her aunt an impulsive hug. "Don't even think of such a thing, auntie. Evan is a horrid child to tease you so. You're perfectly safe here."

Marguerite brightened. "Yes, and Adelaide couldn't be moved in her delicate state. And, of course, I couldn't possibly leave her."

"The cow shed would be far too drafty for an invalid." Evan picked up the plump hand resting on his aunt's purple satin lap and bowed over it. "Forgive me, auntie. It was wicked of me to tease you."

Lenny could barely restrain herself from skipping to the carriage. The duty call to inquire after Aunt Adelaide's health was their last obligation. Now she and Evan were free for their much-anticipated visit to Belfast.

Mary Ann had written frequently in the past weeks of parties and excursions they should undertake and that Henry Joy was very anxious to talk to Evan. She had made only the briefest reference to Thomas Russell, but it was enough to tell Lenny that her friend's affections had not wavered. And, impossible as she knew it to be, she couldn't suppress the briefest daydream of Mary Ann and Thomas with herself and Theobald enjoying a bucolic repast. Even though she knew Tone was in Dublin.

But when Mary Ann welcomed them into the drawing room in Rosemary Lane, Theobald Wolfe Tone stood at the lace-draped casement. The strong light emphasized his aquiline nose and luminous eyes, his brown hair curled just above his ears, and his high black stock framed his face.

"Oh, Mr. Tone! I didn't know . . . that is, I thought you in Dublin."

He bowed deeply. "Indeed, I trust my enemies do so as well."

"Enemies?"

"I have the honor of being the prime agent of those who would bring Catholics and Dissenters together. Therefore, in the view of Dublin Castle, I am a dangerous man. Indeed, I would at the moment, no doubt, be languishing in Newgate Jail if I had not been warned that I must depart or face charges."

Lenny couldn't believe what she was hearing. "You mean leave Ireland—exile?"

Again Tone nodded. "We have this day booked passage aboard the *Cincinnatus* to set sail Saturday for America."

Saturday. Four days. And then there would be a six weeks' ocean voyage between her and her heart. It would have been much better had she not seen him again! She had told herself she was quite recovered of her folly. But now . . . "You said *we?* Who is—"

At that moment three young children romped into the room accompanied by several McCracken pets and flung themselves at the man. "Daddy, Da Da?" The toddler in long skirts clung to his knee while a small puppy barked.

"May we have a picnic? Please say we can." A golden-haired boy of four or five jumped up and down.

"It would be ever so fun, Father. If you say we might." The grave older girl had her father's luminous eyes.

Tone flung his hands in the air. "I have no idea what you're talking about, but what is a father to say to such a brood?" He turned to Lenny. "What do you think, Miss Price? Are they not charming? Could any but a heart of stone refuse any request they make?"

Before she could answer, a tiny woman, delicate and golden as a china figure of a shepherdess, swept in. "Children, don't plague your father. William, Maria, we shall discuss the matter."

472

"Come, my dear, you must meet our newly arrived friends." And Wolfe Tone presented his wife, Matilda.

Lenny had many times sternly reminded herself that he was married, but she had had no idea the fortunate Matilda would be so sweet and beautiful. Seeing her now, surrounded by her children, Lenny felt such a surge of conflicting emotions that it took all her will simply to stand there with a frozen smile on her face.

"Price is the man McCracken has for the paper," Tone continued to his wife. "Sam Neilsen needs help with the editing and—" He looked up at their shocked faces. "Uh-oh, spoken too soon, have I? Well, Harry will tell you all about it in good time. Now, what are we to make of this picnic scheme?" He swooped the youngest high into the air.

It was hard to believe this was a man fleeing for his life. And apparently his presence in Belfast was no secret, for the usual stream of friends, business associates, and political activists continued in and out of Rosemary Lane unabated, as did the plans for entertainment. But what was to happen?

Here was a time when a strong appeal to reason must be made. Lenny had always been aware of how unreasonable her feeling toward Wolfe Tone was. But when was the heart ever ruled by reason? Reason, however, must come into play in the matter of Henry Joy McCracken's offer to Evan. Evan was in need of a job. Assistant editor of the *Northern Star* would be a stimulating situation, putting him at the heart of events. And also in the first line of danger.

Lord Londonderry was furious with the paper, and his son, Lord Castlereagh, was well on his way to becoming a major force in the government. Could offending such powerful people lead to her brother's being exiled as Tone now was to be? Tone's sister was accompanying the young family into banishment. Would Lenny have the strength to support Evan in like manner should he come to a similar fate?

It seemed impossible to think of her cautious brother coming to such a pass. Still, they lived in strange times. Even now the papers reported that Paris was being torn by yet another revolt as starving people ran through the streets shouting, "Bread and the Constitution." One could not be too careful what one chose to become embroiled in. For all that, the talk around Lenny was of nothing but parties and amusements.

The weather was incomparably beautiful when five or six families joined them for an expedition to Cave Hill. Henry Joy had rented a tent, and two wagons were required for servants, food, and equipment. Laughter and conversation rang as bulging hampers produced dish after dish of tasty food and the revelers strolled along the green stretches below the steep hill or lounged on bright plaid blankets.

That afternoon, while the women visited and the children played, the men climbed to the summit of Cave Hill. Lenny and Mary Ann tried to allay Matilda's fears for the future, but it seemed every topic brought out new worries.

Lenny watched Maria help her brother sail a small boat in a meandering stream, then remarked, "The children seem excited about the idea of the voyage."

Matilda shook her head. "They have little notion what lies ahead. Nor can any of us. Of course, our greatest concern is for the children. We have heard how cultureless the Americans are. My husband worries especially for Maria—how a sensitive young lady will fare amidst boorish peasants. And what of the children's education? Giving them an education among such people can only make them discontented in a society wherein learning and talents are useless."

Lenny bit her lip. She had obviously embarked on troubled waters. "Perhaps it will not be so bad as you fear. I believe Philadelphia is quite a lovely city. We have distant relations somewhere thereabouts."

Matilda's blue eyes had grown round with apprehension at the vast unknown she was facing, but she brightened at Lenny's words. "Oh, really? To know someone there would be such a help."

"Evan will give you a letter of introduction," Lenny assured her.

That evening the men returned from their excursion tired but invigorated. They said the climb to the summit had been well worth the effort.

"Amazing view." Tone stretched his long legs in front of him, and his son climbed on his knees. "Belfast Lough all blue at our feet, the sea beyond, the Mountains of Mourne, the Lagan Valley—"

Russell took up the theme. "Perfect sight every direction. Saw all the way to Scotland." Here a friendly argument broke out among the climbers as to whether or not Russell's vision had been enlivened by his imagination.

Lenny saw Mary Ann's eyes on the handsome man. The gratitude she felt that he was not being forced to sail off to wild foreign lands spoke as loudly as any words. And yet, those who remained here were not sailing beyond danger.

There was little time next day to think of life among uncultured peasants or of dangers closer at hand. Preparations went forward for a sumptuous farewell supper. Guests began arriving early in the evening, and soon dining room, drawing room, and every nook between were thronged with guests.

Lenny's main contribution was organizing games for the children. They played *pale-maille* in the garden until it grew too dark for any accuracy in hitting the ball through the series of hanging hoops. And then the men took the mallets and had a riotous round, with most of the balls getting lost in the flower borders. She began herding the children inside for the quieter pastimes of cards and cup and ball.

But all returned to the drawing room when Edward Bunting sat at his harp to demonstrate the newest tunes he had gathered from his collecting journey to the west country.

Lenny had been disappointed that Bunting had not located the Lanark harper, although he said he would be making more trips. But then the harp wove an enchantment over the whole evening, and she became lost in the music. She looked around at the animated faces, lighted by the glow of dozens of candles. She wondered if she would ever again hear the harp played without reliving the bittersweet pain of that evening.

Bunting paused to adjust the tuning on a string, then pushed his glasses back up on his nose. "I want to play for you now a most charming melody I heard an old man playing as he sat by the door of his cottage in Donegal. I sat with the harper for over an hour while the sun sank into the bay. He called the tune 'The Parting of Friends.'"

It was the most beautiful melody Lenny had ever heard. Indeed, the tune was so poignant that she could almost imagine the musician plucking at her very heart. She resisted the temptation to look at Wolfe Tone, for she knew gazing on his fine features at that moment would be more than she could bear. But then she saw Mary Ann looking at Thomas Russell as the candle glow highlighted his wavy hair and warmed his brown eyes.

At that moment Matilda Tone broke into tears. It was obvious she had tried to hold back, but once she started there was no stopping, and the emotion was contagious. Every woman in the room, and many a man too, was in danger of being overcome.

Russell saved the day. He crossed the room and knelt before Matilda, taking her hand in his gentle way. "No, no. This will not do, my lovely mourner. Look beyond the journey to the other side of the picture. You must think not on the sadness of parting but on the joy we shall feel upon your return under happier conditions."

Matilda sniffed and looked up with a wavery smile.

"That's the very thing," Russell encouraged her. "Do not lose your confidence—for such a happy return is sure."

It was advice they all needed the day following, when they stood on the wharf at Belfast Lough and waved their friends away. Especially Lenny. She felt her own heart sailing down the lough and out onto the wide ocean.

She much appreciated her brother's companionship as they

walked slowly back to Rosemary Lane. "I don't understand how this has happened, Evan. How did Dublin Castle know of Tone's affairs?"

Evan shrugged. "Spies, no doubt. Aunt Marguerite is not so wrong to look behind every door."

"But who would do such a thing? Who would be Judas to such a patriot?"

"There are those who would not see negotiating with the French as an act of patriotism."

Lenny sighed. She knew. She had questioned that herself. And yet, when she was in Tone's company, she could not question the sincerity of the man. She turned to her brother. "And have you decided, Evan? Will you undertake the newspaper work?"

"I have given the matter much thought. I have decided to accept."

She squeezed his arm and opened her mouth to congratulate him, but the serious, almost grim, look in his eyes stopped her.

"I do not take this on lightly, Lenny. I fear we are living in more dangerous times than most know. We cover it with picnics and fetes, but the Irish are not so far from the guillotine as they would choose to think."

"Evan, what can you mean? Surely it's all over. There will be no more societies with Tone banished." She found that thought comforting. Her heart would miss the romantic figure, but her head realized they were far safer without the secret activities. If Evan was to work with these people, she would breathe easier knowing there were no antigovernment plots afoot.

But Evan said, "It is far from over. I did not tell you, but when we climbed atop Cave Hill—Russell, Tone, and McCracken stood at the highest point—they swore a solemn oath."

She caught her breath.

"They vowed never to desist in their efforts until they have subverted the authority of England over our country and asserted our independence." Evan paused. "It is noble. Very noble. And very dangerous."

54

Lenny glanced at the small iron and gilt clock that had stood on the mantel of the bawn house for as along as anyone could remember. First, it had been in the old house, which now sheltered cows and pigs, and then on the fine, high mantel of the new Georgian house built higher up. The clock confirmed what she knew. It was time and a day past for Jay to be back.

"Now, no sniveling." His order to Aunt M had been sharp. "I'll be back in three days—to the hour. You can watch the clock."

"But—" The aunt had begun to quiver dangerously.

Jay held up a finger. "One day's ride to Loughall. One day to help our brothers in this spot of trouble." He held up a second finger, then a third. "And one day's ride home."

"But—" Auntie M interrupted her own protest with a loud sniff. "Why must you go?"

"Our Protestant brothers need help. Would you let the Catholics succeed in their nighttime depredations? All over Armagh, the Defenders lie waiting in ditches to murder and destroy every Protestant that appears. We'll have no more of it."

"You make us proud, Jay Calum Lanark." Aunt Adelaide's voice was weakened from long illness, but her determination was as firm as ever. "Proud. Doing your duty as Lanarks have always done."

Marguerite all but smothered him in an engulfing hug. "Take care of yourself, dear boy. Come back to us." Her voice rose. "Dear, dear brave boy. And your father off with the Yeomanry. Who will take care of us—"

"That's what I am here for, Aunt Marguerite." Lenny said. "Fare you well, Cousin Jay."

And she did wish him well in that she wanted him returned home safe and sound. But she deplored the purpose of his venture—to kill. To kill Catholics. Catholics who would then kill Protestants. Protestants who would kill more Catholics . . .

It had been four months since Theobald had sailed into exile. In that time the situation in Ireland and on the Continent had deteriorated rapidly—as had Lenny's own contentment. She told herself over and over, until she feared she spoke it aloud in her sleep, that it was good that Wolfe Tone was gone. Good, certainly, for Tone and his family, who were now far beyond danger. Good for Ireland, who, for all the fine rhetoric, was little ready to undertake establishing liberty, equality, and fraternity.

And good for herself, since her heart could no longer be torn with its infatuation over one entirely off limits. She feared even thinking of him was a sin. What did the Scripture say? Something about "looking" on another being the same as committing adultery with that one? Lenny blushed at the thought. She had nothing of the sort in mind. Still, she could neither stop her mind from filling with pictures of Tone's handsome face nor her heart from aching at his absence.

She did her best to keep busy. Evan was taken up with his newspaper work, and she found the news reports he sent to her engrossing. And now she had the supervision of Lanarks' Bawn to occupy her. That was an ongoing occupation, as Jay's promised three days had come and gone and they had received no word of the skirmish her cousin had so blithely ridden off to fight.

They had heard plenty of the general state of confusion and rebellion in the central counties. Ancient hatreds boiled to the surface. Men attempted to right old wrongs by committing new wrongs. And everywhere French revolutionary ideals were spouted by people who knew very little of actual conditions in France.

But Lenny knew. She set aside her most recent packet of communications from Evan. They included snatches from London and Dublin newspapers, which she would not have otherwise seen. And the news caused all the more turmoil in her breast because, for all her admiration of the person and ideals of Wolfe Tone, she could still find nothing hopeful in the model he had chosen. The flames of war on the Continent blazed ever higher. France annexed Belgium and claimed the Rhine as the boundary of France. Russia joined the Anglo-Austrian coalition to oppose France. The French treasury was empty, inflation rampant. Harvests were poor, the people starving.

It seemed nothing was firm. One *must* believe in something, but what? Lenny sighed and picked up her straw bonnet. It was a beautiful September day. She needed a walk in the fresh air. She had spent far too much time indoors of late. And this was her favorite time of day. Shadows were lengthening, and late-afternoon gold gilded the countryside. She missed her father. His firm belief was always a steadying influence. Even when she didn't accept it herself, she liked to know Archibald's faith held steady in a shaky world.

Lenny walked for some time across the flax field, which some said had been planted by the first Lanark bride. Glimpses of the westering sun shining on Strangford Lough in the distance lifted her spirits. Slowly she angled across the field toward Scrabo Road.

Then she heard the sound she had been listening for ever since her cousin rode off to battle. It was a rider, approaching fast. She listened to the steady pound of the hoofbeats. What a solid, reassuring sound. Should she go to meet him here or return to the bawn to give orders for his supper? Her feet made the decision, and she began running toward the main road.

"Jay, we were so worried . . ."

The rider reined to a halt and dismounted. It was not her cousin.

"Sheldon. I—I didn't expect you. Have you had word of Jay? Has he been wounded?"

Sheldon Ramsey tipped his beaver hat in greeting. Even her concern for her cousin didn't prevent Lenny's noticing the careful fit of Sheldon's dark coat and the polish of his boots.

"We heard of the battle at the Diamond—that the Blearys had gone to help the Peeps—so we thought Jay must be there," he said. "That is why I came—to see if you had any news. Father is most concerned about the outcome."

"That Jay might have been hurt?"

"That, of course. But in the larger sense too. Any undertaking determined to drive the entire Roman population from the area cannot be right. And there's the economic factor as well as the moral—the wreckers on both sides are smashing looms, tearing up webs, tangling tenterfields . . ."

She understood why Sheldon's linen draper father would be concerned. Textiles were the basis for all Ulster's economy. "But you said 'battle.' There's been a battle?"

"Father heard so at the Linen Hall, but there was much talk and few facts."

They walked toward the house as they talked, Sheldon leading his horse. They were almost there when Lenny noted a stir in the yard. A stable lad was leading a horse toward the barn. "Oh, Jay's returned! Come. Now we'll learn all!"

Indeed, Jay stood in front of the fireplace, one arm propped on the mantel in a thoroughly heroic pose, while the Aunts AM hung on his every word.

"Oh, just look," Aunt M cried. "Our dear boy is returned. Dear, dear boy! And a hero too."

"I am glad you're back, cousin." Lenny took a seat on the sofa and smoothed her muslin skirt. "You must tell all. Start again—right from the beginning. What is that orange cockade on your lapel?"

"That is the sign of victory—the sign of the future of Ireland, cousin."

"So you won?"

"Was there ever any doubt?"

A servant lit the candles standing in tall brass sticks on either end of the mantel. They highlighted Jay's broad features and made his blond hair shine silver.

"I must say, though, it was a very near thing. Not whether we would win, but whether there would be a battle at all. Aye, but you should have seen those 'brave' Defenders when we marched to the Diamond right behind the Peep o' Days. The papists had nae realized their opponents were reinforced. We could have ended it right then, of course, but they took the advice of their priests—that lot is always led by priests, you know."

"So what did they do?" Lenny suddenly realized the importance of what she was hearing. Sheldon said Belfast knew nothing but rumors. Here was a firsthand report. She must get all the details and send them to Evan.

Jay laughed. "Turned and ran, didn't they?" He slapped his thigh. "Well, more like agreed to a truce, but it came to the same thing. Left them free to spend the evening in the public house, didn't it? That's all they care about in the end."

"But I thought you said there was a battle?"

"Oh, aye, that was the next day. A fresh body of Defenders arrived from County Tyrone. Determined to fight, they were. And not likely we'd deny them. Captain Sloan had us take our positions on the hill above the Diamond." Again he laughed. "Like shooting ducks in a pond."

In spite of her determination to get all the details, Lenny couldn't help letting her mind wander to what might have been. If Tone's ideals had been put into practice . . . if Irishmen had united . . . if swarms of young men like her cousin, wearing whatever color cockades—or, better yet, no cockades at all—rambled off to the public house together, instead of one lot on the brow of a hill taking aim at the others trapped in the valley . . .

"Thirty, certain. Easily more. Hard to tell, but there'll be a more accurate count when the reapers finish the cornfields by the Diamond." He laughed. "They'll be grim reapers for sure."

"And none of our dear, brave Bleary Boys were hurt?" Marguerite dabbed at her eyes with a lace handkerchief.

"Oh, aunties, you should have seen it. Made your heart proud, it would have. The Peep o' Day Boys led the way—it being home territory to them—straight down the road. We marched right from the Diamond straight on into Loughall to Sloan's Inn. He set us all up refreshments—fine gentleman he is. And that's when we did it—right under the signboard of William of Orange crossing the Boyne."

"Did what?" Lenny was almost afraid to ask. Hadn't they done enough?

"Founded a new organization. For all we beat them so handily, I'll have to confess the Defenders are a well-organized lot. Not just a spot here and a clutch there, the way our side has been. 'We need a disciplined defensive association—one for all loyal men who will pledge to defend the king and his heirs so long as he or they support the Protestant Ascendancy.' That's what James Sloan said, and he almost brought down his own roof by it, the cheers were so great."

Aunt Marguerite applauded with little squeaking sighs and much rustling of silk.

"So the Bleary Boys have become oath-bound?" Lenny asked.

"No, no, no. I'm not speaking of the Blearys or the Peeps. This is something much bigger than any local group. We have founded the Loyal Brotherhood of the Orange Order." He flicked at the ribbon on his jacket. "In sacred memory of King Billy and the House of Orange. Aye, it was a fine sight. All those men, new come from victorious battlefield, sternly solemn as they sat for the reading of the lesson from Scripture, then swearing the oath."

Lenny had been near to the founding of two high-ideal orders now. The United Irishmen had resulted in her heart's dearest being banished to foreign shores and others imprisoned. What would the Orange Order lead to?

She got up and left the room, leaving the questioning of the returned hero to the aunts.

"Lenny."

She had her foot on the first tread to go up to her room when Sheldon's voice called her back. She crossed the hall to him.

"You are as troubled by that as I am, aren't you?"

"Where will it lead, Sheldon? More clubs and organizations? More fighting? There has to be a better answer."

"There is."

"Oh, I know. Preaching and divinity study are all very well for you. I'm very glad you're happy, Sheldon. I once thought the answer was in philosophy and theology, too. But I've seen that doesn't work either."

Sheldon shook his head.

"God wants to be personally active in the life of every one of His creatures. If people would just work with the Creator instead of forming organizations for their own power, we could have heaven right here."

His mention of forming organizations brought her back to the

481

present. "Oh!" She jumped up. "Thank you, Sheldon. I shall think of what you've said. But now I must write to my brother. Evan will be much in need of such firsthand information as Jay's report." She turned toward her room, then stopped after two steps. "But how will I get it to him?"

"You must allow me to be of service. Write your report to Evan. I will carry it to him tonight."

"But it is getting late. And you've had no dinner."

"I had intended to return to Lisburn tonight. Belfast is a shorter ride."

She bit her lip. "Well, yes, it is. And I would be so grateful. I'm sure Cook can give you something to eat while I write."

The next day Lenny took her breakfast on a tray in her room. Uncle Douglas was expected home that afternoon. She would stay to welcome him, then ask Jay to drive her back to Price Manor. She had been away for more than a week now and would be glad to be home.

First, though, she would spend a quiet morning following up her last night's discussion with Sheldon by looking through the volume of sermons her father had sent with her. She picked up the book and looked at it closely for the first time. It was the one Baird Ramsey had loaned to her father. It was a shame she hadn't realized that sooner; she could have returned it with Sheldon last night. But as she still possessed the volume, she might as well read it.

As she turned the pages, she wished the writer were alive today to comment upon the present situation. But since he and Rousseau were contemporaries, such a widely read man as John Wesley must have commented on the French philosopher. It wasn't long before her skimming eye picked up a couple of references to the name she was looking for. She had to smile at Wesley's summation of Rousseau as a "prodigy of self-conceit" and a "consummate coxcomb."

But then she settled into his sermon on the Unity of the Divine Being.

> Almost all men of letters in the civilized countries of Europe extol *humanity* to the skies, as the very essence of religion. To this the great triumvirate Rousseau, Voltaire, and Hume, have contributed all their labours to establish a religion which should stand on its own foundation. . . . And so they have found out both a religion and a happiness which have no relation at all to God, nor any dependence upon Him.

Lenny turned to the small table beside her chair and poured a black stream of steaming coffee into a flowered China teacup, stirred in scoops of cream and sugar, and snuggled deeper into her chair as she sipped. What a thoroughly delicious morning. Then she returned to the book.

> It is no wonder that this religion should grow fashionable, and spread far and wide in the world. But call it *humanity, virtue, morality,* or what you please, it is putting asunder what God has joined. It is separating the love of our neighbour from the love of God. It is a plausible way of thrusting God out of the world He has made. They can do the business without Him.

The rhythm and liveliness of Wesley's words caught her, and she was again fourteen, back at the meetinghouse at Newtownards, sitting on a hard bench between her brother and Sheldon Ramsey. She could still hear the voice of the old gentleman.

> On the contrary, as He created all things, so He continually superintends whatever He has created. He governs all, not only to the bounds of creation, but through the utmost extent of space; and not only through the short time that is measured by the earth and sun, but from everlasting to everlasting. All nature, so all religion, and all happiness, depend on Him; and whoever teach to seek happiness without Him . . .

Lenny looked up. She was imagining things. She had been so reliving that Methodist Society meeting that her mind had added Sheldon's voice to the proceedings. But then she jumped up. There was no mistaking that rich baritone. Sheldon Ramsey had returned to Lanarks' Bawn.

What could it mean? Did Evan need something? Was there more trouble somewhere? She took a quick peek in her glass to be certain her short, dark curls were arranged in a fashionably casual manner and that the skirt of her pink linen dress wasn't too terribly rumpled. Then she rushed to the drawing room.

"You have come back to us, Mr. Ramsey. Is anything—" Her mother had always told her never to enter a room talking, yet she often did. The sight before her, however, was sufficient to cure her of that bad habit forever.

Surely here was the most handsome man God ever created. Thomas Russell, even Theobald Wolfe Tone, paled in comparison to this man's broad-shouldered stature, warm brown hair and eyes, and strong cheekbones. And somehow, the fact that he was dressed in countrified fashion seemed to add to, rather than detract from, his charm.

Both men bowed, and Sheldon spoke. "Ah, and here is the lady of which we were speaking. Carolenn, may I have the honor of presenting your somewhat cousin Franklin Lanark, come all the way from Philadelphia."

Lenny hoped her acknowledgment was warm and welcoming and not as stiff with shock as she felt. "Cousin? How comes this—this miracle?"

The American's laugh was as open and hearty as his appearance. "Why, ma'am, as soon as I met up with your Mr. Tone in Philly and he told me about the great work you folks are doing here to get free of the Redcoats, just like we did back home—and then I read that friendly letter your brother sent me—I knew I just had to come over and help my family."

It took some time for Lenny to sort out all the information in that speech, but at last it became clear that Wolfe Tone had lost no time making his way to the American capital. He had taken lodgings, it turned out, not far from the Lanark townhouse, which house, the effusive newcomer explained, they liked to keep up for his mama and sisters' social doings. But he and his father and brothers preferred life on "the farm," which Lenny soon realized must be far more of a country estate than a mere farm.

Always a man to act on a decision, Franklin had forthwith set sail for Belfast and turned up six weeks later at the office of the *Northern Star,* from whence Sheldon had brought him. "Yes, indeedy, as soon as I read that letter I started packing my trunk. Can't let my cousins fight their revolution all by theirselves, I said. After all, where would America be without the help the Frenchies gave us? Only fair to spread it around a bit."

Lenny looked toward the door. It wouldn't do to have Franklin talking about revolution in this house. Such sentiments could get him placarded if not deported. "Oh, do tell me how Mr. Tone is. How did Matilda and the children bear the voyage?"

Franklin shook his head—a gesture that reminded her of her father's best horse tossing his mane. "Unusually hot summer we had. I'm afraid Tone didn't take to it well at all. I never saw such a man for worrying about his health. Of course, there were quite a few cases of yellow fever—"

"Yellow fever? Matilda? Maria? Baby Frank?"

Again the laugh that was like a fresh breeze blowing through the house. "No, no. Land sakes, none of them got sick—your friend just worried. Said the heat gave him headaches and he couldn't work. Dr. Reynolds's powders didn't seem to do him much good."

The doctor's name was familiar to Lenny. A physician from Tyrone who had been jailed for working for parliamentary reform with the United Irishmen, maybe?

"Quite a society of Irishmen we're getting in Philadelphia, you know. Reynolds's practice is flourishing. And Archy Rowan came over to the land of the free after he got out of that Frenchie prison . . ."

Lenny's head was quite spinning. Apparently her American relative thought she knew far more than she did. And he obviously had no notion of the advisability of keeping a careful tongue in his head if he would keep his head at all. She didn't like to think what the reaction would be if Douglas Lanark, fresh from his maneuvers with the Yeomanry, were to walk in at the moment and hear talk of revolution, United Irishmen, and French conspirators in his own drawing room. She was thankful that Aunt Adelaide had kept to her room, but from the slow flush spreading over Aunt Marguerite's face Lenny could see that the gist of the political sentiments was not lost on her.

Lenny took a breath to speak, trying to think what to say.

But Marguerite outstripped her. "Sir, do you come all this way to insult us to our faces? Or is this some kind of American joke—to talk of odious traitors to test our courtesy?" Aunt M's abundant adipose rolled into motion, emphasizing the intensity of her agitation. "I'll have you know this is a loyal, patriotic household. And with our dear, brave Jay just returned safely to us from the very brink of a battlefield grave." She rolled to her feet, swaths of cerise silk rippling around her. "Sir, this is Ireland. We do not treat our heroes so shabbily here."

Franklin Lanark's brow wrinkled with consternation. He looked from Marguerite to Lenny to Sheldon. "What did I say? I seem to have stepped in a right fine pie."

A noise in the yard below turned Lenny's attention to the window. The master of Lanarks' Bawn had arrived. But Douglas was not alone. He had arrived with a whole contingent of Yeomanry.

"Pie. Yes, indeed." Lenny jumped to her feet. "Our cook makes the best veal and mutton pies in all Ulster. And I'm sure you're starved." She started toward the door as she talked. "Sheldon, you must escort us to Price Manor at once. We mustn't keep my mother waiting. Don't worry about a thing, Auntie M. I've arranged your dinner with Cook. Aunt Adelaide's maid will give her her tonic. I'll send for my box."

As soon as she was at the door, she fled down the back staircase. Fortunately Sheldon and Franklin were following. They were halfway to the main road in the carriage she had earlier asked the stableboy to have ready for her when she finally felt calm enough to explain matters to Franklin.

"You must think me run mad. I assure you, sir, not all Irish are as I must have appeared. But you *must* take more care what you say. My uncle and cousin are staunch for the government, and the countryside is riddled with spies."

Franklin looked quite befuddled. "But I don't understand. Wolfe Tone said the Lanarks were right-thinking folks—member of some committee that supported his views."

Lenny nodded. "The Catholic Committee. Wrong Lanarks. You will soon learn, sir cousin, the great gulf that divides Ireland—and how seldom it is bridged, even by common ancestry. Pray, do not express such revolutionary sentiments abroad. You and the opinions of those you quote will be quite safe at Price Manor. You can feel free to say anything you like there. But you must exercise caution elsewhere."

Fortunately Sheldon then engaged their visitor in conversation, so Lenny was free to sort out her thoughts. They were jumbled still. Through it all, however, one thing rang clear. Wolfe Tone had sent this man to them. Theobald had sent Franklin to her. Whatever he might lack of fashion or social graces—and he did talk so oddly—this man had brought a piece of her heart back to her.

Cook's pie turned out to be beefsteak and ham rather than the promised veal and mutton, but Harriet and Archibald Price made the American visitor just as welcome at Price Manor as Lenny knew they would. And it seemed wonderfully like old times as they gathered around the table. Wimborne had come to call upon Sarah. Sheldon filled Evan's usual place.

As soon as the meal was served and the maid departed, Lenny invited Franklin to continue his interrupted narrative.

He told in some detail how Rowan—the United Irishman who had fled Dublin a few years earlier and been imprisoned in Paris during the Terror—had been liberated by Irish sympathizers within the French Ministry of Foreign Affairs.

"Yes sir. Seems like the hand of Providence, it does, now that Mr. Rowan has your friend Tone introduced all friendlylike to Governor Mifflin and to the French minister in Philadelphia. I don't hold much with French ways myself, but Pierre Adet seems a right enough fellow."

Archibald was also interested in matters of agriculture and religion in America, topics that Franklin talked on as freely as political affairs. Sheldon, who had been as silent as when she knew him early on, was interested in hearing of the lasting results of George Whitefield's preaching a generation earlier. But it was Wimborne who always seemed to bring the conversation back to politics. "And so our friend T-Tone does well, making p-powerful friends in his exile?"

Franklin was pleased to give the present company a happy report.

"And what use, d-do you think, would he make of this Adet?"

"You understand, I've spoken with Tone only once or twice on the subject, but he told me Adet was much moved when he reported how you fine Irish folk desire to break your chains and declare your independence from England. That was the talk that fired me to come lend a hand as well."

Lenny was alarmed again. "But, remember, you mustn't let people *know* you've come as a revolutionary!"

"Sakes, no." Franklin gave his hearty laugh. "Linen merchant, that's my game. Help pay for my keep, it will—and aid the popular French fashions."

Wimborne had adopted the latest French fashion himself. His dark hair, including long sideburns, was cut in the Brutus—a style that made it stand out like hedgehog quills. The effect was heightened by the scarlet silk cloth with which he had swathed his neck. "And may I be the f-first to say how conscious we are of the honor you do us, sir. But do you think the French minister was ap–appropriately moved by Tone's appeal?"

Franklin shifted his broad shoulders inside his brown jacket. "I expect Adet was more moved by the practical side of affairs."

"And that is . . ."

"Well, as I understand it—and being a foreigner, I might have got it wrong—but your Theobald was saying that two-thirds of the English navy is manned by Irishmen and a good portion of her infantry and provisions come from Ireland. He told Adet that if Ireland withheld her support, England could in no way continue the war against France."

Wimborne nodded, a forkful of stewed cucumbers poised above his plate. "Yes, I quite see his argument. For France to invade England would be folly. Whereas, an invasion of Ireland would easily be supported by seven-eighths of its people—the aristocracy alone opposing."

"That's what he said!" In his enthusiasm, Franklin hit the table, and the silver bounced. "Were Ireland to join with France, England would be destroyed and the liberty of mankind assured. That's exactly what he said."

The political talk continued as the men offered assessments of relative French and English strengths. All agreed that France's greatest asset was her General of the Army of Italy, Napoleon Bonaparte. The man's brilliant successes in the war against Austria were making him an independent force from the French Directory government.

But Lenny had had enough and more of politics and military affairs for one day. Her scrape with adventure in spiriting their revolutionary cousin from under the nose of the Yeomanry had left her quite drained once the initial stimulation left. Now she did wish the men could find another topic.

Of course, she was glad her cousin was making such a success, especially with Thorpe Wimborne. She had seldom seen the music master so interested in anyone other than the golden-haired Sarah. Lenny was just thinking that it would be very pleasant to be the one to engage the attention of the rugged American when there was a brief pause in the conversation. She searched for a topic to interest him.

"Gentlemen, you mustn't bore on so. Whatever will our cousin think? And him new come from the American capital." Sarah swept all other conversational comers from the field with the batting of her eyelashes. "Now, you just come with me, Cousin Franklin. I want your opinion on my new harpsichord sonata. You must be polite and tell me that none of the ladies in Philadelphia play so fine. I'm quite longing to hear it's so. And then we'll hear you sing."

Franklin started to protest.

"Oh, none of that, sir. I'll not allow you to have any but a superior voice." With two more bats of her eyelashes, Sarah carried the party into the music parlor.

55

Throughout that winter and on into the next spring all life seemed to be energized by Franklin Lanark's presence. The spark to her days that Lenny thought gone forever when the *Cincinnatus* sailed from Belfast Lough had returned with a greater brightness. Best of all, this leap of the heart into her throat every time Franklin walked into a room could be allowed to be more than a mere schoolgirl crush. She was no longer a schoolgirl, and the American was not married.

However, there was no lack of feminine competition for his attention. Not only did Sarah continue to ply him with her brightest smiles and liveliest harpsichord tunes—which he declared to be incomparable —but also Mary Ann McCracken, whose acquaintance he made as soon as his merchant business was established in Belfast, made no secret that she would be happy to entertain the attentions of Mr. Lanark.

And one of the nicest benefits of that for Lenny was an increased flurry of letters from her Belfast friend.

My very dear Lenny,

I hasten to tell you that we see your brother and cousin regularly, and that they are in good health. Even though Tone remains gone from us, I assure you there is no slacking in our zealous pursuit of the ideals we all hold, though the prospects dim. Lord Castlereagh has turned against constitutional reform. England's peril is too great, he says. And he judges, rightly I believe, that Ulster's Presbyterian element is the real center of genuine republican sympathy.

Just two nights ago a number of activists were taken up. Ten coaches accompanied by a strong escort of dragoons conveyed prisoners all the way to Kilmainham Jail in Dublin. As yet we have met with no misfortune. Though numbers of people here have been taken up, our family has escaped.

M.A. McC

Taken up? The joy Lenny had felt since her cousin's arrival from America almost a year before turned to fear. She had not heard of the arrests. And now she had two to worry over—her brother *and* her cousin. More than once she awoke in the middle of a dream with the sound of iron wheels on cobblestone streets rattling in her ears. Evan and Franklin being carried to jail? And she would never know for certain until the next letter arrived from Belfast.

When the post came the following week, as usual Lenny tore open Mary Ann's letter and skimmed it quickly. When, with a deep sigh of relief, she saw that the worst had not happened, and she settled in to reading leisurely.

My dear friend,

Take heart. We receive reports daily of the growing strength of the U.I. Just imagine—a Scottish regiment at Ballycastle stole the whole of the ammunition and half the arms of the soldiers! All across the counties there are reports of ash trees being felled for pike shafts. I think it's not overestimated that 50,000 men stand ready to join the French when they invade to set Ireland free.

We've heard rumor of 20 cannon, 15,000 arms, 8,000 horses —and so it mounts! I suppose I shouldn't put such things on paper, but it can matter little. The government has as many in its well paid army of spies as we in our United Irish. I do believe that the Inquisition in its worst days was not worse than the laceration of character which is exercised at present. And so the government is sure to know as well as we that Tone is arrived in France. God give him speed!

Wimborne's fine tenor voice filled the room with a romantic ballad sung to Sarah's accompaniment. Lenny had always found it interesting that he never stammered when he sang. And at such times he seemed almost graceful. She hoped he appeared so to her sister, so that Sarah could keep her melting gaze away from Franklin Lanark. Actually, there was little enough opportunity for anyone to gaze on Franklin of late, for he was much occupied with Henry Joy McCracken and the Belfast activists.

Lenny crossed the floor and tossed her letter on top of those in her box. She really must clean those out one day. The lid hardly closed properly anymore.

Letters were so unsatisfactory anyway. Happy as she was to get them, and quickly though she flew to her writing materials to pen an answer, the fact of the matter was that her heart would no more than swell with the assurance that all was well than she would look at the date on the page and the plaguing questions would return. Indeed, they had been well on the *fifth*. But how were they today on the *tenth*? She turned to her brother's writing in the *Northern Star*.

> It is likely true, as is so much said hereabouts, that a powerful revolutionary coalition is arrayed against the government, all wanting to sever the connection with England. But it appears to this observer that, should they succeed, it would be difficult to keep the revolutionaries together. The Catholic Defenders are interested mainly in land. Come to power, they would seek wholesale confiscations. The bourgeoisie leaders favor a government similar to the French Directory—with themselves in charge. Major social upheaval is no part of their agenda. The solid Presbyterian farmers seek popular parliamentary government—freedom of conscience and expression, equality before the law. Getting three such diverse groups to work together would be as revolutionary as driving the English from Ireland would be.

He had signed the article "Belfast Observer," but Lenny knew the authorities would have him as surely identified as if he had signed his name.

Five days later, the letter she had dreaded arrived. It was only a note, hastily scrawled in Mary Ann's hand. "Thomas Russell and Henry Joy taken up. Lodged in Kilmainham Jail. Margaret and I go to them tomorrow under Edward's escort."

Lenny knew she had no right to feel relief when her friend was in such turmoil. But she could not help being glad that Evan and Franklin were still free. At least they had been free three days ago.

And then half of her fears evaporated. Although Evan remained in Belfast, Franklin arrived at Price Manor and settled into Evan's room, made comfortable by Harriet Price, who was thrilled to have a young man to mother once again.

He spent long hours immured in his room, pouring over his correspondence and writing lengthy replies, but he emerged for enough time everyday that Lenny could accompany him on extended rambles to the shore of Strangford Lough or rides to Scrabo. And he talked freely to her of his communications.

She did not ask how he got such letters past government officials or secured the sending of his own. She wasn't sure she wanted to know. It soon became clear, however, that the bulk of his correspondence came from France. Wolfe Tone apparently felt that Franklin, as an American, would be watched less than the Irish radicals.

She was delighted with the news from France. Tone was a colonel in the French army. He had asked for a commission in any Irish expedition the French sent. Franklin showed her Tone's letter, and she read it avidly.

> I requested the commission because, willing enough though I am to encounter danger as a soldier, I hold a violent objection to being hanged as a traitor in case the fortune of war should throw me into the hands of the enemy, who I know would otherwise show me no mercy.

In spite of those ominous words, a soft smile played around the corner of Lenny's lips. "Oh, I do wish I could see him. How fine he must look in his French uniform. I remember how proudly he wore his Volunteer uniform, cut on similar lines."

The next missive was longer. It was a copy of a manifesto that was to be distributed when the French landed in Ireland. Apparently, copies were to be prepared in secret on the *Northern Star* presses and kept under lock and key until the fateful day. It was headed "Address to the People of Ireland."

Lenny read a few lines, then looked up. "Oh, this is moving, indeed. Inflammatory, even. I do hope you keep your room locked, Franklin."

He put his head back and gave a peal of that delightful laughter that could sweep any fear ahead of it. "And who would be interested in the affairs of a bumbling American frontiersman come back to the land of his ancestors?"

She smiled. "I think quite a few more than you might suspect, sir cousin. But I believe it unlikely that Dublin Castle would be taking quite that line of interest."

He looked confused, and it was just as well. Saying more would have been unladylike. Lenny had accepted the fact that she was now of an age where she really must take the proprieties into account. She allowed herself a saucy smile in his direction and continued her reading of Tone's message to Ireland:

> Ireland will never be free, prosperous, or happy until she is independent. My objects are clear and twofold: first, to subvert the tyranny of our execrable government, to break the connection with England—the source of all our political evils—and, second, to unite the whole people of Ireland, to abolish the memory of all past dissensions, and to substitute the common name of

Irishman in the place of the denominations of Protestant, Catholic, and Dissenter.

"It's a fine, stirring work. To my thinking not unlike that of our own Thomas Paine," Franklin said.

Lenny nodded slowly. Yes, it was stirring, but that was part of the problem. She felt the familiar shiver start at the base of her spine. Through repeated experience she had learned not to disregard that warning. She had a kind of sixth sense about such things.

"It seems to me he has turned matters around. Mr. Tone's goal formerly was to unite Irishmen—a peaceable goal, a goal few could fault. But this seems little less than a declaration of war on England." The shiver reached the base of her skull, and she had to exercise great control to keep from breaking into violent trembles.

"No, no, now don't you be worrying, little cousin. When the Frenchies come, everything will be fine. Didn't they help America with her independence? They'll do the same for Ireland. Just you wait. It'll all be over soon. Tone and the French Navy—that's all we need."

Lenny remembered that chill when she heard the news early in the new year. It took her considerable time to sort the reliable information from the hysteria and rumor. It was a confused tale of disorganization and disaster.

When, at long last, Franklin received a letter from Tone, giving an explanation to his fellow United Irishmen, a sort of pattern emerged: On the morning of December 15, after long squabbles and delays, forty-three French ships set sail for Ireland carrying 14,450 troops. Weather conditions were perfect. Expectations of success couldn't have been higher.

But they were not yet out of sight of land when the first disaster struck. Several ships, including the *Fraternite*—carrying expedition commander Hoche—collided. Then they were forced to sail through dangerous waters to avoid the British blockade. Heavy fog blanketed the sea the next morning. The fleet was scattered. Of the original forty-three ships, only seventeen remained together. General Hoche was missing.

They now had only the sealed packet of instructions Hoche had left with his subordinate officers. The instructions themselves were confusing and contradictory. But one thing was clear—their destination was Bantry Bay on the southwest corner of Ireland, not Galway Bay, as had been expected.

At dawn, four days before Christmas, Wolfe Tone sighted the coast of his beloved Ireland. Midday he stood on the foredeck of the

Indomitable as they approached Bantry Bay. He could see snow on the mountains. But there was no sign of welcome from the Irish people. Where were his friends? The Defenders, the Catholic Committee, the United Irishmen? There should be flags, bonfires, small ships sailing out to meet them. Had they not received his communications?

Behind him, the French officers were talking as if the expedition had failed already. And then the French leader gave the order to sail away and cruise off the coast. Tone had been so close to Ireland he could have tossed a pebble onto the land.

The weather worsened during the night. The next day sixteen French ships, including the *Indomitable*, carrying newly promoted Adjutant-General Theobald Wolfe Tone, sailed into Bantry Bay and dropped anchor. That night a driving gale scattered the fleet. Fewer than 6,500 men remained for the Irish invasion. In the face of certain disaster, Tone decided to risk all.

He would lead the invasion. He had no money, no tents, no horses, only four pieces of artillery, and few men. But they would land on Christmas Day and march on Cork. Then Dublin.

That night he prepared another address to the Irish people, assuring them that the French had come as allies to help in their long struggle against England. "Join with France against our common enemy," Tone wrote to his countrymen. "Expel the evils of England's military presence for good."

All night the winds howled. The sea raged. Masts snapped. Ships leaked. Hardy sailors became sick. Tone knew that the same winds that kept them from landing would soon carry the British fleet to lock them in the bay. Driving snow and hail and hurricane force winds accompanied his writing. "I see nothing before me but the ruin of the expedition, the slavery of my country, and my own destruction. I have a merry Christmas of it today."

The next day the fleet that was to free Ireland from her chains sailed for France.

56

Lenny could not remember a more beautiful spring. Every morning a chorus of birds woke her with their rejoicing. Today she dressed hurriedly to be out in the world where the sun shone a clear yellow in a soft blue sky and flowering trees frosted the delicate green of the countryside with mounds of fragrant pink and white blossoms. She took a deep breath and sighed. "Oh, this must be what heaven smells like."

Sheldon Ramsey, en route home for Easter from his last year at university, offered his arm, and they strolled beneath apple trees sifting petals in their way like a gentle snow. "There can be no surer sign of the resurrection than dead wood bursting into flower each spring, can there?"

"How can there be such turmoil and such beauty side by side?" Lenny stooped to pick a few tiny blue flowers, then they continued their walk. "Evil seems so much worse when it is surrounded by such wonder."

She felt Sheldon's eyes on her for several seconds before he answered. Usually she would have wished to share such a stroll with Franklin, but no one but Sheldon would be right for this moment. He always saw things no one else saw, and she could talk to him about things no one else cared about. He never seemed to think she was silly.

"I've been thinking in much the same vein lately. It seems that God's best gifts are capable of the worst perversion."

Dew still hung on the bushes, the sun turning each drop into rarest jewels. Lenny felt she was floating on the surface of all the loveliness, that she didn't want to dig too deeply for fear of jarring the order. But Sheldon's pleasant voice somehow added to the harmony of the moment.

"Such as?"

"Such as man's free will. How much would anything in life mean if we had no ability to choose and strive? And yet, is it not such freedom that allows man to choose evil and do harm?"

She nodded slowly, not wanting to disturb the melody of nature by voicing her thoughts. He was right. Those in positions of power could do the greatest good—or the greatest evil. Those who loved passionately were the most capable of falling into fanaticism.

And in spite of her determination to remain in accord with the springtime loveliness, Lenny could not help slipping into worry that her friends and loved ones might be in just such danger. Henry Joy McCracken and Thomas Russell still in jail, Wolfe Tone in France working for another expedition, her brother writing for an inflammatory newspaper, Franklin Lanark working doggedly for the United Irishmen—whose membership had doubled since word of the French expedition spread. Where would it end?

On that perfect morning, Lenny felt no chill, but the memory of past shivers brushed her like the wings of a moth.

"Your shoes are getting wet in the dew. I must take you in."

When they had returned to the house, Sheldon turned to her in the hall and took both her hands in his. "I shall leave you now. My family is anxious for my return."

"When will I see you again?"

"I will seek ordination when I've completed my degree. I don't know where I'll be assigned. But we shall keep in touch."

She felt just the slightest pressure from the hands that held hers. "Oh, yes. I couldn't bear to lose track of such a friend. It seems I've known you as long as I've known my brother."

He bowed and left without another word.

She watched him go, a small crease wrinkling her forehead.

A letter awaited Lenny at the breakfast table. "Oh, it's from Mary Ann. Posted in Dublin." She picked up a knife and slit the seal, relishing the thickness of it. Two pieces of lovely light blue paper. "I do hope she has good news."

Henry's case still had not come to trial in spite of the best efforts of his solicitor. Mary Ann's brother William had likewise been taken up and was in Kilmainham. That seemed the event that had spurred this trip to Dublin, for Mary Ann had accompanied William's valiant wife, Rose Ann.

Our dear Rose declares she cannot leave her William and is quite determined to stay near him in jail. Our greatest concern is for the health of our prisoners. There is much fever in prison. We are told that a whole society of 52 United Irishmen were taken up by two officers recently. And another group of 21 taken in one house. It is said that both occurrences are the mischief of spies. A man well-known to the family led the officers to the second arrest. He was disguised but easily recognized.

And then, perhaps as relief from all that was crumbling around her, Mary Ann turned to other matters. "We have had very good fortune in selling all the muslins we brought with us, and so our little business flourishes in spite of all."

"Oh, do put your letter down and pass the marmalade, sister." Sarah was unusually pettish this morning. "How can you come to the table with your hair in such disarray? I don't know why Mama permits it."

Suppressing a sigh, Lenny tucked the letter in her pocket and turned her attention to her sister. "Will you be playing your Mozart today, Sarah? I do like that piece so very much."

Sarah pursed her lips. "I can make no progress on my own. Thorpe knows that very well. He had no business to go gallivanting off last week without a by-your-leave. It is much too bad in him."

"And when will he return?"

Sarah tossed her head. "Do you suggest that I should care about the comings and goings of that noddicock?"

There was no soothing Sarah, so Lenny ate her toast in silence, then hurried to her room where she could finish Mary Ann's letter. It was as well she had saved it for a private moment. The remaining contents were not suitable to have divulged before her mother or sister. Mary Ann was considering becoming a sworn member of United Irishwomen.

> Rose Ann is most fervent in her membership and has done great good in concert with other brave females. They collect funds, encourage recruitment, provide comforts, and even carry secret messages. I have a great curiosity to visit some female societies here in Dublin—although I should like them better if they were integrated. There can be no reason for having them separate, keeping the women in the dark. I wish to know if the women have any rational ideas of liberty and equality for themselves.

In a burst of enthusiasm, Lenny clapped energetically. Then, realizing she was wrinkling the paper, she placed it on her star-patterned quilt and carefully smoothed the sheet before she continued reading:

> Is it not almost time for the clouds of error and prejudice to disperse and that the female part of the Creation as well as the male should throw off the fetters with which they have been so long mentally bound? I hope the present era will produce some women of sufficient talent to inspire the rest with a genuine love of Liberty. I hope it is reserved for the Irish nation to strike out

something new and to show an example of justice superior to any that have gone before them. As it is about two o'clock in the morning, I have only time to bid you good night.

Believe me
Yours affectionately
Mary Ann

Lenny sat reliving those happier days in Belfast when she and her friend had enjoyed times together in the pleasant parlor in Rosemary Lane, such moments as were possible between visits from friends and attending civic celebrations. How long ago that all seemed. And how much farther away all they had dreamed of accomplishing appeared now than in those halcyon days of harp music, parades, and picnics.

Depression hung like a dark cloud in the room. The French invasion failed. Tone in exile. Henry Joy and Thomas Russell in jail. In the midst of all that—fresh, even, from visiting her brothers in jail—Mary Ann was able to dream of freedom, justice, and glory. Lenny squared her shoulders. How could she do less?

The cause was dark but not lost. Wolfe Tone's Address to the Irish People would not be delivered, but Evan's passionate articles appeared regularly in the *Northern Star*. Henry and the others were imprisoned in Dublin, but Franklin worked with freedom. Recruitment was sharply on the rise. In spite of its failure, the invasion attempt had inspired republicans with the hope that the French would land and the English government would be easily overturned. And every success of the French army on the Continent brought another upsurge of United Irish recruits.

Lenny looked back at the letter resting in her lap. Ought she not to join a society of United Irishwomen? But was she certain that revolution was the right course? Certain enough to commit her life to it?

The next afternoon Lenny returned from a long ramble across the fields to be greeted with the charming sound of Mozart from her sister's harpsichord. Thorpe Wimborne must be returned. She hurried in, hoping he would have news or at least an amusing tale to tell. Since reading Mary Ann's letter, she had spent most of her time considering what she should do. Still she had reached no decision. She felt much in need of distraction.

When Lenny entered the music room, Sarah's smiles spoke even more loudly than her music. All was well between Sarah and her admirer.

She played on to the end of the piece, concluding with a flourish, before speaking. "The grandest scheme, sister. We are to go to Belfast. Mr. Bunting's book of Irish music has made a great success, and Mr.

Wimborne has kindly procured a subscription for us to attend an evening of Irish music promoted by the Reading Society."

Lenny felt a stab of regret that Mary Ann would not be returned to Belfast yet, but it would be lovely to see Evan again. And, yes, she would be glad of a diversion. Lately she had spent far too much time thinking of philosophy and politics. Perhaps those like her mother and sister, who said such things were not meant for the feminine mind, were right.

Three days later as their carriage rolled along the Belfast road, Harriet Price's feminine sensibilities appeared all aflutter at the prospects before them. "What a wonderful opportunity to view the latest French fashion. We shall call at the dressmaker's first. And then the milliner's." She turned to Archibald beside her. "Husband, you simply must visit the tailor as well. You should bespeak a carrick. I saw a pattern card only the other day for one with three capes. You would be handsome beyond words."

Archibald winked at his younger daughter. "And here I was, fancying I was already handsome beyond words. Ah, but if the matter requires a three-caped greatcoat to make it so, then it shall be as you say, my love."

After the party was settled at the Donegal Arms, however, there was time for only the briefest look-in at the milliners before they made their way to the Assembly Rooms, where they were to meet Evan.

When they arrived, Evan did not seem to be among the numerous music lovers assembled, but Lenny had no trouble spotting a friend. She had not seen Edward Bunting since he had undertaken his second journey across Ireland to collect the tunes that were now successfully published as *Ancient Irish Music*.

It was clear that he was even more on fire with his passion for his country's music than before. "I shall undertake another tour as soon as possible. There are volumes more to be gained," he replied to her inquiring after his plans. "More poetry is needed. We are quite determined to secure original lyrics for every melody. And I have a surprise for you."

"Oh, do tell. What is it?"

Bunting winked behind his small, round lenses. "It wouldn't be a surprise if I told, would it?"

Flipping back the tails of his coat, he seated himself before his harp. "I shall play first for you a tune of that harper, composer, and poet who fills so deservedly large a place in our estimation, Turlogh O'Carolan." Polite applause followed, as his fingers glided over the strings. Then his voice rose, light and clear.

"Where there is music sweetly played
By the bards it is regulated,
Conversing and dancing with wit and diversion . . ."

Lenny enjoyed the lightness and brightness of the Irish poetry, carried by the swing of the music, although she did not find the verse as lyrical as she'd hoped.

Bunting stood and bowed at the conclusion of the number. When the room stilled, he bowed in the direction of the Price party. "I shall now play a most special selection for one group of friends gathered here. Before I set out on my collecting journey, Miss Carolenn Price recommended to me a harper family of ancient connection to her own. I am pleased to report that, although I failed on my earlier trip, this time I, indeed, located Cashel MacHenry in his cottage near Donegal Bay and recorded a tune handed down from his harper forebears."

Amazed, Lenny applauded until her palms stung. She turned to Wimborne. "Did you know? Is this why you brought us here? How did you find out?"

He put a long, bony finger to his lip, and she was silenced as the song began.

"The eagle no longer visits the place of old
But remains forlorn in the lonely glens,
The swan on the coast glides as black as a coal
And her feathers hang down-drooping . . ."

It was a lengthy ballad, the story of a gentleman, John Brown of the Neale in Connacht, who had killed a man in a duel and was forced to stand trial in Dublin:

"The fruits are declined, nor is there dew in the mornings;
There grows neither corn, grass, nor flower as usual.
The bees have ceased looking for honey in their sorrowing,
And if John Brown is lost they will die . . ."

Lenny looked around. What a pity Evan wasn't here for this tribute to their distant relative. Where could he be? What could possibly be so important to have kept him from this? She turned back to the performer for the final verse, glad to hear that the ballad was to have a happy ending.

"Liquor and wine in the middle of the road,
Powder a-burning and shooting like thunder.

The health of John Brown is drunk abroad,
Here he is home alive, *Deo gratias.*"

The triumphant conclusion, however, was obscured by the sound of "powder a-burning and shooting like thunder" coming from outside the Exchange building. Then she heard screams, and everyone ran to the windows.

"What could it be, Father?"

Archibald was too thoroughly occupied with Harriet's and Sarah's hysteria to answer his calmer daughter, and it was some time before Mr. Price and Thorpe were able to convey the ladies through the excited throng in the streets back to their rooms at the inn.

Speculation rang on every side.

"Aye, it's the French! That Bonaparte feller's landed at last!"

"Nae. It's the English. Come to blow us all to kingdom come. I always said it'd come to no good—all that talk of freedom."

"No matter who it is, we'll be landed in the soup. Always are. Always the same, I always say."

Even in the quiet of the inn, the turmoil below the window reached them.

"I sh-shall v-venture forth and see what I can learn." Thorpe Wimborne bowed deeply, his head wobbling.

"I shall go with you." Archibald turned from the window. "That is—" He looked at his wife and elder daughter.

"I can take care of them, Father," Lenny said. "If you will please order a strong beef tea to be sent up. And a maid to warm the bed." She turned to her mother. "Where did you pack your hartshorn, Mother? A fortifying broth will soothe you."

Perhaps an hour later, Lenny finally shut the door on her sleeping mother and sister and was able to sit before the fire, well-stoked by the maid at Lenny's directions. Neither her father nor Wimborne had returned. Where could they be? Had the men in the street been right? Was it the French? Or the English? Had her father become embroiled in trouble? She had heard no more shots, but from time to time, angry shouts from the street still reached her behind the drawn curtains.

A knock came, at first so light she thought it only coals shifting in the fireplace. On the second knock, she sprang to her feet and flew across the room. "Father? Why—" She flung the door open, and a cry rose in her throat.

But a hand, bleeding from several cuts, shot out to stifle the sound.

She pulled the battered figure into the room and bolted the door. "Evan, what happened?"

He sank into a chair before the fire, and she handed him a mug of beef broth. "You look terrible. Shall I send for wine?"

"No, there's no time. I'll have been followed. I had to see you first." He thrust a slip of tightly rolled paper into her hand. "Conceal this well. It is dangerous. When Henry Joy is released—pray God he will be—get it to him. Especially when the rising comes. He'll need it then."

Marching feet and barked orders sounded in the street below. "Soldiers. They mustn't find me here. You mustn't be implicated. Tell no one I was here. Do you hear? *No one.*" He drained the contents of the mug and stood.

"But—no, Evan, stay. I'll help you. Father will—"

"When the rising comes. Do not fail." He was out the door. The room was as if he had never been there. Except for the chill. This time it was around her heart rather than up her spine.

A moment later yelling sounded in the street. "There he is! Take him!"

She ran and threw back the curtains just in time to see her brother marched off between two officers.

She looked at the cylinder of paper in her hand. What could be so important that Evan would risk all to get it to her? Where could she keep it that not even her mother or sister would know of its existence? In passing, she glanced at a small looking glass on the wall, and an idea struck her. Yes, perhaps that would do. She unwound the coiled braid she had affixed at the back of her head with artificial flowers. It was a moment's work. She was just replacing the flowers when her father and Wimborne returned.

She could tell by the look on her father's face that he knew, but she spoke the words anyway. Perhaps if she said them, she would be able to believe it had really happened. "Evan has been taken up."

Archibald nodded. "It's the *Northern Star*. Presses smashed. Premises demolished. The government is determined to smother every spark of revolt."

"Will he be taken to Kilmainham?" Lenny had thought she had sympathized with Mary Ann. Now she realized she had been able to imagine only the faintest glimmer of what her friend had endured all these months. Could she do as well?

57

The flame of sedition was, indeed, smothered, but it was not extinguished. The numbers of discontented Irishmen who bound themselves into an underground revolutionary movement continued to grow. And Irishwomen.

Lenny could hardly let her brother sit in a Dublin jail and not take action herself. She was ready to join. But she did not know what to do. Revolutionaries met only in strictest secret. How did one make contact?

And then Franklin came to Price Manor with a letter from Evan. Lenny choked up at the sight of his careful writing. Nine had been taken up that night and were jailed together.

> We grow daily better acquainted with the jail and can bear the confinement with greater ease. We have got an additional bench to sit on which, with the one we already had, will allow six out of nine sitting at once. And yesterday we got a very great comfort—a wooden bowl to wash in. My watch makes an excellent substitute for a looking glass to shave at.

It was obvious that he had taken great thought to report only matters that would be of comfort to his mother.

"The dear boy," Harriet said in shaky voice. "I am so glad he is keeping himself up. I am persuaded that all things are easier to bear when one keeps up."

It was some time before Lenny could get Franklin to herself.

He looked at her for several moments, as if deciding whether to answer her question. "Are you certain of this, cousin? It's dangerous."

"Do you think I don't know that? I saw my brother taken, remember?"

He nodded. "I do remember. I'll take you. Tell your mother we're going for a drive tomorrow."

"Where shall I say we're going?"

His eyes took on a mischievous twinkle. "Tomorrow is the twelfth of July. Your Uncle Douglas and Cousin Jay will be marching with the Orangemen. Now don't you think anyone with proper family feeling should turn out to watch them?"

"The Orangemen marching?" She had never heard of such a thing.

"Oh, to be certain. Should be a fine sight. General Lake from the English garrison will view the Belfast doings—about seven thousand due to parade, I'm told. They say they plan to make it an annual event. Twelve thousand ready to march in Lurgan. Won't be such big doings in Newtownards, but they've not far under two thousand in the Ards Yeomanry, and most of them are Orange."

"And the United Irish are holding a meeting under their noses?" Lenny giggled.

Sarah came into the room just then, and Lenny batted her eyelashes at her cousin. "Why, Franklin, how kind of you. I'd be charmed."

Sarah sniffed. "Whatever are you two plotting?"

Franklin rose and bowed. "Miss Sarah, I've just invited your sister to view the Orange parade in Newtownards. Would you and your mother care to join us? We'll take refreshments at the public tea house before returning."

"I fear Mama is too overset by Evan's letter. Just imagine—lice in his bedding!" She shivered. "But Mr. Wimborne and I would be happy to join you."

Lenny wondered at her sister's accepting the invitation for her music teacher. She was certain Sarah would prefer to have Franklin's company to herself. Perhaps she had some notion of pairing Lenny with Wimborne so that she could engage the American's attention?

As July had begun hot and dry, the march was a dusty affair, and the Price company was well pleased to repair to the tea house afterwards.

Franklin had had a moment to prepare Lenny for what to expect. Even so, she was amazed at how cleverly matters were arranged. Apparently the Price party was not the only one left tired and thirsty after viewing the demonstration of Royalist solidarity and strength. Almost all of the small, linen-covered tables scattered around the room were occupied by groups of tea drinkers. Franklin nodded to several acquaintances as he ushered his guests to a table near the fiddle player and a bank of potted palms.

Franklin had no more than given their order for Maids of Honor and toasted tea cakes than a gentleman escorted a stylish lady wearing a Roman embroidered dress and classic headband to their table. "Ah,

Lanark, may I present my sister, Miss Balantine? If you'll be so good as to excuse the intrusion. Nothing would do but that she meet my American friend."

Franklin stood and bowed over the lady's hand, then presented the rest of his table, making some vague reference to his having met Sam Balantine at the Linen Hall.

Miss Balantine dimpled prettily and explained her eagerness to meet Mr. Lanark. "You must not think me too forward, sir, but my particular friend has recently emigrated to America, and I so long to hear of conditions there."

Franklin repeated his bow. "If you would care to take a turn around the room, Miss Balantine, it would be my pleasure to answer all your questions."

At the same time Mr. Balantine bowed to Lenny. "And would you care for a stroll until your tea arrives?"

Lenny murmured a pardon to Wimborne, who was deeply engaged in giving Sarah a lecture on the fiddler's technique, and took the arm extended to her. As soon as they were out of hearing of the others she asked, "Is this the way you conduct all your meetings, sir?"

"Almost entirely how it is done in Dublin. Such care is not always necessary in Ulster, but with the increased Orange vigilance we thought it advisable just now."

"It is very clever, but how do you discuss anything?"

Afternoon light from the arched windows lining the south wall fell across their path as Balantine inclined his head toward a group enjoying lively converse over their teacups. "Watch them for a moment."

The strollers had just reached the top of the room when one of the men at the table set down his cup and sauntered to a nearby group. At the same time two women from another party joined the group he had left.

Lenny laughed. "Amazingly clever. Is everyone in here United Irish?"

"No more than fifteen or twenty. There are twenty-five members in our society. Nine in the women's. Smaller groups make for greater secrecy. The others in the room provide our cover. When a mass meeting is desired, we meet under cover of a wrestling match or race meet."

They continued their circuit of the fashionable room, smiling and nodding to acquaintances. They had begun their second time around when Samuel Balantine became very serious. "Lanark tells me you are ready to take the oath. You understand the secrecy required and the risks involved?"

"My brother is in Kilmainham Jail, sir."

"Quite so." He jerked a nod. "Repeat after me: I, Carolenn Price, do voluntarily declare that I will persevere in endeavoring to form a brotherhood of affection among Irish of every religious persuasion . . ."

It struck Lenny as she repeated the words that this was not a vow that should be taken in secret. This should be shouted from the house-tops. She solemnly promised never to inform against any member of this or any similar society and "to work to get rid of rent and tithe and to be free as the French and Americans." It was a lovely vow. Who in this room or in any room in Ireland could not so promise?

But Balantine was not finished. "I further promise on my oath to assist the French in case of invasion."

She thought a second before repeating this. She did not want to promise something she could not in conscience fulfill. Assist the French? Revolutionaries who brought the Terror to their own country? But then, she realized, Wolfe Tone was a French officer. She would be helping her own dear friend. ". . . to assist the French in case of invasion . . ."

"And to overthrow the present government by force if necessary."

Would she take part in violent action? Support the troops if not actually pulling a trigger herself? Would she take such action if it would free Henry, Russell, Evan, and all those imprisoned like them? Certainly she would. ". . . by force if necessary," she finished firmly, head up, eyes snapping.

For the moment there was little she could do except keep Evan's scrap of paper safely concealed and await her opportunity to follow his instructions to deliver it to Henry McCracken. But at least that was something.

That December, Henry Joy and William McCracken were released and returned to Rosemary Lane.

It was as well that her family made no objection to Lenny's visiting friends in Belfast, for she would have made the trip on her own had it been necessary to do so. As it was, the ever-present Thorpe Wimborne, who was coming increasingly to fill the place of a brother in the home in Evan's absence, volunteered to accompany her, declaring himself most anxious to consult with Bunting on a matter of church music.

Once in Rosemary Lane, it was no easy matter to secure time alone with Henry. His imprisonment had left him weak and ravaged from fever and malnutrition so that his mother, sisters, and servants watched over him constantly. He rested, propped against pillows, on the chaise lounge in the drawing room, accompanied by his favorite red hound.

Lenny sat in a corner while Mary Ann plied Henry with fortified broth. Her heart ached as it did every time she looked at the pale, sunken face that had formerly been tanned and rugged. Was Evan so sadly changed as well?

Archibald had made two trips to Dublin to see him and arrange for the best in solicitors to handle his case. Wimborne had gone once, especially to carry provisions and letters. The Price women had been quick to respond with fresh bread, a wheel of cheese, and two thick blankets when Evan mentioned needing such things.

Despite that, she wondered, had this gray weakness settled on her brother? He who was not even a sworn member of the society but merely one who felt honor bound to speak out for freedom and justice? She was glad of the oath she had taken. Nothing would persuade her to pull back now until complete freedom was won. Too many people had suffered.

"You wait so patiently, Miss Price. Did you desire privacy, perhaps?" Henry's voice was firm in spite of the weakness in his body.

Lenny looked up and realized that the others had left. "Yes, I—"

Henry smiled. His smile was all the sweeter from the apparent effort it took him. "I thought so. I sent them away."

"Are we quite alone?"

"Quite. You have something from your brother?"

"How did you know?"

"He sent me a message through another prisoner. 'See my sister for me.' Innocuous enough should it have been intercepted, but I understood."

She had carefully bound up her hair in yellow ribbons that morning. It took several moments to unwind the knotted bun behind the circle of short curls that ringed her face. The paper cylinder slipped to the floor. Before she could retrieve it, there was a knock on the door.

Bunting and Wimborne entered. "We've c-come to cheer you with a song." Wimborne looked even taller and more ungainly next to the solidly built Bunting. But their voices blended perfectly. And in spite of her impatience with them, Lenny had to admit that they had composed a cheerful ditty looking forward to the glorious day when all Ireland should be free. Her attention, though, focused most sharply on the paper by her chair. Was it hidden by her skirt?

When the song ended, Henry's smile seemed forced, but his words were fervent. "I thank you. It would be quite complete, if only my dear Russell were here to enjoy it with me."

Mary Ann reentered just in time to hear the last comment. Her face, which had been so radiant since her brother's return, clouded. "So many have been released, yet he has been there longer than all. Was there any hope of his being granted bail when you left?"

Henry Joy shook his head. "I think they are perhaps harder on him because he was once a British officer. They know how severely we will need such skills when . . ."

The unfinished sentence hung in the air. All knew that the suppressed flame still smoldered. A wisp of smoke here, a spark there. Someday rebellion would blaze. Was the paper on the rug by her foot to be tinder? Or perhaps the very match to strike the blaze?

Mary Ann perhaps sensed some of Lenny's discomfort for she said, "I shall hear no talk of resisting the English just now. We tire you, brother."

"Y-yes. We intrude." Wimborne crossed the room in three long strides. "L-let us leave our honored invalid to regain his strength in peace." He bowed before Lenny, then extended the sweep of his arm to grasp the paper on the floor.

Wimborne followed her into the hall, where he placed the cylinder in her hand with a flourish. Then he dropped his courtly manner and turned to her in brotherly concern. "My dear C-carolenn, I did not wish to speak of it before the others, but we must return to Price Manor immediately. I have just received word. Your father is ill."

They left within the hour, which gave Lenny no more opportunity for time alone with Henry. She thought of leaving the paper with Mary Ann, but Evan had entrusted her to deliver it directly to Henry. And he had emphasized *when the rising comes*. It had not come yet, so there was really no need for impatience. She put up a hand to adjust her high poke bonnet. The message was safe.

When she hurried into the house, she was astonished to find her father at work in his office. "Father, are you not in bed? We were told you were ill!"

Archibald smiled the special welcome he always kept for his younger daughter. "A slight cold, my dear. That is all. But well worth the trouble if it has brought you home to us the sooner."

The note was still in secure keeping when Franklin came to Price Manor one evening in May. He was on his way to Dublin, where a brisk market existed for fine cambrics, he explained, and he knew they would want him to carry provisions to Evan. He had also brought an exceptionally fine bolt of sky blue linen as a gift for the ladies. Sarah and Harriet immediately set to discussing the best method of trimming such fabric, whether with lace, embroidery, or braid.

It was an easy enough matter for Lenny to follow Franklin from the room with the excuse of going to the buttery to choose the firmest cheese for Evan. "There is news. I see it in your face. Is it Evan?"

"News, yes. You can be glad enough Evan's out of it where he is."

"Is it starting? The rising?" It was a warm May evening, but Lenny shivered. "Aren't they to await the French invasion?"

"The French have withdrawn." Franklin looked around to be certain of their privacy. "We will stand on our own feet. It is to be the twenty-third. If all is ready, our people will overturn the coaches leaving Dublin. That will be the signal."

Three days later, the news was on every tongue. The Newry coach had been burned outside Dublin. There was a rustling in the grass across Ulster as men left their barns and fields by back roads.

Lenny too set out. She had a double duty that would allow no delay. The time Evan had alluded to had come. Henry Joy must have his message. Her assignment as a United Irishwoman was to learn all she could of the Yeomanry plans. Visiting the Aunts AM was an easy enough excuse—Aunt Adelaide was poorly again and would be happy to receive Harriet Price's new recipe for vinegarette.

And, indeed, Lenny found the aunts much in need of just such a restorative when she arrived, for Jay and Douglas had both gone off to serve king and country.

"Those odious rebels and insurrectionists, to take all our comfort and support from us!" It appeared that Auntie M was more in need of the smelling salts than Adelaide.

Auntie A was quite complacent. "I don't know why the rabble will persist. They have no hope of success."

"What do you mean, Aunt Adelaide?"

"Douglas explained it all to me before he left. The dear boy didn't want me to worry, so he made the state of affairs very clear. The republicans are without leadership. The government already has their leaders in jail."

Lenny stared. Was this possible? She must come to a Loyalist house to learn the true state of affairs of her own side? "But surely they will have seconds to take over? That is, I can't believe the matter could be so simple." Even as she had approached Lanarks' Bawn, she was quite certain she had seen movement on Scrabo that could have been nothing other than men carrying pikes, hurrying to their post. That scene undoubtedly was being acted over and over again the length of the land.

"You may quite relax, my dear. Two are captured, and—better yet —the rebel leader for County Antrim has resigned. They are entirely leaderless, Douglas was informed."

Lenny needn't ask by whom. All said the government network of spies had tightened of late. "But why did they call out the Yeomanry if there is to be no rising after all?"

"Oh, the rabble always manage to come up with something. Some fellow or other has taken over. As a matter of fact, I believe we know the man—that is to say, he wouldn't be the type we would *know*, but I'm quite certain we met him at the harp festival."

Whom could she mean? That was all so long ago. Who had been there? Everyone, it seemed: Edward Bunting, Wolfe Tone, Thomas Russell—Lenny froze. Henry Joy McCracken. *He* would be the leader. He had the determination and resourcefulness. And Mary Ann's last letter had said he was fully recovered. She held her voice level. "Could it have been Henry Joy McCracken, Auntie?"

"Yes, that's the name. Douglas said he's to lead the insurrectionists. Of course, our army will have no trouble dealing with them, but I will be glad when they are home."

Lenny's mind was in a whirl. *Get it to McCracken when the rising . . .* She had promised Evan.

And she was doubly bound. *To overthrow the present government by force. To overthrow by force . . .* She had promised on her sacred oath. She had not really thought it would come to this. But it had. And she had sworn. She must go to her friends. How could she persuade her family to allow it? The possibility of telling them she was staying with the aunts—and then making her way to Belfast—crossed her mind.

She continued to fret as she hurried her horse toward Price Manor. But when she arrived and saw Franklin's horse hitched to his small gig in the yard, she realized the way was smoothed before her. She didn't even ask him what he had told her parents when she found him awaiting her in the hall.

"You are to come with me," he said.

She hurried to her room to put on her most serviceable dark green muslin dress and wrap herself in a heavy brown mantle against the evening damp. Should she pack a bag? Surely she must—at least for appearances. Harriet Price would never allow her daughter to leave without the proper accessories for any social occasion.

Then an inspiration struck Lenny. She rushed to Evan's room. It was as if he had just left it for an evening's engagement. It seemed she could even smell his special pomade still lingering in the air. Her mother kept the chamber aired and cleaned in perfect readiness for his momentary return.

Lenny flung open the drawers of his chest and pulled out a pair of his stoutest breeches. Shirt, coat, and boots followed quickly into her rush bag. Then she took a deep breath and calmly descended the stairs.

Her mother met her in the hall and kissed her. "My dear, I am so glad you can give comfort to your friends at this time." She eyed the small case Lenny carried. "But you can't have packed all you'll need. Even if your friend is ill, there will still be musical soirees and balls in Belfast."

Lenny thought fast. "To be sure, Mother. But you've been urging me to visit the dressmaker. I can simply order what I need."

Harriet was delighted. "Excellent, my dear, excellent! That way you'll be in the height of fashion." She kissed her daughter again.

A few minutes later, Franklin was urging the horse to a full trot. Then he turned to Lenny beside him on the seat of the light carriage. "It has begun. McCracken is desperately short of men. We are calling up the women to serve as messengers."

"Will you take me to Henry? I already have a message especially for him—"

"Later. The United Irish colonels must have their orders first. McCracken's plan is well conceived. If properly executed, it can compensate for our loss of leadership. But the orders must be delivered. That is vital." He whipped the horse to greater speed.

Lenny held tightly to the edge of the seat as the gig bounced over the rutted road.

"Will you do this, Carolenn? You're not frightened?"

"Of course, I'm frightened. But I have sworn. I will do my duty."

"Good. Then here's the plan: Each colonel is to marshal his troops. They will simultaneously attack any military post in their neighborhood Thursday morning. Speed and surprise are essential. When the local garrisons are subdued, each contingent is to march to Donegore Hill outside Antrim town. McCracken will command from there. The county magistracy is meeting in Antrim Monday evening. We will take them hostage, then march to Belfast. When Belfast is taken, the north will be secure."

Lenny nodded. For what little she knew of military strategy, it sounded a workable plan. If all went well. "But, Franklin, I must deliver my message to Henry Joy—"

"All in good time. The colonels must be alerted. They have only this one night to prepare. You are to take the message to Lisburn. The leader there is a linen draper—fellow named Munro. Fine man with a spirit of adventure. We meet often at the Linen Hall. Short, dapper man. Lives over his shop in the High Street."

Lenny nodded again. "Yes, I met him once. Long ago, but I think I'd recognize him."

"And you remember the plan?" He took her through it again.

"I remember." She repeated it back to him. She shivered but refused to admit that the reaction was from anything other than excitement.

Franklin pulled the carriage to a stop at a crossroad. "I must leave you to go alone from here." He handed her the reins. "I've a horse at the inn just ahead. I go to join McCracken. When Munro has done his

511

work here, come north with him. There'll be more for you to do." He sprang from the gig.

Lenny drove on toward Lisburn, past the extensive bleach fields, where immense quantities of linen were prepared for market. Lisburn was especially famous for the beauty of its damask. But few seemed concerned about this today. Pitchforks and shovels in hand, groups of workers hurried toward town. When she passed the third contingent, Lenny realized that these men, armed with the best they had, must be answering a summons to arms. She would keep her eyes open. Perhaps Munro knew. Perhaps she would encounter him gathering his men even before she got to Lisburn.

At the foot of Prospect Hill, she came upon a gathering. Even as she approached, she could sense the crowd's rapt attention and perceived the intensity with which the man standing just uphill of them addressed the assembly. She tied her horse to a small sapling and approached, surprised to note the number of women present. She was even more surprised when she heard the speaker.

His face was turned away from her, but his words rang clearly, echoing back from the hillside, which formed a natural amphitheater. "England is not the root of all Ireland's problems. Sin is the root of all Ireland's—yea, all the world's—problems. The springs of the human soul are polluted."

What was this? Munro was preparing his troops with a sermon? Then the preacher turned toward her, and Lenny gasped. It was Sheldon Ramsey. That quiet boy who could not hold up his head and say two words together was now a field preacher? She drew closer.

"But man is never far from the cure of this evil that would rob life of all beauty and peace, yea, that would rob life of very life itself . . ." A field preacher of power and poetry.

"God provides the method for healing a soul which is thus diseased. Graciously and gladly, the divine remedy is offered: Know your disease! Know your cure! You were born in sin; therefore you must be born again—born of God. By nature you are wholly corrupted; by grace you shall be wholly renewed. In Adam all died; in Christ you may all be made alive."

They began singing a hymn.

Lenny shook herself. What was she doing here? There would be time for such things when Ireland was free. Now the *rising* was all important. She must perform her duty.

Lisburn was a town of five thousand, and it took her some time to locate Henry Munro's shop. As soon as she showed him the small green ribbon she wore pinned inside her lapel, he bolted the door and pulled the shades.

"Now, my dear, we can talk freely." He led her to a comfortable chair in the back of the shop. The man seemed astounded when she relayed the message. "The French have landed, then? Why do you make no mention of the French?"

"The French have withdrawn their support."

"And yet we proceed? I do not understand. I received word from the Antrim colonels. The decision was to await the French."

Lenny could see, though, that even as he argued against the plan, Munro was formulating his procedure. He paced the floor, gesturing dramatically. He would make a romantic leader in the field, if his sense of glory and adventure did not run too far ahead of his good sense. But perhaps this was a moment that called for brashness and an enlarged sense of honor.

"Yes, yes. I see now. Very right. We cannot have our policies dictated by the French. Certainly we shall proceed. And why should we not? Yes!" He turned toward her abruptly, his arm extended. "My dear young lady, you must undertake further endeavors for your country. Are you ready?"

"I am a sworn United Irishwoman."

"Yes, yes, indeedy. Exactly what we need at this proud moment. All must be summoned. Ride to Saintfield. They will send word from there to all the Ards." He made another sweeping gesture. "I shall establish my camp at Montalto near Ballynainch. Lord Moira's estate. You must take the word."

He turned to his desk and worked so vigorously with quill and ink, not even taking time to sit down, that for several moments Lenny thought he had forgotten her presence. When he suddenly spun toward her with a shout, she almost jumped off her chair.

"There! Done! Ride, young lady. Ride like the wind. We shall meet at dawn. Montalto. Do not fail me!"

"Indeed, I shall not fail. But my horse is tired and hitched to a gig. Do you have a saddle horse I can use?"

Munro looked perplexed. "A horse, yes. A small stableful. But as I've no wife or daughters, I have no ladies' saddles."

Lenny gave a thankful smile at the thought of her bag in the gig. "I shall ride astride, sir."

A short time later, clad in her brother's breeches, her curls tucked securely in a cloth cap the linen draper supplied her, Lenny headed back across the Lagan astride the long-legged Roger. She had only ten miles to accomplish, and she must not call attention to her mission with undue clatter and haste. Besides, it would take her a bit to become accustomed to the strange feeling of the width of the horse's body between her legs. She felt as if her feet were sticking straight out on each side of her.

This near to midsummer, the nights were never truly dark, but the evening shadows lengthened across the lush green land. A thrush sang in a bush to be answered by his mate in the hedgerow. Crickets chirped beside the road. The hay in the field was high and sweet. And on the other side of the hedge, cows mooed gently, bringing back a fleeting memory of old Bessie. Could it be possible that such a world was to erupt in flames in so short a time? Why must people fight, perhaps die? Why couldn't they just enjoy the bounty of the world God had created?

But this would not do. She had a mission. Well across the river and in more open country now, Lenny kicked her mount to a canter.

58

Two days later, as the gold of a June morning burnished the scene, Lenny looked out on the field where Munro's troops assembled. Some seven thousand had answered the call to arms. Unfortunately, few of them were armed with more than pitchforks. Yet it was a proud sight.

If only Wolfe Tone could see this. His dream was coming true. She seldom thought of Theobald anymore, but now she wished he were here—for his comfort, not hers. Still, how comforted would he be? Even in this moment, as they prepared to die side by side for the same cause, how united were the Irish? Irishmen would not even march under the same banner. Catholic pike shafts sported green cloth bordered with yellow, displaying a yellow cross. Presbyterians marched under green flags, ornamented with an uncrowned harp. Nevertheless, they were there, ready to move against the king's army.

Lenny stayed to the back. Still in her man's clothing, she would follow the troops. She might be a woman, but she would be a good soldier.

She saw that two other women served as banner bearers. Clad in green silk, heads thrown back proudly, long hair flying, they made a far different picture than did Lenny. She suspected that they were— she wasn't quite sure of the word—light skirts? ladybirds? fashionable impures? Whatever they might be, today the men called them the goddesses of liberty and reason. And they presented a grand sight with green banners flying over their heads.

Lenny's own presence was considerably less flamboyant. Her orders were to follow the victorious insurgents to Antrim. And there was nothing she longed more to do. At Antrim she would meet Henry McCracken and at last could deliver the message she had guarded so carefully for many months. Even now she seemed to feel the paper cylinder burning her scalp under her snugly coiled hair and Munro's tweed cap.

She counted on her fingers: The battle today. Victory tonight. The march north tomorrow. By this time tomorrow night, she would have fulfilled her brother's commission. She heaved a sigh of relief at the thought.

But then her attention turned again to the field. Unit commanders were relaying Munro's orders to their men.

General Cornwallis's troops were even now marching from Belfast. Cornwallis, whose defeat at Yorktown had decided the American Revolution in favor of the colonists, was now Viceroy of Ireland. They had seen no sign of his men. Yet. But they would. Munro had decided to meet the British head on. An advance Irish troop had already set forth. Munro's army would move forward but not strike until the scouts returned with their news.

Lenny attached herself to a rear guard unit. From there she had a fine view of the Mourne Mountains. They marched through a small wood, where golden sunlight fell in dapples on the shoulders of the soldiers and birdsong cheered them along. Beyond the wood rose the gentle green slopes of Windmill Hill. She drew aside to take a better look at the picturesque windmill atop the hill. The pleasant June landscape stretched around her.

She looked upward—and froze with horror. A scream rose in her throat, but, as in a nightmare, she could give it no voice. She could not tear her eyes from the gruesome sight. The giant arms of the windmill rose up and around in a great circle against the blue sky—a disemboweled republican soldier hanging from one blade.

Cornwallis's men had been there. Munro's advance guard had been dealt with and one grisly sign left as a warning. Others saw it, too, and word flew to Munro.

The warning served only to harden Munro's determination, but not all his men reacted in similar fashion. That night hundreds deserted the Irish camp. At dawn a depleted, desperate remainder marched into Ballynainch, determined to liberate it from British occupation. Three hours later, more than four hundred rebels, including the two standard bearers lay dead in the streets. Munro was taken. The British general ordered the others to lay down their weapons and return to their farms.

There would be no victorious army to escort Lenny northward, but the desperate situation here made it all the more imperative that she complete her mission. Would Henry Joy even know of the disaster in Down if she failed to get word to him? What if he, even at this moment, was waiting for Munro to reinforce his own troops? How were her friends faring? And Franklin. How was her gallant cousin?

She must make all speed to Antrim town. Thirty-five miles or more. And she dare not go the quickest route through Belfast, for the garrison would have it under strict curfew. She could go through Lisburn—if Cornwallis didn't have Munro's hometown under ban. She tried to think. At some point she must cross the Lagan. How was she to cross the river if the British were guarding the bridges? What if she were taken and searched? Would they think to unwind her hair? She had guarded Evan's message for months. She couldn't fail now.

Two hours later she rode through the green Lagan Valley and saw what she had expected. A contingent of red-coated soldiers guarded the bridge. She tugged the cap low over her eyes and hunched her shoulders forward. They had seen her. Nothing to do but plod forward.

"Halt!"

She halted.

"Where you headed, lad?"

She made her voice come from low in her throat. "My master's."

"Oh, aye? Apprenticed are ye?"

She nodded.

"What trade?"

"Linen draper." Then Lenny realized she should have said anything but that. It was the obvious answer for Lisburn, but Munro was a draper. A rider was approaching from the other side of the bridge. She could only hope he would distract the soldier's attention.

But the interrogation continued. "Linen draper? They're a rebel lot. And what master do ye claim that keeps such a fine horse?"

She couldn't think. Dare she make up a name? Would the soldiers know the names of the drapers in Lisburn? She looked around wildly.

"Lenn Price!"

Not for a few seconds did she realize that the angry shout from the approaching rider was directed at her.

"What could have taken you so long? My father sent me after you. He's not patient with slacking apprentices!"

A less stalwart woman would have given all away by swooning with relief as Sheldon Ramsey took over the brunt of the soldier's questions.

"Yes, this lazy fellow is my father's apprentice. Yes, of course, he's a linen draper. Best in the district. Ask anyone. Baird Ramsey—sign of the flowering flax in the High Street." He gave Lenny a sharp look. "Well, come on, lad. You've wasted enough of my time for one day."

They were well away from the bridge before they stopped in a small copse beside the road.

"Sheldon, it's a miracle. How—"

"I thought I saw you when I was preaching. I hoped to talk to you afterwards. Then you were gone. And traveling alone. I thought I might find you at our home, but my father said he had seen you enter Munro's shop. I questioned his stableboy and got enough of a muddled story about a young man riding off on Roger to make a few guesses. I was coming to look for you. We heard about the battle." He leaned across his saddle and took her arm. "Thank God I found you. Come home with me. You look about done for. My mother will take care of you."

"No." Lenny pulled back. "No. I have to go to Antrim."

He looked at her quizzically, then gave a sharp nod. "Aye? Important, is it?"

"Yes."

"And not something I could do for you? You could entrust any commission to me."

"No."

He thought for another moment. "Antrim town? You know there's trouble there?"

"Yes."

"Very well. Come on." He spurred his horse. "We'll have to do something about your clothes. You won't get past the first roadblock like that."

She flared. "I will remind you, sir, that I was doing very well until you interfered. I have been three days among the troops, and no one questioned my presence."

He bit his lip, but the corners of his mouth curled. "I refuse to comment on that. But if you will hear me out, I do have an alternate plan to suggest."

She kept her head in the air but was glad enough to listen. She did realize that Sheldon was not chastising her for her wild appearance or behavior, and she was determined to take him as matter-of-factly as he accepted her.

"If we retrieve your clothes from Munro's," he concluded, "and I don my cassock and bands, I can drive you in father's carriage with no questions asked. We have a strong Methodist Society in Antrim. They furnished one of the largest meetinghouses Wesley ever preached in— and they will help us if we need it."

Lenny was so overcome with his generous offer that she could only nod her assent. She ought to have protested. Sheldon had no interest in politics. There was no need for him to place himself in danger. But it was such a relief to put matters in his hands.

When they reached Lisburn, Sheldon all but carried her into the house, where he presented her to his astonished mother. "She needs sleep."

Lenny was barely aware of the gentle hands that tucked her

between fine linen sheets and snuffed her candle. She sank into blessed oblivion. It seemed a green hill rose before her, crowned with a magnificent windmill. It swept the sky with its long blades. And then, at the next revolution, a female form draped in fluttering bright green, her long red hair flowing on the breeze, swooped heavenward on the tip of the blade. Another, similarly clad, followed her on the next arm. But this one did not have red hair. Instead she had short dark curls and a braided bun. When she rose to the pinnacle of the sweep, the bun came unbraided, and a cascade of tightly rolled secret messages fell like autumn leaves into the hands of red-coated soldiers waiting below. She tried to scream.

"Lenny, Lenny. It's all right. You're safe." Warm, gentle hands were caressing her head, stroking her hair as it flowed onto the pillow. "All's well. Dona fret, lass."

She sat upright with a cry. Her hands flew to the back of her head. Her bun had been unwound, her hair brushed. "My hair! How . . . who . . ."

"My mother put you to bed. All perfectly proper."

"Do you think I care about that? My hair . . . the . . ." What could she say?

At that moment, Mrs. Ramsey, apparently wakened by the commotion, came into the room. "Is this what you're looking for, my dear? It fell out when I undid your hair."

Lenny grasped the cylinder so tightly she feared she would crush it beyond deciphering. Had it been read? Had Mrs. Ramsey shown it to anyone? Or had Sheldon really been the one to undo her hair? She dared not ask. She simply slid down into the bed and pulled up the covers. What terrible indiscretion had she committed—however unwittingly? Could she trust Sheldon? But then, what other choice did she have?

They left at first light. The journey was almost twenty miles over iniquitously rutted roads. In spite of the often harsh jostling, Lenny slept much of the way with her head resting on Sheldon's shoulder, for the remainder of her night had been disturbed by worries over the security of her message.

They were almost to Donegore Hill when she noticed two men sitting dispiritedly by the side of the road. "Stop! I know that man. I'm certain I've seen him with Henry Joy. He'll be able to direct us to the camp."

It took only a few questions to discover that there was no camp. The battle had taken place some three days before. McCracken's force had marched against the garrison of one hundred fifty regular troops,

519

yeomen and civilian volunteers. The battle had barely begun when a contingent of dragoons galloped into the town—reinforcements from Cornwallis.

"Aye, it were a right fine thing. We held against 'em. A brave, pitched battle. And the king's cavalry came off worst."

"We killed fifty of the beggars. More, we did," the other man added.

"That's right, we did. Turned tail and ran, they did. Clattering out of town as fast as could be." He slapped his thigh with a dirty hand. "Pretty sight that were, I can tell you. Finest I ever saw—the back side of all those red coats above the rumps of their horses."

"So we won!" Lenny clapped her hands. All her fatigue and discouragement fled. "That's wonderful! Where can I find Henry McCracken?"

The man shook his head. "Taken to the hills, if he's smart."

"Are they still chasing retreating soldiers?"

"Aye, that they are—with a vengeance. Brutal revenge. Hunted down and shot on sight. Bodies gathered in carts and buried in unmarked mass graves."

Lenny shuddered. That didn't sound like anything her friend would order. "There must be some mistake."

The second man spit in the dust. "No mistake. They do it on purpose. I saw such a cartload myself. 'Where did these rascals come from?' I asked the driver. Bless me, if one on the cart didn't reply, 'I come frae Ballyboley.' But he was buried along with the rest, just as he were—alive."

Lenny buried her face in her hands. "It can't be. It can't be."

"Aye, s'truth enough. English orders. They mean to see there's no more risings."

"English?" Lenny shook her head. "But we won. You said the cavalry retreated."

"Aye, so it did. Right enough. We had the victory fair and clear. Until our own reinforcements arrived. Marched right into the face of the fleeing cavalry. Thought they was being attacked. Flung down their weapons and took to their heels."

His companion continued, "Then Cornwallis's artillery arrived. Pitchforks don't stand long against brass guns. Not likely any Irish will soon go to catch cannon balls on the points of pikes again."

Lenny slumped against the carriage seat. Had Sheldon's hand not been firm on her shoulder, she might have fallen. "But Henry Joy survived?"

"He was standing, last I saw him. And his brother too. Not more than a score fell in battle. It's the hunting down that's the danger."

She drew a shaky breath before the next question, but she had to know. "And Franklin Lanark? Do you know him?"

"The big Yankee, you mean?"

"Couldn't easy miss him, could you?"

Through all the horror of the past days Lenny had not felt the chill that gripped her now. "You mean, couldn't miss him with a shot?"

"Aye, that's the size of it. Not dead, though—the last I knew. Never know how far a wounded man could go in the hills, though."

Lenny glanced away as two riders appeared at the rise of the road. When she looked back to her informants, she gasped to see that they had melted into the copse behind them.

The riders, Royalist soldiers, stopped by the carriage. "You meet any straggling rebels on this road, parson?"

Before Sheldon could answer, the other one laughed. "If you do, tell 'em they've hell to pay for their actions. There's no escaping retribution."

"Apart from the blood of Christ, there's none for any of us. I will gladly tell them, as I tell all men." Sheldon nodded politely. "Good day, gentlemen."

Lenny was too shocked to know what to do. She must do something, but she couldn't think. The reassuring, steady plod of the horse's hooves seemed the only thing she was able to focus on. Even the rough jolts of the carriage were welcome. They helped jar sensation back into her numbed consciousness.

Then she realized Sheldon was turning the carriage. "No. Wait. We can't go home. I—there's something I have to do. I can't think what. But there's something. It's important."

"I'm taking you to your friends in Belfast."

"Yes. That's it. I must tell them—that is—" What would she do now? "Mary Ann will know what to do." She gripped the seat and held on.

When they arrived at Rosemary Lane, it was easy to see that the McCrackens had been informed of the fate of the rising. Even the dogs failed to bound forward with their usual joyful barks.

Mary Ann met them with strained, white face and red-rimmed eyes, but her manner was calm. "We have had no word of my brothers. We are sick with apprehension. My mother and Margaret have taken to their beds, but Rose Ann and I are determined to do something as long as hope lasts. It's just that—" she bit her lip and swallowed hard "—we don't know what to do."

It was an easy matter to get alone with her friend in the subdued household. "My dear Mary Ann, you must tell *me* what to do. I am so torn. Perhaps if I had acted sooner, if I had been less scrupulous about

Evan's instructions—oh, I just don't know." She was determined to be as brave as her friend, but it was difficult.

Mary Ann grasped both of Lenny's hands and led her to the edge of her bed. "Here. Sit. You must tell me all. If I am to advise you, I must know all."

As clearly as she could, Lenny recounted that night at the Donegal Arms when the Royalists smashed the *Northern Star* office and took Evan prisoner. "I tried to give the message to Henry when he got out of prison, but I was interrupted. And Evan had said, 'When the rising comes.' Have I done terribly, terribly wrong?"

"I have no way of knowing without reading the message."

Lenny hesitated. All these months of guardianship had made her overcautious.

"I must urge you. If there is any hope of helping my brothers, you must let me see it."

Lenny nodded. "Yes, and we must help. Franklin, he too—" She focused all her effort on unpinning her hair. The cylinder fell to the floor.

Mary Ann picked up the paper and unrolled it carefully.

Lenny held her breath as her friend read.

In a moment Mary's face lit in a smile. She gathered Lenny into an energetic hug. "Oh, it's marvelous! A miracle! How could Evan have known all those months ago! The very thing. There is hope!" She jumped to her feet and started for the door. "We must find my brothers without delay. I must go to the harbor—"

Lenny was almost afraid to ask. "Am I not to know what it says?"

Mary Ann was astonished. "You mean you've carried this on your person all these months and not read it? What a good, faithful creature you are! Who could imagine such loyalty to duty?" She came back to the bed. "Your magician of a brother has placed in my hand the key to my brother's life. It is the name of a sea captain who will spirit Henry from Ireland in his vessel. Pray God he is in harbor now."

This time she took a bonnet and shawl from the stand by her dresser. "Tell no one where I've gone, but tell Rose Ann to be ready for an outing as soon as I return. She will understand. And tell Cook to prepare the largest hamper for a picnic—two hampers." Again she paused and took Lenny's hands. "Rose Ann and I shall search every hill in Ireland for my brothers. You are so good. Will you help us prepare?"

"Certainly I will. But may I not go with you? My cousin is out there somewhere as well. Out there . . . wounded."

"Yes, of course. If you want to go, you shall. Do you think it possible that I could deny you anything—you who have brought my brothers' passport to life?"

Hours later, however, twilight was creeping over the country, and Mary Ann had not returned.

"What could have happened? Do you think she's been taken up?" Lenny all but whispered to Rose Ann, sitting next to her at the table. The household was attempting to take a light supper of boiled chicken and a molded jelly, but Lenny found that she could no more than play with the stem of her wine glass. She was far too nervous to force anything past her lips.

"Doubtless it is the curfew. She will be lucky to get home at all, now that dusk has fallen. Soldiers patrol every street. *Oh!*" Rose Ann turned to Francis, the quiet older brother who sat at the head of the table because Mr. McCracken was keeping his wife company in her room. "Francis, the name card! If the soldiers come and find guests whose names aren't displayed—"

"I have seen to the matter, my sister. You needn't fear. We will likely be commended for keeping a man of the cloth under our roof."

Lenny was puzzled by that exchange.

"The curfew is rigorous in Belfast," Francis explained. "Each house must display the names of all persons within. All exits from the city are carefully guarded. None are allowed to leave town without passes. The officers will take up all persons who cannot give a satisfactory account of themselves."

Lenny felt the color drain from her face. "We have no passes."

Sheldon smiled his slow half grin. "I did not undertake my profession as a matter of convenience, but it seems that I could have done no better if I had looked to do so. I assume the recommendation of the rector of Saint Anne's will be sufficient? Unlike many of the established church, he has been a fine support to our Methodist societies. He will grant me leave to visit our members."

Just then a rattling of the garden door told them that Mary Ann was returning the back way. The fact that a young lady could not approach her own home in the streets of Belfast told Lenny more forcefully than anything else of the great danger hanging over them all.

The next morning was unusually hot and clear. The three women dressed in cotton frocks and straw bonnets. Sheldon filled the back of the carriage with Cook's ample hampers, taking special care with the one Rose Ann added containing medical supplies. They proceeded openly, as any setting out to distribute aid to the needy in the countryside would do. Soldiers guarding the Antrim Road gave their passes cursory glances and waved the country parson on his way.

"But how do you know where to look?" Lenny asked Mary Ann as they rolled through the open countryside northwest of Belfast.

"I asked myself where they would have gone. The battle was in

Antrim town. They would want to turn toward Belfast. What, I asked, would provide the best cover between here and there—cover they would be familiar with?"

Lenny thought for a moment. Then she remembered. That golden day. It seemed a lifetime ago. The women and children laughing and calling to one another from carriage to carriage. The men riding spirited horses, racing one another and talking bravely of the victorious days ahead for their country. Even the fact that their dear friends were sailing to exile had cast hardly a shadow. And that was where, Evan had told her later, the men had taken their brave vow never to rest until Ireland was free.

"Cave Hill," Lenny said.

Mary Ann nodded.

But for all their attempt to give the impression, the present expedition was no picnic. Their own lives, as well as those of the men they sought to aid, relied on their doing nothing to attract the attention of soldiers patrolling the area or to raise the suspicion of country people who might be glad of a reward for information. Therefore it was necessary that they proceed at a leisurely pace. That suited their purposes well enough, as it enabled the women to scan the countryside, looking for any clue that might tell them a dear one was in hiding nearby. By the time evening fell, however, they had seen nothing.

"Could I have been mistaken?" Mary Ann asked. "I was so certain we would find them here." Again she studied the spot where they had spread their rugs and hampers on that distant, happy day. She sighed.

Lenny thought she had never seen her friend nearer to discouragement as they took shelter for the night in a fisherman's abandoned cottage on the shores of Lough Neagh. Lenny could find little to be encouraged about, either. Mary Ann's logic had seemed unassailable. But perhaps that was the very reason the McCracken brothers would not have taken refuge in this area. No English officer would know about their family picnic, but simply the landmark's location between Antrim and Belfast could make it seem an obvious choice.

What if the men had gone northwest from Antrim into the glens? That would be fine for able-bodied men. But her wounded cousin could not travel so far. She tossed on the straw-filled mattress that was the best the humble cottage could offer. What if they were too late?

The open smile, broad shoulders, and vigorous manner of her cousin rose in her imagination. So much charm and energy couldn't be gone from the world. She had felt much the same when Wolfe Tone sailed from Ireland. Now was the cause of Irish freedom to take her cousin as well? Was the cause to take everyone dear to her?

At last she drifted off into an uneasy sleep. Some time later the sound of rain pounding the window wakened her. Then she realized it wasn't rain but small pebbles pelting the shutter. She shook Mary Ann on the pallet beside her. Together the two women stole to the door and opened it a crack.

A small, towheaded boy stood there. "Gardener sent me. Says he'd be happy of a rose."

Lenny blinked into the morning dimness. Had she heard rightly? A *rose*?

But Mary Ann held a finger to her lips. She turned to her sister-in-law, Rose Ann. The three women wrapped themselves in shawls and crept from the hut without waking Sheldon, sleeping on the far side of the room.

The lad skipped ahead of them and ducked through a small wooden door in the side of the gardener's lodge.

Rose Ann's face lit in a smile of recognition as soon as the elderly keeper of the lodge ambled toward them. "It's Roscoe. He's a United Irishman. He must have been keeping watch."

The old man pulled his cloth cap from his head. "Aye, that's so. And as true a friend to all that's green as ever Ireland had. Put out to pasture like a toothless horse now." He grinned to show that the analogy was apt. "But I've a use or two left for these old bones. And keepin' touch with friends higher up the hill is one o' 'em."

"Oh, yes." It was easy to see that Rose Ann could barely restrain herself from hugging the man. "William. Do you know—"

"Sweet William, is it? That's right, one o' the best flowers in my garden. But it blooms higher on up, nearer the fort."

Mary Ann nodded. "Yes, I was right! I just didn't take my idea far enough. The vow they made that day—it was at MacArt's fort at the very top of Cave Hill. Brian MacArt O'Neill—killed by the English two hundred years ago. Some things never change."

"But do you know—" Lenny began. "My cousin—a tall American. He was wounded."

"I'm just a simple gardener. I know not but flowers and herbs." He turned to a plant with a wide, pale green leaf. "Dock leaf. Very astringent. Very healing." He broke off three leaves and gave them to Lenny. "Happen you'll need this."

The gardener's enigmatic words gave them hope and direction, if little actual information.

Back in the cabin, they breakfasted on oaten biscuits and hard cheese before beginning the climb up the hill. They left the carriage with the caretaker, for the ascent would be precipitous in places. They must proceed on foot, with Sheldon carrying the hampers. And that only added to Lenny's worries. Could a wounded man make such a climb? Yet, if he *had* taken such a refuge, he must not be badly wounded.

The comfort such desolate hills offered was that English soldiers were unlikely to be in so rough and isolated an area. But the going was difficult. They were now some distance from any picnic site, although Sheldon still carried the hampers in hopes of finding men to need the supplies. As Mary Ann approached a shepherd watching over a small flock, Lenny hoped desperately that there would be news. She did not relish the thought of spending the night in the open in such wilderness.

"Be hopeful," Sheldon said gently. "All will be well."

She smiled. Very few things turned out well, she thought. Then she saw the shepherd point and Mary Ann start off, barely taking time to beckon the others to follow.

In the back room of a deserted cottage they found a clutch of huddled fugitives. Rose Ann flung herself into her husband's arms with a cry of delight.

But Lenny's heart sank. Her cousin was not among the small, ragged number.

Nor was Henry Joy, but William knew where his brother was. He had continued farther up the hill to a yet more remote hideout—another two hours' climb. William was giving directions when a soft moan drew Lenny's gaze to a shadowed corner. There a figure lay on a mound of heather.

"Franklin!" She was across the room and kneeling by his side in seconds. Her heart sank when she felt his burning hand. Was she too late to stop the fever? His eyes were bright and glazed, but he seemed to recognize her. One look at the dried blood caking his shirt told her she could not nurse him here.

"Bring me some water." She didn't wait to see if her orders were followed before turning back to her patient.

A few minutes later, Sheldon knelt by her side. He set a wooden pail of fresh stream water on the beaten earth floor and removed his coat. He had taken off his shirt and was tearing it into strips before she understood what he was doing. "You need rags and bandages," he said.

Grateful, she dipped a rag in the cool water and bathed Franklin's face and hands while Sheldon attended to removing the jacket. It took a considerable time to soak the bullet-torn coat loose from the wound, but Sheldon was assiduous. He soaked each area until the dried blood loosened, then ripped free more of the fabric just until it pulled against the skin again.

When at last the mangled shoulder was exposed, Lenny resisted her impulse to gasp in horror and began sponging the wound.

It looked slightly more hopeful when the worst of the blood was cleaned away. The wound was deeper than she had hoped, but at least the ball had torn through at an angle rather than lodging in the shoulder. For all her determination, she doubted that she would have had the fortitude to remove shot from a man's flesh. She placed the old gardener's dock leaves over the wound and bound it all tightly with strips of Sheldon's shirt.

Then they quickly formed a plan. Mary Ann would go alone on up the hill to Henry. Rose Ann would stay in the hut with her William as long as she could. The McCracken women would make their way back to Belfast in a day or two.

Mary Ann gave Lenny a parting hug. "I shall be eternally grateful to you. Take good care of your Franklin, and do not worry about us. I shall send you word when the ship sails and Henry is safe." Her voice caught. "We owe you Henry's life."

Half carrying the nearly delirious Franklin, Lenny and Sheldon began the long, painful trek back down the mountain to the carriage. Then, traveling by back roads, they made for Price Manor. Lenny supported Franklin, clad in Sheldon's cassock, on the seat beside her and held her breath every time the carriage lurched.

She should have felt triumphant at rescuing her cousin, but despondency engulfed her. She had been true to the vow she had sworn; yet the Irish were not united. She had served in the rising; yet it had failed. Were all her efforts to be so meaningless? Reason had failed. Art had failed. Politics had failed. War had failed. What was left?

59

Lenny picked up her long-discarded sketch pad. In the weary, empty days following the failure of the rising, Harriet Price had urged her listless daughter to clean out the drawers under her wardrobe. As it made little difference to Lenny what she did or didn't do, she had as well please her mother. Now she was amazed at the memories the detritus of her childhood brought back to her. When had she made this sketch of the hindquarters of old Bessie? She shook her head at the fond remembrances of the obstinate bovine who had been her favorite of the herd. Bessie was long gone, as were the three calves she had born.

And these pictures she had copied from French fashion cards—the shaggy-haired man in a Phrygian bonnet with a tricolor cockade, the girl in a bonnet of the populace with its three-colored ribbon and rosette—Sarah had worn just such a creation when all Belfast turned out to celebrate the French Revolution in anticipation of the day when Ireland would win its own liberty, equality, and fraternity. Now war continued on the Continent, and France teetered uneasily under the regime called by many the Directorial Terror. She tossed the sketch pad aside.

Perhaps cleaning out her letter box would be more productive. She rose, but she never got to it, for at that moment she heard a shout from her mother in the garden. Lenny took one glance out the window, pulled up her skirt, and dashed headlong down the stairs.

"Evan! Evan! It *is* you! It's a miracle!" She flung herself into her brother's arms just as he dismounted. He was thin and gray and his clothing soiled and rumpled, but he was there, breathing the fresh air, free under the July sunshine. "A miracle!"

Evan returned her hug. "All life is a miracle. I never realized it so until I was nearly deprived of it."

"But how is this come about? Did you stand trial?"

"No. The Crown is resting easier with the rising so thoroughly subdued. And as not even the most cheerful liar among their spies could claim I was ever a member of the Society, my solicitor convinced

His Majesty's counsel that I was serving no purpose as a guest of Kilmainham."

"But that's wonderful! And Thomas Russell? Is he to be freed at last? Oh, Mary Ann will be so very glad! All is coming right for her at last. No one could deserve it more."

At that moment Archibald joined them from his office in the back of the house and swept his son into his arms.

Soon the family sat around the dining table spread with everything Cook could find in the larder and buttery to "put some meat on the poor young master's bones." Franklin, still frail and carrying his arm in a sling, had given Evan a full account of the rising before Evan returned to Lenny's question.

"I am sorry to have to tell you, sister. But there seems very little hope of Russell's prompt release."

She was about to protest at the unfairness of it all when Evan's next words drove all other thoughts from her mind. "There was little enough hope for him, but now it will go harder for all United Irish. I was lucky to have been released and away from Dublin before word reached there that McCracken had been taken. I—" He stopped at Lenny's outcry.

"Taken? Henry Joy? No, it can't be. I gave him the captain's name. They were so grateful. It was all set. He would be well away—" Realizing with horror what she was blurting out, Lenny clapped her hands over her mouth.

"Spies! Dirty, rotten spies." Franklin, still far from his normal strength, had been leaning heavily against his chair, but now he burst forth. "It has been so in all we tried to do. It was as if the English knew our every move ahead of time."

Lenny thought. Everyone knew the country was riddled with spies, but this made them seem so close. Had Mary Ann been followed when she went to the quay? Or did they know all along where Henry was and simply waited for him to come down from his mountain hideout?

Or was the answer even more sinister? Something—someone—closer to home? Impossible. It couldn't be anyone they knew. But the chill persisted. She fled from the table.

The next day Lenny and Evan set out for Belfast. They went straight to the Exchange, where Henry Joy's trial was already in progress.

She held tight to her brother's arm as she looked at the prisoner in the dock. He stood as tall and proud as ever she had seen him. He was suntanned from his time living rough, his hair longer than fashionable but carefully combed. Most outstanding was his composure and extraordinary serenity.

Lenny slipped quietly into a seat beside Mary Ann and gave her hand a comforting squeeze. Mary Ann and her father were the only family members present.

Crown Attorney John Pollock concluded his examination of the witness and requested a brief recess. In a moment, the reason for the unusual proceeding was clear. Pollock requested the aged John McCracken to join in a conference with his son. It seemed the Crown offered banishment if Henry would give incriminating evidence against other rebels, obviously hoping the frail father would encourage his son to do so. It was a request that would be difficult for Henry Joy to refuse.

"I will obey my father," the leader of the rising said.

But John McCracken, frail in body yet strong of courage, would not be drawn. "Harry, dear boy, you know best what you ought to do."

Henry Joy hugged the old man. "Thank you, Father. And farewell."

The sentence was for immediate execution.

The gallows were erected in front of the Market House, the very building where Henry and his brothers and sisters had attended school as children. At five o'clock that summer evening the street was thronged with townsfolk. All windows overlooking the square had been rented to those who wished to observe the spectacle in comfort.

Lenny was thankful for the lace veil of her rose silk bonnet. She drew it over her face and was glad that Mary Ann, walking beside her brother to the gallows, had a similar shielding of embroidered gauze.

Indeed, it was a scene necessitating much protection for a sensitive person. In recent weeks four rebels had been executed in this square, each hanged and beheaded. Their gruesome, sightless heads gaped on tall pikes, staring down on the crowd. Flies buzzed around them as Henry, controlled to the end, bade his sister farewell and, accompanied by his minister, ascended the gallows.

It was the sound of the flies that stayed with Lenny through the coming weeks. The flies and the stench of rotting flesh. Had Henry Joy McCracken's handsome head joined the others as a frightful warning against insurrection? She knew that Henry Munro had been likewise executed in Lisburn. And how many more? It was said that altogether the rising had cost twenty thousand lives. And to what end? She could only be thankful that her brother and cousin were not among that grisly number.

60

There were few United Irishmen leaders who had either not been apprehended or who had not repudiated any association with the ideas of the brotherhood. The movement was dead—but not all who held such sentiments, including Franklin Lanark.

Although Lenny talked to him little about his feelings and kept her suspicions to herself, she was aware that he continued to receive letters from a wide correspondence. However, that was all she knew. Franklin was still too weak to carry on an extended conversation, and, even if he had been vigorous, one could not spend three minutes alone with him without Sarah's interrupting. But most of all, Lenny didn't want to know. She hoped there was no more intrigue brewing. If there was, she was determined to have no part of it.

She had increased reason to suppose all idea of French assistance dead, for everywhere people talked, triumphantly or dispiritedly, of the great victory Lord Nelson had achieved over the French navy in the Battle of the Nile. And yet Lenny felt a familiar chill when she observed the distinctive handwriting on Franklin's most recent letter. Surely Wolfe Tone knew that the cause was hopeless. Surely the news of the disastrous rising had reached him on the Continent.

Her fears and questions lingered. It was October when a veritable flood of answers began. The French had come. They attempted a landing in Lough Swilly but had been blown asunder as they approached the northern Irish coast. The British navy engaged them in battle the next day. The French put up a stubborn fight, especially the *Hoche*—one of her batteries commanded by Theobald Wolfe Tone. Two hundred men were killed on the *Hoche*. The vessel was sinking when it was finally captured. Tone was taken prisoner.

Indeed, Theobald Wolfe Tone was the first prisoner to step onto Irish soil. Rumor said that even then, among the boatload of French prisoners, he might have escaped recognition and capture. Other French officers were sent to England, where they were exchanged for British prisoners. But Tone was marched to Dublin and imprisoned in the castle. And gossip foamed at full spate.

How did the authorities recognize Tone?

An old colleague had seen and identified him when the prisoner boat landed.

Too convenient. The scene must have been staged. The authorities had known which ship Tone was on.

Spies. His plans had been betrayed.

And everyone looked over his shoulder and under his bed.

Waves of news washed northward from Dublin. Word that often traveled so slowly now seemed to race ahead of the event itself.

Clad in the full-dress uniform of a French naval officer, including braid-trimmed blue coat and cocked hat with tricolor ribbon, Tone faced the reading of the charges of treason lodged against him.

He requested permission to explain his actions. And here the rumor mill could found its stream upon fact for his statement was reported in the *Belfast News Letter.* "What I have done, I have done. I am prepared to stand the consequences," he said.

> The great object of my life has been the independence of Ireland. For that I have sacrificed everything that is most dear to man. I have endeavoured by every means in my power to break the connection with England which is the bane of my country. I have laboured in consequence to create a people in Ireland. I have laboured to abolish the infernal spirit of religious persecution by uniting the Catholics and the Dissenters.
>
> I have attempted to follow the same line in which the noble George Washington succeeded. I have attempted to establish the independence of my country. I have failed in the attempt. My life is in consequence forfeited and I submit. The Court will do their duty, and I shall endeavour to do mine.

Asked if there was anything more he had to say, Tone requested execution by firing squad as befitted a soldier. It was denied. He was to be hanged.

That night in his cell, Theobald Wolfe Tone slit his throat with a penknife. Assurance followed quickly that the wound had been dressed and the prisoner was resting. By next day he was much better, and there was little doubt that he would recover.

And suddenly Lenny saw a glimmer of hope. Now, at last, public sentiment, if not actual pity, turned toward Tone. The great regret at his unhappy fate, the sincere commiseration for his wife and family— perhaps they would yet win him a reprieve and banishment.

Lenny fervently hoped so. She thought of the lighthearted girl Theobald's Matilda had once been. How had four years of distress and hardship living in a wilderness changed her? She thought of the golden-haired children she had once led in games in a May garden. She could still see Maria catching her beribboned hoop on a stick and laughingly tossing it to little William. Maria would be leaving her childhood now—if her father's troubles hadn't already robbed her of it.

It was a cold November day, but Lenny, in need of fresh air, was walking in the frosty field. Her breath came in agitated puffs as she recalled old, treasured hopes. How could it all have gone so wrong? Could there still be hope? So many were gone beyond hope.

"Carolenn!" Sheldon Ramsey hailed her from across the field.

Her heart leaped at the sight of him striding toward her. She had not seen him since summer. Did he bring news? Good news, surely.

His face, however, was somber, and her heart sank. "Oh, no. Not more trouble. Is it Tone? Tell me it isn't so."

He took her hand. "I wish I could, Lenny. I know how much you thought of him. Too much for your good."

"I was only a child. So were you."

"Yet I noticed your caring. I always noticed you." He paused, whether for embarrassment over his declaration, she couldn't tell. Then he continued. "Lenny, Tone is dead."

"*Dead?* They said he would recover! Everyone said public sympathy would force the English to grant banishment. You mean they executed an injured man?"

"No, no. He died of his self-inflicted cuts. The wound turned septic. His lungs inflamed."

She gasped and turned away.

Sheldon placed a comforting hand on her shoulder. "It might have been so anyway. There were signs he was unwell before the suicide attempt."

She took a shaky breath. "He was in pain?"

"Yes. And delirious."

"His body?"

"Given to his friends. To be interred privately in his family's plot."

She walked slowly deeper into the field, and, thus dismissed, Sheldon did not follow.

So it was truly all over. She thought back through the whole muddled tale of miscarried hopes, of bravery and treachery, of planning and betrayal. True, it had been the weather that actually defeated the French fleet, but the failure of the United Irish to rally support had aggravated French indecision. Had someone known of the plans and sent out the word to the Loyalists to intercept and confuse the messages?

Then there was the rising. She shuddered at the thought of that fiasco. It was now well known that several Irish colonels had passed their instructions straight to the British. How many spies had told Cornwallis where to deploy his troops, as well?

The whole thing began to form a pattern. Or was it merely that she was in a highly suggestible state because of the death of yet another friend? Had emotional heat simply fired her imagination, or had it cleared her vision to see what had been in front of her all along? Henry Joy had been arrested on his very way to the ship that would carry him to freedom. Unless the captain had talked out of turn, no one knew of the plan outside the McCracken and Price households. And then the fortuitous taking of Wolfe Tone. How many people in all Ireland had known of the invasion plan? There couldn't have been many. And yet she was certain Franklin had received word.

The gripping chill she had learned not to disregard held her frozen. Someone near her had known every time—someone who had access to letters in Price Manor. Worse, someone who had seen what she had carried braided into her hair. She was part of the betrayal herself. Somehow her carelessness with knowledge entrusted to her had led to the disaster. Her friendships, her correspondence, her membership in the United Irishwomen—someone had used all that to betray Ireland. How was it possible that she could be part of the betrayal when her motives were so good?

Think, she told herself. *Who could it be? Who was always there? Always popping up at odd moments? Who could have seen my letters? Franklin's letters? Evan's note?* Names rang in her head. But she could accept none of them.

Mary Ann? Ridiculous. Her friend loved her brother more than she loved her own life. Her whole family was devoted to the cause. Weren't they? What of the less outspoken ones? Quiet Margaret, who always chose to stay home with her mother? Francis, the older brother, assuming leadership of the family from the ailing father? John, the little brother everyone still thought of as a boy, but who was growing up fast?

She was grasping at straws, desperate to think the culprit was somewhere other than Price Manor.

She mulled over Edward Bunting. As organist for the Church of Ireland, his sentiments would likely be Royalist, for all his disavowal of interest in politics. His position as a member of the McCracken household would make him privy to information. And his travels back and forth across Ireland multiple times were a perfect excuse to go into any area, any house, looking for old Irish music.

Having reached the hedgerow bordering the field, Lenny found a large, flat rock and sat down. She would focus on the issue with precision. She began to consider every name carefully.

Franklin Lanark. There was no denying his access to all information and the carte blanche all groups granted him as an American. And who could refuse his winning personality? Yet he had nearly died for the cause. She shook her head.

Another Lanark, perhaps. The Aunts AM would betray anything they knew, that was certain. But it would be without guile or contrivance. Certainly a great part of spy business rested on gossip, but that did not make every gossip a spy.

Douglas or Jay? No doubt where their loyalties lay. And no doubt that any information that came their way would go straight to the Yeomanry and Orangemen. But it would be a straightforward denunciation as good Presbyterians were taught to make in the meetinghouse. Neither her uncle nor cousin would have the patience or wit for scheming.

And her own household? It was more thinkable that the Aunts AM could be spies than Harriet or Sarah. Still, she couldn't deny what a clever cover her sister's empty-headedness would make for a plot. But Sarah had ever been so. This was no contrivance. Nor was her father's solid trustworthiness. Easier to believe Wolfe Tone the traitor than Archibald Price. Or Evan, who had risked so much and nearly lost all to support his friends and country in a cause he was never sworn to.

That left two others—unless it was to be a servant. Her heart leaped at the thought. Yes. Let it be a servant, sneaking around while the house slept at night, reading letters, writing coded messages. But she rejected that hope. How many servants were so literate? Or had the time for such doings? No, she must consider Thorpe Wimborne and Sheldon Ramsey.

Was the ungainly Wimborne as shallow as the goggle eyes he made at Sarah caused him to appear? His jug-handle ears were large enough to hear all whispers. And, like Bunting, he had his music as a passport to any group.

That thought chilled her more than all others, for someone had an even surer pass. Someone had demonstrated its effectiveness in driving her halfway across Ulster and back under the very nose of searching redcoats. She closed her eyes and recalled the night at the Ramsey home when she had wakened, crying from nightmares, to find Sheldon stroking her hair. *Had* he read the note before turning to comfort her?

His habit of popping up unexpectedly was established behavior —behavior she now realized she had come to look forward to more than she wanted to admit. If Sheldon were the spy, would her heart allow her mind to denounce him? That thought caused such pain that she doubled over.

And then a wash of hopelessness dulled the pain. No matter who the informer, what did it matter? Even if it could be proved, what could be done?

She could think of only one person to turn to in her dilemma. Her mind reeling with questions, Lenny made her way back to the house and the small office where she knew she would find her father.

Archibald, slimmer than formerly, his dark hair grayed but his blue eyes no less brilliant for the small wrinkles playing at their corners, gave his daughter a welcoming smile. "Ah, come to see your old father, have you? It's been long and long since we've had one of our grand discussions about the causes of evil in the universe."

Lenny smiled and sat in the chair across from his desk, smoothing the skirt of her simple ivory chemise dress. "Those were good days, Papa. They seem so long ago. Life was simpler then."

She sighed. How pleasant it would be if all one had to worry about were abstract questions of good and evil. "I am beginning to think the Deists are right. God must have put the pieces of the clock together, then gone off and let it run on its own. How else could things be in such a mess?"

Archibald put the tips of his long fingers together and leaned back in his chair. "Oh, my dear, how I have missed our little talks! Only the other day I was reading our fine Bishop Berkeley on that very subject. And I must say your own enervation is evidence against your assertion."

"How is that?"

"All things mechanical, like the clock of your analogy, and all things human, as you yourself, run down, lose their energy, become powerless. The fact that the laws of nature do not do so—that gravity does not lose its hold, that the sun does not fail to shine, that water does not fail to wet—is evidence of an active creative energy behind the world, sustaining all. Parliament could pass all manner of laws regulating rainfall and wind velocity, but they would accomplish nothing. There must be power behind laws for them to work."

Lenny felt too pressed by other matters to explore that thought, but just the fact that her father held it out to her made her feel better. "Thank you, Father. But I need to discuss quite another matter. I have discovered . . . that is, I have reason to believe . . ."

It was so hard to put it in words. In spite of her own certainty, she knew it would sound ridiculous. She took a deep breath. "Father, someone in our close circle of acquaintances—perhaps our own family—is a spy."

Archibald did not so much as blink. "And how do you know this, daughter?"

She recounted all she had so recently gone over in her mind, including the futility of seeking justice against the betrayer.

Archibald nodded. "Yes, you are quite right that the guilty party would be more likely to receive a medal than a jail sentence. Government policy is a strange thing, my dear. But there are a few nuances here you might best consider."

He explained that many were now saying English policy had actually been aided by the rebellion. "Some would go so far as to suggest that England herself had fomented the rising as a means of demonstrating the desirability of having a stable Crown government."

Lenny listened carefully, knowing she would need to think long on the matter to understand the implications of what her father said.

Then he returned to the question of dealing with the spy in their midst. "The only punishment would have to be to deprive him of his standing in the community."

She frowned, not understanding.

"Spies live by their social connections. Public denunciation would ruin him. Exposure, the weight of public opinion, would be its own sentence. Let those who do deeds of darkness in the shadows be revealed by shining the light of truth upon them."

"I see. That would do!" She sprang to her feet and flew to her father to embrace him.

Archibald returned her embrace but held up a warning finger. "But you must be cautious, my dear. Go slowly."

Lenny's face fell. She did not care for slow and cautious.

"You must be very certain. It would not do to name the wrong person. Or to name the right person at the wrong time. Be sure. Wait your time. If you are right, the time will come."

61

And so Lenny bided her time. Of all the difficult decisions she had made in her life, all the actions that had required courage, none had been harder. Certainty required detached observation. To achieve this she must become a detached, objective observer of the two men she suspected. She must pass up no opportunity of being in their company. She would take up her flute again for an opportunity of more discussions with the music master—although almost any excuse would have done, now that Sarah spent all her time with their American cousin and had left Wimborne cooling his heels.

Far more difficult was renewing her theological discussions with Sheldon Ramsey and yet keeping emotional distance. She well knew the dangers of allowing her analysis to be distracted by fond feelings. She had had no idea how much pain she would feel at keeping their relationship purely academic. She was now cut off from her friend by her own decision. He was as lost to her as those who had died. Sheldon Ramsey became to Lenny yet another casualty of the rising.

Many times she asked herself if any cause could be worth such loss. She now realized how close they had become and how much her times with him, infrequent though they were, had meant to her. And yet she must know. She dare not give in to her heart and condemn herself to living the rest of her life shadowed by the ghost of suspicion.

On January 22, 1799, the Irish Parliament in Dublin heard a speech from the Throne proposing that Ireland be united with England under one flag and one parliament. The Crown's timing was perfect. The Ascendancy was still reeling from all the insecurities caused by the insurrection of the year before. The Irish government was entirely dependent on British military and financial support. And it seemed that no one in Belfast, formerly the center of radical opposition, had the spirit to raise an objection.

At such a crucial moment, Lenny knew, spies for the government would have their eyes and ears open for every murmur. She smiled as she sharpened a fresh quill with her penknife. It would be a pity, would it not, when the agent would be so desperate for news, to deny him any tidbit that could be passed on to a superior? If the burning topic of the proposed legislative union could not pierce Belfast's apathy, she would invent a scandal that no ardent Royalist could resist. And let him make of it what he would.

My dear Mary Ann,

How I long to see you, but I fear affairs will keep me closer to home for some months yet. My Aunt Adelaide will achieve the prodigious age of 50 years next month, and, of course, I can't miss the great family festivities.

And then there is this other matter of which I barely dare to speak. You will know, of course, that I refer to the Union. You will have heard of the fanatical opposition being raised to it by the Orangemen. Only last week we heard that in Armagh and Monaghan alone 36 lodges passed declarations opposing the Union. Well, my Uncle Douglas, who is a power in such circles, has a scheme which, when put into operation, is certain to entirely scuttle the government's plan for Union. I dare not speak of it now, but you will hear more within the month, because he leaves on his journey the morning after Aunt A's great party.

She broke off as a housemaid ushered a guest into the parlor. "Mr. Wimborne for you, miss."

Lenny made a great show of hastily and clumsily covering her writing with the blotter. "Oh, Mr. Wimborne!" She managed a confused smile and pushed a curl back from her forehead with the pen still in her hand. "I left my flute in my room. You must forgive me. I was so absorbed—" She flitted from the room.

She was still congratulating herself on her cleverness when, in the midst of her lesson, she looked into the courtyard and saw that Sheldon had arrived, unexpectedly as usual. This would never do. If *he* saw the letter it would spoil her trap. She had determined to use a process of elimination. Only one at a time should have a chance to expose his true loyalties.

She must therefore give Sheldon no encouragement today. She left the drawing room and approached her caller.

"Will you walk with me, Carolenn?" The autumn sun was golden, the air sweet with ripening fruit in the orchard. "Carolenn, I have so long desired . . . that is, I have felt . . ."

"Indeed, I will walk with you—but to your horse. I fear you have not called at an opportune moment, Sheldon."

His hesitance reminded her of the young lad who once hid behind his father's coattails at the Wesley meeting. "That is . . . may I call tomorrow morning? I thought perhaps a stroll by Strangford Lough, a picnic lunch—"

"I thank you, but no. I shall be engaged tomorrow morning as well."

He donned his hat and remounted.

Lenny stood watching until he was out of sight. Then she closed her eyes, but the hurt on his face would not leave her. What had she sacrificed? Could even truth be that important? And yet could life— even a life with Sheldon Ramsey—be built on anything less?

Four weeks went by with no sign of a nibble at her trap. She called frequently at Lanarks' Bawn to ascertain subtly that there had been no officers making inquiries. Certainly Douglas and Jay went about their business as openly as ever. With each day Lenny's depression grew.

It *must* be Wimborne, she reasoned. She knew he had read her letter, for on her return to the desk the blotter lay at quite a different angle than she had left it. But nothing had happened. And that meant Sheldon had to be the spy! For the hundredth time she went over all the names—everyone she knew. It could be no other. If not Wimborne, it was Sheldon. She had already refused him. Could she now denounce him?

Perhaps she could just reproach him privately. He cared deeply for her. That was evident. So a private accusation would have its effect. But then she thought of Henry Joy, of Wolfe Tone, of Harry Munro, of all the twenty thousand dead. And Thomas Russell and how many others still in prison?

Compelling as those examples were, however, the one that brought overwhelming conviction that she must carry on was Mary Ann, who had loved so deeply and so silently and now so hopelessly. She thought of Mary Ann's most recent letter with its unusually revealing reply to Lenny's inquiry about her feelings for Russell:

> It might have been much different had affairs gone otherwise. So much has been lost. So many sacrifices for our vision. I feel my loss is small compared to others. I shall devote myself to my family. And I shall always have the memory of those golden days of hope.

She had said no more, but Lenny ached for her. Certainly Mary Ann McCracken's name must stand at the top of any list of those who had paid the full price for their actions.

And so must the man who had betrayed them pay. The denunciation must be public. In front of all his closest friends.

Now Lenny pushed aside the terrible weight of that decision and assumed her gayest air. It was Aunt Adelaide's birthday, and everyone would be attending the celebration. She understood that Douglas had even arranged for fireworks. And she was glad she had volunteered to help Marguerite with the hostess duties. Passing among the guests with a silver tray laden with small offerings of puff pastry filled with almond paste was the perfect device for following several conversations at once.

It also gave her something to do to cover her nervousness. This was the day. If anything was to come of her plot, it must be now. She had hoped by referring to this event in her letter to prompt some revealing action on the part of the spy before now. But that component of the plan had certainly miscarried, and she fully realized the implication. If Wimborne's reading of her letter had been mere curiosity, that indeed left her with only one option—she must denounce Sheldon Ramsey.

She offered the tray to Sheldon as if he were a complete stranger. He took a pastry with a formal nod and turned back to his interrupted discussion. "I believe that the linen drapers are almost the only group in Ulster convinced that union with Great Britain will be a good thing. My father is quite delighted with the prospects of free trade. And, I must say, I believe it will work if full Catholic emancipation is included in the process as O'Connell insists and Pitt promises."

The puce silk with which Aunt M had swathed herself for the occasion shook alarmingly. "You don't mean to say you're in favor of *popish democracy*, young man?"

Thorpe Wimborne's head wobbled on his skinny neck as he laughed and bowed to her. "You may rest easy, ma'am. Pitt will fold. I believe I can quite assure you on the matter."

But Sheldon held his ground. "I'm afraid I find very little reassuring in the thought that so many of our fellow Irishmen must continue to be deprived of full political participation. I would go quite the other way myself."

"What are you saying? Do you mean you would grant *those persons* more rights?"

Aunt M's look of alarm prompted Lenny to grasp the painted silk fan hanging from her aunt's belt and fan her so vigorously that a pastry slid from the tray in her other hand.

"Indeed, I would grant them the privilege of hearing the faith," Sheldon replied quietly.

Lenny helped her aunt to a chair as Jay Lanark said, "Yes, I have heard of this 'Second Reformation,' as some are calling your Methodist work among the Catholics."

"Not just Methodist, although I'll grant we did begin the work. Presbyterians, Baptists, Anglicans—many are joining us. What could be more sensible than offering preaching, schooling, and tracts to any we believe lost in darkness? Isn't the answer to convert rather than to condemn?"

"Well, I'm sure you know best about that side of things." Jay selected a tidbit from Lenny's tray. "But I believe the priority must be to preserve our Protestant constitution."

Archibald had stood silent throughout the conversation. Now he shook his head, saying, "It is wrong to put too much faith in politics. A constitution does not change the heart of man."

"But it can protect us from the English who would take away the privileges King Billy won for us at the Boyne!" Douglas spoke so forcefully that his words echoed. "This Union business could end our Protestant Ascendancy. And then where would we be, I ask you?"

"The problem is not England. The problem is the evil inside man. The divided human heart is the problem, not divisions in the state. No constitution can deal with that." Archibald spoke in such a soft voice that Lenny hardly heard him.

Apparently Douglas did not. "A fine thing—here's Castlereagh, the first Presbyterian to reach high public office in Ireland for generations, and *he's* the one to sell us out—"

Finally the meaning of this debate struck Lenny. Her father had warned her about the fickleness of political alliances, and now she saw what he meant. Those like her uncle and cousin, who had been most staunchly Loyalist, were now anti-Union. She pondered. So how would that affect the attitudes of the present company regarding a Royalist spy? She tried to think through the intricate situation as the discourse continued around her.

"Just as all systems and powers of human creation will ultimately disappoint and separate us from the original good that God planned for us—" Sheldon now matched Lanark's passion "—just as Rousseau said, we have lost our original freedom and goodness. But we must return to something more original than man's primitive nature. We must return to the divine image."

Lenny's heart felt almost bursting. Sheldon's words were so powerful. Everyone in the room had turned to listen. But it could not continue, no matter how fine his words sounded. No man who had lied and cheated and betrayed his friends could be allowed to go on. She clutched the false letter she carried in her pocket, still hoping . . .

But then she took a deep breath. The sham was all the worse in a man of God. "No! It will not do, sir. I must tell what I know. You did not think you were discovered. But I know. Have known for months—"

Lenny had so focused on getting the words out that she had closed her eyes. She opened them to discover she was proclaiming her words to people's backs. All the guests were hurrying into the hall, where three red-coated officers stood, demanding the arrest of Douglas Lanark.

Lenny was so relieved she could have fainted. Truly, she might have swooned had not a strong arm come around her shoulders. "Lenny, what are you saying? *Who* was discovered? *What* have you known for months?"

She looked up into the warm brown eyes of Sheldon Ramsey. Were it not for the alarm in the hall she would have stayed there without moving. But now she struggled to action. "It is a mistake. I must speak to the captain. He is arresting the wrong man."

Sheldon asked no questions but, still supporting her, moved ahead through the crowd of guests. "Sir—" he approached the army officer preparing to march off Douglas Lanark at sword point in disgrace from his home "—the lady would speak to you."

Lenny pulled the letter from her pocket. "Is this the evidence on which you would arrest my uncle?"

The captain read the paper she thrust at him, then nodded. "Aye, that's what we were told."

"Then I can tell you, Captain . . . er . . ."

"Clarkston, ma'am." He bowed.

"You have the wrong man, Captain Clarkston. This was no true letter but part of a parlor game I invented."

"Game?"

"Yes, I call it 'Spies and Patriots.' Do you not think that a good name? See—" she pulled several sheets from her other pocket "—this is the rest of the game. The object is to trap one who is working against His Majesty's government."

"Oh, aye? That sounds like no game to me, miss." He prodded Douglas with the tip of his cutlass.

"Like a spy himself, my game serves more than one purpose, Captain. And it has worked perfectly to uncover one who has worked at every turn to thwart the interests of the Crown in Ireland."

"Eh? You mean you would give evidence?"

"Yes. But not against Douglas Lanark." She turned with a sweep of her arm and pointed to Thorpe Wimborne. "There is the man I denounce as traitor."

Captain Clarkston looked confused. Murmurs, gasps, and one shrill shriek filled the hall as all pushed farther forward to hear better.

Lenny pressed her advantage. "Do you deny that the Union of Ireland and England is government policy?"

"Nay, none would deny that."

"Do you deny that ten years ago the Crown sent a secret mission to Ireland to ascertain what the reaction might be to a proposal to unite Dublin and Westminster parliaments—and that the envoy reported that the idea of a union would incite a rebellion?"

The officer shrugged. "I've heard rumor of such."

"And do you deny that today such union is little opposed by any but Orangemen?"

The officer nodded and brandished his cutlass at Douglas, growling.

Lenny hurried on. "And do you deny that it was the late rebellion that changed public opinion in favor of union? Do you deny that England secretly *encouraged* the late insurrection to aid such change of opinion?" Now she waited for no answers. She had the full flow of momentum to carry her. "Would it not therefore be that any who sought to prevent the insurrection worked *against* the Crown?" Again she extended her arm toward Wimborne. "And thus, few in Ireland worked more assiduously against the Crown than this man." She addressed her wider audience. "You see before you the infamous Billy Bluff."

Aunt M cried on a rising note. "You mean *he's* the spy in those newspaper stories?"

Wimborne gasped and protested and turned ghostly white.

Lenny hurried on, detailing the saga of the spy in their midst.

When her account ended, Captain Clarkston looked understandably confused, but he lowered his cutlass, allowing Douglas Lanark to step back and be engulfed in puce silk as his corpulent sister threw her arms around him.

"Oh, my dear, dear Dougie, I would have gone to the gallows for you. But what a relief that there will be no such necessity."

Thorpe Wimborne's color began to return, seeping slowly upward the distance of the long neck rising above his collar points and stock. When the purple-red infusion reached his earlobes, Clarkston brandished his sword at the music master.

"Here, come along now."

"N-no. You d-d-don't understand. I was on your side. I r-risked all for His Majesty—"

"Aye? Then I'm sure he'll be mighty grateful. Risked it for bank notes with His Majesty's picture on them, I've no fear. There's little doubt General Cornwallis will want to hear your story. And as ye're such a loyal subject, I know you'll have no objection to obliging him."

The captain barked orders to his two men. They marched off, one on either side of Thorpe Wimborne.

With a swirl of her purple-red skirt, Aunt M swept the guests back into the drawing room, leaving Lenny alone in the hall with Sheldon. Suddenly overcome with a shyness that was entirely unlike her, she slowly raised her eyes to his. "That picnic you invited me to . . ."

"You would find it convenient now?"

She nodded and stared once again at the slate floor.

Sheldon took her hands. "You were uncertain?"

She shook her head. "I was confused. But I was never uncertain as to how I wanted—that is—what I wanted . . . er, *who* I wanted . . ."

"Will I do?"

"Very nicely."

He raised her hand to his lips.

62

As Lenny expected, although Thorpe Wimborne was held only a short time at the garrison, he did not show his face in County Down after that night. Also as expected, early in the next year the proposed union of Irish and English parliaments passed the Irish Commons by a majority of sixty-five votes. A few days later, the Resolution for Union passed the House of Lords by a majority of twenty-five.

Everywhere the likely results of such a move were feared. "It will be destructive to the interests of Ireland." "It will annihilate our manufacturing." "Our taxes will be increased beyond calculation." "It will end the prestige and power of the Ascendancy."

Lenny waited to hear Mary Ann's opinion. She had received only a short note after writing to tell her friend about Wimborne's discovery and disgrace. The note had spent far more ink on Lenny's news of Sheldon Ramsey's having declared for her, and her having accepted, than on any political matter. But now Mary Ann wrote of the Union.

> Is there no other argument against this union than that it will lessen the property of the rich? The question is, what of the sufferings of the poor? If Pitt's support for Catholic Emancipation had not been withdrawn, I should be more sanguine, yet I cling to the hopes that the British Parliament will introduce measures to alleviate the distress and poverty and secure a better administration of justice. I understand there are already measures before the House of Commons to provide asylums for the insane, maintain law and order, and provide for schools for all— so I remain cautiously hopeful. What a fine thing it would be if the changes for which those who are now gone sacrificed all could be achieved by peaceable means.

Lenny saw no reason not to share this optimism, however guarded, as she plied her most careful stitches to the delicate lingerie items her mother decreed she must have for her wedding clothes. Her happiness seemed to soar with every stitch. She had come at last to understand, through all the troubles—indeed it had been the tangled web of turmoil that had taught her the truth—that genuine security lay not in armies, governments, or political power but in the personal faith that she would now spend her life helping others find as she worked beside Sheldon.

She set her sewing aside and picked up the volume of sermons he had brought her only the night before. She turned again to the passage that so summarized the truth all the past events had taught her.

Brethren, countrymen, what shall we do today, while it is called today, to remove the evils we face? Our helps are little worth. Fleets may be dashed to pieces in an hour. Allies may be treacherous, or slow, or foolish, or weak, or cowardly. But God is a friend who cannot betray and whom none can either bridge or terrify. Who is wise, or swift, or strong like Him? And He will send us help, sufficient help, against all our enemies.

Lenny set the book aside and looked across at her sister, stitching in subdued silence. She could not discover the source of her sister's disconsolation. She had held some small concern for Sarah's feelings when she denounced Wimborne, but Sarah had hardly seemed to notice his departure beyond the inconvenience of not having his help on her new Haydn air. Yet there was no denying that something was bothering her.

Surely it couldn't be jealousy that the younger sister was to marry first. Or concern for Evan, who was settling into a law career in Dublin, with help from Mary Ann's relative Harry McCracken. She smiled at the thought of her friend. How like this was to those long-ago days she had spent with Mary Ann sewing less delicate items for the Belfast poorhouse.

At that time she would have thought any wedding garments she might work on would be for her friend. She paused and, as she so often did, raised a thought for the dashing Thomas Russell, immured in the lonely fastness of Fort George. She felt certain Mary Ann still remained hopeful that someday he would be released. Perhaps Union would hasten the day.

Lenny reached the end of the lace edging surrounding a handkerchief and looked up just in time to see Sarah brush away a tear. Lenny dropped her sewing and went to her sister's side. "What is it, Sarah? Do you miss Thorpe? I'm so sorry, I—"

Nothing could have amazed her more than Sarah's laughter. "Thorpe? You dear goose. Why should I miss him?" But the laughter ended in a shaky sigh that threatened to turn to a sob. "It is this hated Union thing."

Lenny had never known her sister to be political. "The Union? You are worried about the imposition of English law on us?"

"Oh, not me. What difference does it make where Parliament sits —whether in Dublin or Westminster or on the Isle of Man, for all I care? But Franklin cannot see it that way." Sarah bit her lip.

"Why should Franklin care? He isn't even Irish."

"That's just the problem." The tears Sarah had been holding back cascaded over each pink cheek. "And now he never will be. He would have stayed—for me. He vowed he would. But he says he cannot. He cannot live without freedom. He says he cannot live under the government his country won their freedom from at such cost. We've argued and argued, but he is quite determined."

Lenny considered the matter slowly. "Franklin is to return to America?"

Sarah nodded. "He is determined to take up the textile trade seriously in Philadelphia."

"I think you might quite like Philadelphia society, Sarah."

Sarah blinked. "You mean you think I should emigrate?"

It seemed a simple matter to Lenny. "I would go anywhere with Sheldon. And I'll gladly divide my trousseau with you. I can't imagine the wife of a Methodist preacher needing so much."

Even as she spoke, Lenny realized how ridiculous the whole idea was. Fashion-conscious Sarah, who never had a thought for anything but the latest bonnet trimming or harpsichord tune, crossing the ocean to settle in the wilds of a new country? "Oh, I'm sorry, Sarah. It was silly of me to suggest anything so absurd—"

She was knocked almost flat by Sarah's ebullient embrace. Then her sister jumped up and ran from the room in such ecstacy that she almost trampled their mother, standing in the doorway.

On New Year's Day 1801, as Mr. and Mrs. Sheldon Ramsey stood on the quay at Belfast Harbor, Lenny waved at the ship slipping into the lough toward the sea. A stiff wind caught the vessel's sails and billowed them into wings carrying Sarah and Franklin Lanark to their new home. Lenny thought it was the most beautiful sight she had ever seen. Behind them the bells of St. Anne's pealed out over the city.

She glanced at the flag atop the pole in the harbor. Indeed, all things were new. The Union Jack, they were calling it. The Cross of St. Patrick, superimposed on the crosses of St. George of England and St. Andrew of Scotland. A fine, bold pattern of red, white, and blue waving against a silvery sky.

"Will it bring peace, do you think?"

"Who can say?" Sheldon pressed her hand.

Lenny returned the squeeze. She had peace in her heart, and that was all one could ask.

63

"I can't do it."

For two days Mary had dithered. Outwardly she held to her determination to leave strife-torn Ireland, where she felt she was beating her head against a brick wall. Every time she questioned the rightness of the decision, she had only to turn on the television, listen to the radio, or scan the day's headlines for confirmation that she did not want to be there. More than two hundred people had been wounded while she drank tea with her friends, attended a lively church service, and read the troubled history of Ireland—which continued to repeat itself with numbing predictability.

Still, in spite of her insistence that they leave on the midweek ferry, she had made no move to pack, to call her cousin or aunt in Scotland, or to cancel the scheduled rehearsal. And now she knew why. Sheldon had held steady. *He* had kept the faith. He—one man— had made a difference. Even in the face of the bad news all around her, Mary did believe it was possible to make a difference. And she had to try. *Give it one final chance,* she told herself.

She heard the soft clomp of Gareth's walking cast coming down the hall toward her room.

"I'll be going along to the Centre now," he said through the closed door.

She jumped up. "I'll go with you. I've got so much to do to get ready for practice tonight." She started digging under a pile of papers for her prompt book.

Gareth came in and gave her a dazzling, if baffled, grin. "What's this? I thought it was all off. I was going to clean out my desk. Well, really to sort everything out with Philip—"

Mary laughed. "You hadn't called anything off, either, had you? We said we were leaving, but I don't think either of us really believed we would."

He still looked uncertain. "Mary, are you sure?"

She sank back on the pastel floral comforter that covered her bed. "I'm sure I want to give it another chance. I'm not sure of success.

Not at all. But I just don't feel right about leaving. And I don't think you do, either."

He ran his fingers through his crisp black hair. "I want you to be happy, Mary."

She jumped off the bed and threw her arms around him. "Gareth, we both know nothing will work if we put what we want ahead of what's right." If she kept saying that, maybe she would come to believe it someday.

"Aye. I just keep hoping they'll turn out to be one and the same thing."

She gave him a quick kiss. "One step at a time. For now we've got our work to get on with."

And trying to get *A Night in Olde Belfast* back on schedule in time for a successful performance was certainly all the challenge she needed at the moment. They had lost almost two weeks. Posters that should have gone to the print room days ago hadn't even been designed yet. She still hadn't found a harpist, and after reading about the Belfast Harp Festival, she felt more than ever that they must have one. Becca and Julie were determined to learn to step dance. And where they would get traditional Irish dresses to fit their athletic American proportions she couldn't imagine.

Even as she walked toward the car, Mary was writing furiously, fearful she might forget some one item that would spell the doom of the whole enterprise. Gareth opened the car door for her. She buckled her seatbelt with one hand while she wrote, "See church hall," with the other. Liam said Noah's Ark had agreed to let them use the room where they held Harvest Festival and Christmas parties. But things had fallen apart so soon after she received that encouraging news that she hadn't followed up on it.

Liam. How could she have forgotten?

"Gareth, has anyone seen Liam? Since Saturday?"

"Not that I know of. Why?"

She told him of the boy she had seen on the news.

"Are you *certain* it was Liam?"

"I was at the time. Now I'm not sure. But either way, I'm worried about him."

And she worried about the program without him. He made the perfect Shawn Bruin. And they needed him to play the guitar. Well, actually Gareth could fill in there—but it would be good for Liam to do it. She had seen such promise in him. She couldn't bear to lose him. The thought of his ending up in prison for paramilitary activity made her sick.

Mary continued to worry about the boy as she pushed furniture against the walls in the entry lounge. She pulled a small table and three chairs to the center to serve as the interior of the Bruin cottage. She barely had time to get things organized before rehearsal. They would practice at the CCC this week. Then, hopefully, they could move to the church hall and build a real set. Sheila promised to take care of the posters; Debbie, who arrived early, said her mom had a friend who could make dresses for the twins. And the solution to their need for a harpist came from a surprising source.

Tommy, who was staying at the Centre again, walked into the room as Mary was asking Sheila and Debbie if they knew anyone who played the clarsach.

"Are you needing a harpist? And why weren't you saying so? Here's me practically engaged to the most beautiful one in all Ireland."

Not only that, but Lila would be stopping by the Centre later, so that Mary could discuss it with her herself. But that relief was followed quickly with renewed worry. It was past time to begin practice, and Liam still had not come. No one had seen or heard from him since he stormed out of the center Saturday.

Mary looked around. The others were getting restless. She would have to start without Liam. "Er—Tommy, I know you wanted to get more of your transcription work done this evening, but would you fill in for Liam?"

Tommy took the playbook she held out to him, as she began giving directions. "OK, Maurteen and Bridget are sitting at the table." She nodded to Martin and Sarah, who were cast as Mr. and Mrs. Bruin. "Gerry, Father Hart is sitting across the table from them. Tommy, Shawn is setting the table for supper." She handed him a couple of magazines to use as plates. "Debbie, use that sofa"—she pointed to one by the wall—"as Marie's settle."

Debbie plopped down, curling her long, slim legs under her, and immediately assumed the character of the young wife completely wrapped up in a book of Irish folktales.

"OK, Maurteen, you're complaining about your daughter-in-law's uselessness."

Mary gestured for Martin to begin. But only half her mind was on the play. Where *was* Liam? Had he been arrested at the riot? Or hurt? Or had he done the unthinkable and joined the IRA? *Please, God, not that.*

"Because I bade her go and feed the calves, she took that old book down out of the thatch and has been doubled over it all day . . ."

The dialogue lurched forward with fumbles and lapses. It seemed worse than their first read-through. It *was* worse, because the time was so much shorter now. And because they didn't have Liam. If they had lost him to the side of violence . . . if all the best efforts of the CCC and "Peace" had failed on this youth who had so much to offer . . .

Maurteen finished his expostulation against his son's wife, and Father Hart attempted to intervene. Gerry made heavy work of Yeats's silver poetry.

"Gerry, I know the lines are a bit obscure, but try to understand what you're saying. 'God spreads the heavens above us like great wings, and gives a little round of deeds and days.' Father Hart is talking about the entire course of human life."

Gerry stumbled on. Yeats had written with a desire to restore the whole ancient art of passionate speech. The poor man must be turning in his grave. Had she chosen entirely the wrong play? She wanted something nonpolitical, yet something essentially Irish, something that celebrated the beauty of the land, its poetry, and its folk legends. If the most gentle and lyrical of all Ireland's poets failed to reach these people, would she just be underscoring the hopelessness of the situation?

She focused on Father Hart's lines, so full of Shakespearean universality. "Life moves out of a red flare of dreams into a common light of common hours, until old age bring the red flare again." She had to believe the beauty of the poetry itself would be strong enough to reach the audience.

"Do not blame her greatly, Father Hart . . ." Shawn Bruin took up the defense of his wife. Tommy did a creditable job of filling in, although he wasn't at all right for the part. "This is May Eve too—"

"When the good people post about the world."

The continuation of the line came from the back of the room.

All heads turned as, completely in character, Liam walked onto the set. "Marie, have you the primroses to fling before the door to make a golden path for them to bring good luck into the house?"

With evident relief, Tommy relinquished his playbook, and the whole scene slipped into place with Liam's lyrical characterization. Debbie truly looked like the mesmerized new bride as she pantomimed strewing primroses with dreamlike grace. Even Gerry, though hardly poetical, was at least clear in his pronunciation: "God permits great power to the good people on May Eve."

Mary relaxed. Liam was back and in excellent form. It had been just another of his mercurial mood swings, she tried to assure herself. The Irish were famous for them. Like their weather, they said—gray drizzle one minute, brilliant sunshine the next. "We have all four seasons in Ireland—everyday," she had heard more than once. Yes, of course, that was it. Still, she wasn't entirely convinced.

On stage the struggle between the mundane and the poetical continued, with Maurteen urging the simple pleasures of the common life: "To sit beside the board and drink good wine and watch the turf smoke coiling from the fire and feel content and wisdom in your heart, this is the best of life."

A knock came at the door right on cue, but it was not a May Eve fairy at the stage cottage. Rather, it was a knock on the street door of the Centre, which Philip had locked for security after Liam's arrival.

Mary's heart lurched as she looked through the glass door. From the simple beauty of sitting before the hearth of a thatched cottage which Yeats's poetry had created, she came tumbling back to the harsh reality of the Troubles. Two uniformed officers stood outside.

As a reflex she looked at Liam. Then she wished she hadn't, for she now noticed what she hadn't before. The blue windcheater jacket he wore was the same as the one worn by the boy she had seen throwing bricks on the news. Were the constables here to arrest Liam?

As Philip came through from his office to open the door, she realized how silly she was. There had been more than two thousand rioters. The Royal Ulster Constabulary would not send two officers to arrest one teenage boy.

Philip took the officers through to his office, leaving the room abuzz with speculation and alarm.

Mary clapped her hands for attention. "It's your line, Father Hart—'by love alone God binds us to Himself and to the hearth—'"

Gerry turned a page in his book. Sarah reached across the table and pointed out the line to him. "Oh, yeah. Er . . . 'to Himself and to the hearth and shuts us from the waste beyond His peace, from maddening freedom and bewildering light.'"

The play lumbered onward. Then even Mary lost her concentration when she saw Gareth leave Philip's office. He returned a moment later with Tommy. The police had come to question Tommy? Tommy, the ex-prisoner who had been present the night of the break-in, who had discovered the theft of the files, who . . . Tommy had been one of the most worried of all. He couldn't possibly have been involved in the vandalism.

Even when Fiona skipped on stage as the fairy child, Mary couldn't wrench her mind from worry over what was going on in the office behind her. She had almost lost track of the action on stage when Father Hart jumped up, threw out his arms, and shouted, "I will have queen cakes when you come to me!"

The set exploded with laughter and applause.

"No, no. What are you doing? That's pages ahead yet," Mary began, then caught the scent of chocolate and heard an unmistakably American giggle.

"Come on, everybody!"

"Fresh chocolate chip cookies!"

Becca and Julie marched to the table bearing a tray of cookies and milk.

Becca turned to Mary. "Can you believe—they've never had chocolate chip cookies?"

"Their chocolate chips here come in *tiny* bags—"

"And their brown sugar is different—"

"And we had to buy the vanilla special. Dorinda said she never uses it."

"Dorinda!" Mary gasped. "You've been baking in the canteen kitchen?"

"Of course."

"Where else?"

"Dorinda said we could."

Mary shook her head. The twins could win anyone over. Dorinda didn't even allow *Sheila* in her kitchen. Even Mary's worries over Liam, the disastrous rehearsal, and the arrival of the police faded somewhat with every bite of crisp cookie filled with bits of melting chocolate.

Moments later, the door to Philip's office opened, and Becca snatched up a plate of cookies. She skipped across the room to the police officers. "Would you like a cookie?"

"An American specialty." Julie followed with glasses of milk.

Mary couldn't believe it when the officers accepted.

A few minutes later, the portly, sandy-haired one was on his third cookie and telling Becca all about his nephew who was a policeman in Newark. Becca wrote down his name and promised to call him when she got home.

With all the conviviality swirling around them, it was easy enough for Mary to slip over to the corner where Gareth, Philip, and Tommy sat, serious-faced. "What did they want?"

"Cookies, apparently." Gareth gave her a half grin.

She didn't respond to his attempt at humor. She was too worried.

It was Tommy who explained. "They've identified a set of finger-prints on the file cabinet."

"And?"

"The break-in wasn't random vandalism," Philip said.

Tommy looked at the floor. "His name is Joe Navan. He was a mate of mine once—before I went to prison."

Mary translated: mate—paramilitary. She looked at Gareth.

"They seem to suspect Tommy was involved. I told them he was with me."

Tommy slapped his knee with determination. "I've got to find Joe. I've got to talk to him."

"No." Philip was firm. "Going back to any of the old group is a very dangerous thing to do. You don't want to get involved with them again."

"You're right, I don't. That's the point. I *am* involved. They took my file. The police suspect me. I have to prove myself."

"Not to me, you don't." Lila was suddenly standing with a hand on Tommy's shoulder, her eyes shining softly at him.

Liam was beside her. "I let her in. Knew it would be all right."

Philip nodded. "Of course."

Tommy took Lila's hand and told her what had just happened. "So you see, I've got to do something. I'm more concerned about proving myself to your parents than to the police."

"But what can you do?" Gareth asked. "You haven't seen Navan for years, have you?"

Tommy shook his head. "Not since before I was at Long Kesh. I haven't had anything to do with anyone from the Army."

Liam came to attention. "You were in the Army—the Republican Army?"

Mary stared. Their gentle Tommy, who spent all day transcribing the Bible for the blind, who loved and was loved by the lovely Lila, had belonged to the IRA?

Tommy saw her face. "That's right. I was nationalist. Most of the fellows here are unionist. It wasn't politics that brought us together—it was Jesus Christ. Once we meet Him, we're together—we're family even if we've just met. At the end of the day, that's the answer."

Mary was speechless. If coming to Belfast was falling down the rabbit hole, this was definitely stepping through the looking glass.

"Can you think of anything you didn't tell the police?" Philip asked. "Anything that would help them find Joe?" he persisted.

But Tommy continued to shake his head, his shoulders slumping.

"Did you know his family at all?"

Tommy shrugged. "I met his da once. He'd been Army. Went to prison. Never recovered from a beating a guard gave him. That's why Joe joined. They lived somewhere out west—Sligo, I think."

"I've an auntie near Sligo," Liam remarked. "She has a B and B."

Philip considered for a moment. "Maybe we should take a run out there. There are people I've been needing to see in Armagh and Enniskillen for the Reconciliaton Union. I've been wanting you to get to work on that, too, Gareth. That's most of the way to Sligo."

"Sligo! How perfect," Mary cried. "That's Yeats country. *Land of Heart's Desire* is even set there. Oh, I wish we could all go—that would help us catch the lyricism of the play if anything could."

Somehow the whole thing snowballed. Someone mentioned that

it would be a good chance to show the twins more of Ireland. The twins said, could Debbie come, too? Mary threw up her hands and said that as they were already so far behind, what difference would missing three more days of play practice matter?

But even while making a joke of it, she was thinking that this might be just the chance she was looking for to get Liam away from the conflicts raging in Belfast—out to the romantic west coast, where, amazingly, he had an aunt.

After the turmoil of the past weeks, it seemed wonderful to be putting the stress and violence behind them the next day and setting out across the rolling green countryside in the minibus. The sun had just risen. The whole world had a fresh, innocent, dew-washed look—just as it must have looked to St. Patrick when he and his band of missionaries came to Ireland.

Gareth sat in front with Philip so that they could discuss ideas for the Ulster Reconciliation Union. The organization wanted to sponsor an event. Something really meaningful. Something that hadn't been done before. But no one had come up with the right idea.

Mary turned to the back where Becca, Julie, and Debbie were singing silly songs. With the fresh air blowing in the windows and the scenes of peaceful cows and sheep in pastures beyond the hedgerows, it was easy to forget that this was a land divided by hundreds of years of violence and prejudice. It was easy to forget the riots, shootings, and burnings. Easy to forget the worries already being voiced that the Londonderry marches scheduled to take place in a few weeks would produce even worse violence across the land than those in Belfast had.

Easy to forget until she looked at Tommy and Liam seated across from her. She had noticed before that they were both the small-boned, dark type of Irishmen that were a heritage of the long-ago incursions of the Spanish army. But not until Tommy's past emerged to stalk him had they shared this intense, haunted look. If only she could understand. If only she could help. Somehow Liam must be prevented from going down the same path to paramilitarism and prison.

64

"There—" Philip pointed across the treetops as they approached the city. "The twin Cathedrals of Armagh. Saint Patrick's and Saint Patrick's."

Mary laughed. "Is there an echo in here?"

"What else would you name a cathedral in the city where Saint Patrick established his monastery? It's the seat of both the Protestant and Catholic archbishops."

They were now traveling along tree-lined, hilly streets. A twin-spired gray stone cathedral stood at the top of a broad flight of stairs on a hill. "That's Saint Patrick's R. C." Minutes later they passed a golden-brown cathedral with a square Norman central tower surrounded by trees on a somewhat lower hill. "Saint Patrick's C of I," Philip explained.

He pulled into a car park. "Our meeting is just down there—corner of Scotch and English Streets, legacy from Armagh being the border town between English and Scottish plantations. Anyway, the rest of you should find plenty to do at Saint Patrick's Trian—quite a good exhibit, I understand."

Mary watched them—Philip, moving with restless energy, forging ever forward, trying to leave no base uncovered to achieve peace for the future of his country; and beside him, Gareth, still limping from his injury, yet with an athletic spring to his walk, carrying her heart and her future with him.

Waiting behind Mary were Tommy, Liam, and Debbie, whose own futures would be determined by the future of Ireland. And because it seemed that, more in Ireland than anywhere else, the past dictated to the future, she turned with the young people to explore another segment of Ireland's history.

The vast exhibit that spread out through six or seven buildings took them first to an interpretive presentation of life here from Celtic, early Christian, and Viking times. They were greeted at the entrance by three lifelike figures of men who had molded Armagh's history: St. Patrick, Dean Jonathan Swift—and John Wesley.

As they viewed the story of Ireland's ecclesiastical capital, Mary wondered that a land that so revered its history had missed the central point of it all. The value of history was to learn by example, to realize who we are, why we are here, and where we are going. The point of history was to learn from the mistakes of the past so that we could avoid repeating them, not so that we could fight the same wars over and over in an attempt to right three-hundred-year-old wrongs.

Behind her Becca and Julie giggled, and Mary was brought back to the present. She looked at Liam, lagging behind, and wished she knew *his* past. She wanted to understand him and help him keep from making the mistakes that so many thousands of young men had made in this land. If only he would talk to her.

They crossed a rotunda, walked along the halls of a former granary that was now a mall of tiny shops, and arrived, as if by magic, at the Land of Lilliput.

"Oh, *Gulliver's Travels!*" Becca gave a little skip and dashed toward a giant figure of the character the Anglo-Irish Swift had created while serving as dean of St. Patrick's Cathedral in Dublin. Then she led the way through the arched door that opened between the enormous Gulliver's knees.

"Costumes!" Julie cried and darted toward a rack of satin, velvet, and brocade outfits.

"Come on, we can be Lilliputians." Becca thrust a robe of pink and purple paisley at Debbie, who pulled it over her head with a giggle. Becca chose green satin breeches and a blue coat trimmed with gold braid.

Julie selected gold lamé for herself and red velvet for Liam.

"Er—that's all right. You go ahead." He backed up.

Mary was sure he wanted to enter into the nonsense, yet he pulled back as if fleeing to safety. She moved quickly before he could refuse. "Of course. Let's. It wouldn't be the same if we didn't costume." She held out a chartreuse velvet turban to Tommy and plopped a black velvet hat with drooping feathers on her own head.

Somewhat stiffly, Liam pulled on the scarlet coat, and they set off for the land of Lilliput. Eventually they went into a theater, where a giant Gulliver told his story with projections and dancing puppets.

When the show was over, Liam led them out, reenacting the Lilliputians parade. He played the air guitar with Becca and Julie behind him on air tambourine and cymbals. At the costume return, obviously playing to the twins' applause, Liam pulled one arm inside his red velvet robe, grasped the cuff of the other sleeve, and with contortions and strangled sounds managed to enact being eaten by aliens. Becca and Julie dissolved in laughter.

Mary, standing across the room, laughed as well, but she was more analytical. How could a boy who could be this amusing be so frighteningly antisocial at other times? This was more than Irish temperament. She turned to Debbie, who was beside her, laughing at Liam's antics. "I wish I could understand Liam. Look at him now—as if he doesn't have a care in the world beyond impressing girls. But sometimes I feel an anger in him that's frightening."

Debbie nodded. "Yeah, I know. He's a really cool guy." She grinned. "Really cool. Most of the time. I think something awful happened to him. I tried to get him to talk to me once, but he wouldn't—just said everything was fine."

As the others finished hanging up their costumes and went into the gift shop, Debbie continued with a wisdom far beyond her years. "I didn't believe him, of course, because I know how it is. That's the first thing the therapist at Courage explained: when something terrible happens to you, it causes pain inside—way down where nothing can get at it to make it better. Most of the time you can just deny it exists and keep it stuffed down. But then sometimes something makes it all boil out, and you just want to go smash your fist through a wall." She shrugged. "At least, that's what I did. Before Mom took me to that therapy group."

"So how can we help Liam? Get him to go to a Courage group?"

Debbie shook her head. "He'll have to be willing to talk about it first. Admit that he wants help."

Mary was still pondering what could be done as they hurried toward the car park. She was afraid they had made the men wait for them. Indeed, Philip was looking at his watch when they arrived, breathless and laughing.

"I hope we haven't made you late for your next meeting," Mary said as she slid into her seat and snapped the seatbelt.

"Should just about make it." Philip put the mini in gear, and they shot forward.

They were quickly out of town and barreling along a narrow, twisting road. Philip must have seen Mary's strained look in his mirror because he laughed. "Don't worry. The secret here is to keep the car between the ditches."

She tried to laugh, but it sounded forced.

Liam turned toward her, grinning and eyes sparkling. "And have you not heard the wee story of the fellow who was stopped for speeding just after he got his driver's permit?"

"No, I haven't." She gripped the armrest as the van crested a hill and plunged downward.

"'And do you realize you were twenty miles over the speed limit, sonny?' the officer asked. 'And what's more, ye weren't in yer own lane —ye were drivin' right down the middle of the road.'

"'Oh, that's all right, sir. I have a license for it.'

"'What do you mean, a license?'

"The lad pulled out his permit and pointed. 'See, it says right there—tear along the dotted line.'"

Mary laughed, but the story would have been funnier if Philip's driving hadn't mirrored the boy's. In an effort to take her mind off the situation, she leaned forward to tell Gareth, in the seat in front of her, about their visit to Lilliput. "We even had breakfast with the Big-enders. Or was it the Little-enders?" Then she thought. "We had boiled eggs for breakfast this morning. Which end did you break, Gareth?"

He frowned, trying to remember.

Mary's view from the seat behind emphasized his high-bridged nose, one heavy, dark eyebrow, and a well-trimmed sideburn.

"I never thought. I guess I usually break the little end because the big end fits best in the egg cup. But I rather think they were served with the big end up this morning."

"Ah, then in Lilliput you would have been shot for treason—or would have had to change sides in the war." But her lighthearted reference wasn't humorous even to herself. Swift was too acute a satirist. Killing people over which street you wanted to march down made exactly as much sense as the Lilliputians' war between Big-enders and Little-enders.

She said something to that effect, and, to her surprise, Liam was the one to answer.

"It isn't just all fighting over marches. The IRA is an army. They're fighting a war. You should understand. It's the same as the patriots in your own Revolution."

Mary was too shocked by the concept to answer. Not two minutes ago Liam had been telling a joke. Now his voice boiled with bitterness. And she had certainly never heard the patriots of the American Revolution called guerilla terrorists before.

"For the sake of argument we'll give them that," Philip replied, this time not taking his eyes off the road. "But if the IRA is going to claim the same respect as a regular army, then they must submit to the same standards of moral judgment."

Liam leaned forward defensively. "What do you mean, moral judgment? They're freedom fighters! That's moral."

"Wait." Philip held up a cautionary hand. "In order to keep from getting bogged down in the emotions and petty details of the moment, any issue needs to be judged by an absolute standard outside itself."

Liam scoffed. "The Bible, you mean? You bigoted Prods don't think Catholics believe in the Bible."

"Liam, I know Catholics believe in the Bible just the same as our lot. But most people don't. The problem with the whole world today is that so few people believe in *any* ultimate standard. So it doesn't do much good to quote the Bible to them. That's why I like to appeal to a more general principle—Natural Law."

Liam looked suspicious.

"Those principles we know to be true by observing nature. Thomas Aquinas—the supreme Catholic theologian, Liam—enunciated them the most clearly of anyone I know. Spent a lot of time reading Saint Thomas in prison, I did."

Liam was quiet, his dark, intense eyes burning into the back of Philip's head.

"One of the things Aquinas did was spell out the principles of what makes a war just," Philip continued. "So if the IRA is going to claim status as a respectable army, not just a terrorist mob, they need to submit to the scrutiny of those principles."

"What about the UVF and the UDA and your lot?" Liam spit out the words.

"They aren't my lot anymore, Liam. Terrorism is wrong, no matter which side of the street it comes from. And counterterrorism can be awfully close to terrorism itself."

"So what's this *just war* of yours?"

"Not mine, Liam. Thomas Aquinas's. And not because he thought up the principles as a good idea to impose on society, but because they are principles naturally observable to rational man."

"Yeah. Such as?"

Mary suspected Liam's caustic tone was a defense to prevent anyone's guessing that he was really very interested.

"There are three principles. One is that you must have a rightful intention."

"Getting the Brits out *is* a rightful intention."

"But the soldiers aren't the British presence in Ulster, Liam. *I'm* the British presence—me and the two-thirds of the Ulster population who came from Scots or English stock hundreds of years ago. We're the British presence. Sending the army back across the water will not eliminate the British presence."

Liam made a scoffing noise.

"Let's back up," Philip said. "I started with the last principle. The first is clearer. Those fighting must have the authority of the sovereign of their nation. The IRA clearly does not have the support or authority of the Parliament or president of the Republic of Ireland."

"Ha!" Liam gave a triumphant crow and turned to Mary. "And your revolutionaries didn't have the authority of George the Third. So that makes the American Revolution an unjust war."

Mary was no philosopher. She didn't know what to say.

But Philip continued calmly. "The second principle, Liam, is that there must be a crime on the part of the enemy. I think we need to concede that Mad George had violated basic rights of the colonists—rights that belonged to them as Englishmen. But we're not fighting the American Revolution."

"No, and you don't have to look far to find crimes the Brits committed against the Irish. Taking our land, for example."

"In the course of the long history of uneasy relations across the Irish Sea, there have certainly been many crimes committed. Cromwell is an example. The Penal Laws are another. But the IRA isn't fighting to defeat Cromwell or to repeal laws that haven't existed for two hundred years. Mostly they're fighting for personal power. And they want to get rid of people whose families have lived here for four hundred years."

Gareth, who had been listening quietly, now spoke up. "Aye, and that's a principle of Natural Law."

Philip shot him a smile. "That's right. One of the five principles of Natural Law is the inborn instinct of man to live in community. Man has a need to form his own community."

"So that's a right that should exist for both Eire and Northern Ireland," Mary said.

"Right again. And we're making good progress toward that today. Trouble is, in the past—even in my own lifetime—I'm afraid the Unionists treated the other side of the street somewhat like King George treated his American colonists. The majority in a community has no right to violate the natural rights of the minority."

Gareth turned halfway around. "That was the principle that prevailed at the Nuremburg Trials. After all, no *statutory* law had been violated in committing those war crimes. But Natural Law had. The courts had to determine that there were higher laws that overrode those in the code books."

Their discussion and Philip's racing driving carried them across the fifty-some miles from Armagh to Enniskillen. They passed enormous brick fortifications with high-tech communications apparatus on the roof that spoke of the precarious position this country town occupied so near the border between north and south. No one stopped them at the barricade, so Philip shifted gears, sped up the hill, and whipped the minibus around a curve. A tractor pulling a load of hay lumbered toward them.

Mary caught her breath.

"That's right. Just breathe in, and we'll get by," Philip called out merrily as he squeaked past the wide load.

As they approached the center of town, however, even Philip slowed down and lost all jocularity. He pointed to the gray stone market cross in the square. "That's where the bomb went off."

"When?" Mary asked. A bombing she hadn't heard about? She didn't see any signs of destruction.

"Remembrance Day 1987. Enniskillen has always been staunchly Unionist. They provided two famous regiments to World Wars One and Two. So every Remembrance Day, the whole town always turned out to the ceremonies at the market cross. Flag-waving, bands, speeches, placing a wreath—the usual sort of thing—but people cared more about it here than most.

"A bomb went off right at the beginning of the ceremonies when everyone was gathered—elderly, schoolchildren, mothers with babies, everyone. No warning was given. This young nurse—Marie was her name—had gone with her father. They were both buried under the rubble. She groped through the broken masonry until she found her father's hand. She said, 'Daddy, I love you.' And died.

"They were a Christian family, and the incredible thing was that, when the reporters interviewed the father, he said, 'I forgive them.' It made national headlines. That father had opportunities over and over again to explain the Christian concept of forgiveness."

Philip shook his head. "I've often thought about that. I've asked myself, what if it had been Ann and me? Could I have said that?" He paused. "I doubt it. I'd like to, but I don't think I could."

"You don't know what you can do until you're faced with it," Mary said softly. But she agreed. She was quite certain she couldn't be that forgiving either.

With one eye on his watch and one eye on traffic, Philip managed to park. "We're way behind schedule—even on Irish time. Meeting's probably about over. We'll hurry along and see what's happened."

Philip and Gareth started up the street at a half trot.

Becca bounded out. "Let's find some food!"

The girls were off.

Then Mary saw that Liam was still sitting inside. "You coming, Liam?"

He shrugged. "Sure, I'll come. I could do with a packet of crisps or something." He got out and locked the door.

The young people bought snacks at a news agent's. Mary picked up a newspaper. They walked up the street and found a stretch of grass along the banks of the Erne that offered a pleasant place to sit. Mary sat leaning against a tree and unfolded her paper. Her eyes went straight to the headline: British Forestall IRA Attack. "Oh, my goodness. Listen to this:

> "A terrorist suspect was shot dead, five men were arrested and some ten tons of explosives and weapons were uncovered in a series of raids in London. Police say the capture has forestalled imminent IRA attacks. The explosives were ready for use, mostly designed for truck bombs like those that wounded more than two hundred people and devastated the center of Manchester . . ."

The newspaper crumpled to her lap. The vision of what could have happened left her too horrified to comment.

Becca and Julie jumped into the silence.

"That is so *stupid*."

"Why would anybody want to blow things up and kill people?"

"Or riot. Can you imagine standing on a street corner throwing rocks?"

"It's barbarian."

Her sisters' tirade had gone on for some time before Mary realized that Liam had disappeared. She looked around. There he was, walking just beyond those bushes. She slipped away quietly, not wanting to attract the others' attention.

Mary had nearly caught up with the boy when he looked over his shoulder. It was a fierce, hooded look that would have warded off any approach if it could. Then he broke into a run.

Mary followed. "Please, Liam. I just want to talk to you."

At least part of him must have wanted to talk, because Mary was certain he could have outrun her if he had really tried. As it was, she caught up to him and, gasping, hung onto his arm. "Don't run off, Liam. They don't know what they're saying."

"I'm not a barbarian!" He twisted and shook but didn't really put enough effort into it to break her grasp.

"I know you aren't. But I also know you participated in the Belfast riot. Won't you tell me why, Liam? I want to understand, and I don't."

He gave her a black look.

"Please, Liam. Help me. It's all so confusing. Please help me understand."

"You can't understand. No one can. Let me go." This time he did pull free. "Why don't you just go home?"

That did it. "Right! Why don't I? If you only knew how much I'd like to. I almost did. Twice. But like an idiot, I chose to stay here because I thought I could *help*. Why I ever wanted to is beyond me at the moment." Her voice rose as she went on. "Just go ahead and throw your life away. I don't care. I tried to help. But there's nothing more I can do." She whirled and started back toward the minibus.

Then she realized Liam was still standing there. Mary Hamilton hadn't been a high school teacher for nothing. "*Liam O'Connor!* Get yourself to that bus." She pointed. *"Now!"*

She walked slowly enough to allow him to arrive first. Philip and Gareth were waiting for them.

Philip shook his head when she asked if they had accomplished anything at their meeting. "We'll have to come back in a couple of weeks. Probably best. We've got another forty miles or so on to Sligo. What time is your auntie expecting us, Liam?"

He shrugged. "When we get there."

Mary feared she had badly mishandled that scene. She had so wanted an opportunity to talk to him. And now that she had calmed down, she knew that half of what she'd said had been untrue. She still *did* want to help him. She consoled herself with the fact that at least he was still with them. She supposed it was something that she had prevented his running away entirely.

Evening shadows lengthened as they drove across Connacht, traditionally the poorest province. As they went farther west, the terrain grew increasingly rough and the vegetation increasingly sparse. The mountains were jagged and bare except for a few gnarled beech trees near the base.

"Isn't this where some of your family lived?" Mary asked Philip.

"That's right. The musical lot. Pity I didn't get any of the talent."

"Do you know where they lived?"

"Not really. Somewhere in this area, or maybe a bit farther north in County Donegal."

For the rest of the drive, Mary scanned the countryside, looking for small cottiers' huts that might have been the sort Philip's ancestors had lived in. Not many were left, but occasionally she spied a small, whitewashed stone building with a thatched roof, probably being used for a barn or storage shed.

Suddenly Debbie cried, "Oh, look! Stop!"

Philip pulled to the side of the narrow road beside a quaint stone cottage. Its thatch was held down all around with wired rocks hanging like ball fringe. There were no flowers, but a row of white-painted rocks in the grass surrounded the house. A black and white collie sat beside a small cart of peat bricks.

"It's the Bruins' cottage. I know it is. One could believe in fairies and good people living there."

And in one of his baffling mood swings, Liam laughed and

entered into the pretending. "See, there's even a barn behind. Probably a book of old tales in the thatch."

Philip drove on, but the cottage had worked a kind of magic, transporting them all back to Yeats's fairy world. Liam and Debbie began bantering in the characters of Shawn and Marie Bruin, even throwing in a few of their lines from the play. Mary wrinkled her forehead in puzzlement. Maybe there was hope yet. Or was this yet another example of Liam's unwillingness to deal with his problem?

It was nearly sunset. The evening light had faded to mellow gold by the time they made their way through Sligo town and on out to an elegant Georgian house on the bay, now marked with an Irish Tourist Board shamrock.

"Liam! This is your aunt's house?" Becca cried.

"Wow! What a place!" Julie joined her sister.

"Na. The guest house is on down by the bay." He seemed uncomfortable at the very suggestion.

"I hope we can see the main house, though," Philip said. He drove slowly along the gravel road. "You'll be interested to know, Mary, that Yeats spent a lot of time here at Lissadell with the daughters of the house. Eva became a rather good poet, and Connie was an actress and became the militant Countess Markievicz. She was elected the first woman member of the British House of Commons, then refused her seat to serve in the Irish Parliament."

Mary looked back at the house. It was perfectly proportioned gray stone against a backdrop of trees. Tall symmetrical windows opened out onto flower-bordered lawns.

> "The light of evening Lissadell,
>   Great windows open to the south.
>   Two girls in silk kimonos,
>   Both beautiful, one a gazelle."

Mary turned in astonishment. "Gareth, I didn't know you knew Yeats. That *was* Yeats, wasn't it?"

"Aye."

His smile warmed her. What else did she not know about this wonderful man? She looked at the ring on her finger. The eternity ring. They would have their whole lifetime to learn wonderful new things about each other.

Around several more curves down the wooded lane, they came to Mrs. O'Connor's cottage. Her lawn ran right down to the bay, where a fringe of tall grass framed the purple water. The world beyond was a soft blend of pink, blue, and lavender as a pale salmon sun slipped behind an island in the harbor.

Becca flung out her arms and twirled down the slope toward the lapping water. "Let's get up early in the morning!"

"Yes, and go for a walk before breakfast." Julie skipped after her.

"We'll see leprechauns."

"And fairies!"

Mary linked her arm in Gareth's as they followed more slowly. "I'd like to see the morning those two voluntarily got out of bed early. But that does sound like a good idea."

He bent and kissed her in front of her ear—which always gave her the most delicious shivers. "Is that a date?"

They stood, arm in arm, looking out over the gently shimmering water.

> "Where the wave of moonlight glosses
> The dim gray sands with light,
> Far off by furthest Rosses . . ."

Gareth quoted. "Yeats could have been standing at this very spot when he wrote that—that's Rosses Point over there."

"What poem is it?"

"*The Stolen Child.* Its theme is like your play. I don't remember much of it, but the refrain is something like

> "Come away, O human child!
> To the waters and the wild
> With a faery, hand in hand,
> For the world's more full of weeping
> Than you can understand."

"Oh, that's so beautiful. And so true. I wish I knew more of Yeats's writing."

They stood side by side in silence until the last of the sun slipped behind the island, leaving only one streak of pink across the purple horizon.

Mrs. O'Connor had bowls of steaming Irish stew and thick triangles of soda bread ready for their supper—which she called tea. While they were eating Mary asked if Lissadell was open.

"Sometimes it is. Can't hurt to ask." Their hostess offered to inquire that evening, but no one had the energy for any more sightseeing.

Full of comforting food and cozy in crisp linen that had been dried in the fresh air, Mary had no trouble sleeping soundly, even though she shared a room with three teenage girls. And as she predicted, Becca, Julie, and Debbie were still soundly asleep, only their tousled heads showing above their douvet, when she pulled on her jeans and slipped out the next morning.

Mary opened the front door and was greeted by the sun coming over Benbulben and a cow mooing in the distance.

Gareth was already on the edge of the walk where the first rays of the sun glistened on a riot of red, blue, and gold flowers growing against the whitewashed walls of the house. He held out his hand, and they turned down the hedge-bordered lane toward the bay.

Sunlight filtered through the trees by the dirt path, gilding the edges of moss, ferns, and long-bladed grasses. Overhead, branches twinkled with sunlight as if sprinkled with gold dust. Even the fence posts glittered. At the foot of the path, she saw that the tide was out and a curving, marshy plain stretched before them. Tide pools shimmered among the tufts of marsh grasses. Snipe and curlew called from the long reeds growing in the wetlands.

They made their way slowly through a world of light and half-light. Mary stooped and picked up a small ivory seashell.

> "Go gather by the humming sea
>   Some twisted echo-harbouring shell,
>   And to its lips thy story tell."

Gareth's softly lilting voice blended with the magic around her, adding to Mary's sense of wonder.

"Yeats again? How do you know so much of his poetry?" Then she saw he was holding a slim, green velour volume out to her.

"Just a wee gift. I thought you might like it."

Mary's eyes misted as she took the book. Such gentle thoughtfulness was so like Gareth. And she ached because their world this summer was so 'full of weeping' that they had had little time for their own love.

But at that moment, with the rising sun warming her head, the rim of the bay shimmering in the distance, and Gareth's eyes smiling at her, she knew it was all there—all the love she had felt for him that had brought her across four thousand miles of ocean to be with him. Their time to be together would come. When their work here was done. She reached for the book, and the sun caught the emeralds on her claddagh ring.

She opened the book and read softly:

> "I will arise and go now, and go to Innisfree,
>   And a small cabin build there, of clay and wattles made;

Nine bean rows will I have there, a hive for the honey bee,
And live alone in the bee-loud glade,
And I shall have some peace there, for peace comes dropping slow.
Dropping from the veils of the morning . . ."

She put her hand in his, and they turned back to another day in the real world. But Mary knew these few moments of magical beauty would be with her forever. And someday she and Gareth would be together in their own peaceful glade.

As she suspected, back at the house all was a hive of activity. Philip hurried his charges to finish the excellent breakfast provided by Liam's aunt and get out to the minibus. They had a full day ahead, indeed. He would allow for a little quick sightseeing, but the main goal for the day was business. They needed to get a line on the illusive Joe Navan—find something to help the police in their investigation.

Mary knew Philip wasn't worried about the damage to the Centre —that had been more than made up by their supportive community. But Tommy needed something to clear himself—as much in his own eyes as in the minds of the police, and most of all to be able to present himself as a good citizen to Lila's parents.

They drove around the bay through a wildfowl reserve to the house they had admired the evening before. Although Mary could sense Philip's desire to get on with his investigation, he drove into the sweeping gravel drive and parked by a small blue car.

"Why don't you all stay in the bus, and I'll go inquire." Mary jumped out, glad for an excuse to get even this close to the house.

She crunched her way across the gravel. She was in the shadow of the house when a very proper English voice from somewhere above her head asked, "I say, can I help you at all?"

She looked up the side of the house. In the middle of the top row of glass panes a head topped by a tweed cap leaned out an open window. "Oh, hello," Mary called up. "I'm from the States. I'm very interested in Yeats. I was hoping the house was open."

"Oh, I see. Well, how many of you are there?"

"Quite a lot. A minibusful, I'm afraid."

"Well, I wouldn't have time to give you a proper tour, but I could just let you have a peek."

"Oh, thank you!" She turned to signal the others.

In a few moments the great doors were opened by a tall, thin man in an old Barbour coat and maroon corduroy slacks. As soon as she stepped into the slate-floored hall, Mary knew why the man was wearing cap and jacket. The cold from the stone floors seeped upward, and she longed for the sweater she had pulled off after her walk by the bay.

But she focused on the antlers, stuffed birds, and other trophies that filled the two-story entrance hall. To their left a red-carpeted stairway swept upward. Before them, double doors opened onto a long music gallery filled with various instruments and ornate chairs and sofas.

"Wow!" Becca burst forth. "Who owns this place?"

Their guide grinned. "Well, I do actually. My great-great-grandfather built the house in 1834, but my family had been here from Elizabethan times."

Mary, who had rather suspected that their guide was the lord of the manor, gulped at her sister's directness. But after all, she had warned him that they were Americans. Of more concern was Liam's reaction to the English landlord. She prayed he wouldn't explode with a "Brits, go home" taunt. She relaxed a bit when she saw that his reaction was limited to a glance of disgust before he lowered his eyes and turned his back on their host.

The great-great-grandson of Sir Robert Gore-Booth led them into the charming lemon and white bow room, where a circle of windows looked out on the south lawn. "These are the windows Yeats referred to when he wrote his poem about Eva and Constance in their silk kimonos."

Then he took them into the dining room, ringed with life-size portraits of family members. He pointed to a gallery of snapshots on the sideboard. "This is Maude Gonne, the actress Yeats was so mad about. And this is Connie when she played Lady Macbeth at the Abbey Theatre . . ."

Mary bent over the picture. "Oh, she must have been very good."

"Well, I don't know how good she was. But she was very keen."

Mary wanted to point out to Liam that this was the woman who refused her seat as first woman in Parliament in order to serve Ireland, but it was Gareth who made a point on the same theme. "You know, Maude Gonne's husband was one of those executed for his part in the Easter Rising. His death had a major impact on bringing about the Irish Free State."

Liam shrugged.

Upstairs they saw the room where Yeats stayed when he was a guest there, but the thing Mary found most interesting was deep in the dingy basement. There the old Victorian kitchen had taken up most of the space under the house. Mary suspected this was not a part of the tour normally offered to the public, since the floor was littered with fallen masonry and broken glass. "Mind your step there," their host warned. "Sorry about that—we're just having some work done."

He led the way to a damp, dimly lit room beside the kitchen. "Now here's a bit I find interesting." He pointed to a white, wooden door, then swung the top part of it back to reveal a wide shelf on the lower half. "My great-grandfather had this cut for serving soup to his tenants during the famine."

A narrow stone stairway just beyond the serving door led to the outside. Mary could imagine emaciated, ragged farmers and their families lining up with their bowls. Behind the half door, great cast iron soup pots still stood on tripods as they must have done when filled with steaming barley and mutton broth. And along the walls were baskets that most likely once held fresh-baked loaves.

"Oh, what a good idea." Mary hoped the object lesson wasn't being lost on Liam: not all the Anglo-Irish landlords had been heartless.

"Yes, one likes to think they did what they could. Terrible, black days those were." Sir Jocelyn shook his head.

Philip nodded. "Terrible for everyone. A third of the landlords were ruined as well."

Again Mary tensed, but Liam didn't say, "Good enough for them," or something worse.

The tour ended. All but Liam thanked their host. She noticed that Sir Jocelyn's eyes twinkled at the twins' effusions.

The two were less effusive, however, a short time later.

Philip turned onto a small lane between green fields, and Mary could just see the top of a square, Norman church tower peeking above a grove of trees.

He stopped and set the hand brake. "This is the wee church where Yeats's grandfather was vicar. And more to the point, where the poet himself is buried."

Becca and Julie were out first and skipping ahead. They were just to the churchyard when two copper and black roosters flapped off the low stone wall.

Becca took off after them. "Look! The sun makes their feathers green!" The birds squawked and flapped ahead of her.

"Becca, we're meant to be seeing Yeats's grave," Debbie reminded her.

"Bor-r-r-ring." She pranced off, laughing.

Julie followed, then darted off to examine a clump of golden flowers.

Shaking her head, yet glad that her irrepressible sisters had been able to grow up in an atmosphere that allowed such freedom, Mary turned to the churchyard filled with gravestones.

Ahead stood a fine, carved cross and, beyond that, the stump of a round tower. But it was a simple stone marker that caught her attention. "Cast a cold eye on life, on death, Horseman pass by." William Butler Yeats had written his own epitaph.

Back in the minibus, Mary knew better than to preach directly to Liam, but she wasn't going to let all this be lost on him. So she directed her comments to her sisters. "I wish you two would pay more attention to Yeats. He was one of Ireland's true greats. And it's so interesting because he was Anglo-Irish, Church of Ireland—his grandfather a vicar, even."

Gareth backed her up. "That's true. And Lady Gregory, who started the whole Irish literary awakening, was English."

"You see, in many ways Ireland would have been much poorer if the Brits had gone home." Mary abandoned any attempt at subtlety.

Liam, hunched in a back corner, appeared not to have heard.

In Sligo, Philip drove to the county library. After a brief consultation with the phone book and some help from the librarian, he came back to the waiting group. "I think we've found the address. Not too far from here. Why don't you all stay here? They have a rather good Yeats display, I understand. Tommy and I'll go see what we can do."

"And you just might care to say a wee prayer," Tommy added as he followed Philip. The spring in Tommy's step expressed the hope he held for what they might be able to accomplish in that visit.

Unfortunately, there was no bounce to his step when they returned an hour later.

"You didn't find the Navans?" Mary asked once they were all back in the van.

"Oh, yes. We found them." Tommy slumped in the backseat. "Sweet old couple. He seems pretty strong physically, but the mind completely barmy. He was never right after that beating, but he's much worse now. He thought I was Joe.

"She seemed pretty sharp mentally—kept telling him, 'No, no, he's Joe's friend,' a decibel louder every time, but it never did any good. She's so frail a puff of wind would blow her over. They haven't seen their son for months." Tommy dropped his head in his heads. "Why can't he stay home and be a good son to his parents? What does he hope to gain by vandalizing the CCC and messing up my life?"

Mary looked at the two young men huddled in opposite corners of the backseat. What a disaster this trip had been. That Tommy could sort things out so that he could propose to Lila seemed more unlikely than ever. And Liam was even more withdrawn and hostile than the first time Mary had met him.

She had been wrong in her decision to stay and try to help. Nothing was working. They should have gone to Scotland.

65

"Come on, come on, come on." Philip restlessly urged the traffic forward as they left Sligo. "We can't be dawdling here all day if we're going to stop at the Ulster-American Folk Park and still be back in Belfast this evening." He zipped around the car ahead and pulled back to his own side as a lorry appeared over the hill.

Mary caught her breath. "What is the Ulster-American Folk Park?"

"Ah, sure, a fine thing. Old World/New World—the largest museum of emigration in Europe. Some forty million Irish Americans in America, you know. Shows how it all came about."

"That will be interesting." Well, it would be, and she appreciated Philip's taking the time to give her a tour. But even as interested as she was in history, Mary was more concerned for the here and now. They didn't seem to be making much progress on the present troubles.

Gareth switched on the radio. A commentator was recounting worries over the upcoming marches in Londonderry, traditionally held in honor of the Apprentice Boys who slammed the city's gate in the face of James II.

"Even worse rioting is expected in Londonderry and Belfast than the violence and deaths produced by the July marches. Nationalist confidence in the British government and police is probably at an all-time low because they see the government as giving way to mob rule. If the saga of this year's 'Glorious Twelfth' says anything about Ulster's future, that future looks bleak indeed."

Gareth snapped off the radio and stuck a tape of Irish ballads in the cassette player, but it was too late.

Even Becca and Julie reflected the gloom.

"That's awful."

"Why do they *do* that?"

"Couldn't they just have a picnic or a concert or something like we do on the Fourth of July instead of marching?"

"Yeah. Parades are pretty boring, anyway."

Debbie tried to explain the unlikelihood of Irish people—from either side of the street—suddenly abandoning a tradition held sacred for hundreds of years.

"But there ought to be something *somebody* could do."

Silence greeted Becca's outburst. It seemed that everything had been tried. And failed.

Just as she had failed with Liam. If she couldn't get through to one boy, how much hope was there for reaching millions?

Two hours later Philip gave his customary glance at his watch and pulled into the parking area at the Folk Park. "Don't want to rush you, but this place covers acres. You could spend all day here, but I've got a council meeting tonight. Er . . . Gareth, while the others have a look around, do you suppose you and Tommy and I could just sit here and go over some notes I made for tonight?"

"Aye. That's fine." He turned to Mary. "You'll be all right?"

"Of course." Mary looked at Liam, who showed no sign of moving. "Liam will escort us—won't you?"

His hesitant response wasn't particularly flattering, but he did come. The twins and Debbie skipped ahead.

They went first to the exhibit telling the story of the two hundred years of hardship that prompted more than two million to emigrate to America. By 1660, Ulster's energetic Protestant population had transformed their area from the most backward of Ireland's provinces to the most developed. Then the Penal Laws forced Presbyterian dissenters to support a church they didn't agree with and debarred them from owning land. The first wave of emigrants set sail for America, where they could worship as they pleased and buy land cheaply.

The second wave washed westward in 1772. Much of Ulster's prosperity had been based on the linen industry. That year the industry collapsed, followed by agrarian unrest, rack renting, and rising costs. Thirty thousand emigrated to the New World in one year.

She couldn't help wondering how her conscripted escort was reacting to this further recitation of Irish woes. Perhaps she would have been wiser to have left him sulking in the minbus. She wanted to say something comforting, but nothing came to her. And his closed countenance was not encouraging.

Mary was glad that her country could have offered a home to so many needy people. She was grateful for the contributions the newcomers had made to her homeland, too: John Dunlop, whose printing house printed the Declaration of Independence and the Constitution; Thomas Mellon, who would one day found the great banking house; Davey Crockett, son of Ulster settlers; fifteen United States presidents of Irish ancestry . . .

The next exhibit was a famine cabin. The one-room shanty built of fieldstones had a clay floor and a straw-thatched roof. Six children slept on a straw pallet.

A guide, portraying a thin, ragged woman, sat in the corner beside the fireplace. In a despairing voice she told the story of her family. "I was born in this cottage. My family had been tenants on this land for a hundred and fifty years. But times changed. Our landlord began grazing more cattle, so he didn't need my husband to farm for him. I had always been a spinning woman, like my mother and my grandmother. But machines started doing that work. We only had half an acre of land for the eight of us, but it produced good potatoes, and we kept a cow. Potatoes and milk. Milk and potatoes. They kept us alive."

Mary looked at Liam uneasily. She could imagine the harsh things he was thinking about factory owners and landlords.

"And then in 1844 a terrible thing happened . . ."

Her story went on, but Mary could take no more. She turned away, feeling drained. Then she realized that Liam had disappeared. What impact had the portrayal of so much suffering had on his easily inflamed emotions? She thought of his running toward the river in Enniskillen and . . .

Mary began to run. The lanes of the outdoor museum twisted among trees and between historic buildings. Which way should she look? Should she call out for him? Surely he would cause no harm to himself at a museum.

Out of breath, she arrived at the replica dock and boarded the *Brig Union,* an early nineteenth-century sailing ship that had carried emigrants to the New World. Had he come this way? She hurried through the tiny "between decks" spaces where as many as five adults and four children had huddled in almost constant darkness for the six-to-nine-week crossing. Typhus had raged in such conditions. In "Black '47" alone, twenty thousand Irish emigrants perished on such "coffin ships."

She ran out the exit and took a deep gulp of fresh air. Here waves splashed the side of the dock, seagulls called, and a breeze ruffled her hair. She was in the New World.

And then she heard Debbie scream.

Mary ran in the direction of the cries, down an American street and across a green patch of frontier land. She could hear the thudding of a heavy object. Debbie's pleas grew louder and louder.

"Liam, *stop!*"

Mary careened around the side of a log cabin and came to a halt. "Liam! No!"

Liam's ax flashed toward a chopping block. Chips of white wood flew in every direction. And so did flecks of bright red blood from a gash in his arm.

575

Had he inflicted the cut on himself purposely? Or had he been cut by flying splinters from his log-splitting frenzy? Either way, he needed help.

"Liam, stop it! You're hurt!" Unmindful of the danger to herself from the swinging ax, Mary threw her arms around him from behind just as the blade sank deep into the stump and toppled the log Liam was attacking. "It's me, Liam. Mary. It's OK. I know you're upset. But we'll help. Please. Please."

Then she felt his shoulders slump, and the ax thudded to the ground. She looked at the wide-eyed girls. "Go get Gareth," she said to Debbie.

The girl hesitated. "But—"

"Go on. I'll be fine."

But Debbie sent Becca and Julie scurrying for help, instead, and put her own arms around Liam, who stood trembling and ghostly pale.

"Sit down before you faint!" Mary ordered. She was thankful to be wearing a white blouse over her turtleneck. She pulled it off and wrapped it tightly around his arm to staunch the bleeding.

Debbie, her own arm smeared with Liam's blood, touched his cheek gently.

He pushed her hand away as if swatting at a fly. "I knew it. I knew Desmond was right. I knew it—but now I've seen it. This is what he was fighting against. The Brits lived in places like that mansion we saw yesterday and sent the Irish off on coffin ships!"

"Who is Desmond?" Mary tightened the makeshift bandage. Liam needed to talk. Whatever he had bottled up for so long had to come out.

"Desmond," Debbie repeated. Her arms still around the boy, she guided him to a log and sat beside him.

"My brother."

"I didn't know you have a brother."

"I don't. He was murdered."

Mary didn't interrupt. Debbie was doing just fine.

"Liam. Tell me."

"Three years ago. We were watching the telly. Doorbell rang. Des went. I heard him greet the guy like he was an old friend. Told him to come in. I got up to go see. Then the shots." Liam buried his head in his arms. "Bam, bam, bam. Just like that."

"Did you see the gunman?"

He sat up. "Saw it all, didn't I? Just standing there, frozen at the top of the stairs while he pumped my brother full of holes. I'll never forget him—the freezin' UVF mongrel." He closed his eyes. "White-blond hair, like an albino."

"Did the police ever find him?" Mary ventured.

"Police!" Liam jumped to his feet and spun around as if he would hit her. "How can you be so bleak stupid? The police're all in league with that lot. You saw what they did last week: 'No, you can't march. No, you can't march. Oh, you want to march bad enough to yell at us? OK, then. Go ahead and march. Don't worry about the people you're terrorizing.'" He sank back onto the log.

"Liam, I'm so sorry about your brother."

"I should have stopped him. I should have gone to the door. I knew Des was in the Army. I should have known the Prod butchers would be after him. But I didn't do anything. I let them shoot him. It should have been me."

"I know." Debbie dropped her head as she spoke. "I know exactly how you feel."

"You know how I feel? You don't know anything! You pampered Prod princess!"

"Pampered!" Now Debbie was on her feet. "You stupid Catholic! That shows exactly how much you know! My father was shot right in front of my eyes. Shot by one of your lot—maybe even by your darling brother! How do you think *I* feel?"

Liam looked as if he'd been struck in the face. "Sorry," he mumbled. "I didn't know. You don't act like anything ever happened to you."

"Because I had the good sense to get help!" She paused. "After I broke my hand trying to slam it through a wall."

They both sat, drained.

Mary took a cautious breath. "Liam, it would do you a lot of good to talk to somebody. You could go to a counselor like Debbie did."

He made a scoffing noise. "I don't need any shrink. I know who I need to talk to."

"Your priest? That's a good idea, Liam. Priests are trained to—"

"Don't be so thick. I need to take Des's place. I need to join the Army!"

"No!" Debbie pulled away with a sob.

Mary sprang toward Liam and clutched his good arm so hard her knuckles turned white. "No, Liam. Don't throw your life away." He wrenched away, and she could see she was getting nowhere. She forced herself to take a deep breath. "Think about Aisling. What happens to her if you join the IRA? What if the same thing happens to you as happened to Desmond? Do you want Aisling to grow up with your nightmares?"

He was silent. At least he was listening.

"So what will she have if you become paramilitary? Maybe you won't get killed. Maybe you'll be lucky and just go to jail. Where will that leave her? At least stick around and see if you can get this youth center built first. Then she'll have a place to play Ping Pong and drink Cokes with her friends while her big brother's in prison!"

Mary heard pounding feet, and the men and her sisters rounded the side of the cabin.

Philip took one look at the situation and helped Liam to his feet. One arm around the boy for support, he led him off toward the car park.

Gareth knelt by Mary. "Are you all right?"

She nodded and dropped her head to his shoulder. Gareth was here. She was all right. "Just take me home." She didn't even stop to think what she meant by that—Belfast, Scotland, America—it didn't matter. Wherever Gareth was, was home. Just being with him filled all her hunger.

GENERATION FIVE

THE GREAT FAMINE
1845–1913

And Moses said, "Fill an omer of manna
to be kept for your generations;
that they may see the bread wherewith
the Lord hath fed you."
For the Lord is good;
his mercy is everlasting;
and his truth endureth to all generations.
Exodus 16:32, adapted
Psalm 100:5

66

Andrew was hungry, but Grandfather was not to be rushed. No matter that Mrs. B would be taking a tray of hot oat bannocks out of the oven for tea even now. Grandfather Lanark seemed to think the potatoes would disappear from the fields if he didn't ride around every acre and look over every ridge of sturdy green plants every day. What was the use of hiring an overseer, Andrew wondered, if one insisted on doing all the overseeing oneself? Especially when one could otherwise be at home enjoying tea.

Sitting easily on his high-spirited horse, seventy-one-year-old Jay Lanark drew a deep breath, expanding his remarkable white beard, and a satisfied smile spread over his wrinkled face. "Yes sir, Andrew, our family has been growing potatoes on this land for two hundred and thirty-five years."

Andrew was surprised he didn't have it down to the number of months and days as well. The fact that Grandfather said "our family" meant that the matter under discussion was one in which to take pride. Any weakness would be referred to as coming from "your family."

Grandfather Lanark made no secret of the fact that it was a sore thing to him that the only heir to Lanarks' Bawn should bear the name Armstrong. Often during Andrew's seventeen years he had been made to feel that it was somehow *his* fault that Grandfather Lanark's daughter had died giving birth to his only grandchild. Always frail and pale, Deirdre had managed to hang onto life just long enough to marry and bear Andrew—after her alarmingly handsome Hugh Armstrong had run off to sea, which was somehow probably Andrew's fault as well.

But today Grandfather was in a mood to focus on the past glories of the Lanarks. "Yes sir. Your great-great-great- . . ." A wave of his broad hand conjured up an unending line of Lanarks standing tall and proud behind the hills of potatoes. "Grandfather Calum Lanark was the first one to grow tatties in all of Ulster. Right here—on this very soil. Now that's a thing to be proud of, my boy." He squinted his pale blue eyes in a faraway look. "Yes sir, someday you'll be showing this field to your son, my great-grandson. A fine thing, family tradition.

Something to build on. Never forget that you're a Lanark through and through."

If only Andrew could forget it. It was a curse. The curse of the Lanarks. But Andrew would not be like the rest of them. He would not be like Grandfather. He would not join the Orange Order, no matter how many times Grandfather recounted the story of his being there when it was formed. "Someday you'll be Grand Master, just like your grandfather," everyone said. He would not. He'd show them.

"Well, speak up, lad. What do you have to say for yourself, eh? Just look at that field. You've never seen a more beautiful sight, have you? Never a better crop. Yes sir. Irish Blacks—the very best. White skin, firm flesh, high yield. Not a better tattie anywhere. You remember that, lad, when you take over the planting of these fields. Don't you be led astray. We'll have none of those white-skinned Lumpers on Lanark land. Oh, they're high yield all right but poor taste."

Grandfather's mouth curved downward. "Only good for animal feed, they are. The wild Irish eat them readily enough, but I'd not have them on my table. Nor the Cup—difficult to digest. Poor keeper too. Now the Apple tastes well enough, if you like your tatties round and mealy, but they're a poor yield. Of course, they can be mighty tasty drenched in fresh butter—"

Andrew groaned silently. Would his grandfather never quit talking about eating?

"Yes sir, you remember that, young man. Just over four more years and you'll be of age. You can sign the papers on your twenty-first birthday. The day you take the Lanark name, you take the Lanark fields too. And you can see to the planting of the best tatties in all Ireland—and take your place at the Orange Lodge."

Andrew urged Rannock forward with a sharp kick of his heels. He hoped Grandfather wouldn't notice that he hadn't responded. The quicker they got around the field, the quicker he could get home to Mrs. B's tea cakes. And the quicker he could get away from having his grandfather's plans for the future dinned into his ears. With luck he could even continue the rounds without their coming to loggerheads. Grandfather was really a grand old man, Andrew reminded himself, as he did several times each day. Jay Lanark had spent most of his seventy-one years standing firm for the things he believed in. And no seventeen-year-old boy was about to change him now, even if that boy was the old man's only living direct relative.

Jay Lanark would never understand his grandson's ideas and desires. So what was the use of annoying him? Besides, Andrew didn't understand himself most of the time. Except for his desire to get home to eat.

But the broad man with the mane of shoulder-length white hair was as immovable as Scrabo Hill, which formed the backdrop of his lands. He would not be hurried. "Aye, a fine crop. I think I'll tear down those old byres and build a fine new storehouse. That's another thing, Andrew, my boy—Blacks store well. Good keepers. New storehouses, that's the ticket. Then we'll keep the crop for the best price. Get top price, yes sir. Build onto the house, too, I'm thinking. We'll have one of those fashionable long galleries. Best houses in Belfast have them—no reason we can't have one, too. But I'll not be filling any room in *my* house with those French and Italian paintings. We'll have good Scots pictures. Raeburn and Mackenzie—they know how to put paint on canvas." His hand thudded on Andrew's slim shoulder. "That's the ticket, lad. Good Scots heritage—never let you down."

Andrew put a hand against his stomach to keep it from growling. If Grandfather was off on the superiority of the Scots, they'd never get home. He toyed with the idea of reminding Grandfather that there had been a time even Scottish skill had failed. But the old man had suffered enough. His beloved wife, Euphemia, died with the birth of their first child—a daughter, not even capable of carrying on the Lanark name. Jay had done his best in naming her Deirdre after the first Lanark wife.

And when it came time for the frail Deirdre to bring Jay Lanark's grandchild into the world, he had insisted that she go to Edinburgh for her lying-in. This was not a matter of fashion—the Anglo gentry in Ireland bought French and Italian art and sent their women to London for confinement. This was good Scots-Irish hardheaded sense. Edinburgh had the best doctors in the world. The only sensible thing was that she have the best care possible for the birthing of the heir to Lanarks' Bawn.

But even the world's best wasn't enough to keep Dierdre Armstrong nee Lanark connected to her thin thread of life. It was evident that she would much rather be with her Hugh, who had been lost at sea. And Jay Lanark had bowed his head and hunched his thick shoulders. If God had not foreordained that his daughter should live, then it was nae man's place to quibble with his Maker. Jay had hired a wet nurse from a poor but respectable family, and Andrew Jay Calum Lanark Armstrong had been borne back to Lanarks' Bawn in the comfortable arms of Elfrith Calder and under the protective eye of Jay Lanark. Under which protective gaze he had remained, lo, these seventeen years.

Grandfather's gaze had ever been loving, if rigid, spiced with occasional flashes of anger and less frequent flickers of humor. But in all those years Andrew had never once doubted his grandfather's deep caring for him or for Lanarks' Bawn. He never doubted that Jay Lanark ever sought the best for both his grandson and his land. And as long as the two interests did not conflict, there would be no problem. But should there ever be conflict, Andrew was in no doubt which held the greater importance for Grandfather.

Thus Andrew knew that his own destiny must always be subservient to Lanarks' Bawn. The matter was as firmly predestined as the question of his own salvation. Andrew had every desire to repay Grandfather's love and make him happy. But he feared growing up to be like him. The hardness of spirit at the center of the man was a fearful thing. And Andrew had no desire to spend the rest of his life at Lanarks' Bawn, either, growing potatoes and marching in Orange parades.

The trouble was, he didn't know what he did want to do. He just knew there had to be something more. Now he shifted his gaze from the potato field to look out to Strangford Lough. He didn't feel the same pull of the sea that his father must have felt. But Andrew felt a great sympathy for what his father must have undergone. Had Hugh Armstrong been forced to spend his days circling endless fields of potato hills when in his mind he felt the roll of the deck beneath his feet? Had the pale Deirdre chosen the only man in the long line of Andrew's ancestry that had burned with imagination and adventure? Was it his father's blood in him that made Andrew so unfit for his preordained life?

Rannock plodded obediently beside Grandfather's horse as they turned down the long side of the south field. Even the Lanarks' Bawn horses lacked imagination. But how much imagination could Andrew claim for himself? It didn't take much creativity to know what he *didn't* want to do. His greatest fear was that at the end of the day he would be just as dull as the more than two hundred years of Lanarks before him. A specter rose in his mind—the brown blob of a Lumper potato. Grandfather was talking on about crop yield. Andrew felt he would go mad if he didn't escape.

All he could do was dig his heels into Rannock's flanks and skim past his grandfather's horse on the narrow path. He could outride Grandfather, but he couldn't outride the brown terror in his own mind. He had to get away before it consumed him.

The swift brown Rannock, however, was more practical. He had no brown blob to outrun. He simply wanted his oats. And so they arrived swiftly at the fine stable that had been Jay Lanark's proudest addition to the estate.

Grandfather was less than a horse's length behind, and they dismounted together. "Now why'd ye do sae daft a thing as to spur away like that, laddie? We'd another whole field to see."

Andrew laid a comforting hand on Rannock. The horse's sides were heaving not only from the run, he suspected, but from the fact that the horse Andrew had raised from a colt had a keen sensitivity to his master's moods. And Andrew was quivering inside.

But honoring Grandfather was one of the hallmarks of Andrew Armstrong's life. He would not blurt out his turmoil. "I'm sorry, Grandfather. I was hungry." And the answer was no prevarication. It was just that there was a hunger in him that had nothing to do with his stomach. If only he knew what it was.

He led Rannock toward the polished mahogany box that bore his name on a brass plate.

"Shall I be taking him for you now?" A freckle-faced lad with a shock of carroty hair skittered out from the shadows.

"Here, now, you be careful, Conor O'Brien, or you'll be startling my horses."

Grandfather's sharp voice was more likely to startle the stable than the boy's exuberance, however. Young Conor's affinity for horses was obvious to man and beast alike. And all five of the blooded animals inhabiting the Lanarks' Bawn stable profited from the careful attentions of this ten-year-old who seemed to leave the stable only for meals.

Andrew smiled at the lad. He could never help looking on Conor as almost a half brother—after all, the same woman had given them both suck. Elfrith Calder had done the unthinkable and married a native Irish, but nine-year-old Andrew couldn't see why they couldn't continue to be friends.

Grandfather, however, was adamant. She'd made her choice and married a wild Irish—she who knew better. And after he had rescued her from that stinking hole in Edinburgh! Elfrith would never be welcome to cast her shadow again on Lanarks' Bawn.

So Elfrith O'Brien went to live with the cottiers along the shores of Strangford Lough, and Andrew lost his mother for the second time. The Irish grew potatoes to feed their families, and around the edges of their two- or three-acre plots they grew oats or wheat as a cash crop. This was a cash poor country, and there was little one needed that couldn't be had by bartering—except for paying the rent. The corn, of course, was for export only. Potatoes, buttermilk, and an occasional bit of bacon was all a soul needed to eat. And the energetic state of the seemingly numberless children playing around the doors of the clustered cottages testified to the nutritional value of the diet.

Andrew handed his reins to Conor. "Yes. Take care of him, lad." He turned toward the house and saw a visitor's horse in the end stall. "Oh, Tammis is here. When did he come?"

Conor shrugged. All his attention was on Rannock. "Half an hour ago. Maybe more."

Andrew hurried to the house. He was always glad to see his cousin Thomas Price. Tammis, with his round, pink cheeks, curling black hair, dancing blue eyes, and impulsive ways, couldn't have been less like the wiry, sandy-haired perfectionist Andrew, who always thought through every decision at least five times. Happy-go-lucky Thomas was the spoiled darling of a large outpouring of cousins at Price Manor Farm. And although he was four years older than Andrew, he could have passed for four years his junior except for his expansive size.

He jumped to his feet as Andrew and Jay entered the warm, brightly lit kitchen where Mrs. B had been plying the visitor with cake and buttered buns. Thomas threw out his arms in greeting. "Aye, and if it isn't Saint Andrew himself, wrapped in his banner of righteousness and carrying his sword of truth."

"What are you talking about, man? And who gave you leave to make free with my kitchen? I'm in the habit of receiving guests in the parlor." Grandfather stood just inside the door. Even his beard frowned.

"Now, don't take on so, sir. It's myself that tempted him in for a nice bit of cake, near perishing with hunger as he was." The motherly Mrs. Berkley intervened from her position in front of the Robinson stove. Although she was younger than her employer, she mothered him right along with the youngsters. Now she picked up a wheat bap chock-full of currants and nuts and handed it to the lord of the manor. "Now, you be telling me, sir. Would a plate of these be suiting you for your tea?"

Grandfather maintained his air of offended dignity, but he took the currant bun. "They will do nicely, Mrs. B." He gave the young men a severe look. "Berkley will serve us when we have all washed."

"Uncle, you mustn't be so hard on the excellent Mrs. B," Thomas said a short time later. They were gathered around the dining room table. A low fire crackled on the grate, taking the nip off the September air. "We'd be happy enough to have her and her good husband at Price Manor. Our Iris is a good enough hand with the pies and puddings, but you do have a treasure here." He took a bite of his third currant bun. "And Berkley could buttle for Lord Londonderry himself."

"Don't talk such rot, Thomas Price. And don't you be telling me how to handle my servants. Now what are you here about?"

Thomas flashed his ready smile, exhibiting an expanse of perfect white teeth. "I've come seeking my cousin's company on a venture."

Andrew had been diligently working his way through a heaped serving of stewed hare. He paused with knife and fork poised over his plate. What was the unpredictable Tammis up to now?

"I'm off to Donegal next week. We need some new brood mares, if we're to make the most of that fine blood stallion my father bought last spring. Thought you might be wanting to improve your bloodlines as well, Uncle Lanark."

Only one thing could bring a brighter light to Jay Lanark's eyes than the Lanark land or an Orange march, and that was the Lanark stables. "Oh, aye? Your da has a line on some good mares out west, does he now?"

"No doubt you've heard talk of the fine offerings at the Rossheely fair last spring."

Jay shook his head. "Fat lot of good that'll do. They all sold. What're you thinking, man?"

"I'm thinking that the word is, there are signs it'll be a hard winter. There's many a small breeder will be glad enough to clear out his stable a bit this fall." Thomas laid a finger aside his nose and tapped knowingly. "So, as I'll be making the trip anyway, I thought I'd just offer to share what promises to be a fine windfall and take young Andrew here along as well. The lad's good enough company."

Andrew held his breath. A journey the breadth of Ireland with Tammis? He could think of nothing he would like better. A vision of shining freedom rose before him—nearly a hundred miles between himself and the stifling walls and fields of Lanarks' Bawn. He opened his mouth to accept.

"Unthinkable. Andrew is needed here."

Thomas laughed, his cheeks glowing pink before the fire. "Oh, come now, Uncle Lanark. Surely not *needed*. Wanted, of course. But not indispensable here, surely."

"We'll be harvesting the tatties in a few weeks."

"Of course. All Ireland will be. Biggest crop we've ever taken in—everyone says so. But you aren't suggesting Andrew is needed for field labor? How many croppies from the clachan owe you service?"

The firelight emphasized the bones of Grandfather's face. "These will be Andrew's fields one day. He needs the practice of supervising."

"Oh, I see. You have my sympathy. I dinna know." Thomas held a hand over his heart. "And here was me, thinking Carlan Dunleer was still overseeing for you. But if he's not . . . well, that's a sore loss, a sore loss, indeed."

Jay struck the table. "I'll not be mocked at my own table by a puppy. Well ye know that Andrew must learn to oversee the overseer. Besides, we're to start a new building project. Hope to have it most completed before harvest. We'll be needing new storage sheds for the tatties."

Andrew wondered if the edge to Grandfather's voice was a warning to himself not to extend the argument, or if it was directed to Tammis and the Price family at large. Jay Lanark held no toleration for the Prices' wishy-washy Methodist ways. If Grandfather had his way about it, he would have as little truck with the Price Manor relations and their Arminian enthusiasms as he'd had with the Seaton Court Lanarks and their popery, before they moved to Dublin or wherever it was they had gone off to. Wherever it was, their going had Jay Lanark's blessing.

Andrew bit his lip and looked at his cousin in appeal. There was nothing to be gained by angering his grandfather further. If an approach to Jay Lanark's love of fine horseflesh left him unmoved, there was no hope. "When do you go, Tammis?" Andrew made no attempt to keep the longing out of his voice.

"Next week. The fair starts end of the month. Take my time traveling, see a bit of the country, I thought. Then get there in time to look all the stock over good."

Jay Lanark's face clearly showed what he thought of young men gallivanting about the country on pleasure trips when they could be at home building bigger barns.

But a few days later, the builder summoned by Jay Lanark arrived, and Andrew dutifully followed along, listening to Grandfather describe his vision for enlarging house and outbuildings. What could stone and boards be compared to the joy of riding across the green beauty of Ireland?

Andrew counted the months in his head. No, counting months made it seem too many. He would stick with years. Four years and two months until he was of age. Then his mother's inheritance would come to him, and he would be independent.

But he couldn't wait that long for a breath of fresh air. Tammis would be leaving in a few days. Andrew felt desperate to find a way to accompany him. But what could he do? He didn't have two shillings of his own. And he wouldn't openly defy his grandfather. All he could do was hope for a miracle.

And obey. For the moment that meant saddling Rannock while Grandfather left the builder with Carlan Dunleer to work out the details. Grandfather would then be ready to inspect the fields—if they could even see them through the mist that was rising thicker all the time. Andrew couldn't remember when they'd had such a cool, rainy summer —even in a land that seldom had anything but cool, rainy weather.

When he entered the stable, the young O'Brien met him with his usual liveliness. "You'll be wanting your horses now? I just gave Rannock a fine brushing. He's a beauty, he is. Best in the stable, I'm thinking."

Andrew let the lad chatter until a direct question required an answer.

"Then what's Joe Maguire about? You'll be having some building, then?"

"Aye. New barn. Room on the house." Andrew usually enjoyed chatting with Conor. Today he answered without thought.

But Conor jumped at the news. "Oh, that's grand. How many men can he be using? Me da, our Paddy, Uncle Des . . . I'll tell them. They'll be here in the morning. They can start the clearing away right off."

The lad's enthusiasm cut through Andrew's abstraction. He had not considered what the news of possible employment might mean in the clachan, and sure it was there was little enough to do on the land until time to harvest the potatoes next month.

"I'll be asking Mr. Dunleer, right enough," Conor concluded without waiting for an answer.

Andrew was in a slightly better mood a short time later when he left the yard a few paces behind Grandfather. It even seemed the mist had lifted some.

They had just turned onto the lane leading to Scrabo Road when a carriage pulled by a fine team of matched grays came alongside and stopped.

The driver, a man with a fringe of brown beard and a well-groomed mustache, raised his high-crowned beaver hat. "Good day to you, gentlemen, and what a happy chance this is to be meeting our new neighbors. Harrowby's the name. Gordon Harrowby. Just settling into the place down the road. You'll know it as Seaton Court, but we're thinking of calling it Harrowby Dale."

He laughed at their blank looks. "We're from Yorkshire, you see. From the dales. It'll remind us of home, like. But of course, as I tell the wife, this is our home now. Fine land here. Fine. The dales are good enough for grazing, but this is crop-growing land. Fine." Gordon Harrowby tipped his fine gray hat in their direction.

Jay Lanark rode toward him, tipped his own hat, and introduced himself and his grandson.

Harrowby then presented his wife, Ellen, a plump blonde woman wearing a fringed black cape and black striped gown. She murmured something pleasant about the attractiveness of the neighborhood.

But to Andrew the time seemed endless until Mr. Harrowby got around to introducing the two young ladies in the backseat of the carriage: his daughters, Wilma and Selma.

Andrew struggled to fix the memory in his mind so that he would be able to tell them apart the next time they met. For of a certain, they must meet again. Often. It did seem that the curls escaping around the brim of Selma's blue-ribboned bonnet were more golden than the brown ringlets brushing Wilma's shoulder.

The young ladies dimpled charmingly and giggled, lowering their eyes.

Andrew sat as if Rannock had taken root, when the carriage rolled on down the lane.

"Well, there you are now, lad. And what do you say to that? Eh?" Grandfather gave him a hearty clap on the shoulder. "Nay, you needn't be telling me what you think. It's plain as a pikestaff on your face." He slapped his thigh sharply, and the horses pricked up their ears. "Twins. Now that's my idea of good breeders. Two for the price of one. You look sharp, young man. Just what this family needs. Too many puny women. Whole family getting weak." He squinted at his slimly built grandson. "Yes sir, need to thicken up the blood." He prodded his horse toward the closest field. "Yorkshire. Hm. Well, that's England, of course, but far enough north—they should do all right."

Andrew let Grandfather's words wash over him as he savored the memory of dancing eyes and flickering dimples framed by the round brim of a straw bonnet. Sometimes the bonnet wore blue ribbons and sometimes green rosettes, but both were charming.

When they got to the first field, he was so lost in his daydream that he had to blink three times to be sure he wasn't imagining the sight before him. Were those potato leaves, which had been so healthy three days ago, really covered with brownish black splotches? One look at Grandfather's face was surer confirmation than anything he saw in the field.

"What is it, Grandfather?"

Jay dismounted and knelt by the nearest plant, cupping it in his hands as a man might hold the face of his beloved. He moved on to the next hill. There he pulled the plant up. The roots were as rotted as the leaves. "I've never seen anything like it."

Andrew left his mount and knelt by his grandfather. "Is the whole field gone?"

Jay pulled up another plant. That one had a few damaged leaves, but the tubers were sound. On further investigation, it appeared that about half the crop was lost. Completely rotted in less than three days.

"Doesn't look like we'll be needing the new store shed," Andrew said at last.

But Jay Lanark was descended from a long, hardy line. "Nonsense, boy. The very time to build. Locals will be needing employment. Besides—" he turned to the field behind them "—did you ever see a finer stand of oats?"

And so it was across the land. Strange black spots appeared overnight, withering more than half the potato crop. But there was no reason for alarm, people said. The potato crop had failed before, they said. Just ten years ago there had been widespread losses all across Ulster. And again in '37. But everyone had recouped the next year. No need for alarm.

Besides, the oats crop was the best anyone had seen for ten years. And Jay Lanark congratulated himself on his fine new storage barn.

"Yes sir, couldn't have come at a better time. England's paying top money for oats this year." He surveyed the foundations that had just been laid for his long gallery. "I heard of a Raeburn going for sale in Belfast. I just might make a start on my collection if I turn enough profit on these oats. Here, now, lad, it's a good time to be neighborly. Mrs. B made pear butter today. You ask her for a jar or two and take it to the Harrowbys."

Andrew jumped to his feet. That was not an order he needed to hear more than once.

"And you tell them not to be worrying. No need to worry. Any losses this year can more than be made up for next year. Nothing to worry about."

67

The next summer, Andrew would consider how prophetic Jay Lanark's words had been.

There had been empty stomachs in many a cottier's hut last winter. Infants had cried at their mother's breasts. Old women, huddling by the turf fire in their black shawls, had inched closer to the grave as the flesh thinned on their old bones. Many a tattie that should have been saved to seed the hillocks on Good Friday had been eaten to keep hunger beyond the doorstep.

But most had survived, and the gray, hungry days were all but forgotten now as fields flourished verdant and vigorous across the island. Everyone's spirits were buoyed by the prospect of an abundant harvest.

And although the croppies, who were never long out from under the shadow of starvation, called these the blue months—the time when winter stores were thin and harvest still a long wait—yet there were pleasures for cottier and landholder alike. And for Andrew that meant the Ballymena Fair. He smiled at the thought of spending the day with Wilma of the brown ringlets. And with the golden Selma. And their parents too, of course, he added hurriedly.

Oh, but Wilma, now . . . The attractions stacked up one upon another as Rannock's hooves plodded down the lane to Harrowby's Dale. He would buy her gingerbread and rock, and they would watch the boys run footraces, and admire the fine sheep and goats and finer still horses, and the travelers would be there with their brightly painted wagons, and there would be music around the campfires, and dancing in the street, and . . .

He turned into the tree-lined yard of the place he still thought of as Seaton Court, admiring the hollyhocks and spikes of lupine and delphinium growing around its whitewashed walls. Fresh gravel covered the open area between house and barns. Gordon Harrowby was a careful man indeed. A man who would be even more careful of his daughters than of his property.

Andrew sat tall in his saddle and endeavored to look reliable.

Thank goodness Grandfather had made the arrangements for the Lanarks to introduce their neighbors to the best fair in County Antrim. Andrew doubted his own courage in broaching the plan—or Mr. Harrowby's willingness to accept. But no one was likely to refuse Jay Lanark anything.

Andrew looked around at the sound of another horse entering the yard. He hadn't expected Grandfather to arrive so soon, since, of course, he must ride around at least the closer of his fields before setting off on the day's outing.

In fact, it wasn't Jay Lanark but a dark-haired rider on a long-legged black.

"Ah, Tammis! A fine thing to see you after these many months." The sight of his cousin brought back the painful memory of last fall's disappointment, though. "And did you have a fine adventure in Donegal?"

Thomas threw back his head and laughed in his open way. "And have we had so little communication these past months? I'd not realized you didn't know. I dinna go, man."

Andrew frowned. "Didn't go?"

Thomas shook his head. "The crop failure. Too expensive to keep the beasts without potatoes to feed them. But it's just as well. With the fine crop this year—" he gestured as if exhibiting a flourishing potato field "—we'll have more than enough for an expanded stable. And last year's shortages will make the prices on horseflesh even better." He tapped the side of his nose and laughed again. "Fancy there'll be some pretty pickings at Ballymere."

Andrew had not known their party had been expanded, but he was glad enough for his cousin's presence, even if Grandfather wouldn't be.

A red-haired serving girl opened the door, bobbing a curtsey. Another O'Brien from the clachan, no doubt. She skittered off to call her mistress.

A moment later Mrs. Harrowby bustled in. The wide lace bertha on her blue dress framed flushed cheeks and a forehead creased in concern. "Oh dear, oh dear, oh dear. Here we are ready to go, and where are those girls? I can't keep up with them for two minutes together." She spun around with a swish of crinoline. "Mr. Harrowby! Where are you, husband? You must come and take charge of your daughters."

Gordon Harrowby entered in velvet-collared redingote and plaid trousers. "Tut, tut, don't fret yourself. The lasses'll be along. Wilma found a bird caught in the hedge. Thinks it's injured its wing."

Andrew relaxed, glad to know she wasn't just avoiding him. "Oh, where is she, sir? I could be of assistance."

"Oh, aye? Out back, then." Mr. Harrowby tipped his head in the direction of the door he had just come through.

Andrew found Wilma on her knees under a tree, a small brown bird cupped in her gloved hands.

She looked up with a small smile. "I'm sorry, Andrew. I can't go to the fair. This poor wee thing's hurt."

Andrew knelt beside her. "Is its wing broken?"

"I can't tell. But it can't fly. It'll die if I leave it."

Andrew felt carefully along the bone of the small wing fanned over Wilma's hand. "I don't think it's broken. I could splint it just in case, but it's probably best just to let it rest. It'll need a dish of water. Where can we put it that the cats can't get to it?"

Wilma thought a moment. "In the henhouse."

"Right." Andrew got to his feet and helped her stand, an act requiring assistance as both her hands were full and her voluminous skirt and petticoats were tangled under her. In a few minutes, however, the wren was safely ensconced in an empty chicken nest. "There now, mission of mercy accomplished. We can go to the fair."

"Oh, not yet, Andrew. I must feed my bunnies." She set to pulling clover from beneath the hedgerow.

Andrew tried to hide his impatience. They would miss half the fun if this kept up much longer. "Can't rabbits do this for themselves?"

"No, these are just wee. I still give them milk too. Their mother was killed in a fearful trap. I searched and searched and was just lucky to find their nest under the roots of the big cottonwood, or they'd all have perished, the dearlings."

Andrew dutifully gave a hand with the bunnies. Then he waited while Wilma checked on a mongrel dog with a sore paw. In spite of his impatience, he did admire her skill with the creatures.

When they rounded the side of the house, Andrew saw that Grandfather had arrived. He did hope their tardiness would not produce too sharp a remark from the old man.

But they were fortunate in their timing. They went in one door just as Selma entered from the garden, her arms full of yellow and blue flowers, her cheeks flushed, a long white apron over her full gingham skirt, and her broad-brimmed gardening hat pushed back on her head. Andrew thought her one of the most enchanting sights he had ever seen. When he glanced at Thomas, he knew his cousin thought so, too. The amazing thing was Grandfather's almost courtly manner as he bowed to the young woman, brushing her hand with his beard.

Thus it was that the party set out in good humor, no matter how tardily, to Ballymere. Mr. Harrowby drove the ladies in the carriage. Jay, Andrew, and Thomas rode escort.

The village of Ballymena, a few miles north of Belfast, nestled in a green glen. Emerald hills clustered around it on every side. They were still some distance from the town when they began to see the barrel-hooped wagons of the "travelers"—red, yellow, pink, green—lining the verge of the road. Some had camped in fields. Flame-haired, green-eyed children, chickens, and scraggly dogs played in the hedgerows and around the wagon ponies' legs. Mothers and older sisters scolded them—children and animals alike—in a strange-sounding language.

Andrew smiled. This was hardly the great escape to the west country he had dreamed of last year, but it was a grand day out, and he never tired of the exhilaration of a fair.

Several tinkers had set up their metalworking trade around the edge of the village. Anvils rang to the sound of hammered iron as horses were fitted with new shoes, cooking pots with new bottoms, and knife handles with new blades.

The visitors stabled their horses and set out. The sounds of penny whistles, fiddles, and bagpipes filled the air with a grand cacophony that had even Grandfather Lanark's toe tapping.

"Rock. Ballymena rock!" A green-eyed girl carrying a tray strapped around her shoulders called her wares.

In a moment Andrew had presented the Harrowby party with long sticks of crunchy, pink-and-white-striped candy.

But Grandfather would not put up with such dillydallying. He cut a straight line through the crowded village to the green, where a wide circle of observers and bidders scrutinized the horses offered for sale. As skilled as the travelers were in metalworking—some said their line went back to the fifth century when itinerate metalsmiths wandered the Irish countryside from the rath of one chieftain to the next—they were even more skilled at horse-trading. In fact, they were so skilled that few of the settled residents would bid for themselves.

Grandfather, however, shook his bushlike beard and raised a hand in refusal as a sandy-bearded man in a tall tweed hat approached him. Jay Lanark would as soon implore a saint to intercede for him as to employ an agent to do his horse dealing.

It was easy to see that Andrew's grandfather had his eye on a very special animal. Andrew saw instantly what a fine addition the little red mare would make to the Lanarks' Bawn stable. And after Jay had looked her over carefully, there was even less room to doubt her suitability.

The tinker showing her held her lead rope loosely and walked her around the ring both ways. Then, lengthening the rope to give her more headroom, he ran her around at a brisk trot.

Lanarks' Bawn had long produced fine pleasure horses. And now, as the little mare showed her fine action and Andrew coupled her in his mind with the long-legged, fiery stallion that was their prize breeder, he could see Grandfather determining to breed horses the rival of Lord Londonderry's.

But his grandfather walked off, shaking his head. "Too delicate. You'd be lucky if she survived her first foaling," he said loudly. He didn't go far away from the circle, though—just to the other side, where he seemingly gave all his attention to a small black cart pony, which he urged Gordon Harrowby to consider for his daughters.

Selma clapped her hands at the idea. "Oh, what a fine thing, Father. I would love to drive a pony cart. I always wanted one in Yorkshire, but it would be even lovelier here for exploring the countryside."

Andrew tugged at his grandfather's coat. The bidding had begun on the red mare.

Jay Lanark hung back. No need to come in at the early stages. Let the others run themselves out. He would know the strategic moment to enter the proceedings. No doubt he had calculated the value of the animal to a fair penny. He also knew many of the interested breeders around the ring and had an equally shrewd knowledge of the depth of their pockets.

The only thing Grandfather obviously hadn't calculated was the wit and quickness of the agents—the "guinea hunters." They bid sometimes in English, sometimes in their strange, coded language, but always with an insouciant skill that was unsettling to one who believed everything in life could be approached with commonsense logic. Jay's one offer was lost in the shuffle. The mare went home with a rival breeder from Bangor who had previously sold three colts to Lord Londonderry.

Andrew turned to offer his arm to Wilma, as much to escape his grandfather's displeasure as in anticipation of enjoying the lively reel he heard coming from the other side of a wagon. But it was not Wilma at his elbow. Rather, he turned into the sandy bush of the guinea man who had earlier been rebuffed by his grandfather. "Fancy yon mare, did ye?"

Andrew raised his eyebrows and shrugged. "Nice animal. A mite small, but nice."

The traveler winked, nodded, and tapped the side of his nose. "Aye. I know where there's a whole stable like that. And better."

"Of the same stock?"

Andrew started at Thomas's question. He hadn't seen his cousin approach.

"Aye. The same."

It was not for nothing that the genius horse traders of the traveling folk were called guinea hunters. A flash of gold passed between Thomas and the man's hand. It as quickly disappeared into the pocket of his flowered waistcoat. "They'll be at the Rossheely fair, first week in August."

Thomas clapped his arm around the fellow's shoulders. "I know the very place. West coast above Sligo Bay. Near the Donegal border."

"Aye. That's the one. Best in all Ireland."

"So I've heard." Thomas gave the man a shrewd look. "You'll not be forgetting me, now, my friend?"

The tinker patted his pocket where Thomas's guinea lay. "Travelers have long memories." He melted into the circle surrounding the horse ring.

The music from across the field was livelier than before. Now was Andrew's opportunity for the dance he had been anticipating ever since plans for the day had been laid. But Wilma was nowhere to be seen. He would gladly have asked Selma to join the reel with him, but his cousin's intentions in that direction were too clear.

"Where has your sister got off to now?" Andrew's question to Selma held a note of irritation.

She pointed to the far side of the field where stood a bright green wagon embellished with yellow scrollwork and red flowers.

Andrew could see Gordon Harrowby's back but not the man's daughter. As Andrew approached the small group by the caravan, however, he spotted the lady. As usual, she was on her knees beside a distressed animal. Andrew sighed as he saw Tammis lead Selma toward the set forming a new square for the reel.

Wilma lifted the colt's right forehoof and turned to the child standing beside her and sucking a grimy finger while tears streaked trails down each cheek. "See there—your pony has a stone in his frog."

The girl's round green eyes grew rounder still at the seemingly incomprehensible words. A boy a year or two older pressed forward.

Andrew picked up a small, sturdy stick and handed it to Wilma.

In a moment her prodding dislodged the stone. "Your pony may still limp for a day or two. The stone may have bruised the tender place, but he'll be all right."

"Here now, lady, sure and don't you be sporting with my sister. I'm after knowing that's no frog."

Wilma smiled and picked up the hoof again, bending it so the boy speaker could see the underside. She tapped the soft, black formation. "See, that's called a frog. It looks like he stepped on a nice, fat frog and it stuck there, doesn't it?" She set the foot down and stood with Andrew's assistance, brushing bits of grass from her skirt. "And next time don't you be making fun of your little sister when she's worried about a hurt animal."

"The older boys and girls were tormenting her for crying over the limping pony. But she stood right up to children twice her size." She took Andrew's arm.

"And you came along and rescued them all." Andrew smiled at his fair friend.

"It's lucky that Father and I were walking this way. The stone might have worked itself in much deeper if it hadn't been removed quickly."

"And it never occurred to you to let one of the tinkers deal with it —or even your father—or myself?"

She looked at him with eyes as wide and green as those of the tinker child. "But I got there first. And I did it perfectly. With your stick. Thank you—it was just right."

He opened his mouth to ask her to join the set for the next reel, but now Mrs. Harrowby approached. "My dears, there you all are. I'm sure I was quite convinced that you'd been stolen by the gypsies."

Andrew started to explain that Irish travelers were an entirely different people from the nomadic Romanys. But Mrs. Harrowby would have known that, and there was no convincing the good lady that it wasn't quite time for them to return home—especially as a rather heavy rain had started to fall.

By the time they reached Lanarks' Bawn, Andrew was in a thorough funk. He was wet through and chilled to the bone. He had given his coat to Mrs. Harrowby when it was obvious that the cover on the carriage was insufficient to protect its passengers from the rain and wind. He had had nothing but a stick of Ballymena rock to eat for the space of several hours. He had not had his hoped-for dance with Wilma, who obviously preferred injured animals to his company. And Grandfather had failed to buy the mare he wanted. How could so many things go wrong in one day?

He flung off his drenched waistcoat and threw himself into a chair before the blazing peat fire Berkley had ready for them. Grandfather entered more deliberately, and Andrew held his breath. All he needed to end the day was a lecture. What had he done wrong now? he wondered. Oh well, he would soon know.

"Andrew, I've made a decision. And I'll brook no argument. I mean to be obeyed in this."

Andrew sighed and ran his fingers through his dripping hair.

"Thomas told me about the fair at Rossheely. I shall have my new mare. I would go myself, but you aren't ready to take charge of the fields."

Andrew choked.

Grandfather cut him off with a wave. "Don't interrupt, boy. You'll go to the fair and buy a mare for me. The best mare in all Ireland, do you hear? I'll not be crossed in this."

Andrew was so dumbfounded that it seemed a full minute before he could manage, "Yes, Grandfather."

68

Andrew's appetite to see more, to travel farther, amused his cousin. "Aye, Andrew, laddie, hunger for adventure's a fine thing. But not when ye put it before filling your stomach."

Andrew grinned. He was always ready to eat. "Right. We'll stop wherever you say. Under that tree ahead, maybe? But Tammis, I'd no idea the land is so grand. I knew seeing it would be fine, but Lough Neagh is near the size of the sea!"

Even through the mist enveloping land and riders, the low, marshy surrounds of the lough were visible. Two large waterfowl flew by, their rasping call drawing replies from nests among the reeds and grasses.

Thomas swatted at a buzz of midges. "Aye, it is more of an inland sea. But is this truly your first time away from Lanarks' Bawn?"

Andrew drew in a deep breath. "Aye, for any great time or distance without Grandfather."

Thomas gave a shout of laughter. "You're a sturdy lad, Andrew Armstrong, a sturdy lad. Living with your grandfather. My mother, God rest her soul, used to say, 'That man is so rigid I'm surprised he can bend his knees to sit in a chair.' But then, we're promised that tribulation worketh patience. Maybe that's why I'm so impatient—not enough tribulation."

But even Thomas's impatient stomach had to wait longer. By the time they reached the beech tree, rain was falling beyond the ability of its thick leaves to shelter travelers. And it was almost a mile farther along before they found a rocky outcrop with sufficient overhang to offer protection.

Mrs. Berkley had left nothing to chance in preparing for the young master's journey. Andrew pulled a loaf of brack, a boiled chicken, and a small, round cheese from his saddlebags. "Don't bother opening yours, Tammis. There's more than enough here for two— even with your appetite."

Thomas pulled a jug of cider from his pack. "Aye. Hunger is a bad thing, but thirst is worse."

They leaned against the rocky wall to enjoy their meal while the horses grazed along the bank of a stream.

"Well, there should be full stomachs in every cottage hereabouts come October." Andrew gestured to the fields before them. Potato plants spread broad leaves over every ridge and extended down into the furrows as well. Such vigorous top growth gave promise of fine, firm-fleshed tubers growing thick under the brown earth. This year, little space around the edges of the fields had been given to growing oats and wheat. Cash crops were a luxury. Potatoes were the thin line of existence for man and beast. And after last year's widespread crop failure, there was even less margin for survival than usual.

Thomas nodded. "Aye. A good thing the promise is prosperous. The blue months have been bad for the croppies this year."

Andrew chewed a mouthful of crusty wheat loaf stuffed with currants and paused to ponder. His vittles had always appeared as if by magic on the table on schedule. He had never before given the matter consideration. "What do they do?"

"Those that can, go over the water to work. Some scrutch flax for landlords here. Those with wracking rights—like the cottiers along Strangford—pick the shellfish out of the seaweed. Some of the kelp's edible, too."

Andrew made a face. "*Urgh!* Have you ever smelled that stuff? Bad enough when they manure the fields with it. Can't imagine eating it." No wonder, then, that Conor O'Brien had been so eager to secure work for his cousins and uncles.

He sank his teeth into a chicken leg. After a few moments of chewing in rhythm with the sound of rain dripping from the ledge overhead, he asked, "Will we go to Armagh? I hear it's a fine city."

Thomas nodded. "It is that. But out of our way. We'll find an inn near Craigavon before dark."

"But we've no hurry, have we? We could go tomorrow."

Thomas's laughter echoed inside their rocky shelter. "Oh, aye. And while we're at it, we'll just nip on down to Dublin. And maybe you'd fancy seeing Cork? Or taking a wee run over to London? It's little wonder Jay Lanark kept you on a short lead. We've horses to buy, man!"

Tammis put a wedge of cheese back into its cloth and stood up. "Afterwards . . ." He gave his young cousin a wink. "We'll be for seeing what might develop. But we'd best be getting on down the road now if we don't want to be spending the night under a dripping rock."

Whatever Tammis had in mind, he apparently didn't want to talk about it yet. But there was plenty to occupy Andrew as they carried on westward. His mind had been held captive by the narrow world of the Bawn. Now that he was beyond it, his thoughts roamed. The few sermons he had managed to pay attention to in meeting had once satisfied any curiosity he might have felt about matters of infinity. But now he wondered. "What do you think about it all, Tammis?"

"All what?"

Andrew shrugged. "Creation. God. All that."

Thomas was quiet for a while. He gazed around in every direction, then looked upward as if trying to see beyond the clouds. "Oh, I reckon the Almighty's up there. Not sure what He's doing, though. Don't think about it much."

Andrew nodded. "Me either." Mostly he had avoided such questions, for whenever Andrew thought of God, a picture of Jay Lanark's face came to him. And if the Almighty was as rigid as Grandfather, Andrew could see little use in religion. He didn't need another set of rules. But sometimes one did wonder.

It was after noon five days later when they passed their first red tinker's wagon and knew they were nearing their goal. The only room to be had in town was a small, dark hole upstairs at the public house. It smelled of must and stale smoke, and the husk-filled mattress was lumpy and damp. But they were glad for it. And, Andrew thought, they'd be spending little enough time in it anyway.

The opening day of the fair was called "gathering day" because the travelers from far and wide made special effort to gather here at the liveliest horse fair in Ireland.

The cousins had no more than finished their morning porridge when they heard a great stirring in the street. Pipes, drums and whistles, shouts, calls, and laughter combined to bring them running from the inn into High Street. There a fine procession greeted them. The street was jammed with about equal parts of viewers, paraders, and children with pets running alongside.

At the center of all the hoopla was the largest, shaggiest goat Andrew had ever seen. His grand curving horns spanned at least three feet, and bright ribbons streamed from horns and hair alike. Red-haired, barefoot girls in long skirts skipped and danced before the creature, clapping their hands and strewing the path with flowers.

"*Rí Síogai!*" The shout went up wherever the goat passed, chewing placidly on a mouthful of daisies.

Andrew was thoroughly bewildered, but Thomas shouted and cheered with the others. "What's it all about?" Andrew asked as the commotion passed on down the street.

"The fairy king. King of the fair."

"A goat?"

Tammis shrugged. "Something about a goat giving warning to the sleeping town when their enemies were attacking."

They joined the crowd accompanying the procession. "How do you know so much about all this?"

"Grew up listening to my great-aunt's tales. She lived with us after her husband died. I adored her. She could tell tales to outdo any *seanachaidh*. She had married a Methodist preacher. They traveled all over the island, holding meetings." Tammis's cheerful face was soft with remembrance. "Aye, Auntie Carolenn knew everything. And hearing her tell about it was as good as being there."

Andrew kept trying to remind himself that they were here on business. There were horses to be evaluated, bargains to be sized up and argued over, deals to be struck. He daren't return to Lanarks' Bawn without the best broodmare that ever graced Irish soil. But it was hard to keep one's mind on business when there were so many distractions.

Tammis seemed unusually drawn to the musicians who filled every nook of High Street and meadow with lilting tunes.

Surprisingly, it wasn't the livelier pipes and fiddles that attracted him most but the gentler harpers and the lone singers. Thomas could even be in the midst of inspecting a likely piece of horseflesh and break off to talk briefly to a passing musician.

Andrew bought a large square of spicy, warm gingerbread for a penny and wandered down a winding lane where barkers vied with one another to lure passers-by to games of chance. He risked a farthing on the proposition that he could point out which of three walnut shells had the stone under it. He was certain he had not taken his eye from the correct one. But when he pointed to the shell in the middle, it was empty.

He shrugged and walked on. Sellers offered trays of ribbons, pins, polished shells, every geegaw imaginable. A little girl offered straw St. Bridget's crosses for a ha'penny. An old woman with three teeth missing called out to passers to buy her Celtic crosses, "Pure gold as the living sun, and blessed by Saint Patrick himself."

Andrew paused.

"Sure and you'll be wanting one to give to your lassie. You'd not go home without a fairing for her, would you, now?"

Andrew smiled and looked over the tray. The woman's words were true enough. For all the fun and excitement, an awareness of the fair's missing element had been growing on him all day. Wilma Harrowby was the width of Ireland away from him. Rossheely Fair was maybe three times the size and merriment of Ballymere, yet without Wilma's company it lacked luster. And the street dancing held no attraction at all.

He paused over a tray of ribbons and beads, thinking how fine the emerald satin bows would look holding Wilma's shining ringlets.

But he hesitated. He mustn't spend all his money until the horse-dealing was done. It wouldn't do to be outbid because he had spent his purse on fairings. He watched a juggler, then started back toward the horse meadow.

He had just caught sight of Tammis and was hurrying toward him when the clear, pure trill from a harp stopped him dead in his tracks. It sounded like the warble of a lark amid a cacophony of crows.

He followed the sound to where a thin old man in a faded green jacket sat caressing a harp of highly polished black bog oak. A length of canvas provided a sort of shelter from the intermittent rain. A large brindled hound lay at his feet. Children raced by, adults passed laughing and talking, donkeys brayed, sheep bleated, but the ancient musician—wispy white hair falling to his shoulders and skin as thin and pale as paper stretched tight over his high cheekbones—seemed unaware of anything but his music.

The small bowl beside his chair contained only two farthings and a ha'penny, but the otherworldly appearance of the man and the angelic sound of the harp gave the impression that he had little need for anything as mundane as money. Just the same, Andrew tossed twopence in the bowl, not even thinking about horse-dealing.

The tune went on for a long time, as if the player's fingers were singing repeated verses in his head, each with a slight variation. But at last the melody ended on a rising glissando, and the air fluttered off on butterfly wings. Andrew stood barely breathing as the harper's fingers stilled on the strings.

Then a young girl, perhaps fourteen—no more than sixteen, certain—came from behind the tent. She took the harp gently from the frail hands and replaced it with a steaming beaker. "Here, now, *Seanathair*, I've a fine mussel stew for you. Drink ye all of it. It'll keep the chill out."

"Aye, you're my thanks. You're good to me, child."

Andrew saw then that the old man was blind. But his granddaughter's eyes were wide and round, and even from where Andrew stood, he could see they were bright as emeralds. And her cloud of red-gold hair was a light in the overcast day. She glanced at the silver coin among the coppers, then at Andrew, and flashed him a smile. He turned reluctantly to the horse ring.

Thomas was a different person from the carefree companion who had laughed his way across Ireland. Now he was all business. He sized up every horse in the field and asked sharply judged questions of all the other men who were standing around, likewise examining the prospects.

Andrew considered how strange it was that the easygoing Tammis was suddenly so focused, while Andrew, usually so intense, was romping about the fair like a child. But little matter how childlike he might feel. He had a job to do, and he couldn't leave it all to his cousin.

"What have you seen, Tammis? Anything worth bidding on?"

"Oh, decided to look at the horses, did you? Thought I'd seen the back of you for good. Thought maybe you'd run off and joined the travelers."

"Just looking around, Tammis. But I'll settle now."

"Eh, well . . . then you might take a look at the little filly over there. A first cousin to the one your grandfather wanted at Ballymere —if not a sister."

Andrew walked around her, not letting his interest show too clearly. "Aye, she is. Only better developed in the hindquarters. Should breed good." Grandfather had taught him what to look for in horses as well as in women.

Behind them a pelter of bidding rang out as a little cart pony was run around the ring by his handler. The showing and bidding would go on all day. This was only the opening. The serious buying would begin tomorrow. Then they would need their guinea man. But the sandy-bearded Gabriel, he of the tweed stovepipe hat, was not to be found.

"You'll never see his shadow again," Andrew said over their pot of greasy lamb stew at the inn that night. "Probably got so roaring drunk on your gold that the whole thing went right out of his head."

Thomas bellowed the easy laughter that had returned when he left the business side of the horse fair. "Sometimes I could swear I hear Jay Lanark speaking out of your mouth, cousin."

Andrew's brown eyes flashed. He hit the table to chase away the image of Grandfather. *A true Lanark at heart, just like me.* "No. I'm nothing like my grandfather."

Thomas held up his hands. "Whoa, easy. I'd no mind to anger you, man."

But Andrew wondered. The last thing in the world he wanted was to grow up narrow and rigid like Grandfather Lanark. But was it happening anyway, in spite of his determination to get away from all the legalism that inhabited the bawn? "No. Grandfather would never have given a coin to a harper." And tomorrow he would go back and buy those ribbons for Wilma.

Thomas was instantly all attention. "Harper? I saw no harper worth tossing a coin to. Just an endless procession of tooting whistles, caterwauling pipes, screeching fiddles, and banging bodhrán." He shook his head. "I think you must have dreamed your harper as an escape from the clamor."

"Nay, not a bit of it." And Andrew told him in detail about the musician and his granddaughter.

"Aye." Thomas nodded. "Now I understand the sudden liking for the harp."

Andrew smiled. The day had been all that the grand gathering of the Rossheely Fair should have been. But tomorrow would be different, he promised himself. Tomorrow he would attend to the business of the little red mare with the finely rounded rump. He would bid as skillfully as any guinea hunter. He'd seen it done. He knew what to do. And for once Grandfather Lanark would be proud of him.

The next day he saw that the crowd at the horse ring had at least doubled, both in the number of animals being offered and in prospective buyers.

Andrew held true to his determination. In spite of a gnawing in his stomach for a tasty bit of gingerbread—and several fleeting thoughts of listening to harp music and gazing at emerald eyes—he examined every mare as thoroughly as Grandfather himself would have done. And at the end of it all he was satisfied that the little red filly was the one for Lanarks' stable. He had already named her—Fairling.

Throughout the morning, Thomas had bid on several beasts, but Andrew knew his cousin was waiting for a certain chestnut mare to enter the circle.

And then he felt more than saw a flutter off to one side. A man in a flat tweed cap brought Fairling into the ring. Remembering Grandfather's nonchalant stance at Ballymere, he held back, just on the edge of the inside circle, and let the bidding start. He had to judge the matter just right. If he tipped his hand and entered in too soon, he would just run his own price up and encourage others to go higher than he could afford. If he held off too long, he could have the bid stolen from under him as it had been with Grandfather—although now he was certainly glad that had been so.

In spite of the cool air, Andrew felt sweat break out at the back of his neck. What if he muffed the whole thing? Grandfather would never give him a second chance. The bidding crept up. He held his breath and again mentally counted the pound notes in his pocket. What if the bidding surpassed his limit before he even had a chance to bid? Perhaps he could attempt to talk the winner into trading the filly for Rannock. Would Andrew have the heart to do that?

Then he realized that the bidding had slowed. The auctioneer in the middle of the ring cleared his throat. Andrew started to open his mouth.

But no sound emerged. A large, freckled hand with red hairs on the back clamped over Andrew's mouth and drew him backwards into the crowd. He struggled. He tried to punch backward, but the larger man's grip held. It mattered little. The mare went to the last bidder.

Andrew's assailant spun him around and held him by the shoulders, just out of reach of the lad's spitting and kicking.

Then Andrew recognized the man through his blaze of fury. More accurately, he recognized the hat and beard. "What do you think you're doing? My cousin engaged you to *help* us! Is this the way you repay his generosity?"

"Aye, it is. I'm thinking you should know that mare was a twin. And the other one was born blind, a weakness this one could carry, too. You'll be wanting a proven broodmare, I'm thinking. I've found you a deal—two for the price of one."

He led the way beyond the field to a quiet corner where stood a bright green wagon painted with distinctive yellow scrollwork and red flowers. Andrew recognized it. Beside it, back in Ballymena, Wilma had cared for a pony's forefoot.

On the other side of the wagon stood a sleek, proud mare giving suck to a long-legged foal that couldn't be above a few hours old.

"See what I mean?" the guinea man said. "More interesting things elsewhere than the sale yard sometimes."

"Aye." Andrew had to admit mother and child were beauties. But it wasn't only the double value price that appealed to him. He was most struck by the fact that the mare's red-gold coat was the exact color of the harper's daughter's hair. He handed the agent another golden guinea.

"Leave it to me." The man ambled toward the wagon, stroking his bush of a beard.

There was nothing for Andrew to do there. Indeed, his presence would be a detriment. He nipped down a winding side street and bought the green ribbons for Wilma. And now he had time to wonder about the harper. Was he even still here? And the emerald-eyed granddaughter. It was testimony to the intensity of Andrew's concentration that this was the first thought he had given the matter since the bidding began.

But now that he'd left the noise of the sale ring, it wasn't long before his ears picked up the sweet note he was listening for. The length of canvas on poles, forming a tent roof and back, stood in the same place.

And there was *Thomas*, his head thrown back, laughing at something she of the red-gold hair had just said to him. Even the harper smiled at his cousin's infectious laughter. And the girl joined in like a chiming of golden bells. Andrew stood frowning.

Thomas turned and threw his arms wide. "Andrew Armstrong, the very lad. Come meet your Cousin Bridget!"

Andrew didn't move. Could even Thomas have worked that fast?

"Aye, man, I'd not told you, because the chances were so sparse, but I was determined that, if I ever got near to Donegal, I'd seek out the MacHenry relations Great-aunt Carolenn always told me about."

It was a long, involved tale. Some early Lanark daughter had run off, enchanted with a harper. It seemed that Carolenn Price had traced her ancestor with the aid of an acquaintance who traveled about collecting Irish melodies. Andrew couldn't follow the convolutions of the story, but all that mattered was the enchantment of listening to Bridget MacHenry's voice with the sounds of the *cláirseach* shimmering behind.

Shortly the men must needs turn to practical matters. For all that it was a bargain, the foal presented certain problems. Until its wobbly legs gained strength, it couldn't travel far in a day. It certainly couldn't get out of sight of its mother, or they would both go quite wild.

The next morning, Thomas returned triumphant from the sale ring with his white-footed chestnut mare. Once more the canny guinea man had struck a bargain that presented a happy solution. The traveler had convinced the mare's seller to include a soft leather saddle—which led Thomas to suggest that they might offer their newfound cousins a ride home.

The distance was short enough on horseback, even with a new foal following, but a long walk for an ancient blind harper. And Andrew had the pleasure of discovering that Bridget's eyes looked even more like cut gems when they were bright with gratitude.

So their return journey began with a northward detour. The slim old man sat stiffly erect—his cherished black bogwood harp in a bag slung over his shoulder—atop Thomas's new mare. Bridget rode bareback astride the foal's mother, her full green skirt pulled up to reveal slim white calves. Even though it was a matter of only a few miles, they stopped frequently to allow Fairling to suckle.

It was on the third of these pauses that Andrew looked out across a nearby potato field, and the sight chilled him. Something was wrong. Connacht was known for its thin, rocky soil. It produced crops poorer than any other in the island—that was why most of it was left to the native Irish. But this was something far worse than sparse growth. This was something sinister.

The potato leaves, which should have been broad and lush green, were curled and black spotted. The blight had struck again.

The little party that had set out in such high spirits arrived at the harper's cottage silent and tense. How bad was it? How widespread?

Last year, less than a third of the crop had survived. What would happen if this failure was as severe? The Tory government had repealed the Corn Laws, allowing wheat and oats to flow into Ireland and be sold cheaply. But would this cheap, imported grain be adequate to feed a population formerly totally dependent on the potato for survival?

And then Andrew saw their cottage. He had expected little. He found less. The one-room building was all of a piece with its surroundings. Its stone walls had been gathered from the earth on the spot where it stood. The timbers supporting its roof had been dug from the nearby bog. The roof thatch had been harvested from the fields, and its inside walls no doubt were blackened with the smoke of burning peat—likewise cut from the bog.

It appeared that Bridget, who had lived there all her life, saw it for the first time through the eyes of another. "I'm sorry. I didn't think. I was so happy for *Seanathair* to have a ride home. But it's all right. There's the lean-to. Dermot and I will sleep there. You can have our pallets. The brychans are warm."

Andrew should have said he wouldn't consider taking her sleeping place, but he was too stunned. He merely nodded and entered the hut.

The floor was beaten earth. Turfs burning in the fireplace at the far end of the cottage filled the room with warmth and also with smoke, which stung his eyes. A bare wooden table was to the right of the door and the room's single window over the table. An iron rush holder stood in the window.

Bridget pulled a dried rush from a basket by the fireplace and lit one end. She stuck the other in the holder and motioned for their guests to take seats on the bench beside the fireplace. "Sit you down."

Andrew looked about desperately. What could he say? Then his eye lit on the straw weavings—one beside the door, one by the fireplace. "Oh, what fine crosses." Every cottage in the clachan had similar ones, but the intricacy of these was particularly skillful.

Bridget smiled. "The Bridget crosses. I'm after making them. They keep the evil out the door and the hearth safe from fire and ravagement." She turned to Brendan MacHenry. "Now, *Seanathair*, you must give our guests a song while I boil the kettle." She placed the *cláirseach* in his hands and settled him on a stool.

The brindled Madoo nestled against the old man, who stroked the dog's crisp hair before caressing the harp.

The moment his fingers touched the strings, the dark pushed back, chased into corners by silvery notes. Andrew felt warmed, his stomach less empty. It wasn't as bad here as he'd thought. The cabin was snug against the weather. Thomas had given Bridget a full saddlebag to provide their supper and many meals beyond their going. They would sleep well tonight. And tomorrow they would see that the blight was not so widespread. They would find it isolated to only a few fields, a shortage that could easily be made up for with imported corn.

Bridget sang to Brendan's tune as she put oatcakes on the griddle to bake and held strips of bacon over the fire in a long-handled iron frame until the edges browned and curled. The fat sizzled as it fell on the hot peat bricks.

But suddenly the heavy wooden slab door slammed against the stones, and a hard-muscled young man about Andrew's age entered with a bellow. The abrupt shattering of the atmosphere was as if an angry bull had rampaged through the entrance. "And what are ye after doing, *Deirfiúr?*"

Andrew knew only a few words of Irish, but he realized that the angry young man—he must be the Dermot to whom Bridget had referred earlier—had called her sister.

"As ye can see if the drink has left you with eyes in your head, we've guests, *Deartháir.*" She called him brother.

"Aye, and you'd drink, too, if you'd been in the fields these three days instead of off fairing." Dermot held a flat-bottomed wooden trug in his arms. He dumped its contents on the floor. The potatoes hit the hard earth with a sickening splat. A rancid stench filled the cottage.

"Go wash, Dermot. We've food for tonight, and you'll feel better with something solid inside." She scooped the rotten lumps back into the carrier and threw them out the door.

It was a tense, silent meal. Dermot took his plate to the corner and sat on a brychan. Bridget ate standing up, since the bench and stool were occupied.

Andrew cast about in his mind for something hopeful to say. "Seems Peel will have to send to America for more of their maize. That made up for last year's losses—surely it will see us through again." He felt a hypocrite before the words left his mouth. He had eaten no American maize. But Conor O'Brien had talked of the strange flat corn cakes his sister baked from the grain brought in by the British. And grain was not as complete a food as the potato. Relying on it as the whole source of nutrition had resulted in violent outbreaks of scurvy and dysentery.

Dermot jumped to his feet and nigh split the table with his fist. "There'll be no more American maize. Or anything else. Where have ye been, man? It's all that's talked of in the dram shop. Peel's government fell. Lord Russell has vowed to stop all distribution of grain. No more subsidized food. With the potatoes rotting in the field again, that means no more food, period." He banged out of the cabin as wildly as he had flung himself in.

Andrew looked around the dismal cottage, still reeking with the smell of rot. What would they do? The MacHenrys and the O'Briens and millions like them across the land? Life was hard enough at the best of times. Could they survive another winter without potatoes and with no subsidized grain? Months and months on boiled kelp and mussels—for those who could get them? He tried to think what he could do. He thought wildly of giving Bridget the mare and foal, then realized that would be a liability—more mouths to feed.

In the end he emptied his pockets of all but the few coins he would need for his return trip.

"I couldn't take it. It wouldn't be right. Charity—" She backed away from him.

"Not charity!" He spoke angrily, then cast about wildly in his mind. What could he say to convince her? "Not charity. Payment. Payment for—" For what? He glimpsed the harp in the corner by his stool. "Music. Payment for music . . ." He faltered, then he knew. "For your grandfather's music. When you've time, you must write it down. It's valuable. People will buy it—"

Her brittle laughter stopped him. This was not the golden bells he had heard from her before. "I can't."

"You can't write?"

"I can, then. A little. Father Lynch taught us at the hedge school. But I can't set down music."

He saw the problem, but he wouldn't give up. "You must learn the tunes then."

She looked from him to the coins in her hand and to him once more. She nodded. "Come you back, then."

They left early the next morning, anxious to be gone before they stressed the meager household further. Besides, it would be slow going with the wobbly colt.

They were half a field away. Bridget was still standing by the door waving when Andrew turned Rannock and spurred back. In front of the cottage he drew up and thrust a hand into his pocket. He pulled out the emerald satin ribbons. "They match your eyes." He didn't look back as he galloped off.

And so began the nightmare trek across the land that less than a week before had been magically beautiful. Every mile they rode, it seemed the fields grew blacker and the atmosphere thicker with the stink of decomposition. By the time they reached home, the very air was brown with hunger.

69

"'The supply of the home market may safely be left to the foresight of private merchants'!" Andrew crumpled *The Northern Whig* and dashed it to the floor. "Supply of the home market! What home market? Has the man ever been to Ireland? Doesn't he realize these people have no money to buy his private corn?"

Jay Lanark crossed his feet on his stool before the fire. Outside, a howling wind rattled the windowpanes. "Don't get overheated, lad. And I'll thank you not to rumple my newspaper. Lord John Russell has the best economic advisers in the kingdom."

"Economic theory be—" Andrew strangled at a warning look from his grandfather.

In spite of Andrew's agitation, Grandfather remained relaxed, stroking his ample beard. "If you'd calm down long enough to read what's left of my newspaper, you'd see that the government isn't just cutting back on the distribution of subsidized food. There's to be a major extension of public works as well." He nodded complacently. "That's as it should be. The poor must work for their food just like everybody else. Not the government's place to affect economic conditions. State handouts will only make the people dependent on the government. And it's perfectly sound economic theory that Irish property should pay for Irish poverty."

"Fine, then. Let it pay. Let Lanarks' Bawn pay. Reduce your rents!"

"Aye, I will. Just as soon as Lord Londonderry reduces mine."

"The Marquess of Downshire has reduced his rents by thousands of pounds. And promised his people free seed for spring planting."

"Aye, but he's not *my* landlord, is he? And if His Highness of Downshire chooses to pauperize himself, it doesn't follow that the rest of us need do the same. Use your common sense, lad. The rents are fixed with due regard to bad seasons as well as good. I don't hear anyone arguing that I should collect higher rents when the harvest is good. And now I have to pay iniquitously high rates on these lavish and wasteful public works."

Andrew began pacing, his fists clenched. "All right. Forget the rents. Forget the economic theory. These people are starving. I don't just mean not enough food or poor quality food. I mean *no* food. Nothing to eat but boiled seaweed! How can people like this be expected to pay free market prices for imported grain?" His voice rose with every sentence.

It had been four months since Ireland had been stunned by the failure of the second potato crop. Not just a bad harvest. Not just heavy losses. Total failure. There was hardly a potato in Ireland, a land where two-thirds of the population was totally dependent on that single item for sustenance and a healthy man was accustomed to eating ten pounds of tatties a day.

The new government in London had reversed Peel's compassionate response of the year before. However, even Russell's government realized that programs of road building would not be enough in the hardest-hit west country. So the government established corn depots along the Atlantic seaboard as far north as County Donegal. Andrew could only hope that Brendan MacHenry's family would have a share of the supplies that the paper said were to arrive next month. If the people could survive that long. And the winter storms had set in— worse storms than even the oldest residents held in their memories.

Andrew strode stiffly from the room. He and his grandfather had had the same argument every night for months. Andrew still had made no progress.

Yet he couldn't entirely blame his grandfather. Andrew himself would have had no idea how dire the situation was if he hadn't seen it with his own eyes. It was one thing to be told the crops failed and people were hungry. It was another thing to spend days riding by black, desolate fields. To sit inside a cabin and realize that the food he gave them was all they had. To wonder if they were surviving even now. To smell the black rot with every breath one took. Andrew knew the stench would never leave him.

But if the government measures were inadequate and Grandfather Lanark could not be shaken from his comfortable fireside, at least Andrew had his own strong arms. He would use them carrying what he could to the clachan. He strode downstairs to the kitchen. "Mrs. B, I want you to load every basket we have with bread and meal while I hitch up the cart."

He turned without waiting for an answer. But once beyond the shelter of the house, he'd gotten no more than ten feet toward the stable when the wind whipped blinding snow in his face. Driving to Strangford would be impossible in this.

Back in the kitchen, he found both Berkleys arranging supplies on the long, scrubbed table in the center of the room. "It'll have to wait until tomorrow, Mrs. B. The storm is fierce."

"Aye. As you say, sir. But if you'll permit me, this isn't the way to be going about it."

"What do you mean?" he flared. "Don't tell me you're going to lecture me on market economics, too!"

"I don't know anything about that, sir. But these Quaker people, they have the right of it, to my way of thinking."

"Oh? And what's that?" Andrew didn't mean to sound so caustic, but he had been preached at quite enough for one night.

Mrs. B, however, didn't flinch. "Soup boilers. Make soup, let the people come. Hot on the spot, no questions asked. Public works is all right. But how would Lord John Russell like to build a road on an empty stomach? That's what I'd like to know."

"Mrs. B, you're a genius!" Andrew threw his arms around her full form. "You could instruct Parliament."

From that moment Andrew was determined to do something. If Irish property was to pay for Irish poverty, then he would see to it that Lanarks' Bawn did its share, in spite of Grandfather Lanark's intransigency.

He knew that many landlords were taking vigorous action, giving what employment they could to all who applied. To be fair, even Grandfather had made some movement in that direction until bad weather halted construction on the long gallery. Now, the second crop failure seemed to offer a propitious time to start again. As there were no potatoes to harvest, the laborers had as well be put to work gathering stones to build walls—but stones could not be pried from frozen earth.

Grandfather, following the example of Lord Londonderry, refused to join the numerous County Down landlords who had waived part of their year's rents. Ten percent off the one pound fifty per acre annual rent could mean the difference in survival to the clachan. And some landlords had gone so far as to wipe off a half year's rent and promise free seed for spring planting.

It was a hopeful prospect if the cottiers survived until spring, Andrew considered as the wind flung another blast of snow against the windows. He was stopped for the night. He felt helpless, but there had to be something he could do against the horror of hunger and despair pressing down on their land.

His mind flicked westward to the bare, black interior of a stone cottage. It had been four—almost five—months since he had left Bridget with all the food and cash he had. How long could such supplies have lasted? How long had it been since any in the MacHenry hut had gone to sleep with a full stomach? Was the frail old Brendan even still alive? Did he have strength left to play his harp?

And Dermot. There had been disturbances in places where supplies of food for distribution had been quickly depleted. Had that angry young man taken part in such brawls and had his head broken for it?

And Bridget. He could not think of her apart from her gleaming hair and eyes and golden laugh, knowing that such would be the first sacrifice to the god of hunger. Famine ate the shine off life first. Then it gnawed in the darkness.

But Andrew would light a candle. Somehow.

The next morning, the snow lay six inches deep on the level. Mostly it lay in drifts reaching halfway up to the windows and leaving the roads blocked. It was two days before Andrew could take the loaves of bread, jars of preserves, and bags of meal and beans to the clachan.

Conor O'Brien was the first person he saw. It seemed that even the lad's freckles had faded. "I'm right sorry I haven't been up to the horses. I was after walking through the fields, but Da said I'd get stuck in a drift. I wouldn't have, though."

"He was right, Conor. You help me with these bags, then you can get up to your horses. They'll be right glad to see you." It was a pleasure to see the light come to the boy's eyes at the sight of food. "Go ahead and eat a bun now. It'll give you strength for carting the others."

The bap disappeared almost whole into the boy's mouth. Andrew knew what Conor had had for breakfast. He could smell the boiling seaweed.

He heard an infant crying inside the cottage of Elfrith and Seamus O'Brien. Since outraging Jay Lanark by marrying her papist, the girl from Edinburgh had borne nearly a babe a year. As near as Andrew could remember, more than half of them had survived, so this cottage must house six or more hungry mouths. He knocked on the door.

It was opened by a girl of four or five.

At the end of the room Elfrith sat by the fireplace, a weeping babe on her lap. Had he not known, he would have thought this hollow-eyed woman to be the grandmother.

"I've brought some supplies to help you through the cold spell." Andrew set a basket and his largest bag of meal on the table.

"That's verra kind of you, Andrew Armstrong."

"Only fair." He smiled. "You once fed me when I needed it." He meant the remark as a kindness. He hoped the difference in station wouldn't add to her embarrassment. She had made her choice. "Where's Seamus?" Only the younger children were in evidence.

"Gone to the mill in Newtownards for the weaving."

"Aye." Andrew nodded. "That's good."

The fact that the economy of this area included linen and cotton weaving and the growing of wheat, oats, and barley would help them through this disaster if anything would. There seemed nothing more to say, so Andrew bade his former nurse good day.

He was turning the cart onto the main road when he spotted the Harrowby carriage approaching. He pulled to the side and waved. It had been long since there had been any opportunity for socializing. To his surprise, Wilma herself was driving.

"Are you coming to the meeting? What a fine thing. I'd hoped to see you there."

He had to admit he had no idea what she was talking about.

"The relief committee. There's fine plans under way. We must do all we can. Selma would have come, too, but mother's not well, so she stayed with her."

"Then you must allow me to drive you." As Harrowby's Dale was closer than Lanarks' Bawn, Andrew left his cart there, and they went on together into Comber.

The meeting was in progress when they entered. The speaker, a portly gentleman with long, thick sideburns and a black silk stock above his white waistcoat, was one of the guardians of the Newtownards workhouse.

"The poor and destitute are pressing on the workhouse beyond its powers of reception. Our numbers have nearly doubled, and the walls will hold no more. The lamentable fact is that the workhouse is inadequately equipped to discharge our obligations to the poor. Our Board of Guardians has voted to submit a petition to the House of Commons asking permission to distribute food to those in need without their having to be admitted to the workhouse. It is our belief that such outdoor aid can do much to relieve the distress."

But the speech that had been delivered on such a full head of steam ended on a doubtful note. "I must report, however, that we deem it unlikely such permission will be granted."

A pinch-faced man in a black frock coat jumped to his feet. "You much relieve my mind, sir. Outdoor relief, indeed. Encourage dependency and promote pauperism, that's all you'll accomplish. If they need aid, let them come to the workhouse. That's the system. These people have to learn to live with the system."

"Many of them would rather die."

Andrew wasn't well enough acquainted with clerical garments to know whether the speaker was from the papacy or prelacy. But from the drawing back he sensed in the hall, it was certain the man wasn't Presbyterian.

"Then let them make their choice. It's a free country." The first speaker flipped the skirts on his coat and resumed his seat. There was scattered applause.

But the tall cleric stood firm. "The entire poor law and workhouse system is particularly alien to the native Irish. The peasantry here is tied to the land with a special feeling—as a mother for her child. Entrance to the workhouse requires giving up the lease on the final two or three acres that have sustained their family for generations. It is the loss of hope and dignity—the final damnation."

Heads nodded or shook in about equal numbers.

"Not government's business to run around the country feeding people. Let them work for it." The frock-coated man's features grew sharper yet.

Andrew was on his feet, a retort rising in his throat, when he was cut off by the chairman's ushering a small woman in a plain black dress and bonnet to the front of the room.

"You couldn't have given our special guest a better introduction, my friend. The chairman flashed a toothy grin at the pinch-faced speaker. "Mrs. Emelia Foxe has come to us from the Religious Society of Friends to speak about the very thing you suggest—voluntary soup kitchens."

It was a moment before Andrew realized how neatly the chairman had turned the man's own speech against him. He resumed his seat and joined in the welcoming applause for the lady, who managed to look pleasant in spite of the fact that she didn't smile.

"Gentlemen." Then seeing a few other women present, she added, "And ladies. I am no stranger to dealing with the problems of poverty and hunger. I come to thee from Liverpool where I have spent many years feeding the families of out-of-work dockers. And I want to assure thee all that many in thy position on the other side of the water are not insensible to the struggles thee face. Many British charities are vigorous in their dedication to collecting funds and sending contributions to committees in Ireland. But we of the Society of Friends prefer a more direct approach.

"It is our goal to establish a network of soup boilers the length and width of Ireland. People so ravished by hunger that they are scarcely able to crawl cannot break stones to build roads."

Andrew burst into applause and did not stop when narrowed eyes and raised brows turned toward him.

Emelia Foxe's voice reached to the back of the hall without strain. "For each soup kitchen we establish we will supply a boiler and money to buy ingredients to fill those pots. We have many workers, but we need more. We would invite those who would like so to do to join us."

A jumble of questions and replies echoed around the room:

"And who will receive this charity broth?"

"Aye, good question. Must keep in mind there's many good Protestants going hungry as well."

"But most Protestants have fishing rights, at least."

"And whose fault is that if it isn't the shiftless Irish themselves? Lived on an island for two thousand years and never developed a fishing industry—I ask you!"

"Gentlemen, gentlemen." The chairman banged on the table before him until water sloshed from his glass. "Mrs. Foxe has the floor, gentlemen."

Emelia Foxe's only indication that she was aware of the dissension in the room was an almost imperceptible raising of her chin. "Indeed, gentlemen, thy points are well made. Let me assure thee that we have the strictest order for distribution of our relief."

Some of the more agitated speakers leaned back in their chairs. The pinch-faced man nodded and folded his arms across his chest.

Now, for the first time, Mrs. Foxe did raise her voice. "Our soup kitchens will be open only to hungry people. *All* hungry people." She looked directly at her sharpest challenger. "With no preference on the ground of religious persuasion." She took her seat quietly amid the hubbub that followed that announcement.

"Not Christian. Charity begins at home. We must feed our own first. Bible says so."

"It's not right to encourage those people in their heathen idolatry."

"If they're too lazy to break rocks, then that's their choice. The public works are there. Let them work. I pay my rates—blasted steep ones, too."

With the meeting at an end, the hall quickly cleared of speakers airing such sentiments. But there were others who stayed.

Throughout the proceedings, Andrew had become aware of Wilma's drawing closer to the edge of her seat. Now she sprang to her feet. "Isn't she magnificent! I knew there had to be something I could do, but I had no idea what." Without waiting for Andrew, she crossed the hall to the small group surrounding the small Quaker woman.

"We will open kitchens in Comber and Newtownards next month. We should be happy, indeed, of hands to help prepare and serve the soup. We would also be grateful for additional contributions of food or money."

A variety of questions rose.

"A most sustaining soup," the speaker replied to one. "Perhaps thee would care to see." She pulled a handful of papers from the black bag she carried and handed them around.

Andrew read the recipe over Wilma's shoulder:

> 1 oxhead
> 28 pounds turnips
> 3 1/2 pounds onions
> 7 pounds carrots
> 21 pounds pea meal
> 14 pounds Indian cornmeal
> 28 gallons water

Nutritious, indeed. A boiler of such a soup distributed daily would do much to relieve distress. He would enjoy working beside Wilma in the effort. And yet, as he thought of the rancor that still hung in the corners of the room, it seemed that even those with full bellies suffered from their own form of desperation. It was hard to define what bothered him. It seemed frivolous to worry about matters of philosophy in the face of the suffering that pressed down on their land. And yet he had seen in his own grandfather, as in some of the speakers tonight, a joylessness that no soup boiler, however nutritious the ingredients filling it, could feed.

There had to be a better answer to the problem of human suffering than a potato.

70

Just one potato. If only she had just one. Bridget hugged her brychan closer to her and edged toward the banked turfs. She'd been dreaming she walked in the field, feeling the soft brown earth under her feet, smelling the clean, fresh air as the sun shone on row after row of healthy green leaves. And then she had gone in and boiled a great black pot of tatties to set before Dermot and *Seanathair* with the sweet butter she had churned that morning and a cool jug of fresh buttermilk.

Sure and it had been sweet, but the memory made the clawing of her stomach all the worse. She listened to the howling wind whip snow against the side of the cottage. Would the weather be too bad for Dermot to work tomorrow? All labor on the roads had ceased when snow gripped the land in as tight a hand as the blight had last summer. And so the last drops of life were being squeezed out of Ireland between the strangleholds of famine and frost.

While summer lasted, there had been much she could do to fill the MacHenry cook pot. Nettles and dandelions were never so nasty as seaweed. Berries grew in the bog. And she had become clever at trapping birds in the hedgerow. But that all seemed as long ago as the days of digging tatties from their bed. Now there were only rocks to crush. And today there would not even be that, as there had not been yesterday or the day before. And anyway, one could not make soup from rocks.

She reached beyond the edge of her pallet to where Madoo slept beside Brendan. Her fingers closed in its long gray hair, only a slightly darker shade than *Seanathair*'s. How many winters had they spent huddled beside the fire, keeping each other warm, man and dog? As long as Bridget could remember—since the days when Madoo was a squirming pup begging to have his pink stomach scratched. And then Brendan had been able to see to do it. The memory brought tears to Bridget's eyes. All so long ago. How could it be so long? Everything so changed.

She knew she was putting off the inevitable moment. Now she understood how *Seanathair* could go so far away in his mind for such long times, and she was glad he had that escape. But that could not be her way. She was the woman. She must have something in the cook pot if Dermot was to have strength to crush rocks and if *Seanathair* was to live through the winter. She crossed herself with a plea that the solution offered for today wouldn't be a blow that would kill him.

"Come on, boy. It's time." Her brychan still wrapped around her shoulders, she took the knife normally used for cutting seed potatoes in happier times. The wind wrenched the door out of her hand, but she managed to close it before kneeling with her arms around Madoo. She would have liked to go farther away from the hut, but she dare not in the snow.

She knew where to make the slit. The animal was too weak even to cry out. He settled his head on her lap as the warm blood ran into the snow. It was as if he knew he was giving himself for *Seanathair*. It was the last thing he could do for his lifelong companion.

Even as scrawny as the creature was, they would be fed for a week, perhaps two. First the roast. Then the bones and entrails boiled for broth. If *Seanathair* would eat. She did not know what she would say to him.

He woke when the smell of roasting meat filled the cabin. Bridget watched his sticklike fingers search the pallet and earthen floor beyond for a clutch of stiff, brindled hair. Then the thin old nostrils quivered. His whole body stiffened to a sitting position, the hands still searching in empty air, the nose smelling.

Bridget left her spit-turning to fling herself into her grandfather's arms. "*Seanathair*. It's so sorry I am, *Seanathair*. So sorry."

He patted her back. "I know, *Cailín*, I know, girl." He said no more about it. But when she put a meaty bone in his hands, silver tears trailed from his blind eyes.

Later he took up his harp. It had been long silent. The second crop failure had taken all music from the land. But a *shanachie* must hold wake for his loved ones. And hearing his songs, for the first time in months Bridget thought of the debt she owed to Andrew Armstrong. She had done nothing about the learning of Brendan MacHenry's songs. The hunger had driven all thought of anything but survival from every mind.

But now she thought of the kind stranger from a different world who claimed some sort of relationship to their family. The whole matter had sounded like a tale of the fairies. Perhaps Andrew Armstrong himself had been but a fairy's conjuring. But no fairy would leave coins. And it was that brass and silver that had made all the difference. Andrew Armstrong's coins were to thank for the MacHenrys still having thatch over their heads.

Even in front of the fire, Bridget shuddered, thinking of their many neighbors who had been evicted when they had no means of paying their rents. Turned out on the roads with the snows coming. Staring into the glowing peats, she could see it all again. Weeks before the constabulary came with their signed notices from Lord Grangeton, one could feel the fear. The smell of the terror was as sharp and rancid as that from the bins of rotted potatoes. Families huddled inside, wondering if they would be next. For none of the croppies in their clachan or anywhere the length of the Atlantic coast had been able to pay their rent. Some landlords were lenient. Lord Grangeton was not.

And so the constabulary would come. To two or three huts a week, sometimes to as many as one a day until an entire area was cleared out.

"Aye, and Erskine enjoys every one of them." Dermot, his mouth still warm with a swig of last year's poteen—for there had been no potato peelings to make whiskey in the hidden stills this year—would curse Lord Grangeton's overseer. "Can't wait to get us all cleared out, he can't. Wants the land for grazing. You think he has the constabulary smash the cabins just so no one can live in them again? Nae. Doing his work for him, they are. Nice, smooth pastureland as far as the eye can see, fattening cattle for the English market to feed fat Englishmen and fatten his purse—that's Grangeton's goal."

Whatever the landlord's goal or his overseer's, it came to the same thing: the constabulary in a circle around the door, banging hard enough to break it down if they didn't open. The smell of fear coming out before the ragged family emerged from their black hole, clutching each other and what few rags they could hold around themselves. Some tried screams, some prayers, some physical resistance. The reply was always the same and always swift. Families whose people had lived on that land, in that cottage, for time out of mind were no more than a few yards down the road before battering rams had scattered the stones that had provided the only shelter they had ever known. The last glimpse any of them had of their home was black smoke curling from the thatch of the fallen roof.

The lucky ones were done first, before the workhouse was full. Officials did what they could. They threw up shacks in the workhouse yards to provide some shelter, but the buildings in every county were so filled there was barely sitting space on the floor. Only death made room for newcomers.

Bridget forced her mind back to *Seanathair's* song. She must keep the songs in her memory. If Andrew Armstrong should ever return for his payment, she must have it for him. All of *Seanathair's* songs of saints and fairies, of beauty and hardship, of people, animals, and plants, she must remember them. For Andrew, yes, but more for *Seanathair*. His songs were himself. To preserve his songs would be to preserve the man.

She would sit on the pallet next to him just as Madoo had always done. "Teach me the songs, *Seanathair*." Then sometimes hunger rose like a black fog in her brain, and she hadn't strength even to hear the words. But after a time, when the weakness passed, she would turn to her grandfather, who had let the harp droop to his tattered brychan. "I'll fetch a cup of kelp broth, *Seanathair*. Strength it will give you for another song."

And sometimes she must needs crawl to the pot because there was not support in her legs to hold her. Yet even so weak in body and in spirit, Bridget carried on until fear closed in again. Was there anything to carry on for? Was the land itself dead? Had the very dirt died like the countless bodies it covered?

Where would it end? When they were all dead—every last person in Ireland a corpse? And who would bury the last one? Would God send a rain to wash the land clean then? Or would it ever be thus, world without end?

One morning she woke to hear a bird singing in the hedgerow. It was a faint, hungry-sounding warble, but it penetrated the stone walls of the cottage and reached Bridget's heart like a glimmer of hope. Just two weeks ago there had been a heavy snowfall. Yet this faint trill said that somehow they had survived another winter. Perhaps the land would be green and fertile again as it had once been.

But then a sound far louder and more penetrating than the bird's entered the hut. It was the far too familiar wail that struck her with terror every time she heard it. She went to the door to watch the pitiful sight pass across the frozen earth.

Eight or nine keening people—rag-covered sticks—followed an old/young man whose stooped shoulders told more than the bundles he carried of the desperation that pushed him to his destiny. But it wasn't fear for the departing stranger that gripped Bridget. It was fear for her brother.

The road to the bay ran past their door, and Bridget never failed to notice the quiet way Dermot looked at the emigrants trudging down the path, belongings tied in pitiful bundles, their relatives following along, wailing as if seeing them to their graves. And, indeed, the partings were called "American wakes," for those who set out to cross the water in the overcrowded, creaking ships to America or Canada or New Zealand were as lost to their families as if they were dead. Even if they survived the voyage, they would not be returning to Ireland. Ever.

Bridget clutched at her heart as if she could grasp the fear and fling it from her. Dermot and *Seanathair* were the only family she had ever known. She knew she must lose the frail old man someday. But Dermot, the big brother she had trailed after since she took her first steps—what would she do without him? Her first fears upon waking every morning—even before she feared there would be nothing at all for the pot that day—was that she would find *Seanathair* dead on his pallet or that this would be the day Dermot would tell her he had booked passage. Winter storms had slowed the emigrations, even as they increased the hunger, for the ships could not sail. So people lay in their huts and breathed their last, rather than dying on one of the coffin ships.

But a bird had sung this morning. Bridget turned from the sorrowful group disappearing down the road and gathered the strength to look her brother full in the eye. No matter what she saw there, she must face it. "It will be better now, Dermot. Even today, perhaps, the works will be starting again."

"Aye." His tone was always bitter now. But perhaps it relieved the pain inside. "Oh, aye. Those with strength to lift a hammer will do so. Building roads that go nowhere and lining them with famine walls—as if one could wall out the famine!" He spat.

"We can buy seed, Dermot. We must have seed."

This year it would be a pitiful handful, if tubers for planting were available at all. But they must be, or there would be nothing to go on with. Planting seed so there could be a harvest was the very essence of hope. It was seed that made life go on.

Planting time had always been her favorite. Memories she thought lost came back to her. Springtime when she was a child. She almost thought she could remember her mother, a fair woman with a babe in one arm, another wane tugging at her apron, and her belly rounding under her skirt . . .

She returned to thoughts of planting. Always she and Dermot had worked together, pushing their feet in rhythm on the blades of their loys, turning the first long, thin spade of sod on St. Patrick's Day to make beds for the potatoes. A new crop, no matter how sparse, meant new hope. No matter how deep the hunger, how far off the harvest, seed in the field meant life.

Planting had always been a communal thing. All the croppies from the helter-skelter cluster of stone cottages that dotted Lord Grangeton's estate gathered to hear Father Lynch begin the labor by blessing the fields. As soon as he was gone, Daddo O'Casey, the only man in the clachan older than Brendan MacHenry, would spit into the wind and toss a handful of straw into the air to keep the storms at bay, while his daughter Mairead crumbled a sweet cake to appease the fairies. And then they would all turn to their digging.

But this year, even if they could obtain seed, it would be different. The O'Caseys had been among the first to be evicted. Only four or five of the huts on the estate remained with their walls unbroken and their thatch intact. Grady Erskine was a thorough man.

A few weeks later, on the day Dermot came in with a handful of seed potatoes, Bridget and her brother put their backs to turning the beds. It was a lonely process, for fear is an icy companion. And the apparition of the coming months was always before them. Even in the best of years, the blue months were there to be gotten through. And now the phantom of *what if* hung over everything. What if they couldn't hang on until harvest? What if they hung on but couldn't pay the rent? What if . . . no, the specter of another crop failure was too bleak to imagine.

On Good Friday Bridget planted the few ridges of potatoes that her seeds would fill. And Dermot returned to his futile, endless road building.

"Dermot!" Bridget could not give words to the fear that gripped her at her first look at him only two hours later.

Sure and he was returning too early in the day, for didn't the works crews stay at their shovels and sledgehammers until dark? But it was more the manner of his return than the hour of it. She had not seen such anger in him since the day he had heard of Lord Russell's policy that Ireland would export the only food that could feed its people. What could have happened to make him react in such anger now? She feared to ask.

"Dermot? What is it?"

"The public works are to stop."

"When?"

"Now. Whole system to be done up by summer. Government decided men should stay home and work their fields to produce this year's harvest."

"But that's months away!"

She started to signal him to speak more softly—she didn't want to worry *Seanathair*. But it was no use. The old man sat on a bench against the sunny wall of the house. His eyes were blind, but his ears were keen. *Seanathair* knew.

"What will we do?" she barely had strength to ask.

"The government will provide soup. We are to be given tickets."

Even if the stirabout of boiled Indian corn would keep them alive, soup tickets would not pay the rent. Only the few precious barley seeds Bridget had planted around the edge of the field could do that. If the heads made well. If the rain and sun came at the right time. If the potatoes were good so they could sell the barley. If—if—if. Survival was always a thin line. But never had their whole existence hung by such a spider's thread.

A curl of black smoke caught her attention. "Faith, is it the O'Malleys? Have they been evicted now? How can that be? They planted their potatoes not two weeks ago."

Dermot shook his head. "It's not the constabulary this time."

"Then—"

"It's the fever."

"The whole family? Cathal? Finola? The wanes?" Last week Finola had taken to her pallet with the bloody flux—one of the common signs of famine fever. But the whole family? Bridget slumped to the ground. Who would be next? Would the fever take them all like that? Had they survived two winters of famine and escaped eviction only to be carried off by the dropsy?

A soft tune reached her ears, more as if the harp strings were moved by the wind than by Brendan MacHenry's fingers.

No. Bridget squared her shoulders. No. She would not give in. As long as there was breath in her, they would survive. She and her family and the songs they had made for hundreds of years—they would survive, and Ireland would be the better for it.

71

That spring of 1847 Andrew was quite certain he had found the answer to many of his longings. Indeed, as satisfying as he had found working with the Quaker Society to be throughout the dark, cold winter months, he realized that the light and warmth he felt was from quite another source than the ever-simmering soup boilers.

Wilma came into the kitchen of the renovated warehouse, her soft brown hair curling around her face, her cheeks flushed from the warmth of the pot she had been stirring. She wiped her hands on the long white apron that swathed her full skirt and hugged her tiny waist. "There now, Andrew." She gave him a smile that made him think the answer to her happiness lay in the same direction as his. "You can open the doors. The soup is ready."

He moved toward the heavy wooden doors creaking with the weight of hunger pressing against them. "And the loaves?"

"Aye, the last batch done."

The ovens were manned all night by Quakers come from England to bake the bread they distributed with the soup.

Andrew lifted the bar, the doors groaned open, and the line moved forward. That was perhaps the most disheartening aspect of this work, watching how the line grew longer every week—and moved more slowly. When they began last November, the hungry people had pushed and hammered against the doors until Andrew sometimes feared a brawl. But now they didn't have the spirit to fight or complain. The gray line of ghosts shuffled forward, each shadowy specter holding out a battered tin cup or cracked bowl.

Andrew ladled thick porridge into each container presented to him as Wilma put a crusty brown loaf into the birdlike claws held out to her. The line wavered as fog blowing over the bog. The wraiths shifted, and Andrew filled another bowl.

So on for hours. It would continue until they came to the end of the line or the bottom of the pot. When the wooden ladle scraped on the black iron and not another grain of cornmeal could be scratched off, Mrs. Foxe's Society of Friends took charge, washing the vessel and refilling it with the prescribed meat, vegetables, meal, and water to be ready for the process to start all over again the next day.

Today as every day—for Wilma insisted on working without a break, and Andrew would not let her face the task alone—Andrew soon shifted his thoughts from the dismal scene before him to the happier time he anticipated. Flashes of guilt caught him out for contemplating his own joy in the face of so much suffering. And yet how could it be otherwise with Wilma beside him? Soon he must speak to her. He was almost certain of her answer. How could she not return his favor when he felt so much for her? She must feel something for him beyond gratitude for his help and companionship.

He would speak to her tonight when they were driving back to Harrowby's Dale with the shared satisfaction of having helped so many people survive yet another day. Knowing that together they had kept absolute starvation at bay for another few hours, they could relax from their labors while others prepared for the next day's battle.

Or should he speak to her father first? Again, he did not despair of success, for Mr. Harrowby had ever made him welcome at Harrowby's Dale. Andrew had known a worrying time last winter when Mrs. Harrowby was too sick to leave her bed. Would Wilma have to put her own happiness aside to care for her mother and keep house for her father? For Selma, who had taken on that task so naturally when first Mrs. Harrowby fell ill, was now looking forward to her own wedding. Thomas Price had not been so slow in the asking as Andrew Armstrong had been.

All through January, Andrew had worried. But when the last of February's snowstorms melted, Mrs. Harrowby had left her bed. Everyone's spirits rose. And Selma had ordered a length of white silk from London. Thomas's successful suit no longer appeared as a barrier to Andrew but rather a good omen.

Yes. He would speak. Tonight.

"Oh!" A sharp cry from Wilma jerked him from his daydream. "That poor woman!"

Andrew handed his ladle to one of the kitchen workers and hurried around the serving bar.

He had seen it before—indeed, the incidents seemed to be coming more frequent—but he could never accustom himself to the idea of people's being so starved that getting food into their stomachs made them faint. The woman's three children were crying and pulling at her, terrified.

He moved the children aside and put a piece of bun in each pair of grimy hands. "Here now, your mother will be all right. Let her rest."

He turned to the oldest girl. "When she wakens, see that she takes only small bites. Why haven't you come before?"

The baffled looks that met this speech told him his effort at communication had been wasted. The family spoke only Irish. He expressed his instructions by pantomime, then resumed his serving.

"Will she be all right?" Wilma asked.

How could he answer that? Would any of them be all right? What was the use of recovering today only to starve tomorrow? He shrugged and tipped a scoop of meal into the bowl held out to him. "They seem to be wandering poor. Most likely come down from the mountains. Her husband probably died."

"Then they don't have any place to stay."

Wilma spoke matter-of-factly. They were all past any level of shock at a new horror. Whenever it seemed things couldn't get worse, they got worse. And all the time Andrew kept in the back of his mind the fact that eastern Ulster was the least hard hit of any of Ireland. Bad as things were here, they were worse elsewhere. And as the destitute drifted in from other areas, the situation worsened here.

As always, such a thought made him wonder about Bridget. Western Connacht was the most devastated area in Ireland. Had she managed to survive? He had not forgotten that he told her he would return. But that was not possible. Not now. Everything had stopped when the hunger descended upon the land.

"What will they do?" Wilma repeated, bringing Andrew's focus back to the little huddle of bones and rags on the floor.

"Workhouse."

"Andrew, no!"

The ultimate horror. The end of all hope. But what else was there? Looking at the scene before him, Andrew could think of nothing else. The outside aid provided by voluntary soup kitchens was sufficient just for those with their own cabins. Only the workhouse provided sleeping shelter as well as food. "They won't object. They have no property to surrender."

Wilma nodded. "We can take them when we're through here."

Andrew groaned. That would take at least an hour more. Maybe two. The woman and three squalling children in the carriage. And then, after facing the dismaying facts of the workhouse, he and Wilma would both be drained emotionally and physically. He could not speak of their future happiness tonight.

"Andrew? They canna walk there."

The woman had wakened from her faint. The oldest child was spooning bits of meal into her mother's mouth. Apparently Andrew's pantomime had been successful. But the woman only half sat up, and her scrawny throat looked too frail even to swallow the stirabout.

He sighed. "No. They cannot walk."

Andrew had regularly heard reports of the appalling workhouse conditions. People held out too long before resorting to charity. They were so seriously undernourished by the time they entered that the workhouse was nothing more than a place to go to die. As he stopped the carriage before the iron fence surrounding the gray stone building, he recalled vividly the most recent report: "The great majority of new admissions are moribund when brought to us."

The somber guardian reporting had been replying to a charge that the death rate in the workhouse was unacceptably high.

"The country is rampant with disease. Many have been known to die on the road, others even as they are lifted from their beds to the cart to be brought in. Many are sent for admission merely that coffins may be provided for them at government expense."

As a matter of fact, the Board of Guardians had received complaints from the parish authorities that the graveyard was filling up with pauper dead from the workhouse. A separate burial ground for paupers was necessary. And still the workhouse bulged with 750 unwashed bodies while an additional 100 inhabited the fever hospital attached to it. A house of horrors, indeed. And yet, there was nowhere else for the destitute to go.

The woman huddled in the back of the carriage looked at him with famine-hollowed eyes. She descended listlessly when he indicated. The children clung to their mother silently. The youngest, barely two, never took her thumb from her mouth. Their skin was blotched and cracked from scurvy. The little boy scratched constantly at the lice living on his scalp.

The gray-uniformed matron at a table inside the door announced, "We've no place to put them." She paused. "But from the looks of things, they won't be here long." She thrust a form at Andrew.

He glanced at the information requested. "I don't know. I have no idea what their names are or where they came from."

The exhausted woman shrugged. "Then put down your name. We have to have some identity. They can sleep in the attic tonight. If they're alive tomorrow, we'll worry about it then. Probably the usual story— husband wouldn't leave his land, so he died on it. Then his family comes to the workhouse. Always comes to it in the end."

It was as well that Andrew had already decided he wouldn't speak of his heart to Wilma tonight. He was too drained to talk at all. And apparently she was too. Yet her presence was a comfort. He felt her warmth, her small person. Beside him. Where he wanted her always.

Perhaps it was the fatigue that made him wonder, *Will that be enough?* Would having Wilma to wife fill all his heart's desires? He had certainly been right in his conclusion that food and pleasant surroundings were not the key, for in the midst of all the suffering they dealt with daily, he had found unspeakable happiness in her company.

So, surely, having that companionship sealed for life would be the answer. He would have the deep, settled joy inside himself that would preclude his turning into the sour, rigid man his grandfather was. Wilma's love could keep him from that if anything could. With Wilma he could defeat the Lanark curse.

A freezing rain started to fall before they reached Harrowby's Dale. He pulled the carriage as close as he could to the door and hurried Wilma inside, holding his coat over her bonnet and mantle. At the door he urged her to take care of herself. "Have a hot drink and a meal and stay warm and dry. Sleep well, Wilma. This work is too hard for you. You must rest."

Her hand rested briefly on his arm; her eyes still smiled after the exhausting day. "Dear Andrew. Don't fuss. I'm fine. It gives me such pleasure to help these poor creatures. I only wish I could do more. I draw strength from the work."

There was little that could have lifted his spirits when he entered the bawn that night, but the sight of Thomas Price sitting before the fire where he had expected to encounter only his scowling grandfather made the fatigue roll from Andrew's shoulders.

"Tammis! What a welcome sight!" He clasped his cousin's hand, then flung himself into a chair and propped his wet boots on the hob.

Berkley appeared as if by magic with a dry coat and a tray of cold meats and cheeses.

"Thank you, Berkley. Just what I need. Ah—and a bowl of spiced punch." He drank deeply. "Perhaps I'll live to fight another day." He leaned back in his chair.

Jay Lanark scowled at his grandson. "Don't know what you think you're doing, serving soup like a kitchen maid. Not so sure I hold with this whole volunteerism thing, anyway. The *Whig* says indigents are pouring into Belfast—attracted by the reputation of local charities. Bad enough having to take care of our own. We'll be overrun. And they bring disease. Importing contagion and demoralization we are."

Andrew was too exhausted to mount a reply. And in spite of the brutal attitude, there was just enough truth to what his grandfather said to give him concern.

"We pay crippling rates to keep the workhouse open," Jay Lanark continued. "That ought to be enough. Only collected seventy-five percent of my rents this year. And Price here telling me he waived half of his—besides feeding his croppies." He shook his head. "We'll all be bankrupt soon. Then who'll pay to keep the workhouse open? That's what I want to know. Be standing in your soup line myself, that's what. Alongside Lord Londonderry, no doubt. If the gentry can't pay their rents, the whole system'll crumble. You'll understand one day, boy. You'll see it my way."

"Never!" Andrew spit out the word like a poisoned dart.

His grandfather laughed. "You say that, but you'll see. It's your destiny. You're a Lanark. You're preordained. You can't escape it."

Andrew had heard the same speech every night for two years. He turned to his cousin. "Tammis, I hear I am to wish you joy. A length of ivory satin on its way from London, even. When's the happy day to be?"

Thomas heaved a sigh, seemingly to clear the air of acrimony before turning to his own situation. "Late summer we're talking about. Aye, and it can't come too soon for me." A small smile curved his generous mouth. "But I don't know. Can't help wondering if we should put it off for a more auspicious time."

Andrew stopped with a slice of roast mutton halfway to his mouth. "Put it off? Man, if I were in your position, I'd be counting the days—if not the hours."

Thomas ran a hand through his thick black curls. "Aye, I am that."

"Then, why—" Andrew had seldom seen his lighthearted cousin so doleful.

Thomas looked into the fire. "I don't know. It's just that it seems callous when so many are dying."

"What's their dying to do with it? Can you save them by staying single? Will your marriage make their pain worse? On the contrary, when there's so little happiness in the world, it's our responsibility to do what we can to bring in a little joy. Anything to cut through this gray mist of sorrow hanging over the land."

"Gray mist of sorrow—cousin, you're a poet." Thomas paused. "Maybe there is something in what you say. And yet—this matter of the *Swatara*, now—it seems things just get worse and worse."

"What matter? What's the *Swatara?*"

Grandfather had sat silently smoking his pipe. Now he burst back into the conversation. "Ha! Well you might ask, lad." He scooped the newspaper from the hearth rug beside him. "Here now, read this and learn a thing or two. You'll see what I was telling you. Disease and desolation—as if we didn't have enough of our own, now we're importing it by the shipload. Right into Belfast harbor."

Andrew took the paper and shifted position so that the firelight fell more directly on it. Disease was the topic of the day, even above famine itself. Widespread hunger was pressing down on much of Europe—although not with the desperation of Ireland, because only Ireland had relied on a single crop for almost all of its food supply. But particularly alarming news was the highly contagious nature of the plague-breath. The peasantry's emaciated condition left them highly susceptible to the ravages of disease, but gentry and merchants were falling victim to the pestilence as well. In Cavan alone, seven *doctors* had died.

Ah, there was the item Tammis had referred to. The *Swatara*, a vessel chock-full of emigrants to America, had for the second time been buffeted by contrary winds and forced back into Belfast harbor. Only after some of those aboard had been allowed ashore had it been discovered that typhus fever had been festering in the cramped below-deck quarters. The article quoted a campaigner for public health, Dr. Andrew Malcolm: "I have the gravest concerns that the fever may sweep from the port throughout the town. The results of such an epidemic at this time could be unthinkable."

Andrew let the paper slip from his hand. How was it possible for things to get worse? The stench and noise of the overcrowded workhouse rose in his nose and ears—and then he saw Wilma, holding a crying infant while a little boy stood beside her and scratched at lice. Body lice carried typhus.

Wilma must be warned. She took enough risk just working at the soup kitchen. It seemed everyone took risk simply living in Ireland. She must not, however, expose herself further by going to the workhouse again. He would speak to her first thing.

The next day she met him smiling, her rosy brightness chasing away his midnight alarms. He had barely handed her into the carriage when she turned to him.

"Selma and Mother are to go to the dressmaker today. We spent half the night with Selma looking at the *Journal des Demoiselles* and looping swaths of silk over her in different manners." She clapped her hands. "Oh, you must think us terribly frivolous to be thinking of such things when people are starving, but it was so lovely to spend a few hours just laughing and daydreaming as we did so often—before." She sighed. "Can it really have been only two years ago?"

Andrew smiled at the pleasant sight of a young woman thinking of dresses and future happiness. All life had stopped when the famine struck. Even those with food in their bellies had put normal activities aside to fight the hunger choking life out of their land. But his friends had found a gleam of light in the dark. And he was glad.

"You are the least frivolous woman I know. I would as soon apply the term to Emelia Foxe. And I am delighted you spent a pleasant time with your sister. If we sink with the famine victims, who will be left to minister to them?" He could see his answer much mollified her concern.

She gave him the smile that revealed her dimples. "And what do you think? Should my gown be of lavender or yellow?"

Andrew had never been consulted on a matter of fashion before. A few flowers surviving beside the lane caught his eye. "Yellow is very pretty."

She laughed but did not seem displeased.

He had not forgotten his determination to warn her to stay away from the fever-ridden workhouse, but he could not bring himself to introduce such a dismal topic. He did not want those dimples to disappear.

Besides, there would be time. After all, he was driving. He simply would not take her into an infected area. The soup kitchen was carefully scrubbed with lye soap every night by the meticulous Quakers, and he could guard her from actual contact with those she served. Perhaps they should even start washing their hands after working with the famine victims. Some advanced thinkers such as Dr. Malcolm were beginning to advise that. But in the meantime he could enjoy Wilma's smiles.

A few days later Andrew went down to breakfast to find his grandfather brandishing the *Belfast News-Letter*. "Ha, and what did I tell ye?"

"Indeed, Grandfather, quite a few things. But I'm sure you'll inform me as to which particular one you are gloating over this morning."

"Epidemic in Belfast. Knew it was just a matter of time. From that ship, no doubt. Town full of emigrants and starving hordes from the countryside. What do they expect?"

Grandfather continued on about how the newly established Board of Health had ordered sheds put up beside the Frederick Street Hospital and a temporary hospital erected near the workhouse—and how Dr. Malcolm warned of worse to come.

But Andrew wasn't listening. How could he have let the matter lapse so long? He had to get to Wilma. He had to warn her. He hurried to the stable.

No, warning wasn't enough, he decided as he urged his horses along the lane. Wilma must give up the soup kitchen work, at least until the epidemic was past. There would be something else she could do for the poor. Sew for them. Raise chickens and give them eggs. But she must be kept safe. Why, oh why, had he waited to broach the subject? He would see that she stayed safely home today.

The Harrowby front door opened at his first knock. "Oh. Selma."

He had been so prepared to launch into his lecture to Wilma that he was tongue-tied at the sight of her sister. He struggled to regain his manners. "How is our radiant bride today?"

"Oh, just step in and have a look!" Selma dimpled almost as prettily as her twin. Tammis Price was a lucky man. She held out the sketch of a dress. Rows of lace ruffles surrounded the wide shoulder line, and the full skirt was lace from fingertips to the floor.

"Um . . . very pretty."

"Yes, isn't it!" Selma hugged the picture. "It was Queen Victoria's wedding dress. I'm thinking I'll have it copied."

"Yes. Very pretty. But—forgive my abruptness—but I must see your sister."

"Oh, yes, she left you a message."

"What do you mean? She knew I'd be calling for her."

"That's why she left the message. She said to tell you she'd meet you later at the kitchen."

"But I don't understand. Where is she?"

"She went with that Quaker woman—Mrs. Foxe."

"Yes, yes—"

"To buy supplies for the boilers. The kitchens are so inundated, they are starting double shifts."

"But where did they go?"

"To market, of course. Newtownards, I think. Or Belfast, maybe. A grain ship was coming into port—"

"Why didn't you stop her?" He turned on Selma with such vehemence that she dropped her fashion sketch. "Why didn't someone—"

"Did you ever try to stop Wilma when she'd her mind made up? Mother isn't well, and father's in the fields. I—"

He waited to hear no more. But halfway down the walk he turned back. "When did she leave? How long ago?"

Selma frowned, considering. "Half an hour. Maybe more."

He jumped into the carriage and sprang his horses. There was a chance he could catch up with them on the road. Belfast. Had the girl no sense? Going to a crowded market in a town raging with typhus. Why, oh, why had he let things go so long? If anything happened, it would be all his fault.

The road to Belfast was a nightmare. And, as in a nightmare, Andrew felt a desperate urgency to hurry, yet could barely move. The road was choked with traffic going both directions—those going to the city seeking food, shelter, and medical aid, and those coming toward him, fleeing the pestilence, no doubt. A few carriages trotted smartly along, whenever possible passing lumbering farm carts. But most of the traffic was on foot, clumps of ragged humanity, clinging together for the strength to move forward. A few pushed hand barrows. Most carried pitifully small, tattered bundles—all their earthly possessions. Victims of eviction with no place to go.

Andrew's heart leaped as he passed a clattering wagon. There— just ahead—was a small black buggy of the style favored by Quakers. The two-wheeled carriage was pulled by only one horse, so Andrew's fine pair could easily overtake it if he could just get around this group shuffling in front of him. And the old man pushing a handcart. And . . . He flicked the reins and urged his horses forward.

"Hello!" He drew up beside the carriage and leaned around its tall, straight side. "Thank goodness I caught you—" He broke off when two bearded men in plain collars and flat, wide-brimmed hats stared at him from inside. Without another word, Andrew sped past the buggy in spite of the narrowness of the road.

At last he clattered over Long Bridge spanning the River Lagan and made for High Street. How would he ever find anyone in this milling mob? A ship just in, Selma had said. He turned toward Chichester Quay. Indeed, the harbor was full of tall-masted vessels, some with sails furled. How many of their holds were stuffed to the deck with fleeing human beings? Rumor said it wasn't unusual for a third of the human cargo to die en route to their new homes. Still, the billowing sails offered hope to those able to scrape together money for passage. And some landlords, no longer able to support tenants who were unable to pay their rents, paid the passage for their people.

Something was wrong here. It took Andrew several minutes to figure out that it was the lack of sound. In the heart of this busy port, choked with people, there was a strange silence. Hunger-weakened people moved as in a stupor. They had no energy for conversation. The predominant sound was an eerie mumble, sounding more like moaning wind than human voice.

Determined to search the market on foot, Andrew found a vacant hitching post for his team. Bags that could well contain corn were being unloaded at quayside. A great crowd was gathered around. Was Wilma in the center of those people? Breathing their plague-breath?

Looking intently at every face that happened to be framed by a round bonnet tied with black ribbons, Andrew paid little attention to the placement of his feet until he tripped over a scrawny figure and almost fell. He started to offer assistance to the fallen man, then reeled back. The man was dead. Andrew looked around for someone to help.

An old man sitting on a stump nearby shook his gray head. "Don't bother yourself. He's been there all morning. Dead cart'll be along by evening." The man gave a gap-toothed imitation of a chuckle. "Be more to keep him company by then."

Andrew backed away. Where *was* Wilma? Her name rose in his throat. It was all he could do to keep from shouting it.

Then a sound rose just ahead from around the sacks of grain being stacked on the quay. It was just an angry rumble, like threatening thunder, but in the atmosphere of enervation and futility it rang loud.

"Corn. From America!"

A rock struck the shoulder of a dockworker guarding the precious hoard.

"Aye. To keep my family alive!" A man lunged forward with a stick.

They were futile gestures. The dockworkers would not yield their grain. But it was enough to start a riot. Hunger-crazed men would not be denied the possibility of a few more days of life. The dock erupted in a swell of flailing clubs and hammering fists.

Andrew started to retreat. Then he saw two female figures. He pressed forward. "Wil—" A heavy stick caught him on the side of the head. His knees buckled. His last sight was of dirty, roughshod feet as the paving stones rushed up to meet him.

"Aye, man, and that's a nasty one all right," a soft Scots-Irish voice burred near Andrew's ear. He flinched as the ointment the man was applying stung his wound. "Easy now. Ye've a fine gash there, but it'll heal."

Andrew opened his eyes. His skull was being bandaged by a handsome man with a broad forehead, wavy hair, and clear gray eyes.

"Malcolm, Dr. Andrew Malcolm," his attendant introduced himself. "I must say, you don't seem the sort to be brawling."

The object of his frenzied hunt returned to Andrew. "Wilma!" He started to jump up but was overcome with dizziness.

A firm hand on his shoulder pushed him back.

"Just sit a minute until your head clears. You'll be right soon."

"My friend. I must warn her—the epidemic—" But he calmed and told Dr. Malcolm about his chase to keep the ladies from exposing themselves to danger.

The doctor nodded. "Aye. Ye're right about keeping away. The papers understate it—don't want to start a panic. We're faced with no mere epidemic. This is a plague. Mark my words, this will be a plague in comparison with which all previous pestilence will seem trivial and insignificant." He paused. "Unless Almighty God in His wisdom chooses to spare us."

Andrew struggled to his feet. It didn't seem that the Infinite Wisdom had chosen to spare them much of anything.

72

It was late afternoon before Andrew could attempt driving the ten miles home. They would probably be finished at the soup kitchen now. What had happened? Had Wilma returned safely? Or had she and Mrs. Foxe been caught in the riot? Had they failed in their errand to purchase grain? Was the kitchen even able to open?

He attempted whipping his horses to a trot. But the road was as congested as it had been that morning, and now traffic was moving even more slowly.

In spite of the few starvelings sitting on the pavement, a pall of desertion hung around the warehouse soup kitchen as if it had never been open. Heavy with weariness, weighted down by the very hopelessness in the air, Andrew hitched his team and shuffled to the door, dreading the news he must face.

To his surprise, the door opened readily. And there she was, wearing her deep purple dress with a white apron over it, her dark hair curling around her face.

Wilma took one look at him, dropped her broom, and rushed to him with her hands out. "Oh, Andrew! My dear. What has happened to you?" She put a careful finger to the bandage. "You're hurt. Come, sit down."

It was not his injury that made his knees weak but the relief of seeing her. He sat. "I went to Belfast. To warn you. Selma said—"

"Belfast? We didn't go to Belfast. Merely to Newtownards."

He gripped the edge of the bench for support. "I can't tell you how thankful I am to hear that. The epidemic—plague, they're saying now—Wilma, you can have no notion of the horror—people lying dead on the street—" He straightened up and grabbed her shoulders. "Wilma, you must not go near it. I want you to give up the soup kitchen work."

She gasped in protest, but he hurried on. "You are too dear to me. There are others who can do this work. You must not expose yourself." He took her hands. "My love, I've been slow to speak of so many things. But today when I thought I might not find you again, when I was surrounded by such horror, I determined that, if God would give me a second chance, I wouldn't delay. You must cease this work. And you must marry me."

After a moment's hesitation, Wilma let out a trill of laughter. "Yes. Yes, Andrew, that is exactly what we must do. Not quit the kitchen —we'll talk about that. But we must marry. I saw that this morning, too. It's as if—" she hesitated, then pressed on"—as if we are living in the midst of a dread, silent dissolution that's harder to fight than the hunger itself. But we must fight. And we can be stronger together."

It was fortunate they were alone in the room, for nothing could have stopped Andrew's taking his beloved into his arms at that moment.

They were driving toward Harrowby's Dale, Wilma's bonneted head resting on his shoulder, when she said, "See, it's as if things are somehow better already, isn't it? I don't mean just for us—but as if I can give the new hope I feel to others. We can beat it—this—this unseen ruin creeping around us."

"Yes. We can. We will." He smiled tenderly at her. Somehow, just in the time since they had declared their love, she had become infinitely more precious to him.

She sighed and snuggled a hand under his arm. "I saw it all so clearly today in Newtownards. It was so awful in the workhouse. I asked about that family we took in. The little boy is the only one still liv—"

"What?" Andrew jerked his team to such an abrupt halt they were almost thrown from the seat. "You went to the workhouse!"

"Why, yes. It's part of the Friends' program—to take comfort to—"

"No, Wilma. No!" he exclaimed, as if he could change the facts by denying them.

"I know—I had hoped for better news, too. The mother and her babes dead. A small defeat in the face of so much death. But forgive me—I did not want to talk of defeat tonight. Tonight we are to hold the doom at bay."

Andrew shook his head against the crush of inevitability. He had struggled to protect her, but his best efforts were less than the wind. When she bade him good night in the hall, her eyes were so bright. Then the darkest thought of all struck him. Were they fever-bright?

And then the situation that could get no worse got worse. Several shiploads of Irish emigrants were turned back from Glasgow and other British cities. Regardless of where they had come from, all were dumped into the most convenient port—Belfast.

Fourteen thousand people crowded Belfast's hospitals and workhouse. Hundreds, for whom no provision could be found, huddled on the streets. Dr. Malcolm reckoned for the *Belfast News Letter* that one out of every five persons in the city was attacked by the plague. "In the delirium of this frightful malady they are left exposed in the streets or abandoned to die in their filthy, ill-ventilated hovels."

Fever penetrated every part of Ulster. Public works closed down. Soup kitchens struggled to continue with less than half their volunteers. Many finally shut their doors, leaving the starving, fevered victims to die clutching their empty bowls.

The plague reached its peak in July. On the first day of August, Wilma died.

Perhaps the worst of it was that Andrew could not mourn. All human passion had withered. He knew that was the end—there was no feeling, no meaning to anything. There was no food for his soul hunger. Physical hunger could be fed with wheatmeal. But the hunger he'd thought could be fed with love mocked any attempt at satisfaction.

His love lay in the grave. And famine in the heart was more severe than any in the stomach. There was no food for the hunger he felt. If there was nutrition that could give meaning to life, how was it that the further he searched, the hungrier he became?

Or perhaps that was the answer—merely to hunger on until one reached the void.

Or maybe this was the void.

Maybe they were all dead.

Dead. And in hell.

73

The old saying had been "To hell or to Connacht." Bridget's ancestors had chosen Connacht. But was there a difference?

She clasped the trug to her chest, enfolding the final digging of her small harvest, and tried to calculate. Did she have fifty pounds? Certainly the small mound in the lean-to was less than a hundredweight. In the days before the famine, Dermot alone would have eaten this many tatties in two weeks. But now it must keep them both for a whole year.

The autumn of 1847 had yielded its harvest. The potatoes—what few there were—were sound. The fever epidemic had run its course, and the government had declared the famine officially over. How could it be over when people were still starving—the workhouses still overflowing—the destitute still dying on their doorsteps? Yet, the government said it was over and halted its distribution of soup. Two months earlier, three million people had been fed by government ration tickets. Now there were no more tickets. And no more soup.

Bridget turned to stow her basket of brown diamonds. A hairless brown dog wandered across the field, its backbone protruding like the teeth of a saw. It glared at her with a wolfish eye, then slunk away. The birds that had twittered last spring sang no more. The soul of the land was faint and dying.

Dermot had said that. It was rhetoric from his Young Irelander meetings. But maybe they weren't so far wrong. Dying. Or already dead.

She selected two large potatoes and one small one and went into the hut. She would boil them for dinner. They could drink the cooking water for supper. Inside the door, she froze.

She hadn't thought it possible to feel a new fear, but the sight of Dermot gathering his few belongings into a woven rush basket stabbed like a knife through her heart.

"Dermot, no! I've tatties. A whole mound. We've enough. There's no need for you to leave." In her desperation she lied, pouring out words neither of them believed. "We've made it this far. Don't emigrate now. The ships are death pits—better to go directly to the trench in the churchyard."

He gripped her arm and shook her until she stopped on a sob. "*Wheesht*, woman! Who'd have thought ye had the energy to set up such a howl?"

"But—"

"I'm not taking ship. I'm going to *Dublin*."

She sank to the pallet where *Seanathair* lay, hollow-eyed and cadaverous, hardly making a ridge under the brychan. "As well take a coffin ship, then. There is nothing in Dublin. No land for crops, no space in the workhouse, not even kelp to boil—"

Dermot wrinkled his nose against the seaweed smell permeating the cabin. "Aye. If I wanted kelp would I go to Dublin?"

"But what's in Dublin?"

"The future."

"There is no future."

Now the bitterness that had sustained Dermot in the worst moments surged in his speech. "You talk like all the others. Like the Irish have always done when they didn't have someone to lead them."

Bridget sighed. She had heard it all too many times before. "O'Connell's dead, Dermot. Let him rest."

"O'Connell! Aye, rest. That's all he did at the end, anyway."

"He won emancipation for us."

"Oh, aye. The Great Liberator. He earned the title well enough. Then turned around and bargained with the enemy."

"It's not the time for a rising, Dermot." If anything could make her think it might be better for her brother to emigrate it was talk of a rising.

"But the time is coming. Soon. Next year is forty-eight. Fifty years since Wolfe Tone's rising. Time indeed. Time to break this fiendish union with Britain."

She could only shake her head. She had no more strength for arguing. The rock crushing, building roads to nowhere, had taken every ounce of mental and physical energy from the men who were left. Now when they met at the crossroads, it was with empty hands. And so they talked of the Brotherhood of Young Ireland.

Daniel O'Connell had died last spring, while making a pilgrimage to Rome to pray for Ireland. But his break with the Young Irelanders had been complete before that. Now the way was clear for those calling for the taking up of sword and pitchfork. The spirit of Wolfe Tone walked the pages of *The Nation* and made its way into the hearts of those who could read or who would listen to it read aloud.

"We've a new leader. Smith O'Brien, descendant of Brian Boru.

He's visionary enough to see clearly through the film of suffering encasing this land. New ties have been forged in the fires of the famine. If anything good can have come of this, it's that the horror has effected a purge in the gentry. Attitudes have changed. Attitudes hard as iron can be hammered on the anvil of freedom."

At such moments, Dermot displayed his descent from a long line of *seanachaidh*s. And there was no arguing with him once the poetry rose.

Bridget got up wearily. "I'll cook extra tatties for ye to eat on the road." She calculated how many *Seanathair* was likely to need. She could send the rest with Dermot. She had raised them for him.

It was as well, she considered. She had not told Dermot that the few pecks of barley she sold had paid only half the rent. But Dermot would go to Dublin with his Young Irelanders, and there would be enough potatoes and paid-up rent to last until she took *Seanathair* to the churchyard. Then she would go to the workhouse. Unless she was lucky and the fever took her farther away.

She took the St. Bridget's cross from the wall just inside the door and placed it on the top of his bundle. "The God of St. Patrick and Ireland watch over you, Dermot."

"And may the same God watch over you."

That winter was the coldest yet. There were deep snows in February. What if *Seanathair* died now? Who could dig a grave in such rock-hard ground? As the old man's breath came more shallow and ragged, Bridget found herself more and more obsessed with the thought. The mortal remains of generations of MacHenrys rested in the churchyard. She would not have the finest of them tipped into a famine pit. Perhaps, if he could just hold on a bit longer . . . the thaw must come soon.

That was all she cared about. Her final goal would be reached then, and she could give up the struggle. In spite of everything, she managed a smile. She had done it. A handful of small potatoes remained in the basket. Brendan MacHenry would die with his own thatch over his head. He would be laid out and waked by his own granddaughter. Father Lynch would lay him in St. Finian's churchyard . . .

And then? Her plan had been to go to the workhouse. But too many had sought their last refuge there. If the snows went off soon enough, it would be better to stay here and eat grass. Many had chosen to die with a green mouth in the open field than with fever in the poorhouse. Perhaps she would make that choice as well.

Several days later she lay on her pallet, thinking the same thoughts round and round, except that the thoughts came less clearly now. Often she didn't know whether she slept or daydreamed, whether it

643

was day or night. It made no difference. She would listen for *Seana-thair*'s breath, then sink back into her stupor.

But this time she did not sink back. There had been a sound, and it was not *Seanathair*. It was a knocking. She dragged herself to the door.

"Father Lynch. You're good to come."

"Bless you, daughter. And how is himself?"

It had become a ritual. And at every visit she had replied, "He breathes." But tonight she said, "Have you your stole, Father?"

"Indeed, I have. It's time, is it?"

She nodded.

The priest took his stole out of his pack, kissed it, put it over his shoulders and knelt by the barely breathing form. He made the sign of the cross. "God the Father—"

Bridget gave the response, "Have mercy on Your servant."

"God the Son—"

"Have mercy on Your servant."

"God the Holy Spirit—"

"Have mercy on Your servant."

"Holy Trinity, one God—"

"Have mercy on Your servant."

"Jesus, Lamb of God—"

"Have mercy on him."

"Jesus, bearer of our sins—"

"Have mercy on him."

"Jesus, Redeemer of the world—"

"Give him Your peace."

Father Lynch placed a crumb of wafer on the tongue that had once sung so fair to make children dance and men weep. "Lord, have mercy."

"Christ, have mercy."

"Lord, have mercy."

Bridget had no idea how long she sat there after Father Lynch left. Perhaps she dozed. Or perhaps the cabin actually grew warm with a soft light. Perhaps a breeze or a moth's wing ruffled the strings of Brendan MacHenry's harp. Or perhaps the angels really sang a heavenly welcome for the *sheanachaidh*. But whatever the truth of the matter, Bridget knew it was time.

She moved slowly but with determination. She must find the strength for this one last thing. Tugging with both hands, she pulled the table to the center of the room. That task done, she found strength for the next and went to the small trunk in the corner. She was glad she had kept it—her grandmother's wedding veil. Many a time she had thought of trying to sell it. She would have offered it for rent had *Seanathair*'s breath outlasted her final payment. But that had not been necessary. She covered the table with the fragile lace, then turned to bathe the body, more frail than even the veil.

She had washed his shirt and dried it by the fire only last week. His hair and beard lay smooth under the furrows of the comb. She had no candles, but she had been careful never to be without a supply of rushes. Now she lit one to place in the window and one for the holder on the shelf. The light flickered on the silvery hair and ivory lace, giving an otherworldly atmosphere to the scene. Bridget would not have been surprised if *Seanathair*'s body had simply floated to paradise with the soul that had already departed.

She knelt by the side of the table. "O God, whose only begotten Son, by His life, death, and resurrection has purchased for us the rewards of eternal life . . ."

Bridget blinked at the morning light when Father Lynch pushed open the cabin door. She remembered that *Seanathair* was gone. There was nothing left. Nothing in the whole world. "There are three potatoes in the basket, Father. You must give them to the poor." She would not be needing them. Grandfather's bones would go in the pit today. Perhaps she could just lie there with him when no one was looking. It would save their having to carry her from the field.

Father Lynch signed Brendan MacHenry's forehead, lips, and heart with the cross, then turned to Bridget. "You have done well, my child. He looks fine."

"Aye. He was always beautiful. But, no—" the old worry gripped her with the return of the full light of day "—no, you cannot take him yet. He must have his own grave." She looked around wildly. "My loy. It's sturdy. I can dig the grave."

"No, child. You—"

"Father Lynch, I can. I can. *Seanathair* mustn't go in the pit. I can do it. The ground can't be frozen that hard. I—I'll—"

The old priest grasped her shoulders to calm her, and she slumped against him. "Go calmly, my child. There's no need."

She tried to struggle but was too spent.

"The digging's been done. By his own kin."

"Dermot?" She looked around. "Dermot's come back? Oh, thank You, Jesus, Mary, and Saint Patrick."

But the figure who entered the cabin just then was not her brother. She shrank behind the priest at the sight of a stranger in black coat and crepe armbands.

"Aye, it's little wonder that ye nae recognize me, Bridget Mac-

645

Henry. We're sore changed, all of us. But I said I'd return. I'd no notion it would be under such circumstances, though."

Father Lynch put an arm around Bridget. "He says his name is Andrew Armstrong, come from County Down. He said he was kin. I'd no reason to doubt him."

Bridget nodded. "Aye. It was the shock. It's as he says." She made a weak gesture for the men to sit on the bench and all but collapsed on her pallet. "It's been long."

Andrew nodded. "Aye. Several lifetimes." And silence filled the space between each word. "I've come with the Quakers. They set up boilers—run soup kitchens. The government quit, so many landlords are bankrupt, but the Quakers carry on."

She looked at his sober attire. "So you've become one of these—these—what?"

"No. No, I'm not anything." The sadness in his voice was like the mourning of the sea.

While they talked, Father Lynch busied himself poking up the turfs, filling a kettle with water, and boiling the last potatoes.

Andrew explained that when the Friends Relief Committee received a shipment of boilers and supplies from England, they decided to send them to the west coast where the need was most severe. Thinking of the MacHenrys, Andrew had offered to drive his wagon. He would be in the area a few days, making deliveries to volunteers.

Bridget nodded. A few days. Then she must go on living a few days more. Then a worse thought struck her. If there was to be a soup kitchen in their village, she must eat. To refuse would be to commit suicide. And suicide was a sin. But she didn't want to go on living. Why couldn't Andrew Armstrong have waited just a few more days? Then it wouldn't have mattered if manna had fallen from heaven. She would not have been obliged to stir herself to eat it for fear of her immortal soul.

Was even such a thought sin?

"Eat this in remembrance of him."

She obediently opened her mouth. Then she realized Father Lynch was holding out a potato, not serving Communion. Yes, she would eat in *Seanathair*'s memory. She would need strength for the funeral.

Father Lynch and Andrew Armstrong wrapped Brendan MacHenry in his brychan and placed him in the coffin that Andrew brought in from his wagon. That a miracle was taking place dawned slowly on Bridget. The digging of the grave was enough. She had never even thought of a coffin. But Jesus—or Mary—or the fairies had sent Andrew with a fine pine coffin as well. She made no attempt to hold back the tears.

Bridget jostled between Andrew and Father Lynch as the wagon lumbered over the frozen ruts and the coffin bounced in the back. But to her the ride was as smooth as a flight of angels' wings. Piles of snow still lay on the shaded side of St. Finian's, but she did not feel the cold. She stood beside the fresh-turned mound as the men lowered the coffin.

Father Lynch held his prayer book. "A reading from a sermon by Saint Anastasius of Antioch. 'To this end Christ died and rose to life that He might be Lord both of the dead and of the living. But God is not God of the dead, but of the living. That is why the dead, now under the dominion of one who has risen to life, are no longer dead but alive. Therefore life has dominion over them and, just as Christ, having been raised from the dead, will never die again, so too they will live and never fear death again.'"

74

The words entered Andrew's dulled brain. *So too they will live and never fear death again.* He supposed something like that had been said at Wilma's funeral, but he had been too numb to hear. Now he listened more closely.

"'When they have been thus raised from the dead and freed from decay, they shall never again see death, for they will share in Christ's resurrection just as He Himself shared in their death.'"

The words brought a tinge of warmth to his frozen heart. Even if they weren't literally true, they made beautiful poetry. The very concept that hope could exist in religion or art was in itself hopeful.

The service continued, but now Andrew did not resist it as the frozen earth had resisted his digging that morning. He let the words float around him as he would a *seanachaidh*'s tale, as he had once listened to Brendan MacHenry.

"Concerning those who are asleep, do not be sad like men who have no hope . . ."

Bridget nudged him, indicating that he should join her in the response. "For if we believe that Jesus died and rose again, God will bring forth with Jesus all who have fallen asleep believing in him."

"Do not weep for the dead, do not mourn them with tears."

This time Andrew listened to his own response. "For if we believe that Jesus died and rose again, God will bring forth with Jesus all who have fallen asleep believing in him." A pretty big *if*, but still—nice words.

They were nearly back to the cabin when Andrew heard clangs and thuds coming from the MacHenry hut. Two uniformed, helmeted constables blocked the way to the door. Three ragged laborers swung sledgehammers and a battering ram at the stones and turf that had housed generations of MacHenrys.

Bridget gave a piercing cry, such as she might have been expected to emit at her grandfather's grave, then returned to her dazed silence.

"Here now! What's this?" Andrew jumped from the wagon seat with a shout.

A pinched-looking man in a tweed cap confronted him. "Grady Erskine. Lord Grangeton's overseer," he announced himself. "Rent past due. Thought they'd cleared out. Save us the trouble of throwing them out. But I read the eviction notice anyway. The constable here will swear to it. Things always done by the letter of the law on Lord Grangeton's land."

"I've no doubt." Andrew had no trouble matching the hardness in Erskine's voice.

The overseer drew a crumpled paper from his back pocket. "'Hear ye, hear ye. The queen's business is now in progress, to ensue forthwith, and not to be interfered with—'"

Andrew pushed the paper aside. "You've no need to read the riot act to me, man. I've no intention of interfering with you or Her Majesty. But Lord Grangeton owns only this cabin and the land it's on. If his lordship is so careful about the letter of the law, you'll be knowing that the tenants' personal property is theirs to take." He advanced toward the door as he spoke, and the constabulary moved aside.

Andrew's shoulders slumped. It had been a small victory. But what could there be in this hovel worth taking away? He started to take Bridget's brychan, then considered that it would inevitably be full of lice. He chose the empty potato basket instead. The two iron rushlight holders went in, the bit of lace on which the mortal remains of Brendan MacHenry had lain, the St. Bridget's cross from beside the fireplace. "To save the hearth from fire and ravagement," she had said in lighter days. It hadn't worked.

He was ready to leave when he saw the harp in a shadowed corner. He picked it up and ran his fingers over the satiny black wood. Then he strode to the rig and placed the treasure in Bridget's lap.

Even before he was on the wagon seat again, Erskine signaled his men, and the blows resumed on the cabin walls.

But now it was not only the pounding of battering ram on stone that accompanied their departure but also the silver warble of Bridget's fingers on the harpstrings.

He looked at her in amazement. "I did nae know ye played!"

"I didn't. *Seanathair* showed me. And now the gift is passed. It is only for its owner that the *cláirseach* sings its true sweetness."

"And did your grandfather teach you his songs as well?" It had all been long ago, on the other side of the famine wall, that long-ago time and place when life had been good and sweet and filled with song. And he had asked Bridget to gather songs for him.

"Aye. I had no paper. So I got them by heart."

Andrew looked at the child on the seat beside him, clutching the few possessions that were all she had in the world. What was he to do with her? She had said Dermot was somewhere in Dublin—gone off to join the Young Irelanders. Should he take her to her brother? Enough careful questioning in pubs should unearth his whereabouts—if he hadn't already gotten himself jailed or knifed in some sectarian squabble.

The answer was easy enough for tonight. Father Lynch had offered Andrew hospitality. His first impulse had been to refuse—surely there would be an inn, however mean, in a nearby town. But now he was glad he had accepted. When the priest learned Bridget had been evicted, he would give her a sleeping place as well. And perhaps for longer than tonight, Andrew mused. Perhaps she could serve as housekeeper for the elderly priest. Yes, that would be a fine solution. He clucked to his team with renewed spirit.

Andrew's optimism lasted until he saw the priest's home. It was barely more than a hermit's cell, built in the ancient style with cobblestones stacked to form a steeply pitched roof. But it was warm and dry and there was room—barely—for the three of them to sleep on brychans before the fire.

Father Lynch went straight to the question when they told him of the eviction. "And what will you do now, my child?"

It was obvious from Bridget's widened eyes that she had given the matter no consideration. "I—I don't know. I had thought to die when I'd buried *Seanathair.* Now . . ." The barrenness in her voice filled the space.

At least, Andrew knew what he was to do for the next few days. "I have a list, Father—of the places the Society of Friends want to start soup kitchens. I'm to deliver the supplies. Their workers will arrive soon—mostly on foot, I expect. Anyway—" he drew a sheet of paper from his pocket "—could you give me directions to some of these? The villages on the top of the list are on my map." He took out the crumpled document. "But I can't locate some of the others."

Father Lynch studied the list by a flickering rushlight. "Yes, your journey is well organized for you." He traced the path on Andrew's map. "These two are quite near—you can be there by midmorning tomorrow. But Finn Birne is being a piece farther on."

As he talked, Andrew jotted notes of landmarks.

"Aye, it's rough going here, the descent very steep. I'd not attempt it myself except on foot, but—" Father Lynch spread his hands. "I'll ask St. Patrick to give you special protection on your mission of mercy."

The priest frowned before going on. "There are people there who've had naught but seaweed and mussels for three years. If they're still alive . . ." He paused at the last name on the list. "Inish Malin. Aye.

You'll be hiring a boat, then. See you set out in fine weather. If it's not too blustery or the mists too heavy, you'll do."

Andrew was not encouraged by the tone of doubt in the cleric's voice. He looked to see how much Bridget had taken in of their conversation and saw that she had none of it. She slept curled before the fire. In the dim room with the fire glow on her, the dirt and ravages of the past years were softened. He could see glimmers of the red-gold child who had once entranced him with her bell-like laughter. Her vulnerability and aloneness struck him anew.

He saw that Father Lynch observed the direction of his gaze. "I'll take her with me, Father. She can stay in one of the villages with the Quakers. They can give her soup, and she can give them songs. This will be something new for even as advanced a group as the Society of Friends—a soup kitchen with a *seanachaidh*."

Having arrived at that happy solution, Andrew settled himself as comfortably as he could for the night. Rolling in a brychan on a beaten earth floor was all very well for people accustomed to such things. But Andrew Armstrong was not. He smiled at the thought of Grandfather's seeing him now. Jay Lanark had been irate at his leaving. But that made little enough difference to Andrew. Nothing had made any difference since Wilma's death. So why shouldn't he take soup boilers to the west coast? One place was as empty as another.

And now he had another chore. He would deliver Bridget along with the kitchen supplies. And then he would return to the emptiness of Lanarks' Bawn.

The next day, when he explained his decision to Bridget, she neither objected nor stated acquiescence. She merely stored her rolled brychan neatly against the wall and ate the small bowl of stirabout the priest set before her.

Andrew left a bag of meal with the priest, and they set out. The first two villages were as easy to find as his guide had assured him they would be. But the plague and fever had found them equally accessible. A few destitute beings leaned against run-down huts with scanty thatch. Andrew would hardly have thought to dignify the collection with the title of clachan, much less village, in spite of the presence of the requisite smithy and dram shop. Leaving Bridget in either place was unthinkable. They rattled on.

The trail grew steeper and rougher. As they crossed the Black Gap, Andrew recalled Father Lynch's admonition that this land was best crossed on foot, and he hoped that the meager track wouldn't peter out on them. By evening, though, they were descending with a view of Donegal Bay spread before them. This looked better. Surely

651

Bantooley would be just the place to establish Bridget along with the soup boiler.

And perhaps it would have been, as it was a somewhat larger village that boasted its own church. But the Quaker workers had not arrived yet, so the equipment must be left with the priest. And Andrew would not—could not—leave his young cousin without speaking to the Quakers in whose care he meant to leave her.

And so they went on.

On the second day she asked shyly, "Should I be teaching you the songs so you'll have them when you go?"

Andrew sighed. The publishing of songbooks was something else the world had left on the other side of the famine wall. But these were some of the first words Bridget had volunteered since they departed from Grangeton. It would be as well to encourage her.

Her light melodies did not smooth the roads, but it seemed that the horses stumbled less on the ruts. And Andrew realized how much he had missed the presence of music in the world. In the old days— days before the Great Hunger—he had occasionally gone to church with Grandfather. Although the metrical psalms were monotonous to his ears, they were music. And there had been harpers and fiddlers and pipers at fairs. And children had sung in the fields and clachans. He had forgotten the sound of it all.

And the birds had sung! Those few birds that had survived the harshness of the winters and escaped trapping for food had faced their own famine as the earth was wiped clear of berries, seeds, and even bugs for human consumption.

But here, for this brief space, there was melody in the air. Andrew consulted his map. The last place was an island. That should be perfect for a *seanachaidh:* green, with sandy coves and wild, rocky outcrops. A place with ancient memory of legendary *selkies* and water fairies.

Yes. It was a good thing none of the other villages had suited. Inish Malin would do far better.

Three days later they arrived at the westernmost tip of the peninsula, where Donegal Bay faced the open waters of the Atlantic. The dark mound of an island showed offshore, silhouetted by the setting sun.

Andrew approached a party of wrackers. "Can you tell me, is that Inish Malin? Where can I get a boat to ferry us out there?"

Sticklike children hid behind their mothers' tattered skirts. A young boy made a sign against evil. A girl fled, screaming.

Bridget touched his arm. "They aren't understanding yourself." She spoke to them in a lilting flow of Irish.

The children came out from hiding. A stooped old man gave a few words of reply.

Bridget turned to Andrew. "Aye, it's for being Inish Malin. But they have no boats. Fishing isn't allowed them. Lord Malinmore keeps the boats."

She turned back to the kelp gatherers while Andrew considered what they should do. He had hoped to make his last delivery tomorrow and start home—although the thought of going home to the gray emptiness of the world without Wilma was not enticing. Except for the comfort of his bed, there was little to choose between Father Lynch's cell and Lanarks' Bawn.

He looked at his map. They were twenty miles from Glenties. They could go there tomorrow. He had often heard the Glenties Union talked of at relief committee meetings. Run by the British Association, they fed eight thousand children a week. Surely they could use an additional boiler and another willing worker—for he did not doubt that Bridget would be willing. That was a better choice than some unreachable island. If he couldn't get there, then neither could the Quakers. They had probably gone to Glenties as well. On that decision, he folded his map.

But before he could announce his new plan, Bridget tugged at his arm. "Come. This way."

He would have demanded an explanation, but she returned to her Irish jabber with the people, who began escorting the newcomers down the beach.

At the shore, all but one fell back. "Desmond—Des," a black-haired youth introduced himself. It appeared that he would be their guide to somewhere.

At the coastline, the sand gave way to a shale-covered path that grew more and more rugged until Andrew feared he would lose his footing and slip into the water. Suddenly it appeared that was what Des had done, for his dark head vanished from sight. A moment later, however, Andrew followed the sharp turn in the trail and saw that their guide had merely ducked into a cave in the side of the cliff. And there lay a sturdy rowboat.

Bridget explained. "People have hidden boats here since the time of Cromwell, when all the priests were driven out. They spirited priests to Inish Malin and slipped them back under cover of dark to say the Mass. When the potatoes failed, they fished at night." She shrugged. "It was little enough to choose—death from the law for fishing without rights or death from hunger by not fishing."

Andrew would have preferred to wait till morning, but Desmond would take the boat out only under cover of dark. He should go back and get the boiler and sacks of meal and vegetables he was to deliver In case the Quakers were there, ready to set their kettles boiling. But the thought of traversing that trail again—and the return laden with supplies—made him decide to go ahead and just make the arrangements. He would bring back one of the islanders to take over the equipment if the Quakers hadn't their own boat. Yes. He nodded to himself and got into the small, rocking craft. That would do very well. Get Bridget settled in her new home. Best to do that first.

The pale half-moon gave only a cold light, and the few stars showing served to highlight the darkness around them. When they reached the island shore, the dark seemed thicker yet.

Through Bridget, Andrew had asked about the island's population and was told there were more than a hundred the last anyone knew. But that had been some time ago, as no one had come from the island during the winter storms.

Andrew felt a prickle at the back of his neck. It was *too* dark. Even with the village asleep, there should have been a glow from banked fires or a wavering rushlight indicating some sleepless soul.

He jumped when a marsh bird, startled from its nest, flew low over his head, crying.

Bridget moved closer. "Des says we must leave before sunrise."

"Nonsense. I paid him more than his whole village has seen in a year. I need to talk to these people—have you talk to them, at least."

Unless there was an educated priest on the island, this was going to be more awkward than Andrew had imagined. And he had no intention of tackling such obstacles in the dark. The only thing he would undertake before daylight would be finding a protected spot to doze. Fortunately he had a few brimstone matches in the little tin box in his pocket.

But even when they crowded around a small blaze built at the foot of a standing stone above the beach, he mostly had only disgust to keep himself warm. Disgust with himself. How could he have gotten into such an awkward situation? It was more than awkward. And more than disgust with the dark, the isolation, the language barrier, the penetrating cold. He couldn't define it, but as he huddled deeper inside his voluminous MacFarlan coat, he began to feel an eeriness creeping over him.

Something was . . . wrong. He hesitated to use the word "evil," and yet he could think of no better. And Bridget? What of his plan to abandon her here?

But he wasn't abandoning her. He was bringing her to a new home. A place of beauty and poetry, where she could run free in the grass and play her harp by the seaside. Of course he was. It would all look better in the morning.

He must have dozed in spite of his agitation, because a rim of gold was gilding the sky to the east when he opened his eyes.

For their breakfast he had only a few hard biscuits in his pocket, left over from supper last night. It was unlikely they could buy food in the island village, but he would try. When he set out on this journey he had had no idea of the isolation—or desolation—of such villages as he had visited in recent days. And there was little to be hoped for from this island unless the Quakers had established their work ahead of him.

He looked across the expanse of open green. He should have known better than to expect animals in the fields. If ever there had been any, they would have been eaten in the first year of the famine. Yet it seemed *something* should be moving. The stillness had a breathless quality in spite of the breeze blowing in from the sea.

How would people have fared here? he wondered. In spite of the Irish dependence on and preference for potatoes, there should have been no shortage of fish. Could they have survived all these years on fish and seaweed alone? He looked around. Wind-ruffled grass was the only thing that told him he wasn't beholding a painted scene. There was no sign of tilled soil. Still, it was a week or so yet till St. Patrick's Day—they probably wouldn't start until then.

Bridget came up from the shore. He was pleased to see that she had washed herself. That was a good sign. She was coming back to life and making ready to settle into her new home. Des refused to leave his boat, so Andrew held his hand out to Bridget and the two of them climbed the winding path to high ground, where scattered stone buildings stood well away from shore.

The closer they drew to the buildings, the more his nervousness increased. What if the Quakers weren't here yet? What would he do with Bridget? The language was no problem to her, but he couldn't leave her in an isolated, starving village without the protection of a charitable society. And he had no desire to spend more time here than necessary, awaiting the others' arrival.

Bridget seemed to feel none of his reluctance. She almost skipped ahead of him on the path. Even in the few days of eating the proper food Andrew had brought, she had gained strength. And today, after her early bath, her hair seemed to have regained some of its original color when the sun shone on it. She stopped before the first cottage. The door stood open.

"Wait!" Andrew wasn't sure why his command was so sharp. He just knew the stillness leaped out to crush him. The silence shrieked.

He pushed open the creaking door and entered. The form on the pallet had been female. It was a mother, clutching the body of a small child.

Andrew clasped a hand over his nose and mouth and backed out, shielding the sight from Bridget behind him. "Don't." He stopped her as she started to move around him. "They're beyond help. We'll go on and find a priest—or someone."

A small stone church stood on up the footpath. Andrew surveyed the churchyard with growing uneasiness. He noted the number of mounds that seemed new since last autumn. The grass had not sodded over them yet. There was a half-dug grave off to the right. Perhaps that was for the woman in the cabin. And yet the dirt around it didn't appear to be new-turned.

Bridget cried out, and he turned to see her pointing. The last shreds of a black cassock told him that the corpse they saw was once a priest. Fallen, too weak to get up, on his way to administer last rites to another, perhaps? The man had been so for some time, for the sea gulls had left little of his face. Andrew put an arm around Bridget and turned her away. "We must go. I must get you away from—from this island of death."

But she did not yield to his movement. "No. We cannot leave." She knelt by the priest, as he had doubtless knelt by so many others. "Our Father . . ."

Andrew stood stiffly by until she completed the prayer. "Now," he said. "Let's go. This whole place is dead." The enormous horror of the situation had been slowly dawning on him since they arrived at the cove last night. He had known then that something was wrong.

He wasn't a superstitious man. He didn't really believe the dead walked. And yet he looked uneasily over his shoulder. Stone and turf cottages and cabins straggled around in every direction. There were twenty, maybe thirty, buildings, some having little sheds or byres behind them. How many of them were not cottages but tombs? How many of the inhabitants of this once-busy village had received proper burial in the churchyard before the rest simply lay down on their pallets and never found the strength to get up again? The wind made a moaning sound.

Bridget was still kneeling.

"Come." He pulled her to her feet.

"Aye, I was after forgetting myself." She gave a little shake. "Yes, there is so much to do." She started across the churchyard toward another hut.

"Where are you going? The boat is this way."

He might as well have saved his breath. "We must check every cottage. I will say an Ave for each one." She turned back and grabbed his arm, her eyes wide with concern. "Do you think many died without absolution?"

Andrew swallowed his impatience. All he could think of was getting away from this ghastly place. And here she was, worrying about some religious mumbo jumbo. "It appears the priest was the last one on his feet, apparently in the process of preparing a burial. He probably lived long enough to perform—all the necessary rites." He really had no idea, and he couldn't think it would make a whistle of difference. But he was pleased to see that he had said the right thing. The fear in her eyes subsided.

The next few hours were a catalog of horrors. Andrew had no idea where Bridget got her strength—physically or emotionally. She moved steadily from hut to hut, inspecting each interior. When the huts were not empty, when dead eyes looked at them from ragged brychans, when gaping mouths greeted them, she never gave in to fright or disgust but merely knelt at her prayers as calmly as if she were in church.

Andrew, however, did not have the comfort of religious ritual. He saw the dark stains around the corpses where the body fluids had soaked into ragged blankets and dirt floors. He saw the gleam of bones where skin had decomposed. He saw the maggots, the lice, the ants. And he smelled the putrefaction.

Dust thou art, to dust returneth. The phrase ran over and over in his mind. Was this the end of everything—for everyone? Death had looked so much prettier for Wilma, resting on a lace-edged linen sheet in Harrowby's Dale and laid to rest in the Comber parish churchyard with the reading of the beautiful words of the Book of Common Prayer. Even Brendan MacHenry, lying on the table with the rushlight reflecting on his white beard—there had been dignity, an acknowledgment of the human spirit created in the image of God. But this abandoned waste was horror upon horror.

Bridget saw it through to the end. "There." She closed the door on the farthest-out cottage, near to the back side of the island. "There are three men unburied, counting the priest, five women and two little ones." She thought for a moment. "I suppose the babes would weaken and die first, so most would have been buried."

That thought seemed to comfort her, but Andrew was thinking of the nightmare for those last few on their feet. How many of their hundred-some neighbors, friends, and family would they have had to bury? And now it was over for all of them.

The concept of walking out into a black void terrified him. One always thought of life continuing. One cultivated land and built homes

657

and barns for one's posterity; one worked for laws, churches, schools for one's children. But for Inish Malin, the void had descended.

They were more than halfway back across the water to the mainland when Andrew realized that he, at least, did have a future, and therefore he must make plans. Bridget was fully prepared to tell the local priest all that needed seeing to on the island. He must leave word for the Friends workers. Then inspiration struck him. He would leave the boiler and supplies with Desmond. If any people needed a regular nourishing soup it was the wrackers on Donegal Bay. It could keep this village from going the same way Inish Malin had.

But Bridget . . . He looked at her now. The sea breeze tangled her hair as she told Des about his island neighbors. And Andrew faced the truth that had been growing on him for days. He could never leave her here, the ward of some charity. She was kin. She was part of his past for generations, the past that could make the future live, if they were not all to go the way of Inish Malin.

And suddenly he had the perfect solution. He would take Bridget to Lanarks' Bawn. There was room and enough. Mrs. B could use the help of a pair of young hands. And Elfrith O'Brien could teach her the lessons she had missed in the spotty education of the hedge school. He rather liked the idea of the woman who had mothered him serving as surrogate mother for Bridget as well. That would make them more than cousins. Almost brother and sister.

75

Andrew was hungry. He didn't even know what for. Certainly not for another piece of meat. He pushed away the roast joint surrounded with vegetables and swimming in gravy.

Berkley tottered in, his head wobbly on his thin neck. "Shall I pour your port for you now, sir?"

"No, no. I'll get my own."

Andrew jammed his chair back so impatiently that it slammed against the wall. He wouldn't let Berkley touch his best liquor—the old coot shook so that he could hardly hit the glass when he poured. Why hadn't he gotten rid of him years ago? And Mrs. B too. His food would be uneatable if Bridget didn't come over from the clachan daily to keep things at Lanarks' Bawn in order. He was glad he had brought her here—even if her coming had sparked his last—and worst—fight with Grandfather.

He strode into the parlor just as the clock on the mantel chimed three. Funny old clock. It had been there forever. Probably came over with St. Patrick. But how could it be so late already? He turned to the sideboard. No, it wouldn't be port. He wanted something stronger. It seemed he did most of the time now.

He poured a full glass, sloshing a little himself, then flung himself onto the dark plush sofa and put his booted feet on the marble-topped table in front of it. He stole a glance at the clock as if to catch the hands in the act of racing ahead.

Eleven years. How was it possible for the wind to blow so fast? People spoke of the sands of time, or of the years running like a river, but Andrew knew better. Sand and water had substance. They could be held in one's hand—no matter how briefly. Their movement could be measured. But time could be held and measured only by the mind of God. He took a deep drink from his glass.

Eleven years ago he had returned from the west coast, hungry and tired, his senses numbed by the horrors he had encountered. He had brought with him one spark of light in Bridget and her *cláirseach*. And Jay Lanark had thrown her out.

"There have been no papists sully the portals of Lanarks' Bawn in the near to three hundred years since my ancestor built it. I'll not be the one to let the Devil in now."

Andrew had tried argument. How did Grandfather know what had happened here for two and a half centuries past? It was quite likely there had been more than one Catholic under this roof. The Seaton Court Lanarks had been Catholic—and they were descended from the same ancestors. There were even rumors that the O'Briens—who were welcomed enough as stable hands—had had Lanark blood at some time in the past. As did Bridget MacHenry herself. And he wasn't asking Grandfather to adopt the girl—just give her a bed in the servants' quarters and let her earn her keep helping around the house.

As for being "papist," at least Bridget believed in Jesus, whereas Andrew—if he ever stopped to think about it—had his doubts. He had said something of the sort to Grandfather Lanark back then. Now he took another long sip of his drink and closed his eyes to savor the burning sensation in his throat.

The picture that filled his mind was not one to be savored, however. Grandfather's face loomed large, turning red, then white, in Andrew's memory. "She may call herself a follower of Christ, but her allegiance is to the antichrist in Rome!"

Andrew had tried. "But Grandfather, aren't we the ones who say it's not a matter of sacrament or ritual—only a matter of what's in your heart that counts? Aren't we the ones who say it's one's own personal faith that matters? Aren't we the ones who should be willing to listen to the testimony of others?"

"Those in the darkened grip of Rome can have no testimony."

"But—"

"I'll hear no more on it, boy. She goes out."

Andrew had spent his whole life—nearly twenty-one years—resisting his grandfather. He had always thought that when he came of age he would revolt, claim his inheritance, leave Ireland perhaps. Certainly leave Lanarks' Bawn. But he had just returned from a grueling trip. He was exhausted—physically and emotionally. Was that the night Jay Lanark won?

No, because Andrew had not changed his name or joined the Orange lodge then. Grandfather's victory had been the next year when he died and Lanarks' Bawn and his Orange sash passed to Andrew. Andrew had begun sitting at the head of the table, and riding around the fields daily, and doing all the things he said he would never do. Somehow he had become everything he had said he would never be. He could see it in himself and hated it in himself, and yet he could not stop himself. And now he was thirty-two, and he might as well be sixty-two. Or eighty-two. It was all the same.

He lunged to his feet and refilled his glass.

The cut crystal bottom was clear of amber liquid when Jay Lanark's gloating countenance appeared again. "You're a Lanark, boy. Just like me."

Andrew threw his glass at the apparition. "No! I'm an Armstrong. And I'll stay Armstrong. You haven't won yet!" For a moment he thought he heard the phantom laugh. Yes, he had managed to defy his grandfather in that one thing. He hadn't changed his name. But he knew it was a hollow victory.

A form appeared at the door. Andrew's hand gripped a cushion to throw, then realized it was Berkley. He was nearly as much of a shade as Grandfather, but still above ground. "Mr. and Mrs. Price, sir."

Andrew came to his feet, wishing he were steadier. "Tammis! So you haven't forgotten your old cousin?"

If Thomas Price had seemed Andrew's junior a few years ago, now it was doubly so. Thomas, with the fair Selma on his arm, was the image of everything Andrew had once hoped for himself.

He waved them to a chair. "Tea, Berkley. Hot and strong." Whether or not his guests felt the need, Andrew certainly did. He turned to the visitors. "How are the children?"

Andrew settled back and awaited the tea that would help clear his head, knowing nothing would be required of him beyond a nod and a smile as Tammis and Selma told the latest accomplishments of nine-year-old Robert, a strapping rider, and seven-year-old Wilma, a budding talent on the pianoforte.

Thomas and Selma had waited the required year of her family's mourning for Wilma and then had married as planned. Since then, Thomas had expanded the prosperity of Price's Farm with an ambitious horse breeding program. He now sold thoroughbreds to many of the Anglo-Irish across the island. The little chestnut mare he bought at the Rossheely Fair had dropped some of his best colts.

Andrew had toyed with the notion of undertaking a similar endeavor, but it seemed too much effort. The fields produced well, and he put more land into flax when the linen industry expanded again. Besides, Grandfather had not engaged in breeding as a business enterprise. There. He'd done it again—submitted to the tyranny of the dead. Perhaps that was because *he* was dead. In truth, *he* had died in the famine, too.

"And Wilma, the clever lass, has begun on her second sampler."

Selma was talking about wee Wilma, not her namesake, but

Andrew still caught his breath. How different life might have been if they hadn't all died.

Berkley entered with a rattling of teacups. Andrew sprang to take the tray from his hands before it all landed on the floor. "Will you do the honors?" He gestured for Selma to pour out.

Thomas took a long sip of the well-sugared drink his wife handed him. "Ah, lovely." Then he set down his cup with a satisfied sigh. "Sorry we can't stay longer. But we just came by on our way in to Newtownards. Thought you might like to go to the prayer meeting with us."

Andrew frowned. "What prayer meeting?" This was a Monday. Weren't prayer meetings usually held on Wednesdays?

Selma leaned forward, just as he had seen Wilma do so many times. "It's for the revival. So many have feared it might pass us by. The schoolmaster has a real burden for Newtownards. He has started weekly united prayer meetings—and open-airs and cottage gatherings."

"Has he now? I've read there's been a lot of ranting and singing going on. Can't see why folks would want it on their own doorstep, though." Andrew all but scalded his throat with a gulp of tea intended to keep down just such a harsh response as he knew Jay Lanark would have made. "Dashed untidy, that's what it is. Fanatics and imposters." The *Northern Whig* had treated the whole affair with biting sarcasm.

"I'm sorry to hear you feel that way, cousin." Tammis got to his feet and held out a hand to Selma. "We won't bother you further on the subject. But I can assure you the physical manifestations are but a small part—a very small part—of the Spirit's moving. Changed lives, that's what it's all about."

Andrew laughed as he followed them toward the door. "I'll believe that when I see results beyond the sway of emotion. Until then, the only praying I'll do is that the enthusiasts stay away from here."

When his callers were gone, he returned to his chair with such force that he upset his teacup on the side table. He reached for his crumpled newspaper. When Grandfather died, Andrew had no intention of replacing his reading of the more moderate *Belfast News-Letter* with the *Northern Whig*, but the *News-Letter* subscription ran out first, and he had just gone with things as they were. It was easier that way. It seemed that was the way he made most of his decisions anymore—holding to the line of least resistance.

The headlines screamed at him. "Conviction! Convulsions! Epilepsy! Insanity!" And that was the complimentary part. The paper was reporting events in Ballymena near where the first religious awakenings had taken place in mid-March. Some three thousand Presbyterians, Episcopalians, and Roman Catholics standing in heavy rain had joined in prayer and singing. Many were stricken prostrate in anxiety over their sins, while others knelt in the mud to pray over them.

And thus it had continued for more than two months. There were daily meetings for praise, prayer, Scripture reading, and exhortation, attracting thousands—*and in the busiest time of the year,* Andrew thought. When they should be working in their fields, shops, looms, and kitchens. What would all this praying do to commerce? That's was what he wanted to know.

Another article quoted a Presbyterian minister from Lisburn, who professed himself to be a good friend of the movement but was nonetheless disturbed over the manifestation of stigmata and other miraculous revelations claimed by some. He explained some of the more ingenious methods of generating these "miraculous" marks, such as writing upon the arm or hand with starch, then rubbing over the area lightly with iodine of potassium.

Andrew muttered over the depths to which people would stoop to gain money or attention—and the avidness with which such antics were greeted by the mob. "I am a believer in the great and glorious Revival," the good reverend had said, "but, since it is as much the duty of a gardener to pluck the weeds as it is his office to plant the flowers, I could not let this fanaticism and imposture to pass."

And rightly so, Andrew thought as he strode from the room, disgusted over all the hubbub. He had delayed far too long over matters of no importance when he should be riding around his fields. Grandfather Lanark would never have waited until the shadows were so long before making his daily inspection tour. Although Cal Dunleer had taken his father's place as overseer, Andrew held firmly to the farmer's foot in the field as being the best manure.

A short time later he was surveying his property with satisfaction. He had put three new fields into flax production this year, and, looking at the rich stand of shoots greening the land, he could tote up the profits in his head.

A few years back, the Ulster linen industry had nearly been wiped out by the cheaper cotton being mass-produced in Britain. And then there was the famine and its subsequent emigration—it was said one million had died and two million had emigrated. The loss of three million workers was the last straw. Wages rose until linen-spinning all but perished. That would have been the end of it had not the industry been rescued from collapse by the appearance of the power loom.

Power loom weaving did, of course, put skilled weavers out of work, but it was good for the flax-grower, so Lanarks' Bawn again grew flax.

Andrew kicked Fairling to a trot and rounded the hedgerow bordering the field. He was looking across the way to his closest barley field when a feminine voice made his mount shy sideways. Andrew raised his hand to reprimand the horse but halted mid-swing when he saw it was Bridget. Aye, she would be on her way back to the clachan from seeing to the scrubbing in the kitchen. One of the young O'Briens came in to scivvy, but she needed supervision.

"And is it yourself, Andrew Armstrong?" Her smile managed to be sweet and saucy at the same time.

"And who do you think it would be?" He hadn't meant to bark at her, but after the closeness they had shared during the days of death and starvation, the difference in their station always stung him. Sometimes Andrew could almost convince himself those times had been nothing more than a nightmare; that famine, plague, and pestilence had never swept this fair land. But there was Wilma's grave in the churchyard. And here was Bridget, bringing all the memories back with her.

"And isn't it Fairling that I've known from a wane." She stroked the horse's satiny neck. "Ah, but what a fine horse you chose at the Rossheely Fair, Andrew Armstrong. And here's me forgetting myself and stepping out to frighten the creature."

Andrew started to make a noncommittal remark and ride on, but Bridget continued.

"Sure and I wouldn't have been so wool-gathering, but I was thinking how I should speak to yourself."

"Well, that should be easy enough—you seem to be doing very well right now."

"Aye, but it's not so easy a matter. I would be going to Belfast."

"Belfast? What would you go *there* for? Is Elfrith needing something? I can get it for her when we take the next load of flax to market —been holding some for the price to rise."

"No, I mean to stay for a time."

"What!" This time it was Andrew's shout that made Fairling shy. It was unthinkable. Who would see to his meals? "Impossible! Mrs. B needs you."

"Mariad O'Brien will help her."

"And what, pray tell, do you think you'll do in Belfast?"

Bridget took a letter from her pocket and handed it up to him. He raised his eyebrows at the fine, crested paper. Paper with the imprint of the Linen Hall Library. Why would anyone be writing to Bridget on stationery like this?

It was from a Mr. Robert Young, a member of the Belfast Society for Promoting Knowledge. He professed himself to be an enthusiast for the collection of Irish music and songs. He had made a careful study of Bunting's *Ancient Irish Music*, the final version of which had been published nearly twenty years ago, and had come upon some tunes of Cashel MacHenry. Somehow he had traced the relationship to Bridget and wanted to know if she had any more songs.

"What tangled faradiddle is this? You can't be haring off to Belfast to see this Robert Young fellow. You don't know anything about him. I'll reply to this for you. Explain it's impossible."

"It's good of you to offer to trouble yourself, but there's no need. I've already done the replying."

"But that's impossible. You don't write well enough to be corresponding with some chap from the Society for Promoting Knowledge."

"Oh, but Elfrith was after teaching me. And I'm so grateful. It's a fine skill. Still, I'm glad I didn't have the means earlier, or I might not have got the songs by heart from *Seanathair*."

Andrew blinked. Was this the scrap of a child he had brought back from the ravages of death in Connacht? She'd been nothing but hair and bone and large round eyes. How long had it been since he'd seen her? *Really* seen her—as more than a cog in the household gears that saw to the setting of his meat in front of him? She had filled out remarkably. Her red-gold hair fell halfway to her waist. A memory of her singing stirred.

He thrust the letter back at her. "Aye. I'll be going to market the end of June. You can ride in with me." He spun Fairling around on the narrow path. "And you'll return with me. I'll not leave you with a stranger." He didn't wait for a reply.

Why had the encounter disturbed him so? He should be glad enough to have Brendan MacHenry's songs collected. He had thought of doing something like that himself once. Once—on the other side of the famine wall. Could he ever have been so caught up in music and poetry? It was a good thing he had taken over matters here before he lost all the business sense Grandfather had instilled in him. He used to waste time looking for a meaning to life—for some great answer to the problems of universal suffering and despair. And the answer had been here all the time. Right under his feet. Work. That was the answer.

Grandfather Lanark would be proud. *You're just like me, boy. You're a Lanark.*

This time Andrew didn't chase the shade away. Instead, he smiled at it. So, in the end Jay Lanark was right. And why not? He had been about everything else. All right, Andrew would make the final submission. When he was in Belfast, he would go to see his lawyer. He'd change his name to Lanark. Grandfather's death had allowed him to take over the fields without changing his name. But now the time had come. Let Grandfather have his victory. Let him gloat in his grave. He had little enough else to do there.

Andrew couldn't understand why the road to Belfast was so choked with traffic. Wednesday was always a busy market day, but that could hardly explain this crush. His irritation grew as they drew closer to the city. When they came to the bridge, where all the traffic poured inward, he had to wait some time even to get a place in line to cross. It was worse on the other side.

It had been his intention to let Bridget off at the Linen Hall Library and go on, collecting her again when he was finished at the market and with his attorney. This was to be the day Andrew Armstrong would become a Lanark *de jur* as well as *de facto*—in law as well as in fact.

And why not have his first name stricken as well? he thought as he waited a chance to turn right out of the flow of traffic. He had never thought much about the fact that his second name was Jay. Bitter laughter rose in his throat. That was it. Let Andrew Armstrong be dashed. He would become Jay Lanark.

However, there was no question of turning north. It was as if the globe had tilted and the whole population of Belfast—nae, of Down and Antrim—was being poured into south Belfast. There was nothing to do but follow along.

There was little use even in holding the reins. His team was forced along with the flow. Andrew's grim laughter turned to fury. How dare the fates so conspire against him? What right did all these people have to be going wherever they were going and interfere with his plans?

But Bridget bounced with delight on the seat next to him. "And have you ever seen a finer thing, Andrew Armstrong?"

He wanted to snap at her for calling him that, but he pretended to be absorbed in his non-driving.

Large numbers of people, many of them singing, poured from the Botanic Rail Station. There must have been special trains laid on for this event—whatever it was.

"Wherever so many people are going must be worth seeing," Bridget said. "And just listen to that fine music. Do you know the song?" She began humming along with a jubilant party just emerging.

Andrew had to admit that, although he had never heard the tune before, it was catchy. He struggled to apprehend the words. It was something about news—but this could hardly be a conference of journalists. Finally he sorted out the refrain: "What's the news? Whene'er we meet, you always say—What's the news?"

The carriages moved at about the same pace as the groups on foot, so he had ample time to listen. The song seemed to go on interminably. They must have been on their second time through the ditty when he realized he was listening to a gospel song:

"Oh, I have got good news to tell:
My Saviour hath done all things well,
And triumphed over death and hell,
    That's the News!
The Lamb was slain on Calvary,
    That's the News!
To set a world of sinners free,
    That's the News!"

And then it dawned on Andrew. This vast crowd—ten thousand, fifteen thousand, maybe more—was funneling into Belfast's Botanical Garden for a mammoth *revival* rally. And he was stuck in the middle of it.

He observed the people more closely, wondering what fanatics looked like at close hand. Apparently no different from anyone else, unless they were better scrubbed. The throng seemed to be made up of well-dressed, respectable-looking people carrying Bibles and hymnbooks. Except for their singing, they were as quiet and orderly as if they were going to meeting. But no Presbyterian would sing such songs in church.

Indeed, Andrew wasn't certain such singing could be truly Christian. It wasn't a metrical psalm. Could God be truly praised in any other voice? Still, he had to admit it wasn't entirely unpleasant.

Bridget, now thoroughly caught up in the spirit of the day, was singing in her clear, lyrical voice, "All hail the power of Jesus' name," along with a group on the other side of the street.

At the end of Botanic Avenue, drivers were simply leaving their carriages and proceeding on foot to the green sward between the pavilion and the conservatory. Since they were packed in so tightly, the horses could hardly wander off.

There seemed little reason not to follow. As they walked into the garden, Bridget tugged at his arm and pointed upward to the spreading tree branches. "Oh, look, Andrew. The wee wanes are like Zaccheus."

He gave her a blank stare.

"Are ye not knowing the story? Father Lynch told it often—about the man who couldn't see Jesus, so he climbed a tree—"

"Yes, yes, I know the story. But there's little telling what those youngsters will be seeing."

Anything could happen if a crowd this size got out of hand. And from what he had heard of the excesses of other prayer gatherings, Andrew was inclined to expect the worst. Someone thrust a card into his hand. Andrew felt his brows knit in a scowl as he read a printed prayer. "Grant, O God, we beseech Thee, a still greater outpouring of Thy Spirit upon our country and dominions; so as to cause a deep and wide revival of living faith in Christ, working by love and bringing forth all the fruits of the Spirit. . . . Be to our country a wall of fire round about her and the glory in the midst of her." He crumpled the card.

A man in a black robe with white bands stood on the pavilion steps and held up his hands for silence. The singing stopped, and the vast crowd quieted. The man was introduced as chairman of the meeting, Mr. John Johnston, Moderator of the General Assembly of the Presbyterian Church.

Andrew strained forward. It was all but impossible to hear. As best he could tell, the speaker welcomed them to "this great united prayer meeting which had been arranged to give information about the progress of the revival and to offer prayer for the abundant outpouring of the Holy Spirit." The man voiced praise that across Belfast, and much of the surrounding area, factories and shops had been closed in order to allow people to attend.

Andrew scowled again. Factories closed? On a Wednesday? And what about the spinning of flax—*his* flax—and the looming of linen? Did they have no orders to fill? Did they not care what happened to flax growers if they let the cotton industry get further ahead of them?

Apparently they cared more immediately that people be able to hear the proceedings—which few in the wide reaches of the gardens could do. To that end, the crowd was then divided into twenty or so groups, each with its own leader. When things were sorted out, Andrew saw with some relief that the Rev. Mr. Johnston was to lead their group. If he had to be exhorted by some ranter, it had as well be a proper Presbyterian.

Andrew certainly felt a kinship with the man's opening words: "My brothers and sisters, I must confess that, at first, I was unwilling to preside at this great gathering for fear that it might lead to excesses and give occasion to the enemies of true faith to point at improprieties."

Well, if he had to exhort, he couldn't have chosen a more appropriate subject than avoiding excess, Andrew thought.

Their leader continued. "Let us set the Lord God before us and so realize His awful presence in this place that good may be done and God may be glorified. We are especially met to do homage to the Holy Spirit, whose convincing and converting power has been so strikingly manifested amongst us for these several months. Let us not resist Him."

He had barely finished speaking when a girl who could not have been yet twenty years old faced the group. She was not a pretty lass, but there was a shine about her that was most refreshing. In plain words, spoken in a clear voice, she told that she had found peace on the previous Sabbath evening and that she was happy in the Lord. "Come to Jesus," she concluded, almost as an afterthought.

The effect of her simple invitation was like an electric shock. People all around Andrew dropped to their knees. "Lord Jesus, have mercy on me, a sinner" and similar cries came from all directions. On every side, people exhorted those who were seeking salvation, others wept and prayed aloud for mercy, some praised God for salvation, some were singing, "He took me from a fearful pit, and from the miry clay, and on a rock He set my feet . . ."

Bridget stood with hands clasped, tears streaming down her face.

Andrew tugged roughly at her arm. "Come on. I've seen enough."

She startled as if waking, crossed herself jerkily, and turned to him. "Oh. Yes, enough. Oh, yes." She followed him as he fought his way through the throng.

Movement became easier as they neared the edge of the garden, but untangling the carriage was another matter. By the time they were moving, it was too late to accomplish anything at the market—if they had even held one. Imagine canceling market day for a religious gathering. Andrew's disgust knew no bounds.

They were making their way slowly back southward, having veered considerably out of their way in an attempt to avoid traffic, when Andrew heard that blasted song again, "What's the News?" A group of young voices shouted out the question.

The answer came from their fellows on the other side of the pavement. "Oh, tell them you've begun to pray, that's the news!"

They seemed to be boys from some factory or home or school, all under the leadership of a man in clerical garb. At the end of the song they formed into a more orderly procession and began a new hymn:

> "Here we suffer grief and pain,
> Here we meet to part again,
> In heaven we'll part no more.
> Oh, that will be joyful,
> Joyful, joyful . . ."

The final joyful was cut off by their black-suited leader. "Boys, boys, that's fine singing, that is. But I'd ask ye to pass quietly here now."

Those in the back were still singing, unable to hear him, so the portly man jumped up on a cart beside the pavement and held out his arms. "Boys! Boys, hear me. That's a fine testimony to the power of the Spirit burning in your hearts."

Several cries of "Praise Jesus!" interrupted him.

"That's fine, but I'd have ye quieten now. Ye'll be noting we're approaching Durham Street, and I'm fearing our singing might be of disturbance to our Catholic neighbors. I ask you to desist. Let us bear silent witness to the love and courtesy our Savior asks us to show to one another as Christians."

The boys nodded assent, and the minister jumped down and set forth with a wave of his hand. "I'll give the signal when ye can start again, lads, when we're in the Shankill. We are not to provoke one another to wrath."

Andrew was soon able to turn eastward, but what he had just witnessed impressed him more than all the prayers, songs, exhortations, and phenomena he had heard or seen. Upwards of forty boys marched toward the Falls in a quiet, mannerly order, many with radiant smiles on their faces, and not a hint of a song or slogan that might be deemed provocative to that solidly Catholic neighborhood.

So could there be something beyond emotion to this business of being stricken by the Spirit? He laughed and whipped up his team. Only two weeks until the Glorious Twelfth. Then they would see.

76

This year promised to be something special in the way of Orange marches. It was an anniversary year—the tenth anniversary of Dolly's Brae, when thirteen hundred Orangemen from around Castlewellan had chosen to march through an exclusively Catholic neighborhood with drums, songs, and loaded rifles. They had been met by a thousand Catholic Ribbonmen armed with pitchforks, pikes, and muskets.

No one ever knew who fired the first shot, but at the end of the day, the thirty or more corpses lying in the road were all wearing green ribbons.

Then, only two years ago, intense sectarian rioting had raged for ten days in the very area of working-class Belfast through which those revival boys had walked in silence.

So they would see, indeed. Andrew mused as he set out Grandfather Lanark's orange sash for Mrs. B to press. This year his lodge would support their brothers in County Antrim by joining the march from Ballymena to Toome. It promised to be as fine a gathering as any that celebrated the glorious anniversary of King Billy's victory. Finer than most, since the Ahoghill Old Fair was to be held nearby with liquor flowing freely to wet a man's throat after miles of dusty singing, and plenty of good card games and rousing cockfights for lively entertainment after the march.

Andrew couldn't remember ever having looked forward to a Glorious Twelfth more than he did this year. Now he understood the pleasure Grandfather Lanark used to take in such doings. He was certainly in the mood for a rousing march. A good loud band and a few rounds of singing "Ye Loyalists of Ireland" was just what he needed to shake off the depression he had been in for weeks.

The prayer meeting Tammis and Selma had invited him to had apparently borne fruit in Newtownards and Comber. Nightly prayer meetings were attended by upwards of two hundred people all around the district. Andrew had even seen people kneel down in the Newtownards marketplace. Whenever there was a meeting announced, people dropped their other activities and went—anytime or anyplace. Even on

Scrabo. Andrew grimaced at the thought of the open-air meetings being held almost in his backyard.

But that was better that than those in town, where weavers stopped their looms at the sound of singing and women dropped their muslin or went off to join the audience with their hoops in their hands.

Well, they had their revival. And much good it might do them. What any of them would do when the linen industry collapsed, Andrew couldn't imagine. And all for a lot of psalm singing.

Still, he had to admit that the revival songs had more life to them than the metricals. If there was any long-lasting result of all this brouhaha that he approved of, it would be the newly installed organ in the Presbyterian Church. No sense letting the Methodists have all the good songs. But an Orange band and a good pounding of Lambeg drums could beat any organ he ever heard, and Andrew had never been in a finer mood to raise his voice.

> "Remember your allegiance,
> Be this your Battle Cry,
> For Protestant Ascendancy
> In church and State we'll die!"

He sang at the top of his voice as he drove northward the next day.

> "Ye Loyalists of Ireland,
> Come, rally round the throne!"

He had started through the ballad again when he began to wonder if he had his directions wrong. The lodge master had been very clear about the matter. They were to meet at Broughshane to form for the march. But as he drew near, something seemed amiss. He heard no booming of drums calling all loyal marchers to order, though the area seemed lively enough. Indeed, there were people everywhere, including the usual clutter of children and chickens that lined every march route.

He was almost there before he heard a boom. And it was not the cadence of a Lambeg drum. It was the booming voice of a man addressing a large crowd all besashed in vibrant orange.

Andrew couldn't understand how he could have arrived late. He hurried forward, not wishing to miss the Loyalist Charge or any last minute instructions

"And so I can tell you that all are knit together in one holy band of Christian fellowship. The Presbyterian not annoying the Episcopalian, the Episcopalian not vexing the Presbyterian. I thank God that, in every convert I have spoken to, all their sectarianism fled and their love to the human family was such that if they could gather all their Roman Catholic neighbors in their arms and carry them up to the third heaven, they would do so."

Andrew frowned. This was the strangest Loyalist Charge he had ever heard. He stood apart from the group and listened.

"I tell you, gentlemen, this brotherly love is a hallmark of the revival. I would say, even, that it is *the* hallmark. Neighbors once at variance now embrace each other. Animosities have passed away. Where there has been enmity, now there is love. Where there was revenge, now there is forgiveness . . ."

Jay Lanark's orange sash rested heavy around Andrew's shoulders as if it had stones attached to the ends. He had come to march for the power and industry that had made Ulster prosper, for the traditions his grandfather had lived for, for the values and lifestyle he held to and sweated for every day. He had not come for a revivalist rant.

Andrew turned on his heel and returned to his carriage. If they wanted to march for prayer and sermonizing, let them. If they wanted to sing psalms instead of Loyalist ballads, let them. He'd have no part of it. He knew where the real action would be anyway. Why wait until after the march? He'd get an early start. A good cockfight could take a man's mind off anything, and people came from miles around to the sport at Crea Rocks.

He wasn't disappointed. A rowdy crowd was gathered about the ring, cheering. Andrew put his money on a long-tailed Rochester Red to beat a scrappy-looking Wendham Gray. The Red attacked viciously, but the Gray was a stayer. The Red drew blood three times before Wendham stumbled and Rochester could move in for the kill. Andrew, who had been leaning over the pit in his enthusiasm, drew back to wipe the sweat from his brow and discovered he was spattered with blood.

He wiped his palm on his handkerchief quickly before any should see. The stigmata phenomenon had been disproved. He wanted nothing to do with even the looks of any such thing.

The next pair of cocks were paraded around the ring by their owners.

And then a group of newcomers caught Andrew's attention. He stared. What were three *parsons* doing at a cockfight?

But the matter soon became clear. As Crea Rocks was annually the scene of carousing, cockfighting, and cardsharping, it seemed the revivalists had scheduled a service here. And looking beyond the cockpit, Andrew judged that nearly two thousand people had responded to their call. He turned back to place his money on Shaker's Blue as the enthusiasts began singing "What's the News?" That song again. He tried to shut it out and concentrate on the cockfight.

"For us He bowed His sacred head,
For us His precious blood was shed,
And now He's risen from the dead,
That's the News!"

Andrew's cock was dragged from the pit, a mass of blood-soaked feathers, by the time the song ended. He turned to escape from the whole reddened area but could not shove a path through the throng that now tightened up the better to hear the preacher.

The parson announced his text. "Before the cock crows, thou shalt deny me thrice."

Andrew almost expected to hear an accompanying crow from the cockpit. The silence that followed was more chilling.

"Peter was in the same predicament as Paul later found himself when he wrote, 'For what I would, that do I not; but what I hate, that do I.' Perhaps some of you—nae, nae, all of us—all have found ourselves hating what we do, doing the very thing we said we would never do—"

Andrew nearly knocked to the ground the woman behind him in his effort to flee. What right did that preacher have to single him out? What did he know about what Andrew Armstrong did and did not want to do? How dare he accuse him of hating what he did? He *wanted* to be like his grandfather. Of course he did. Jay Lanark had been a fine man. And Andrew had decided more than to be like him. He would *be* him.

What I would, that do I not; but what I hate, that do I. The words rang in his head until he would have thrust his hands over his ears had the crush of the crowd given him room.

He had just forced his way to the back when a young red-haired woman approached him with a smile. He would merely have brushed past her had she not looked so much like Bridget. As it was, he took the card she held out to him and jammed it into his pocket.

By the time Andrew reached Lanarks' Bawn, he wasn't sure whether he was hearing Lambeg drums, thunder, or the pounding of his own heart, but whatever it was, he had to exorcise the ghosts that compelled him. Perhaps that was it—who would have thought one could hear the feet of marching ghosts?

Was it only because it was the Glorious Twelfth that he felt driven by all those who had died in the '41, at Drogheda, at the Boyne, in the 1798 Rising, and in the Potato Famine? All those of *both* sides? Even as the thought formed, he sensed a glimmer of hope breaking in. The very fact that he could ask such a question must mean that Jay Lanark hadn't won after all. For Andrew's grandfather there had been no question of there being two sides to any matter. If Andrew could question the Orange position, he was not Jay Lanark. And if he wasn't Jay Lanark, Andrew Armstrong could ask his own questions and find his own answers.

With the drumming still pounding in his head, he made his way to his study and took down the large, crumbling Bible from the highest shelf. The fact that he had to blow a cloud of dust from the cracked leather cover was further evidence of Mrs. B's waning vigor. And of Jay Lanark's absence. Grandfather had regularly taken down the volume to point out the name of every Lanark so carefully inscribed there: Calum who had built the Bawn. Dougal, his son who had fought with Cromwell. David and Graham, father and son who had fought at the Boyne . . .

But now Andrew focused on something Grandfather had never pointed out. Other names were there as well: Rory, who had married a Catholic and gone to live at Seaton Court. Isobel, who had married an O'Brien. Katrina, who had married Robert Price. And Aileen . . . That was the one who had run off with the MacHenry.

As his family tree lay spread out before him, it was as if his own life branched and blossomed. It wasn't necessary to follow one narrow path to be true to his heritage. He wasn't predestined by birth to a course of action or of thought. That was exactly what he had once said himself when arguing with Grandfather.

He had tried to find purpose in carrying on the Lanarks' Bawn tradition—with all the rules and rigidity he had once tried to reject. But one could not only reject. One must also accept—open oneself to meaning, to direction, to a higher power and purpose than oneself and one's own rules. One must embrace life and life's Creator.

Putting his hand in his pocket, he felt the card that girl had given him. It was headed "My Covenant." He read it through. Slowly. Three times.

> I take God the Father to be my God.
> I take Christ the Son to be my Savior.
> I take the Holy Spirit to be my Sanctifier.
> I take the Word of God to be my Rule.
> I take the people of God to be my people.
> I dedicate my whole self to the Lord.
> And I do this deliberately.
>   and sincerely.
>   and freely.
>   and for ever.

He had just signed and dated the card when there was a light knock at the door.

"Come."

The threatening storm had rolled on, taking the dark clouds with it. Now the deep golden sunlight of a summer evening shone through the tall windows lining one side of the room. It fell on Bridget as she entered. The fact that Andrew was no longer hungry had nothing to do with the fine roast duck surrounded with potatoes that she was carrying.

Andrew took the platter from her and set it aside. Then he turned back to embrace Bridget and his new life.

77

Mary put the manuscript aside, stretched, turned on the radio, and reached for her hairbrush. She had just time to get to the CCC for play practice. She did hope it would go well this evening. It had to. In the almost two weeks since they had begun again on the project they had made considerable progress but not nearly enough. She would describe their successes as uneven at best.

At least Sheila's posters were brilliant. And the young people had distributed them all over Belfast. Which would be great if their production was good. If it wasn't, it would just mean that many more people would watch them fall on their faces.

Liam seemed to have steadied since the scene at the park. He hadn't accepted the counseling Courage offered, but neither had he joined the IRA—so far as anyone knew. She had to be thankful for that.

She gave a final, swift glance to her image in the mirror: slim-fitting jeans, long-sleeved white shirt over a navy blue turtleneck, sleek golden hair. She slung her brown leather bag over her shoulder and reached to shut off the radio, then paused as the announcer's voice caught her attention.

"As the twelfth of August nears, tensions mount over planned marches in Londonderry and Belfast. Authorities say they fear the Apprentice Boys' marches may produce an even more violent confrontation than the sectarian violence that erupted over July's traditional Glorious Twelfth marches. Spokesmen from both communities—"

Mary snapped off the set. She had enough to worry about. She was glad that the church was holding special prayer meetings, and she knew that other congregations were doing the same. She just wished she had more faith. No matter how hard she tried, she couldn't shake the feeling that the whole country was on a giant treadmill, destined to repeat the same rounds of violence over and over.

On the M1 to Belfast, Mary shifted Sheila's little car to a higher gear, but she couldn't shift her mind out of its depression. Were she and Gareth on a giant treadmill, too? She envisioned each of them running round and round in interlocking wheels. At the moments those wheels touched, their love flared a sure, bright flame. But the eternal turning of the days kept flinging them apart so that they made no progress. Sometimes it seemed each turning pulled them further apart.

One of the things she loved most about Gareth was his compassion—his deep caring about these people, his work for them and the future of this country. She gritted her teeth. She tried, she really tried, to be as selfless as he was.

At the CCC she braked and shifted down to make the turn into her parking space.

Inside, she was met by a buzz of activity. This was to be their last rehearsal at the Centre. Next week they would begin rehearsals at Noah's Ark. That cheering thought gave her a sense of progress.

A CD player lilted out a lively Irish melody while Fiona directed a line of step dancers. Mary smiled, noting how quickly Becca and Julie had caught the basic technique, even if they weren't as light on their feet as Fiona. Debbie appeared to be a natural. Her long, slim shorts-clad legs moved effortlessly, and her dangling silver earrings swung in rhythm. It looked as though that was one part of *A Night in Olde Belfast* that Mary didn't have to worry about.

Sheila hurried across the room, her countenance shining like the gold silk blouse she wore. "Good news! We've just had a reply from the Development Council. They are terrifically interested in what you're doing. They're sending a whole delegation to the program. If we pull this off, it means we're almost assured funding for the youth center."

"Oh, that's great!" Mary tried to match her excitement and put out of her mind the niggling fear that said, *Yes, but if you fizzle, that'll tear the whole thing.* She approached the dancers, clapping her hands. "Super! You're doing a great job. And I've got some really great news." She looked around. "But where are the rest of our musicians? I want to tell everyone at once."

Where *were* the musicians? Why were they dancing to recorded music? The musicians needed more practice than anyone else. Liam here and Martin she didn't worry about, but Tommy had missed many practices lately, and Lila's harp was really what held the whole thing together.

As if they had heard her question, Lila came running down the concrete stairway that led from the upper offices. Tommy followed her, one hand gripping the bannister, the other held out in a pleading gesture. Neither carried instruments. When Lila reached the lounge, Mary could see that her eyes were red and puffy.

Tommy came directly to Mary. "You tell her. Tell her it's not about me—it's for the kids."

Lila shook her head, tears still glimmering on her dark lashes. She turned back to Tommy with both hands out. "I've told you and told you—it's not me you have to convince. It's my parents. They're afraid—"

Tommy put his hands on her shoulders. "Lila, you're twenty-one years old. You're old enough to decide whether you play your clarsach in a program or not."

She shivered. "But Da says the IRA might . . ." She swallowed. "They might disrupt the whole show!"

"And your parents think I'm working with the Army." He turned his back to her, his hands gripping both sides of his head.

"No, they don't—" she started, then stopped. "Well, the police said—"

Liam rose from the floor where he'd been sitting, idly strumming a few chords. "There it is, man. See, it doesn't matter what you do—you'll get blamed for it anyway. It's better to act."

"Liam," Mary said. "You promised."

He shrugged. "Said I'd do the show. Didn't say what I'll do after."

The show. That brought Mary back to her job. "Wait, everybody. I've got good news. Please. If we can just work together for a few more days. Just till the middle of August." She sensed Lila edging toward the door. "Please. Just for tonight. If we can have a really good rehearsal tonight, then maybe we can work something out." She turned toward Lila. "Please, we really need you."

By a combination of Mary's cajolery and Sheila's good news the moment was rescued, and the rehearsal went on. They finished the musical numbers and were just beginning the play when the outside door opened, and Philip and Paddy O'Reilley walked through to Philip's office. Mary hoped the serious look on their faces wasn't a harbinger of more bad news.

She turned back to the action in the Bruin cottage. The characters lacked the magical lyricism Yeats's poetry required for the play to be a success. But at least they all seemed to know their lines. That was a major hurdle crossed.

Liam fell to his knees, mourning Maire's death, and for an instant Mary felt her throat tighten. Yes, the magic was there—mostly too far below the surface to be seen—but it was there. If only she could bring it out.

Behind her, the office door opened. Paddy came out first. Mary's spirits rose. The old twinkle was back in his eyes and a broad smile on his ruddy face. "Well, there's good news and bad news and good news. But what did you expect? This is Ireland. First bit of good news is that Philip has been invited to speak at the peace rally in Dublin this weekend."

That announcement was greeted with enthusiasm. But then an uneasy quiet settled over the room. He had said bad news too.

"I won't mess you about. The bad news is that plans for cross-border cooperation programs have bogged down." Such announcements were so normal that reactions amounted to shrugs and raised eyebrows. "The one for a youth camp is the one I feel worst about. I'd worked hardest on that, and we had a good program set up—one that some of you boys and girls would maybe have liked to join. That's why I'm appealing for your help now."

Warning flags went up in Mary's head. They didn't need another failing project to rescue. They had more on their plate than they could begin to handle now. "Can it wait until after the show, Paddy? We've got those people from the council coming—"

"Aye, that's why we need to do this now. It'll clinch the leisure center sure if I can tell them how your young people banded together to work cross-border as well as cross-community."

"Paddy, there isn't time—"

He wasn't listening. "All I need is the leaders from each side of the street." He looked at Debbie and Liam. "Just a quick trip to Dublin. I've got it all set up. And since Philip says he needs to meet his URU people in Enniskillen anyway—"

Paddy bounded on, explaining, while Mary groped for a chair. She needed to see a map to be certain, but she was pretty sure Dublin was anything but on the way to Enniskillen. This would require at least two, probably three, days away. Right when they were in such a critical time crunch.

"Oh, can we go to the peace rally, too?" Becca never missed anything.

"Dublin! Cool!" Julie was always right behind her.

"Gareth and Liam can bring their guitars. Imagine singing *Bind Us Together* at a peace rally!"

The twins seemed to have taken over the peace rally plans. The next thing Mary knew, they would be getting up an Irish/American exchange and putting her in charge of it.

In the end, the same group that had journeyed to the west coast crowded into the blue minibus and joined Paddy's expedition south the next day. Mary wasn't quite certain how it had all come about, and she didn't know why Tommy was there, but she suspected it might have been a compassionate move on Philip's part to get him away from his girlfriend troubles.

Oh, well. Things were out of her control. She might as well enjoy herself. She'd tucked Philip's final manuscript in her bag. If nothing else, she might have time to get some reading done while the others were in meetings.

She was really pleased to be getting to see Dublin. Besides, she could always hope that the scheme might result in some time alone with Gareth. She looked at him, sitting next to her on the seat but a hundred miles away mentally.

He looked back with a sigh. "I wish I could think of something."

"Something for what?"

"The Ulster Reconciliation Union meeting in Enniskillen."

"The one you missed last time."

"That's right. They want to promote a nonpolitical, really grassroots program—something that will make a change inside people—where, of course, it all has to start. But no one has been able to come up with a fresh idea."

Mary laughed. "Sounds like they're looking for a revival." Then she paused. "Seriously, I just read about an amazing one here in 1859."

Gareth nodded. "Yes—but again, that was mostly only on one side of the road. Anything that doesn't reach all the people won't work."

"What about this peace rally?"

"Oh, aye. A fine thing. But it doesn't go deep enough. We need something more."

Mary wished with all her heart that she had something to offer.

They passed the enormous security installations on the border at Newry. She could sense Liam tense as they stopped at the checkpoint, as if he were already IRA and feared inspection. Then they headed straight south toward Drogheda.

She considered the troubled lives in their one small vehicle. How much of that was a legacy of "the curse of Cromwell"? Fortunately, no one else seemed to be thinking of that particularly gloomy subject.

Philip did, however, take a westward turning off the motorway. "We'll just take a little jaunt up here, since I know Mary's interested in history."

It wasn't Cromwell he had in mind. "King Billy's Glen," Philip said. They drove up a beautiful meadow where a smooth, swift-flowing river ran a silver ribbon through the deep emerald. He pointed out the knoll to the northwest where King James's troops had massed. Today the only activity was two little black water hens that scurried through thick brush to their nests alongside the river.

Philip and Paddy were at their usual jovial bickering over the long-term results of the Battle of the Boyne, but Mary concentrated on the scenery. The glen was grown solid. Ivy and moss clung to oak and elm. Sheep grazed in the meadow beyond. She had seldom seen a more secluded, peaceful scene. There was no interpretative display, no visitors' center, no audiovisual presentation. Just green grass, silver water, and cream-colored sheep. And a large green and orange sign with flags fluttering atop, proclaiming "Boyne Battlefield Crossing, 1690."

"There was a stone obelisk down by the river at the place King Billy crossed. But the IRA blew it up in 1922." Philip offered the information without comment.

A few minutes later the Boyne was behind them, and Paddy was pointing out the window to a tall, bare mountain streaking by. "Ah, and there now's the Hill of Slane. And isn't it a grand sight? The very spot where St. Patrick lit the Pascal Fire on Easter Eve."

"Oh." Mary hoped it was a reasonably intelligent sounding oh.

"And just down here—" they whipped around a corner and turned onto a southbound road "—you'll see Tara in just a minute."

"OK."

"Ah, there. The green hill through the trees."

Well, everything was green through the trees. But one mound did seem taller than the rest.

"Home of the High Kings of Ireland for centuries. And doesn't the very name conjure up images of the glories of a civilization long silenced? It was from here that King Laoire saw Patrick's flame on Slane. The High King had Patrick brought to him in chains, because the king had forbidden anyone to light a fire that night. But when the druids saw Saint Patrick's fire, they said it was a flame that could never be extinguished. Laoire gave Patrick permission to preach Christianity in Ireland—so it's seeming the druids knew what they were talking about.

"There's not a lot to see there now—not with the physical eye, you understand. But for those of us with an eye for the spiritual—ah, well . . . And there's the Lia Fail still standing in the center of it all."

"Oh! The Lia Fail!" Now he had Mary's attention. She smiled as Paddy waxed eloquent over the ancient Stone of Destiny, which cried out its approval at the inauguration of a true High King. She had spent a whole summer tracking the Stone of Scone, which some believed to have come from the Lia Fail, and she well knew that particular piece of Irish history.

Paddy barely had time to catch his breath before he pointed out the other side. "And there's New Grange." And since Paddy never needed much time to catch his breath, he went on, telling her about the stone age grave—older than the pyramids.

Well, it was interesting. And she appreciated his pointing out the sights, when he would probably have rather been talking strategy with Philip. She had started her summer anxious to learn all she could of Irish history. But now she was feeling just a bit overdosed—especially as the more she learned of history here, the more she understood how deep the problems around her today were.

She suddenly felt she would rather simply focus on the present—even if it led only to shallow, short-term solutions. Right now she would settle for any solution that would just last long enough for Gareth and her to get back across the Irish Sea to Scotland.

They crested a small hill, and Paddy threw out his hands. "Ah, and isn't that a sight to gladden the heart of any true Irishman—even one from occupied Ireland?" It was a sign of the depth of their friendship that Philip smiled in assent as Paddy continued. "'Dublin's fair city'—*Dubh Linn*. That's meaning the Dark Pool to those without the gift of the Gaelic. And running right through the middle, the River Liffey—the River of Life." Paddy glanced at his watch. "Ah, fine. Ye did a brisk job of the driving, Philip. We'll just have time for a wee ride about before our meeting."

Philip raised an eyebrow. "That Irish time, Paddy? You know how I feel about being late to meetings."

Paddy laughed. "Ah, if it's Irish time you're on, we'll have time for a meal." He turned to Mary. "You know what they say: the Irish have just one meal a day—all day." Then back to Philip. "That's it, just turn down O'Connell Street here. The colleen will be wanting to have a wee peek at the GPO."

Philip shook his head. "Only in Dublin would the General Post Office be the first place you'd take a tourist."

It was, however, a magnificent building with an impressive portico lined with enormous Ionic columns.

"The scene of the 1916 Rising," Paddy said in the same tone of voice he might have used concerning an ancient church. "It was the main stronghold of the volunteers fighting for independence." He pointed to the middle of the street. "Ah, and we'll just take a wee peek at the Parnell monument."

"You'll be spending all day showing her statues of your troublemakers, Paddy." But Philip paused as requested before a fine stone column topped by a bronze flame. At the base was the statue of the powerful member of Parliament who led the fight for Irish Home Rule in the late nineteenth century—until a scandal with a colleague's wife brought his downfall.

At the next embellishment to Dublin's main thoroughfare, however, Paddy did not suggest they stop. He merely waved a freckled hand at a fountain splashing forth water over the head of a marble female. "Aye, a bit of local art more popularly known as The Floozie in the Jacuzzi.

"And the Abbey Theatre is just a block up there."

"Oh!" Now he had Mary's full attention. How she would love to see *The Playboy of the Western World* or *Juno and the Paycock* at the very theater that gave them birth.

At the foot of the street, Paddy pointed out further statues, but Becca had a low tolerance for historical sights. "Where's Molly Malone?"

"Aren't there any shops?" Julie seconded her sister's restlessness.

"Just you wait. Along here in a minute—some of the best shopping in the world." Paddy O'Reilley wasn't given to understatement.

Across O'Connell bridge, bustling Grafton Street's tangle of colorful shops and pubs were crowded with patrons being serenaded by street musicians, all watched over by a life-sized bronze statue of Sweet Molly Malone pushing her wheelbarrow of cockles and mussels and calling, "Alive, alive-o."

"Now, we'll let you out right here," Philip said. "Sweet Molly makes a good meeting place. Say in two or two and a half hours." He pulled a map of the city from the glove box and handed it to Mary. "You're centrally located here."

She found Grafton Street, then followed his finger to the west. "Right here at Christ Church Cathedral is *Dublina*, a reconstruction of life in medieval Dublin. Twins might enjoy that if they get tired of shopping."

"Or run out of money—which is more likely." Mary winked at her sisters.

"Back over here—" he pointed to the east of Grafton "—is the National Museum. Some of the finest Early Christian art in existence: Saint Patrick's Bell, the Tara Brooch, Viking relics . . ."

Mary could see her sisters' eyes glazing over. "That's all right, Philip. Thanks."

"Ah, but for my money, the Book of Kells is the best thing in Dublin," Paddy spoke up.

"Oh, yes. I'd love to see that!"

Philip pointed to Trinity College on the map. "Right there. Easy walking distance. But you may have to queue. Very popular exhibit."

Mary's face fell. She would gladly stand in line for as long as it took to see the world's most beautiful book. But there was little chance she could talk Becca and Julie into the idea.

Tommy must have seen her disappointment. "I'm not really needed at your meeting, am I, Philip?" he said. "I could show the girls around. Leave Mary free to see what she wants."

Philip not only agreed but, even better, suggested that Gareth join Mary, since his main purpose in coming was to attend the Enniskillen meeting tomorrow. So she watched her sisters happily trip off with their escort in search of fish and chips.

Mary and Gareth walked along the crowded sidewalk hand in hand. To their left was the Ionic-columned Bank of Ireland, built in the eighteenth century to house the Irish Parliament. Across the street, they turned toward the Corinthian portico of Trinity College.

But in jarring contrast to the classical architecture, here they were confronted with reminders of the turmoil on this small island. A black and white sign strapped to a lamppost blared: "Dublin's prisoners —Britain's hostages."

Mary wasn't even sure she understood what they were saying, but the sentiment was the same as that which moved the rebels to the action that leveled O'Connell Street nearly a hundred years ago. She breathed much easier when the next three lampposts held announcements of the peace rally to be held that evening in Phoenix Park.

Then they entered the wide quadrangle of Trinity College.

"Oh, my." Mary looked at the queue snaking past the buildings that surrounded the grassy square. But she really didn't mind. It was a beautiful day, and she was sharing it with the man she loved. It was good just to be standing there chatting about nothing much in particular. Just being together.

They talked about their hopes for the success of the peace rally—especially that it would get good media coverage. Then Gareth told her a little of what he hoped to accomplish at tomorrow's meeting. She smiled and agreed. But at the moment she felt she would have smiled and agreed to anything he chose to say.

And then they were at the library.

Mary was disappointed to learn that the famous Book of Kells wasn't actually made by Saint Columba's own hand. It was probably done by monks from Iona when Viking attacks drove them to Kells in the year 807.

But there was no disappointment when she walked around the well-lighted glass case containing the actual book. The ancient tome had been rebound with each gospel in a separate volume so that more could be displayed at one time. The pages were turned weekly. Mary tried to calculate how long it would take a person to see the entire work at that rate, but she abandoned calculations to lose herself in the detailed beauty of the page displayed before her.

Even after they left the college and sat in a quiet shop over afternoon tea, she couldn't quit thinking about the beauty of the work she had seen and the endless hours of devotion that had been poured out by countless monks working in the most primitive of conditions. The overwhelming thing was not the time involved, the infinite attention to detail, or the rich creativity, but rather the love for the Word of God that the production of such a treasure exemplified.

And then they had to hurry back to Molly Malone to meet their group.

Spirits were high in the minibus. Debbie and Liam had apparently impressed the committee with their enthusiastic talk about their youth councils and how they were working together to build a leisure center. Apparently Liam had kept his sympathies for the IRA well hidden. She could hope he had even had a change of heart. Debbie was glowing about what a fine idea she thought the exchange program was. She would love to spend a summer living in Dublin.

She was even more enthusiastic when Philip turned into Phoenix Park. "Oh, this is beautiful! What a great flower garden. My mum would love it."

Paddy explained with the considerable pride of a born Dubliner that this was the largest enclosed public park in Europe. And there was the residence of the president of the Republic of Ireland. "And the American ambassador's residence . . ." He turned in his seat with a wink for Mary.

By now the traffic was increasing enough that even Philip was forced to slow down. A green double-decker bus draped with white ribbons lumbered in front of them, bringing people from downtown to the park. Philip found a parking spot, and they joined the crowd funneling toward a high, white cross. Somehow that made the spot seem perfect for a peace rally. What better symbol of peace and unity?

A smiling, red-haired young mother with a fat baby in a pram and three young children smiled at Mary. The little girl closest to her held out a white ribbon.

"Oh, thank you!" Then she saw that workers everywhere were handing out ribbons. She was delighted to be part of the intent throng, all wearing white ribbons and waving homemade peace posters. "Give Us Back Our Peace" "Ceasefire" "No More Bombs" It was particularly poignant that so many of the signs had apparently been made by children. And it was important that this was in the south. A vast majority of these people would be avid Nationalists, like Paddy. But they did not support the violence that had torn their island for thirty years.

The CCC delegation edged as close to the speaker's platform as they could, and Mary looked around, wondering how many people were there. Thousands, surely. As far as she could see there were hopeful faces, white ribbons, waving posters.

A beautiful black-haired girl went to the microphone and sang "Lord, Make Me an Instrument of Thy Peace." The response following her song was warm and encouraging, but there was a seriousness to the occasion that kept down any of the elation usually shown at a concert.

The mood was neither jubilant nor militant, as Mary had rather expected it to be. She almost had the feeling of being in church.

The event was thoroughly ecumenical. Father Eamonn, a Catholic priest, prayed for the victims of violence and that God would grant political leaders on both sides of the divide "the serenity to accept the things they cannot change, the courage to change the things they can, and the wisdom to know the difference." Many in the crowd responded with fervent amens or crossed themselves.

A Presbyterian pastor spoke, followed by a Methodist minister, then a Church of Ireland archdeacon, all expressing the deep desire of their people for peace. And then Philip took the stand, and Mary pressed farther forward.

"There is good news!" His proclamation was met with smiling, though reserved, anticipation.

"The peace we all seek is possible. But we must seek it at the right source. Not in politics, not in arms, but in the One who has called us to live in peace. There will be a political settlement—soon, we hope. But there have been political settlements before. None have lasted. Lasting peace won't be just a political settlement. Lasting peace must start with each one of us. The Prince of Peace will give us peace within ourselves to give to others and to spread over our land.

"When there is peace in the heart, there will be peace in the home. When there is peace in the home, there will be peace in the nation. Pray for the peace of Ireland. But first, pray for God's peace within your own heart."

He turned to Gareth and Liam, who stood on the platform with him, carrying their guitars. "Bind us together, Lord. Bind us together with cords that cannot be broken . . ."

Most of the crowd seemed to know the song, and those who didn't picked it up quickly. "Bind us together with love."

They were on the second time through when people began taking one another's hands. "There is only one God, there is only one King . . ." And then, with hands locked, people raised their arms, swaying in rhythm with the song. "Bind us together with cords that cannot be broken."

The rally ended with a full minute of silence. All across the largest park in Europe, thousands of people bowed, seeking the love that would bind them together.

At every exit, workers offered pages of the peace book for any who wished to sign a petition urging all leaders and people to work for peace. Mary wholeheartedly wanted to sign. Her one signature wouldn't make any difference to Irish leaders. But it made a difference to her. It was a concrete act, putting her name on the line. It would make her feel more a part of these people. But she didn't know about the proprieties. Perhaps one had to be a registered voter.

She approached the table. "Is it all right for an American to sign?"

"Oh, and is it your first trip to Ireland?" A ruddy-faced man smiled at her.

Mary said that, indeed, it was her first visit.

"Well, may it never be your last!" He held out a pen, and Mary thought of the irony that the Irish were the most welcoming, accepting people in the world—to everyone but each other.

78

They were perhaps an hour out of Dublin the next morning when Philip stopped in the center of a small town. "And would you like to take a wee peek at what's left of Saint Columcille's monastery?"

"You mean we're in Kells?" Mary had read about the monastery yesterday at the exhibit, but she'd had no idea they would be driving through the town.

"That's right. Thought you'd like to see where the book was made."

"Oh, yes, thank you." She bounded out and up the narrow street.

Kells had been raided four times by Vikings after the monks had fled there to escape Norse raids on Iona. But in the warm gold of an Irish summer morning it was easy to recapture the peace of the place that had given the world The Book of Kells.

Mary was fascinated by St. Columcille's House, which was really a tiny church. A plaque said that Columba had founded the monastery around the year 550, before he established work on Iona. And monks who returned here from Iona two hundred fifty years later produced the famous book. Dark green firs encircled the churchyard, and invisible birds sang from their boughs, just as they must have hundreds of years ago.

As they returned to the minibus, Mary couldn't shake the feeling that had been pushing at her and growing in intensity ever since she'd seen The Book of Kells. It had been increased by the devotional atmosphere of the peace rally yesterday. She ran a finger over the white peace ribbon she still wore pinned to her lapel.

A gentle floating mist bathed the countryside as they continued their trek northward across rolling farmland. Mary sat in thought beside Gareth, trying to find a focus for the thoughts chasing around in her head: Kells, the monastery and the book, the timelessness and power of the Word of God, the contribution of His ministers who had achieved things of lasting value, the longing of the people expressed at the rally yesterday.

It was odd, the change the past twenty-four hours had made in her feelings. Now she agreed with Gareth—everything they had been working on was too shallow. A cross-border exchange, *A Night in Olde Belfast,* even if they had dozens of peace rallies, something more was needed. All the things they had been working on were good things. But they were so . . . so . . . well, for want of a better word, they were so secular.

Maybe self-centered was a better word. They were working for themselves, for each other to some extent, but they needed a higher purpose. Art, music, folklore, and history all were part of what made Ireland special, but these would not make a lasting difference. The more she thought, the more uneasy she became. Had she missed something fundamental in her whole summer of work?

As they crossed the border back into Northern Ireland, she turned to Gareth and tried to express her troubling, confused thoughts.

He listened, then nodded. "I know. I keep trying to define our goals. I don't mean just the youth center or the production but the meaning behind them. What do you really want, Mary?"

She thought for a moment. "Well, I guess the same thing everybody in Ireland wants—peace and unity. You know—'Bind us together.'"

"Right."

"But singing about it isn't enough. There's something else we must do. And I don't have a clue what it is."

Gareth pulled out a note pad. "I didn't sleep much last night—had this afternoon's meeting on my mind. I got to thinking about one of the theologians we studied at university. Maurice was his name. He believed that the unity of mankind can be expressed only in worship, because that is where we make our common acknowledgment that God is our heavenly Father and that we are therefore brothers."

She nodded. "That makes sense. We sort of had that feeling at the rally when everyone held hands and sang."

"And Maurice believed that this unity could best be experienced at the one part of worship that is the Christian's highest privilege, the supreme moment in worship that is a reenactment of Christ's sacrifice for all mankind . . ." He paused as if waiting for her to supply the word.

"Communion." She said it slowly. "Yes." Then she frowned. "So? Christians take the sacraments all the time."

"In their own churches. In their own way. But not together."

"Together? You mean believing Catholics and Protestants? In the same service?" The concept was breathtaking. "I don't think that could be done. Catholics have very strict rules about that. My cousin married a Catholic. He couldn't even take Communion at his own wedding. Really upset my aunt."

Gareth sat back. "Yep. But if there were some way it *could* be done, just think how powerful that could be." He leaned forward to the font seat and explained the idea to Philip and Paddy.

Both were intrigued, but neither had a solution. "Interfaith rallies, prayer meetings, and song services are done rather often," Philip said.

"The BBC did an interfaith thing a few years ago. 'Songs of Praise.' My mom was involved," Debbie said from the backseat.

"Was she, now?" Paddy asked. "I was there myself. Fine singing that night, even with the C of I. Everyone knows the Methodists can sing. But this idea of taking the Eucharist . . . now that's a different matter."

"That's what makes the idea so special," Mary insisted. "The most sacred moment in all Christian worship through the ages—for all believers to put all differences aside and gather around the Lord's Supper . . ."

But no one could see how it could be done.

It was midafternoon when they drove across the bridge, through the security barricades, and into Enniskillen. Philip stopped in front of the hotel. "Hope they have room for us."

"Shall I go ask?" Mary slid her door open. "Two rooms enough? Boys and girls?"

As soon as she opened the hotel door, she heard music coming from the back. Probably the bar. The lounge television was also booming. There were people everywhere. A young man in a side room raised his glass and called a salute to someone in the lobby. A group of gray-haired women sat trying to hold a conversation over the blare of the TV. A little girl in a flowered dress and shiny patent shoes skipped down the stairs beyond the desk. She was followed by a pair of little boys in white shirts and short dark pants.

Mary picked her way through the crowd to the woman at the desk. "Do you have any rooms for tonight? We need two."

"Oh, Lord love you, dearie. We've aplenty. And don't you worry about all this. They'll quiet down. Not staying here, they aren't."

Mary smiled. "What is it? A wedding?"

"No, no, love. It's a funeral."

"Oh." She told the manageress what they would need. "But I can see you're busy. We've got some things to do, so we'll check in later."

The men had their meeting to attend. The twins spotted a pizza parlor. And Mary, who had been gripped on their last time through Enniskillen by Philip's account of the Remembrance Sunday massacre, wanted to get better acquainted with the town.

If one didn't know of the outrage that had occurred here, she thought, the casual passer-by would think this merely a more than usually tidy town square. The storefronts had been rebuilt, the war memorial replaced. She walked around, trying to imagine what the massacre must have been like. She had little success building the scene in her mind, although the threatening rain did provide a somber atmosphere.

After circling the square twice, Mary stopped at a news agent's and found a book Philip had told her about. Then, as it was long past lunchtime, she found a quiet tea shop and opened the book while waiting for her scone. The cover showed a smiling young woman with warm brown eyes and wearing a nurse's cap.

It was tradition. Gordon Wilson and his daughter Marie always went to the wreath-laying ceremony at the war memorial cenotaph on Remembrance Day while Mrs. Wilson prepared Sunday dinner. The ceremony on November 8, 1987, was exactly like all the others—the band, the flag, officials to lay the wreath, all the town turned out to honor their war dead. Until eleven o'clock.

A bomb exploded directly behind the Wilsons. A three-story building crashed down on them. There had been a moment of sinister silence, then shouting, moaning, screams of agony. Gordon and Marie Wilson lay buried beneath several feet of rubble.

"She held my hand tightly, and gripped me as hard as she could. She said, 'Daddy, I love you very much.' Those were her exact words to me, and those were the last words I ever heard her say."

Mary's tea cooled, untouched, as she read on. Eleven people had been killed. Sixty-three injured, nineteen of them severely. And that night Marie Wilson's father gave the BBC interview that rocked the world.

"I have lost my daughter, and we shall miss her. But I bear no ill will. I bear no grudge. She was a great wee lassie. She loved her profession. She was a pet. She's dead. She's in heaven, and we'll meet again. Don't ask me, please, for a purpose. I don't have an answer. But I know there has to be a plan. If I didn't think that, I would commit suicide. It's part of a greater plan, and God is good. And we shall meet again."

Reaction to the outrage came from President Reagan, Pope John Paul II, the Soviet news agency TASS, the lord mayor of Dublin, the rock group U2, and on and on. But none had the impact of those words from the quietly grieving father. Loyalist paramilitaries admitted a few days later that they were planning massive retaliation but were stopped by Wilson's words.

Mary turned to the family photos in the middle of the book, but her eyes were too blurred to see them properly. How could he do it? How could anyone have that much grace? As at the first time she heard the story, she asked herself what her response would be in such a situation. She hoped she would never have to find out.

She had spent far longer in the tea shop than she had thought possible. But it seemed the Reconciliation Union meeting had gone on overtime as well. She was hurrying toward the hotel when she saw the men approaching from the other direction.

As always, her eyes sought out Gareth first. He was so alive. Even after a long day, his eyes were shining. She linked her arm in his. "How did the meeting go?"

"Ah, it was brilliant. A priest there said he'd heard of something like that being done at Catholic/Protestant weddings. They call it an Agape Service."

Mary thought a moment. "Yes, I like the name."

"So did the Reconciliation Union people. They appointed committees to work on it—everything. Now I if I could just come up with a way to make it really nationwide. This can't be a hole-in-the-corner event—not if it's to accomplish its potential."

Mary still wasn't convinced that anything could make the kind of difference he was looking for. But Gareth was so elated, she didn't want to be a wet blanket.

He talked on, explaining his hopes and ideas, then paused to make a note. "Ah, that's good. I want to remember that in the morning."

"What's in the morning?'

"We're having another meeting."

She groaned. "You're meeting again?" Why couldn't they get on with things? Why did everything have to be so slow? She felt as if she were caught in a time warp trap—and the more she knew about this place the more she felt that way. Reading that book today had brought it home to her again. Over and over and over again, the 1641 Rising, the 1987 Enriskillen massacre, events just kept repeating themselves. The merry-go-round would never stop. She wanted off.

"Mary, I know how you feel about this, but please be patient just a little longer. Getting everyone together around the Lord's Supper really *could* be the beginning of lasting peace. It's worth our total commitment."

She wasn't going to take up that argument again. "I'm tired. Just show me to my room."

The request sounded simpler than it turned out to be, however. The wake continued full swing. The manageress was distracted four or five times before she actually led them up the stairs. And it was considerably later than that before she had them sorted out into workable rooms. The first she took the women to looked very pretty with its rose-covered comforters. But when Becca tossed her backpack on one of the beds, a leg collapsed, and it crashed to the floor.

"Well, now, that's no problem. The room next door is empty. You can just have it." So the manageress went back downstairs to get the keys, then went off to lead the men up another flight of stairs.

When Debbie turned down the cover on the bed she and Mary would share, the sheets were damp.

"Oh, I don't believe this." Mary started for the door.

"Wait." Julie stopped her. "The mattress pad is dry. Why not just pull the sheets off and sleep under the comforter?"

Mary was too tired and hungry to argue. It had been a very long day. She decided to give her hair a brush, then realized her bag was still in the mini. "Oh, Becca, toss me your brush."

"Yeah, here. Then let's go eat."

"Yes, hurry, I'm starved!"

"How about fish and chips?" At least her sisters were normal.

Mary finished with a quick flip of the brush and tossed it back to Becca. "I'll go ask if there's a chip shop somewhere close."

She met Tommy in the hall. One glance at his face stopped her. "What's wrong?"

"Ah, Mary, I'm sorry to tell you this."

"What?"

"I just called home. The show—the kids—they were working on the sets at Noah's Ark. Seems some kind of fight broke out. Frightened some of the daycare children. I'm not sure what happened, but Lila sounded pretty upset. Anyway, it's definitely off."

Mary put a hand over her face to hide her reaction. She should have been upset. After all the effort she had put into that program, this should be a blow. Instead, she found it blessedly liberating. Now she could leave. Now there was nothing she had to stay for. Except Gareth. And he could finish his work at that meeting in the morning. He could turn in his proposal, and they could leave. She closed her eyes and for a moment could hear the seagulls and feel the breeze on her face as they stood together on the ferry.

She hurried down the hall to find him. She was at the stairs when she met the men coming back down from above.

"Plumbing broken," Philip announced.

Everyone trooped upward and found a room with working taps at the back of the fourth floor. At least the cold water worked. No one felt like asking for more. Except for directions to the chip shop.

Philip and Tommy started out, taking the key to turn in at the desk. But Gareth sat on a bed, still bent over his notepad.

"Oh, come on, Gareth. You can make your notes later. Everyone's starving." Mary's protest was none too patient. She wanted his attention so that she could tell him the good news—that their work here was done.

694

But he seemed anything but finished. "You go on. I'm not very hungry. I want to work on this."

"Gareth, I have great admiration for your drive and devotion. But this is silly. You've done your part. You got the idea started. The committees can carry it on. They've done interfaith services before."

"That's the point. It isn't just another service. It's Communion."

"So?"

He took her hands and sat her on the edge of the bed next to his. "Mary, I guess I forget how new all this is to you. The Lord's Supper is a love feast that all believers are commanded to participate in—together. It's a memorial of His sacrifice on the cross."

"I know that."

He gripped her hands tighter, his eyes shining. "And in Communion we come to the table as members of His family—and we recognize each other as members. Members of Christ. Believers are one."

"That's great, Gareth, it really is. And I expect it will happen—someday. But can't you get it through your head that such reconciliation is not going to happen *now*? I spent all summer on that program. Tickets were selling well. The development council was coming. The kids knew their lines. And now it's all off—just like that. These people can't work together. They never have. They never will. Not even believers. So you might as well come eat fish and chips with us." She might have saved her breath to cool her chips.

It was as if he hadn't even heard her. "There's so much to do. And the time is so short."

"You mean you expect violence at the Londonderry marches?"

"Who knows? It may not wait that long."

"What do you mean?"

He came to his feet. "The peace process is too slow. Tempers are too short. That was true even before things bogged down over the marches. The word is that there's a power struggle within the leadership of the IRA. The peace faction there may not be able to keep control." He returned to her side in two quick strides. "Mary, I do understand your impatience. You were so good to come here at all. And I know it hasn't been easy."

Easy? She stood. It had been the hardest summer of her life. And she had accomplished nothing for all her effort. The sooner she got away from here the better.

"Please try to hold on a little longer." He drew his hands together, hers between them, as if folded in prayer. "It isn't just that I need to make some notes. What I really want—need—is to spend some time praying."

She made a sound of contempt, then was sorry when she saw how that reaction hurt him.

But he didn't back down. "We only have a window of time. That window may be closing."

His words chilled her. And perhaps because she was frightened, she reacted in anger. She jerked her hands away and turned from him. "Good! Let it slam shut. It serves them right—the whole lot of them!"

"You don't mean that."

She turned back, her hands on either side of her head, as if to suppress a scream. "Gareth, I'm sorry. I know how much this means to you. But I'm not a sanctified saint. I can't accept this 'not my will but Thine' stuff. And I've had enough. I worked hard on that program. I was committed to it. But they can't even work together long enough to put on a music and drama show. It's just stupid, blind optimism to think they'll come together politically *or* religiously."

She strode to the door. "I've had it. I can't take any more." She jerked the door open. "I'm sorry, Gareth. I'm sorry." She pulled the ring from her finger and threw it behind her as she fled.

79

In the glaring, overheated chip shop where she caught up with the others, Mary tried to push Gareth's words out of her mind. Most of their group were crowded into one large booth. Tommy and Liam, the last to receive their orders because they waited for a fresh frying of haddock, sat on the counter stools facing the window. She doused her steaming cod filet in salt and malt vinegar, then closed her eyes so as to enjoy the first bite more fully. Crisp, golden batter; tender, juicy fish. There was nothing like it.

She really couldn't think about the scene with Gareth right now. One corner of her mind was screaming, *You broke up with Gareth. You threw his ring at him. You just ended everything you've dreamed of for four years.* But another part of her tried to argue that now she was free. Free of her commitments to him. Free of her commitments to Ireland. Free to leave and be her own person.

She tried to concentrate on the salty, vinegary taste of the fish. She was starving, and this was about the best fish she'd ever tasted. So why was it so hard to swallow?

A chrome stool clattered onto the linoleum floor, and her eyes snapped open. She dropped her fish back onto its bed of chips as Tommy flung open the door and darted up the street. Liam bolted after him, shouting obscenities.

It was several minutes before Tommy returned, shaking his head. "Lost him."

"What was that all about? Who were you chasing?" Philip demanded.

"Joe Navan."

"What? Are you sure?"

"Haven't seen him for five years, but I'm sure. I've even seen him carry packages just like that for the Army." Then Tommy seemed to realize what he'd said. "Oh, God!"

He had spoken the words as a prayer, but Mary was too shocked to pray. Tommy had chased an IRA member, carrying a package that could be a bomb—going in the direction of the hotel.

"Gareth!" She wasn't sure whether she had whispered or shouted.

She only knew she was on her feet, running. Out of the corner of her eye she saw Philip dashing toward the phone box across the street.

Then all she saw was dark streets blurring past her and the look on Gareth's face when she threw the ring at him. All she felt was the hardness of the pavement as her feet slapped against it and the searing dryness in her throat as air rasped in forced gulps.

She had to get there in time. She had to warn Gareth. And the others. Pictures flashed before her eyes: a little girl in a party dress, singing as she skipped down the stairs; a group of grandmothers, gray heads bent together as they shared old memories; a young couple, laughing over a joke; a new mother sitting quietly in a corner nursing her baby.

And then the scene twisted in her mind. The music didn't come from the television but from a school band. The flowers weren't a funeral wreath but a memorial to fallen soldiers. It was Remembrance Sunday 1987.

No. Gareth must not wind up buried under piles of rubble as people had that day. No warning had been given then. This time one would be. She shouted at the empty store fronts as she raced past. "Bomb! There's a bomb!"

Then her feet faltered to a stop. Where *was* she? She didn't remember any of these shops. There should have been a cinema and a news agent. Then turn right and there would be the town square with the war memorial. The hotel was only a little farther on. It had to be.

Her sides heaved, and her lungs were bursting. But she could keep running. She could do anything to save Gareth. Her whole life—everything she cared about was in that hotel room that might explode into a million fragments at any moment. She must get to him. But which direction should she run?

She looked wildly up and down the deserted street. Should she go back to the chip shop? By now she wasn't certain where it was. She thought she had only taken one turning. But she must have become confused and taken more.

She heard a car engine. Headlights approached from around a corner. She dashed into the street, waving her arms wildly. "Help! Please! There's a bomb—" The car roared by. They must not have even seen her.

At the foot of the street the car turned left. Did that mean there were people that direction? She had no better idea. She ran, her ears straining for the one sound she dreaded most—the tearing explosion that would tell her she was too late.

She headed up a new street, telling herself she had seen these buildings before. Sure she had. The tea shop was just in the next block. Maybe. She could find her way easily to the hotel from there. *Please, Lord. Please. Let this be right.*

But how long did she have? Worry circled in her mind. Maybe they would set the bomb to explode in the middle of the night. Of course, they would. In hopes of getting everyone while they slept. Or maybe they didn't want to kill people—just frighten them. Demonstrate the power of terror. Maybe the IRA would issue their own warning. Sometimes they did. Maybe a warning had already been sent. Gareth and all the guests could be safely away when she got there. She didn't even need to be doing this.

But no argument could stop her running. She sped around a corner, and there it was. How on earth did she get here? This was the back of the hotel. But, thank God, however she got here, it was still standing, tall and square against the black sky. She glanced upward at the top floor where Gareth's room was. There was a light in his window. "Gareth!" she shouted.

The alley door was unlocked. She stumbled into the black kitchen, sending pans crashing. She pushed through a swinging door and across the dining room. "Gareth!" She hit a table set for breakfast. Glassware shattered. The hotel was still. Her own voice echoed back at her as she sped up the narrow back stairway, screaming, sobbing, choking. "Gareth! Gareth!"

He would hear her. He would come. They would run. Together. Hand in hand. Away from this place of fear and violence. This would show Gareth she was right. He would come with her. They would be together just as she had dreamed. "Gareth! Gareth!"

Up another flight of stairs. How many more could there be?

"Mary!" Gareth's voice.

There he was—at the top of the next turning. They leaped toward each other. The next moment they were in each other's arms.

"A bomb! There's a bomb!" Even as she said it she was starting back down, pulling at him. She wanted to explain, but there wasn't time. And she had no breath. Second floor. Around and down. First floor. Around and down. Back through the dining room.

Halfway across the kitchen, she stumbled into the pans she had scattered earlier. She grabbed wildly at the counter but couldn't stop her plunge. Gareth's arms came around her. He bent over to lift her to her feet.

The blast knocked them to the floor, Gareth on top of her.

Silence. Why was it was so quiet? Then there was a great crash as pots, kettles, and crockery fell around them. As if in slow motion, she heard each thing clatter, bounce, and settle.

The wall beside them wavered and creaked, then split with a great crashing and pelted down over them.

GENERATION SIX

THE BIRTH OF NORTHERN IRELAND
1914–1921

We . . . will give thee thanks for ever:
we will shew forth thy praise to all generations.
I will sing of the mercies of the Lord for ever:
with my mouth will I make known thy faithfulness
to all generations.
Thy seed will I establish for ever,
and build up thy throne to all generations.
(Psalms 79:13; 89:1, 4)

80

"I found this in the mini, Mary. Shall I read to you?"

Gareth was speaking to her. Mary struggled for consciousness.

"It'll help pass the time." The voice came again. Not Gareth.

But this time she recognized it as Philip's. She nodded. As long as she didn't have to open her eyes, she didn't care.

***

When would they ever quit bickering? Nora Armstrong tucked an escaping dark lock back under the narrow brim of her pink straw hat and sighed. Didn't they realize she needed to be at the theater in just three hours?

Nora was certain everyone was correct in declaring that this day, 5 August 1914, would remain in all their memories as historic—far beyond the family gathering to celebrate the baptism of Nora's nephew. But no matter how historic this day was for Ireland, for Britain, for the world, she did not choose that it should also become infamous in the history of the Ulster Literary Theatre as being the first time an actress ever missed her own opening night.

This was the day Nora had dreamed of since she was eight years old and had first been taken to a production of one of her cousin's plays celebrating the Renaissance of Gaelic culture. She had spent the succeeding twelve years dreaming of being an actress. It seemed she had attended every play staged within a twenty-mile radius of the bawn, and reading—usually aloud to her longsuffering family—every play she could get her hands on. Then, just a few weeks ago, all that roleplaying turned into serious rehearsals when she won the lead role in Pedar O'Brien's *Princess Deirdre*.

Now she looked in appeal at the slim, intense playwright standing with the other men of their family on the far side of the bawn's elegant long gallery. But it was clear that Pedar's mind was turned with the others to consideration of the momentous news that had descended on them.

Thom Armstrong, her father and the silver-haired patriarch of the clan, had made one brief stop that morning on the way from the baptism at the First Presbyterian Church to the family reception at the Armstrong home. He had spent less than five minutes inside the Post Office. But it had been long enough. He returned as ashen as if he had aged ten years in those few minutes.

Nora saw again her father walking with slumped shoulders through the gray drizzle, his dark overcoat blowing about his legs. He settled himself on the driver's seat and picked up the reins, but in spite of the stamping of his fine pair of blacks, he remained still. At last he cleared his throat and turned stiffly to those in the carriage.

Nora was seated by her mother with sixteen-year-old Eric—for once not making jokes—on the end of the seat. Across from them, her older brother Lanark glanced at his wife, Brenda, holding their newly baptized Mitchell Campbell Armstrong.

Father held all their eyes as he said in a hushed, steady voice, "England has declared war on Germany."

From that moment, the day had taken on an air of unreality. Perhaps they had taken a wrong road. Perhaps this was the Ulster Arts. Perhaps *this* was the play. The story of the Celtic princess was reality— war was the fantasy. But the arguments of her father, brothers, and cousins broke in on Nora with undeniable certainty.

Her favorite cousin, Stuart Price, shook his head, reminiscent of the thoroughbred horses he raised. "There will be trouble here—you can count on it. There are always those who believe that England's trouble is Ireland's opportunity." He looked at Pedar, who made no secret of his Nationalist views.

"*Och*, trouble, all right. And England will be the one making it. They'll use the foreign threat as an excuse to sweep Home Rule under the carpet. But it won't do. Ireland has worked too long for her freedom to let go of it now." Pedar's ardent dark eyes glowed in his thin white face.

"Those Fenian Nationalists better not try anything. No sir! I did not sign the Ulster Covenant only to knuckle under to threats from Kaiser Wilhelm or any of his kind!" Thom Armstrong thundered with such vehemence that wee Mitchell stirred in his mother's arms and stretched out a tiny fist.

"Right you are! And my grandson agrees with you!" Harlan Campbell, father of Lanark's wife and partner in one of Ulster's leading shipbuilding firms, bellowed.

"Hush, Father, you'll wake him." But Brenda's protest went unheeded.

No one had ever managed to rein in Harlan Campbell, and few had ever tried. He slapped his son-in-law on the back. "That's a fine bairn you've produced there, son. And as soon as he's old enough to hold a pen, he can sign the Covenant of Resistance to Home Rule, too."

And so ran the arguments, around and around. Prime Minister Asquith had introduced the Home Rule Bill in Parliament in April 1912. But under an Irish Parliament, there would be no security for life or property, no fair play for the Loyalists. Ulster could not continue to prosper without the commercial confidence provided by union with England. A Dublin Parliament would be dominated by farmers, who would be incompetent to administer industrial Ulster and unconcerned about its welfare. Nationalists would tax the north too heavily . . .

Again and again, Nora's father returned to the Covenant. Six months after the Home Rule Bill was introduced, Sir Edward Carson had led a great Ulster Day rally. All over the province, Protestants had signed the Covenant, pledging themselves to stand by one another to defend their cherished citizenship in the United Kingdom and to use all means necessary to defeat the conspiracy to set up a Home Rule Parliament in Ireland.

When Home Rule passed the Commons in November of that year, Asquith was castigated as being a traitor. An Ulsterman in the House had hurled a book at Home Rule supporter Winston Churchill. Although the bill failed to pass the House of Lords, Ulster prepared for the worst. Sir Edward Carson led the effort to form a provisional government. They readied an army—the Ulster Volunteer Force— recruited from men who had signed the Covenant. The south of Ireland responded by forming the Irish Citizen Army and the Irish Republican Brotherhood from the old Fenian Brotherhood. They began training their men in a shooting gallery.

And so for two years Ireland had teetered on the brink of civil war. Now, this past spring, the Home Rule Bill had passed the Commons for the third time. It only required the royal signature to become law.

"There can't be any other answer. War will put Home Rule on hold."

Nora couldn't tell by Stuart's voice whether this prospect relieved or worried her cousin.

But her brother Lanark seemed to find cause for optimism. "You should be happy enough, Price, with the amount the army's sure to be paying for horses. And never mind about all this Home Rule business. Carson struck a deal with the government. When it is implemented— after the war—there will be some special accommodation for Ulster."

Was that all they could think about? Nora wondered. Their country was at war, but all anyone could think about was what will this mean to Home Rule? Surely war with Germany would have farther-reaching effects than those on Irish government and the prices of horses and ships. Still, her own concerns were not primarily the far-reaching matters of Europe or Britain or even the Irish troubles, either.

Her thoughts were focused on the people who comprised all those dearest in life to her. What of her father and brother, who had signed the Covenant and joined the UVF? Father was too old to march off to a battlefield. But what of her handsome brother, or even that lovable nuisance, the freckle-faced Eric? Lanark had gone to work with Campbell & Wilson Shipbuilding the day he and Brenda returned from their honeymoon, and Eric was already talking about running the bawn farm with his father after attending university. But war could smash all those carefully laid plans.

And the gentle Stuart Price, her idea of the perfect country gentleman, who was so maddeningly slow to speak to the fragile Victoria Raglan, daughter of an old Anglo-Irish family, whom he had met at a horse show a year ago. What would war mean to Stuart and Victoria?

Nora looked at Vicky now, standing behind the men. Her delicate, white-stockinged ankles barely showed beneath her ice-blue peg-top skirt.

"Well, I shall join the Women's Unionist Association." The wavering of the ostrich feather topping her charmeuse hat gave the only indication of the fervor with which this slip of a girl spoke.

Nothing else, not even the whimperings of wee Mitchell Campbell Armstrong, had made the slightest impression on all the male bombast. But Victoria's simple sentence silenced them.

"Victoria!" Stuart gasped after a moment. "Why on earth would you do a daft thing like that?"

"It isn't the least bit daft. You men belong to all sorts of Unionist Associations and volunteer forces—" She turned to Pedar, who had made a protesting sound. "And don't you be sounding so full of righteous indignation, Pedar O'Brien. You have your Gaelic League. Don't be trying to tell me it doesn't have political overtones, too."

Having silenced him, she turned back to Stuart. "Women have long seen—far clearer than you men, it seems—that a crisis was imminent. There was sure to be civil war in Ireland or conflict in Europe. We women can do our part. We can raise funds, organize nursing courses, help prepare hospitals—"

The shock on the face of her quiet, refined mother was not sufficient to prevent Nora from bursting into applause and jumping to her feet. "Bravo! Well spoken, Vicky! And I shall join you. If there's to be trouble, every woman should have nursing skills."

"I'll thank you to remember yourself, daughter." Thom Armstrong glared at her. "I'll have no suffragette nonsense in this house. Nor the Gaelic League either." He turned his glare on Pedar.

In spite of the fact that the Gaelic Renaissance in Ulster was fostered largely by Protestants, such patrons were entirely unrepresentative of the mass of Ulstermen such as Armstrong, who was horrified by the very suggestion that his cultural identity should not be with England but rather with some misty Irish past. And he was alarmed by the growth of a movement that implied he was some kind of an outsider.

"I'll have no one suggesting to me in my own house that I'm no true Irishman. My people have been here for over three hundred years. We built this whole province. My family and others like them. Transformed it from an uncultivated wasteland populated by a few huddling savages into one of the most prosperous parts of Great Britain. And we did it by hard work, not by singing to our harps in some barbarian tongue."

Nora knew better than to attempt to answer back. Only because of her mother's support and her older brother's insistence that the best course was to let her get "that stage nonsense" out of her system had Father agreed to allow her to be in this play. That and the fact that such leading Protestants as the Bishop of Down and Sir Roger Casement were among those who promoted the revival of Gaelic culture in Belfast. But now Nora wondered what the war would mean to the Gaelic Renaissance, to Pedar's plays, to her own career?

One thing was clear. No matter that international events might cut her career short, she was determined that the announcement of the war would not mean she would miss her opening night. "Pedar, we must be going." She emphasized her quiet words by tugging at his coat sleeve.

The men had returned to talk of politics and would likely have ignored her exit had not her irrepressible younger brother jumped to his feet, his blue eyes snapping, his freckled face screwed into a grin. Eric made a deep bow and gestured to her with a flourish. "Ladies and gentlemen, I give you Nora Armstrong, Ulster's own Maude Gonne."

"Oh, Ellen Terry, surely." Victoria caught the nuances and did her best to repair the harm of Eric's joking, but the damage had been done.

Eric's mention of Maude Gonne echoed in the room. The Irish actress was even better known as one of the founders of revolutionary Sinn Fein than for her ethereal beauty and her success in the plays of William Butler Yeats.

"I'll not have that revolutionary named in my house!" Thom Armstrong's heavy eyebrows pulled together threateningly. "Nor will I have my daughter turned into a Fenian."

Following her dramatic instincts, Nora rushed across the room and gave her father a quick hug. "Ignore the brat, father. You know you've taught me soundly."

"Humph." Armstrong sounded skeptical, but he let her go.

Nora spent at least the first half of the hurried drive to Belfast wondering what she really did believe about issues of Unionism and Nationalism.

All she had ever thought about was the theater, and in Ireland the theater meant Gaelic Revival. She had always focused on the part of the revival that looked to Ireland's unique past—far back into the mists of time before the English, the Spanish, the Scots (who, confusingly, had originally been Irish), before even the Vikings had come to trouble the waters of this green island. But for all that the movement had been largely started by Protestant Anglo-Irish, there were those in the movement, such as Maude Gonne, who drew from the past to project into the future—a future they defined as an independent Ireland. At any cost.

Poetry and art aside, though, what *did* she believe about political policy? It was a fair question. After all, the whole flowering of Irish drama in the past decades had been in response to nationalistic promptings. If faced with a demand to choose, would she, like Maude Gonne, join a revolutionary movement for that culture?

Nora forced herself to laugh at the ridiculousness of her own thought. She must be more overwrought about her opening than she had realized. She must focus all her thoughts and energies on tonight. And tonight there were no questions for Nora, no decisions for Nora to make. Tonight she was Deirdre.

81

Nora slipped the simple white, almost-Grecian gown over her head, then bound a chain of small, white paper flowers in her hair. There had been talk when they arrived at the theater—*ought* the play to go on? Would anyone come? But the play had gone on, and the audience, she could tell from the muffled buzz from the other side of the drawn curtain, had come. This was not a night to be alone. This first night of declared war was a night for people to draw together, to share memories and present strengths that would take them into the future.

And perhaps no play could have served as a better vehicle for this than Pedar O'Brien's telling of the greatest love story of Celtic legend. In broad outline, the story was still that of the Celtic princess who fled to Scotland with her lover rather than stay in Ireland and marry the High King of Ulster. But in a larger sense it was a much different story. Pedar's play, more explicitly than John Millington Synge's *Deirdre of the Sorrows*, made Deirdre a symbol of Ireland, forced to abandon the true soul of her homeland by those in power, a symbol of survival of spirit against great odds, a symbol of courageous action and a statement of faith that could mean hope for the future.

All that in the person of one slim girl. Nora refreshed her lipstick, which did not need refreshing, and retouched her powder, which did not need retouching.

"Curtain, Miss Armstrong." The call girl stuck her head in the open doorway of Nora's dressing room, then disappeared.

And Nora couldn't go on. Her feet were lumps of iron welded to the floor. Her throat felt swollen three times its normal size. She couldn't breathe, let alone speak. What was she doing here? She was no actress. How could she get out? She must escape.

"Deirdre."

She turned at the sound of the name and blinked three times before she recognized Pedar, stiff in his tuxedo and high white collar.

"You are perfect, my lovely princess." He raised her hand to his lips and kissed it.

The rivets fell from her feet, her throat returned to normal.

Pedar led Deirdre to the stage and left her in the care of her nurse, who was seen draping the princess in her wedding veil when the curtain rose. Deirdre waited until the welcoming applause of anticipation stilled before tearing the veil from her head. "No, Lavarcham, I will not be married to Conchubar."

"But you must, lady. He is all-powerful, and he will give you gold, fine buildings, servants . . ."

"He will give me his servants to be masters over me, you mean. He will build his fine buildings on my land, the green, fertile fields my father gave me. He will give me tawdry gold only after he has taken from me all I have of value. He will take my soul."

"No, no lady. King Conchubar is very religious. He has many priests."

"They are not my priests. They do not minister truth to my soul. I find no peace with the priests of the High King of Ulster."

Offstage a rousing blast sounded on an oxhorn.

"Oh, do hurry, lady."

The nurse reached to replace Deirdre's veil, but the princess tore it from her hands.

"Yes, we must hurry, Lavarcham." Deirdre flung herself on her couch. "Tell the king I am ill. Tell him I must have a priest—my own priest."

Lavarcham dithered.

Deirdre sat up, gesturing urgently. "Go. Tell him he must not come in until I have seen my priest. And then bring Patroclos to me. I will have no other. Go!" She fell back on the cushions as the servant fled.

For a moment the stage was still, held in the grip of waiting. Would the king force an entrance? Or would Deirdre have her moment of solace? It was a tricky moment dramatically. If the audience broke their attention, the dramatic tension would be lost. It was up to the actress, lying silent on her couch to keep them riveted.

The soft sigh of relief from the audience at the entrance of the druid priest and his acolyte told that no mind had wandered from Deirdre's plight. And at the end of act one, when the acolyte revealed himself to be Deirdre's beloved Naise and they fled together into the night, the ardent applause told of the enthusiasm for the play.

Pedar met her backstage with open arms. "My dear. My lovely, lovely Deirdre!" He hugged her with the same intensity he brought to everything he did. "You are wonderful. You have brought to my play so much more than I put there."

She laughed and pushed him gently away. "Not at all. I brought out exactly what was there. What you put there." She paused. That was perfectly true, and yet, there was more. "What you put there, and what generations of Irish people who have loved this story and this land have put there—along with the hopes and dreams and fears that every member of the audience brought with them. I felt it all while I was on stage. It was as if every *seanachaidh* who ever told the story was there on the stage with me."

"I love you." Pedar clasped her in his arms again and gave her a kiss that was far beyond mere appreciation of artistic expression.

And all through the second act, when the lovers came together in an embrace, it was part Deirdre in Naise's arms and partly Nora in Pedar's arms and partly the heart of Ireland in the arms of her true soul mate—her heritage. Act two ended with a bittersweet tenderness born of the rapture of the lovers and the regret that such happiness could be found only in exile. And the knowledge that such joy could only be short-lived.

The tears streaming down Deirdre's cheeks as the curtain fell had little to do with stagecraft. And she heard many sniffs from the audience.

Again Pedar met her backstage, but this time it was with a subdued intensity. He ushered her gently to her dressing room, solicitously poured a glass of water for her, and stood facing away from her, even though she went behind a screen to change to her black act-three gown. She sensed that if Pedar spoke one word it would produce a tidal wave that would fill the room and drown them both. She all but held her breath, fearing to say anything that might cause the dam to overflow.

"Two minutes." The call came from the narrow hallway outside the dressing rooms.

Nora emerged from behind the screen in her flowing black gown and paused at the mirror to adjust the raven scarf over her hair. Her dark eyes, huge with their rings of khol, looked back at her, amazed that her skin could be so white, her lips so red. Who *was* that woman in the mirror? Could the real Deirdre have looked like that?

She turned toward the door to find her way blocked by Pedar. She started in surprise.

He held out his hands as a supplicant. "Marry me." It sounded nearly a prayer.

In response to some deeply hidden instinct, she raised her hand and made the sign of blessing over him. He stepped aside, and she walked to the stage.

What had he said? Had Pedar proposed? She stood waiting in the darkness of the curtained stage. *Pedar?* Growing up, she had thought of him as a cousin—although the relationship was so distant as to be almost nonexistent. She had always hero-worshiped this older man as an artist. His plays had inflamed her passion for the theater. There was no one she admired more. No one with whom she felt more artistic kinship. No one to whom she owed more for this chance to fulfill her dreams. And yet . . .

The gas footlights flared as the curtain rose. She closed her eyes for an instant and took a deep breath. She was Deirdre once again.

Act three was the inevitable playing out of the tragedy. The destruction set in motion by the lovers' flight came upon them as Conchubar of Ulster marched in with his army. Deirdre and Naise resisted return to Conchubar's kingdom, but the High King's power was overwhelming. Even once back in his domain, the lovers did not submit. They gathered supporters to stand against the tyrant.

And yet Conchubar triumphed. It could not be otherwise. In this world, power is supreme. With his kingdom in flames behind him, Conchubar killed Naise. Then he turned to the still defiant Deirdre.

"No!" Magnificent with her tall stature swathed in ebony robes, Deirdre held aloft the knife she had taken from Naise's fallen body. "Hear me, Conchubar the mighty. For you are mighty and terrible indeed. But there is One mightier than you. There is One above all, who wreaks vengeance on the unjust and serves justice to the nations. The High King above all has promised that no more will the captive people be a reproach among the nations."

Conchubar backed away from Deirdre's advance.

Her voice rang with a prophet's passion. "Fear not, O land! Exult and rejoice! For He above all has done great things. He has promised, 'I will restore you the years the locust has eaten. You shall eat and be filled. My people shall nevermore be put to shame. And you shall know that I am in your midst. I am He and there is no other. My people shall nevermore be put to shame.'"

Deirdre stood still and silent for three heartbeats, then plunged the knife deep in her breast with one final, defiant word. *"Freedom!"*

The silence of the theater reverberated.

The shout came first, then the applause. Naise raised Deirdre and led her downstage. Beyond the footlights, she could see the faces of the first few rows, faces alive with sorrow and hope, determination and passion. And Nora understood what she had done.

She and Deirdre and Pedar and all the cast and the Deirdres of all time had given this audience a gift. On this night when all the world had turned gray, she had lit a candle for them. For a brief time the worry, fear, and horror that closed in around them were held at bay. She had created a ring of light—given them a glimpse of their own courage from times past. She had helped them find that courage that ran so deep in all Gaels—courage that would carry them through the dark of the future.

At last the curtain fell for the final time. On the other side, the theater was emptying slowly as people went out into the night. On her side of the curtain, Nora stood alone as everyone scurried to their next task.

Pedar came to her then, embraced her, and held her for long moments. She felt his heartbeat, the rhythm of his breathing.

Finally, he pulled back and regarded her at arms' length, shaking his head gently. "Never. Never did I imagine my words could soar so far above my own vision."

But then the world crashed in on them. Reporters wanted interviews. Friends offered congratulations. Strangers wanted autographs.

Hours later, Pedar drove her to her boardinghouse off Clarence Street. He stopped the carriage in a small pool of gold from a gas streetlight and took her hands. "Nora, my dearest, my timing was inexcusable. Forgive me. But please allow me to repeat my petition. I love you. I have loved you since you were eight years old and came to me with shining eyes and whispered that you wanted to act in one of my plays. Do you remember that?"

"Yes, of course, I remember. Tonight has been the fulfillment of all my dreams."

"And of mine." He kissed her hands—fingertips first, then the palms. "Since that moment you have been all my heroines. Every one I created, I saw you playing her."

"Including the role of wife." She said it gently but with a hint of teasing. This scene would call for far more careful handling than any on stage.

"Say you'll marry me, Nora. I know I'm nearly twice your age, but I swear I can make you happy."

She leaned over and placed a tiny kiss on his cheek. "I would never doubt that for a moment, darling Pedar."

"Then you will?" He engulfed her in an embrace.

"No, my dear, I won't."

"But—"

"For your sake. You deserve a far better wife than I could make. You deserve a wife that has the passion for you that I have for the theater. I knew tonight. I had always hoped, dreamed. Always knew I wanted to act and thought I could. But tonight I knew."

How could she explain to him what she felt at curtain call? The sense of mission that she had something to give to her audience . . .

"Pedar, I don't entirely understand it myself, but tonight I knew I had done something important. And I want to go on doing it. Never in all my dreams, my playacting, my rehearsing, has anything been so glorious. Life can hold nothing more wonderful for me."

"Yes, of course. I understand fully. Don't you think I feel the same way—about my work and yours? And just think what we can accomplish together. Marry—"

She silenced him with a gentle finger on his lips. "No. I'm a very total person. When I give myself to something, I give all of me. I must give all of myself to my acting. There would be nothing left over to give to a husband—even one as dear as you."

He was silent. The drizzle that had begun the day started again, spattering against the side of the carriage.

"Pedar, talk to me of the future. We must go on, giving the world and our art our very best—working together. Tell me about the future."

"Dublin," he began hesitantly. "It will be a year. Two years. But the Abbey is the pinnacle. We'll work with Yeats, Martyn, Lady Gregory—" His voice suddenly took on a new ring, devoid of the note of supplication it had held earlier. Now she heard confidence, woven round with wisps of dream. Now he grasped her hands with far more enthusiasm than he had in the role of entreating lover. "Tomorrow I will post a copy of *Princess Deirdre* to Lady Gregory. If she likes it I—we—will be on our way."

82

"Will you be home for Easter, Nora?"

She looked from the green and rose floral wallpaper of her mother's sitting room to her mother herself. Eileen Armstrong looked even more like a fine porcelain figurine today than she usually did. Always her mother had embodied the full definition of a lady in Nora's mind: understated elegance, unflappable manners, always putting the needs of others first. Still Nora heard the wistful note. Her mother would do nothing to stand in the way of her daughter's success, but she would so much like to have her here at the bawn, nestled in the heart of the family.

Nora gave her an impulsive hug. "No, Mama, not Easter. The play opens just before. I won't be home sooner than midsummer—unless I'm a terrible bomb."

"I'm sure there's very little chance of that, after all your successes in Belfast. I just don't see why . . ." She ended with a shrug.

"There's no other theater in Ireland like the Abbey—no other in the world, for that matter. I'll be working with Ireland's greatest talent. They've developed an entirely new style all their own. They've fused the best elements of romanticism and realism—lyrical, poetic speech presented with simple, natural acting. And it's pure Irish."

"Yes, darling." Eileen Armstrong squeezed her daughter's hand, then rose from the sofa. "But do take care of yourself. These are such troubled times."

And Nora knew that was as close as Eileen Armstrong would come to making a scene. Troubled times, indeed. Times when a daughter might think of staying at home to be of comfort to her family. She was not spared the stab of guilt such thoughts might be expected to produce.

All through the 1915–1916 winter, the German war effort had been focused on a fifteen-mile strip of land just inside the French-Belgian border—that demarcation now being called the Western Front. It was apparent that Germany's strategy was to bleed France to collapse, after which Great Britain would have no effective military ally in

715

Europe. From there, Germany believed, it would be an easy step to bring Britain to terms.

Just two months ago, Britain had passed the Military Service Act and had begun conscription, as well as beefing up efforts at enlistment in Ireland, which was not to be conscripted. The deal that Ulster leader Sir Edward Carson had struck with the British government at the outbreak of the war not only postponed implementation of Home Rule until after the war but also assured special consideration for Ulster. Part of Ulster's accommodation had been the formation of her own Army Division, the 36th Ulster. Men were enrolled from the Ulster Volunteer Force, and their initial training took place in Ulster.

All that had been months ago. Since that brave day when the local enlisted men marched off, led by a fife band and followed by most of the residents, the North Down toll had risen: Their first wounded. Then the first casualty. Then second and third, and the number continued to mount.

So far—although they had lost many acquaintances and friends—the Lanarks' Bawn family was unscathed. Lanark was unlikely to enlist. He was giving all his effort to shipbuilding for the Royal Navy and his wife was expecting again. Nora held her breath, though, when she thought of her younger brother. Eric would be ready for university this fall, and she well knew how close to the surface such lads' patriotism boiled. If only it could all be over before Eric was old enough to join up.

She glanced at her mother's knitting basket, where a nearly finished woolen waistcoat testified to Eileen's efforts with the Newtownards Ladies' Association. And now the guilt stabbed more deeply. What was *she* doing to help? Nora wondered. Pedar insisted that the work of artists was important. It gave people moments of beauty and inspiration and helped them see beyond the war to a world worth rebuilding. She hoped he was right. She often questioned Pedar's high view of art, and yet she loved to hear him espouse it.

Eileen smoothed her ivory lace skirt. "Shall we go down? Surely we've waited long enough for our tea. Your father has had more than enough time to finish his cigar by now." It was tradition for the Armstrong ladies to retire after dinner to allow the men their cigars and port before the tea tray went into the parlor.

"And time to win at least one argument," Nora added with a laugh. "Let's go so he can take a few pot shots at me." She started toward the door.

"My dear, you know how much your father loves you. It's just his way." And it was Eileen Armstrong's way to want to soothe everyone's feelings.

"I know, Mama."

"It just seems everyone's nerves are so on edge. And everyone is simply exhausted with working night and day doing everything we can. The shipyards are working around the clock. It's a miracle Lanark managed to come to dinner tonight. And your father is run off his feet supervising in the fields. We've close to doubled our linen production. There's so much needed for uniforms, and now they're talking of needing airplane fabric. I must be at the church hall first thing in the morning to pack the boxes of donated supplies we've gathered for our boys—mittens, sweets, pencils . . ."

Nora took her arm. "I know, Mama. And I'll try not to add to your worries by fighting with Father."

That was easier said than done, however. The men were in the parlor before them, and Thom Armstrong had already worked up a full head of steam. He was railing at Pedar about the disloyalty of his fellow Gaelic revivalist Sir Roger Casement. "The Germans—gone to the Germans, he has!" Thom shook the *Belfast News Letter* in Pedar's face.

"I understand that was to work with Irish prisoners of war." The playwright's reply was mild.

"Oh, aye. Work with them all right. Working to recruit them to fight against England. 'The enemy of our enemy is our friend.' How dare he? The swine!" He rounded on Nora as she entered. "Here, see this, girl? One of the founders of your Literary Theatre. What have you to say for yourself, associating with the likes of that?"

"I never met the man, Father. But if I did, I would tell him I think he's a traitor and a swine." She hoped the statement, and the brilliant smile she followed it up with, would mollify her father. And most desperately she hoped that he would not use the matter to attempt to keep her from going to Dublin.

Perhaps her words did satisfy him, or perhaps he knew his daughter too well to try to divert her from her course. Perhaps he understood that, although she stated her decisions in softer terms, Nora had inherited her strong will from him. Whatever the reason, Thom changed the subject, turning to ask his oldest son about the possibility of Campbell & Wilson adding airplane production to their shipbuilding.

"Airplanes!" Eric had just jumped into the conversation with eager questions when the maid ushered in two newcomers.

Nora stared at the uniforms both wore. Victoria's was soft gray with a white apron. Her only decoration was a red cross on her small white cap. "Vicky, you're a real nurse!" She bent to hug the girl, who looked even tinier under all her stiffly starched cotton.

"I loved my nursing classes with the Women's Unionist Association, so I decided to really do something with it. Especially since Stuart—"

She faltered as she turned to him. Her smile was brave, but Nora was certain there were tears in her eyes.

Stuart Price stood tall in a khaki wool uniform crossed with a gleaming white Sam Browne belt, and on his cap was the special badge of the 36th Ulster Division. He grinned almost bashfully. "Aye. Raising horses for the army was all very well, but I did feel I might be doing a bit more."

"Dear boy." Eileen put a hand on his shoulder. "Dear, dear boy." Her hand slid down his arm to squeeze his hand. She said no more.

Even Eric, who generally met everything in life with a laugh, was subdued. "'I would be true for there are those who trust me, I would be strong for there is much to suffer, I would be brave for there is much to dare.'"

He quoted from the pledge card that had been given to the first company of Newtownards Volunteers to join the Ulster Division. There were now some 850 Newtownards men serving in France, and the entire Ulster Division numbered nearly 35,000. Holding the Western Front was becoming grim business, and daily the home front realized more and more how much their own survival depended on that thin, fifteen-mile line.

Eric recovered from his somber mood quickly. His blue eyes twinkled, and his freckles seemed to dance as he slapped his cousin on the back. "You're a dark one, you old dog. Don't you be thinking we haven't heard plenty about how good-looking those French girls are."

The remark garnered more laughter than it deserved. Everyone seemed relieved for a chance to break the tension.

Stuart put his arm around Victoria and pulled her close. "Glad you brought that up, Eric. Vicky and I have something else to tell you."

Nora clapped her hands and squealed. "You're engaged! At last!" She darted forward to embrace them both, then stopped in confusion as they both shook their heads.

"Not so fast, my impetuous cousin." Stuart grinned at her. "You're not the only one allowed to be impetuous. And I'm not quite the slow-top everyone thinks me to be. Vicky and I aren't engaged—we're married."

Now the room that had been so grave a few minutes before erupted in celebration. Thom rang for the maid to bring glasses and a bottle of his best champagne, and the bride and groom took turns telling about their decision to be married by special license at the Newtownards City Hall.

"Stuart's division leaves next week for training. We didn't want to waste any time," Victoria explained. "We've known we'd get married since the day we met at that horse show. At least *I* was certain. But it always seemed we had all the time in the world. Now . . ."

As her voice trailed off, Stuart jumped in. "Actually, it's all worked out very well. Vicky will be nursing at St. Bart's in London while I'm in Seaford, so we'll still be able to see each other on weekends."

"And when Stuart goes to France, I shall volunteer to go to LeHavre with the nursing corps. So it's all for the best."

Nora wondered if part of Victoria's emphasis on the rosy aspects of the situation was really to convince herself. But she matched the new bride's smile with no hint of skepticism.

"That all sounds very jolly, indeed. But who will be seeing to Price Manor, young man?" Thom Armstrong wanted to know. "You have responsibilities here as well. Can't just be dashing off to France in a blaze of glory and let everything go to rack and ruin at home."

"Don't worry, uncle. The Price stables will be in more capable hands than anything you've seen yet." He turned to his wife of a few hours. "Tell them, Vicky."

"My Aunt Meg is one of the best horse breeders in all of County Armagh, and she'll be bringing some of her prize stock as well as her daughter. With Meg's knowledge and Irene's energy you won't be able to see the stables for the dust they'll raise." She chuckled. "And my father can relax for the first time since his brother died and Daddy took Uncle Charlie's widow and daughter under his wing."

"Yes, I do believe it sounds as if you've worked everything out very well." Eileen raised her glass to the newlyweds.

Nora replayed that scene in her mind later that night in her room. How lovely that, in this uncertain time, Stuart and Vicky had taken such sure steps. And how lovely that with so much unhappiness in the world they could be happy—at least for a little while. And their happiness sprang from more than just their marriage. They were also happy because they had made choices to take action for their country. Vicky's fund raising for the WUA had been important, as was Stuart's work producing horses and crops. No one would have faulted them had they stayed securely at home. But they had chosen to answer the call to duty in a more personal way.

Again, Nora couldn't help asking, *What about me?* She truly believed that the things Pedar was saying through his plays were important. The Ireland that had produced the Book of Kells had cherished art and learning and preserved it for the world. Ireland could be like that again. That was the Celtic Revival he envisioned. Nora was convinced no other actress could communicate that vision with quite the same passion she brought to her roles.

Still . . . She fingered the silken fringe bordering a pillow, then tossed it on the floor. Was she a coward, hiding behind her misty vision when the real battles that must be fought were military and political? What if the Western Front didn't hold? It was unthinkable, but sometimes the unthinkable must be thought. What if Germany overran France? Then England? Then Ireland? What would that do to any hopes for renewing Ireland as a land of faith and culture?

Head up, shoulders back, she crossed the room and faced the mirror at her dressing table. She looked at her reflection honestly, objectively, as if studying a character for a role. Was she being shallow? Was she running away from her duty? And if the answer was yes, then what *was* her duty?

83

Nora was still asking herself that three days later when she arrived in Dublin, though the intensity of the asking faded as she lost herself in the wonders of the city. She had been to Dublin only a few times in her life but loved it more each time. Even in early March, it met her with open arms and both hands full of daffodils.

She left her room behind Trinity College, peeking in at the green serenity of College Park but not taking time to stop. As she continued along the classical Corinthian front of the college, the cries of buskers and fishwomen reached her from Grafton Street where they pushed their two-wheeled carts up and down. Traffic swept around the curve of College Street, led by a clanging electric tram closely followed by a crush of carriages, cars, and horse-drawn, double-decker coaches.

She crossed the bridge over the Liffey and looked down on the boats and barges filling the river. She wished she had time to dawdle, but she must hurry. Of all the times in her life, she who never liked to be tardy for anything did not want to arrive late on her first day as a member of the Abbey Repertory Company.

Sackville Street was even busier than College Green had been. Nora wondered if people ever got used to all the bustle and noise. Belfast had seemed hurley-burley after the quiet of Lanarks' Bawn, but it was nothing compared to Dublin, often called the second city of the Empire. She glanced up Sackville, toward the General Post Office, wishing she had time just to dash up to the next corner and mail letters to her mother and Victoria. But prudence dictated that she turn right onto the quieter Abbey Street.

For all the stature it was gaining in the world of arts, the Abbey Theatre, built in 1904 at the expense of an American patroness, was a disappointment architecturally. Its drab, gray stone exterior was little relieved by its one outstanding feature—an art nouveau canopy.

Nora couldn't have cared less what it looked like, however. She knew what it stood for. Unlike other theaters—which had been built to house the performance of plays—the Abbey had been built to house the spirit of a people. The National Theatre Society was dedicated to bringing together Ireland's great literary forms—narrative, lyrical, and dramatic—and to producing new plays in a manner accessible to all the people. And she was to be part of it all.

She pushed through the door and crossed the darkened lobby, dimly aware of the black-and-white tiled floor and wood paneled walls. Beyond the grilled ticket windows was the doorway to the theater. She went on into the darkened auditorium. It wasn't a large theater. She guessed it would seat about five hundred people. Still, if they played to full houses, several thousand would see their plays in the course of the usual fortnight's run.

At first the two men on the stage did not see her. It was clear from the intensity of their voices and emphasis of their gestures that *Princess Deirdre* had met a clash of artistic wills even before rehearsals began.

Pedar stood in the center of the bare stage. The harsh overhead lighting made his features seem thinner and sharper than ever and his eyes darker and brighter. "And furthermore, if I had chosen to write my play with musical accompaniment, I would not have chosen a harp!"

The other man was only of middling size, but next to the pared-to-the-bone Pedar he seemed large. The perfect oval of his face was broken by a long, thin mustache. "The harp is the symbol of Ireland," he said.

"Aye, but an Ireland balancing uncomfortably between manor house and cottage. The harp only flourished under aristocratic patronage. It would do at Conchubar's court, but the exiled lovers would have pipes—if anything."

"The singers and minstrels—"

Nora caught Pedar's eye as she approached the spill of the stage light.

"Ah, Nora, come meet John Ervine, your director."

Since Nora's joining the company had been something of a package deal with *Princess Deirdre*, which Lady Gregory was anxious to bring to the Abbey, she had not met any of the other artists yet. She knew the acclaimed director only by reputation. She started to acknowledge the introduction, but Pedar rushed on in a tone of dismissive disgust.

"It seems that Yeats's latest interest is Japanese Noh drama, which involves the accompaniment of musicians, so we are to have music with all our plays."

"Not all. That would be ludicrous. But I see this play—one that has been brought down to us by our great bardic tradition—as one where the links with our artistic past can be strengthened by subtly suggesting the presence of a *seanachaidh*."

As if on cue, an evocative melody floated to them from offstage. Ervine gestured with a flourish. "Eoin, center stage."

The man who emerged from the backstage gloom carrying a small harp was tall and slim with auburn hair. Fanciful as it seemed, he gave Nora the impression of a birch tree in autumn. It was an image that was enhanced as Ervine made the introductions and the musician bowed slightly as if blown by the wind.

Nora wrinkled her forehead at the name. "Eoin MacHenry? My grandmother's name was MacHenry."

He shrugged, his long, loose limbs stirring the image of graceful branches. "Unlikely to be a connection if I've the right of it that you're from County Down, Miss Armstrong. I'm Dublin born and bred for two generations, and from Donegal before that."

"Call me Nora, please. And I'll not be so easily put off. My grandmother was from somewhere in the west."

"*Och*, it was no attempt to put you off, be assured. It's just that I'd not be assuming where I'm not welcome." Eoin's smile was pure Irish laughter drawn from a clear, babbling brook.

Nora couldn't hold back a mirthful trill. "I don't think that would be possible, Eoin MacHenry." She caught Pedar's scowl out of the corner of her eye.

"Eoin is our harpist," Ervine said, unnecessarily.

Now Pedar's scowl deepened to an open frown. "The words make their own music. We need no more."

Ervine ignored him. "Ah, and here are the others." And the director introduced the rest of the cast.

Norton Riley, who was to play Naise, had an athletic build that made one think him a more likely footballer than actor, but his boyish grin showed promise of the appeal he would have as a romantic hero. Anna Fitzgerald was not much older than Nora, but her short, plump stature had a comforting quality that was just right for Deirdre's nurse. There was nothing about the unassuming Bernard Vance, however, that made Nora think he could embody the tyrannical presence of the King of Ulster—not, that is, until he acknowledged the introduction and his powerful voice rolled forth. The director went on through the company as he moved a few straight-backed chairs downstage for the first read-through.

And soon all artistic and personality conflicts were set aside as they began spinning the complex strands that would ultimately weave the complete web of dreams for entrancing their audiences.

And, indeed, the music of the harp was part of that weaving. Eoin sat on a low stool on the apron of the stage and played only a hint of rhythm or melody at times of greatest intensity or most serene calm. But even those few notes were enough to tell Nora that this would be a very different production than the one she had been part of in Belfast.

This would be John Ervine's interpretation of his own vision. The director took control, and the playwright was relegated to the back of the auditorium.

It was a much longer rehearsal than Nora had expected. And when it was over she was more tired and hungry than she had expected. After all, she had only sat there and read. And yet she was emotionally drained.

"May I take you to dinner, Miss Armstrong?" Eoin MacHenry offered his hand to assist her from her seat.

She certainly hadn't realized she would need any assistance, but she laughed as she stumbled against him. "Oh, my goodness, I've been sitting too long. I would like to have dinner with you—but only if you call me Nora."

He turned to pack his harp in its wooden case, and Pedar came down the aisle. "We must hurry, Nora. Must change for the party."

"What party?"

"Edna St. George is giving a salon—something for the war effort —I told her I would bring you."

"I'm sorry, Pedar, but I didn't know anything about this. And I've made other plans."

"What—" Before he could ask what plans, Eoin returned and offered his arm. Pedar spun on his heel and walked back up the aisle.

Eoin took her to a small pub off Grafton Street, where she had the general impression of dark wood, smoke, and raised voices. Thankfully, there was a small room for dining off to the side. The high backs on the benches gave the feeling of privacy. Eoin ordered pints of Guinness and large plates of Irish stew for them both.

As soon as they were served, he held his mug aloft. "Ah, 'tis said an Irishman drinks only on two occasions. When he's thirsty and when he's not." He took a deep drink. "Now, tell me all about yourself, my pretty cousin."

"So you'll allow us kinship, will you?"

"I'll allow us anything you'll talk to me about."

And so they talked. Nora was fascinated with his flashes of wit. They sometimes reminded her of the teasing of her younger brother. Then, as quickly, the humor would be replaced by an incisive remark, usually directed to the glories of Irish music or to hatred of the English, for those seemed to be the two themes that held his thoughts. But whether he was being bitingly political, fancifully artistic, or giving a charming compliment, Nora was attracted to Eoin's intelligence, energy, and sense of fun. She was eager to get to know him better.

Somewhere in the conversation, the name Brendan MacHenry was mentioned, and Nora remembered. "Yes! That was the name of my grandmother's father—he was a blind *seanachaidah*. Some of his songs have been published."

"*Och*, that's right. So you are real Irish. I should have guessed. Deirdre's in your blood. I never knew much family history. My grandfather was killed in some Fenian bombing when my father was a wane. Tell me about my great-grandfather."

Nora crumbled her last piece of soda bread into the empty stew plate in front of her. "I wish I could. My father never talked about that particular bit of our family history. I would hardly know about it at all if it weren't for Pedar." She paused. "Eoin, I hope you and Pedar can come to terms. You know, he's some sort of cousin, too. And you have so much in common. But tell me about the rest of your family."

Eoin shrugged. "My father's named Brendan as well. I have a younger brother, Conor. Wants to be a priest." He paused. "That's it." And that was all Eoin MacHenry chose to say on the subject.

Nora felt that she would be prying to ask more, so she turned her queries to the Abbey company. "I'm so looking forward to meeting Lady Gregory."

"You'll be meeting Augusta the Great, don't be worrying on that score. The grand duchess will likely be showing up at rehearsal some night with one of her famous barmbrack fruitcakes."

Nora arched an eyebrow.

"Forgive me. She's true enough the great lady. The Abbey wouldn't exist without her energy and her money. Sometimes I think she keeps this whole place going by the sheer force of her willpower, especially now with Synge dead, Yeats off in London, Maude Gonne nursing in France . . ."

"So?"

He shrugged. "So nothing. Sometimes I feel a little overpowered by her, that's all. Just me, I expect—natural reaction of the Irish Catholic peasant to the Anglo-English overlord."

"Even when you're working for the same thing?"

"Are we? That's what I'd like to know."

Nora sensed that another door had just shut. Obviously, her complex companion partially achieved his impression of being a tree in the wind by a certain amount of bending to the prevailing forces. That bending prevented his being broken.

She was leaning against the back of her seat, laughing at some offhand remark of his when two men approached with what struck her as assumed nonchalance. They greeted Eoin.

When it became clear that they weren't just passing through the room, Eoin introduced her to Terrance, the thin dark one with a scar on his chin, and to Patrick, with the round face and pale hair with streaks of red. Terrance said little, Patrick nothing, yet it appeared to Nora that some communication had passed among the three men.

When they left, Eoin returned to being the charming companion he had been earlier, but he soon came to his feet. "What am I doing keeping you out past all saints' hours, and you with rehearsal in the morning?" He held out a hand to help her from the booth.

"And you've rehearsal, too, I believe?"

"Aye, but I can play the harp if I can breathe. A bit more's required of you."

They walked along the dark narrow pavement to her boarding-house and up the three steps to the green door. He waited while she unlocked the door before bidding her good night. Mrs. Murray had very firm rules restricting boarders' guests in the house.

The door clicked shut behind her, and she stepped across the small foyer to the stairs.

"Nora." The parlor door to her left flung open.

"Oh! Pedar, you startled me." Visitors were not allowed, but fellow boarders could use the parlor at all hours, providing they disturbed no one else. "What are you doing up?"

"Waiting for you, of course."

She laughed to hide her irritation. "Pedar, I don't need a nanny." Was he jealous of her friendship with Eoin? She had thought the clash between the two men was only on artistic grounds, but that would not explain this. Pedar had asked her to marry him only once more during the past eighteen months and had taken her refusal well. She thought the matter closed. She hoped so.

"Maybe not a nanny, but you need a warning. I'll not have you drawn into any Fenian conspiracies. Besides all the other arguments I could make, it would ruin your art."

She didn't know whether to laugh or be angry. She settled for scorn. "Don't be ridiculous. Nothing could be farther from my mind. I've never had a political thought in my life." She started for the stairs, then spoiled her exit by turning back again. "But one could hardly argue that Maude Gonne or Constance Markiewicz have spoiled their art with their Nationalist activities." She warmed to her subject, stepping back into the parlor. "As a matter of fact, if Maude Gonne hadn't been known as such a passionate Nationalist, much of the symbolism of her portrayal of the old woman in *Cathleen ni Houlihan* would have been lost."

"Yes, that's exactly my point. Think what you're saying, Nora. Think of what we're trying to say in our plays."

Her mouth fell open. "*Our* plays? Your plays, surely, Pedar."

"You are always part of my vision, you know that." The room fell silent. The last tram rattled and ground its way homeward two streets over. He moved as if to take her hand, but didn't. "I don't stand for an Ireland forged by bullets, nor do the plays I write and you act in. If you should be drawn into an activist conspiracy, it would ruin everything."

She took breath to argue, but he held up a hand.

"Oh, you could still mouth the words, but you could no longer *be* the meaning. True art cannot be a lie. In the end, the person the artist is will speak louder than any words."

Her head was beginning to ache. This was no time for a philosophical discussion on the aesthetics of artistic truth. And yet, as if in support of his premise, the force of his personality would not release her. "The person is more powerful than words, and words are more powerful than bullets."

"Exactly." Even in the deep shadows of a room lighted by one shaded lamp, Pedar's eyes glowed with the fire of passion. "My vision is for an Ireland that cannot be achieved by armies or diplomats. No treaty can ignite what I would have enkindled in the hearts of all Irish." Now he did take her hands. "Stay with me in this, Nora."

And then he was the one to exit, leaving her alone on the worn plush couch, trying to sort through her thoughts. Was Pedar speaking for Ireland and for his art, or was he using them as another man might use money or power to entice a woman to romantic interest? Was he lashing out in jealousy at Eoin with the tool closest to hand, or did he know something secret of the musician's political connections?

She had to admit there had been moments during the evening when she had questioned whether Eoin was not something more than the charming will-o'-the-wisp she had first envisioned him to be. In most of Ulster, certainly in Lanarks' Bawn, one believed all members of the Sinn Fein party could be recognized readily by their horns and cloven hooves. She had been in Dublin less than a week, and already she knew matters were not so simple.

But whatever Eoin's views on the best method of achieving Home Rule—and there was no doubt he believed in it—by no stretch of her imagination could she picture him as a bomb-throwing Fenian or a gunrunning member of the Brotherhood.

And whatever the truth, she was determined to learn the facts.

For the next two days, Eoin's smile warmed her with its usual grace, and his lilting harp offered the perfect pace to the play. But the harpist melted into the darkness of the auditorium before the last of the bardic strains accompanying Deirdre's final speech ceased echoing.

Then, after three weeks of frustrating starts and stops, came the day every company prays for. For the entire space of the first act, everyone got his cues on time, each character filled the space blocked for him at the proper moment, and even the prompt girl couldn't see her script for the tears in her eyes. Ervine released them an hour early. And for once Eoin seemed to be in no hurry.

A gentle April sunshine drew them out of doors. "Have you been to Phoenix Park yet?" he asked.

She hadn't, and there was no place she would rather spend a late spring afternoon. At the corner of Abbey and Sackville Streets they clambered to the top of a double-decker pulled by four black horses sporting plumes that bobbed with each step. The coach rolled along the quay while the afternoon sun shone on the Liffey and highlighted the dome of the Four Courts, center of Ireland's judicial system.

At the entrance to the park, they left the conveyance and walked slowly through the People's Garden, where a blaze of yellow and red primroses alternated with beds of tulips.

Nora took a deep breath of the wonderful fresh air. "I really had no idea Dublin was so lovely."

"And have you not been here before?"

"Oh, yes, a few times, strictly guarded by my father, of course. Somehow it rather lacked the sense of freedom I find here now."

They laughed together, and Eoin suggested that, should she be feeling homesick, they might go to the zoological gardens, which were noted for their lions.

Amid all the lightheartedness and beauty, it took her some time to get the topic around to politics—although it never took any Irishman too long to take up the subject. She stuck carefully to questions of a general nature, never anything that would imply she thought him to be a revolutionary. Of course, she didn't think that. And if he were (silly notion), she wouldn't want to know.

"But I don't understand why anyone would be interested in revolution now. What's there to fight for? The king signed the Home Rule Bill. It's all done."

"Yes, all the words are on paper."

"Is that all? I thought John Redmond had a provisional government all organized—ready to take over as soon as the war ends."

"And isn't that just the crux of the matter—'as soon as the war ends'? There are those who grow restless. Impatience can be a strong unifier."

Unifier, maybe; but motive for *killing*? She had heard her father rail against the Irish Republican Brotherhood, a renegade Fenian army. Its insurrectionary tradition included a long list of dynamiters and convicted gunrunners. And of late, an Irish Citizen Army had been organized to guard the newly emerged labor unions.

Nora shivered. In the middle of that sunlit spring garden she suddenly had a picture of Ireland's peaceful green fields as riddled by unofficial armies as the Western Front. That was silly, of course. Whatever was thought of in the north and whatever special considerations Sir Edward Carson might carve out for Ulster, Home Rule had passed. "Surely most Nationalists are reasonable enough to await the natural course of Home Rule. John Redmond—"

"Redmond recruited twenty-seven thousand Irishmen for the British Army as a gesture of Irish goodwill!"

Nora started at the contempt in his voice. She even turned to look at him. "What could possibly be wrong with good will? There's little enough of it in the world. And surely the British are more likely to give us what we want if we show willingness to work with them. If we're friends, rather than enemies—"

His laugh broke through her words. And the amazing thing about it was that he wasn't jeering or mocking. He was genuinely amused, and his infectious laughter caught her up as well, although she had no idea what she was laughing at.

Other strollers looked at them and smiled. Some even gave a little chuckle as well. This was a world living on the knife-edge. Any excuse for mirth was welcomed.

At last Eoin wiped his eyes. "Oh, my darling, innocent Nora. I hadn't realized until that moment how much I love you. I must say that would be a fresh approach—make friends with the English by giving them everything they want and at the end of the day say, 'Now, please may I have my lolly?'"

Her face fell. She turned away from him. "Eoin, you are laughing at me. I realize I don't know anything about politics, but I—"

He put his arm around her and spun her around. "No, no, Nora. My darling, I could never laugh at you. I've known you only a few weeks, and already I realize I'd sooner laugh at my own ability to breathe. But I'd also sooner try to make friends with the lions in the zoo than with the English."

As if on cue, a roar issued from one of the big golden cats pacing back and forth in his great iron cage.

They skirted the display of carnivores for which the Dublin zoo was famous and went on to a lake, where pelicans and flamingos sunned themselves on green banks rimmed with purple and yellow iris.

Eoin took her hand. "You see, my sweet innocent, committing the Irish Volunteers to the British war effort reduces the pressure on England to implement Home Rule. By his act of 'friendly cooperation,' Redmond may have undercut everything Irish men and women have struggled for since 1801."

"I would like to understand, Eoin. I truly would."

But for the moment it was impossible to believe that the fate of nations, including their own, was hanging in the balance as men, many of them Irish, died in France. Two boys in knee pants and sailor shirts skipped by, rolling hoops. A dark-caped nurse pushed a shiny black pram down the walkway, followed by two little girls in white frocks and straw hats.

"All right, I'll try to explain." He took up the subject of a rising as casually as if they had been discussing the thematic structure of a new play. "This is nothing you'd read in the *Irish Times,* you understand, but the word on the street is often a lot closer to the truth than what you read."

Nora nodded.

"About a year ago a few of the IRB met in secret and pledged to mount an insurrection sometime during the war. Their goal being not just Home Rule but Ireland's total independence."

"*Total* independence?" Home Rule was a shocking concept to an Ulsterwoman. Total independence was as unthinkable as atheism. "But who wants anything so radical?"

"I'm just giving you the background. Most Nationalists are content with the concept of Home Rule and support the patient approach of Redmond's Irish National Party. Twenty-seven thousand volunteers wouldn't have marched off to France in reply to his appeal if they didn't."

"So?"

"Redmond's recruiting drove a split in the Irish Republican Brotherhood. Some of the IRB broke away to form another group—the Sinn Fein Volunteers."

"But I thought Sinn Fein was just political."

"The founders—Arthur Griffiths, Maude Gonne, the Countess Markiewicz—they're political. The Sinn Fein Volunteers were just formed to keep up the pressure for Home Rule. The thing is, a lot of the more revolutionary members of the IRB joined, too."

"Took the chance and infiltrated, you mean?"

He shrugged. "You could say it that way."

"And so now?"

"So now you hear things—in pubs and the like—talk of a rising. That's the background."

"But you aren't worried, Eoin?"

He shook his russet head.

Questions flitted across her mind like blown leaves. How did he know so much about secret meetings and infiltrations? How did he feel about such insurrectionist activity? How did his political leanings affect her feelings for him? They were questions to which she had no answers.

And then, in one of those right-angle turns that conversations sometimes take, they were talking about their younger brothers. Conor, it seemed, was just a year older than Eric. He was in his first year of training for the priesthood at Maynooth.

Eoin grinned. "Amazing, isn't it? My grandfather was a Fenian bomber, and here's Conor and me—a priest and a musician."

"And what about your father?"

He must not have heard her question, because he said, "Tell me about your brother."

She sighed. "I wish Eric were someplace safe like seminary. He'll go to university this fall because he isn't old enough to enlist, but if the war isn't over soon . . ."

Eoin squeezed her hand, and she gave him a wavery smile. Then she went on to tell about Stuart, safe for the moment training in Sussex—but for how long? And Victoria planning to go to France as a nurse. And . . . She was totally amazed when she looked around and realized how long the shadows were getting. She laughed. "What a chatterbox. I must have told you my entire family history."

"Well, if you've got the right of it, it's seeming it must be my family history, too. But Nora, there's no way on this earth I'll be thinking of you as a cousin."

They stood at the foot of the Wellington Testimonial, an impressive obelisk higher than a two-story building. But Nora's mind was on the man beside her. The tenderness in his voice touched her more than anything else. That and the fact that she felt such a closeness to him. The relationship she wanted with Eoin MacHenry was far closer than that of cousin.

And yet how were such feelings possible? Aside from the fact that Eoin was the most fascinating man she had ever met, she hardly knew him. And most of the things she knew about him were ones that should drive them apart. All the Nationalist ideas he had explained so passionately were, at root, abhorrent to her. He was descended from a line of Fenians. She from a line of Orangemen. He was Catholic. She was Presbyterian. Still . . .

84

And then it was the second week in April. *Princess Deirdre* was to open that weekend. Lady Gregory would give one of the first-night suppers for which she had become famous and which had done much to promote public relations for the Abbey. The theater ever teetered on the brink of financial ruin and would have plunged down that sheer precipice many times had it not been for the great lady's willingness to leap into the breach with her personal fortune and effort.

Since that golden stroll in Phoenix Park, there had been many similar and increasingly intimate occasions. And she was coming to know Dublin better at the same time she tried to absorb every morsel of Eoin MacHenry. They visited the elegant Christ Church Cathedral and, just down the road, the even larger and statelier St. Patrick's, the national cathedral of the Church of Ireland, which Cromwell used as a stable and where Jonathan Swift was now buried. They visited the lovely little park St. Stephen's Green, surrounded by elegant mansions. They visited Trinity College, which Nora never tired of visiting, always picturing Eric as one of the black-robed undergraduates they met strolling across the green or bent over books at one of the long library tables. And such a library it was, housing the Book of Durrow, the Book of Armagh, the Book of Kells.

And the ancient Irish harp often called Brian Boru's.

"Of course, it isn't anything near old enough to have known Brian Boru, but, ah, it's a grand instrument," Eoin said.

Nora, in accord with him as she was, could feel the aching tingle in his fingers to run his hand over the satiny wood and to pluck the ancient strings.

Suddenly she grabbed his arm. Why hadn't she thought of it sooner? She couldn't modulate her voice to an appropriately sepulchural level for a library, so she steered Eoin out into the soft evening rain. "Eoin! The harp! I have it! Well, that is, my family does. Grandmother Deirdre brought it with her from Donegal."

Eoin looked at her as if she had just produced St. Veronica's veil. "Brendan MacHenry's harp?"

"Aye. Brendan's and Cashel's and however many MacHenrys before them. It's of black bog oak, much darker than Brian Boru's—"

He stopped her babbling with a kiss full on her lips. "Nora Armstrong, I love you. Marry me."

Three black-capped heads halfway across the green turned at her laughter.

"Eoin, you don't have to marry me to get the harp. It's yours by right. Oh, if only we had it here for you to play for opening night. But there's no time to go north before—"

The gowned men applauded when Eoin kissed Nora a second time.

"Will you listen to me, adorable one? I didn't say a thing about the harp. I said, I love you. I've known it for weeks—been dying to tell you for weeks. Actually, I have told you. Every time I played for Deirdre and Naise, I was playing for us, putting all my love into the notes. But just now when you came so alive in there in that narrow dark room, surrounded by all those dusty books, and you lit up like the finest crystal chandelier because you'd thought of something to make me happy—oh, Nora, my darling . . ."

"Yes, yes, silly. Of course I'll marry you." Catholic-Protestant, Nationalist-Unionist—neither mattered. Eoin-Nora was all that mattered.

"But what shall we do? Our families—I mean, at least, my family—" Catholic and Nationalist might not matter to her, but there was no way she could present Thom Armstrong with such for a son-in-law. Then her laughter was a bright waterfall of excitement, and she clapped her hands. "Yes! We'll be like Deirdre and Naise. We'll run off to Scotland. Or Australia. Oh, it doesn't matter, just so we're together." And somehow she would get the harp for him as a wedding present.

Now he became serious. He grabbed a handful of his wavy hair and pulled as if he would take it out by the roots. "Oh, what was I thinking? I wasn't thinking, that's all there is to it. Oh, Nora, it will never work."

"It will. It has to. We'll make it work." The matter was simple to her. Just do it. When the pieces fell and the dust cleared, there would be time to do what could be done to clear them up.

"Nora, there are things—things beyond our control—" He closed his eyes and took a deep breath. "Right. You must meet my father."

"I'd love to. And Conor as well." Then she stopped. But would Conor want to meet her? How would an ordinand or acolyte or whatever he was called react to a having a Presbyterian sister? And Eoin's father, would he be as unwelcoming to her as her father would be to Eoin? At last her voice was subdued. "I-I hadn't thought about your father, Eoin. You've talked about him so little. I guess I thought he was dead."

"Come on."

At the top of Grafton Street he hailed a cab. It took them around Dublin Castle, that bulwark of British administration, and on to St. Nicholas Street. It was an area Nora had seen briefly when visiting the cathedrals, the area known as the Liberties because in past times it had been outside the jurisdiction of the Lord Mayor. But other than noting its insalubrious, overcrowded conditions and the apparent misery of much of the population, she had gone by as quickly as possible. It had certainly never occurred to her that anyone she knew could live there. Certainly not Eoin.

They turned up Back Lane, which ran in front of Tailor's Hall. Eoin explained that the narrow, crowded houses had once been a colony of prosperous Huguenot weavers. "Five thousand people were employed at the looms here in the late eighteenth century."

The cab stopped, and Eoin handed her down to the dirty pavement. Without another word he led the way up a dark narrow stairway. At the first landing, he opened the door into a dim hall that offered a choice of closed doors. One showed a light in the wide crack underneath.

Eoin opened the door slowly.

"I tell you, MacHenry, the rejuvenating power of blood is what's needed. A blood sacrifice is necessary to liberate Ireland." The voice that floated to them so clearly was as well-projected and as sharply enunciated as if the speaker were accustomed to addressing a lecture hall full of people.

Eoin stepped backward and started to close the door. But it emitted a sharp squeak.

At the sound, a head of thick white hair, which was all Nora could see of the room's occupants, jerked up sharply. "Eoin, is that you, lad? Come ye in then. It's Paddy here for a visit. Paddy never forgets a brother, though there's not many these days that remembers an old war horse put out to pasture like myself." The voice wavered uncertainly, and the speaker's left hand groped along the arm of the chair.

Nora was so close to Eoin that she heard him swallow. "Yes, Daddy, it's me. But I've a friend with me. We'll come back later when you're not busy."

"And when am I ever too busy for my own dear boy? And would you be backing off down the stairs without greeting Paddy Pearse? And where would you be today if himself hadn't seen you through your lessons?"

Eoin's shoulders slumped. He stepped in, and Nora followed.

The room was small and poorly furnished but clean, almost stark in its impeccable neatness. No books or papers on the floor, no stools or small chairs out of place, nothing askew that a one-armed, blind man would be likely to trip over.

Eoin gripped the left hand his father held out to him and placed it in Nora's. "Daddy, I want you to meet Nora Armstrong. She's from the theater."

"Saints forgive us. What are you thinking of, boy? Help me up. I'd not be having the lass think me so mannerless I'd meet her seated." With her hand still in his, Brendan MacHenry's only way out of the deep, upholstered chair was with his son's help.

"Hello, Mr. MacHenry. I'm sorry about bursting in on you at such an awkward time—"

Brendan shook his leonine head. "Sure and there could be no such thing as an awkward time to be visited by one with the voice of an angel."

"And she's as beautiful as her voice, Da," Eoin added.

"You've no need to be telling me that. The blind have ways of seeing things you'll never understand." MacHenry was a handsome man in spite of the puckered skin around his eyes and the burn scars that ran down his right cheek. "My dear—" he squeezed Nora's hand "—you must meet my oldest friend, Paddy Pearse. The only one of my old mates that still brings me the news. But then, we were knowing Parnell together, and that's a special bond."

Nora turned and got her first look at the man she had heard speaking earlier. He had a high, narrow forehead, dark hair, and thin lips. Even before she shook his hand, she thought: *writer, schoolteacher.* "How do you do, Mr. Pearse. We heard a little of what you were saying when we came in." The words had sounded alarmingly revolutionary, but it was only fair that he know she had heard.

The men resumed their seats as Nora and Eoin crossed the room to a tattered sofa.

"Aye. Blood. So I was saying. It was ever so. In all the great sagas, in the myths of all people, in our own Christian faith. The power of blood to renew, to sanctify. There can be no birthing without it. So we cannot hope to birth a new nation without shedding blood. The old heart of the earth needs to be warmed with the red wine of the battlefield."

Pearse extended an arm as if giving an oration. "Ireland requires a sacrificial act. An act of beauty and bravery which will inspire the Irish people to overthrow British rule once and for all."

Was the man a fanatic revolutionary, a visionary priest, or a poetic scholar? Nora couldn't tell, but there was no doubt that he believed in what he was saying, and he said it well.

The conversation became comfortably general for a while, then

Brendan rose to make tea. Nora jumped up to help him, although she could see his tiny kitchenette was arranged so that he could manage on his own when alone.

A short time later Eoin suggested they should be going. On the street he looked for a cab, but Nora insisted that they walk. She felt an almost compulsive need for exercise, and walking would give them more time to talk.

As soon as their strides found an easy match, Eoin said, "I am sorry about throwing you in at the deep end, but I thought it best. You needed to see for yourself so you could understand."

"Eoin, your father is charming."

"Yes, that's what I wanted you to see. You had to experience him so you could understand."

"What is there to understand? I knew from day one that our backgrounds were as different as day and night. But what does that matter?" Even as she protested, Nora felt a tickle of fear at the back of her neck. Eoin was too serious. What was he really getting at? He wasn't asking her simply to understand the differences in their backgrounds. Something far more profound was taking place here. "Eoin?" Her hand had been resting gently on his arm. Now she gripped it. "What do you want me to understand?"

"Why I joined the Brotherhood." He said it so calmly.

They were several paces on down the pavement before it fully hit her. Eoin was a member of the Irish Republican Brotherhood. Her father and brother were Orangemen. Their love was Romeo and Juliet come to life. And she had a terrible premonition that it could well end just as tragically.

"I did it for him. For Da."

Now that the truth was out, his natural flow of words fell smoothly. "My grandfather Dermot—your grandmother's brother—and his young wife (although the term is probably merely honorary)—were killed in a dynamite explosion that was part of some hopeless rising. My orphan father was a wane then, but he was essentially taken into the Brotherhood. Grandfather's fellows became father, uncles, brothers to wee Brendan. He was making bombs for them by the time he was twelve. And he was good at it. He'll tell you himself straight; he makes no apology."

Their footsteps echoed against the dim walls of buildings as they turned off Ship Street to Stephen Street, skirting the back side of Dublin Castle. Nora felt an instinctive desire to shush Eoin, as if the British garrison in the castle could hear them.

But he continued in his steady way. "It was Da's anguish the night he heard of Parnell's fall—betrayed and run out of office by his own people, the very people Da had worked beside for years. That was much of Parnell's genius, you know—he gathered the revolutionaries around him, gave them offices in the Nationalist party, made them believe they could achieve their means peacefully. He was too successful, too much of a danger to British control. So they got at him through his only vulnerability—his beloved Kitty."

Nora had heard of the moral outrage both England and Ireland poured on the formerly revered party leader when he was named as co-respondent in the divorce of Katharine and Capt. William O'Shea.

"And so Parnell's fall was Da's fall, too. When he heard Parnell had been ousted from his own party, Da was so upset he got careless. Got too close to an open flame with some explosive powder. Blew up right in his hand. It was a miracle he wasn't killed—and my mother upstairs as well. She was expecting Conor at the time."

Eoin was silent until the noise of Grafton Street reached them. Songs and raised voices spilled from pubs. Children and old women wandered the pavement along with dogs and cats and a pair of hens that must have escaped from some back street coop.

"My mother took in laundry, cared for Conor and me and for Da for twenty-three years. And said the rosary every day of her life. She was a saint. Her death two years ago was much harder on Da than losing his arm and his sight to the bomb.

"Paddy Pearse came to her funeral. No one in the Brotherhood had been around for years. Paddy came back up here with us afterward and told Da about the Volunteers—MacNeill was just organizing them then. Well, it was obvious someone had to carry on the tradition, and Conor was going to be a priest . . ."

Nora tried to sort it all out. It made sense, given his family tradition. Weren't they all products of their background? No matter how far one strayed intellectually or geographically, the background was still there. "Yes, so you joined the Volunteers."

"I wanted you to understand. Be warned. In case . . . in case anything—"

"Eoin—" now the chill she had felt earlier turned to an icy blast "—Eoin, are you telling me there's going to be a rising?"

"And do you think I'd be blabbering if there were?"

"You could trust me!"

He looked at her in the light of a street lamp. "I know. But, thank God, it won't be necessary."

"Won't be necessary to trust me?"

"Won't be necessary to prepare you for a rising."

As they resumed walking, she could tell he was considering, balancing his next words, deciding how much he should tell. At last he shrugged. "*Och*, little difference it could make. You'll see it all in the newspapers soon enough. Does the name Sir Roger Casement mean anything to you?"

"The traitor who went to Germany to recruit Irish prisoners of war to fight against Britain?" She tried to keep the scorn out of her voice. She didn't want to sound like her father.

"Yes, and I didn't suppose you'd be a fan of his."

"Well, I suppose I should give him his due. He did help start the Ulster Literary Theatre."

Eoin brushed that aside with a nod. "You'll think less of him when I finish—and perhaps of all of us—but there must be honesty between us. We can handle disagreement but not dishonesty."

"Yes, yes. Go on."

"Well, when Casement was in Berlin, he sought German help for an Irish rising. He had been absolutely appalled by his fellow Ulstermen when they opposed Home Rule. He saw that no provisional government, no sort of shared rule, would work. It had to be total separation from Britain. And that could only be accomplished by revolution. So he got Germany to agree to help us as a means of getting at England."

Nora nodded. "'The enemy of my enemy is my friend.' I know."

"Germany made him all kinds of promises—leaders, troops, weapons."

Nora closed her eyes. What was she hearing? German troops in Dublin? Were these people mad? Did they think German domination would be preferable to English rule?

"Then Germany reneged. They're afraid such a bold act against England would bring America into the war."

She was so relieved she almost sagged against him. She felt that Ireland's narrow escape had been her own. What if, even now, a German warship were sailing toward Ireland loaded with soldiers and guns? She saw the green hills and fields sinking into the ocean. But they had been spared. "So there'll be no rising?"

Eoin shook his head, and she couldn't tell whether he was discouraged or relieved. "No. When he heard of the German betrayal, MacNeill canceled the Volunteer maneuvers."

She still felt it hard to believe what she was hearing. "You mean it was all planned?"

He nodded. "Easter Monday. Volunteer maneuvers in Phoenix Park. We were to launch the rising from there."

They were at Mrs. Murray's door. Nora was suddenly so tired she could hardly drag herself up the stairs to her room. She felt battered, as if she had been through a bomb explosion.

Where had it all begun? At Trinity College, with Brian Boru's harp. And Eoin had proposed. And she had accepted. Hadn't she? She meant to, but now she could hardly remember what had been said. It seemed years ago when she'd met the charming, pitiful Brendan MacHenry, heard the strange, frightening words of Patrick Pearse. And then, a generation of Irish history jumbled in her mind, new information and viewpoints bumping against pieces of stories she had always known. Parnell. Casement.

She pushed her palms against her temples to stop the throbbing and threw herself on her bed. Where would it end? They had been spared a bloody revolution on their own doorstep. This time. But what about next time? Or the next? This was Ireland. There would always be a next time.

85

"My darlings, my chicks! What a triumph! I knew it would be, of course. That's why I knew I had to bring *Princess Deirdre* to the Abbey."

Lady Augusta Gregory, her short, rather bulky figure draped in the black mourning that she had worn since her husband's death in 1892, pulled Nora and Pedar forward. "Come, you must meet all my guests and let them fawn on you. That's what they come to these opening night suppers for, you know. I like to tell myself it's for my food and hostessing abilities, but they want to meet the celebrities."

Nora started to protest that Lady Gregory was a celebrity herself, but the lady swept them into the elegantly appointed salon of the hotel where she stayed when she was in Dublin. She was never long away from Coole Park, her County Galway estate, and her next words revealed that this occasion would be no exception.

"Tomorrow I must rush back to Coole to spend Easter with my chicks."

Nora had heard how the lady doted on her three grandchildren, especially now that her son Robert was commanding a squadron in the Royal Flying Corps.

But tonight the world was all theater. Lady Gregory leaned close to Nora's ear and pointed to a young man whose sturdy tweed suit stood out in a roomful of tuxedos and evening gowns. "Be sure to have a few pleasant words with Timothy O'Connell. He's with the *Irish Times*. We need all the good press we can get."

Already Nora understood why the lady had such a reputation for her enormous energy. Some found her a bit imposing, but her ability to accomplish her goals was truly awe-inspiring.

Lady Gregory turned to Pedar. "Now, tell me about your ideas for the play you're working on. We do Lennox Robinson's *The White-Headed Boy* next—a comedy will be a good billing after the drama of *Deirdre*. Then a revival of something of Willie Yeats's with my *Workhouse Ward* as a curtain raiser—you would make a splendid Honor Donahoe, Nora, my chick. Can you have your new play ready for us by summer, Pedar?"

Pedar launched into his ideas for *The Vale of Avoca*. "I want to show how, even in pre-Viking times, it was necessary to withdraw from the concerns of life to find oneself, to find God, to find Ireland . . ."

Meanwhile, Nora drifted across the roomful of beautifully dressed, chattering people toward the sumptuous buffet.

"Bravo, Miss Armstrong."

"Moving performance."

"You were wonderful, darling."

Nora smiled and thanked each one. She dipped a small curtsey to a group who applauded her approach. Much as she enjoyed the admiration, however, Nora kept moving. Something more compelling than the buffet of chicken, salad, fruit, and cake drew her.

She had never thought of Eoin as shy, but now as he stood just apart from the cluster of theater-goers who were lavishing praise on him, Nora realized that his slight reticence was also part of his charm. A smile that communicated paragraphs passed between them before both turned to do their duty to their public.

It was considerably later in the evening before they could actually speak. And even then it was of the play.

"We have a convert," Nora said. "Pedar was delighted with the music. Has he admitted it to you yet?"

"No, but verra pleased I am to be hearing it." Eoin grinned. "I like the work."

"Well then, you'd better be polishing up your repertoire from the sixth century. He's doing Saint Kevin next."

Eoin's face lit up. "*Och*, yes. Glendalough is for being the most beautiful place in all Ireland. Have you been there?"

Nora hadn't.

"Then we've a date. Tomorrow, after rehearsal." He saw Tim O'Connell approaching with his notebook out. "And, Nora, we'll talk more then about—about us." He backed away, leaving her with the reporter.

"Congratulations, Miss Armstrong, and congratulations to Dublin. You're a grand addition to our theater." The journalist's pale blue eyes smiled at her from behind silver-rimmed glasses.

They chatted easily about Nora's background, her reaction to life in Dublin, and her interpretation of Deirdre. Then O'Connell slipped in his stinger. "As an Ulsterwoman yourself, Miss Armstrong, would you like to comment on the arrest of Sir Roger Casement?"

Nora stared. "Casement? In Germany?"

"Indeed, no." O'Connell flipped his long brown hair out of his face. "I don't suppose you've had a chance to see the evening edition of the paper." He pulled one from the inside pocket of his jacket. "German Ship Intercepted Off Tralee. Casement Arrested. Weapons Seized."

Nora shook her head. "I don't understand. I had heard . . . There were rumors going around that—" What could she say?

The reporter nodded. "Rumors going around that Germany was going to support a Nationalist uprising."

"Yes, and then that Germany had refused. So what was Casement doing off the coast of Tralee with a boatload of German arms?" She looked around in confusion, then smiled with relief as she saw Pedar coming back. "Oh, good. Here's someone you can ask for a comment."

Pedar was always willing to discuss political philosophy. He rarely did anything else. His theories were the underpinnings of all his plays.

"Ireland will never be the land she once was, and can be again, if we insist on violence as our means. We can never outdo England in firepower. Nor can we force our way at the negotiating table to which all battles of arms must eventually come. Ireland can only find her true self and take her true place in the world by returning to her moral foundations."

A hush had gradually spread across the room as Pedar's voice carried beyond their small circle. More and more heads turned their way until the small, intense playwright was addressing the entire roomful of Dublin's social elite.

"Ireland cannot be the strongest nation among nations, nor the wisest, but Ireland can be the most moral. The bedrock has been covered with centuries of silt, but it's still there. The cornerstones are moss-covered and slimy, but they can be unearthed."

Pedar O'Brien was as capable of holding the limelight as any of the actors who performed in his plays. He closed his eyes slightly and rocked to the rhythm of his own words. Nora almost thought she could hear Eoin's harp, but it was the melody of the words themselves.

"I see a green island with a river of grace running down the valleys and trees of life on either side. Their leaves shall serve as medicine for the nations. Blessing shall answer blessing. And the years the locust has eaten shall be restored. Nothing deserving a curse shall be found there."

Pedar paused and seemed to come out of his poetic trance. Now his eyes were fully open and snapping with intensity. He leaned forward as the energy of his body served to propel his words. "If you meet force with force, answer bullets with bullets, you end with a river of blood running down the streets. Is that what you want?" He paused three beats. "Which is it to be? Ireland must choose—a river of grace or a river of blood."

In the silence following the poet's outpouring, Nora and Eoin looked at each other, communicating their shared relief in their secret knowledge that Dublin had been spared its river of blood. Dublin could sleep well tonight. The rising had been called off.

On Easter Sunday, Nora woke to a triumphant awareness of new life. Bells rang from cathedrals and church towers. She ran to her window and threw it wide, reveling in the rays of early sunshine and the moist fresh air made vibrantly alive by the joyous reverberations. *Risen, risen, risen.* The bells proclaimed it over and over again.

And suddenly Nora wanted to fly and sing with the birds. She wanted to dance in the green and proclaim with the bells. She wanted to embrace all of life. In this world so fraught with war and revolution, she wanted to swim in Pedar's river of grace.

As he spoke that night, she had thought how different his vision was from that of Patrick Pearse, who lauded the necessity of blood sacrifice. But now, Easter morning, she saw that their views were not so separate. A blood sacrifice had been required. But it had already been paid. No more blood need be shed. All that was left for us to do was to wash in the river of grace that flowed so freely from that sacrifice. To attempt to make our own blood offering would be to trample on the one already made.

The Presbyterian Easters of her childhood had been subdued affairs, focusing more on the sacrifice of Good Friday than on the joyous new life of Easter morning. In her exuberance, Nora grabbed her hat and followed the sound of the bells to Christ Church. And there, in the beauty of the Eucharist, she saw the whole pageant of Christ's atonement reenacted. She approached the altar with tears streaming down her cheeks. She had never experienced a more glorious Easter. Never before had she experienced the reality of Christ so palpably.

"The body of our Lord Jesus Christ keep you in everlasting life." *Amen.*

"The blood of Christ, the cup of salvation." *Amen.*

Easter Monday, Nora sprang out of bed with a singing heart.

Eoin had told her that he would be taking his father to Maynooth so that they could celebrate Easter Sunday together with Conor. But he would be back today. He would see her at cast call, where Ervine would go over his notes and they would work through any changes he might want, although they were sure to be minor after the triumphant opening. Then, since the theater was dark on Mondays, she and Eoin were to go to the most beautiful spot in Ireland, just the two of them, to talk about their future.

Passers-by gave her odd looks as she made her way toward the river, but she simply couldn't keep the smile off her face. She paused halfway over the bridge and looked down at the swirling Liffey. "River of Life" it meant. Everywhere she saw metaphors. And she breathed a prayer of thankfulness that the Liffey could be a river of life—of grace, as Pedar saw it. They had been spared the river of blood. Casement had been arrested with his pitiful cache of outmoded German guns. O'Neill had called off the maneuvers that were planned to launch the rising. She shuddered at the thought of how close their escape had been. Even now the flower-bordered expanse of Phoenix Park would have been filling with grim-faced, armed volunteers. The park, where children played and nannies strolled with their charges, would even now have been ringing to the sound of barked orders and booted marching feet.

Her smile faded to the serenity of deep gratitude for the good things in life as she continued on across the bridge and started up Sackville Street. She was just ready to turn onto Abbey Street when a commotion ahead caught her eye. Something seemed to be going on at the Post Office. She had walked fast. It was barely noon, and cast call wasn't until one o'clock. She had time to investigate.

A small, apparently baffled crowd of shoppers, street urchins, clerks, and shopkeepers milled around the pavement. Many people merely glanced at the onlookers, then passed by with a shrug. Easter Monday was a holiday for most. Everyone had his own plans. Nora was about to leave as well when she caught sight of a familiar tweed-clad figure.

"Tim O'Connell, isn't it?"

He looked up from his scribbling and pushed his glasses back up on his nose. "Oh, Miss Armstrong! I'm honored." He rubbed a smudge of pencil lead from a finger and extended his hand.

"What's going on here?"

"That's what I'm trying to find out. The old man on the bench over there swears an army marched up the street and took over the GPO." He turned to a newsboy. "Come here, young man. Tell me, did you see what happened?"

"Aye, guv'nor. Seed it all myself, I did." The lad held out a grubby hand—O'Connell slipped a copper into it—and the boy gave a satisfied nod. "They come from up there." He pointed to the top of Sackville Street.

"Who?"

The boy shrugged. "Some army, I guess. They wore green uniforms."

"How many?"

The boy looked vague. "Hundred, maybe. Nah—more like fifty." He shrugged again. "A bunch. Marched right sharp, though. Came right down the street. Not much traffic today, but nothing stopped

744

them. When they got to the GPO, they just turned sharp right and marched in."

It sounded ludicrous, and Nora was about to laugh when a shot rang out from inside the building. A handful of frightened postal workers burst through the doors and darted across the street.

O'Connell managed to detain one of them, a white-faced young man in a celluloid collar and three-piece pin-striped suit. "Can you tell us what's going on in there?"

The man mopped at his forehead with a voluminous handkerchief. "It's a revolution. They've taken over."

"Who?"

He shook his head in bewilderment. "Them that's inside. The ones with the guns. They're in uniforms, so they must be real." He paused and brightened. "But they aren't German. I'm sure." Then his relief turned to confusion. "So who are they?"

"We heard shots. Was anyone hurt?"

"I don't think so. There weren't many in today—janitor, a few clerks, one man buying stamps. We all ran." The sound of another shot echoed across the street. Their informant fled. A lady clutching a stack of brown parcels she had apparently been intending to post ran out shrieking, followed by a few more of the staff.

The onlookers drew back, some peering around nervously for cover. More strollers joined them. "Is it the Kaiser?"

"Nah, Bolshies, I think."

"Bolshies? What are they wanting with our Post Office?"

"I've got a son serving at the front. How will I get his letters if the Bolshies take our GPO?"

Then the great brass door in the center archway opened and several of the occupiers marched out.

Tim O'Connell nodded when he saw the uniforms. He turned to the lady worried about receiving letters from the front. "It's all right, old mother. They aren't Bolshies. See those heather green uniforms? They're Volunteers. The Irish Citizen Army."

"You mean they're our own people? Then why were they shooting? They could stand in line like the rest of us!"

Then one uniformed man emerged from the group under the portico and held up his arm for attention. Nora recognized him immediately, but she couldn't believe it. Patrick Pearse? The schoolteacher poet who had sat rehearsing his symbolic visions with his blind friend only a few days before—what was he doing here?

And she began to understand. She was amazed she could have been so slow. This was the rising. The rising that had been called off. The rising Eoin told her would not be. But it was.

"Irishmen and Irishwomen!" Pearse seemed to project his voice as far as he could.

But it still was necessary to move across to the west side of Sackville to hear him clearly. Even as they walked, Tim O'Connell scribbled in his book.

Pearse's opening line was in Gaelic, but he switched quickly to English. "I proclaim the Provisional Government of the new Republic of Ireland to the people of Ireland!" He paused, obviously expecting applause. But there was far more head-scratching, frowning, and shrugging than cheering.

"Even as I speak to you, our forces are moving across Dublin. In all this great city, the centers of power are ours: The Four Courts, the Custom House, even that great bastion of tyranny Dublin Castle. All will belong to the Republic of Ireland."

He held both arms out and proclaimed, "Our troops have redeemed Dublin from many shames and made her name splendid among the names of cities. The dead of generations from which Ireland receives her old tradition of nationhood summons her children to her flag. We, the Irish Republican Army, strike for freedom!"

Most of the onlookers had turned away in confusion or boredom when Nora noticed the tall man in the heather green uniform behind Pearse. It was really his movement that caught her eye. His features were largely hidden under the brim of his cap. But there was no mistaking that birch-tree-blown-in-the-wind motion of Eoin MacHenry.

Until now she had been only confused, batting it all around in her mind. Eoin had told her the rising had been called off. The Germans reneged. MacNeill canceled the Volunteer call-up. Casement was arrested with his cache of weapons. Eoin would not have told her of the plans if they had been in process. This could be nothing but a terrible mistake. This wasn't happening.

But now she saw Eoin—standing grim-faced in uniform, and she knew she was the one who had been betrayed. He had lied to her. After all his protestations of love and trust and understanding, Eoin had lied.

Anger welled up in her. She would have it out with him. Now. She had given him her heart. She had never felt for another person as she had for Eoin. And he had trampled on her feelings, somehow using her love for his devious Fenian ends. She couldn't see what he could have hoped to gain by deceiving her—perhaps inside information from the north? But one thing was clear: he who had sworn there would be total honesty between them had vowed there would be no rising. And there he stood in his uniform, backing the self-proclaimed commandant of the Irish Republican Army.

She started to lunge toward the steps of the GPO. If he wanted blood, she would give him blood. His own.

"Whoa!" Tim O'Connell threw both arms around her waist and pulled her back. "You don't want to go in there. It's dangerous."

"Let me go!" She struck out wildly. "It'll be dangerous for Eoin MacHenry if I get my hands on him." But when she looked up, all the uniformed men had exited stage center and locked themselves backstage behind the brass doors.

She looked at the clock below the central window. The whole thing had taken barely half an hour. Nothing had happened, yet the history of Ireland had changed. Her whole life had changed. And she wouldn't even be late for cast call. She wouldn't be late, but Eoin MacHenry wouldn't be there.

If Pearse was right and the center of Dublin was occupied by revolutionary insurgents, would there even be any more performances? Even as she turned toward Abbey Street, gunfire erupted in the distance. She broke into a run and arrived at the theater gasping.

Pedar and Anna Fitzgerald, the actress playing Deirdre's nurse, met her in the lobby and both threw their arms protectively around her.

But Nora tossed her head, flinging tendrils of dark hair out of her face. "I'm not frightened. I'm angry. What do they think they're doing? Marching around Dublin like tin soldiers shooting at old women! What's going on?"

They moved into the auditorium where the rest of the company huddled at the edge of the stage, sharing information and rumors.

Pedar had come in later than the others and had recent news. The insurgents had actually taken Dublin Castle. Believing MacNeill's orders calling off the rising to be definitive, the garrison had been given the day off. The Volunteers, a few armed with old pistols but most with pikes, had surprised the single guard and shot him. Then they fled in panic at their own success.

There would be no rehearsal, but no one wanted to go home. By common consent they walked to a pub farther along Abbey Street, where a steady stream of customers kept the latest reports flowing. The rebels had occupied something like fourteen buildings, including the Imperial Hotel and Jacob's Biscuit Factory.

Nora's anger was swamped with incredulity. Biscuit factory? How, by the wildest stretch of imagination, could a hotel and a biscuit factory be military targets?

Two others from the company entered the pub and were hailed to their booth. The boy athlete Norton Riley and the unassuming Bernard Vance had taken a stroll up Sackville to see things for themselves. They came in laughing and shaking their heads. "Aye, it's a truly Irish matter. The Dublin rabble will be the Dublin rabble till the sound o' the last trump."

Bernard paid appropriate homage to his pint before explaining. "Formed a barricade, the rebels did—all across the front of the GPO. Must have emptied every office in the building of its furniture—desks, chairs, tables, cabinets, piled higher than two men."

"Aye, I'd have been fair pressed to kick a football over it."

Nora was confused. "Do they think a stack of office furniture will keep the British out?"

Pedar laughed. "Sure and our schoolmaster has spent too much time reading Victor Hugo. The students in *Les Misérables* built a grand barricade in the streets of Paris to which all the citizens rallied. I expect all Dublin is expected to rally to this one."

Norton nodded. "Aye. Well, give them credit. It worked."

"You mean Dublin is rallying to the cause?" Nora was amazed. She had seen no signs of popular support for the rebels.

"I wouldn't be for saying they've exactly rallied to the cause—but they rallied to the furniture, all right." Bernard paused for another drink. "Dismantled the whole thing. Carted every single stick of it away with them."

Everything she heard made Nora more disgusted with the rebels in general and with Eoin in particular. What was he thinking? How could he be so stupid?

Apparently the insurgents had little strategy beyond occupying buildings. According to most accounts, something like fifteen hundred of the IRB and Citizen Army had answered the call. That meant maybe one hundred rebels occupying each building, most armed with pikes. What did they intend to do? Eat biscuits? Throw cups of Imperial Hotel tea at the British when they fought back? And they would fight back.

Or would they? The Brits would see how ridiculous it all was. Why not laugh them out rather than shoot them out? But the British were unlikely to laugh at anything that might make them look foolish or weak, especially in German or American eyes.

She knew they would retaliate. At that thought Nora's anger rose again. What was Eoin doing in the midst of all that? His quick wit and intelligence were such a large part of what she had loved about him.

The anger turned to fear. Eoin had lied to her and behaved foolishly, but she didn't want him shot. And then, in this game of emotional shuttlecocks, fear for him turned back to anger. She would have it out with him. He might be barricaded against the British but not against her. She and Eoin had a date for today. She would jolly well keep it.

She left the pub without a word to anyone and marched up Sackville Street. She was vaguely aware of the crowds milling up and down the pavement, discussing the days' events, waiting to see what would happen next, but she saw nothing in detail through the red haze of anger. She had no idea how she would get into the blockaded building, but if she had to pound on the doors until the British came to shoot holes in the walls she would do so.

"Here you are then, love. You can be for carrying the bowls. Wouldn't do to be having our brave lads eating their soup with their hands, would it now?" A broadly built country woman thrust a basketful of assorted crockery into Nora's hands and turned to heft an enormous soup pot off a cart.

Then Nora saw what was taking place. A clutch of women, probably wives, mothers, and sisters of the Volunteers, were seeing to it that their men would not go hungry. The doors of the GPO opened wide for the women bearing baskets of bread and pots of soup. Nora entered with the others and did her duty distributing her load of cracked bowls.

"Nora, what are you doing here?"

She thrust a bowl into Eoin's hands. "That's what I've come to ask you."

One look at his strained face told her he was as hurt and confused as she was. All her notions of railing at him drained from her. She jerked her head toward the women ladling soup from steaming pots. "On with you. Get your supper. Then we'll talk."

They sat on the cold terrazzo floor behind a marble pillar. She waited until he had wolfed half of his food before she attacked. "You lied to me."

"No. No, Nora. I have never lied to you about anything. And I never will."

Her laugh was brittle. "I'll admit it was the most brilliant piece of strategy of this whole thing—probably the only brilliant piece of strategy. But letting Dublin Castle get word that it had all been canceled did put them to sleep. The only thing I can't figure out is why you thought I was important enough to bother disinforming *me*. Surely you don't think I have ties to the Brits just because I'm an Ulster Protestant."

Eoin plunked his bowl on the floor and grasped her shoulders. "Now you listen to me. And you get this straight. MacNeill canceled the rising. I am a Volunteer. He was my commander. That was final."

"It looks it."

"It was final until Pearse called us up."

"I thought MacNeill was your commander."

"Pearse is my friend. He spent Sunday night at our house, for goodness' sake. Do you think I could refuse to march out with him? Do you think I wanted to refuse?"

"I don't know. I came to find out what you want. I thought you wanted me."

"Oh, God . . ." It was a prayer. He covered his face with his hands. "I want you so much . . . I want you more than I want heaven."

"But not more than you want Ireland?"

"Wanting you—loving you—makes me want Ireland more. I can only love you fully, I can only be what you truly deserve in a man, if I can be a free man. We need a free Ireland for *us*, Nora."

"Are you trying to say you did this for me?"

"I did it for you. For myself. For Da and Dermot and Brendan— for all the MacHenrys. For all the Macs and the O's for all the hundreds of years they've writhed under British rule. For all the lovers, like Deirdre and Naise, who were torn apart by the tyranny of an oppressor."

Eoin's kiss was the grandest fusion of tenderness and passion she could ever experience. He put all the pain and all the passionate longings of generations of his people into that moment.

After an eternity he pulled her to her feet, still locked in his embrace. They walked to the front door of the GPO as if alone in a daisy field.

At the door he cupped her face in his hands and looked at her deeply, hungrily. "Nora, my darling, beautiful Nora. I can't thank you enough for coming. You'll never know—" He bit his lip and swallowed before kissing her again. "But don't come again. This might look like a comic opera, but it isn't. The British bullets will be very, very real."

He held the door open for her.

86

By Tuesday night the British had their forces in place. Everyone had known they would send in troops. That was expected. But the sheer size of their weapons had never been seen before. Not this side of France. Dublin had become the new Western Front. There were howitzers in Trinity College. A gunboat up the Liffey. Banks of artillery in Phoenix Park.

And then the bombardment began.

Nora thought of Stuart in France as she listened to the boom of the great guns. She crept to her window and looked out. A glow of light to the north told her that a section of Dublin was ablaze. The new high-powered shells that the British lobbed on the second city of its empire were incendiary, but no one ventured out to extinguish the fires, only to loot. Civilian casualties were running to the hundreds. Thousands.

On the third day, Nora knew she had to do something or she would go crazy. She only dimly recalled the training she had received in the few Women's Unionist Association classes she had attended with Victoria. But at least she could say she had been trained. Besides, in the desperation of the moment, willing hands were all the credentials anyone needed.

And all the time she bandaged wounds, held lights and pans for attending doctors, and spooned water into fevered lips, she wondered, *Where is Eoin in all this?* The GPO had to be one of the main British targets, as that was Pearse's headquarters. Still, the shelling was so widespread that it seemed Dublin and her people were the targets rather than the rebels.

She attended to old women and young children with cuts and contusions from shattered glass and falling masonry and tried not to find comfort in the fact that all the shells weren't falling on the building Eoin occupied. But with every face she held a lamp to, every head she sponged of blood, she wondered if the next patient would be Eoin. That was silly. These were all civilians. The rebels were inside their fortifications, sitting there with pistols and pikes, while firebombs fell on their heads.

On Saturday, Patrick Pearse, Commandant of the Irish Republican Army and head of the Provisional Government of the Irish Republic, surrendered.

Nora couldn't believe the blessed relief of quiet. The calm was incredible. No booming artillery shook the ground under her. She kept finding herself tensing, expecting the next scream of shells. She tried to carry on with her duties—the endless rounds of bedpans to carry, stacks of linen to wash, dressings to clean, bowls of broth to spoon.

Strangely, she had worked above fear for all those days of the bombardment. It was as if her system were on some kind of automatic drive. But now, with the word that it was over, the questions flooded back, all but immobilizing her. Soon she would know. She wondered how she would hear it—that news that told her whether or not she was still alive. For Eoin held her heart. If he was dead, she would be dead.

For the past four days and nights, news had traveled swiftly, always bringing word of something she didn't want to hear. Now, when she was desperate for news, the world stood still.

At last Anna rushed in, her red hair streaming about her round face. "The Volunteers—they're being routed from their buildings."

Nora closed her eyes. At least that meant they were still alive. Some of them. "Where are they taking them?" Even as she asked, she thrust her tray of bandages into Anna's hands and untied her apron.

"Being marched to Kilmainham Jail I heard."

Nora was halfway down the stairs. "Thank you, Anna. Thank you."

Nora had walked the route over the river every day for almost two months now. Today, a cab or a coach was out of the question in the disarray in the streets. And with the congestion of traffic trying to make its way around demolished buildings, she was much faster on foot anyway. Sackville, one of the finest boulevards of Europe, lay in rubble. Smoke rose from blackened heaps. She coughed and choked on the ash in the air. Climbing over piles of debris, she felt as if she were clawing her way up a mountain.

It made no sense. Neither side made any sense. The rising—to gain what was already promised and signed—made no sense. The British reaction—shelling a city they had already promised to give to its own people—made no sense. But then, when did things ever make sense in Ireland?

The classical facade of the GPO stood out like a grotesque stage set against all the destruction around it. The back part of the building had been demolished. The front remained, a silent, accusing witness of all that had gone on there. She looked around with a desperation of questions. Supreme over all, where was Eoin?

Then in the distance she heard the bark of military orders and the angry shouts and boos of a crowd. Just as Anna said, British soldiers were marching those routed from the GPO off to Kilmainham.

She had to see Eoin. Once he was sealed behind those stone walls, she might never see him again.

As she raced toward the sound of the crowd, an idea took shape. If the populace of Dublin was finally roused against the British for their vengeance wreaked on the city, if people were already gathered to cheer for the Volunteers and jeer at the British soldiers, could they be moved to do something more? Even if it was nothing more than distract the soldiers long enough for her to speak to Eoin. Maybe stone-throwing might be enough to allow Eoin to escape. She would take him home. Home to Lanarks' Bawn, whose walls had ever served as fortress and haven.

The sound of the crowd grew louder. She was gaining. She darted down a narrow street. Maybe only two or three more blocks. Then she was stopped. The end of the street was blocked with a pile of rubble from a bombed building. She looked around. She would lose too much time going back. She clawed her way up the heap of debris. She was nearly to the top when the stones rolled under her feet, and she slid backward. She screamed more from exasperation than from pain. She was beyond feeling cuts and bruises.

"Sure and ye're needin' help, lady. Just grab hold."

Two street urchins atop the rubble thrust a pole at her, and she seized it, sobbing with the effort to breathe. In a moment they had hoisted her up and over. She slid down the far side, leaving her long brown wool skirt in tatters.

"Ye're wantin' to catch the Brits, are ye now?"

She nodded.

"Right then, and aren't Seamus and I for knowing the way?"

They led her through a zigzag of back alleys and in and out of buildings. Only street arabs born and bred in such a rabbit warren could possibly have found their way. Fear of losing her escorts kept Nora running far beyond normal endurance.

And then they emerged into the light of day, and she stood panting. Behind them was the Four Courts, damaged, but still standing. To their left, the river. And then she heard the harsh, shouted orders of soldiers marching their captives to jail.

With an almost hysterical cry, Nora hugged her urchin escorts. "We did it! Thank you! We beat them! Here they come now!" She pointed in the direction of marching feet. "Quick, pick up lots of stones!"

The boys were delighted to obey. It took them only seconds to fill their arms. Then Nora led them toward the jeering mob.

"Shall we be throwing now?" Seamus fingered a broken brick.

"No, wait. I have to find him first. When I find him, we'll throw at the soldiers, so he can escape."

"The Brits got your man, do they?"

She nodded, but she was too intent on looking to talk. She recognized many of the faces that marched by, some dejected, some defiant, most bloodied, all exhausted. Patrick Pearse was near the end. But nowhere was the dear, tall sapling form she so hungered to see.

She pushed ahead through the mob toward the front of the marchers. She must look again. She couldn't have missed him. They were marching slowly, held back by the men's fatigue and the necessity to press through the angry crowd. She looked until her eyes ached. She would not, could not, overlook Eoin. Her heart would make that leaping, electric connection it always did when he entered a room, before her mind registered his presence. But she felt no spark of recognition for any of these defeated patriots. Pity, but no spark.

But she had to make sure. She waited for the rearguard to catch up, then shoved her way through the throng. "Patrick! Patrick Pearse!" She had never been more thankful for her commanding height or her actor's ability to project her voice.

From the middle of the rear marchers, Patrick Pearse looked at her.

"Eoin? Where is Eoin?"

Pearse shook his head. It was as if one of the British soldiers had turned and fired at her.

"That the one you want us to throw at, miss?"

"No. No." Nora shook her head. She considered throwing an armload of stones at the soldiers who had . . . had what? What had they done to Eoin? Where was he? Had he miraculously managed to escape? Was he even now waiting for her at her boardinghouse? Or was he lying dead in the rubble of the GPO with a British bullet in his heart? Or was he trapped under the debris? Wounded, perhaps, but still living? In their triumphant rush to march the insurgents off to jail, had the Brits overlooked the most precious of all their captives?

For the first time, Nora really observed the scene around her. And the truth suddenly struck her. The mob was not booing and hurling expletives at the British. They were haranguing the rebels! "Troublemakers!" "Bring the Brits down on us!" "Sure and they're German sympathizers. And isn't my own dear boy fighting in France this very minute?"

A storm of emotion overwhelmed her. Why, why, why all this devastation? It could be argued that Britain was punishing Dublin for turning against them. But obviously the people of Dublin had not so turned. The people jeered the *rebels*—blamed them for bringing this destruction down on their heads.

But above all the conflict of nation against nation, even Irish against Irish, Nora knew one overwhelming certainty. She must find Eoin.

There was an outcry as two small ragamuffins began hurling stones indiscriminately at soldiers, prisoners, and observers, but Nora turned away.

"Whoa, where you going? Can I help you?"

She had all but walked into a tweed-clad form. The late afternoon sun glinted off his silver-rimmed glasses. "Tim O'Connell!"

He stuck his notepad in his pocket and held a hand out to her.

"I need to go to the GPO. The soldiers don't have Eoin. He must still be there."

O'Connell put his arm around her shoulders, which had begun to shake. "Are you sure? It's an awful mess."

"I know. I have to."

"Right." Still supporting her, he led the way to a quiet street the other side of the Four Courts. "Look what I've got for the day."

Even in her fatigue and worry, Nora smiled. "A car!"

"Convinced my editor I could do a better job covering the news if I could get around quicker than on my old bike."

Nora almost collapsed onto the cushions.

Tim drove a confusing route to skirt the demolished areas, but even then he had to make his way around uprooted trees and the carcasses of burned-out automobiles.

At the GPO, police had cordoned off the area and declared a curfew. They were doing their best to keep the crowd of curiosity-seekers at bay. For the first time in the whole nightmare day Nora had to fight tears. Was she to be kept out? Not allowed to look for Eoin?

Tim gave her hand a quick squeeze. "Chin up, old girl. Leave it to the silver-tongued press."

Nora didn't hear what he said, but he flashed his press card with a courteous smile, and in a few moments she was standing on almost the same spot she had stood four days ago when Eoin had kissed her.

Eoin, where are you? Was he somewhere in the middle of this burned out rubble? He must still be alive, because she was still breathing. *Eoin, where are you?* She started clawing at the rubble with bloodied fingers.

It was Timothy, jotting notes for his story, who heard a groan. "Hey, there's someone in here!"

Two large policemen left their guard duty to help them dig, but Nora felt she was moving more pieces of the broken marble pillar than all three men.

"Eoin! Eoin, it's me. I'm coming!"

When they uncovered the broken form of a man in a heather green uniform, one of the policemen held her back. A carved ceiling beam imprisoned him beneath the rubble at the same time that it protected him from it. The policemen shook their heads. "We can't shift that beam."

"Aye, and it'd be for naught if we could."

Stifling a sob, Nora fell to her knees and gently lifted the head of autumn-leaf hair to her lap. She tried to wipe the dust and dried blood from his face with her fingers but managed only to streak him with her own blood. She dropped her face to his. She would kiss the blood away. Love would accomplish what nothing else could do.

Murmuring endearments, she ran her fingers through the springy russet hair. She told her fingers to memorize the feel, for they would never touch anything so wondrous again. And then she cupped his face in her hands as he had cupped hers at their last parting. "Go to God, my love. He will care for all."

The beautiful, warm lips parted in a smile. She didn't cry out when they relaxed with their final breath.

87

The statistics were grim. Sixty-four rebels, 134 Crown forces, and 220 civilians had been killed in the Easter Rising. Two thousand six hundred fourteen were wounded. Dublin had sustained three million pounds worth of damage.

And across the city, across Ireland, the people blamed the rebels for being fools. John Redmond, leader of the moderate Irish Parliamentary Party called the movement insane. The failed rebellion had produced the exact opposite of the effect the insurgents had hoped for. Seldom in their history had the Irish people stood more united behind the British.

Then the firing squads went to work. The stone walls of Kilmainham Jail reverberated with shots as the captive rebels were dealt with. Patrick Pearse was the first. Idealistic to the end, he declared, "We shall be remembered by posterity and blessed by unborn generations." At last Pearse had achieved his terrible beauty of blood sacrifice. His own blood had been some of the first to spill in the glorious defeat he sought.

And then, slowly, the mood of the country began to change. Nora surveyed the stack of newspapers Tim had brought her. The *Irish News* from Belfast was the first to call for a halt to the executions. A few days later, two Dublin papers added their voices. She looked at the recent issue of the *Irish News*. The toll of executions had reached fifteen, and Sir Edward Carson of the Ulster Unionists called on the government to intervene to stop the shootings.

But it was too late for the British. The fifteen executions had accomplished what four days of fire-bombing had failed to do. They had turned Irish opinion in favor of the rebels.

Nora, still numb with disbelief that the service she had just attended in St. Colum's church had really been Eoin's funeral Mass, could only think of the unreasonable needlessness of it all. Her mind played over and over again the desperate heroism of the past days.

Such a wonderful, poetic drama it would make. But this was no drama. Her fallen hero would not rise after the drop of the last curtain and lift her to her feet.

She listlessly crossed her room to the bureau. This play had finished its run on the world's stage. For her the theater would be dark forever. And she could not imagine what she would go on to. She was now fully convinced that Pedar's vision was the best way. The only real victory must be accomplished without bullets. But she despaired of that ever being possible in Ireland. And she did not want to stay in a land where reason could count for so little.

A knock sounded on her door, and she jumped. These days any sudden noise made her think of gunshots. "Come." She tried to steady her voice and steel herself for whatever might come next. Then she relaxed with a smile as a familiar form entered.

"Oh, Pedar. I was just thinking of you."

He smiled, although the fierceness never left his eyes. "Aye? Kind thoughts, I hope."

"Always, Pedar, you know that. I was thinking that you're the only one who could make sense out of all that's happened. You could write a play—"

"Aye. When it's all over. If it ever is." He took her in his arms and held her.

For an instant she was afraid he would again ask her to marry him, but then she felt the difference in his embrace. He held her like the cousin he very nearly was. With relief she returned the hug. Pedar was the friend she needed. He always would be.

He drew back, his hands still on her shoulders. "Nora, I've a surprise for you. A visitor."

"Who?"

"Your brother. Eric."

"*Eric?* Here? Why didn't you bring him up?"

"He thought it best to wait downstairs. I told him all about everything. He didn't know how you'd feel . . ."

Nora turned toward the door. "That silly boy. Did he come to register for university?" She paused. "Oh, I hadn't thought. Is everything all right at Trinity? I heard the British installed guns in the green?" Not waiting for an answer, she rushed down the stairs to where Eric awaited her in the parlor.

Sun fell through the lace-curtained windows, highlighting his beloved freckled nose and thickly lashed blue eyes. She almost knocked him off his feet with her embrace. He had filled out in the months since she came south, but she was still taller.

"Eric! How good to see you! How is everyone? I've had no news of the family for ages." She dragged him to the sofa and threw a velvet pillow out of the way so they could sit together. "I suppose the family sent you to check up on me. I'm probably the one thing in Dublin still in one piece." She paused. "Outwardly, at least."

"I know, sis. Pedar told me what you've been through. That's why I—" He hesitated.

"Tell me about everyone." Seeing Eric's dear, freckled face suddenly made her family seem so close. She had been so caught up in events here that she had shut them out of her mind. Now she realized how dear they all were, how much she missed her father's ranting and her mother's porcelain figurine serenity, her brother Lanark's slightly pompous pride in his shipbuilding. "How's Brenda? And wee Mitchell?"

"Wee Mitchell is nae so wee. He'll do the Armstrongs and Campbells proud. And Brenda is blooming like a ship at full sail. She'll be well delivered and on her feet in time for Vicky's foaling. Mother says she can only handle one new grandchild at a time."

"Wait!" Her head was spinning. Brenda had been expecting when Nora came to Dublin. But Victoria? "Vicky and Stuart are having a baby? I thought they were in England."

Eric laughed. "Don't tell me they've made such an Anglophobe of you here that you think the Irish can't conceive children in England? Eric grinned, and his irrepressible blue eyes danced. "I understand Stuart had a long weekend pass before he was shipped to France. When Victoria discovered she was expecting, she came back to Price Manor. If that baby is as good stock as the horses that aunt of hers is turning out, she'll be just fine."

In spite of his hopeful words, Nora shivered. Stuart in France. She had heard little war news lately, but she knew it was bad. She recalled that Vicky had planned to go to France, too. Nora certainly understood the impulse to want to be as close to her man as possible. Especially as a nurse—to feel that she might be able to do something. "And what of you, Eric? Trinity next term? Have you matriculated yet?"

He hesitated. "No, actually, I came to Dublin—" He shifted his position on the sofa. "Well, you see, Campbell & Wilson are starting to make airplanes now. Absolutely smashing Sopwith Tabloids—seventy horsepower. They can fly seventy-five miles an hour. It won't be long until we can fly long-range night sorties behind the enemy lines. It can make all the difference—"

"Eric! What are you babbling about? What does this have to do with your coming to Dublin?"

"I've joined the Royal Flying Corps. I'm off next week to flight school in Hendon." He ducked his head. "And it's no good your telling me I'm too young. That's why I came down here to enlist—where no one knew me. They never questioned my age."

It was later that night that Nora sorted it all out. Eoin's funeral had brought a sense of closure for more than just the life she had hoped to share with him. There was nothing more for her to do in Dublin. She wasn't sure there was anything more for her to do in Ireland. The rising and the British response to it had put an end to any idea of a peacefully accomplished Home Rule and to her dreams of living in the ideal Ireland Pedar envisioned. The bullets and firebombs that had rained down here had put an end to such dreams. And they were still raining down in another land—targeted at Irishmen in France as well. There were nearly ninety thousand Irish, about half from her own Ulster, serving in the fiercest areas of fighting. Eric soon to be among them. Stuart there already. In the thick of the worst of it as the Germans moved slowly but steadily toward Verdun, pushing the Allies ahead of them and walking over their bodies every step of the way.

Nora shivered. Victoria couldn't go to LeHavre as a nurse, but *she* could.

88

One July, 1916. Nora looked at the water-spotted paper calendar tacked to the wall near her bed as she crawled out, bleary-eyed and shivering after a short night. In spite of the early morning chill, she opened the small window at the end of the row of cots and leaned out for a breath of fresh air. A lingering mist covered the ground, but the sun would soon burn through. A few birds chirped in the hospital garden below.

She listened, straining her ears. Of course, it was only in her imagination that she had heard the roar of the mighty Allied guns during the past days. The Western Front was nearly a hundred miles to the northeast. But reports of the bombardment were so vivid that she believed she *could* hear them at times. Or was it her remembered nightmare of the siege of Dublin?

For a full six days, British artillery had pounded the German positions with the greatest concentration of shellfire in history. The hospital buzzed every hour with heartening reports. Men brought into the hospital from the front told of the great clouds of smoke the howitzers produced, of the dust and debris their falling shells flung into the air. There could be little left of the German positions. Such a massive attack would have cut the coiled banks of German barbed wire—reported to be thirty yards thick in some places. It would be a simple matter for the 36th Ulster, along with the other Allied divisions up and down the line, to push the enemy back at last.

The men had been securely dug into a labyrinth of trenches now twenty-five miles long. But soon—some thought it would be today—the 100,000 men of the Allied forces, including the 35,000 of the 36th Ulster, would leave their trenches to cross the two-mile-wide strip of No Man's Land to attack the Germans face to face.

Nora thought of Stuart, standing so tall and proud in his uniform with his darling Victoria beaming shyly by his side. She thought of Davy Smyth and Andrew Russell and William Brown and Robert Doggart and the other young men she had known from Newtownards who were now serving in that cauldron of fire, smoke, and dust. A ray of

761

sunshine struck a poppy below her window. A bird trilled. Surely the guns must be silenced. The world could not feel so peaceful otherwise.

She wondered what her family was doing at home. Not much doubt about her father and Lanark. Today was the anniversary of the Battle of the Boyne. They would be donning their orange sashes and marching to the cadence of Lambeg drums. Her gentle mother would spend the day praying that there would be no trouble at the marches, as Vicky would be praying for Stuart's safety.

She wondered as well, as she had so frequently in the past month since joining the nursing corps, what she was doing here. And the answer came back the same as always: She had nowhere else to be. Eoin was gone. The best she could do was to spend the vast emptiness stretching before her in trying to save other young men so that other women wouldn't have to face similar emptiness.

She turned to the day's routine, first making her own cot in perfect neatness as every other bed in the row. Emma, who slept in the bed next to hers, would soon be coming in, her shoes and uniform hem damp with dew, her hands full of wild flowers. She always spent the minutes just before she went on duty, gathering flowers to brighten the wards. And whenever she had a spare minute she would spend it singing to her patients—especially those with head and face wounds, which trench warfare produced in such vast numbers.

Nora had no energy or spirit for flower gathering or singing. For her, simply making it through each day was a triumph. As she went out, those on night duty came in, too exhausted to more than nod at her and fling themselves onto their beds.

So she began another day of carrying trays and pans, trying to make men with arms and legs missing a little more comfortable, feeling the pulses of the faint, each time praying she *would* feel a pulse, rewrapping bandages. And the ambulances moved steadily back and forth, bringing new cases who had arrived at the train station from the front.

Trench warfare dictated a system of medical care different from any used before. The wounded went in a continuous stream from first-aid stations in the field to evacuation hospitals ten miles back from the lines, and within twenty-four hours to base hospitals such as the one at LeHavre. There were no women nurses in the field hospitals. If there were, Nora would have volunteered. As it was, all she could do was wait for each new trainload to arrive.

There was never much waiting. This war, unlike any other before it, did not have well-defined battles that demanded collecting and caring for the wounded at the end of the day. In this war, a single battle lasted for days. The dead were buried as best they could be or not at all. The wounded were rescued under fire. There was always a stream of wounded, sometimes swelling, sometimes thinning, but never ceasing.

The day was almost over. Since morning, Nora had moved like clockwork from one job to the next, from one bed to the next, from one man to the next. She had hoped to write a letter to her mother today, but she knew that in the end she would be too tired. She would eat her supper in the dining hall—in her first week there she learned that, even when fatigue had driven her far beyond any sense of hunger, she must eat—and then she would fall into her bunk.

Sometimes she thought she could kill for a cup of tea—or more precisely, a tin mug, as it was served here. Steaming hot, brewed strong and black, fortified with rich milk and scoops of sugar. It was all that kept her going.

She was on her third mug, and the fatigue and tension were just starting to ease, when the word went around. There had been a major battle along the River Somme. Nurses were asked to volunteer for extra duty. Nora shook her head. She couldn't possibly.

Then she heard: the 36th Ulsters were one of the hardest-hit divisions. Stuart. Nora volunteered. She was sent to the station to tend the wounded as they came off the trains and waited for ambulances.

A short, blue-eyed nurse, her white cap framing a round face, smiled at Nora. "And it's fine we can be together, these being our own dear boys."

She had forgotten that Emma was from Belfast.

Nora gasped when the big arc lights at the station revealed their patients. The stretchers lay four deep. Emma was sent to the walking cases—although they were long past walking. A few sat, cradling their heads between bent knees. Most lay huddled together on the cold cement. Their arms and heads were bandaged, their clothes were soaked with blood, and everything was caked with mud.

Nora turned to the first of the stretcher cases and rearranged the man's splinted leg, trying to make him more comfortable. He attempted a smile. "Ta, miss."

The next man was unconscious. The bandage had slipped almost off his head, exposing a gaping wound. She had no clean bandage. But rewrapping the cloth already wet with blood was as unthinkable as it would be useless. She pulled off her apron and rebound the wound. And on down the row. The cases shifted like the tide, as those carried off to waiting ambulances were replaced from a newly arrived train that filled the station with great clouds of white steam.

She turned from adjusting a sling for a man with a shoulder injury and knelt beside a stretcher to check an abdominal wound—

probably from a bayonet. It was a miracle he was still alive. The man groaned and shifted. The fresh red stain seeping through the bandage sent a dreaded danger signal.

"Matron!" Nora called her supervisor.

The woman shook her head at sight of the hemorrhage. "Apply pressure here. Firm and steady. If that stops the bleeding, stay with him and keep it up. It's all we can do."

Nora knew that translated, "If it doesn't work, spend your time on one there's hope for."

He was breathing. That meant there was hope. The wound was low and not as ragged as many she had seen. While keeping the pressure steady with her right hand, she felt for his pulse with her left. Yes, reasonably steady, and he didn't feel fevered.

The stretcher-bearers bustled up.

"Matron said I was to stay with him."

The carriers grunted. It was up to her to keep pace with them.

She feared the jolting of the ambulance would start the hemorrhaging again. Her patient groaned with every jostle, but the rag under her hand remained white. In the dim light she peered at the identification disc around his wrist. She noticed his division first: 10th Irish. He wasn't from Ulster, so what was he doing here? Then she remembered hearing that as the forces thinned, the English, thinking all Irish the same, had lumped the divisions together.

And then she saw the name: Capt. Shane Lanark. Lanark? Her older brother hadn't joined up. No, no, Lanark was this man's *last* name. Could he be a cousin of some sort? Shane? The similarity to Stuart made her heart flip. Then she realized how ridiculous she was being. It was just coincidence. The man's sharp-nosed, high-cheekboned, aristocratic features suggested no family resemblance.

At the hospital she all but fainted from fatigue when a doctor took over her charge. The supervising matron ordered her to bed. She slept all morning.

When she went down to lunch the next day, a hush hung over the dining hall. Nurses, doctors, staff personnel were talking in whispers. Nora joined Emma at one end of a long table. The girl's sweet, round face looked shrunken with more than the exhaustion that had become routine. "What is it, Emma? What's happened?"

Emma shook her head and fought for control. "It's so awful. Our poor boys. Thousands killed. Whole companies wiped out . . ." She buried her face.

Although her stomach was churning, Nora forced herself to eat. Thousands of dead meant even more wounded. She must eat in order to deal with them. She shoved the sugar bowl at Emma. "Take another scoop. You'll need it."

Throughout the day Nora got bits and pieces that formed a picture in her mind. The Ulsters had started the day with prayers and hymns, then celebrated the Battle of the Boyne by putting orange lilies in the bands of their tin helmets. Many wore Orange sashes over their uniforms. One company even had a Lambeg drum. They marched up and down their trench, beating it. It was considered a grand omen that the day's battle should fall on the anniversary of Ulster's greatest military victory.

One of the stories a wounded man told her was of the company commander from the West Belfasts. "Took off his Orange sash, he did, swirled it over his head, and shouted, 'Come on, boys! No surrender!' I didn't think I could make it up the scaling ladder until then. 'Ladders of Death' we call them. And they were." He gasped as a spasm of pain from his wounded shoulder gripped him.

She gave him a drink of water.

"I was huddled against the side of the trench. Word came down the line 'Ten minutes to go.' *Ten minutes to live*, I thought. I wanted to pray, but I couldn't. I wanted to think of someone—my mother, my sister, my sweetheart, but I couldn't. I was shivering all over. My legs felt as if they were asleep."

Once he'd started, the lad couldn't stop talking. Nora realized how desperately he needed to get the horror out. She stood and listened.

"We crouched around the base of the ladders. I was sick and faint. 'Three minutes.' Then a blast of whistles. 'Over the top with the best o' luck. And give 'em fury.'"

It was the famous phrase of the Western Front.

"But I couldn't do it. I knew I'd be shot for a traitor. But I couldn't move. Then Major Gaffikin shouted, 'No surrender!' and I was over."

The men were to advance in units across No Man's Land. They were told it would be an orderly advance and would meet little resistance. They were told that the six-day bombardment had cut the barbed wire and smashed the German trenches. They were told that the British guns had knocked out most of Germany's formidable machine gun emplacements. They were wrong.

"The first twenty feet were the worst. Then I was running through the lanes our fellows had cut in our own barbed wire. I knew I was running because, when the men on either side of me would fall, I passed them. The Germans sprayed the whole place with shrapnel, but some of us made it. Somehow we made it. The Schwaben Redoubt, that was our target. One of the fiercest of the German machine gun nests in the whole line. And all the time they were firing at us, firing at us . . ."

Nora wiped his face with a cool, damp cloth. "There now. You can tell me the rest later. See if you can get some sleep."

But he clutched at her hand and held on. "No, no. You've got to hear the lot of it. It's important."

Nora nodded and held his hand.

When he saw she wasn't leaving, he quieted. "I was crouched in a dugout. There was an explosion. A man's torso—one of ours—flew through the air and plopped beside me. I shot three Jerries—but it didn't help that poor nod.

"I could have shot a whole regiment of 'em and laughed—but not as individuals. I came on one Jerry—about my own age, bad wounded. It was against orders, but I gave him a drink from my canteen.

"Then I found one of our men. His arm was shot clean off, and his whole front was open. He wanted me to kill him. But I couldn't do it. I wanted to. He was in mortal pain. But I couldn't do it." At last he fell quiet. Little sobs shook his body, although his eyes remained dry. He began rocking himself in rhythm to his sobs.

Nora sensed she was no longer needed, and she moved off. She wondered how many times Private Granger would have to tell his story before the horror of it began to fade.

One thing became clear throughout the day. The loss had been unthinkably staggering—someone calculated sixty thousand British, which would be two men for every yard of the front. And for all that, no ground had been gained.

There had been one victory, however. The Ulstermen had taken the Schwaben Redoubt. At the end of the day they had been required to fall back, but the most destructive of all the German machine gun emplacements was destroyed. It seemed unlikely that any family in the province would be left unbereaved, but Ulster had her victory.

It was late that night before Nora had a chance to inquire about her abdominal injury case from the night before. "Captain Lanark?"

The orderly looked over his lists. "Third floor. Ward two."

Nora smiled for the first time that day. He was still alive.

Just barely. He was fevered now and muttering incoherently. "Stay down. Down! They're shooting! Have to go back. Go back. No! Wire isn't cut. Never get through. Oh, my God! My God! Run! God help him!"

The best she could do was to give him a drink of water. So many supply ships had been torpedoed that they were desperately short of medical supplies.

It was three days later before Nora could get back to ward two on the third floor. She approached, her shoulders stiff with dread. She did not want this case to end as so many had in the past weeks. She did not want to think of Captain Lanark's family receiving a wee brown envelope bearing the dreaded news. She wondered if her family had received such a message. She had kept a careful watch on the patient lists. The fact that Stuart was not in hospital might mean that the miraculous had happened. Or the worst.

And Eric? It was little use asking about him, other than in prayer. There was no telling where the flying corps was being deployed. But she had heard patients talking about seeing planes like mosquitoes in the sky. And then puffs of smoke from the antiaircraft artillery, like balls of cotton. That was how they could tell whether it was a German plane or one of their own. White cotton puffs meant the Allies were shooting at a German plane. German antiaircraft shells puffed black cotton at Allied planes. *Oh, Eric.*

She took a deep breath, raised her head, and entered the ward as she had once made her entrance on stage. Captain Lanark was on his cot. His thin face was whiter than his sheets and drawn with pain. But he was breathing. She thought him asleep, so she approached quietly, but he opened his eyes. She had not realized they were such a startling blue. The hands lying limp at his side were long-fingered and fine.

His thin lips attempted a smile. "Hello, nurse. Have I been making trouble again?"

There were few enough attempts at humor. It was important that one not go unrewarded. "I expect you have. They only send me to sort out the incorrigible ones." She pulled up a stool and sat by his bed. "Actually, I'm off duty. I came by to visit, if you feel like it."

"Well, I don't know. I have a pretty busy social calendar." He turned the full gaze of his cornflower eyes on her, then frowned. "I've seen you before."

She nodded. "I stayed with you the night you came in. And I was up once before, but you were . . . asleep."

"No, I mean *before.*" He struggled to sit up, but the pain convulsed his features. He fell back against the pillow, gasping. "Sorry. Got to learn not to do that. Can't move."

She was gripped with concern. "Can't you move your feet? Can you feel anything at all?"

"Oh, yes. I didn't mean that. Just meant the pain." He managed a smile. "Still, I expect it'll go away. One of the lucky ones, for sure." He continued puzzling over her. "You're Irish, aren't you? Are you from Dublin?"

"County Down, actually. But I was in Dublin this spring." In Dublin for Easter. It sounded so poetic. Daffodils in the park . . .

"I was there then, too. Home on leave."

"What did you do? *Before*, I mean."

"Before I took the king's shilling? I was a lawyer. Family tradition. Then joined that patriotic volunteer lot that responded to Redmond's call. 'Show our loyalty when England needs us. She'll give us what she's promised when it's over.'" He shook his head. "I don't know now. You were there at Easter?"

"I was there." She shut her eyes against the memory. "And you?"

"I left Monday morning, before it all began. I didn't get the letter until I was back in France. There was nothing I could do."

The ache in his voice told her his reference was personal. "Your family?"

He nodded. "Our home was firebombed. Mother. Father. Kid brother. All inside."

The silence of despair was overwhelming. She had to say something. "Do you have any other relatives?"

"An uncle. Keeping the law practice going." He closed his eyes again. "Do you ever wonder what it's all about? What there is to go on for?"

Yes, she did. But even in her most despairing, she never completely abandoned the vision. She tried to tell him about Pedar's plays, about being at the Abbey.

"Yes!" he almost shouted. "*Princess Deirdre.* That's where I saw you. Our whole family went. Together. My mother cried—"

She went on, telling him everything. The Rising. Eoin.

"Aye." He looked at her long. "I'm sorry." He brushed her hand. "And that's what brought you here? One might think you would have had enough disaster."

"I think maybe that's what it means to be Irish. Never to come to the end of disaster."

Although Nora was off duty, the ward matron soon spotted a pair of idle hands and sent her on an errand. It was two days later before she could get back to Captain Lanark. She hoped she wasn't deluding herself with the thought that his face had a bit more color in it. But she was sure his smile was brighter.

"And here I was, just thinking about yourself."

"Well, I don't suppose you've a lot to do." She slid onto the stool. "And what is it you were thinking, then?"

"I need to tell you I think we might be kin." He said it as if it were very bad news.

"Yes, I think that's likely. Lanark is one of my family names, and it's not especially common. Actually, my home is called Lanarks' Bawn from the old times."

"Yes, I know. I would have sorted it out sooner when you said you were the actress, but my mind's a bit foggy these days, and I wanted to be sure."

"Sort what out?"

"When my regiment was put into the Ulsters, most of them weren't too happy about it—my men being mostly RC and all that, although I'm C of I myself. But the captain of the next regiment was friendly. He caught my name and said *we* were probably kin. In the course of things, he told me about his cousin the actress. Right proud of you, he was."

Nora felt numb. She didn't want to say it. If she didn't say it, it wouldn't be true. At last she dragged the words out. "Stuart Price?"

"Aye, that was him."

"Was."

Shane Lanark nodded. "I'm sorry, but I need to tell his family. It's doubtful they'll get an envelope. There wasn't much left to identify. Missing in action is so hard to bear. I don't want to leave his wife with that."

"He told you about Victoria?"

"Aye, and about the wane. I'm so sorry to have to tell you."

"I kept trying to tell myself it was good news that he didn't show up here wounded. But really, I knew. That's about the only hope—to be wounded long enough to keep you out of the action." Then, after a long silence she said. "You'd better tell me."

"It's pretty grim. Are you sure you can bear it?"

"I think one of the worst parts of all I've been through is that I'm numb to horror. I don't think there's anything left that can shock me."

"Still, it's pretty rough." He reached for her hand.

She wasn't sure whether he was offering comfort to her or seeking it for himself.

"We had one advantage from the first. We were on the edge of Thiepval Wood, so our first line was hidden from German view. Price's regiment was right next to mine. I admired him as an officer. Took good care of his men. They didn't mind following him, because they trusted him. We lined our men up on a sunken road running along No Man's Land. We were lucky. Our stretch of wire was mostly cut." He shivered. "Some places it wasn't and . . . well . . ." He fell silent a moment.

Nora knew. She had heard stories of men trapped on the barbed wire. Held there writhing as bullets riddled them. She was relieved when he continued.

"Anyway, the Jerries were slow coming out. We had a sharp fight and captured their front trench. Unfortunately, the advance of the Thirty-second on our right had broken down. When they fell back, the Jerries in Thiepval village turned their guns on us.

"But we'd taken one German trench—we figured we could take another. Besides, our Irish spirit was roused. By mid-morning we'd captured the Schwaben Redoubt and five hundred Germans taken prisoner. We were feeling pretty good, I can tell you.

"Even so, casualties had been stouter than we'd expected. Instead of a brigade, we had only two small parties to launch the attack on the German second line. Price's lads and mine. We were close enough to see into Jerry's trenches. We could have taken the whole thing." He shook his head as if denying the memory. "We were so close. That's the heartbreak."

Nora squeezed his hand, waiting, picturing Stuart as she would always remember him.

"The Jerries build their trenches with a kind of chimney pipe to act as an air vent. We'd seen quick enough on the first line that they made perfect rabbit holes for dropping grenades down them. A few men could sneak through the barbed wire and clear most of the trench that way. Price opened his last pack of grenades, just ready to hand them out for the attack. That's when it happened." He squeezed his eyes so tightly shut that his whole face scrunched with the effort.

"We were ahead of schedule. Our support artillery behind us didn't know we were there. They opened fire on the trench. We were pinned down. One shell exploded so near us it jiggled the pins out of some of our grenades. Barbed wire in front of us and artillery fire falling all around us—we all froze while the grenades sizzled. I shouted to my men to run—I figured they had a better chance with the artillery than with a case of exploding grenades. But Price was the hero. He—he saved us all. He—"

Nora knew. She could see it. "He threw himself on the grenades." It was what Stuart would do.

She suddenly realized that the whole ward was silent. They had all been listening. Now men turned their faces to the wall. Someone blew his nose. Another sniffed. "Aye," still another said. "He should get the Victoria Cross."

"And the devil of it was we had to retreat. I could see right across into the German line, but there were too few of us. It was no good. We had to go back."

And that was the heartbreak of the Battle of the Somme. It finally bogged down in mud four months later. More than 600,000 Allied casualties and more than 400,000 German, and the lines had not moved ten feet in either direction.

Shane and Nora worked together for several days composing letters, one to Vicky, one to her family. It was all they could do for them for the moment.

Nora refused to think about the fact that she had had no news from Eric for weeks. But she couldn't entirely suppress the fact that pilots arriving at the front were said to have a three weeks' life expectancy.

It was a warm, sunny day with a hint of approaching autumn in the air when she walked Shane to the harbor in LeHavre to board the boat that would take him back across the Channel. He had been posted to office work in London. She resisted the impulse to cling to him. "You must come to Lanarks' Bawn when this ghastly war is over. If it ever is."

"I don't know, Nora."

"But you must, if only for a few days. It would be such a comfort to Victoria to talk to you in person. And you can see Stuart's child." She couldn't understand his reluctance. "Please. Please come." She could make her desire to see him again no plainer.

But still he didn't reply.

"I can show you the place your family had. Seaton Court it was called, I think. Although I don't know why—probably for some earlier owner. Now it's Harrowby's Dale. It's a grand place—" She broke off. Why was he looking at her so oddly?

"It sounds grand. But I think it would be best if we didn't see each other again." He said it gently, but with an air of finality.

The sound of the water lapping against the stone pier was suddenly very loud. The sun warming her head burned very hot. "I—I don't understand. I thought we . . . That is, we . . ."

What *had* she thought? They were kin of some sort, but too distant to count. They were friends, companions who had shared a dreadful experience and in sharing had helped each other survive. But . . . Suddenly she realized how much more Shane was to her. She realized that her thoughts of Eoin had changed in recent weeks.

She still thought of him. She would always think of Eoin. And always with the vision of a tall, graceful young man bending to her, his russet hair blowing in the wind, her whole heart warming to him, her whole being singing with just being in his presence. The shortness of breath, the racing pulse, the toes-over-top love that had sent her skipping to the theater every day just to see the wonder of his smile. No, she would never forget any of that. Always she would cherish the memory of Eoin MacHenry.

But of late the pain had faded. No longer did her throat close and her eyes fill with tears for seemingly no reason. No longer did she wake in the night unable to breathe for the pain in her heart. Now she knew that she could live again. Just as Stuart had given Shane his life, so Shane had given her life. And now he was telling her he didn't want to see her again?

And then it struck her. "Oh, of course. Why didn't I realize? You should have told me. Of course, you would have someone else." She took a deep, shaky breath. It was the hardest role she had ever played. "I hope you will be very happy, Shane Lanark."

Shane kissed her briefly on the cheek. "And you, Nora Armstrong. You be happy." He gazed at her for a long moment. "Deirdre was the most beautiful thing I ever saw." He turned and walked up the gangplank. He never looked back.

89

In March of 1917 America entered the war, and General Pershing and his brash Yanks brought new life and hope to the bogged down Allies on the Western Front. And more fighting. More wounded for Nora to tend with her mechanical efficiency.

That was all she was left with since Shane had gone—just the mechanics of getting through each day. Stuart Alexander Price had been born the previous November. Nora was named godmother. And she had acknowledged Victoria's letter. Mechanically.

In October 1918 Germany was finally defeated, and Nora set about with the rest of the nursing corps preparing to evacuate the last of their patients and turn the hospital over to French civilians. Emma went out every day singing, all but skipping from ward to ward and filling every room with autumn flowers. Nora had constantly to repress a desire to hit the irritating child.

In June 1919 the Treaty of Versailles was signed. Part Six of the treaty provided for identification and return of all prisoners of war. Including Eric Armstrong.

The day Nora learned that Eric would be home when she got there, she embraced Emma, who had taken care recently to stay out of Nora's way. "My brother's alive!" Nora waved her mother's letter like a flag. "Three years. I haven't seen him for three years. I was so sure he was dead. Every time I thought of him, I could see those little puffs of black smoke and hear the plop of shells. And then the black smoke was coming from his plane and—" She buried her face in her hands, shivering.

Then she threw out her arms and cried, "But I was wrong! It didn't happen that way. Or maybe it did." She looked back at the letter crumpled in her hand. "'Shot down over Luxembourg,' it says. He was wounded. Maybe it did happen just the way I saw it. Only he survived. He was captured, but he survived!"

"I'm so happy for you. Truly, so very happy."

But she saw tears shimmering in Emma's round blue eyes. "Emma, what's wrong?" She had never seen Emma Duffy show any emotion but eternal cheerfulness.

"I'm just happy for you. You've had so much unhappiness. No one deserves good news more. I don't want to spoil it."

"Emma, tell me."

"It's just that my own brother won't be coming home. None of them, actually. There were four. But Eddie—he's the one I'll miss the most. And Mam will, too. He could always make her laugh. There's just us now, Mam and me."

"Emma, what a selfish pig I've been, only thinking of my own unhappiness when there's so much of it in the world. And you always doing so much to make everyone else happy. No one ever suspected— I never thought . . . Emma, will you forgive me?"

"Sure and there's nothing to forgive. You've been a grand friend."

"Yes, we have been friends." In the past months—years, even— since she had lost Eoin and Stuart and Shane—she had grown more and more inward until Emma was her only friend. Only Emma smiled at her and chatted with her as if she was a human being and not the machine she pretended even to herself to be.

And now she had Emma *and* Eric, and back home there would be wee Alex, who would hardly be wee anymore. Perhaps life could go on. "Emma, you must come visit me. Lanarks' Bawn isn't all that far from Belfast. You must come. And bring your mam."

The Treaty of Versailles put an official end to the slaughter of the Great War, but blood continued to flow in Ireland.

The battles there were unconventional, but already the conflict was being referred to as the Anglo-Irish War. And no matter how Nora longed for peace, even at her welcome-home dinner the conversation focused on conflict and killing. If it hadn't been so discouraging, Nora might have found all the contention comfortingly familiar.

"Have you heard what those Sinn Feiners have done now? Ruddy fools have refused to take their seats in Westminster. They're forming their own assembly in Dublin—the Dail Erienn, they call it. Civil war, that's all there is for it. What can they hope to gain?" Lanark Armstrong had filled out considerably in the time Nora had been gone, but his voice hadn't mellowed a bit. He seemed to be practicing one of his political speeches on the family.

Nora and Eric looked at each other across the table and shrugged. Neither had a clue what their older brother was ranting about.

Still, it was so good to be home. Nora gazed around the table. Brenda, sitting beside Lanark, looked the perfect wife and daughter of Belfast shipbuilders. Her blonde hair was swept back and piled high on her head. Her smart black georgette frock was in the new short length that ended just below her knees. Young Mitchell and his wee sister, Melinda, were well cared for by their nanny, leaving Brenda free to cultivate politically important friendships.

"Our poor, dear boys returning from the trenches are having a dreadful time finding jobs. Lady Londonderry has come up with the most splendid idea. She has decided to build a series of new gardens at Mount Stewart and hire veterans to do the work."

But Brenda's offering hardly brought peace to the table. The subject of employment was always volatile.

Thom Armstrong, his mane of white hair still striking even if it had thinned in the past three years, leaned forward and hit the table. "Aye, and whose fault is it if there's no jobs to be had? Who chose to stay safe at home and take up all the jobs our valiant fighting men left behind? I ask you. Catholics and socialists—that's who." He turned to his elder son. "Mark my words. If you don't expel these disloyal elements from the shipyards, you'll have no need to be worrying about the Sinn Feiners. You'll have enough trouble on your own hands."

"Eric, Nora, it's so wonderful to have you home again." Her mother smiled at them from her end of the table.

Nora appreciated Eileen's attempt to bring calm, and she gave an appropriately soothing reply. But actually she found the political discussion interesting—if they could just stay on one topic long enough for her to make sense out of it. She might as well have been dropped on some strange island in the South Pacific where the natives spoke English but none of the words made reference to anything she understood.

She picked Lanark as being the most likely to give her a cogent explanation. "Is it the Home Rule issue again, then?" In spite of the Easter Rising in the south, the war had put the entire issue of Home Rule on hold in Ulster. Now the war was over. She sighed. Were all the old battles to be fought yet again?

"Indeed. Only now they're not calling it Home Rule. Nothing will do for those rebels deValera and Collins but an independent Irish republic."

"Who?" Eric asked.

Nora remembered the names well enough from the Rising, but in those days Eric had spent all his time dreaming of flying airplanes. Eamon deValera was an American-Irish mathematics teacher whose battalion had been the last to surrender in the Rising. Only his American birth had spared him from the firing squad. She knew less about Michael Collins—just that he had taken part in the Rising and been jailed.

Lanark scowled. "Plaguey Fenians. DeValera's president of this upstart provisional government of theirs, and Collins runs the army."

"An army again?" Nora shuddered. Hadn't there been enough fighting?

"Aye, Michael Collins—the man most wanted by the British." Even Thom Armstrong's voice was hushed at the terrible thought of another war—this one on their own island. "Collins's troops practice guerilla warfare—ambush the Royal Irish Constabulary. Now the British have sent in special forces to reinforce the RIC—they call them the Black and Tans for their cobbled-up uniforms."

"And so it goes," Lanark said. "Reprisals for reprisals. Meeting terror with counterterror. Where will it end? British have to do something, of course. We don't want Sinn Fein bringing their war up here. But these new auxiliaries don't seem to be subject to any regular military discipline. I'm not sure playing the enemy's game by his own rules —or lack of them—is the best way. Likely to bring disaster in the end."

"But what do they want? Has the government reneged on their promise to implement Home Rule after the war?"

"Little chance we'd be so lucky," her father broke in. "Cram it down our throats, they will. What does Ulster want with their own Parliament? Isn't the English Parliament the finest in the world? You mark my words. The British want to dump us, that's what. We fought their war for them. Look at all we sacrificed at the Somme." He paused long enough for everyone at the table to think of Stuart.

Nora and Eric looked at each other, their expressions clearly saying they would rather not remember the Somme.

"They'll force a Parliament on us, like it or no. Just you watch. And that rabble in the south just make matters worse."

Lanark returned to his slightly less-heated explanation. "Sinn Fein says they'll settle for nothing but an all-Ireland Irish republic, sovereign and independent of England."

The statement left the table in silence until, finally, Nora broke it. "All Ireland. Meaning no special consideration for Ulster? But surely Lloyd George hasn't agreed to that."

David Lloyd George had succeeded Asquith as prime minister in 1916 and had been a highly effective wartime leader. The question now was whether or not the Welsh Wizard could be as effective on the matter of Irish settlement.

"Lloyd George has assured Craig there will be no change in the laws regarding Ulster without our consent."

"Er . . . Craig?" Eric rubbed a hand over his face. It was clear he felt even more at a loss than Nora did.

"Sir James Craig succeeded Edward Carson as head of the Unionists."

Nora was glad Lanark's reply to Eric was succinct. The experienced nurse in her had spotted marks of fatigue and pain in her younger brother. He had spoken little of his experience as a prisoner of war, but she had heard tales of men being mistreated and starved. The prominence of the bones in Eric's face gave silent evidence to what he had endured. She pushed back her chair and said softly, "Eric, wouldn't you like to come upstairs with me?"

His look of gratitude changed to a scowl, however, when she reached to assist him from the chair. "I can do it. I'm slow and awkward but not completely helpless." Gripping the edge of the table, he pulled himself to a standing position and limped from the room.

Eric's terse explanation of his experience had included the information that he had managed to land his damaged Sopwith in a cow pasture, but it had flipped over. He regained consciousness in a prison camp. He'd done his best to set his smashed knee himself. Other prisoners scouted the camp for stout sticks for him, and a French officer had sacrificed his shirt to tie on the splints. It had all more or less healed, and Eric got around reasonably well, in spite of the pain whose presence he refused to admit.

Nora reclined on the couch in her room while her brother threw himself on her bed. "Oh, Eric, what kind of a world have we come home to?"

"Much the same kind we left, apparently. Last time I saw you, we were in the middle of a bombed-out city. Then I spent two years dropping bombs on cities so the Germans would quit dropping bombs on ours. And now the Black and Tans are shooting people to try to make the Sinn Feiners stop shooting people." He flung an arm over his eyes.

Nora shook her head. "What a pair we are. And we're the survivors. Though I wonder if there really *are* any survivors. Pedar used to go on and on with such beautiful theories about love and beauty and peace for the nations. Peace that flowed like a river down the streets of our cities and the leaves of the trees for healing." She closed her eyes. "I used to believe it would be true someday. I could see it—the Lagan in Belfast, the Liffey in Dublin—the image seemed quite perfect. Until a gunboat sailed up the Liffey."

The silence in the room threatened to become oppressive.

"Oh, Eric, what will we do now? We're still young. You're only nineteen, for goodness' sake. I'm twenty-five, even if I do feel fifty-two. What are we going to do with ourselves? Will you go to university?"

He gave a bitter laugh. Her lighthearted Eric, the one who could always make the world smile. The war had smashed far more than his knee. "And what would I study? I thought once I'd study divinity."

Nora gave an exclamation of surprise.

He shrugged. "Yeah. Daft, I know. But I used to think there were answers, purposes. And I wanted to help people find those answers and purposes."

She nodded. "I know. Like Pedar and his plays. I felt the same way about acting. It was a kind of preaching, playing roles that could help people see truth." She was quiet for a long time. "Haven't you thought of anything you'd like to do?"

"Don't laugh—"

"I wish I could remember the last time I laughed."

"OK, then. Do laugh. But there was something I started doing in prison camp. I couldn't get around much, and there wasn't much of anyplace to get around to. So I sort of started writing."

"Writing what?"

"Making up stories, poems. Mostly in my head. Once in a while we'd get a scrap of paper from somewhere, and I'd write something down."

"Well, by all means, then, you must keep on." She turned to her desk and pulled out a thick pad of paper.

Eric took the notebook with him when he limped off to his own room.

When Nora happened to see it a couple of weeks later, however, the paper was still pristine. She wanted to help him. But she couldn't even see how to help herself.

The one bright spot in all their lives was young Stuart Alexander Price. His mother brought him over from Price Manor at least once a week, and Nora found herself doting on her godson more each time— his ivory skin, his golden curls, the small hands that held so tightly to Auntie Nora's when she took him for a walk. She realized she was becoming quite silly over the child, but she couldn't restrain herself from making excuses to visit Victoria.

Only rarely did Nora give in to feeling sorry for herself because she would never have such a child of her own. At least she held firm in the daytime. Her dreams were harder to control.

One night she dreamed of Eoin as a child running through a field of daffodils that must have been Phoenix Park. And then Eoin was there as a man, and the child was running to him. Only now the child was Alex. And the man was Shane. She woke, her pillow wet. Did that mean Shane had married the girl who was waiting for him, and they had a son? She hoped so. She desperately hoped so. She wanted to think that somewhere someone was as happy as she had been for a moment in that dream.

The south staggered on under the turmoil of civil war. Royal Irish Constabulary men were being shot from behind hedgerows and the Black and Tans exacted brutal reprisals for each ambush. The north debated the Better Government of Ireland bill that Lloyd George had introduced in the British Parliament early in 1920.

With an eye to winning a seat in the proposed Northern Ireland Parliament, Lanark Armstrong took to the hustings to promote support for the bill among the people of Ulster. The family—all except his father—accompanied him to a rally at Ulster Hall. Thom Armstrong staunchly refused to countenance any suggestion of a separate Parliament.

The great hall, lavish with gilt carving, rang to the strains of the national anthem as attendees raised their voices with that of the magnificent organ on the dais. "God save our gracious king, God save our noble king. Send him victorious, long to reign over us . . ."

Sir James Craig gave the opening speech, making perfectly clear that there was absolutely no way Ulster would be forced into a free state with the south. "We are part of that great British Empire on which the sun never sets. And the sun shall not set on Ulster."

The crowd cheered.

"We are plain people. Plain, hardworking people who love peace and industry. The attempt by those in the south to separate us from our motherland is at its heart an attack against Protestantism. It is an attempt to establish a Roman Catholic ascendancy in Ireland. It is an attempt to begin the disintegration of the Empire."

As applause for the speaker filled the hall, Nora wondered. Was he talking about the same group of poets and idealists she had known in Dublin? Well, not exactly, of course—most of those were dead. Perhaps the new Sinn Fein leaders were different. Or perhaps perceptions were really that disparate in this small land. Perhaps those who suggested a divided Ireland were right. It was an unconscionable thought. But perhaps it was the only way.

Craig continued, "I know my responsibility as your leader, as leader of the Ulster Unionists. I know my responsibility, and I accept it. And I enter into a compact with you, as my predecessor Sir Edward Carson did, that with the help of every one of you and with the help of God, we will defeat the most nefarious conspiracy that has ever been hatched against a free people."

Lanark Armstrong spoke next, and it was an amazing speech. Nora had no idea her brother had such a gift for oratory. He began by giving a roll call of Ulster's war heroes, those who had been awarded the Victoria Cross for bravery and others who performed outstanding valiant acts, including the account of his own cousin. Nora's eyes were wet as were most others in the hall.

"These deaths serve to give resolution to any waverers. There is now no way any person in Ulster can honorably accept a Parliament with those who rebelled against England in her darkest hour. To do so would be to turn our backs on these, our honored dead."

Even as Nora wiped her eyes, she wondered again. What about the forty five thousand Irishmen from other provinces who had fought in the war? What about those from the south, such as Shane, who had been attached to the 36th Ulsters at the Somme?

And yet it was a magnificent speech. "Let no one ever forget that the men of the Ulster Division did more than simply kill Germans when they stormed the Schwaben Redoubt. The Ulster Division sacrificed itself for the Empire. The Ulster Volunteer Force has won a name which equals any in history. Their devotion deserves the gratitude of the entire British Empire and the loyalty of their beloved province to remain a solid part of that Empire for which they died."

The audience was on its feet, Nora with them, cheering. She wasn't entirely certain about the implications of all he said, but it was a grand moment. She had had so little to exult over lately that the experience was like heady wine.

The final speaker was Bonar Law, an Ulster Unionist who had fought Home Rule since the first bill was introduced. Raising a clenched fist, he proclaimed, "I here give solemn warning to those subversive forces that would attempt to force Ulster out of the Empire. Ulster will resist, by force if necessary. I can imagine no length of resistance to which Ulster can go in which I should not be prepared to support them."

Again the applause was thunderous.

But Nora's burst of euphoria had, leaving her sober. His words were ominous.

A voice with an ironic twang said close to her ear, "Peculiar situation, wouldn't you say? Ulster is so loyal she will take arms against the Crown to prove her devotion to the Crown."

Nora all but threw her arms around the familiar tweed-jacketed shoulders. "Tim O'Connell, it's yourself!"

"Indeed, Nora, me love." He stuffed his notebook in his pocket to take her hand in both of his.

"What are you doing in Belfast?"

He grinned and pushed his glasses up on his nose. "Same thing I always do. There's some that makes the news; there's some that reads the news. But without us poor hacks in the middle writing the news, there'd be none."

She laughed. Here was someone from her old world, from the days of elegant suppers and poetic plays. Someone from before the guns of risings and wars. Someone who seemed unchanged by it all. "Oh, Tim, that's grand. But what brought you to Belfast? Surely you have news enough in Dublin."

"Never a dull moment. He who is tired of Dublin is tired of life. But a lowly scribe like myself goes where his editor sends him. And our Belfast man quit. So here I am, until a new scribbler can be found."

"Pardon me, but do I understand rightly that you're looking for a writer?"

Nora turned. She had not realized that Eric was standing directly behind her. She started to introduce him, but the two young men brushed such amenities aside as they jumped straight to the heart of the matter.

The *Irish Times* needed a writer in Belfast. Eric was a writer—at least he wanted to be—and he was a fast learner. Tim would be delighted to teach him the ropes and give him a recommendation—the cousin of Pedar O'Brien should have no trouble learning the craft of words.

"Delighted to help the brother of a friend. Especially when it'll get me back to the heart of the action." Tim clapped Eric on the shoulder. "Come with me now. I'll show you how I put my story together and telegraph it to Dublin. This rally will be in the *Times* tomorrow."

Eric took to journalism with such vigor that even his limp was less pronounced. And whenever he could get home, his up-to-the-minute information fueled family discussions for days.

Certainly there was plenty of news in Belfast. Loyalist forces were preparing to meet increased pressure by Sinn Fein to force them into an all-Ireland republic. Sectarian warfare flared in Londonderry with shootings, bombings, and riots. Protestants burned Catholics out of their homes. Catholics burned Protestants out of their homes.

As IRA attacks spread northward, the Ulster Unionist Council in Belfast decided to revive the UVF. Meanwhile, those such as Lanark Armstrong, who put more faith in the political approach than the military, debated the pros and cons of Lloyd George's Government of Ireland Bill. The measure proposed two Irish Parliaments, one for the six northeastern counties, to be called Northern Ireland, and another for the other twenty-six counties, to be known as Southern Ireland. Both sections would still send representatives to Westminster, which would hold ultimate authority. There was to be, as well, a council made up of twenty representatives from each of the two Irish Parliaments, which would seek to establish a Parliament for the whole of Ireland.

While all the men of the family were absorbed by the debate, Nora turned her attentions more to Victoria and Alex. She was pleased to see some of the bloom returning to Victoria's cheeks, if not the sparkle to her eyes. Vicky was becoming more and more involved in Methodist Society charity work among the poor. The delicate fragility that had been so much of her appeal was now sticklike thinness, but her sheer determination to get on with life by helping others was doing her good.

Vicky must have been watching for Nora's approach. She came out the front door of Price Manor in a short green dress with a dropped waist. A tiny cloche covered her blond curls. "Nora, I'm so glad you've come. I've got something to show you. I wanted you to be the first."

Alex, now close to five, appeared behind his mother and grinned at the sight of Auntie Nora.

She bent down and opened her arms for him. "Sorry, Vicky, I do want to hear your news. But I have to greet my darling first."

"Oh, don't mind me. I know who's important in my son's world. But now, come see."

Nora offered Alex a hand to hold as they crunched across the gravel toward the barns.

Sturdy Meg Raglan emerged from the stables, a rope halter in one hand, a nosebag of oats in the other. "Humph!" She snorted like one of her prize thoroughbreds. "All a lot of nonsense. A passing fad. And don't you be scaring my horses, young woman."

Vicky smiled at her aunt, who did such a brilliant job of both horse breeding and running Price Manor. "Don't worry, Aunt Meg. Is Irene around to watch Alex? I'm hoping to talk Nora into joining me at the mission today."

Nora felt the small fingers tighten around her own. She would much rather spend the day playing with Alex. But she knew the urgency of the mission work. Unemployment and poverty among the returned soldiers, especially the disabled, were appalling. She hated the sight of war-crippled men standing in the gutter selling matches. Nora felt guilty for her idleness. Victoria was quite right. There was work to be done, and it was time Nora started doing her share. "Of course I'll go with you, V—"

She stopped mid-word as they rounded the building. "Vicky! A motorcar!" Nora ran her hand over the shiny dark green surface of the little Austin. "But can you drive?"

"Oh, yes. It's really quite easy. The man who sold it to me taught me. It's absolutely amazing. It goes fifteen miles an hour—we can be in Belfast in less than an hour!"

Indeed, Nora felt quite breathless when they arrived at the mission shortly before noon.

Methodist workers had spent all morning packing baskets of provisions to be distributed to the poor of New Lodge and beyond.

"See how wonderful it is to have an automobile," Vicky said as she loaded the rear seat with food packages. "We can accomplish so much more this way."

Nora held some misgivings about going into the New Lodge area until she saw how grateful the women were to receive their packages. The winding streets were lined with row upon row of narrow dwellings, spilling over with children. Time after time, a careworn mother with a babe in her arms would thank them for the food.

"I wouldn't be taking it for myself, as I've no way to be paying you. It's for the wanes." "Aye, it's thanking you I am. My man was gassed and wounded in the trenches." "I'll not be taking charity. It's just a loan, like, until my man can get his job back at the docks."

And so they went on down the street. Nora had no idea their load would seem so pitifully small when the car was empty and row after faceless row of houses had gone unvisited.

They were heading back toward the main road when she heard the angry rumble of distant thunder. The car was open-topped, and she was looking around for some kind of protection from the weather when the sound came again. Then she realized it wasn't thunder. She was hearing the roar of an angry crowd.

A small boy ran down the sidewalk, shouting. A group instantly formed around him, but Nora couldn't make out his news.

They were almost to the corner of Crumlin Road and York Street when Nora spotted a familiar figure. "Oh, look! It's Eric. I think he needs a ride."

Vicky swerved expertly to the side of the pavement, and Eric jumped into the back. "What a spot of luck! Can you turn up here and drop me near the docks? There's trouble at the shipyard."

"Trouble? Is Lanark in danger?"

"I shouldn't think so. Apparently it's mostly a matter of stone-throwing at the railway embankment." He settled back in the seat as Vicky headed north. "What a day this has been! Twenty-four fires there've been. All of them malicious."

Nora turned around to face him. "Was anyone hurt?"

"Two looters wounded by the police. This dockyard thing looks worse, though."

"What happened?"

"That's what I'm trying to find out. The report is that the riveters at another shipyard had a meeting at noon and swore to drive all disloyal workers from the docks. They apparently marched into Campbell and Wilson and pelted rivets at the Catholics and socialists. Of course, that set off a riot."

"How dreadful." Nora shivered as the angry sounds became louder.

"Stop here." Eric pointed. "I'll get out on the corner. I don't want you girls coming any closer." He scrambled over the side. "Now turn around and go straight home. This is only the beginning. Things are sure to get a lot uglier—fast."

"Yes, we will. But Eric, you be careful."

He laughed as he started off toward the angry shouts. "Don't worry. I've seen lots worse."

Victoria was turning around to make for the Newtownards Road when the street in front of them suddenly burst into a wall of flame. Rioters were throwing petrol over vehicles parked on each side of the street and setting them ablaze. She screamed and braked so hard that Nora almost slammed her head against the windscreen.

"Quick, turn down here!" Nora pointed to a narrow side street offering a tunnel of quiet.

They had gone no more than a few yards when Nora saw an all-too-familiar sight. An ex-soldier in a tattered uniform, his left sleeve empty, dark glasses over his sightless eyes, was tapping his way along. A collecting tin hung around his neck.

Just then an angry crowd roared around the corner, shouting and waving sticks as they rushed to join the main brawling body. No fewer than three of the rioters slammed into the soldier, knocking him to the pavement. Others trampled over him and raced on.

Nora was out of the car before Vicky had come to a full stop. She knelt over the man. "Here, let me help—" A blast knocked her to the pavement. Her body sprawled across the fallen soldier. She heard the crack of her own head on the cement.

90

Nora woke slowly, swimming in pain, and struggled upward through waves of blackness, straining to reach the pinpoint of light at the top. If she could fight her way to the surface, she would be able to breathe and see. The temptation to sink backward was nearly overwhelming. *Just give in to the forces pulling downward.* But, no. The light. She must reach the light.

"Nora. Nora, come on. Can you hear me? Open your eyes if you can. Nora?"

She was sure she recognized that voice. Why couldn't she put a name to it?

"Come on. Wake up. Please, Nora." It was her brother. But Eric was lost in the war. His plane had been shot down. Why was she in bed? She was on duty. They had a whole ward of new head injury cases from the Somme. One of them might be Stuart. Stuart might need her to nurse him. No, it wasn't Stuart. Stuart was dead. It was Shane. Shane needed her. She needed Shane. She groaned.

"Nora, wake up." That was a woman's voice. Of course. It was Emma in the next bed. Time to go on duty. She would wash her face while Emma picked flowers. Emma was always so cheerful.

She opened her eyes. "Emma. Why do you have that scarf on? Where's your cap?"

"It's a new uniform, Nora. This is the Royal Victoria. We're in Belfast, not France."

"It's France. Shane just called me." Nora struggled to sit up, but the pain in her head was too sharp.

"Sorry, sis. It was only me." Eric gave her a strained smile.

"Oh. I remember." It all came back slowly. "I was with Vicky. There was a riot. We stopped to help a vet—" She closed her eyes against the pain. "Where's Vicky?"

The silence in the room chilled her. Eric took her hand.

Emma embraced her. "I'm so sorry, Nora. Can you bear another loss?"

Nora let the tears fall and the blackness cover her. It wasn't until the next day that she could sit up and hear the details. No one knew where the bomb had come from, but it had been thrown directly at Vicky's car. Nora, on the pavement with the soldier, had been concussed, but she would be all right.

"You can go home tomorrow," Emma said. "Doctor Jones wasn't too happy about letting you go so soon, but Eric told him you couldn't miss the funeral."

"Alex will be needing you," Eric added. "Mother is with him now. But next to his own mother, he loves you best, you know."

The tears came again. That poor wane—to lose both parents before he was five years old. After a time she was able to say, "Thank you, Eric." She even attempted a smile. "You've been so good. You've hardly left my bedside, have you?"

"I have some. You've slept a good deal of the time."

"And Emma. It's so good to see you again. I didn't know you'd gone on with your nursing. You never came to visit me."

"I know. I didn't want to lose touch, but Mam seemed to need me every minute I wasn't here."

"I think you might be seeing a bit more of her now." Eric grinned. "I've . . . uh . . . been attempting some persuasion."

Emma smiled and ducked her head. "Oh, get on with you now."

Nora managed another weak smile. *In the midst of death we are in the midst of life.* Indeed, they were in the midst of death. Victoria, the young widow, leaving behind those with a new grief. And what of the families of the Catholics and other Protestants killed in this most recent spate of rioting? Even as the questions rang in her mind, Nora saw again the shy smiles Eric and Emma exchanged. Still there was the eternal cycle of love and renewed life.

One must go on with the living. Stuart was gone, Victoria was gone, but Alexander remained. Hope for the future remained. Those such as herself, who had seen the ravages of war and violence, must endure for the tender young if there was to be any hope at all.

She would do her best to endure for Alex.

"The Lord is my shepherd; I shall not want. . . . Yea, though I walk through the valley of the shadow of death, I will fear no evil: for Thou art with me . . ."

Alex's fingers gripped her own. She knelt beside him and engulfed him in her arms as the Rev. Mr. Wesley Carlton committed "the body of our beloved sister Victoria Isabella Price to our loving heavenly Father's care."

Alex sniffed. "Is Mummy really in that box?" He was such a thinker.

"No, my darling. That's only the part of her she used here on earth. Now she's in heaven, and everything is much nicer there."

"My daddy's in heaven. Is she with my daddy?"

"Yes, she certainly is. She loved the Lord Jesus."

The child screwed up his face, considering. "Does her in heaven have a new dress?"

"Maybe something like that. Only much better. Dresses get soiled and wear out here. Nothing in heaven will ever wear out."

He looked relieved. "That's good. Mummy didn't like it when I ripped my shirt."

Nora pulled him closer and watched as the casket—such a tiny one, it could have been a child's—was lowered into the ground. Around them the Price family graves stood witness: Archibald and Harriet, Evan, Thomas and Selma, Stuart's father, and Stuart's mother, who had died at his birth. But there was no grave for Stuart Price. His earthly remains were somewhere in France in a field that was slowly grassing over and coming back to life—just as these poor remains would someday.

The breeze ruffled the minister's robe. "We go now, though sorrowing for our departed, in the certain hope that neither death nor life, nor angels, nor principalities, nor things present, nor things to come, nor powers, nor height, nor depth, nor anything else in all creation, will be able to separate us from the love of God in Christ Jesus our Lord. Amen."

Nora attempted to stand, still holding Alex, but she stumbled in the attempt. A hand caught her elbow, and an arm around her waist brought her firmly to her feet. "Oh, thank you. I—" Nora turned, thinking her assistant was Lanark or her father.

"Shane!" She all but stumbled again.

He led her apart from the crowd standing about the grave. "I've a lot to explain, Nora. I'm so sorry. I would ask you to forgive me for being such a coward. But—"

To Nora's amazement, Alex unwound his arms from her neck and reached for him.

"Uncle Shane."

"He knows you?"

"I've been keeping touch ever since I got back from France. I came here straightaway to tell Victoria in person all that we tried to explain in the letters we wrote. I wanted to be sure she understood what a hero Stuart was."

"Yes, of course. That was important. But why didn't she tell me?" The answer was already forming in Nora's mind. Shane and Vicky? But he'd had a girl waiting for him in Dublin.

"I told her not to tell. You see, I saw right off that—as wonderful as all the women of Price Manor were, this lad needed a man in his life. So I did what I could for him. I've come up several times—as often as I could get away from the office."

"And never came to see me? Never a hello? Shane, I understood that you had someone at home that you were coming back to, but—" She bit her lip and turned away. She ached to tell him how hard that knowledge had been to bear. But she didn't dare. "I just don't understand why we couldn't be friends. Why would you have to sneak? I realize you must be married with children of your own now—"

His face paled, emphasized by his black coat and hat. The thin lines pain had etched in his face deepened. "Nora, that's just it—the crux of the whole matter. If I thought I could have children of my own I would have pursued the matter long ago." He looked at her deeply. "Before I left LeHavre, Nora."

She was too shocked to answer. Not an old girlfriend? Not Victoria? Shane was free? He wasn't wholly well, perhaps. Not complete, as many put it. But he stood before her, his own dear self. Unmarried. And what had he said? He would have spoken in France. He would have spoken to her. It was she!

It took all her willpower simply to stand there outwardly calm. Her mind whirled. Perhaps the greatest shock was not that matters should be so, but that she hadn't guessed earlier. She was a nurse. She knew his injuries. And his assumption could well be correct—although one could never be sure. She looked at him, trying to communicate with her heart what the lump in her throat would not let her say. She touched his arm lightly.

The small, bright blond head next to Shane's sagged onto his broad shoulders as the child relaxed into sleep. It was the most beautiful sight she had ever seen. All the willpower in the world couldn't keep the tears from spilling down her cheeks.

"Ah, Nora, I'm sae sorry. But that's why I let you think I had someone else—why I kept my friendship with Price Manor a secret. I—"

"You wanted me to be free."

"Aye, that. I knew you'd find a fine fellow—someone who could give you wanes as beautiful as yourself. I didn't want to stand in the way of that. But it was nae so selfless, really. The fact is, I couldn't face the pain of seeing you and not taking you in my arms."

"And do you really think I'd rather have another man than yourself, Shane Lanark—on any terms?"

Yet, even in the joy of the moment, finding the fulfillment she had thought never would be hers, the conflict of duty hovered in the back of Nora's mind. Not three days ago she had pledged herself to rearing Alex. Would her marrying Shane and going away mean yet another loss for the child who had already lost so much?

She was learning that in this life loss was inevitable. As Alex's godmother, she must choose which he was to lose—her presence or his home. Three generations of Lanarks had practiced law in the little office behind the Four Courts in Dublin. A dozen or more generations of Prices had lived at the Manor. She could take neither's heritage from him.

And though it broke her heart, she never doubted but that her choice would be Shane. Meg and Irene Raglan would rear Alex with the same first-class efficiency that they expended on their prize bloodstock. It was an imperfect solution, but they lived in an imperfect world.

Her hand reached to caress the child's curls.

91

"To live together in the holy estate of matrimony . . ."

Assassination Squad Kills 14 British Officers. Entire Special Intelligence Team Slain. Even as Nora, elegant and slim in white satin, repeated her wedding vows, the desperate headlines of the past weeks hovered somewhere in the back of her mind.

"Will you love him, comfort him, honor and keep him, in sickness and health, for better or worse . . ."

Brits Retaliate for Killings. Twelve Shot at Football Match.

"Be faithful to him as long as you both shall live?"

IRA Destroys Convoy of British Soldiers in West Cork.

"Oh, gracious and ever living God, look mercifully upon this man and this woman who come to You seeking Your blessing . . ."

British Burn Cork City Centre in Reprisal.

"Grant that, by Your Holy Spirit, Shane and Nora, now joined in holy matrimony, may become one in heart and soul and live in fidelity and peace for the sake of Jesus Christ our Lord."

As Nora joined in the last "Amen," she looked up into Shane's steady face, and her fears faded. Whatever the future, no matter how grim the next headline, they were one. They would face it together in the strength of the grace of God, who had joined them together. She turned then with a radiant smile to her family gathered in the small chapel.

The organ postlude began, and bride and groom led the way into the uneasy sunshine of an Irish December. Emma and Eric as groomsman and maid of honor emerged just behind them.

The wedding dinner was served at the hotel. That is, dinner would be served after the traditional toasts, and Nora knew that meant the meats would be cooling while the men of her family all had their say. She reached for Shane's hand under the table as Pedar stood. As the acknowledged family bard, it was his place to offer the first toast.

"To the bride and groom. That their love for each other may be a seal upon their hearts, a mantle about their shoulders, and a crown upon their foreheads. That the love in their home may reach out into the wider community. And that such love, which comes only from above, will plant a seed of restoration that will spread throughout this land. That the years which the locust has eaten will be restored. That the kingdom of Him whose throne is in the heavens will rule over all."

Nora reached out a hand to Pedar. "That was beautiful. I wanted to respond, 'World without end, amen.' But don't you get discouraged when it seems no one else shares the vision?"

Pedar laughed. "Ah, but that's the *seanachaidh's* consolation. My job is only to speak the words. I keep the vision alive with the words. And so I'll keep on speaking and writing until the vision becomes reality, no matter how long it takes. That's the thing about the written word—it'll be here beyond me."

Nora brushed the veil back from her face and stood to kiss him.

"Aye, a kiss from the bride—that's for luck!"

Everyone cheered.

Then Lanark rose to welcome his new brother-in-law into the family—and to thank him for taking his sister off his hands.

After the good-natured laughter, however, he got to more serious matters in the true spirit of an Irish politician, who could never let any occasion pass without making a speech. "And so, when Ireland goes to the polls next May in her first truly representative election, I know you'll all remember our sacred and worthy cause and rally round to shatter our enemies and their hopes of a republic flag. The Union Jack must sweep the polls."

Nora cringed. Shane was that rarest of creatures, a nonpolitical Irishman. Still, he was from the south.

But Shane's response bore no hint of any kind of politics. "I cannot be thanking you enough, Lanark Armstrong, for giving me your sister and for giving me a family. You see, Pedar, already your prophecy is being fulfilled. The family that was lost to me is restored good measure and manyfold in you grand folk. May it truly be so for all that the locust has eaten in this land."

The room rang with cheers, and Nora felt that, with such a husband, all losses could be restored indeed.

Through that Christmas season and on into spring, the sheer joy of being with Shane was enough to make Nora think all had been restored. It was such joy to wake every morning and feel her husband's arms around her, to open her eyes and see his dear face next to her on the pillow. It seemed that every time he smiled at her the pain of the losses she had known faded just a bit more. At such times it was easy to believe all would soon be right with the world.

On the other hand, there were times when Nora would crumple the newspaper to the floor, sick with the things she read there. "Black and Tans burn 49 houses in Balbriggan. Observers accuse troops of drunken violence."

At other times matters were more hopeful with talk of truce and negotiations. Then the discouragement would begin again when it seemed that the only choices for the British government were to escalate the war or to sanction terrorism by acquiescing to rebel threats.

Worst of all for Nora were matters much closer to her heart. Those were the mornings when she woke to the memory of Alex's eyes when she tried to explain to him she was going away. The child had shown extraordinary courage for a five-year-old. His lip trembled, and his eyes glistened, but he did not cry.

She and Shane had talked of it time and again, and always they came to the same conclusion. They must visit Alex soon. But Shane seemed to get ever further behind with his work. And so they had not yet made the trip.

Then came the day in April when Nora woke with a desire to see the daffodils in St. Stephen's Green. Shane had gone to the office early to finish writing some wills, so she left a note and set out on her own. The walk through streets she had first discovered with Eoin held a bittersweet poignancy. She cherished and clung to the feelings, because she would share them with Shane. That was one of the best things about their marriage. They could talk about everything—old loves, old agonies. Everything became more bearable and more meaningful as it was shared.

And Shane, who had lost so much in the Rising, understood her feelings better than anyone else could. Dear Shane. He bore no love for the rebels who started the trouble nor for the government whose firebombs had killed his family. But in his refusal to be bitter he set the pattern for the restoration of peace. His love made it possible for Nora to continue praying with faith.

St. Stephen's Green today, however, was not a restoration. A few daffodils struggled to bloom in the ragged grass, but the charming bridge that had once curved over the crescent pond was gone, a casualty of the Rising. Piles of rubble lay in place of many of the dignified homes that had surrounded the park. The area was depressingly derelict.

Nora turned and ran, not really noting which way she went, just knowing she had to escape the ghosts. The way led uphill, and she was short of breath when a harsh voice barked at her.

"Halt!"

She looked up and found herself facing two armed men clad in the infamous tan pants and black coats that had become the symbols of fear and oppression in the city.

"'ello, luv. What's a pretty lady like you doin' 'ere with all these papists?"

Nora stood very straight, which made her taller than one of her challengers. "If you'll excuse me, I happen to be a Protestant. But I'm not aware that it's against the law to be a Catholic."

"Oh, the lady doth protest that she's a Protestant." The shorter one stepped forward.

Nora started to back away. She could smell the liquor on the man's breath when he laughed.

"And just what brand are you, then?"

Nora hesitated. She had been raised Presbyterian, as everyone at Lanarks' Bawn had been since there was such a thing as Presbyterian. But Shane was Church of Ireland, and they worshiped there now. Did that make her Episcopal? It was the hesitation that undid her.

"Oh, not so sure about it, are you? Now, a good Protestant girl like yourself should know her prayer book better than that."

She wanted to turn and run, but both men held rifles.

The black coat came menacingly close. He put a hand to the top of her bodice. "Now, let's just see here if you're wearing some of your heathen symbols under that fine frock—a rosary or a Saint Christopher's medal, maybe. No sense in praying to any virgin to help you now."

Nora screamed, but in her own ears the ripping of her dress rang far louder. She scratched, hit, kicked until the tall one got behind and locked her arms in a painful grip. She screamed again. Her attacker landed a hard slap across her face that left her cheek stinging. He reached for her slip.

Her third scream brought a crowd of onlookers. Most stood huddled on the edge of the pavement, muttering darkly. A couple of urchins threw stones at the men. One missed and hit Nora. A trickle of blood ran into her eye.

"Attention!"

At the barked order from behind them, Nora felt her arms loosened.

An officer of the Royal Irish Constabulary, which the Black and Tans were supposed to be supporting, strode up with his polished blackthorn stick. "That will do. Bender, Finchley. Your orders were to search pedestrians for weapons."

"Sir. That's what we're doing, sir."

Nora was struggling to pull her dress together and wipe the blood from her face when a man jumped from a car and came running.

"Nora, Nora, what have they done to you?"

Shane took her in his arms, and she collapsed against him. "I thought I'd go mad looking for you. Your note said Saint Stephen's

Green, and there's trouble there. Then some street arabs started yelling there was more trouble up here. Whatever made you come through the Liberties?"

All she could do was cling to him, shaking. He almost carried her to the car.

They didn't talk until they were home, sitting in the kitchen with a pot of tea and Nora wrapped in a soft flannel dressing gown.

She tried to explain what had happened, but the words stuck in her throat. The humiliation of having her dress ripped from her in the middle of the street. The man's rough hands that had left bruises on her arms. The fear of worse—so much worse. And her sense of alienation from the city she had once loved so much. She couldn't explain. All she could do was shake her head.

"I know, my darling. Living here is awful for you, isn't it?"

The idea that he sensed her feelings was such a relief that she found her voice. "Oh, thank you for understanding. I didn't want to say anything. This is your home. Your work is here. But it's all so—so alien. It isn't like it used to be at all. I thought I could take up life here —like before the Rising. I even thought of meeting my old friends at the Abbey—seeing Pedar sometimes . . ." She took a long drink of tea. "The war changed everything."

"And you miss Alex."

Now the tears that she had been holding in check fell, and Shane held her until the sobs subsided.

"I was afraid to say anything. I didn't want you to think I cared more for him than for you." She hiccupped. "But I feel so guilty— abandoning him for my own happiness—"

"Of course, I understand. I miss him, too. I've been thinking about this for some time. That's one reason I've been working such long hours. There were things I had to get finished up before I could leave the practice to Uncle Finlay."

"Why would you leave the practice?"

"To open another one in Newtownards."

"But—"

"You're not the only one who came home to find everything changed."

And then Nora understood. She had thought of their apartment as his home, but it was only where he'd lived when he came back from France. His home was gone, too. Even her presence here with him had probably just highlighted the futility of trying to recapture the past. Shane needed a new start, too.

"What do you think, Nora? Do you want to go home?"

Belfast had perhaps never seen a greater day than 22 June 1921, for that day King George V opened the first Northern Ireland Parliament. While Michael Collins, Arthur Griffith, and Eamon deValera were busy shuttling between Dublin and London, negotiating their own treaty for an Irish Free State, Belfast was busy draping every street with bunting and painting miles of pavement and lampposts red, white, and blue.

The Better Government of Ireland Act was to serve as the constitution of Northern Ireland. In the south, Sinn Fein had rejected the "Partition Act" out of hand. And even in Belfast, King George would be addressing only the Unionist MPs. The Ulster voters had returned 40 Unionists, 6 Sinn Feiners, and 6 Nationalists. In the south, Sinn Fein had won 124 seats out of 128. Northern Sinn Feiners and Nationalists had refused the Belfast Parliament and taken seats in the Dublin Dail.

As one who had been elected to the Parliament and would take his seat enthusiastically, however, Lanark Armstrong was able to secure passes for his family to attend the reception for King George and Queen Mary after the opening ceremony.

Nora had often heard what a lovely lady Queen Mary was, and she was not disappointed. Her hair piled atop her head, the queen was elegant in an ivory lace gown and pearl choker necklace. But Nora was surprised when King George stood to address the hall. He was a much smaller man than she had imagined. He was nonetheless splendid in black uniform with heavy gold epaulets and wide gold braid on cuffs and pants legs.

"This is a great and critical occasion in the history of the Six Counties, but not for the Six Counties alone, for everything which interests them touches Ireland . . ."

Nora turned to the tall man beside her and smiled at those dear features that she had found so beloved ever since that dreadful night on the LeHavre station platform five years before. His blue eyes smiled back at her, but now the little crinkles at the corners were smile lines rather than marks of pain.

But as she looked at him, she suddenly felt a pang of apprehension. She had been anticipating the moment the speech would be over and she could drag Shane to a quiet corner. They had had no time together all day, and here they were in the middle of a crowd of hundreds. But how would Shane react to what she must tell him?

Nora swallowed her impatient fears, though, and wrenched her attention back to her sovereign.

"I speak from a full heart when I pray that my coming to Ireland today may prove to be the first step towards an end of strife amongst her people, whatever their race or creed . . ."

No one could agree with King George's sentiments more than Nora, but she did wish he would hurry. She looked again at Shane, who seemed thoroughly engrossed in the speech. How could she get him out of this crowd? Was there any quiet corner in the whole city today?

"I appeal to all Irishmen to pause, to stretch out the hand of forbearance and conciliation, to forgive and forget, and to join in making for the land which they love a new era of peace, contentment, and good will."

Beautiful words. It was a new era, indeed. And no one was more aware of newness than Nora. She could simply wait no longer. No matter how memorable King George's words were, hers would be more memorable to her husband. She turned to whisper in his ear.

But at that moment the king concluded his speech. "The future lies in the hands of my Irish people themselves." The applause was so deafening that it was several minutes before she could make Shane hear her.

And then he didn't believe he had heard. "What? Nora, darling, I can't have heard you right."

"I think you did. It's quite true, my love. You are going to be a father."

"I'm what?"

"You're going to be a father!" She didn't realize how loudly she had spoken until several heads turned their way with broad smiles. But the unwanted attention lasted only moments because all were again caught up in cheering for the king. And then, right there, with half the population of Belfast squeezed into Ulster Hall, Shane Lanark took his wife in his arms and kissed her.

"Jolly good show, what ho! Took all his fences like a champion, didn't he?"

Nora, emerging from her husband's embrace, blinked at the energetic Meg Raglan and tried to form a reply. But of course. The woman was referring to His Majesty.

"Yes, yes, indeed."

Nora and Shane exchanged winks and joined in the continued cheering. No one need know they were cheering for quite another matter. The crowd spontaneously broke into singing the national anthem, and at the end of the song, Shane and Nora moved to the side of the room where Irene stood with Alexander.

"I saw the king!" the boy cried as Shane swooped him up and held him at eye level.

"Aye, that's a fine thing. And did you hear his speech?"

"I didn't understand it much. Auntie Irene said it means people are going to quit hurting each other like they did Mummy. She said everybody is going to get along now."

"Did she now? That's a fine thought, indeed." Shane sighed. "It seems we've done the best we can do at the moment, Alex. But I fear it will be left for you and your children to find the real solution." He ran his fingers through the child's curls. "And I fear there may be more than a little bloodshed yet before it can be achieved."

Nora rested her head on her husband's shoulder, one hand on Alex and one hand on her abdomen. *Let it come. For the children. Let the peace come flowing like a river and the leaves of the trees be as medicine for the healing of the nations.*

92

Who could have foreseen how much blood was to be shed? How many children had been maimed and killed in the past eighty years? And still there was no river of peace. Mary raised a bandaged hand to the throbbing lump on her forehead as Philip let the notebook fall to the floor.

"Do you want a sedative?"

She had refused any but the mildest painkillers for her scrapes and bruises. But now pain radiated down both sides of her face. Maybe just one more dose . . .

"No."

Philip nodded and left the room.

No, she would not be drugged into unconsciousness, no matter how comfortable that sounded, for at any moment Gareth might open his eyes. And they would be just as beautiful, as alight, as full of love as always. And she would not miss that moment.

And so she had sat by his bed all night. Waiting. Listening to Philip's voice to keep herself awake. She had to tell Gareth the moment he became conscious. She had to tell him how much she loved him. She had to tell him how he had saved her by covering her with his own body as the whole world crashed in on them, falling and shaking and splintering in an endless waterfall of boards and masonry. She had felt none of it. She had been aware of only one thing. Gareth was there, protecting her.

Any minute now, he would open his eyes and smile, would assure her that everything would be all right. It had to be that way. Anything else was unthinkable. It wouldn't be much longer. He would talk to her soon. And everything would be fine.

Only a few people interrupted her all-night vigil. There had been the nurse and doctor, bandaging her and assuring her she would be sore and bruised for many days but that she was all right.

And then the police. What did she think she was doing, crossing the police ribbon?

She had insisted there had been no barricade across the alley.

798

That is, none that she saw. She had been so terrified for Gareth, so focused on reaching him, that she could have probably run through a brick wall without noticing.

She learned that the police, alerted by Philip's call, had acted swiftly to evacuate the hotel. Mary still felt sick to her stomach at the thought of what might have happened had Tommy not recognized his former IRA mate. But all had been moved to safety. Only Gareth had been missed. Because the others had left the key at the desk, they had thought his room empty. And Gareth had probably been so deep in his prayers that he hadn't heard anything.

God, that's Gareth. You can't let anything happen to him. She kept trying to pray, but her petition always ended up more an argument than a prayer.

The door on the other side of the room opened, and a nursing sister in blue uniform and white cap came in. "Your sisters are here. Would you like to come out and speak to them?"

No. She couldn't leave Gareth. But she sighed and got up slowly. It was only fair. They must have been terrified. They needed to see that she was all right. She paused at the bed and took Gareth's hand, so pale on the sheet. "I'll be right back," she whispered.

She had never seen Becca and Julie so subdued.

Julie held out a white paper bag. "Debbie said they always bring grapes here."

"But we knew you'd rather have chocolate."

"And I'd rather have you two than even chocolate." Mary hugged them. "And thank you for coming too, Debbie."

The three girls fell silent as the lift door opened and Paddy and Tommy came into the hall, looking grave. Mary caught her breath. Had the matron told them something about Gareth that she didn't know? But apparently they didn't know anything new, either, because Paddy's first question was, "How is he?"

She shook her head, then forced a wavery smile. "He'll be OK. I'm sure he will. But what about you? What did the police—"

"Just come from the *garda*, we have," Paddy answered. "And very grateful they are to our Tommy here for his quick work."

"Oh, that's good. So they got Navan?"

"Oh, aye. And a cellar full of bits and pieces of bomb makings. Of course he denies everything, but that fellow says more than his prayers. They'll sort him out."

"Good." Everything would be fine. She just had to keep reminding herself.

And then the lift opened again. Almost before Liam shot out ahead of Philip, Mary could feel waves of hot rage emanating.

Tommy met Liam and started to put a hand on his shoulder.

Liam jerked away. "Dirty stinking Prod. You said you were Army. Sucked me in to believe in you. Made me think you understood."

"What are you talking about, Liam?" Paddy demanded. "And where were you last night? We were frantic that you might have been in the hotel, too. Thank God you found him, Philip. Why did you run off?"

"I saw him, too, didn't I?" Liam shouted accusingly. "You didn't think I'd know. But I do. I don't know what your blazing game is, but I know your lie. And I'll see you don't get away with it."

Now Paddy took Liam by both shoulders. "All right now. Just tell me, lad. Tell me what this is all about."

"I saw who you ran after. And he wasn't any IRA bomber. He was UVF. If that's the guy who set the bomb, it was set by Prods trying to blame it on our side. Dirty stinking trick—just the sort of thing they'd do."

Paddy held Liam tightly. "This isn't helping anything, Liam. There's some mistake—"

"There's no mistake. That's the Prod that shot my brother!" Liam yelled. "I'll kill him! Just like I should have done the first time."

This time Paddy shook him. "I don't know anything about your brother. But Navan is IRA. They claimed the bombing!"

Liam wrenched away, then turned, his back against the white wall. He looked wild, frightened, like a cornered animal. "You're crazy, man. I saw him!" He closed his eyes, as if looking at the portrait painted on the inside of his eyelids. "That face. That white hair. *Bam! Bam! Bam!* And there was Des bleeding all over the hall. I should have stopped him. It should have been me." With a sob he lunged toward the lift again.

Debbie shot forward and tackled him with both arms. "Liam, don't. Listen to what they have to say. Running off won't help. You have to face this—all the pain. I know—I know what it's like. But you can't run!"

Liam looked like a wildcat ready to spring. But he stood.

Tommy spoke. "I see what's going on. Liam. All these years you've thought Desmond—"

"Don't you dare use his name!"

"You thought your brother was shot by Loyalists. And since he was IRA, that's a logical conclusion. But don't you see—there's another answer." Tommy spoke with the authority of one who had been on the inside.

"You going to tell me the *Army* shot him? That the Irish Republican Army shoots their own men?"

"That's exactly what I'm telling you, Liam. And think. You know it, too. It's in the news all the time. Kneecappings, beatings. Every army deals harshly with deserters, doesn't it?"

"Desmond was no deserter."

"Not in his own eyes. Not any more than I am. But that's how the IRA would look at it. If De—if your brother wanted out, they would go after him—just like they tried to come after me."

"You saying that's why they stole those files?"

"That's right. To find any former Army members. The IRA only has one retirement plan."

"So why are you walking around? You've been out for months. They could have got you anytime."

"Not easily while the cease-fire was in place. This new wave of violence gave them a perfect excuse. I thought I'd be OK since I'd been at Long Kesh. Ex-prisoners aren't as useful. I think the thing with Joe was more personal."

The others kept talking, but Mary was frantic to get back to the hospital room. She realized all this was important to these people, but Gareth was the only one who mattered to her, and she had been gone from him too long.

She backed quietly away and slipped through the door. Gareth lay just as she had left him. She could barely see him breathing. The green line on the monitor looked thin and weak to her, but it still showed a heartbeat. *Please, God.*

Philip followed her in and put his hand on her shoulder.

She leaned against him for a moment. "Oh, Philip. He will be all right, won't he? I was so awful. I yelled at him. I threw his ring . . ." She choked.

Philip put an arm around her and held her.

The confession—it felt so good. She had thought she would never be able to admit to the guilt she felt over that parting scene. "I wanted him to give it all up—to leave Ireland. I wanted him to see how hopeless it all was. But he just wouldn't agree. He cared so much. He loved these people so much."

She went cold at her own words. She had spoken in the past tense. She whirled to look, but the monitor still emitted its little row of tiny green bleeps. They weren't fainter or slower than before. Were they?

A nurse came in on quiet, crepe-soled shoes. She took one sharp, disapproving glance at Mary and Philip, then turned to check the tubes giving Gareth blood and glucose. "You'll both have to leave now—until I'm through. And then only one," she finished severely.

Mary picked up the notebook that still lay on the floor by her chair and followed Philip out of the room. She was thankful that the hall was empty. The others were probably continuing their discussion in the hospital's tea room.

She handed Philip's manuscript to him. "So that's how it all came about—this poor, divided land." She shook her head.

"Yes, the Anglo-Irish Treaty of 1922 created the southern twenty-six counties as the Irish Free State. They had a constitutional relationship with Britain similar to that of Canada."

"So when did that change?" Mary wasn't sure she cared. She hardly listened to the answer, but anything was better than the cold, white silence that let in the chilling fear.

"It was always an uneasy relationship. DeValera became president of the republic. At one point he proposed to the U.S. minister to Ireland that the northern Unionists could be sent to the British mainland in exchange for the Irish in England, who could 'come home' to a united Ireland. The minister replied that the suggestion was 'about as practicable as expelling the New Englanders from Massachusetts.'"

Mary smiled, mostly as an indication that she heard. She appreciated Philip's attempt to lighten the atmosphere.

They both glanced at Gareth's door.

It remained firmly shut, so Philip continued, "The Irish government declared Ireland an independent republic in 1949. British Prime Minister Atlee promised that no change would be made in the status of Northern Ireland without Northern Ireland's agreement."

Mary's mind wandered, though she was grateful for the reassuring drone of Philip's voice.

"Then in 1972, after months of incredibly bloody episodes, Direct Rule from Westminster was imposed on Northern Ireland . . ."

Mary didn't need to hear about any more 'incredibly bloody episodes.' Almost subconsciously she put her hands over her ears. "I've tried to understand. You know I have. But the irony of the most religious land in the Western world being the most violent will never be comprehensible to me."

And then, blessedly, the door opened behind her.

She ran to the nurse. "Sister—"

The stiff white cap barely moved, the shaking of her head was so slight. "We hope for the best." She started to move on, then stopped. "Oh." She pulled a small envelope from her pocket. "You'll want this."

Clutching the envelope, Mary fled into the room. She had to see for herself that the little green light still monitored a beating heart. That the world still existed. For a world without Gareth would be no world at all.

Standing by the bed, she opened the envelope and tipped its contents into her hand. It was a golden circle with two hands clasping a heart, and it felt as if it would burn her palm. She relived the moment of ripping it from her finger and throwing it at Gareth. Now she could visualize Gareth as the slamming door still vibrated, crossing the room to pick up the ring and slip it on his little finger. The ring he had called an eternity ring. The ring that pledged their love forever.

She grasped the hand lying limp and still on the bed. She couldn't stand to think of the medics pulling off the ring as they prepared him for surgery. Holding his hand, gently she slipped the ring back on his finger, bent, and kissed it. Then she carefully twisted it off and put it on her own finger.

"There, Gareth. It's where it belongs. Where it will stay. Always."

Still holding his hand, half standing, half resting on the edge of his bed, she lay her head beside his on the pillow. "Gareth, I love you so much. But you know that. What I want to tell you now is that you're right. About commitment. Gareth, I want you to know. Can you hear me?"

"Mary." His arm moved to encircle her.

"Oh, Gareth. All summer I've fought and struggled for us to have a chance to talk about us. And Ireland kept getting in the way. And I was so angry because you put Ireland ahead of me. And now I see I was doing the same thing that's at the heart of all the strife here. It's all selfishness—putting 'my rights' and 'my needs' above everyone else's —even if it means going to war over it."

The warmth of his arm was the most delicious thing she had ever felt. She didn't want to weary him with her talking, and yet, she had been so afraid she wouldn't get to tell him this—or anything else. She snuggled closer.

"What I mean is, I wanted us to work out a solid plan—get our lives organized. Now I know there's no need to work anything out. It's like Gordon Wilson said after his daughter died—'I don't have a purpose. I don't have an answer. But I know there is an answer.'"

She thought she saw a smile on his lips. "That's enough for me, Gareth."

She felt intense joy and peace as she thought of the years ahead, not having to struggle to achieve her own goals but simply living in submission to God's will. With Gareth. She thought she felt his lips move.

"Just hold me, Gareth. Don't try to talk."

It felt so good. She never wanted to leave the shelter of his arms. Here in this haven all fears for Ireland, for the future, for the two of them were held outside the three circles of Gareth's eternity ring around her finger, his arm about her shoulder, and God's love around them both. "We'll have time, Gareth. Lots of time."

And then it seemed that Gareth was holding her hand and they were on the deck of a boat sailing to the jewel-like island of Iona. "Aye, lassie, we've time. Come." And they were running through the green and purple Highlands, laughing as they jumped from column to golden column at the Giant's Causeway, then walking quietly in a silvery, dew-sparkled morning along Sligo Bay . . .

His arm fell from her shoulder. She awoke. And she knew she was alone in the room.

93

She was so cold. The nurse had put a heated blanket around her. Someone had placed a cup of steaming tea in her hands. But she would never be warm again. All warmth had gone out of the universe.

She wanted to rage. She wanted to scream. She wanted to deny that the unthinkable could have happened. But speaking her denial would be to admit that it had happened. Screaming would make her wake up. And she wanted to stay asleep.

Gareth would not waken again. Why should she? Raging would move her back into the world of anger and violence. Better to stay here, isolated in her frozen world.

"Mary."

How dare they speak to her? How dare they try to break the ice? Didn't they know what had happened? Didn't they know that ice was all that was left?

"Mary."

She raised her eyes. Somewhere her mind registered that this was Philip.

"Mary, I know it's a terrible thing to trouble you just now. But they thought—if you might just say a word—or if they could just film a wee bit. Because you're an American, and you signed the peace petition, and you've been working for reconciliation, it could be important, Mary. It might make a difference."

What was this man saying to her? And why was she nodding her head? How could she be nodding without cracking the ice? But she just kept nodding.

That bright light. Turn out the light. It will melt the ice.

All those people were in the room, and Philip kept talking. Something about peace. Reconciliation. He was saying something about Gareth. A great vision for something that would outlast the coming political settlement and make any such future settlements unnecessary. An agape service. All believing people coming together—all across Ireland. North and south. A great epiphany.

Epiphany? Didn't that have something to do with joy and celebration? She had felt joy once, just before the lights went out. Before the ice came. But she couldn't remember why she had felt it. Or what it felt like.

Now the glass eye of a black camera was pointing at her. A woman holding a microphone asked her a question. Something about how she felt. How did they think she felt?

And then from the dim recesses of her frozen mind came a memory. The memory of Gordon Wilson saying, "I bear no ill will, I bear no grudge." More than once she had wondered how she would react if faced with a moment like that. She had wondered if she could rise to such a pinnacle of Christlikeness. Could she be sweet and forgiving and radiate the love of God?

She couldn't even imagine such feelings, let alone express them. Yet, the ice began to crack. The embalming barrier broke, and all the anger and anguish it had been holding at bay flooded in. "I forgive" was the last thing she could say!

She wasn't sure whether she was screaming or whispering. It took all her effort just to get the words past her rigid throat and lips.

"This has to stop. This can't go on! How many more have to die? I've spent months trying to understand. And I *don't* understand. I can't even think about the differences that cause such senseless . . ." She tried to say "killing," but the word wouldn't come out. "If I think about it, I'll go crazy. I can't think about people who have been hating each other for hundreds of years." She shrugged back inside her blanket, letting her hair fall around her face.

In the distance she heard Philip concluding the interview. "In order to make some kind of sense out of this tragic death, I'm asking everyone across this island to attend . . ."

The next three days were a blur of pain. Back in Belfast, Mary slept intermittently. Always she would waken after an agonizingly beautiful dream to a world without light. Anger and denial fought each other to control her responses. And she was too numb to care which ruled.

Around her everything was a quiet, organized bustle. Life went on as Philip, Sheila, and her sisters saw to the thousands of details that needed to be dealt with. Philip was especially intense. He worked long hours on the phone and at meetings, forging ahead with the plans that had been set in motion in Enniskillen.

She nodded when he told her that the Londonderry marches had occurred without incident. "That's good," she replied.

"It's a miracle," he said. "Someone has been praying."

"That's good."

That morning Mary awoke to a blessedly silent house. It was Sunday. Everyone must be at church. She pulled on a soft, white terrycloth robe and made her way to the kitchen. She had just clicked on the kettle when the front door opened. Were they back already? She glanced toward the clock on the wall. No, it was too early.

"Mary, ye poor lass, I came as soon as I could."

The canister of tea bags clattered to the floor. It couldn't be. But it was Gareth's voice. She whirled with a cry.

"Mary, I'm sae sorry. Sae sorry." He held out his arms.

"Davie." She put her head on the shoulder of Gareth's brother.

"I came for the service. And to offer what comfort I could."

"What service?" The funeral was to be in *Glasgow*. That was the one thing she had been adamant about. She would go on the ferry with the—with Gareth. Philip had made the arrangements. They were going tomorrow. She and Gareth were going back to Scotland together.

"The agape service this afternoon. It's amazing. Everyone is talking about it. They're even holding them in Scotland and England in support of unity here. I think some in the States too." He held her at arms' length and offered her a smile. "And your interview was what sparked a lot of it. But I'm sure you've seen all that."

She picked up the scattered tea bags as David recounted her interview on the BBC. Yes, she remembered a bright light focused on her. She remembered people moving around with cameras and microphones. She supposed she said something, but she couldn't remember what. And, yes, she did know about the agape service today—in a vague sort of way. They had told her that Gareth's dream of a great reconciliation service was going to be fulfilled. Someone had even said some nonsense about its giving meaning to his death. As if anything could do that.

The kettle boiled.

David took the bags from her hand and moved to make the tea.

Sometime later Becca and Julie came in. "Aren't you dressed yet?"

"Don't you know we have to be early?"

"We have special seats down front."

Mary didn't resist as they herded her down the hall. Becca produced a plain black dress from somewhere. Julie brushed her hair and insisted she put on a little lipstick and blusher. "The BBC will be there, you know."

"Everyone is coming."

Sheila came in with a little black hat for her to wear. "Hope you don't mind, but this is Ireland, you know."

Mary nodded and made appropriate comments. It was easier that way.

Even going early, Philip had to park the mini some distance from the cathedral. Bells began ringing as they started up the sidewalk.

They were almost to the churchyard when she noticed a group moving toward them. Then she recognized them. Liam, Debbie, Sarah, Gerry, Fiona, Martin, Syd—the young people she had worked with all summer. It seemed a lifetime ago. They approached shyly, as if glad to see her but embarrassed.

Little Aisling, her saucer-round blue eyes shining and soft hair cupping her face, let go of Liam's hand and walked up to Mary. She held out a handful of daisies and zinnias. "We're ever so awful sorry." She looked down.

Mary took the flowers. "Thank you."

Debbie came up next. "We—we've been talking . . ." Her words ground to a halt as the toe of her shoe ground a hole in the grass.

Liam took over. "We—all of us—we feel awful about not working together before. We see how stupid it was. Yesterday I went to this thing that Debbie's mom sponsors. I—uh, it's cool."

"Please. If you possibly could, we'd work really hard."

"We can't do it without you." Voices spoke out confusingly.

"What we mean," Debbie tried again, "is that we really do want to work together. We really want to put on the show and everything. We know you have to go to Glasgow. But if you could come back—"

"We wouldn't let you down," Sarah finished.

Come back? Tomorrow morning she was taking the first ferry to Scotland, and that was that. Come back to Ireland? To all this trouble—violence—pain?

There was an awkward silence. Then Liam rubbed his hand over his hair and cleared his throat. "You kept telling us we had to quit focusing on our differences and start looking at our similarities."

"And you said we had to approach the situation in love, letting God's love speak when we didn't have any of our own," Debbie added.

Mary wondered when had she said *that*.

"And it seems that we had more of our own than we realized." Debbie and Liam smiled at each other.

Now everyone seemed to be awaiting her response.

"Thank you for the flowers." She forced a smile at Aisling. "I think we should probably go in now."

Philip and Sheila led the way. David put a hand lightly on her waist to guide her as people came from every direction toward the open doors of the church. They were about to enter when she saw Tommy.

He was bending down to talk to a frail, elderly woman in a wheelchair. Behind her stood the silver-haired man who had been pushing her chair, his hands still on the handles. He would have been handsome had his head not lolled as if he were partially incapacitated.

Philip stopped to speak to them, too. It was obvious that the man wasn't quite clear about what was going on, but the woman, though feeble, seemed mentally very sharp. Then Philip said something that jogged Mary's memory. Joe Navan's parents. The father mentally disabled from a Loyalist beating in prison.

She took a step backward. What were *they* doing here? Come to raise sympathy for their son in prison? Surely she wouldn't be expected to speak to the parents of the man who had killed Gareth.

But she had to listen. The birdlike lady with the curly gray hair and shining bright eyes spoke in a clear voice. "My dear, we grieve for you. We had to come to tell you. We felt we had to ask your forgiveness."

If David hadn't been there with an arm protectively around her she might have turned and fled. What did these people expect of her? The teens wanted her to come back. The parents of an IRA bomber wanted her forgiveness. For killing Gareth? She backed another step, shaking her head. Then David led her into the church.

It was blessedly dim. Candles flickered on the altar. The organ played a familiar Bach piece, but she couldn't think what it was. The stained glass windows glowed jewel-like.

She followed Sheila into a front pew and knelt when Philip lowered the kneeling rail. She tried to pray, but no words came. Instead, she raised her eyes to the three arched windows behind the altar. On the left, Christ prayed in the garden, prepared to die for the sins of the world He loved. On the right, Christ, the sacrificial lamb, gave Himself as an atonement for mankind. In the center, surrounded by jubilant reds and golds, Christ rose triumphant.

And then she recognized the organ prelude, "Sleepers, Awake." Yes, someday those who slept in Christ would awake and rise triumphant over the grave as He had. There was comfort there. She supposed.

The procession began. The central aisle was scarcely wide enough for four robed clergymen to walk down side by side, but they managed: Catholic, Church of Ireland, Presbyterian, and Methodist, very close together.

As they began the first hymn, bells tolled from the tower, and for just a moment Mary had a sense of connectedness. All across Northern Ireland, in Londonderry, Armagh, Enniskillen; people down south, in Dublin, Kells, Sligo; across the water in Scotland, England, Wales— everywhere bells were tolling like this, and believers, Catholic and Protestant, were going to church together. Right now they were singing, praying, listening to Scripture and to words of peace.

The hymn ended. They sat for the first reading.

"Anger and wrath, these are abominations, yet a sinner holds on to them. The vengeful will face the Lord's vengeance, for He keeps a strict account of their sins. Forgive your neighbor the wrong he has done, and then your sins will be pardoned when you pray. Does anyone harbor anger against another, and expect healing from the Lord: if one has no mercy toward another like himself, can he then seek pardon for his own sins?"

The coldness and hostility of the past days seeped back to grip Mary. The Scripture spoke of forgiveness and mercy. But she could think only of the wrongs. She could dwell only on her loss. How could she ever have cared about these people? Would this service never end? What a ridiculous idea it all was. It was accomplishing no more than the "peace rally." A nice gesture, but an empty one. She twisted the ring on her finger. It was all she had left. Who would have thought eternity would be so short?

And then came the reading from the Gospels: the story of the unforgiving servant. "I forgave thee all that debt, because thou desiredest me: shouldest not thou also have had compassion on thy fellowservant, even as I had pity on thee? And his lord was wroth, and delivered him to the tormentors, till he should pay all that was due unto him. So likewise shall my heavenly Father do also unto you, if ye from your hearts forgive not every one his brother their trespasses."

The words sank in, as if from a great distance. *Torment if we don't forgive.* And wasn't that exactly what was happening? They were tormented in Ireland today. Tormented by violence because they hadn't forgiven the past. Mary looked around her and was shocked at the number of hard faces she saw even here. People sat stiffly, some scowling. It wasn't working. There was no love in this agape service.

Now it was the Presbyterian cleric's turn. A green stole over his white robe, he led the collective prayer. "Grant that all those who do confess Your holy name may agree in the truth of the holy Word of God and live in unity and godly love. As we all gather here today, each one professing Your name, help us to put our differences aside. No matter what we think on other issues, help us to make peace for the sake of Your name. Amen."

"Lord, hear our prayer." All answered in unison, some kneeling, some standing, some crossing themselves, some with hands folded. Each group, it seemed, defiant in its own worship form.

Mary glanced at the order of service. The Message of Peace was next. Someone had gotten around the sermon/homily controversy. And again, each clergyman took a turn addressing the congregation on the theme of peace.

The bald, black-robed minister with the white Geneva bands spoke on the need for Christians to act with divine love. "Agape love means we love others because God loves us. Agape love unites us to God through Christ. Agape love doesn't cut us off from others. Agape love is the way God loves us and the way we are to love other people."

The cleric in the green stole urged everyone to allow agape love "to flow into you and through every situation. This kind of love comes only from God and should be the supreme focus of every Christian life. Love is more important than our rights."

Mary shifted on her seat. Her bruises were still sore, her cuts raw, although she seldom thought of them because of the sharper ache inside. But now it seemed that all the pain, coldness, and hardness were coming together in her.

The next preacher, tall and magnificent in a red robe with a gold pectoral cross, told a story. "One day last week as I approached my church for morning prayers, I happened to glance up at the cross on our spire. It just so happened that a small, black bird had alighted on one end of the transverse bar of the cross. A large brown bird sat on the other end. The birds were separate. They were some distance apart. But they were being held together by the cross. The cross is what holds us together."

A short man with gray hair and gold-rimmed glasses, wearing a white, lace-edged chasuble over his black robe, continued. "In coming closer to Him we come closer to each other. That is the meaning of our coming together at this great gathering at the Lord's Table. You will be coming with different understandings, different expectations, as you partake of these sacred elements. But you will be blessed. And we will all be drawn together.

"For even as we recognize that we differ on the meaning of what is happening, as we participate we are symbolizing our respect for each other as brothers and sisters in Christ. We are one."

And then, as if the whole service hadn't been ordeal enough, a young woman with a guitar stood to one side of the platform and led them in singing "Bind Us Together."

It should be Gareth up there, playing his guitar, his eyes shining with the love and excitement he brought to everything he touched. He'd been the most truly alive person she had ever known. Alive to God and alive to a radiant vision of all He could accomplish in this world.

But no more.

No, she couldn't take Communion with these people. Not with Tommy, who had belonged to the IRA. Not with Liam, who had thrown petrol bombs at marchers. Not with Joe Navan's parents, who . . .

811

The elements were prepared by the respective clergymen, and each with his assistants took his place by the cathedral altar. The first group of communicants went forward.

She shouldn't have come. She sat, looking straight ahead as all around her moved. There was barely room for Philip and Sheila to squeeze past as they made their way to the altar. But Mary had no option. She couldn't move. She was turned to stone.

She saw a group to her right walk forward together. Fiona, Gerry, Sarah, Martin—all of her kids from the Centre. She couldn't help remembering the sullen antagonism she had encountered that first day. Yet here they were now, taking Communion together. *And* asking her to come back. She withdrew from the thought as from barbed wire.

Then she saw Liam and Debbie, the two most acrimonious opponents, coming from their own situations of hurt and loss. Now they approached the altar hand in hand.

She looked away. But there was no escaping the scene around her. The animosity she had sensed earlier—each group bristling—faded as people moved toward the Lord's Table. It wasn't the speeches, the prayers, or the songs. It was recognition of the broken body of Jesus Christ that accomplished the miracle.

Tommy and Lila went forward next, along with Lila's parents. The four of them were smiling. No doubt that they would soon be taking Communion together at Tommy and Lila's wedding.

The four didn't go directly to the altar, however. Instead they turned aside to where Mrs. Navan sat in her wheelchair beside a pew. Tommy offered to push her. Lila held out her hand to the doddering Mr. Navan.

But then Liam, waiting for a place at the altar where the red-robed priest was serving, spotted the parents of the man who had shot his brother.

Mary saw him recoil as the Navans approached. She held her breath. Surely he wouldn't cause a scene here. But would he refuse to take Communion at the same table with these people? After having come so far, would Liam turn from complete healing at the last moment?

She was amazed at the intensity of her caring. *Don't let him pull back now.* And then she realized that this petition for Liam was her first since she had begged for Gareth's life.

Liam backed away from the altar, turned, strode down the side aisle. And stopped in front of the Navans. Then Tommy nodded and stepped aside.

Liam pushed Joe Navan's mother to the altar. He knelt between her and her husband—the man whose own paramilitary activity had led his son down such a tragic path.

"Mary?"

She started as David touched her arm. Had he been waiting for her?

"Do you want to partake?"

And suddenly she knew that she did. She didn't *feel* any of the love and forgiveness that she had seen demonstrated all around her. But she *wanted* it.

And then she was moving toward the altar. On each side of her, as far as she could see, people knelt together. People of differing Christian faiths, but one God and Savior. This had been Gareth's vision. Gareth had died praying for this. She all but fell at the altar.

"We offer and present unto You, O Lord, ourselves, our souls and bodies, to be a reasonable, holy, and lively sacrifice unto You, humbly beseeching You that all we who are partakers of this holy Communion may be fulfilled with Your grace and heavenly benediction.

"We commit our lives and all that we possess to You. By the merits of the most precious death and passion of Your dear Son, we live in hope of Your will being done on earth as it is in heaven. Assist us with Your grace, that we may continue in holy fellowship and accord with one another and do all good works as You have prepared for us.

"Through Jesus Christ our Lord, to whom, with Thee and the Holy Ghost, be all honor and glory, world without end. Amen."

Mary still knelt. As the Communion bread dissolved on her tongue, so the hardness inside her dissolved. She was at one with these believers around her. She was one with Christians everywhere. Just as she was one with Christ.

And then the cup. The blood of His sacrifice poured out for her. The warmth of the wine spread down her throat. Her whole body seemed warmed by His presence. The ice melted. And now she knew she could say yes to whatever God might ask of her. She was completely His.

She could accept life without Gareth. As long as He was guiding, she could go on.

She raised her eyes to the window that showed Christ triumphant over death. The sun shone through the glass, bringing light and warmth down upon her. She bowed her head once more. "Yes. Anything You ask."

Mary returned to her seat for the final blessing. Now she really understood the words the priest pronounced: "The peace of God, which passes all understanding, keep your hearts and minds in the knowledge and love of God, and of His Son Jesus Christ our Lord. And the blessing of God Almighty, the Father, the Son, and the Holy Ghost, be among you and remain with you always."

Then she raised her voice with all those in that church and in all such services across the land in the final "Amen."

Mary filed out of the church slowly, caught in the glow of the transformation she felt. She wondered if the new person she was on the inside showed on the outside. She stepped into the golden light of early evening. It was as if she were walking into a whole new world.

And there they were, waiting for her. The group she had come to think of as "my kids." The young people who symbolized the future of Ireland. They stood together—bound to one another with love. They were waiting for her answer. Would she come back to this land she had been so anxious to leave? Would she again take up the work that had cost her so much? Today's service was a beginning—but even after a political settlement came, it would take years of struggle to build a stable peace. Was she willing to make that kind of commitment?

And she realized she had already answered those questions. Back at the altar she had said yes to anything Christ asked of her.

She walked toward the anxious group with her arms open.

She had just finished hugging each of them—some of them more than once, ending with Liam and Debbie in a three-cornered embrace, when Becca and Julie came darting across the churchyard from the phone box on the corner.

"We just called home."

"We talked to Mom and Dad—and Brutus!"

"We made the varsity team!"

"And Sharon had her baby!"

"Whoa! Wait!" Mary held up her hand. "One at a time. Sharon and Brad—"

Becca jumped up and down, clapping her hands, her short brown hair flopping. "Yes! And Mom had the number, so we called Edinburgh and talked to them both. He's only about two hours old, and we heard these tiny little squeaks on the phone."

Now Julie pushed her head of blonde curls forward. "Sharon said he was nursing—that he's already an enthusiastic eater. And he has masses of black hair."

Suddenly both girls fell silent. Julie looked at the ground. Becca put her hand on Mary's arm. "Mary, they've named him Gareth. Gareth Lindsey Hamilton. They want you to be his godmother."

Mary swallowed. "I'd be honored. And I'll do everything I can to see that he grows up to be as fine a man as his namesake—in a world of peace and love."

As the chimes rang from the church tower above them, Mary turned and saw the trees edged with gold.

The Reconciliation

"Of peace and life now eat," His love invites.
In holy hush of expectation kneel.
"Come, take," the church through strife-torn time recites.

"Rejoice! His potent sacrifice requites
Our sin." The celebrant prepares the meal
Of peace and life. "Now, eat," His love invites.

The breaking echo pierces sharp. The white
High-elevated Host makes the offer real,
"Come, take." The church through strife-torn time unites

In silent reverence. Bowed with acolytes,
As if at that supper long ago, I feel
The peace and life I eat. His love invites

Us to recall His grace, which heals all lives.
The saints' communion joins in the appeal,
"Come, take." The church through strife-torn time unites

In wafer on my tongue, His flesh so light,
While wine of blood burns strong and stays to heal.
"Of peace and life now eat," His love invites.
"Come, take." The church through strife-torn time unites.

DFC

HISTORICAL NOTES

Although the case is disputed, the noted Ulster historian Jonathan Bardon (see References) says on page 190 of his definitive *A History of Ulster*, "The earliest authenticated reference to potatoes in Ireland dates from 1606 when Hugh Montgomery's wife gave Scots land for this crop at Comber, still the best known center for potatoes in Ulster." Bardon's reference for this is Jonathan Bell and Mervyn Watson, *Irish Farming 1750–1900* (Edinburgh, 1986), p.112.

James Hamilton did, indeed, spy for the Crown using the cipher. There is no evidence, however, that he was responsible for the fires that plagued his rival settler.

The story of Cromwell at Drogheda is one of the most hotly debated issues in the long, troubled history of English/Irish relations. The fact that Cromwell put the entire garrison to the sword, except for a few Royalists who were transported to Barbados as slaves, is not disputed. Whether or not he executed weaponless men who had surrendered their arms, believing quarter had been promised, is in doubt. After careful study, the argument that made me decide that the garrison was, indeed, unarmed was that put forth by J. B. Williams in the magazine *The Nineteenth Century and After*. Cromwell lost between 65 and 100 men. His troops killed upwards of 3,000 of the flower of the Royalist army—seasoned soldiers. Such statistics seem possible only if the garrison was killed "not resisting," as some reported at the time. The extent of civilian losses is less well documented, but it appears certain that there were many.

The extent of English/Scottish deaths and torture in the 1641 Rising are also debated. Reported deaths range from as low as 2,000 to more than 150,000—more than the entire population of the plantations at that time. Every atrocity I portray is taken from a sworn deposition, although not necessarily from County Down. Whatever the actual losses, it is certain that Cromwell believed the worst and, however illogically, used that as an excuse for the war that earned him the title "Hammer of Ireland."

And it's the same today. Whether or not Cromwell committed the atrocities history has accused him of, we are living with the attitudes formed by generations who believe he did. That is the true "Curse of Cromwell."

Mary and Gareth's story is based event by event on the summer of 1996. As I wrote that part of the story, it was the first time in my life to write a historical novel that required reading the morning newspaper to see what my characters were doing that day.

The CCC is based on an actual center in Belfast, and all major characters in the modern story are based on real people—dear, gracious friends whom I thank from the bottom of my heart, where a little bit of Ireland will always live.

DFC

REFERENCES

An Address to the Church of England Evidencing Her Obligations Both of Interest and Conscience to Concur with His Gracious Majesty in the Repeal of the Penal Laws and Tests. Pamphlet. 11 September 1688. Original is in Linen Hall Library.

Ashley, Maurice. *The Greatness of Oliver Cromwell.* New York: Macmillan, 1958.

Bardon, Jonathan. *A History of Ulster.* Belfast: Blackstaff, 1992.

Bennett, H.S. *English Books and Readers 1603-1640.* Cambridge: Cambridge Univ. Press, 197.

Bishop, Patrick, and Eamonn Maillie, *The Provisional IRA.* London: Corgi, 1987.

The Book of Common Prayer. Eyre and Spottiswoode, 1968.

Buchan, John. *Oliver Cromwell.* Boston: Houghton Mifflin, 1934. Pp. 471–90.

Carson, John T. *God's River in Spate, the Story of the Religious Awakening of Ulster in 1859.* Antrim: W & G Baird. Second edition. Baird, 1994 "What's the News?": 121; Prayer Card: frontispiece; Decision Card: 125; Johnston's sermon: 57; "Oh, That Will Be Joyful": 58. Published by the Presbyterian Historical Society with the authority of the Board of Communications, Presbyterian Church in Ireland, Church House, Belfast.

The Case of the Protestant Dissenters of Ireland with Respect to the Sacramental Test Humbly Represented to the Legislature. Pamphlet. 1723. Linen Hall Library.

Christian Prayer: The Liturgy of the Hours. New York: Catholic Book, 1976. Source for graveside service in Generation 5.

Coonan, Thomas L. *The Irish Catholic Confederacy and the Puritan Revolution.* Dublin: Clonmore & Reynolds, 1954.

Curtin, Nancy J. *The United Irishmen, Popular Politics in Ulster and Dublin, 1791-1798.* Oxford: Clarendon, 1994.

Dangerous Consequences of Repealing the Sacramental Test. Pamphlet. London: Roberts. Linen Hall Library.

Dolan, Josephine. *History of Nursing.* Philadelphia: Saunders, 1968. 320–21.

Elliott, Marianne. *Wolf Tone, Prophet of Irish Independence.* New Haven: Yale Univ., 1989.

Empey, Arthur Guy. *Over the Top.* New York: Putnam's, 1917.

Foster, R. F., ed. *The Oxford History of Ireland.* Oxford: Oxford Univ., 1989.

Fox, Charlotte Milligan. *Annals of the Irish Harpers.* London: Smith, Elder, 1911. Lyrics of Irish harp songs are based on this careful study, which was dedicated to "The Right Hon. The Earl of Shaftesbury, K.C.V.O., K.P., President of The Irish Folk-Song Society."

Fraser, Antonia. *Cromwell, The Lord Protector.* New York: Knopf, 1973).

Gilby, Thomas, editor and translator. *Saint Thomas Aquinas.* Philosophical Texts. New York: Oxford Univ., 1960.

Haire, Robert. *The Story of the '59 Revival with Some Methodist Sidelights.* Belfast: Nelson & Knox, n.d.

Haller, William. *The Rise of Puritanism.* New York: Columbia Univ., 1938.

Haythornthwaite, Philip. *The English Civil War 1642-1651.* N.p.: Gladford, 1983.

Higgins, Paul Lambourne. *John Wesley: Spiritual Witness.* Minneapolis: Denison, 1903.

Hone, Joseph. *W. B. Yeats*. London: Macmillan, 1942.

Kohfeldt, Mary Lou. *Lady Gregory*. New York: Atheneum, 1985.

Knox, John. *The Book of Common Order*. Vols. 4, 6. *The Works of John Knox* collected and edited by David Laing. Edinburgh: The Bannatyne Club, 1966. (Formal prayers in Generation 2 were adapted from this source.)

Letter from a Distinguished English Commoner to a Peer of Ireland on the Repeal of a Part of the Penal Laws Against the Irish Catholics. Pamphlet. London: Keating, 1785.

Leyburn, James G. *The Scotch-Irish, a Social History*. Chapel Hill, N. C.: Univ. of North Carolina, 1962.

Lloyd-Jones, D. M.. *The Puritans: Their Origins and Successors*. Edinburgh: Banner of Truth Trust, 1987.

Macdonald, Lyn. *Somme*. London: Joseph, 1983.

Macrory, Patrick. *The Siege of Derry*. Oxford: Oxford Univ., 1988.

Magee, John. *The Heritage of the Harp*. Belfast: Linen Hall Library, 1992.

Maguire, W. A. *Belfast*. Staffordshire, U. K.: Keele Univ., 1993.

Maxwell, Constantia. *In Ireland Under the Georges*. Dundalk: Dundalgen, 1949.

———. *Irish History from Contemporary Sources, 1509-1610*. London: Allen & Unwin, 1923.

———. *Country and Town in Ireland Under the Georges*. Dundalk: Tempest, 1949.

McCavery, Trevor. *Newtown: A History of Newtownards*. Belfast: White Row, 1994.

McConnell, Charles. *Carrickfergus: A Stroll Through Time*. Carrickfergus: Carrickfergus Publications, 1994.

McNeill, Mary. *The Life and Times of Mary Ann McCracken, 1770-1866.* Dublin: Figgis, 1960. I have been as accurate as possible as to the spirit of Mary Ann's biography. She was an energetic correspondent, and, although most of the letters in this novel are fictionalized, her passionate statements on the rights of women are taken from the first letter she wrote to Henry Joy in Kilmainham Jail on March 16, 1797 (p.127). Evan's letter is based on one William McCracken wrote to his sisters (p.120). Mary Ann's comments on the Union are from a letter to her cousin (p. 202).

Middlebrook, Martin. *First Day on the Somme.* New York: Norton, 1972.

Miller, Perry, and Thomas H. Johnson. *The Puritans.* Vol. 1. New York: Harper & Row, 1938.

Millin, S. Shannon. *Sidelights on Belfast History.* Belfast: Baird, 1932.

Mitchell, T. Crichton. *Meet Mr. Wesley.* Kansas City, Mo.: Beacon Hill, 1981.

Montgomery, William of Rosemount. *The Montgomery Manuscripts, 1696-1706.* Extracted in "Glimpses of Old Newtownards," no.1, Ards Historical Society. Pamphlet. N.d.

Notestein, Wallace. *The English People on the Eve of Colonization, 1603-1630.* New York: Harper & Brothers, 1954.

Packer, J. I. *A Quest for Godliness, The Puritan Vision of the Christian Life.* Wheaton, Ill.: Crossway, 1990.

Phelan, Brian. "The Treaty." London: Thames Television/Screen Guides, 1991. Pamphlet. N.d.

Powell, S. *The Advantages Proposed by Repealing the Sacramental Test.* London: N.p., 1733.

Reid, William. *Authentic Records of Revival Now in Progress in the United Kingdom.* London: Nisbet, 1860. Reprint 1980, Wheaton, Ill.: Richard Owen Roberts.

Ryken, Leland. *Worldly Saints, The Puritans As They Really Were.* Grand Rapids: Zondervan, 1986.

Sheehan, Sean. *Dictionary of Irish Quotations.* Cork: Mercier, 1993.

Stevenson, John. *Two Centuries of Life in Down, 1600-1800.* Belfast: White Row, 1920.

Van Der Zee, Henri and Barbara. *William and Mary.* New York: Knopf, 1973.

Wesley, John. *His Journal* and "The Case of Reason Impartially Considered." Sermon LXX from *The Works of John Wesley* on Compact Disc. Franklin, Tenn.: Providence House, 1995. I have put no words in John Wesley's mouth that were not his own.

Williams, J. B. "The Nineteenth Century and After." Periodical. Vol. 72, July-Dec 1912. London: Sampson Low.

Wilson, Gordon, with Alf McCreary. *Marie, A Story from Enniskillen.* London: Marshal Pickering, 1990.

Wilson, Ron. *A Flower Grows in Ireland.* Elgin, Ill.: Cook, 1976.

Yeats, William Butler. *The Land of Heart's Desire.* New York: Macmillan, 1907.

————. "The Stolen Child," "The Lake Isle of Innisfree," "In Memory of Eva Gore-Booth and Con Markievicz," in *The Poems.* Edited by Richard J. Finneran. New York: Macmillan, 1983.